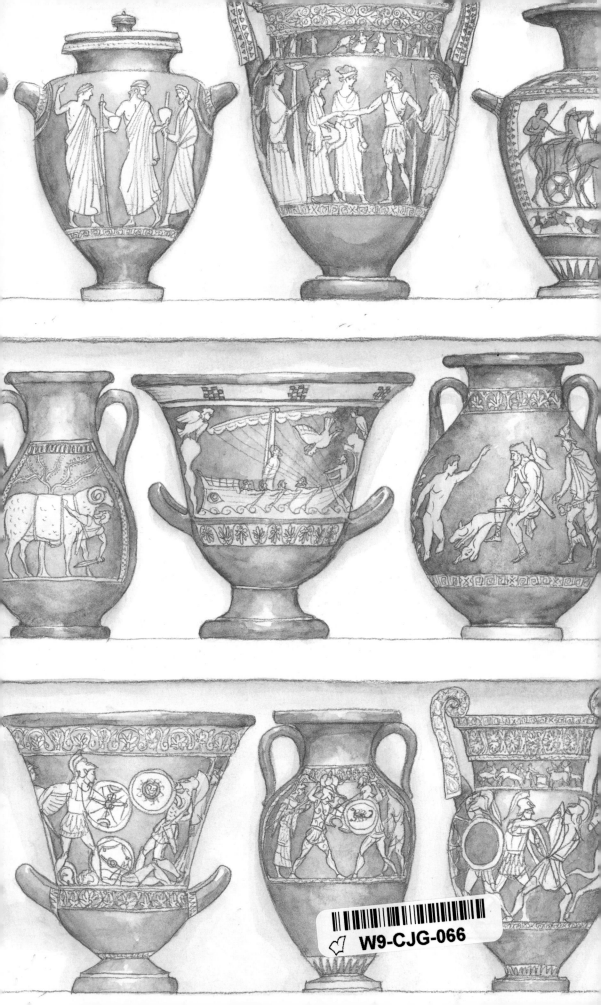

THE
ODYSSEY

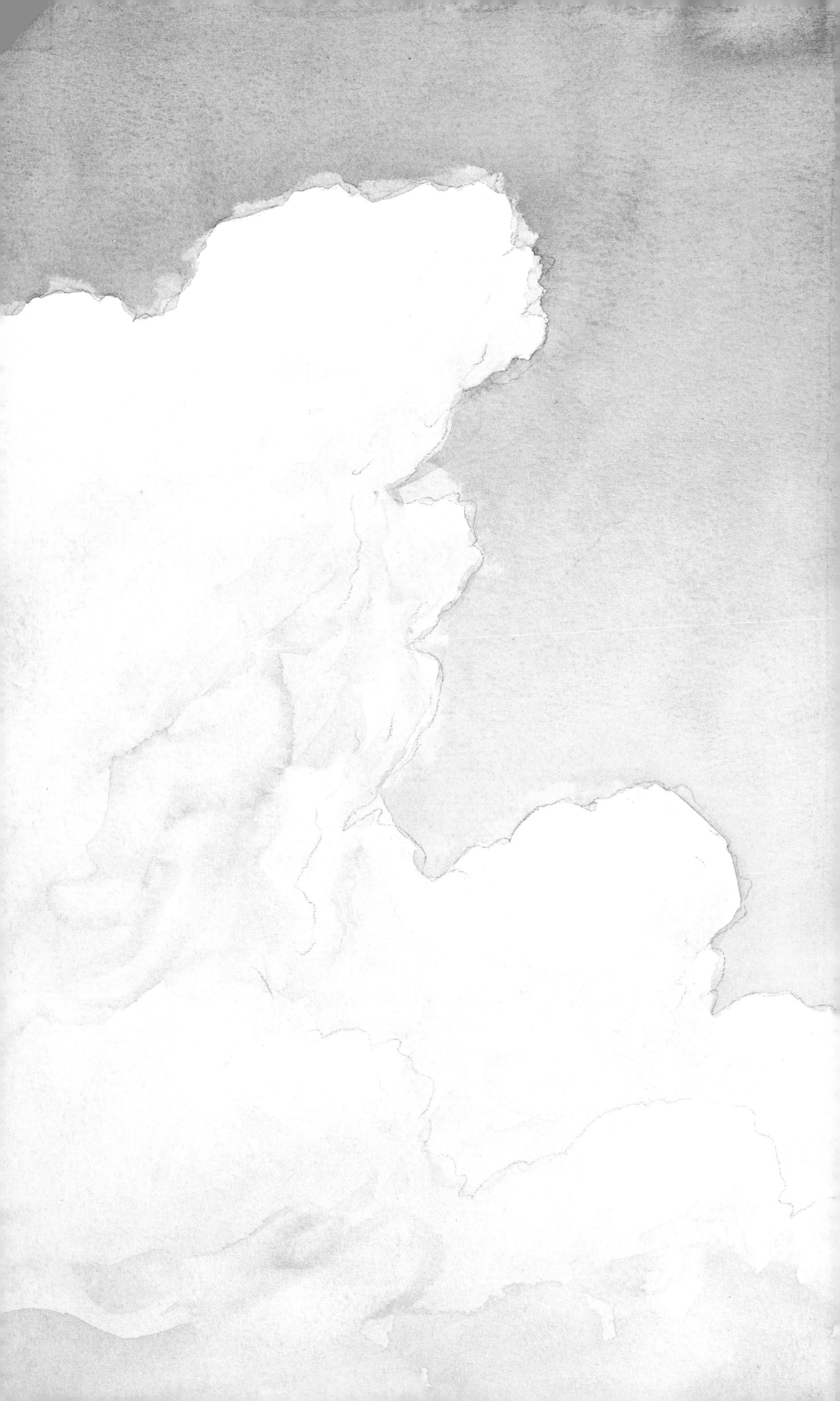

THE ODYSSEY

A GRAPHIC NOVEL BY GARETH HINDS

CANDLEWICK PRESS

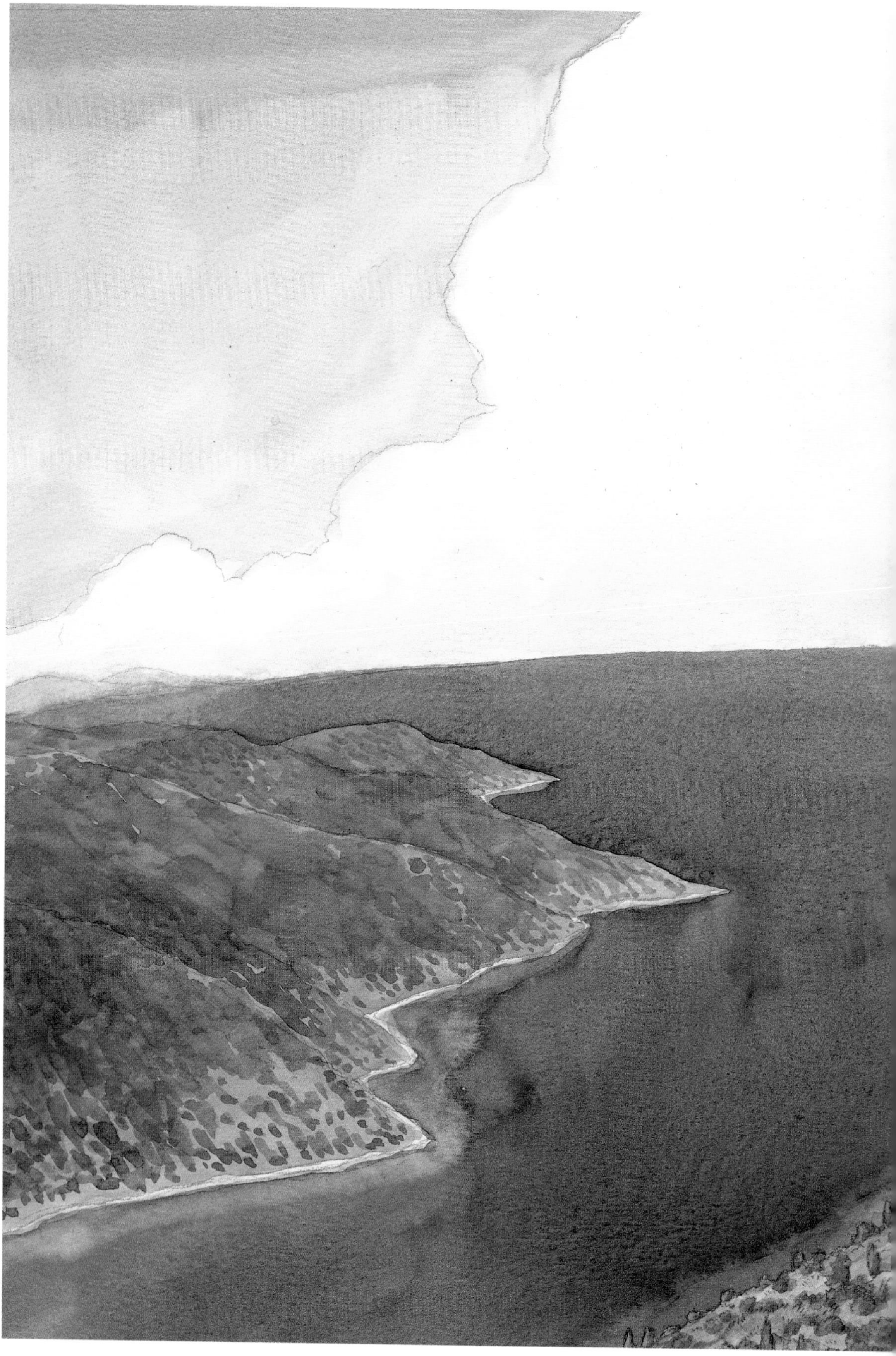

Book 1 — Ithaca and Olympus

Sing to me, O Muse, of that man of many troubles, Odysseus, skilled in all ways of contending, who wandered far after he helped sack the great city of Troy. Sing through me, and tell the story of his suffering, his trials and adventures, and his bloody homecoming.

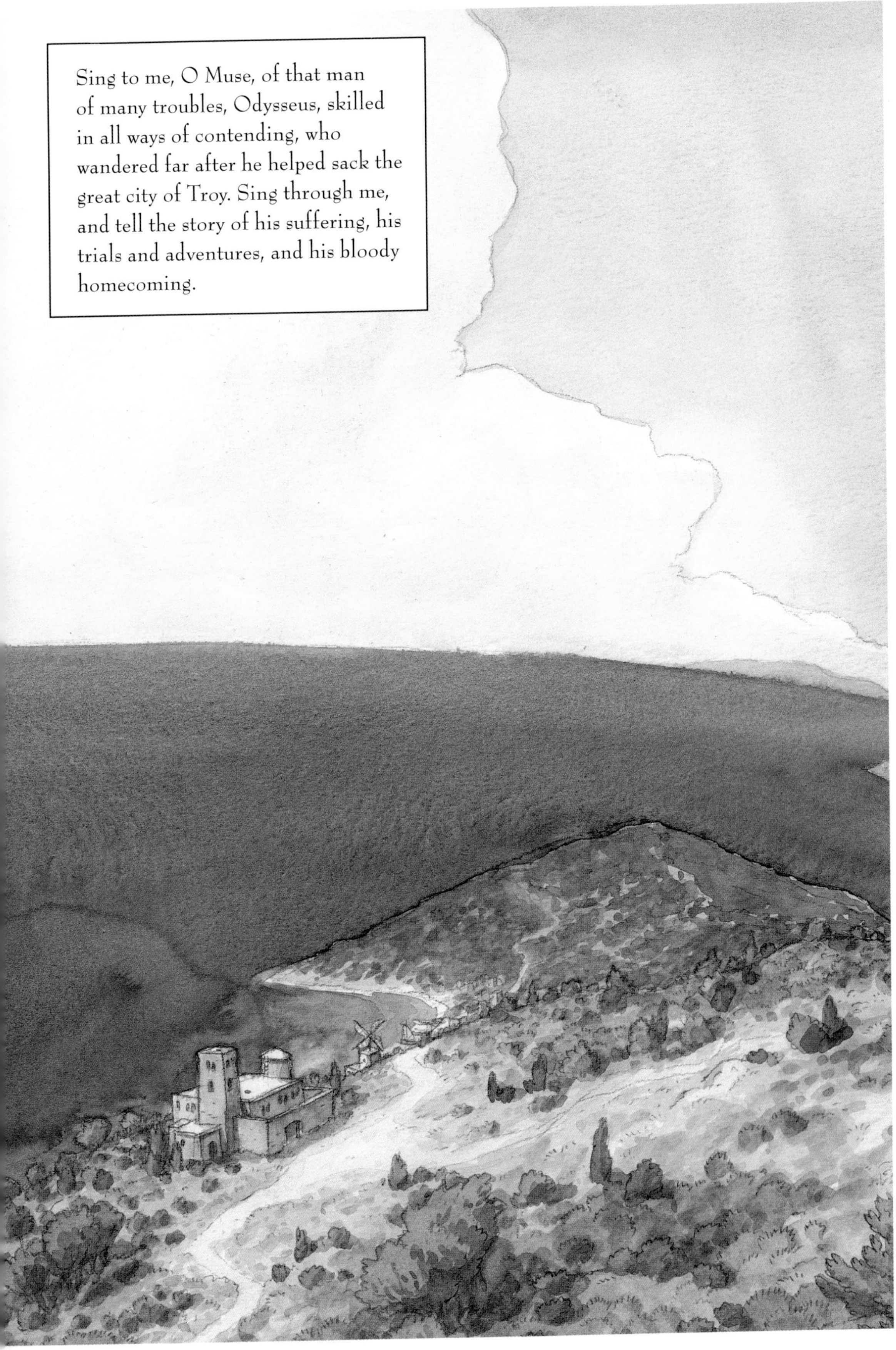

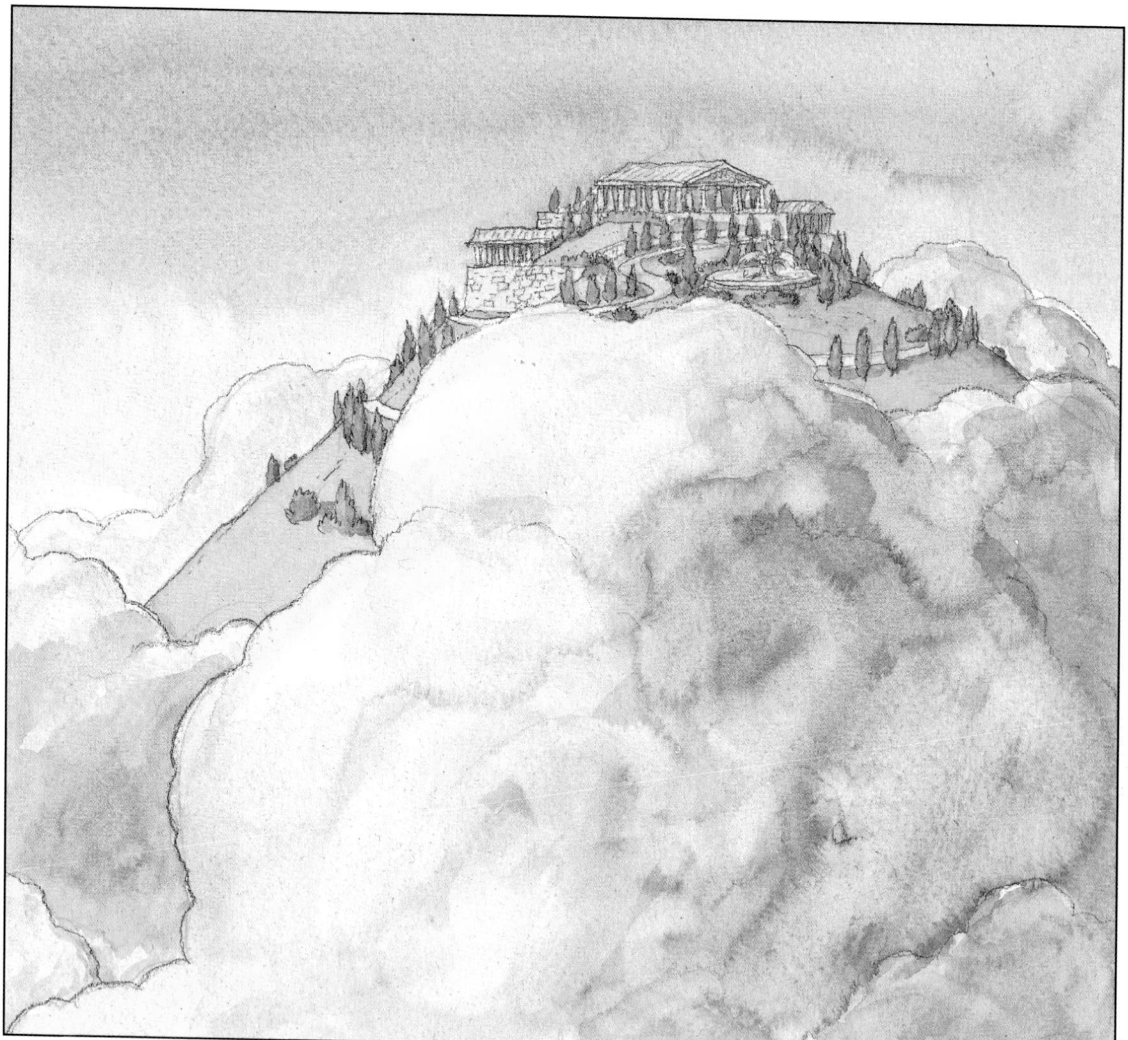

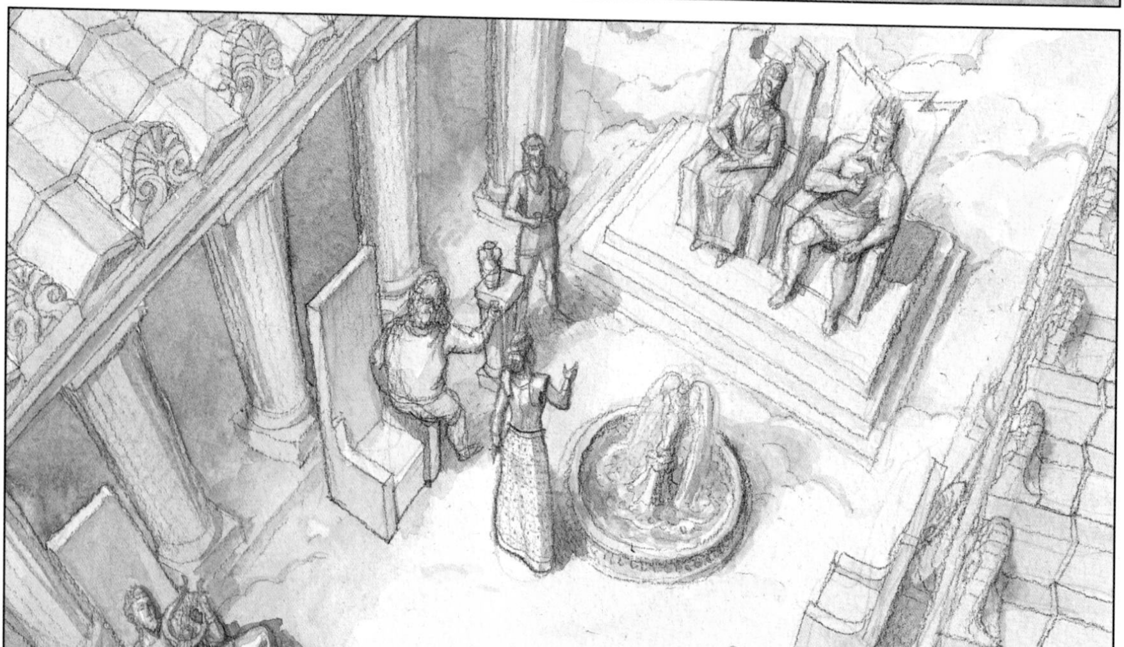

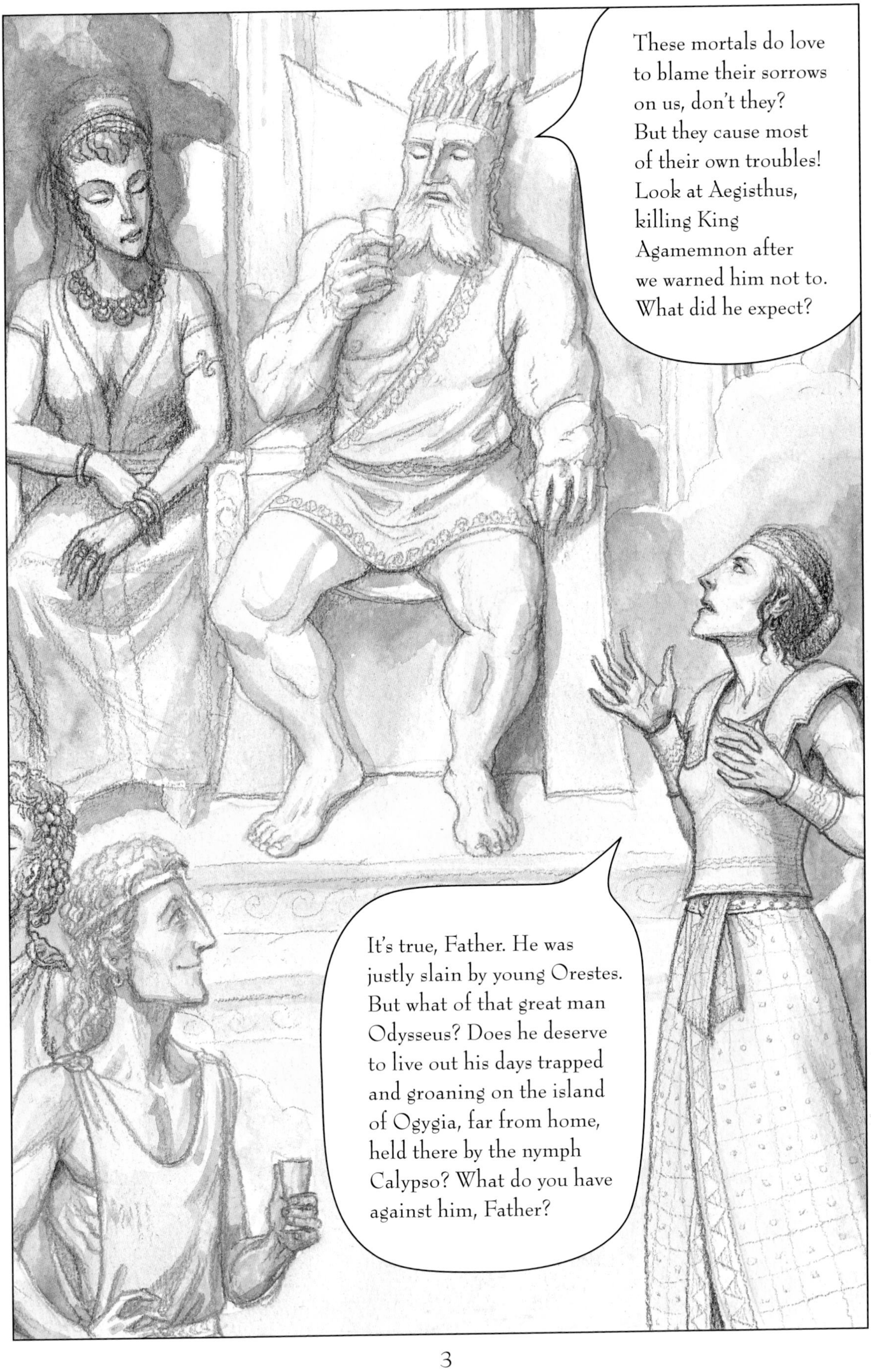
These mortals do love to blame their sorrows on us, don't they? But they cause most of their own troubles! Look at Aegisthus, killing King Agamemnon after we warned him not to. What did he expect?
It's true, Father. He was justly slain by young Orestes. But what of that great man Odysseus? Does he deserve to live out his days trapped and groaning on the island of Ogygia, far from home, held there by the nymph Calypso? What do you have against him, Father?

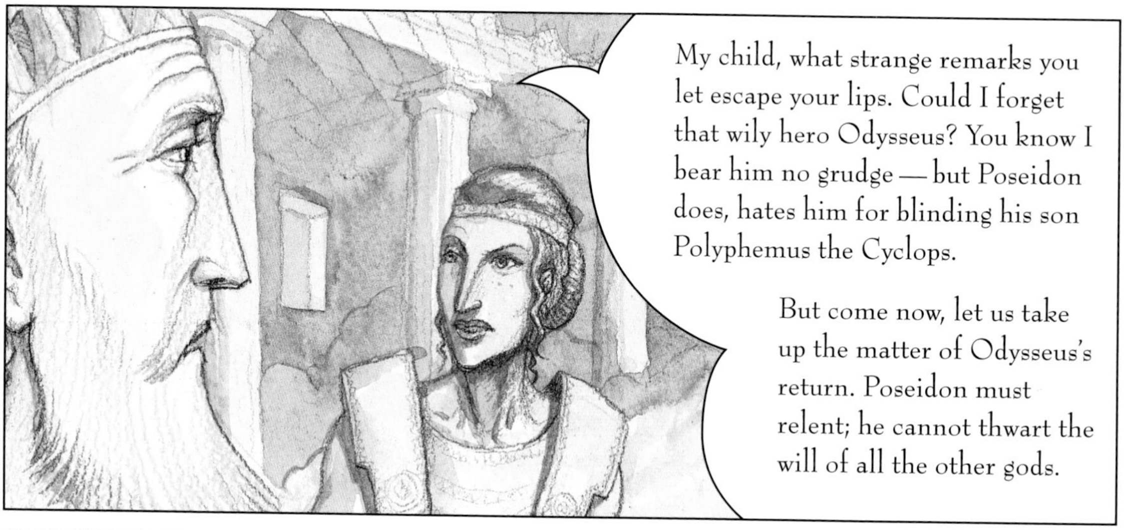
My child, what strange remarks you let escape your lips. Could I forget that wily hero Odysseus? You know I bear him no grudge — but Poseidon does, hates him for blinding his son Polyphemus the Cyclops.
But come now, let us take up the matter of Odysseus's return. Poseidon must relent; he cannot thwart the will of all the other gods.

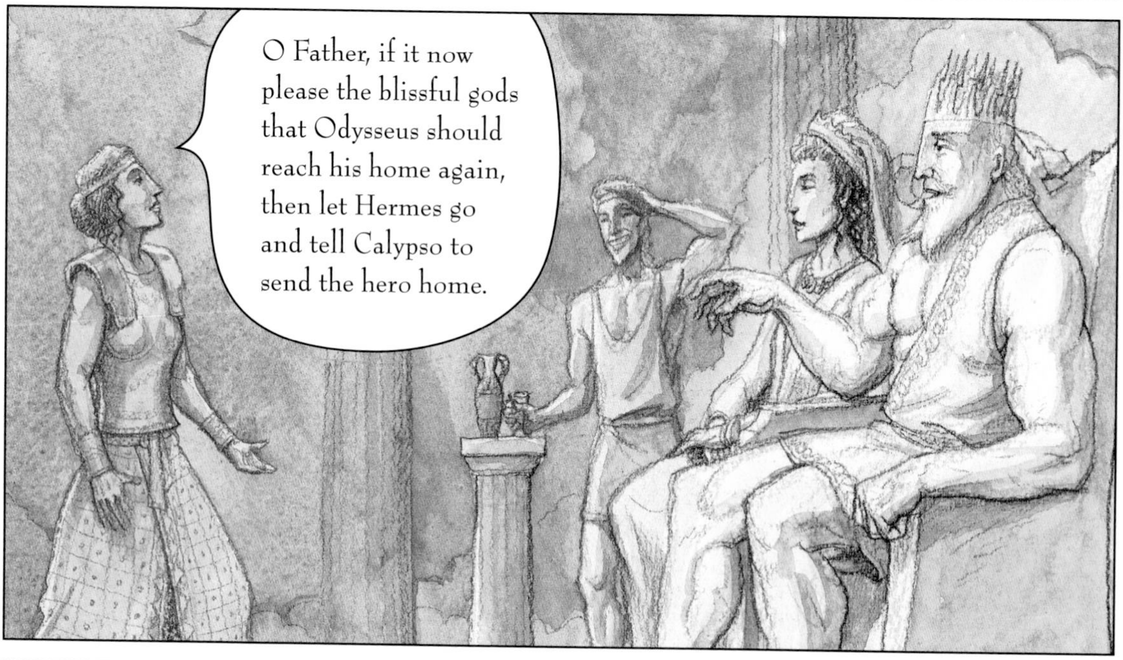
O Father, if it now please the blissful gods that Odysseus should reach his home again, then let Hermes go and tell Calypso to send the hero home.

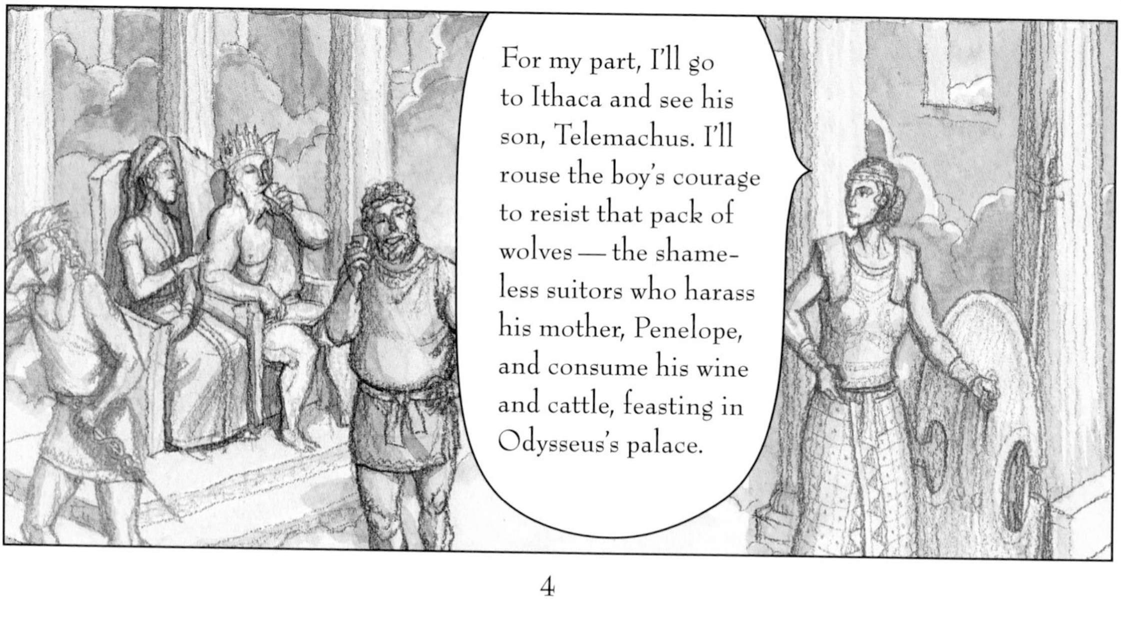
For my part, I'll go to Ithaca and see his son, Telemachus. I'll rouse the boy's courage to resist that pack of wolves — the shameless suitors who harass his mother, Penelope, and consume his wine and cattle, feasting in Odysseus's palace.

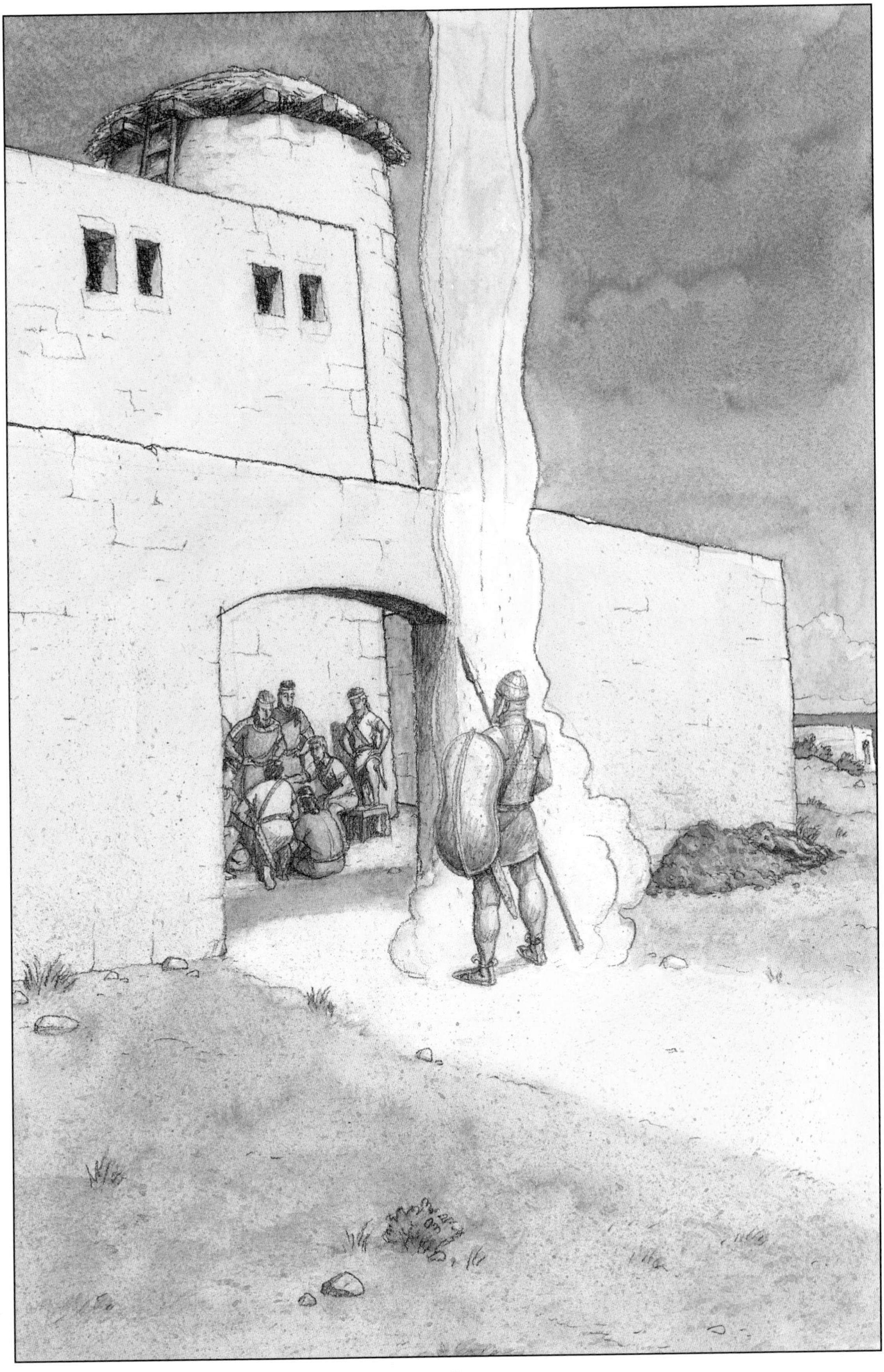

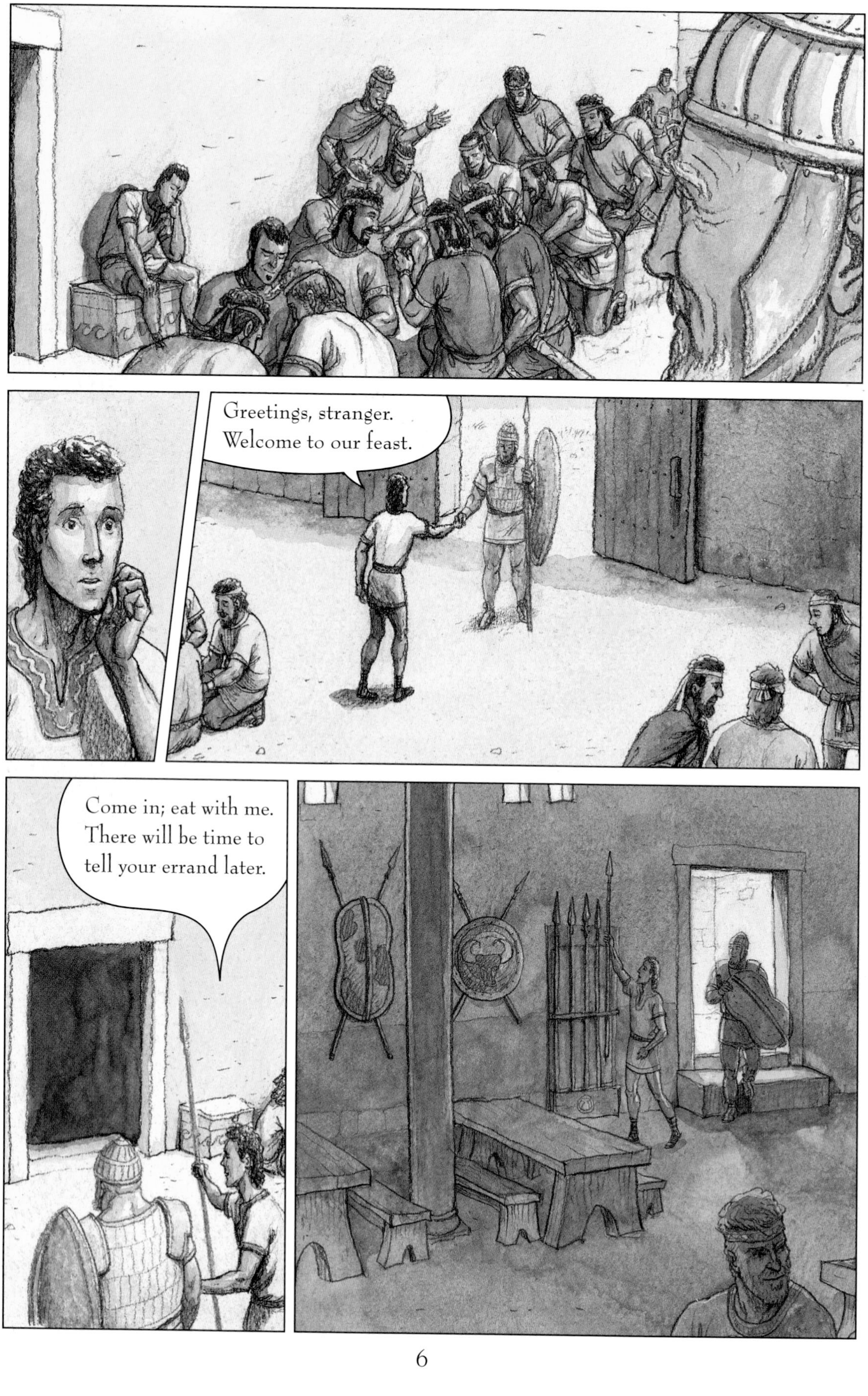
Greetings, stranger.
Welcome to our feast.
Come in; eat with me.
There will be time to
tell your errand later.

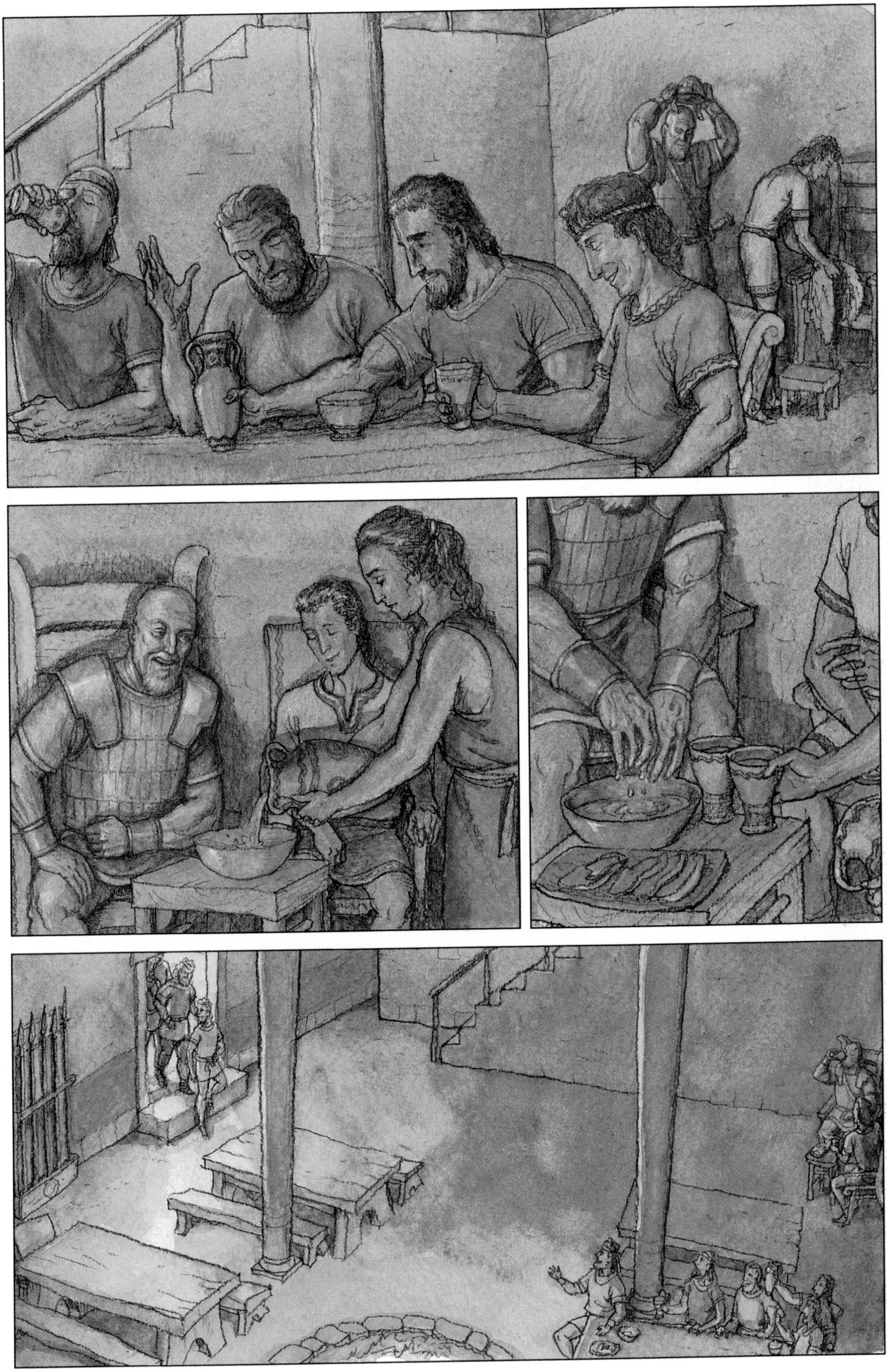

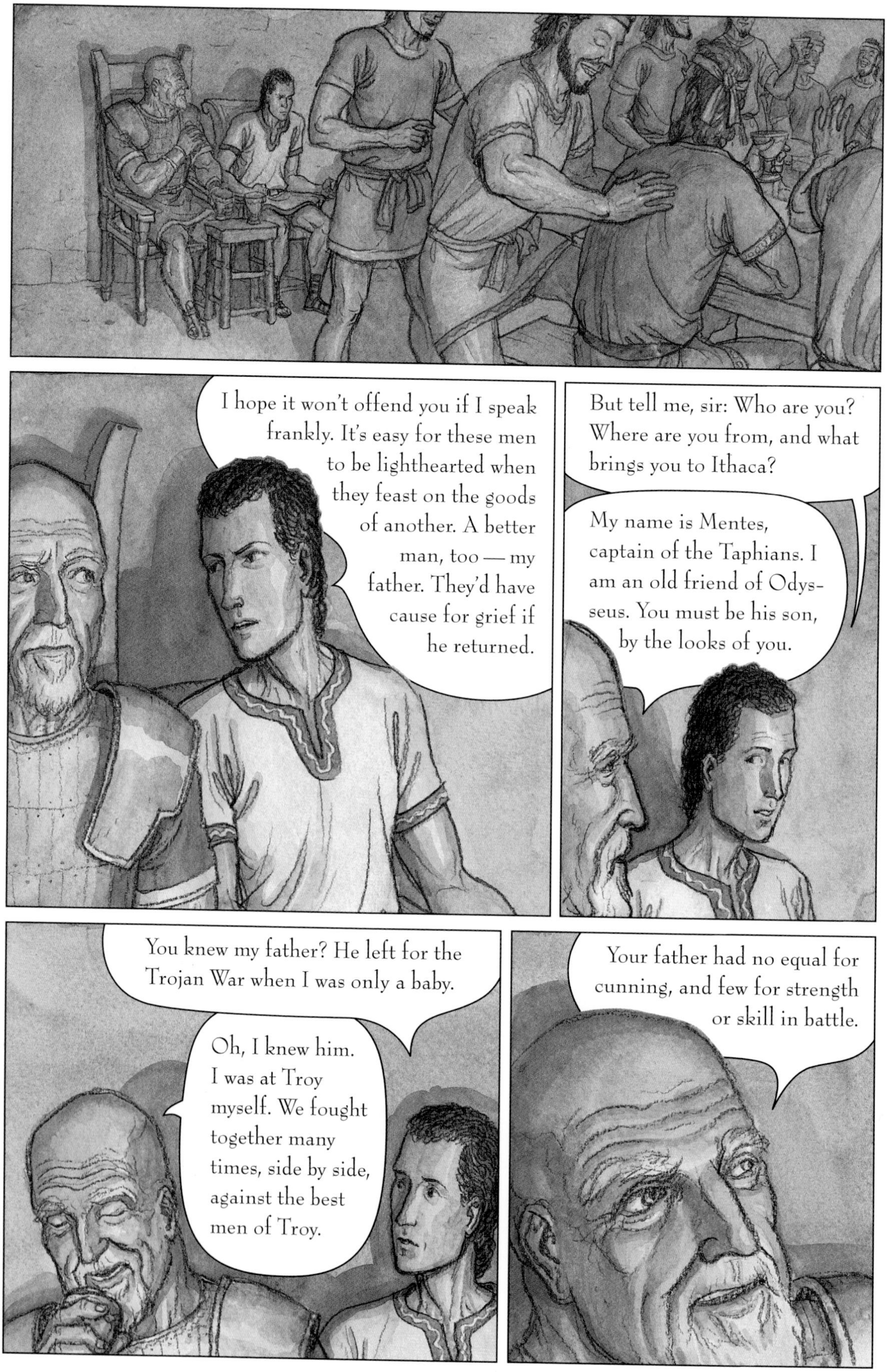
I hope it won't offend you if I speak frankly. It's easy for these men to be lighthearted when they feast on the goods of another. A better man, too — my father. They'd have cause for grief if he returned.
But tell me, sir: Who are you? Where are you from, and what brings you to Ithaca?
My name is Mentes, captain of the Taphians. I am an old friend of Odysseus. You must be his son, by the looks of you.
You knew my father? He left for the Trojan War when I was only a baby.
Oh, I knew him. I was at Troy myself. We fought together many times, side by side, against the best men of Troy.
Your father had no equal for cunning, and few for strength or skill in battle.

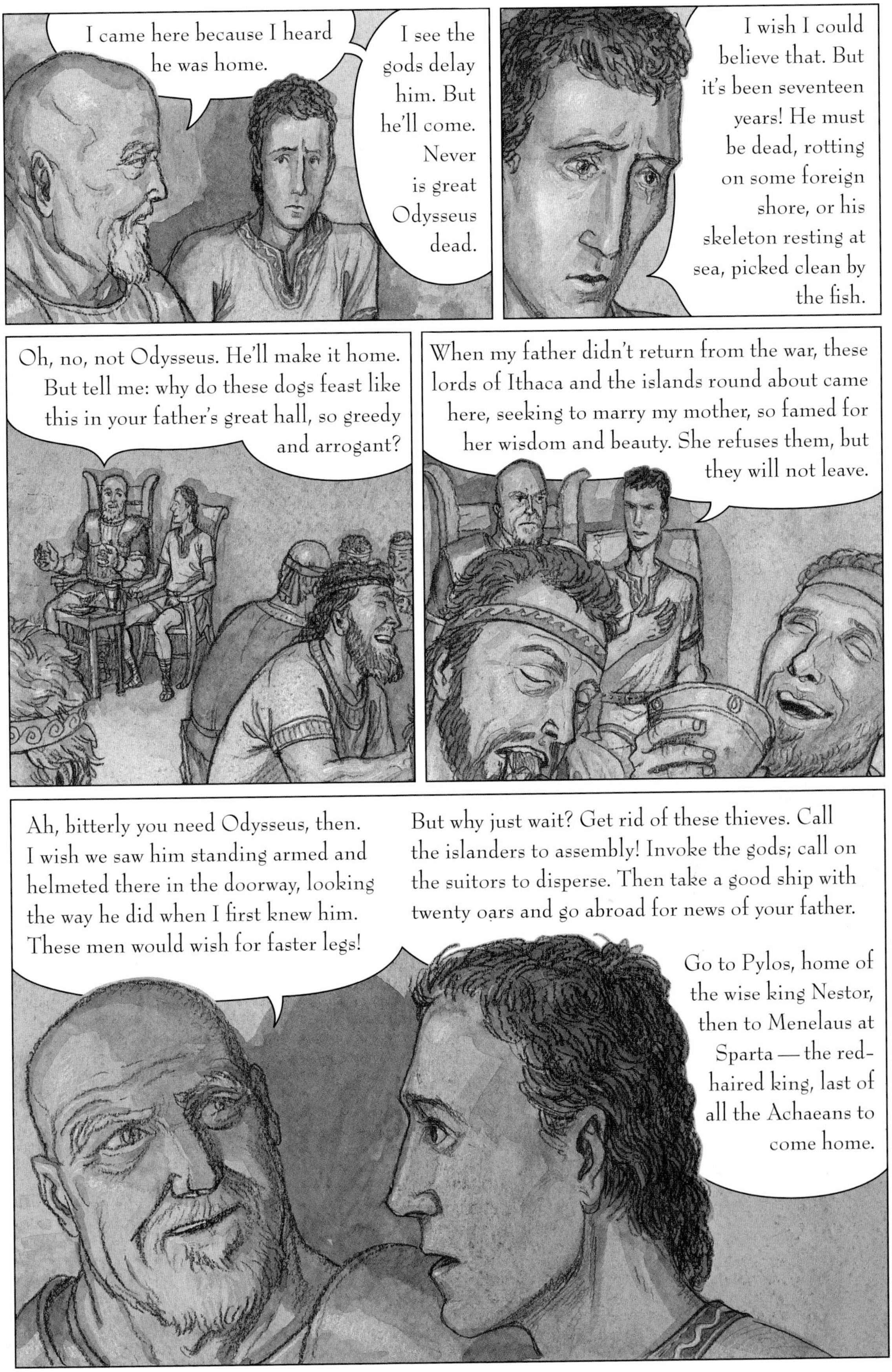
I came here because I heard he was home.
I see the gods delay him. But he'll come. Never is great Odysseus dead.
I wish I could believe that. But it's been seventeen years! He must be dead, rotting on some foreign shore, or his skeleton resting at sea, picked clean by the fish.
Oh, no, not Odysseus. He'll make it home. But tell me: why do these dogs feast like this in your father's great hall, so greedy and arrogant?
When my father didn't return from the war, these lords of Ithaca and the islands round about came here, seeking to marry my mother, so famed for her wisdom and beauty. She refuses them, but they will not leave.
Ah, bitterly you need Odysseus, then. I wish we saw him standing armed and helmeted there in the doorway, looking the way he did when I first knew him. These men would wish for faster legs!
But why just wait? Get rid of these thieves. Call the islanders to assembly! Invoke the gods; call on the suitors to disperse. Then take a good ship with twenty oars and go abroad for news of your father.
Go to Pylos, home of the wise king Nestor, then to Menelaus at Sparta — the red-haired king, last of all the Achaeans to come home.

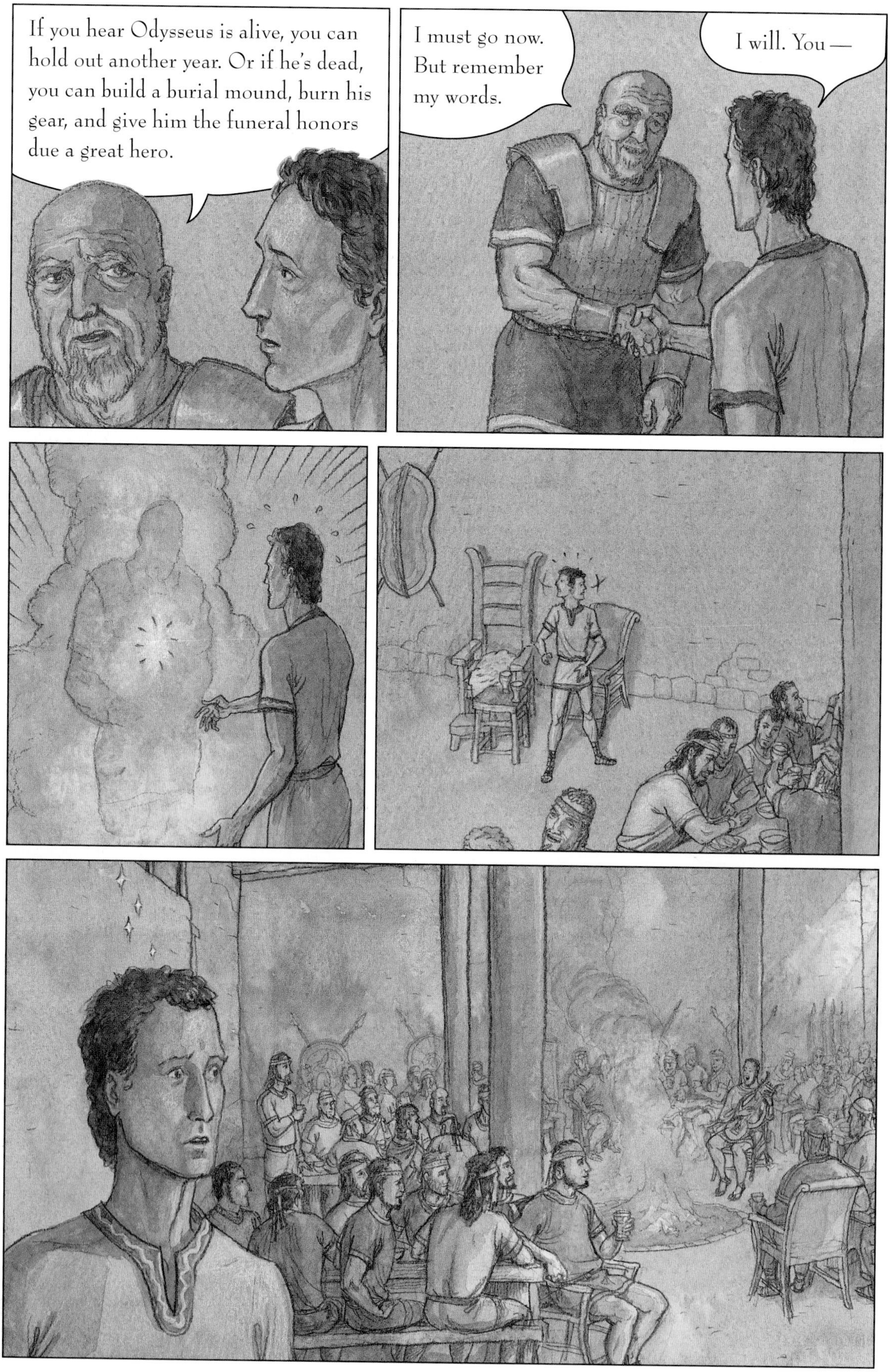
If you hear Odysseus is alive, you can hold out another year. Or if he's dead, you can build a burial mound, burn his gear, and give him the funeral honors due a great hero.
I must go now. But remember my words.
I will. You —

Phemius.

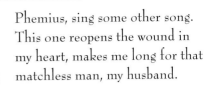

Phemius, sing some other song. This one reopens the wound in my heart, makes me long for that matchless man, my husband.

Mother, let the bard follow his muse. Poets are not to blame, but the gods who decide men's fates.

You should make yourself listen; he tells of others besides Odysseus who lost their lives, never made it home from Troy.

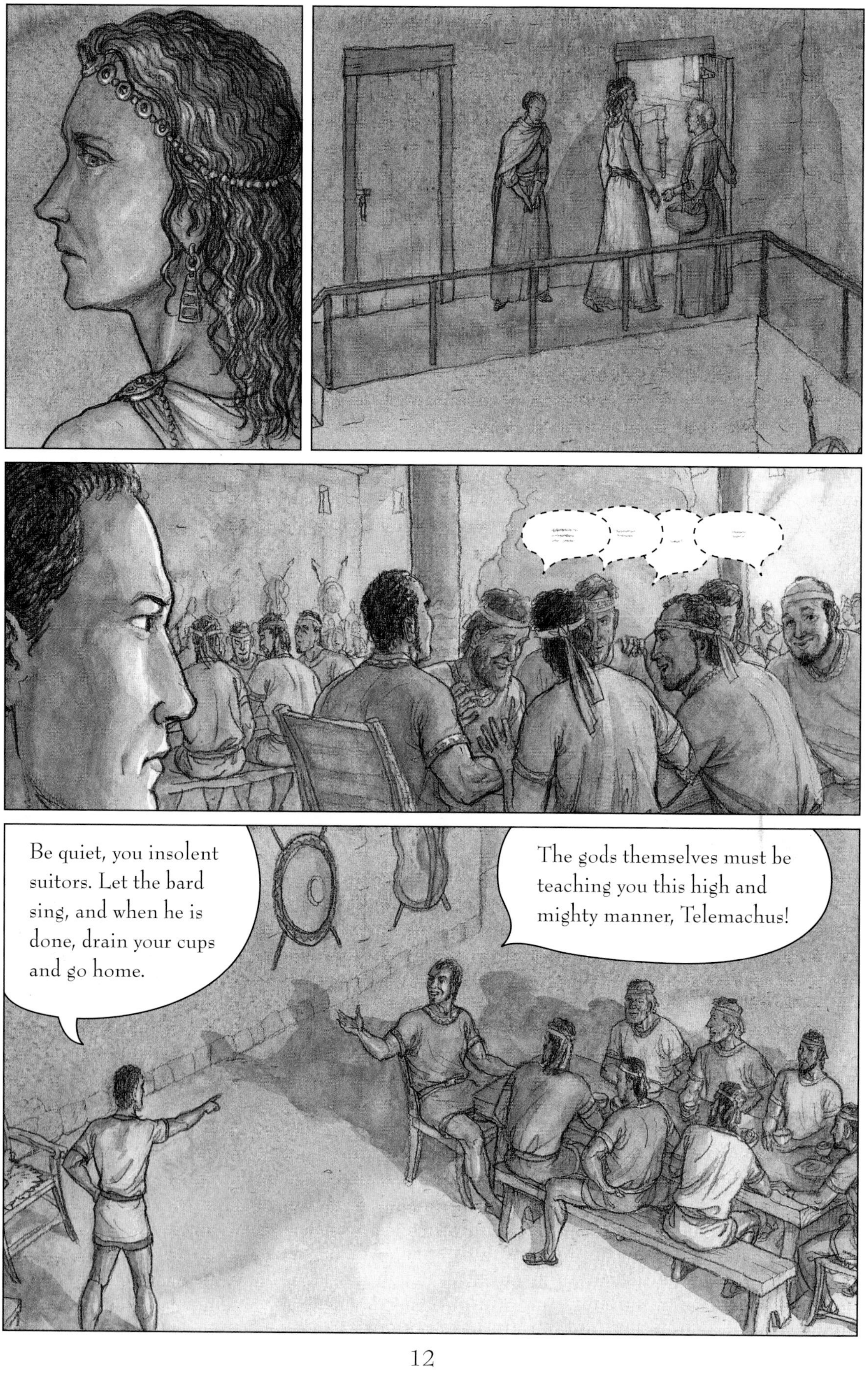
Be quiet, you insolent suitors. Let the bard sing, and when he is done, drain your cups and go home.
The gods themselves must be teaching you this high and mighty manner, Telemachus!

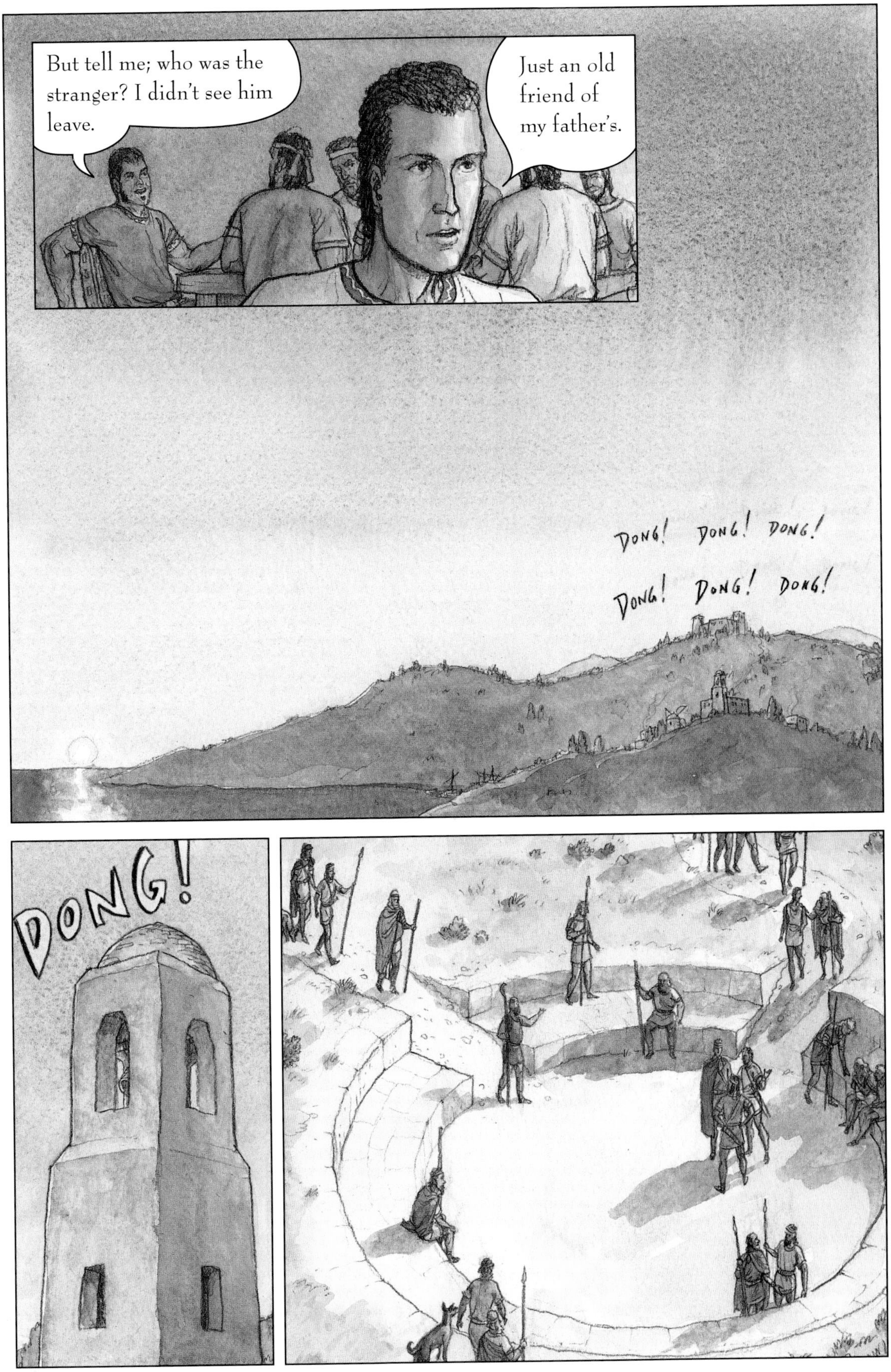
But tell me; who was the stranger? I didn't see him leave.
Just an old friend of my father's.
DONG! DONG! DONG!
DONG! DONG! DONG!
DONG!

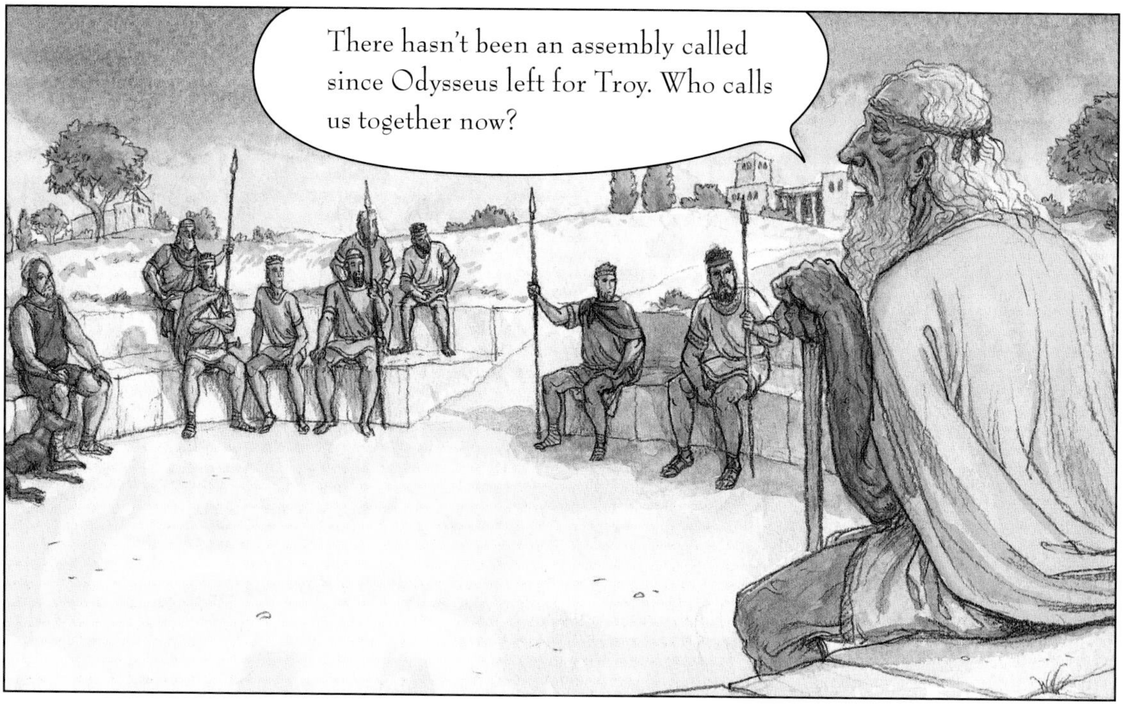
There hasn't been an assembly called since Odysseus left for Troy. Who calls us together now?

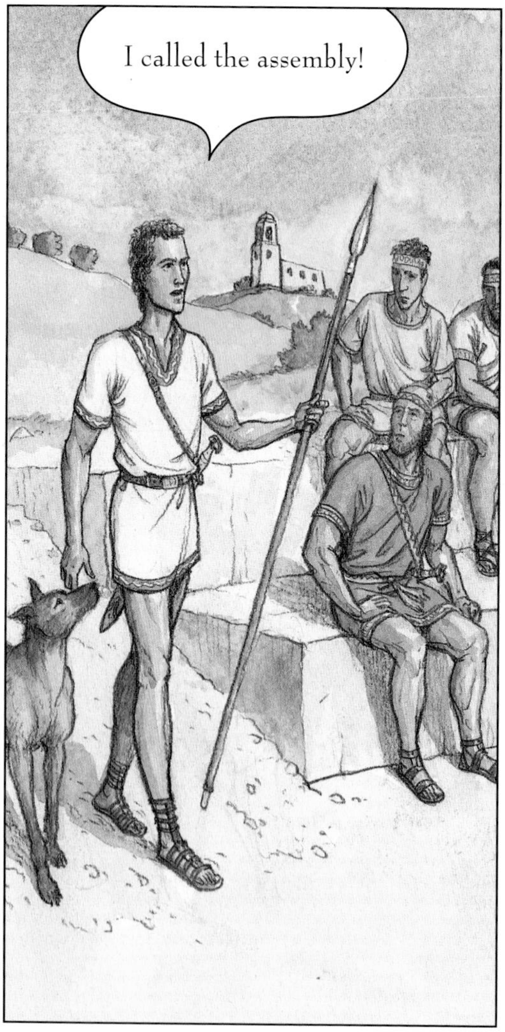
I called the assembly!

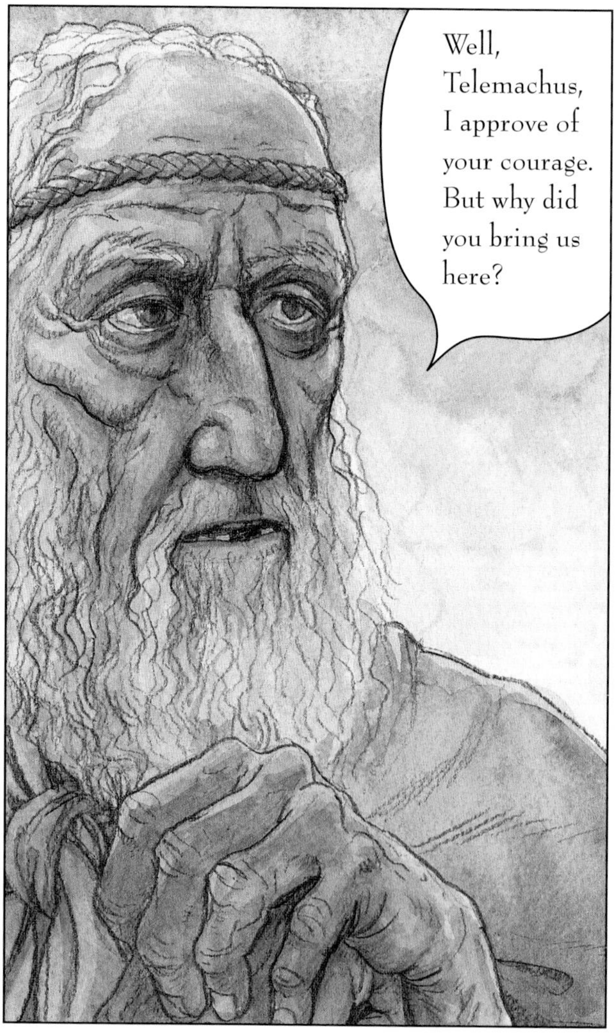
Well, Telemachus, I approve of your courage. But why did you bring us here?

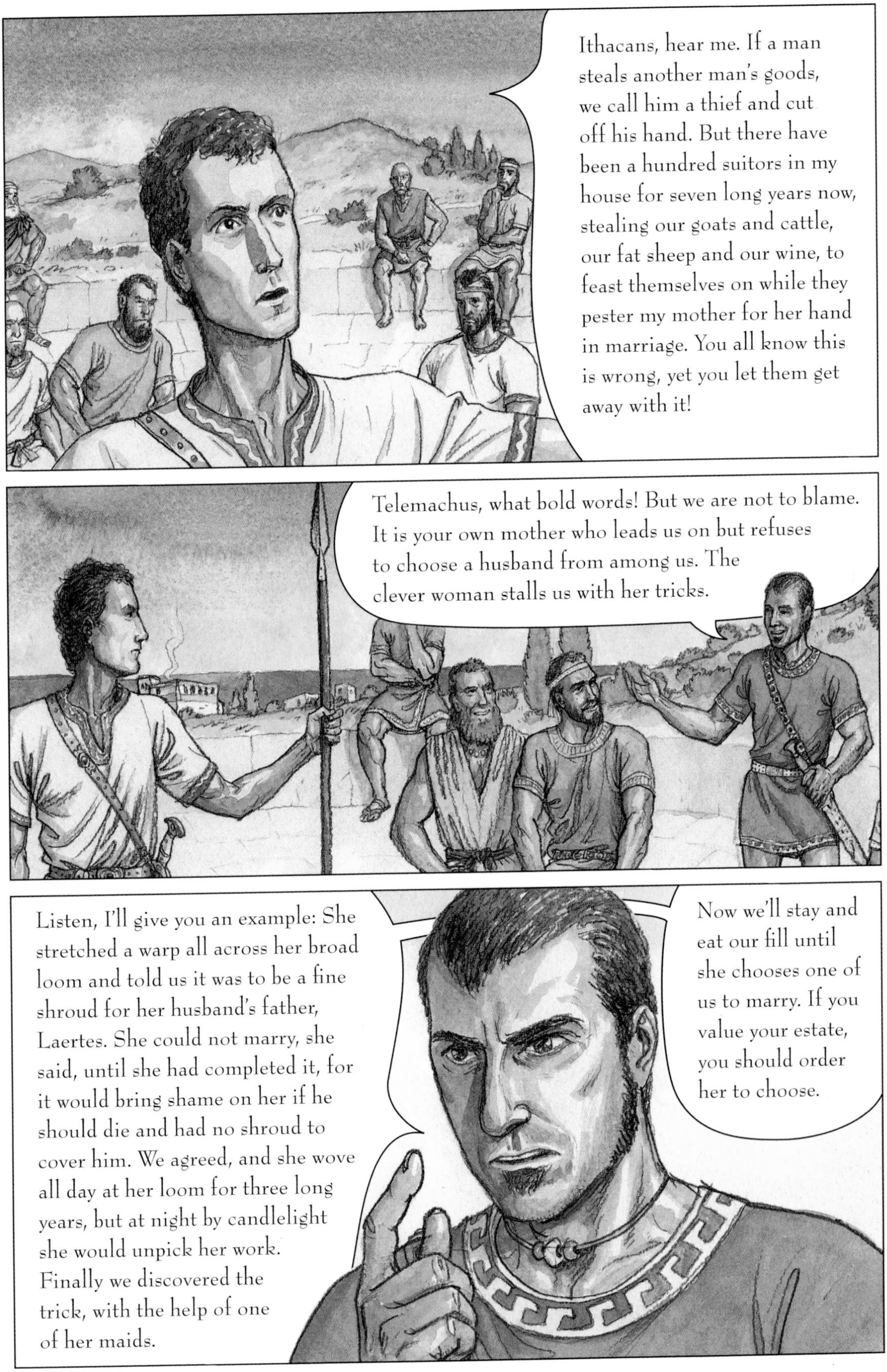
Ithacans, hear me. If a man steals another man's goods, we call him a thief and cut off his hand. But there have been a hundred suitors in my house for seven long years now, stealing our goats and cattle, our fat sheep and our wine, to feast themselves on while they pester my mother for her hand in marriage. You all know this is wrong, yet you let them get away with it!
Telemachus, what bold words! But we are not to blame. It is your own mother who leads us on but refuses to choose a husband from among us. The clever woman stalls us with her tricks.
Listen, I'll give you an example: She stretched a warp all across her broad loom and told us it was to be a fine shroud for her husband's father, Laertes. She could not marry, she said, until she had completed it, for it would bring shame on her if he should die and had no shroud to cover him. We agreed, and she wove all day at her loom for three long years, but at night by candlelight she would unpick her work. Finally we discovered the trick, with the help of one of her maids.
Now we'll stay and eat our fill until she chooses one of us to marry. If you value your estate, you should order her to choose.

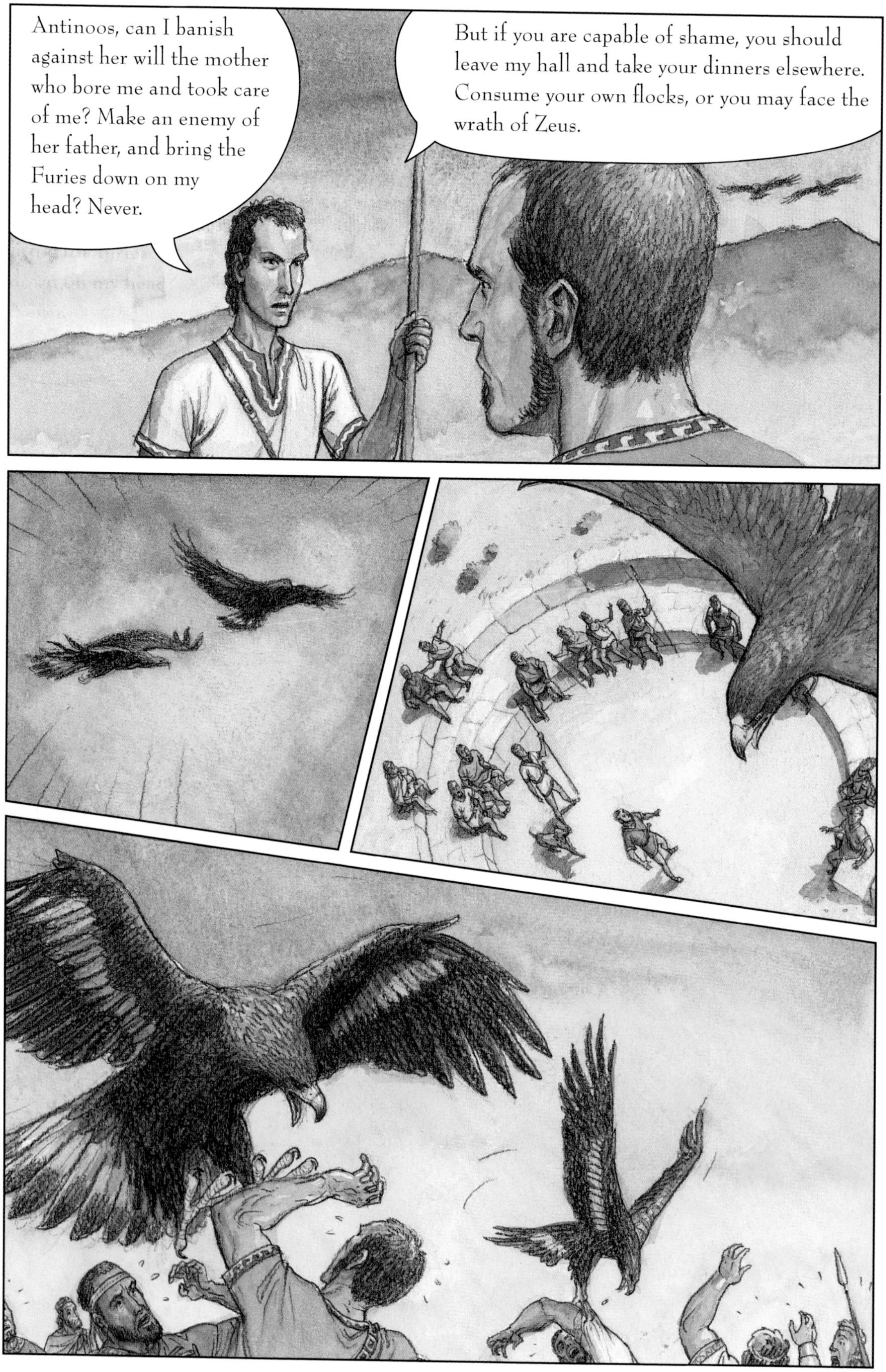
Antinoos, can I banish against her will the mother who bore me and took care of me? Make an enemy of her father, and bring the Furies down on my head? Never.
But if you are capable of shame, you should leave my hall and take your dinners elsewhere. Consume your own flocks, or you may face the wrath of Zeus.

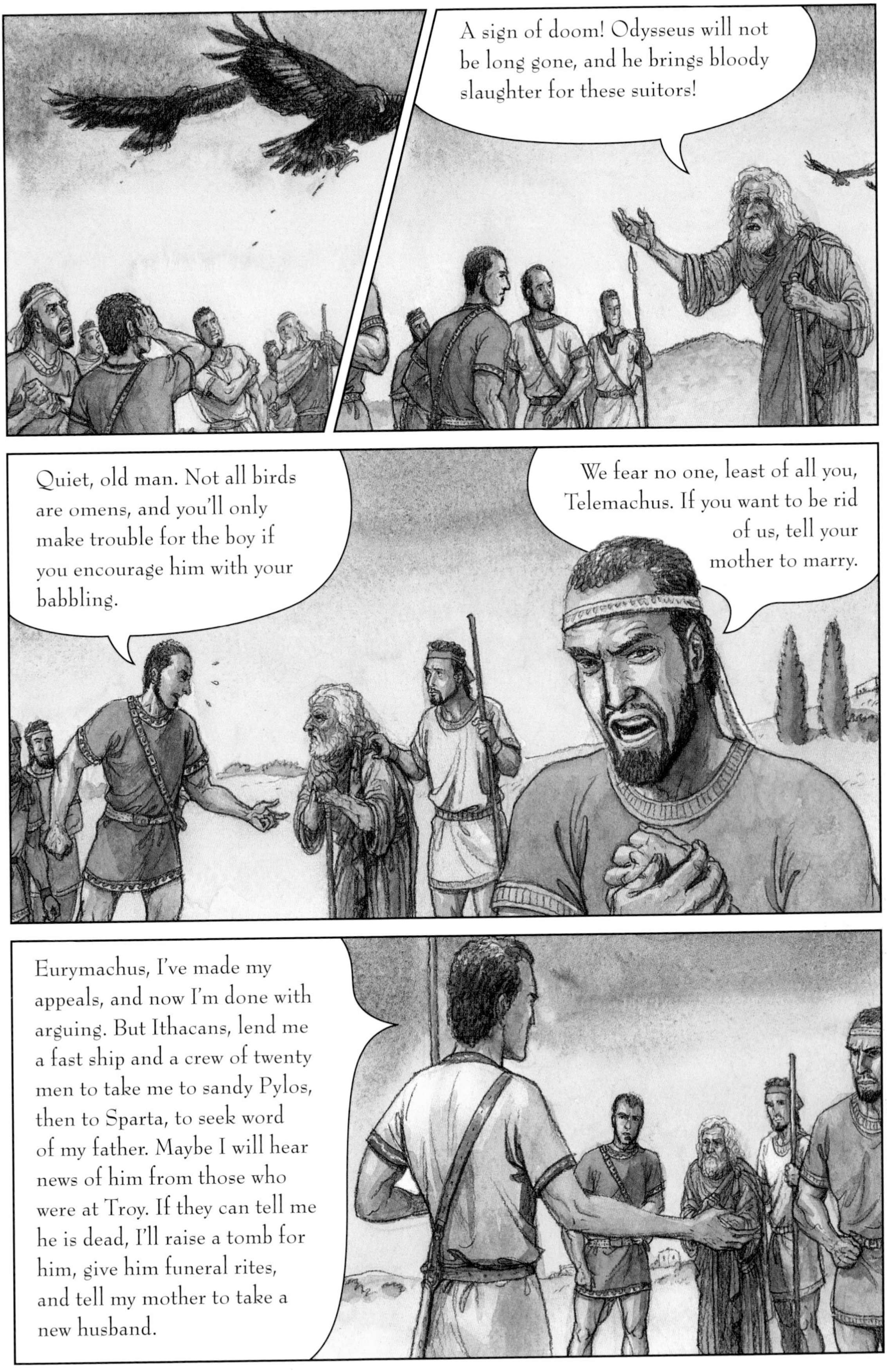
A sign of doom! Odysseus will not be long gone, and he brings bloody slaughter for these suitors!
Quiet, old man. Not all birds are omens, and you'll only make trouble for the boy if you encourage him with your babbling.
We fear no one, least of all you, Telemachus. If you want to be rid of us, tell your mother to marry.
Eurymachus, I've made my appeals, and now I'm done with arguing. But Ithacans, lend me a fast ship and a crew of twenty men to take me to sandy Pylos, then to Sparta, to seek word of my father. Maybe I will hear news of him from those who were at Troy. If they can tell me he is dead, I'll raise a tomb for him, give him funeral rites, and tell my mother to take a new husband.

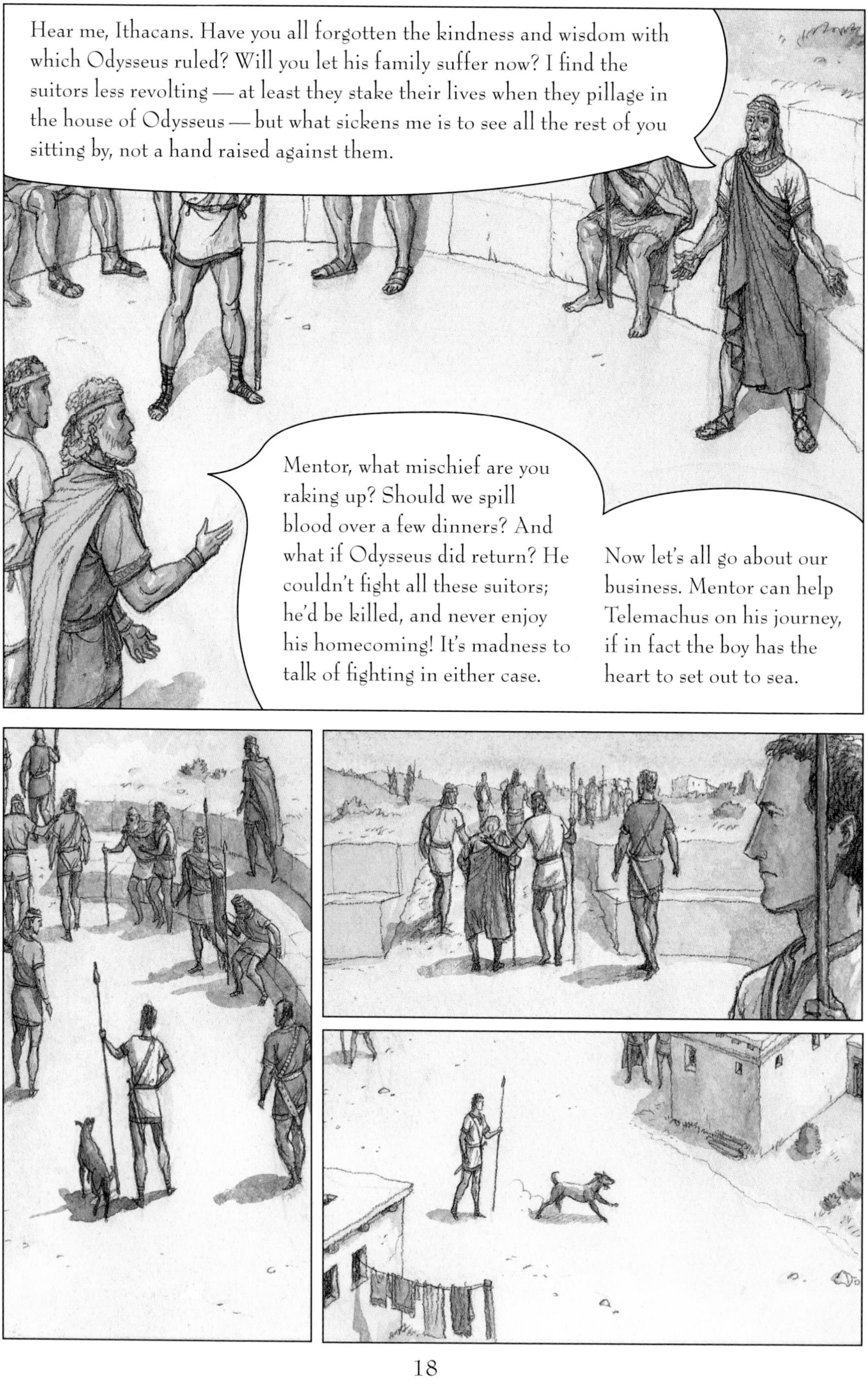
Hear me, Ithacans. Have you all forgotten the kindness and wisdom with which Odysseus ruled? Will you let his family suffer now? I find the suitors less revolting — at least they stake their lives when they pillage in the house of Odysseus — but what sickens me is to see all the rest of you sitting by, not a hand raised against them.
Mentor, what mischief are you raking up? Should we spill blood over a few dinners? And what if Odysseus did return? He couldn't fight all these suitors; he'd be killed, and never enjoy his homecoming! It's madness to talk of fighting in either case.
Now let's all go about our business. Mentor can help Telemachus on his journey, if in fact the boy has the heart to set out to sea.

Whatever god visited me yesterday and told me to take ship in search of my father, help me. The Achaeans will do nothing.

Never fear. I sailed beside your father in the old days, and I'll find you a ship and help you sail her.

Go on home and join the suitors, but gather up provisions, wine in jars and barley meal — the staying power of oarsmen — in watertight bags. I'll find sailors to man the oars.

It's a rare son who measures up to his father, and only one in a thousand is a better man — but you have the heart and wit to win through.

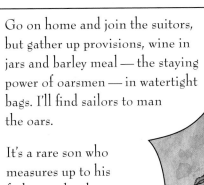

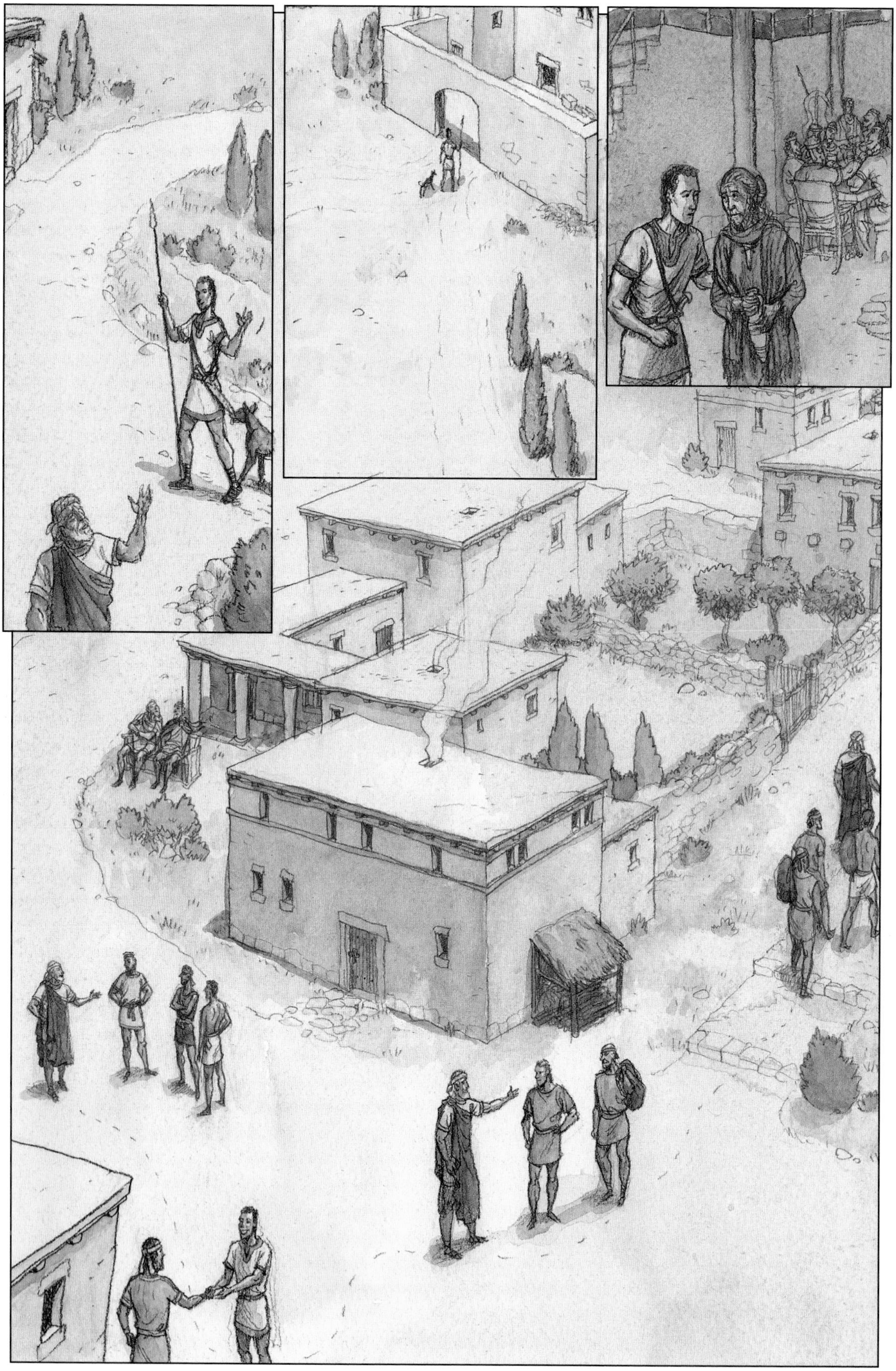

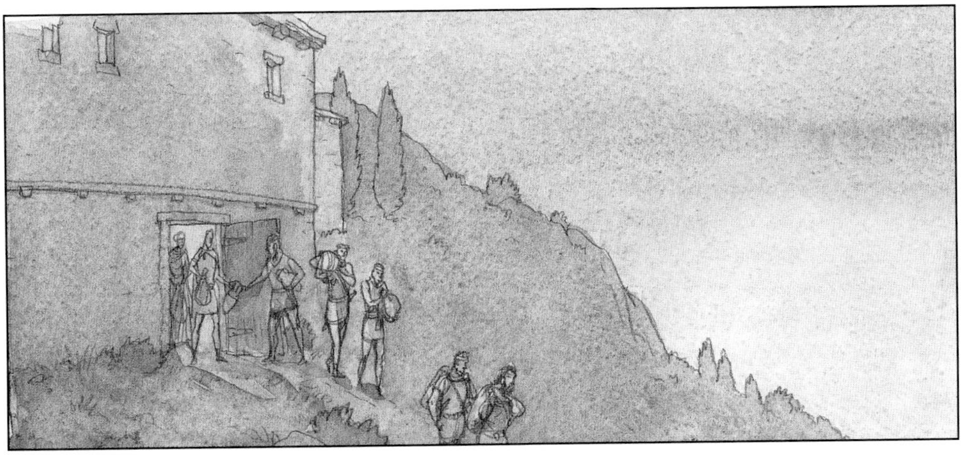
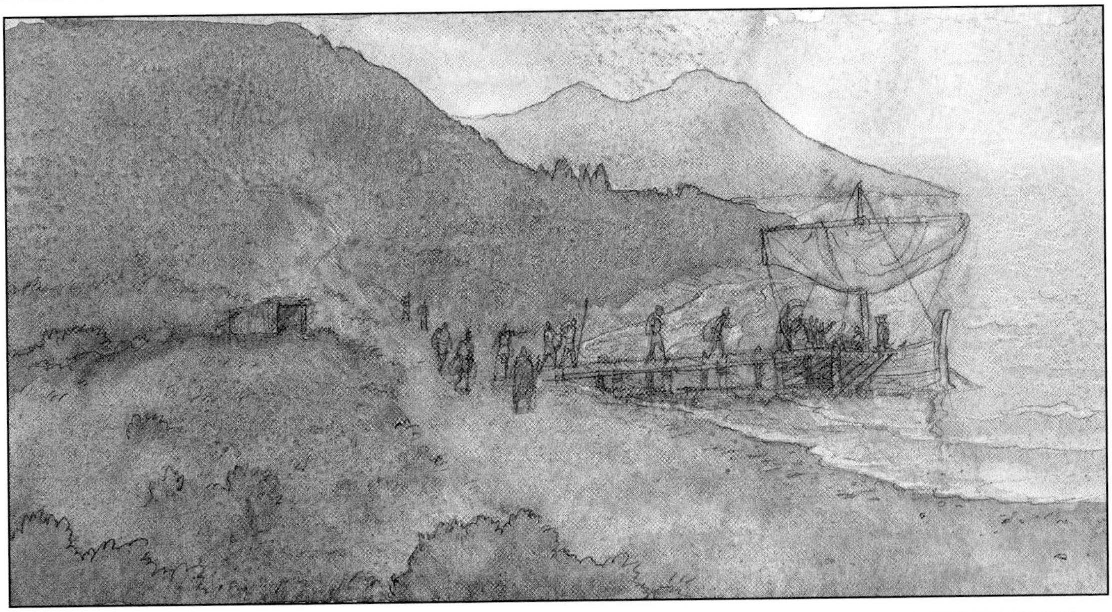
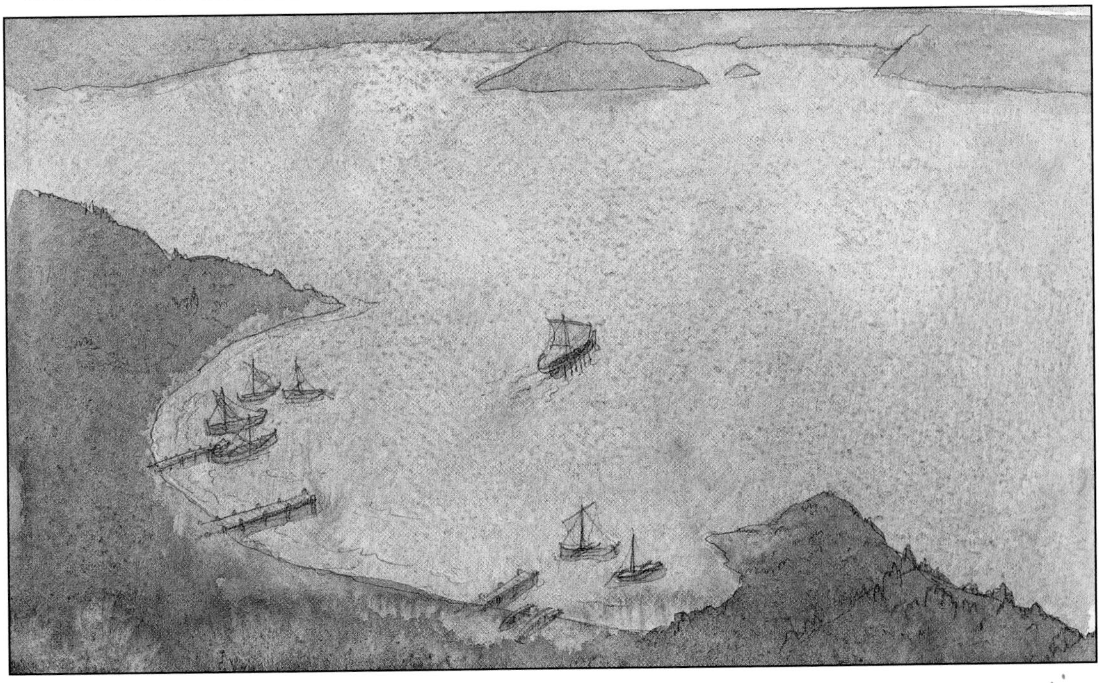

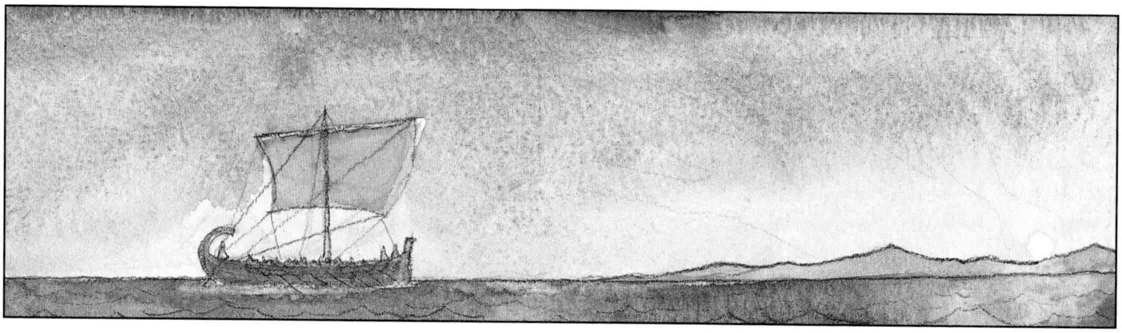

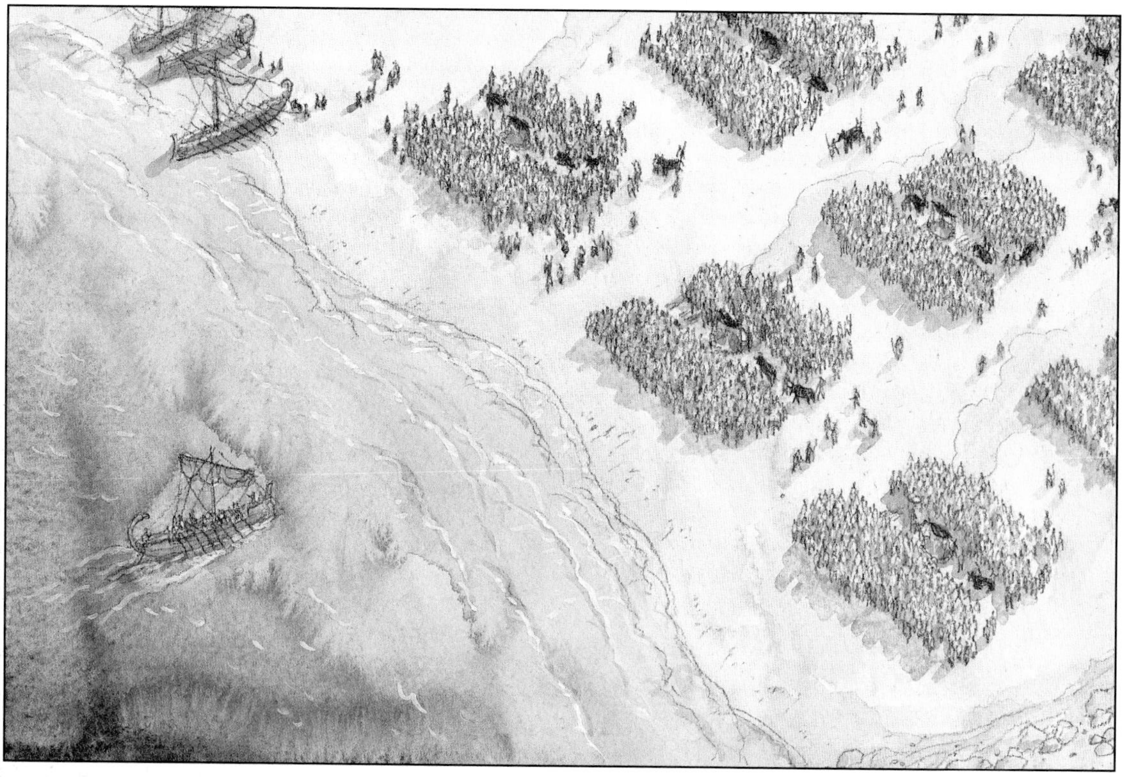

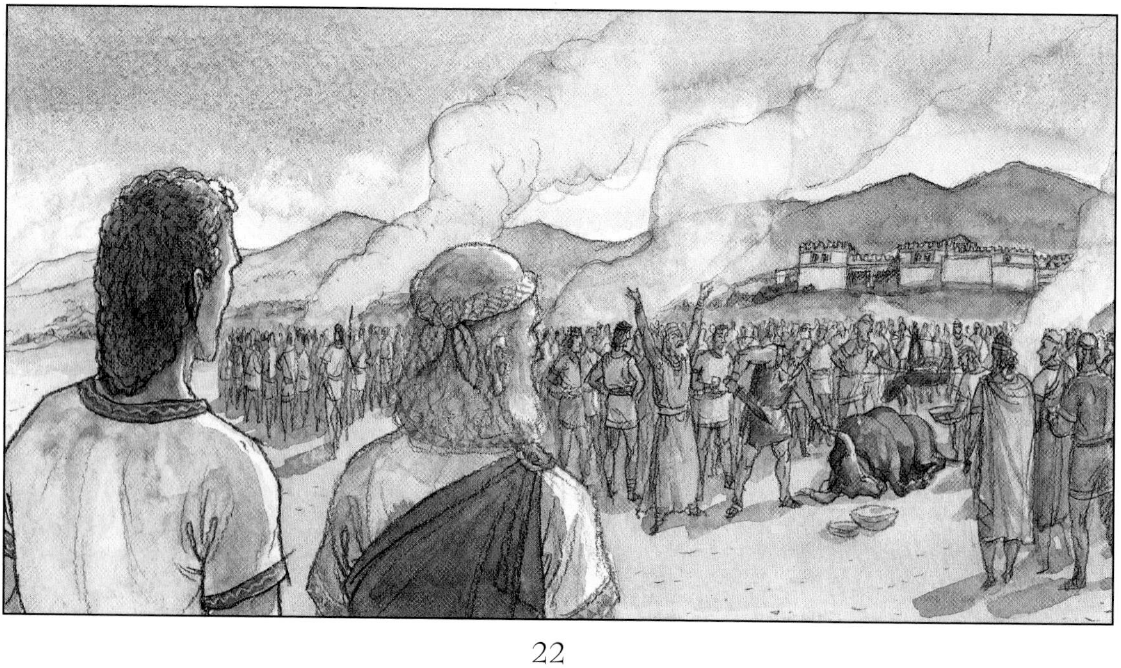

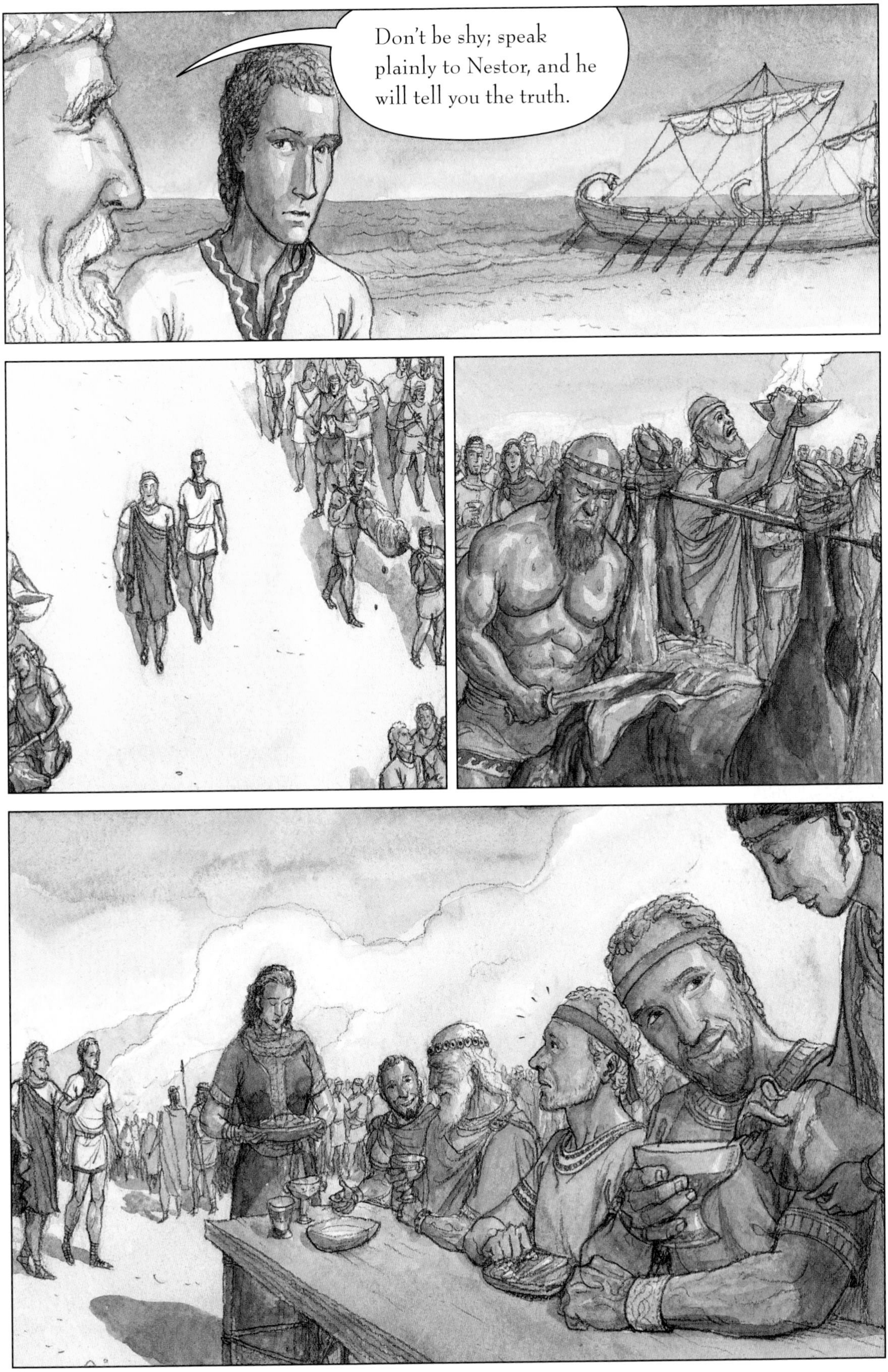
Don't be shy; speak plainly to Nestor, and he will tell you the truth.

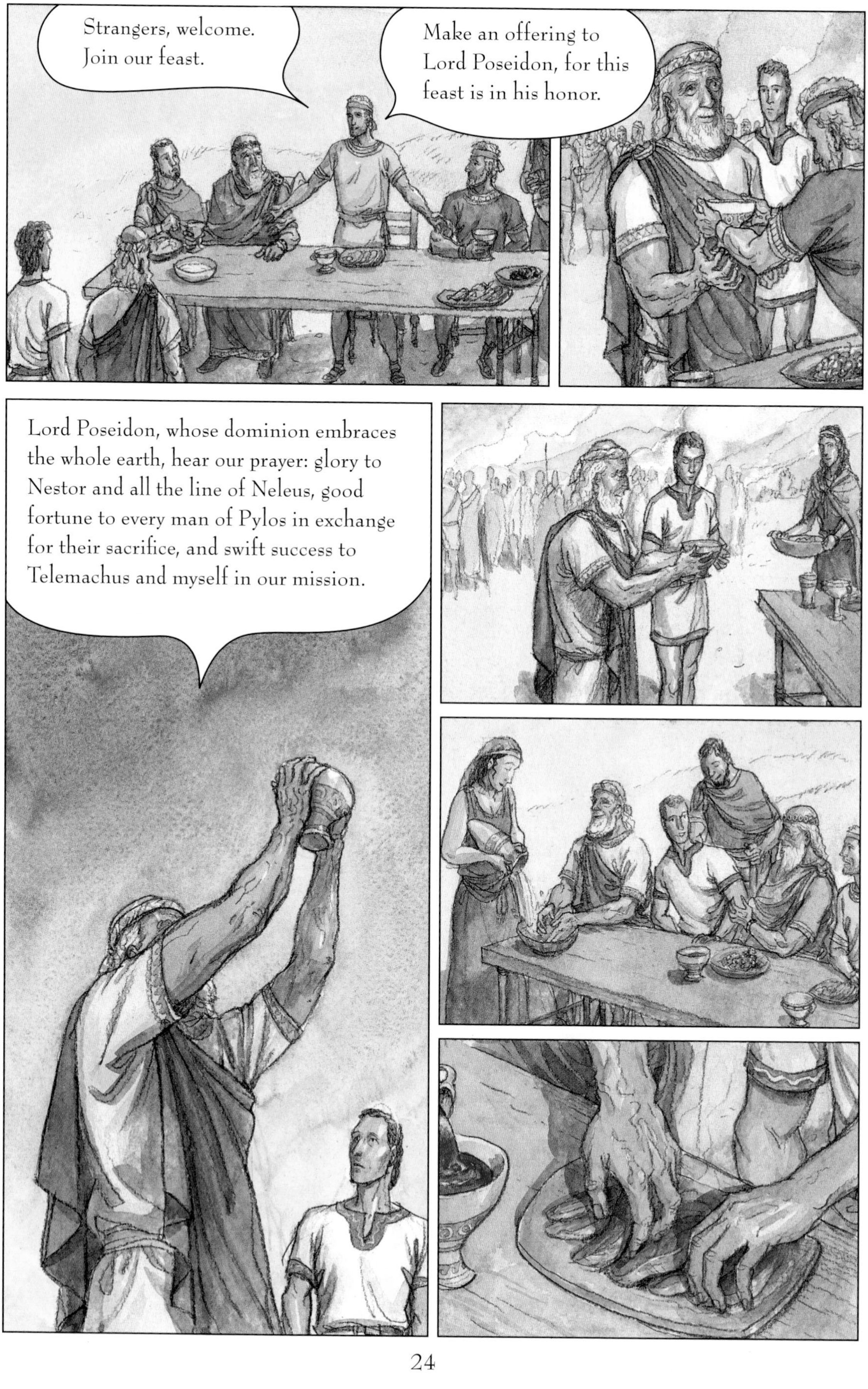
Strangers, welcome. Join our feast.
Make an offering to Lord Poseidon, for this feast is in his honor.
Lord Poseidon, whose dominion embraces the whole earth, hear our prayer: glory to Nestor and all the line of Neleus, good fortune to every man of Pylos in exchange for their sacrifice, and swift success to Telemachus and myself in our mission.

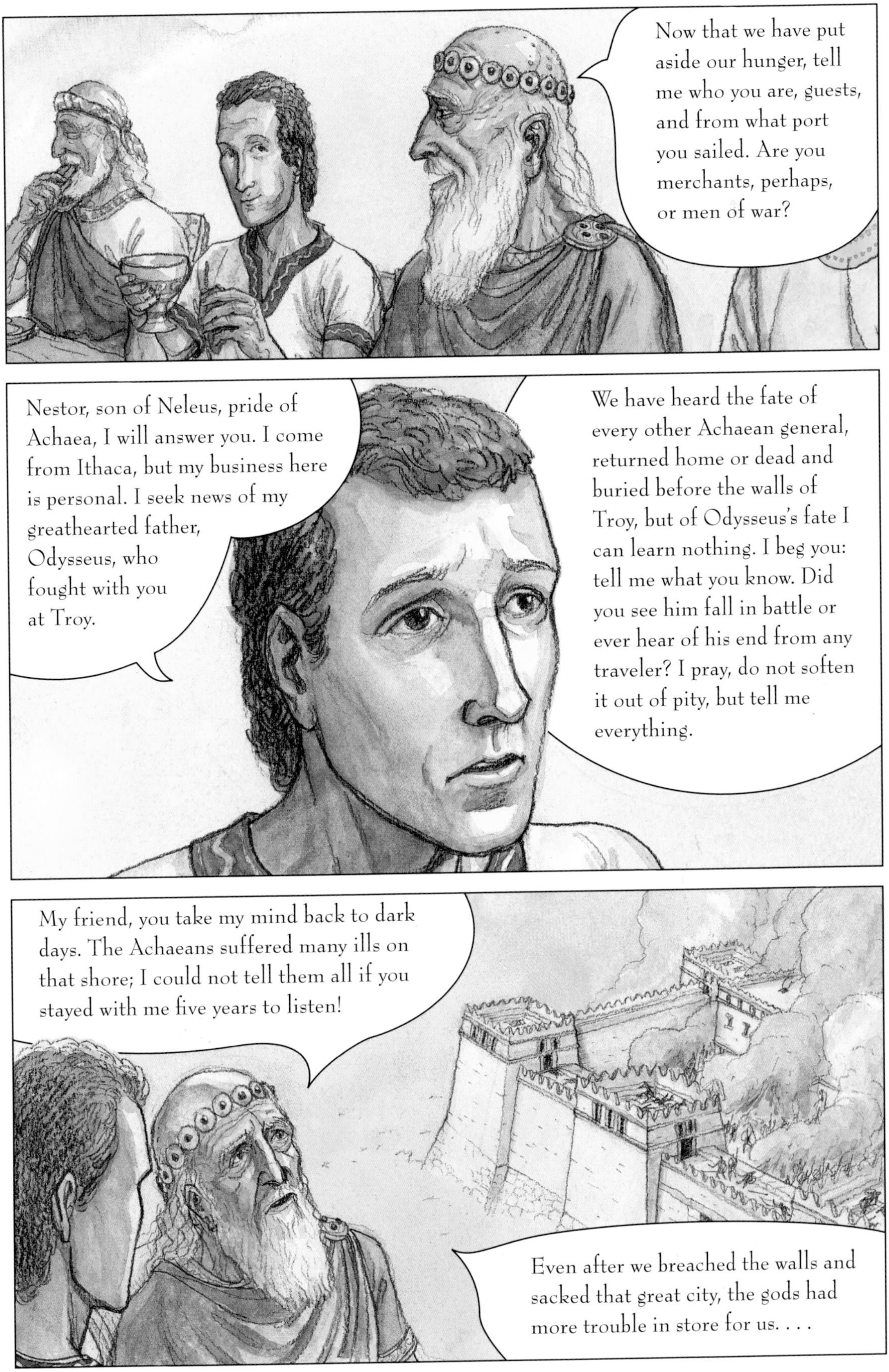
Now that we have put aside our hunger, tell me who you are, guests, and from what port you sailed. Are you merchants, perhaps, or men of war?
Nestor, son of Neleus, pride of Achaea, I will answer you. I come from Ithaca, but my business here is personal. I seek news of my greathearted father, Odysseus, who fought with you at Troy.
We have heard the fate of every other Achaean general, returned home or dead and buried before the walls of Troy, but of Odysseus's fate I can learn nothing. I beg you: tell me what you know. Did you see him fall in battle or ever hear of his end from any traveler? I pray, do not soften it out of pity, but tell me everything.
My friend, you take my mind back to dark days. The Achaeans suffered many ills on that shore; I could not tell them all if you stayed with me five years to listen!
Even after we breached the walls and sacked that great city, the gods had more trouble in store for us. . . .

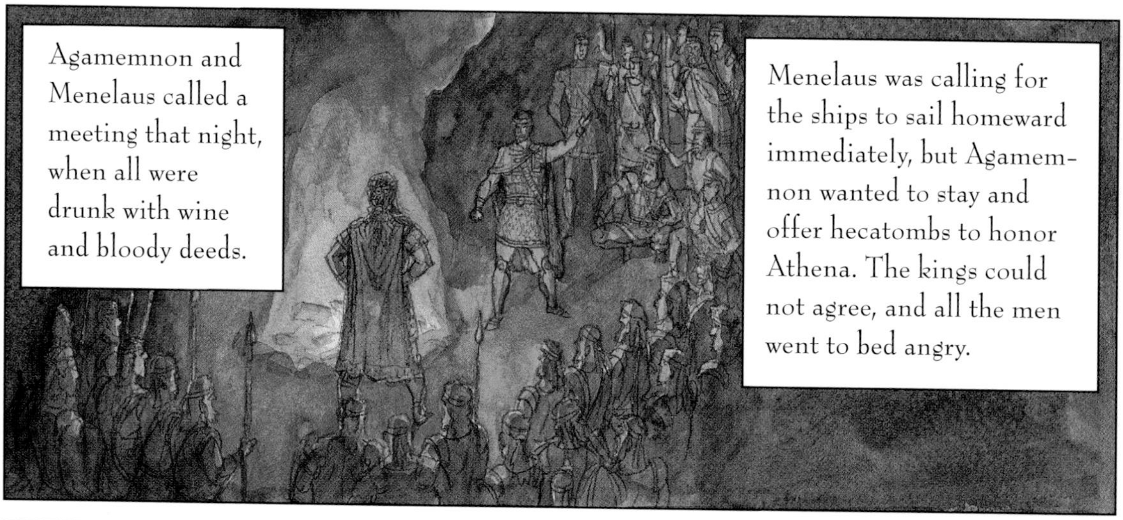
Agamemnon and Menelaus called a meeting that night, when all were drunk with wine and bloody deeds.
Menelaus was calling for the ships to sail homeward immediately, but Agamemnon wanted to stay and offer hecatombs to honor Athena. The kings could not agree, and all the men went to bed angry.

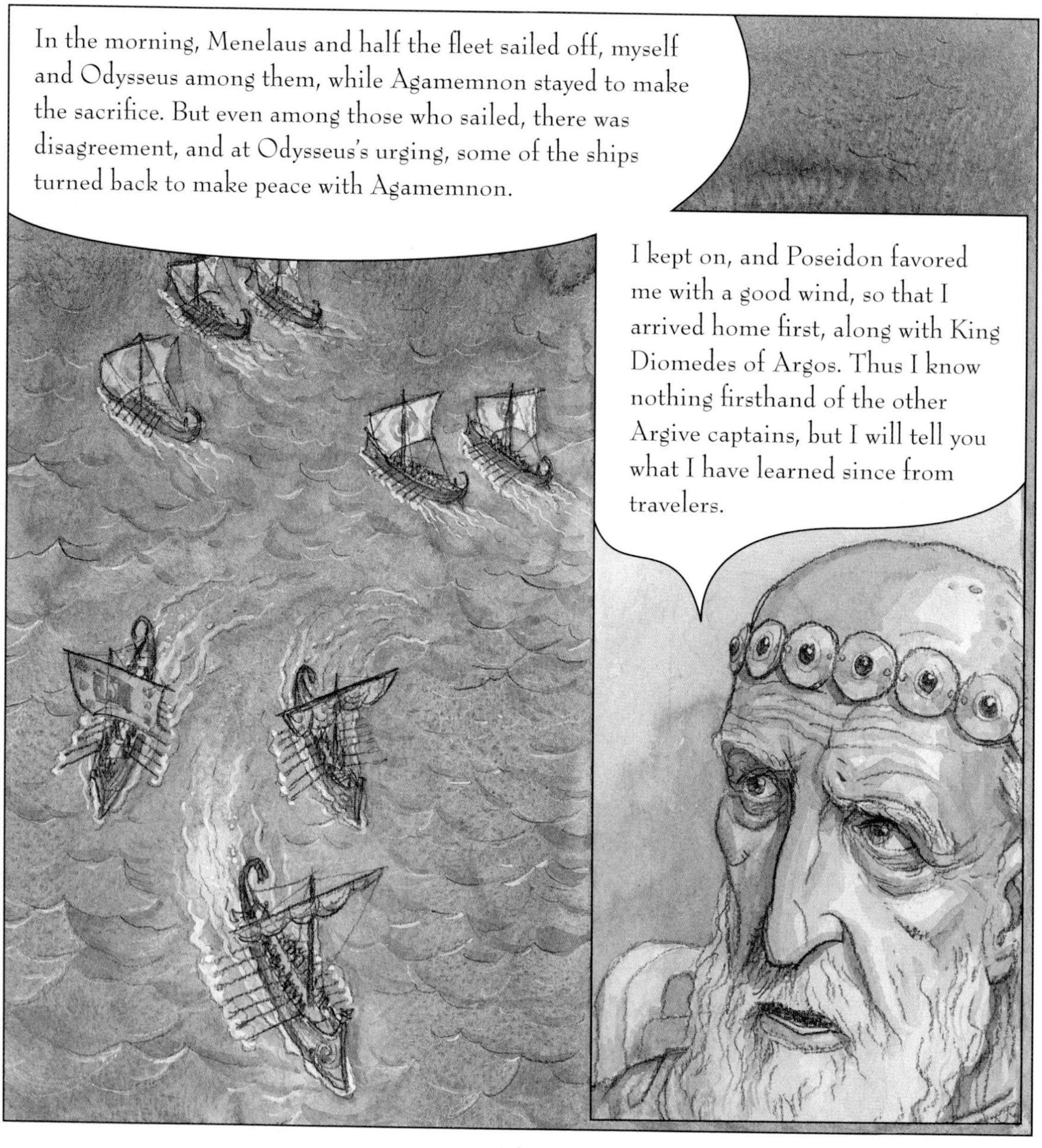
In the morning, Menelaus and half the fleet sailed off, myself and Odysseus among them, while Agamemnon stayed to make the sacrifice. But even among those who sailed, there was disagreement, and at Odysseus's urging, some of the ships turned back to make peace with Agamemnon.
I kept on, and Poseidon favored me with a good wind, so that I arrived home first, along with King Diomedes of Argos. Thus I know nothing firsthand of the other Argive captains, but I will tell you what I have learned since from travelers.

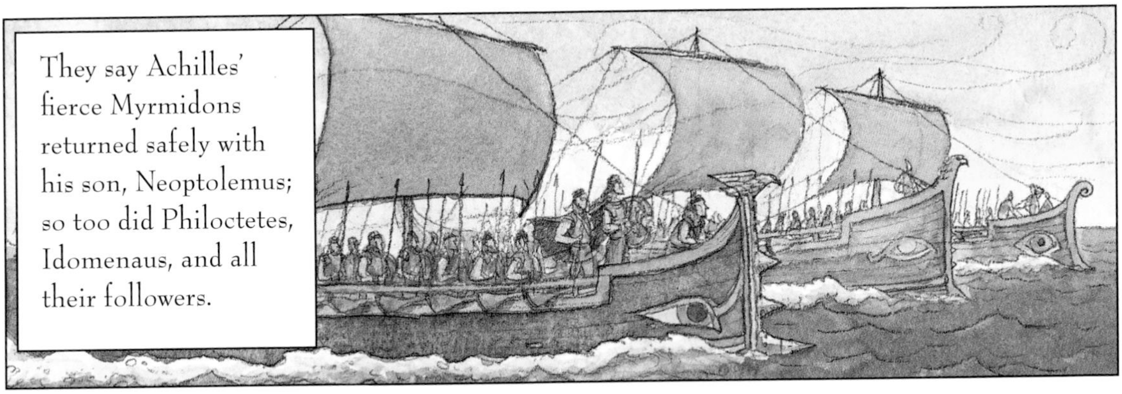
They say Achilles' fierce Myrmidons returned safely with his son, Neoptolemus; so too did Philoctetes, Idomenaus, and all their followers.

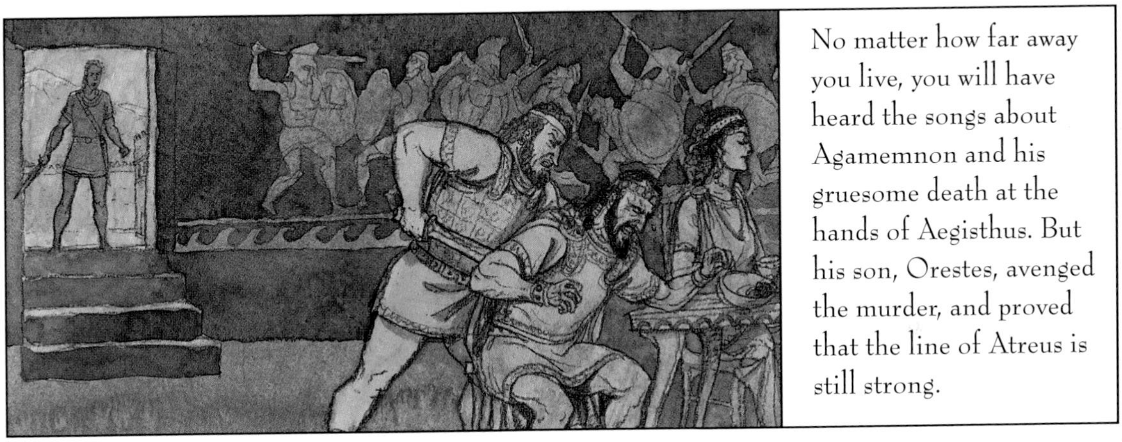
No matter how far away you live, you will have heard the songs about Agamemnon and his gruesome death at the hands of Aegisthus. But his son, Orestes, avenged the murder, and proved that the line of Atreus is still strong.

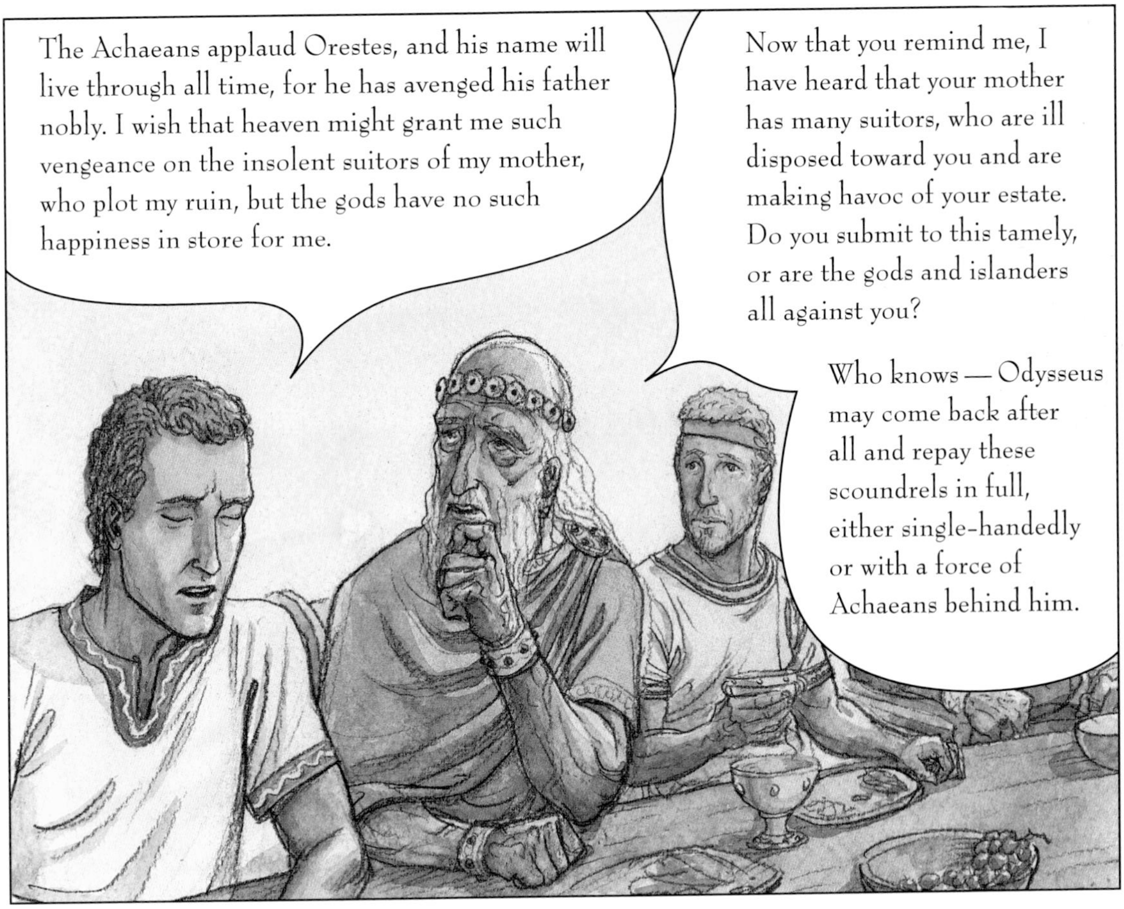
The Achaeans applaud Orestes, and his name will live through all time, for he has avenged his father nobly. I wish that heaven might grant me such vengeance on the insolent suitors of my mother, who plot my ruin, but the gods have no such happiness in store for me.
Now that you remind me, I have heard that your mother has many suitors, who are ill disposed toward you and are making havoc of your estate. Do you submit to this tamely, or are the gods and islanders all against you?
Who knows — Odysseus may come back after all and repay these scoundrels in full, either single-handedly or with a force of Achaeans behind him.

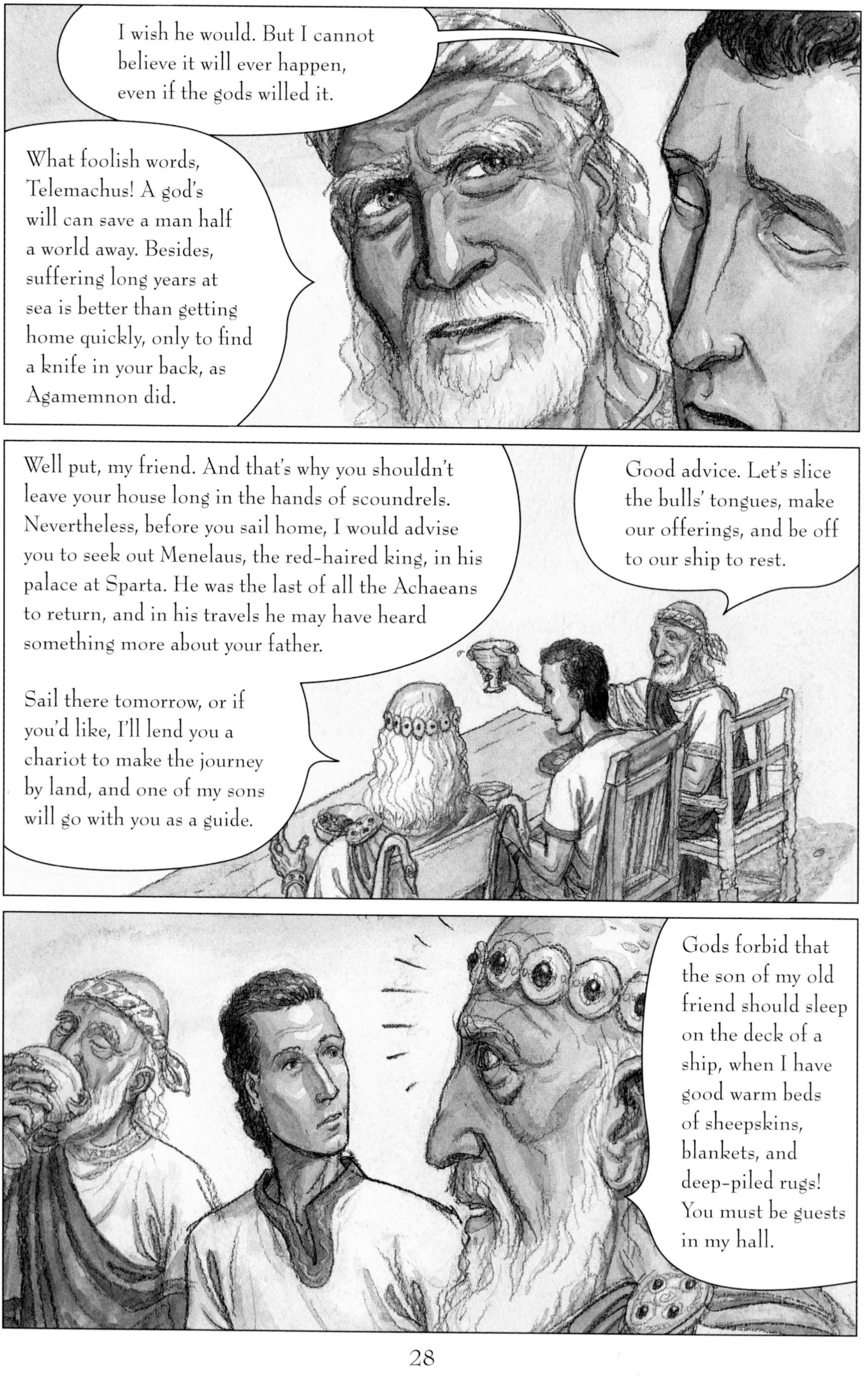
I wish he would. But I cannot believe it will ever happen, even if the gods willed it.
What foolish words, Telemachus! A god's will can save a man half a world away. Besides, suffering long years at sea is better than getting home quickly, only to find a knife in your back, as Agamemnon did.
Well put, my friend. And that's why you shouldn't leave your house long in the hands of scoundrels. Nevertheless, before you sail home, I would advise you to seek out Menelaus, the red-haired king, in his palace at Sparta. He was the last of all the Achaeans to return, and in his travels he may have heard something more about your father.
Sail there tomorrow, or if you'd like, I'll lend you a chariot to make the journey by land, and one of my sons will go with you as a guide.
Good advice. Let's slice the bulls' tongues, make our offerings, and be off to our ship to rest.
Gods forbid that the son of my old friend should sleep on the deck of a ship, when I have good warm beds of sheepskins, blankets, and deep-piled rugs! You must be guests in my hall.

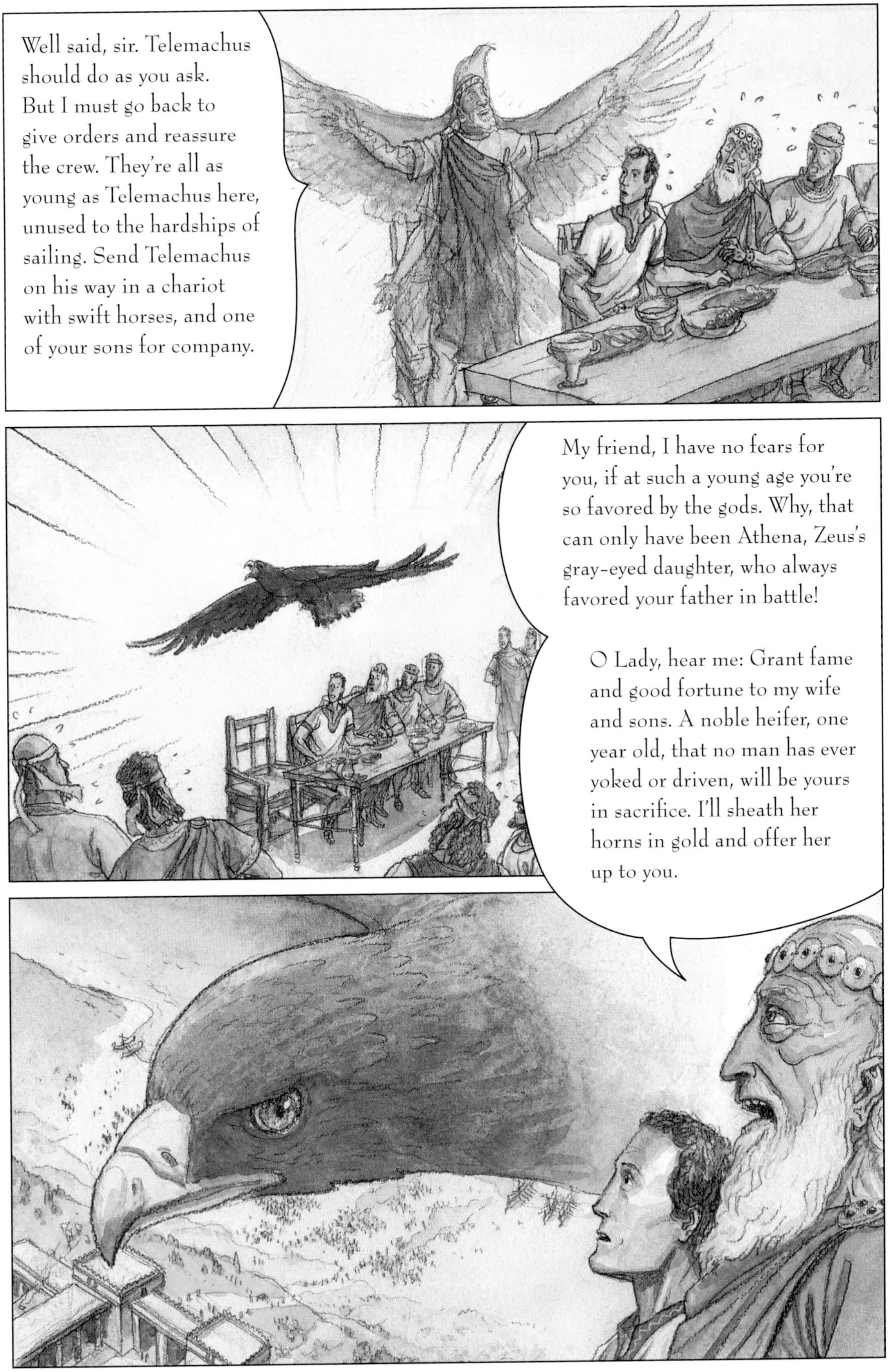
Well said, sir. Telemachus should do as you ask. But I must go back to give orders and reassure the crew. They're all as young as Telemachus here, unused to the hardships of sailing. Send Telemachus on his way in a chariot with swift horses, and one of your sons for company.
My friend, I have no fears for you, if at such a young age you're so favored by the gods. Why, that can only have been Athena, Zeus's gray-eyed daughter, who always favored your father in battle!
O Lady, hear me: Grant fame and good fortune to my wife and sons. A noble heifer, one year old, that no man has ever yoked or driven, will be yours in sacrifice. I'll sheath her horns in gold and offer her up to you.

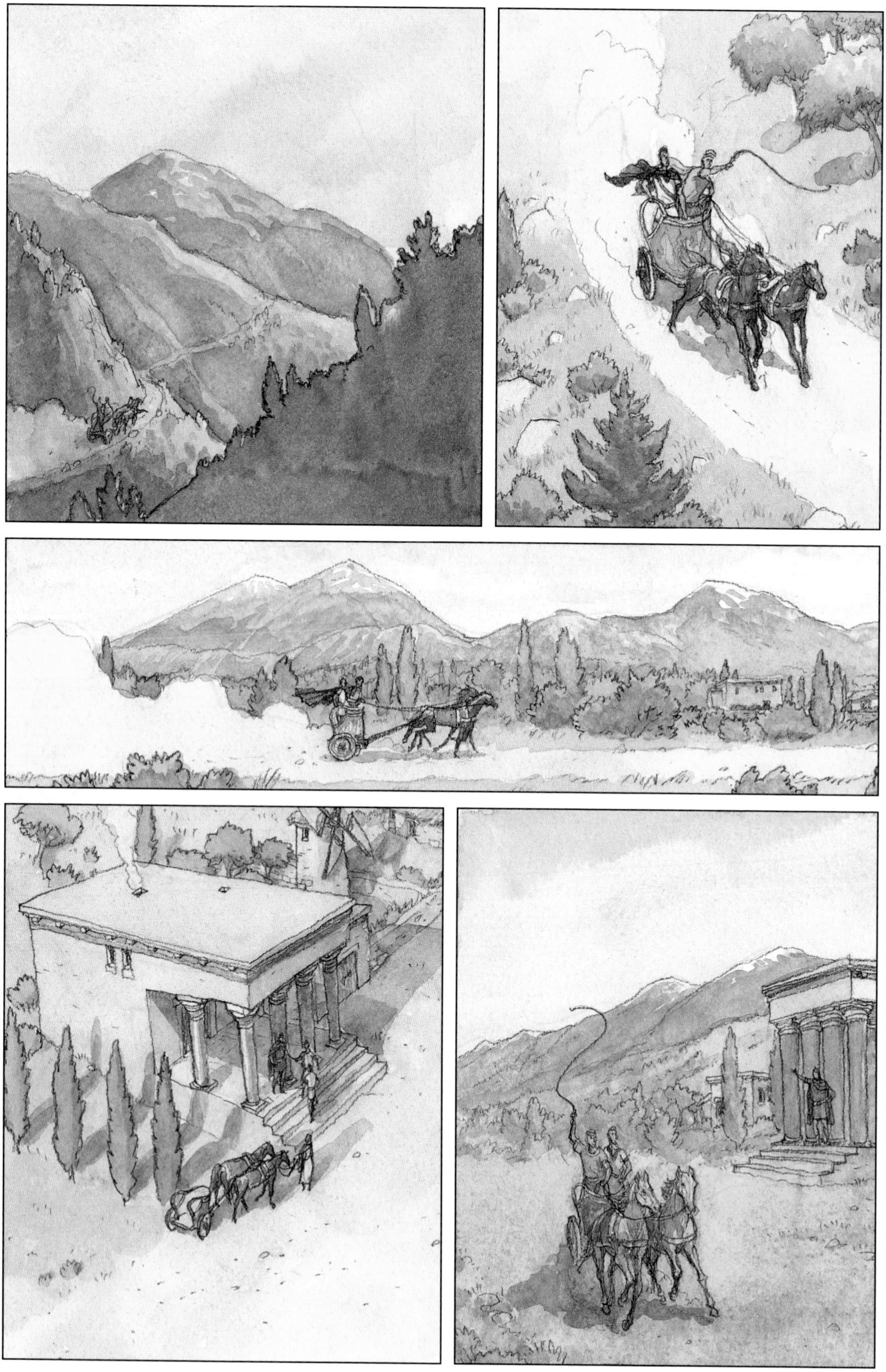

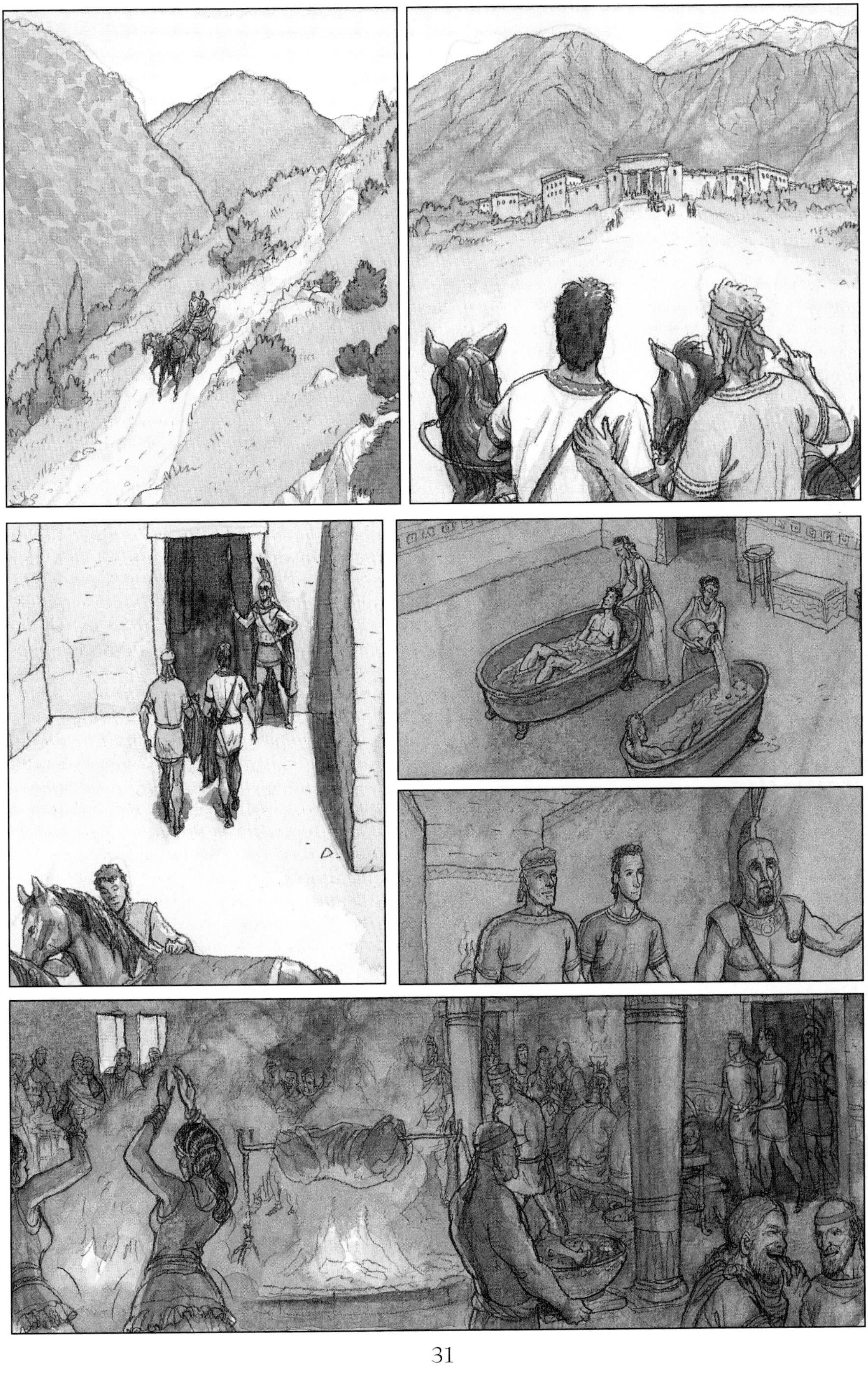

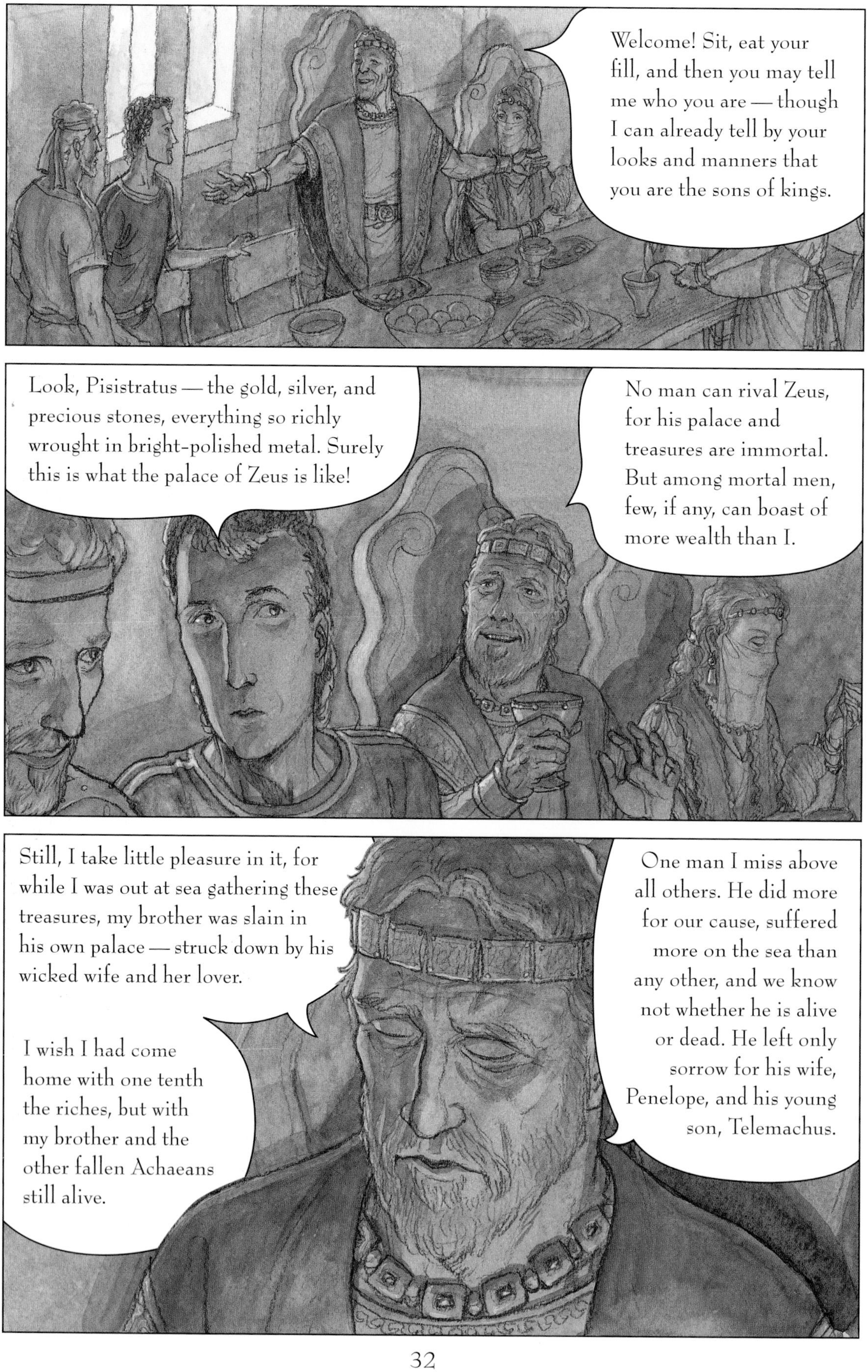
Welcome! Sit, eat your fill, and then you may tell me who you are — though I can already tell by your looks and manners that you are the sons of kings.
Look, Pisistratus — the gold, silver, and precious stones, everything so richly wrought in bright-polished metal. Surely this is what the palace of Zeus is like!
No man can rival Zeus, for his palace and treasures are immortal. But among mortal men, few, if any, can boast of more wealth than I.
Still, I take little pleasure in it, for while I was out at sea gathering these treasures, my brother was slain in his own palace — struck down by his wicked wife and her lover.
I wish I had come home with one tenth the riches, but with my brother and the other fallen Achaeans still alive.
One man I miss above all others. He did more for our cause, suffered more on the sea than any other, and we know not whether he is alive or dead. He left only sorrow for his wife, Penelope, and his young son, Telemachus.

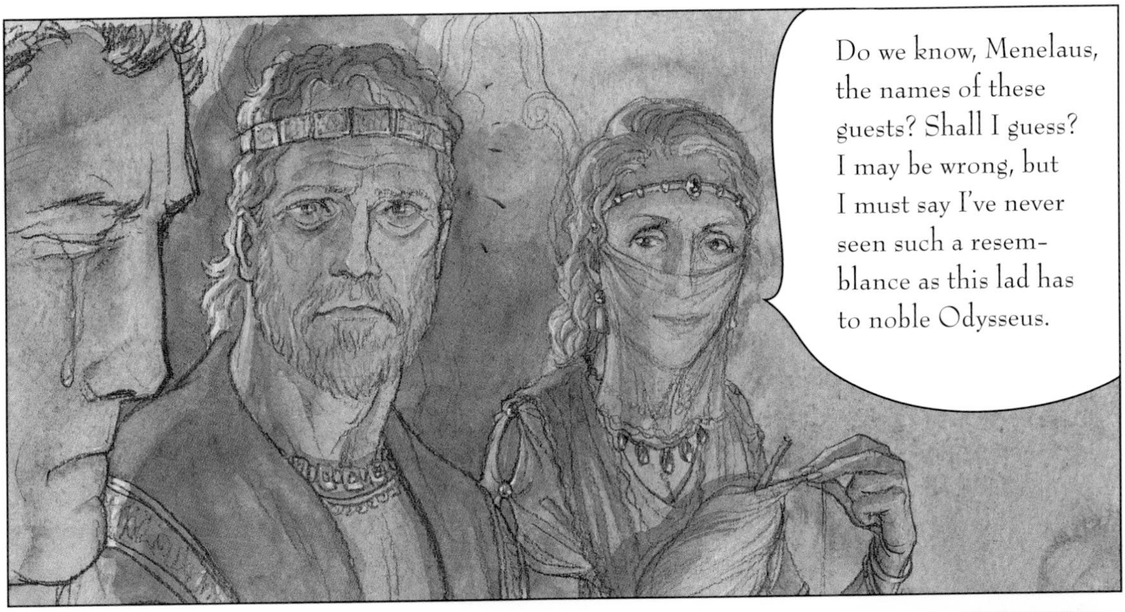
Do we know, Menelaus, the names of these guests? Shall I guess? I may be wrong, but I must say I've never seen such a resemblance as this lad has to noble Odysseus.

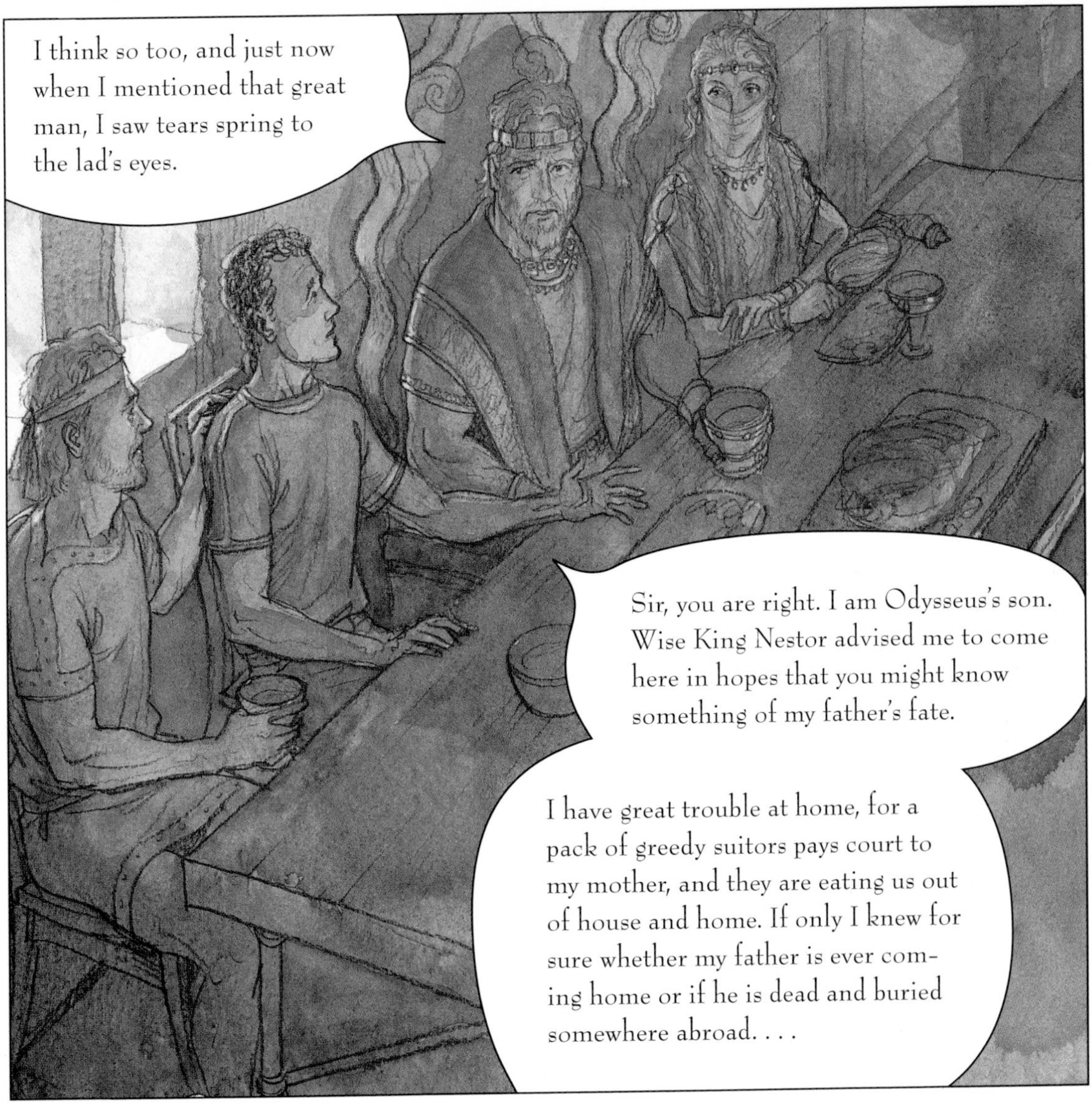
I think so too, and just now when I mentioned that great man, I saw tears spring to the lad's eyes.
Sir, you are right. I am Odysseus's son. Wise King Nestor advised me to come here in hopes that you might know something of my father's fate.
I have great trouble at home, for a pack of greedy suitors pays court to my mother, and they are eating us out of house and home. If only I knew for sure whether my father is ever coming home or if he is dead and buried somewhere abroad. . . .

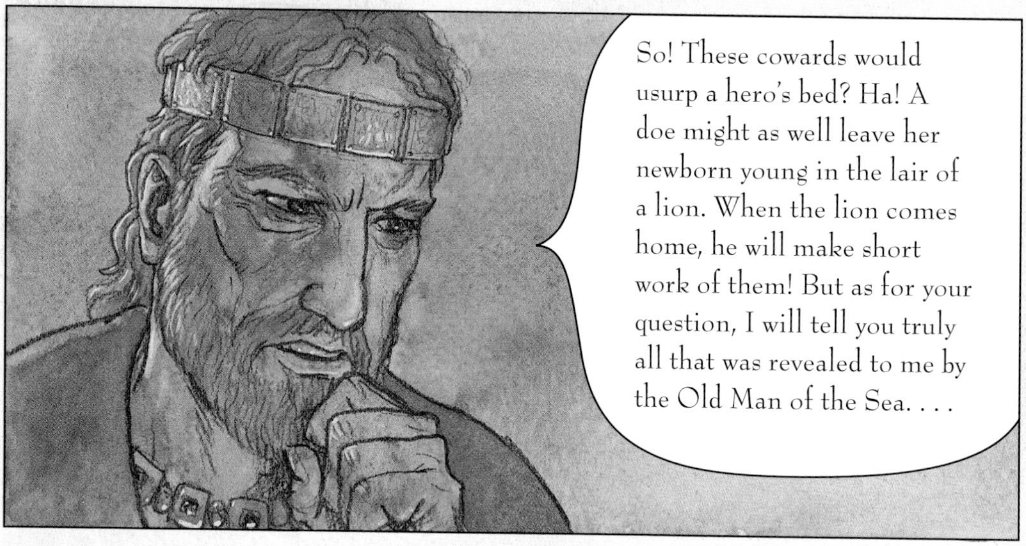
So! These cowards would usurp a hero's bed? Ha! A doe might as well leave her newborn young in the lair of a lion. When the lion comes home, he will make short work of them! But as for your question, I will tell you truly all that was revealed to me by the Old Man of the Sea. . . .

I was returning from Troy by way of Egypt, and I stopped to make a sacrifice to the gods. But my hecatombs must not have satisfied them, for one day out from Egypt, we were becalmed upon the island of Pharos. For twenty days, not a breeze stirred, and our provisions were soon exhausted. The men would take hooks and spread out on the shore in hope of catching fish, while I sat alone on a rocky outcrop. Then a strange woman approached me.

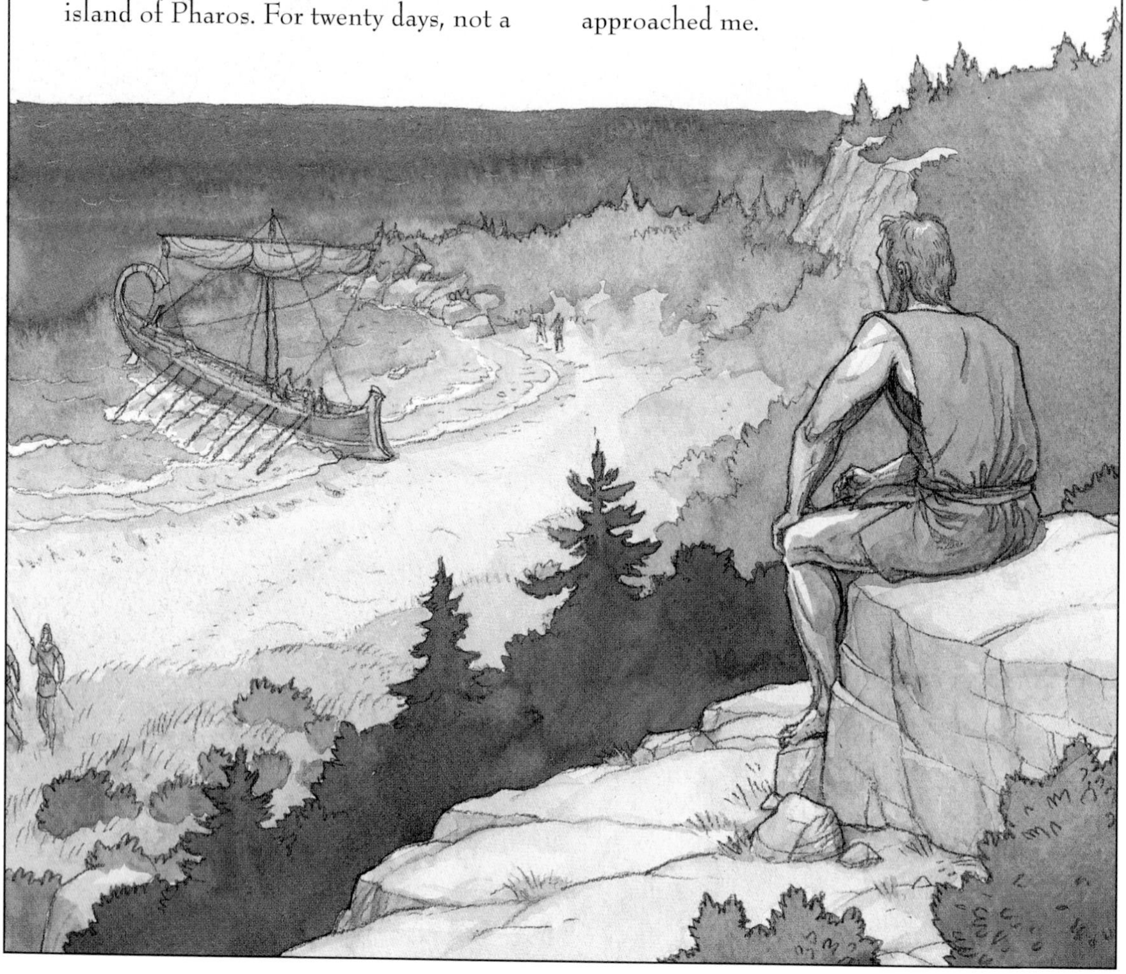

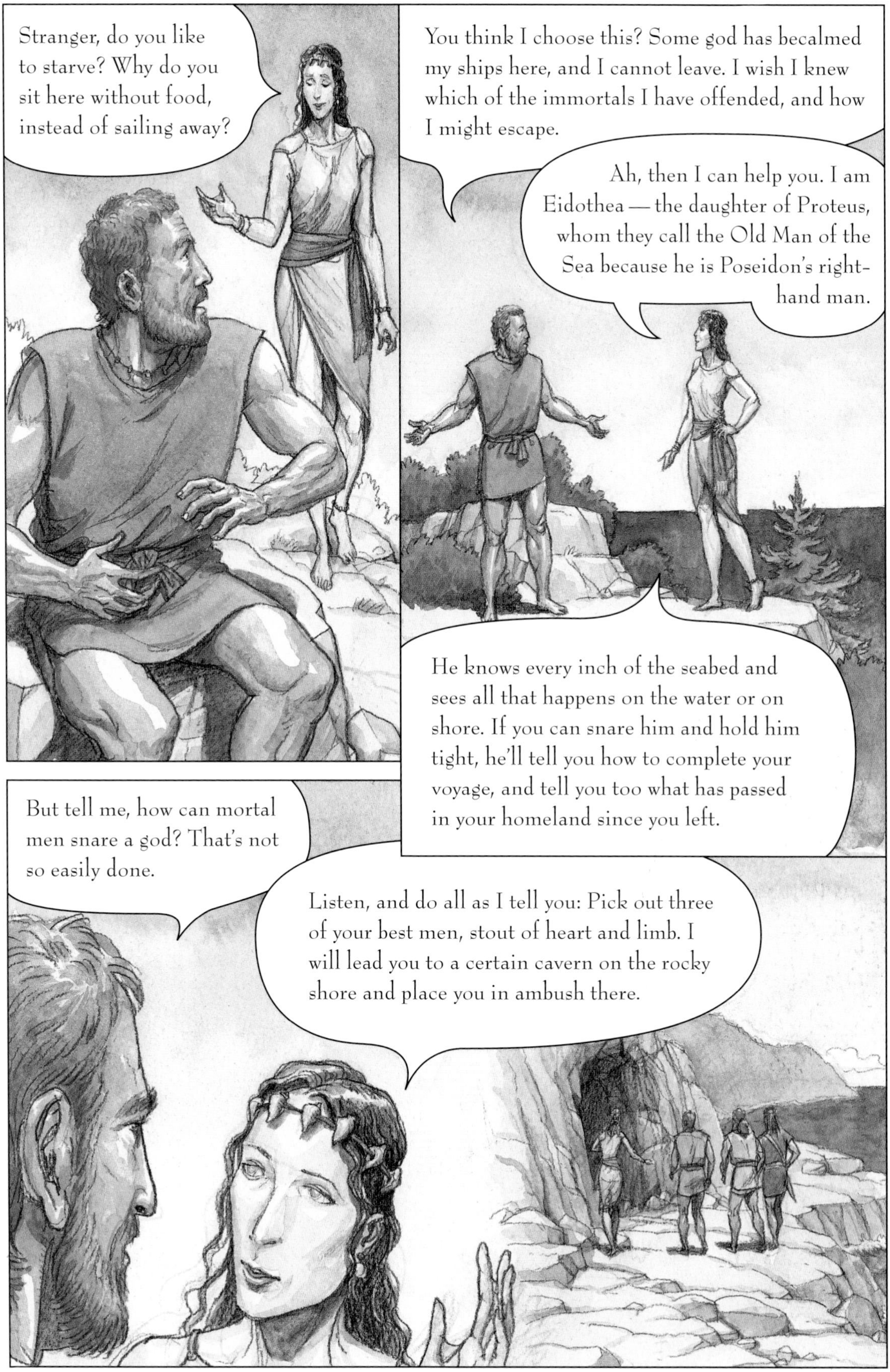
Stranger, do you like to starve? Why do you sit here without food, instead of sailing away?
You think I choose this? Some god has becalmed my ships here, and I cannot leave. I wish I knew which of the immortals I have offended, and how I might escape.
Ah, then I can help you. I am Eidothea — the daughter of Proteus, whom they call the Old Man of the Sea because he is Poseidon's right-hand man.
He knows every inch of the seabed and sees all that happens on the water or on shore. If you can snare him and hold him tight, he'll tell you how to complete your voyage, and tell you too what has passed in your homeland since you left.
But tell me, how can mortal men snare a god? That's not so easily done.
Listen, and do all as I tell you: Pick out three of your best men, stout of heart and limb. I will lead you to a certain cavern on the rocky shore and place you in ambush there.

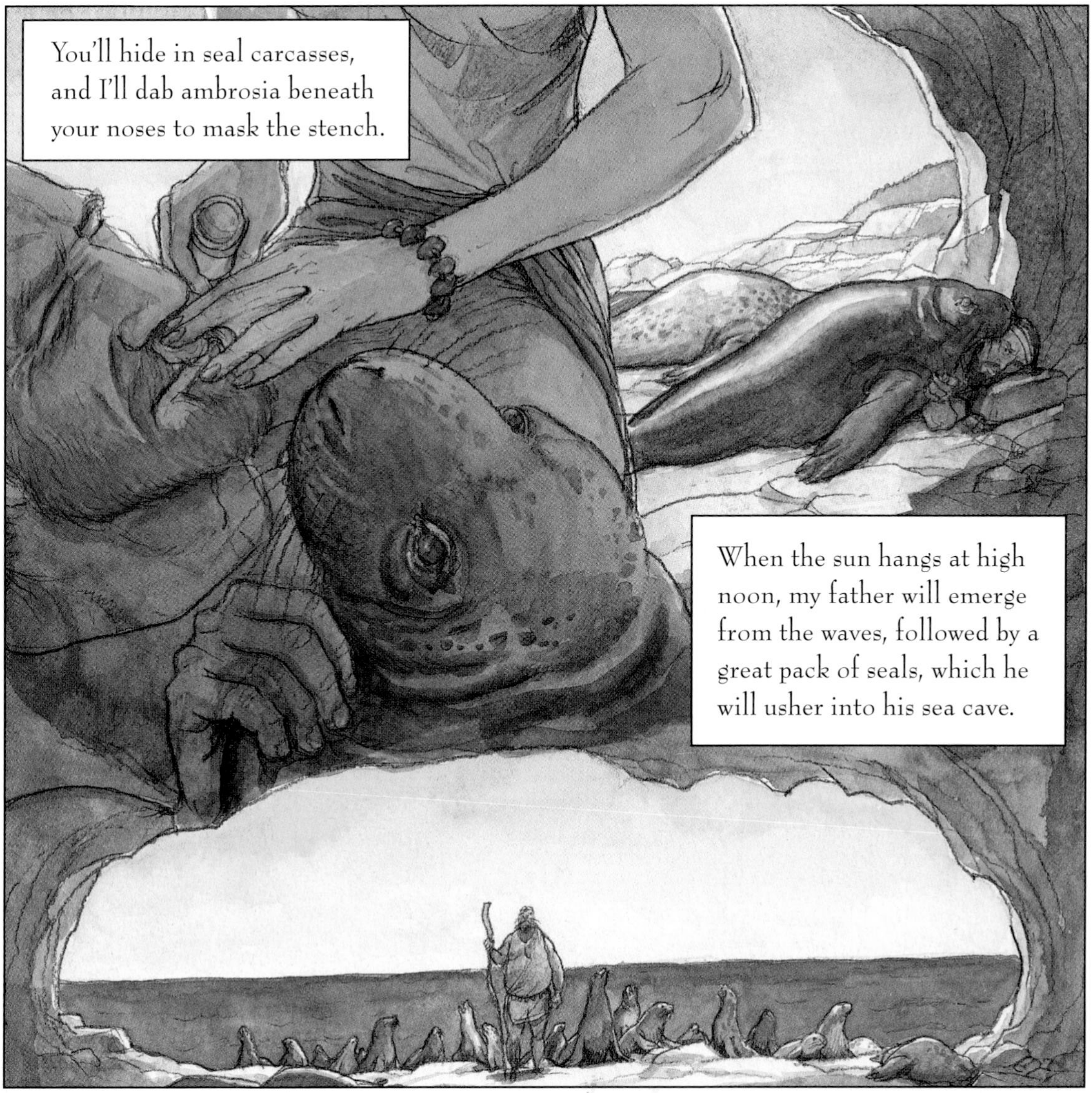
You'll hide in seal carcasses, and I'll dab ambrosia beneath your noses to mask the stench.
When the sun hangs at high noon, my father will emerge from the waves, followed by a great pack of seals, which he will usher into his sea cave.

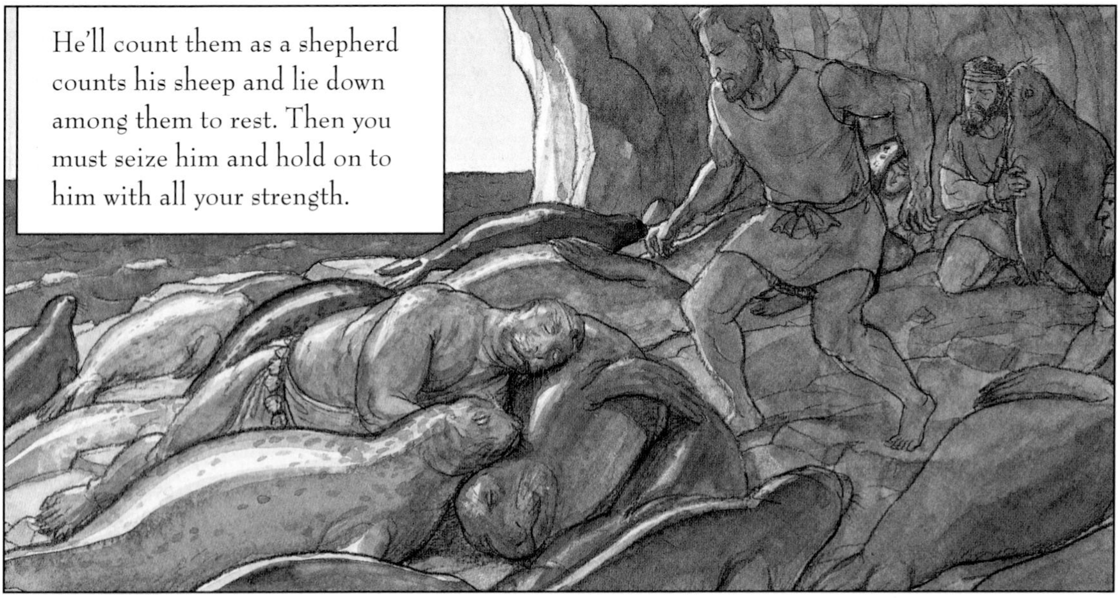
He'll count them as a shepherd counts his sheep and lie down among them to rest. Then you must seize him and hold on to him with all your strength.

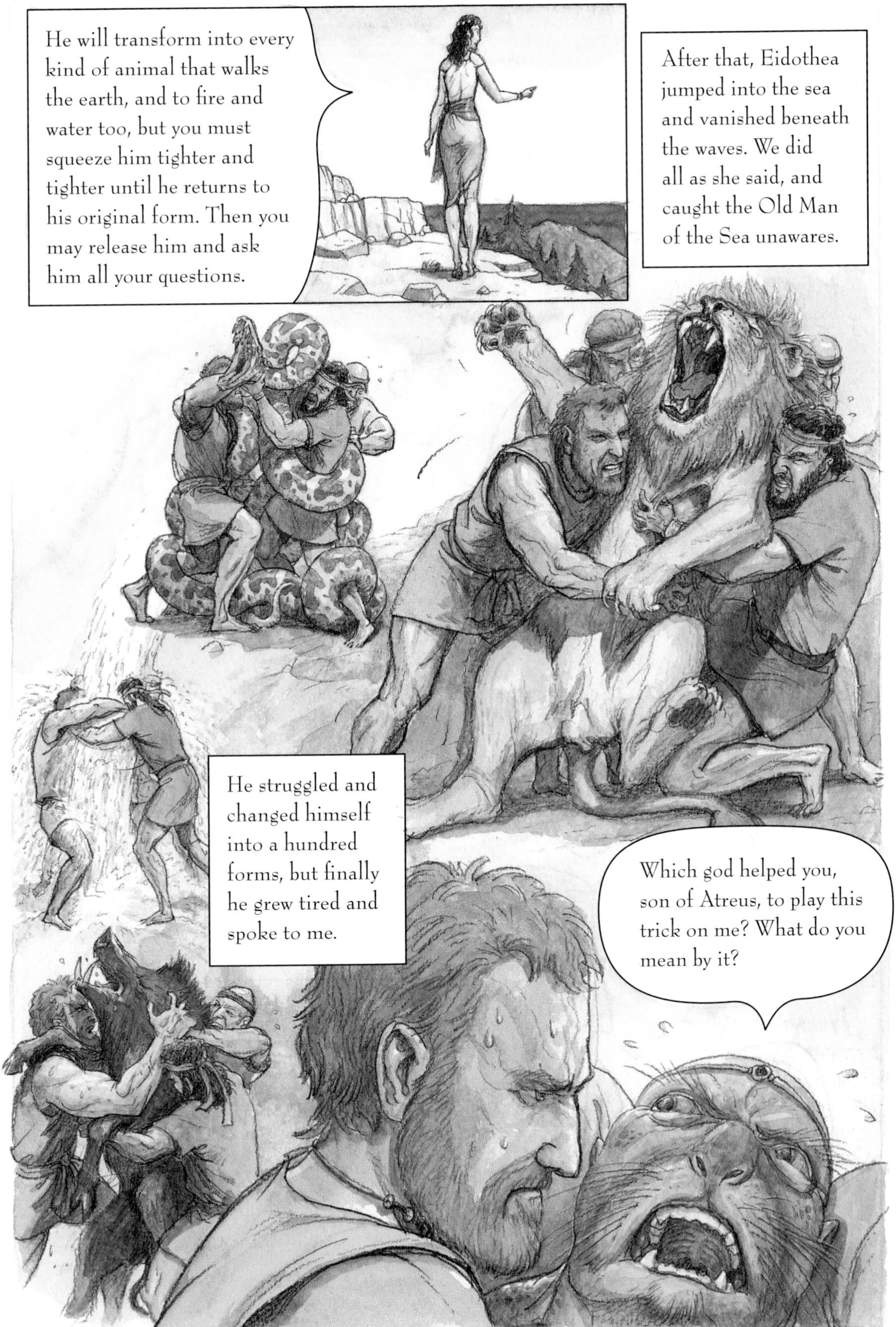
He will transform into every kind of animal that walks the earth, and to fire and water too, but you must squeeze him tighter and tighter until he returns to his original form. Then you may release him and ask him all your questions.
After that, Eidothea jumped into the sea and vanished beneath the waves. We did all as she said, and caught the Old Man of the Sea unawares.
He struggled and changed himself into a hundred forms, but finally he grew tired and spoke to me.
Which god helped you, son of Atreus, to play this trick on me? What do you mean by it?

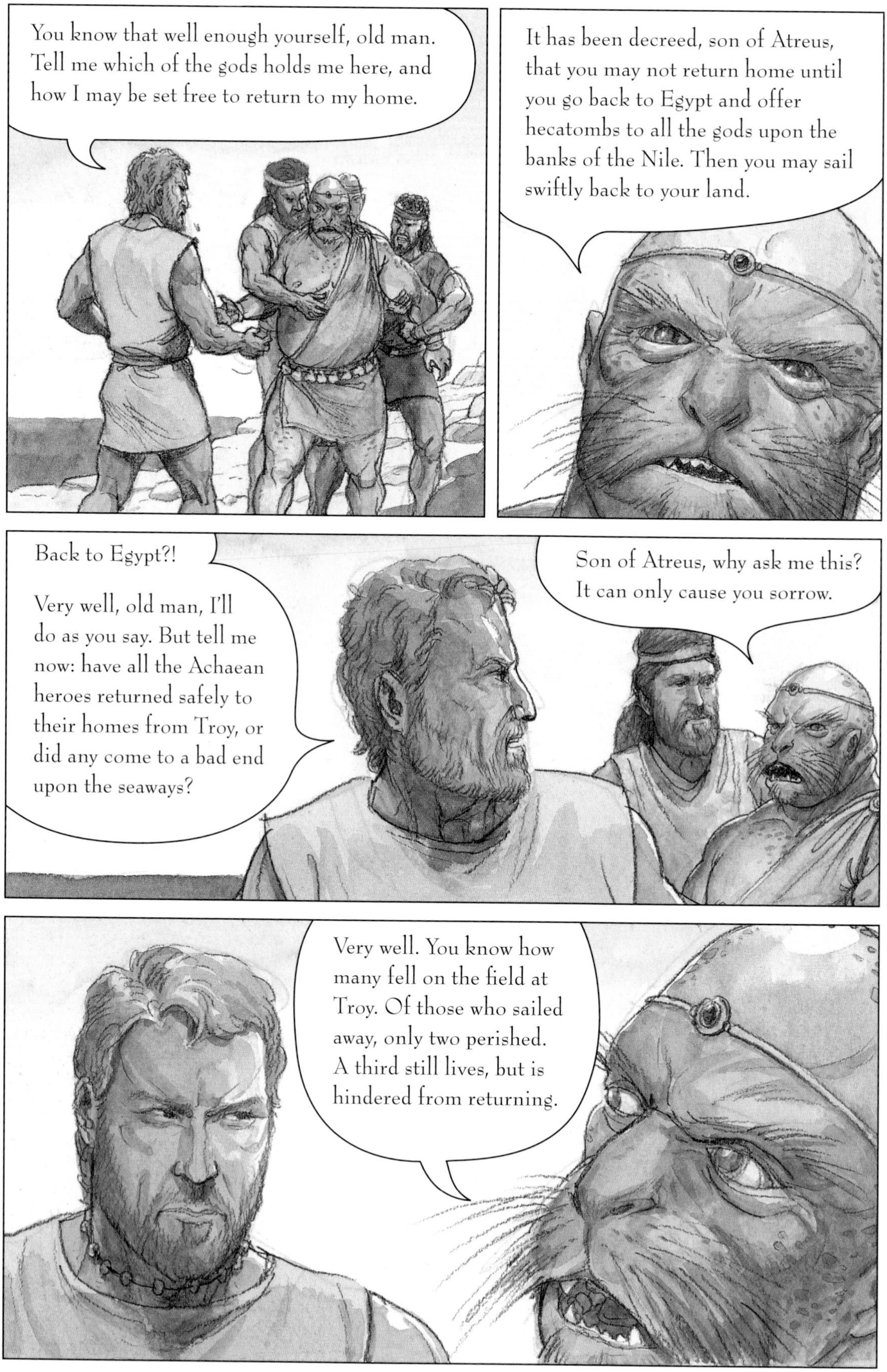
You know that well enough yourself, old man. Tell me which of the gods holds me here, and how I may be set free to return to my home.
It has been decreed, son of Atreus, that you may not return home until you go back to Egypt and offer hecatombs to all the gods upon the banks of the Nile. Then you may sail swiftly back to your land.
Back to Egypt?!
Very well, old man, I'll do as you say. But tell me now: have all the Achaean heroes returned safely to their homes from Troy, or did any come to a bad end upon the seaways?
Son of Atreus, why ask me this? It can only cause you sorrow.
Very well. You know how many fell on the field at Troy. Of those who sailed away, only two perished. A third still lives, but is hindered from returning.

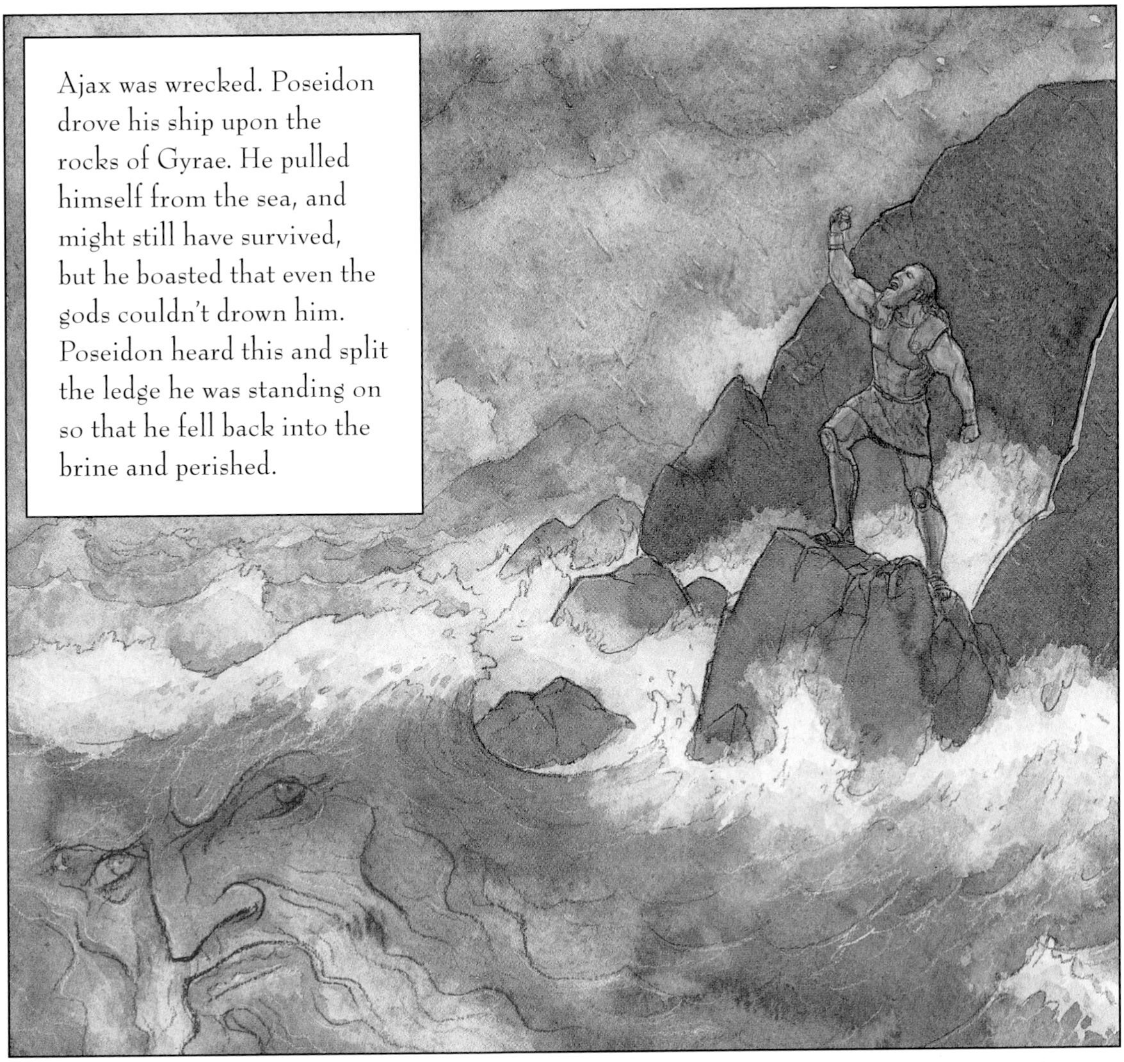
Ajax was wrecked. Poseidon drove his ship upon the rocks of Gyrae. He pulled himself from the sea, and might still have survived, but he boasted that even the gods couldn't drown him. Poseidon heard this and split the ledge he was standing on so that he fell back into the brine and perished.

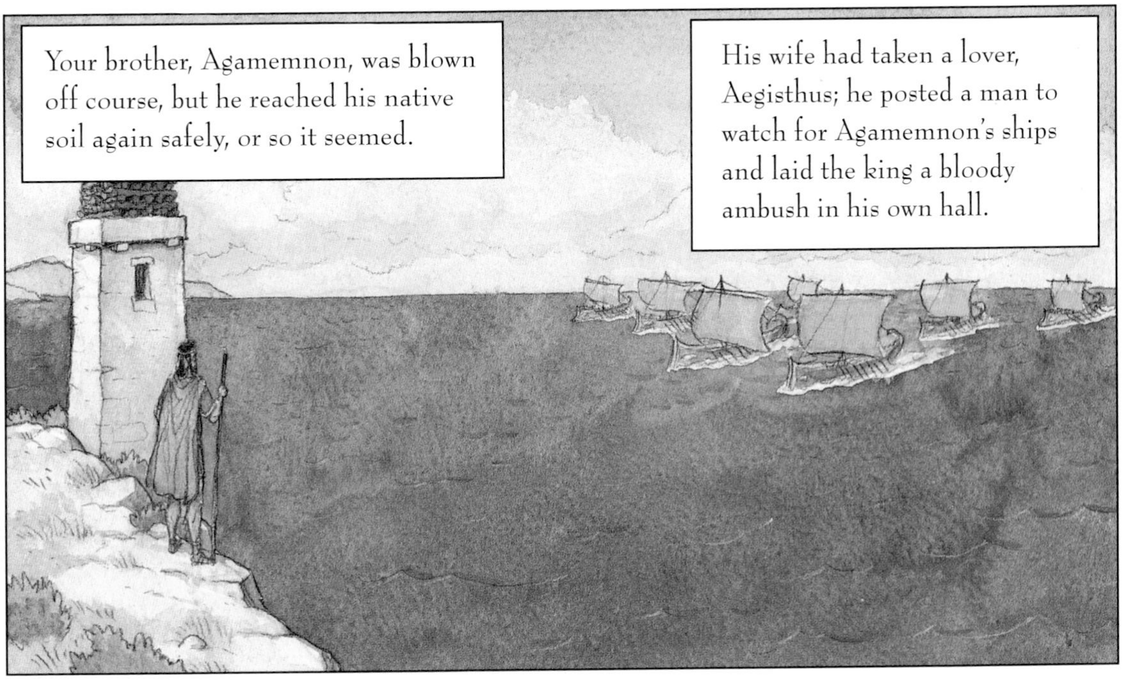
Your brother, Agamemnon, was blown off course, but he reached his native soil again safely, or so it seemed.
His wife had taken a lover, Aegisthus; he posted a man to watch for Agamemnon's ships and laid the king a bloody ambush in his own hall.

In the midst of the welcome feast, Aegisthus's men sprang out and slaughtered your brother and his men. They fought well, but all went down to death.

Take comfort, for your nephew Orestes took revenge and killed Aegisthus. If you sail quickly, you may arrive in time for the funeral.

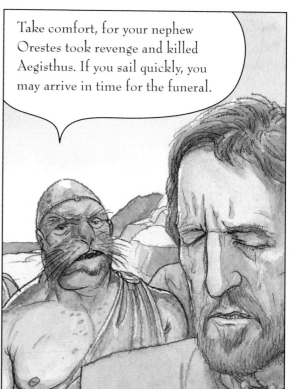

Tell me about the last man, the one who is still at sea.

The third man is Odysseus of Ithaca. I have seen him on an island, deep in sorrow, trapped in the caves of the nymph Calypso. She keeps him there for her pleasure, and he has no means of escape, no ship or crew to take him home.

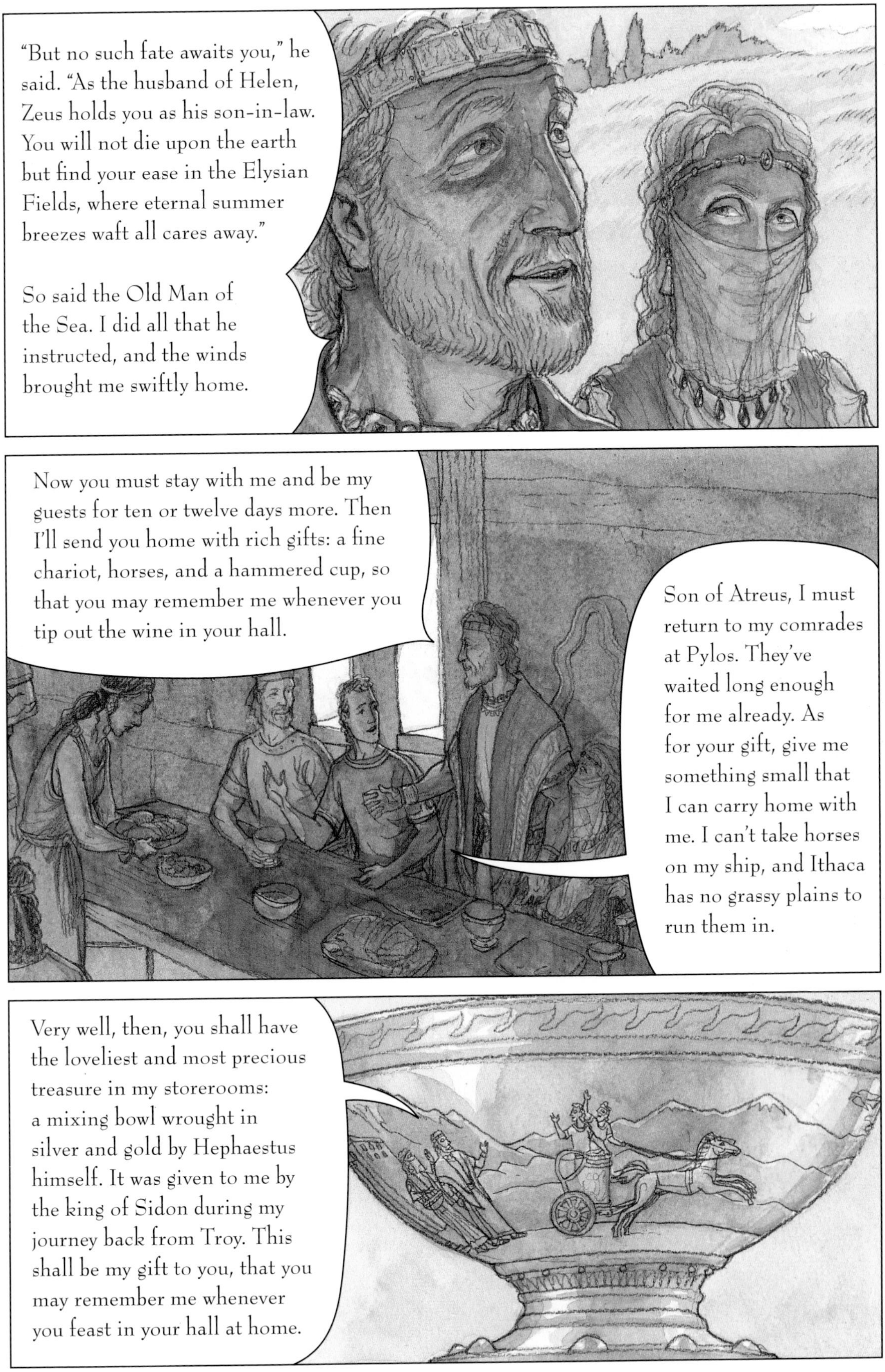
"But no such fate awaits you," he said. "As the husband of Helen, Zeus holds you as his son-in-law. You will not die upon the earth but find your ease in the Elysian Fields, where eternal summer breezes waft all cares away."
So said the Old Man of the Sea. I did all that he instructed, and the winds brought me swiftly home.
Now you must stay with me and be my guests for ten or twelve days more. Then I'll send you home with rich gifts: a fine chariot, horses, and a hammered cup, so that you may remember me whenever you tip out the wine in your hall.
Son of Atreus, I must return to my comrades at Pylos. They've waited long enough for me already. As for your gift, give me something small that I can carry home with me. I can't take horses on my ship, and Ithaca has no grassy plains to run them in.
Very well, then, you shall have the loveliest and most precious treasure in my storerooms: a mixing bowl wrought in silver and gold by Hephaestus himself. It was given to me by the king of Sidon during my journey back from Troy. This shall be my gift to you, that you may remember me whenever you feast in your hall at home.

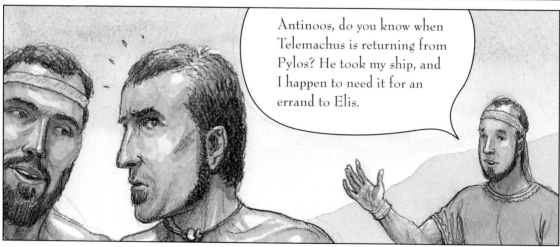

Antinoos, do you know when Telemachus is returning from Pylos? He took my ship, and I happen to need it for an errand to Elis.

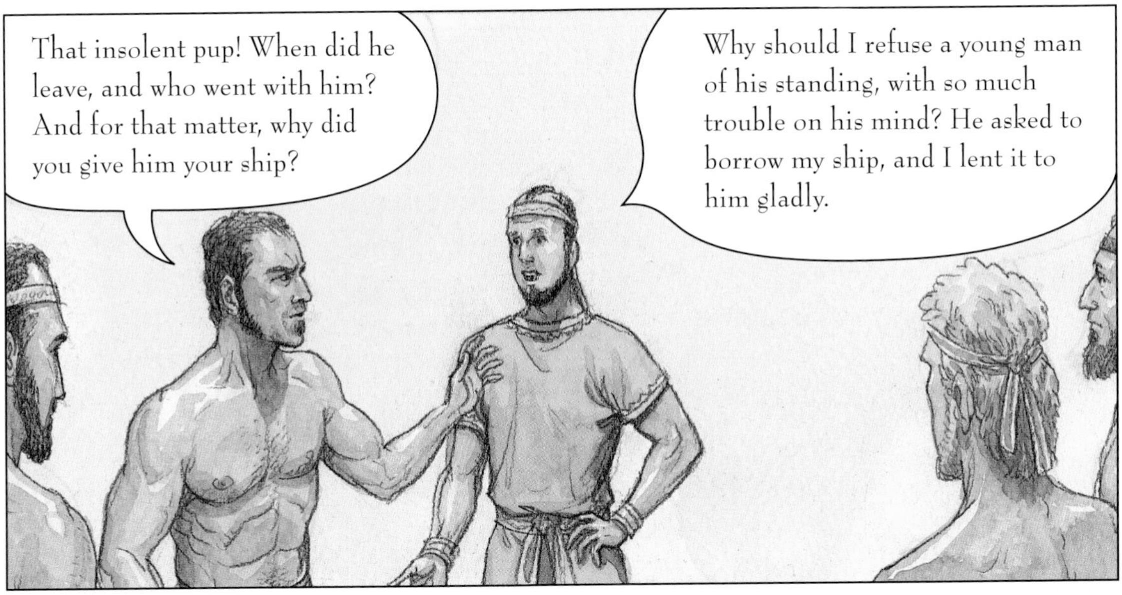
That insolent pup! When did he leave, and who went with him? And for that matter, why did you give him your ship?
Why should I refuse a young man of his standing, with so much trouble on his mind? He asked to borrow my ship, and I lent it to him gladly.

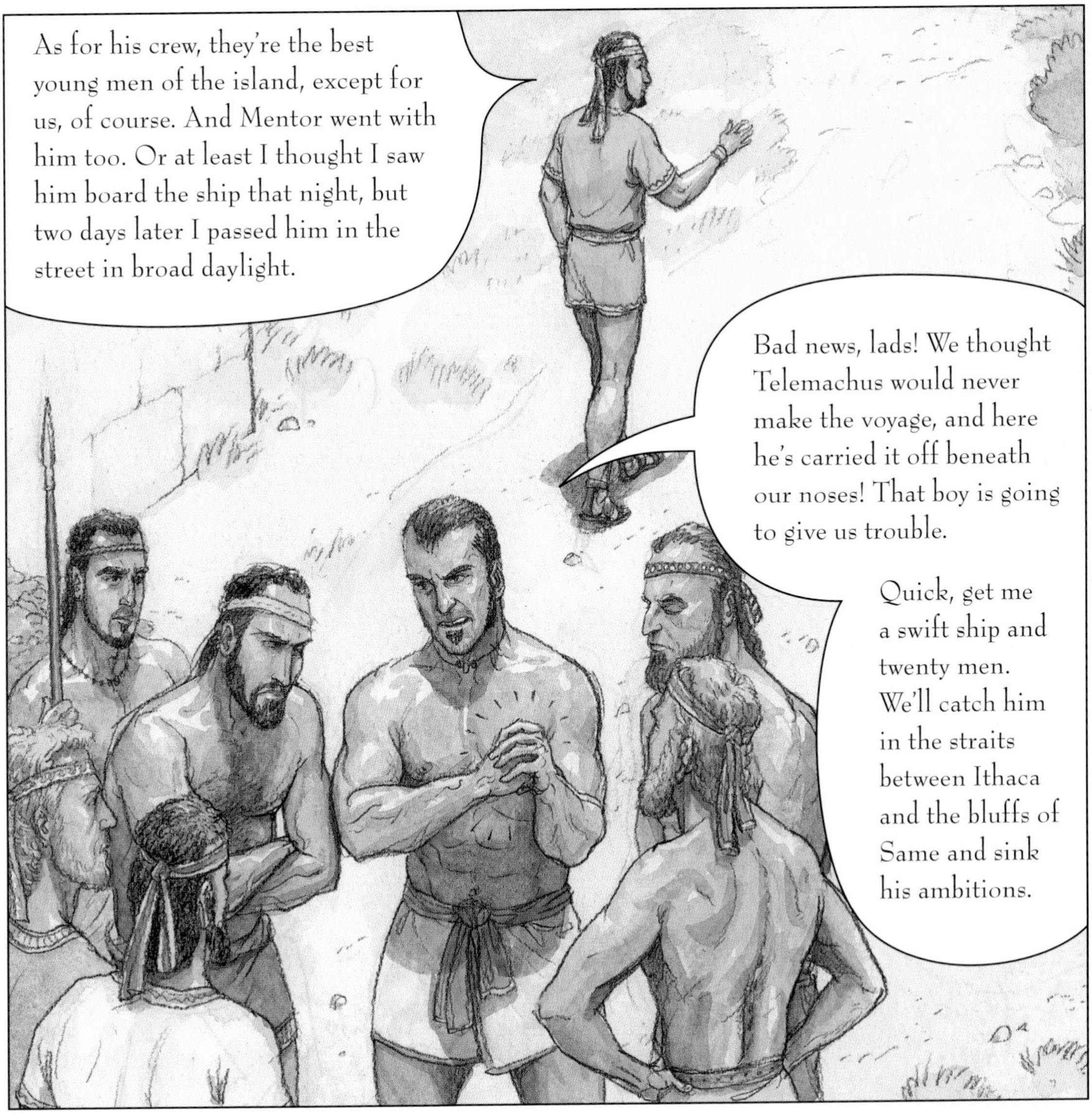
As for his crew, they're the best young men of the island, except for us, of course. And Mentor went with him too. Or at least I thought I saw him board the ship that night, but two days later I passed him in the street in broad daylight.
Bad news, lads! We thought Telemachus would never make the voyage, and here he's carried it off beneath our noses! That boy is going to give us trouble.
Quick, get me a swift ship and twenty men. We'll catch him in the straits between Ithaca and the bluffs of Same and sink his ambitions.

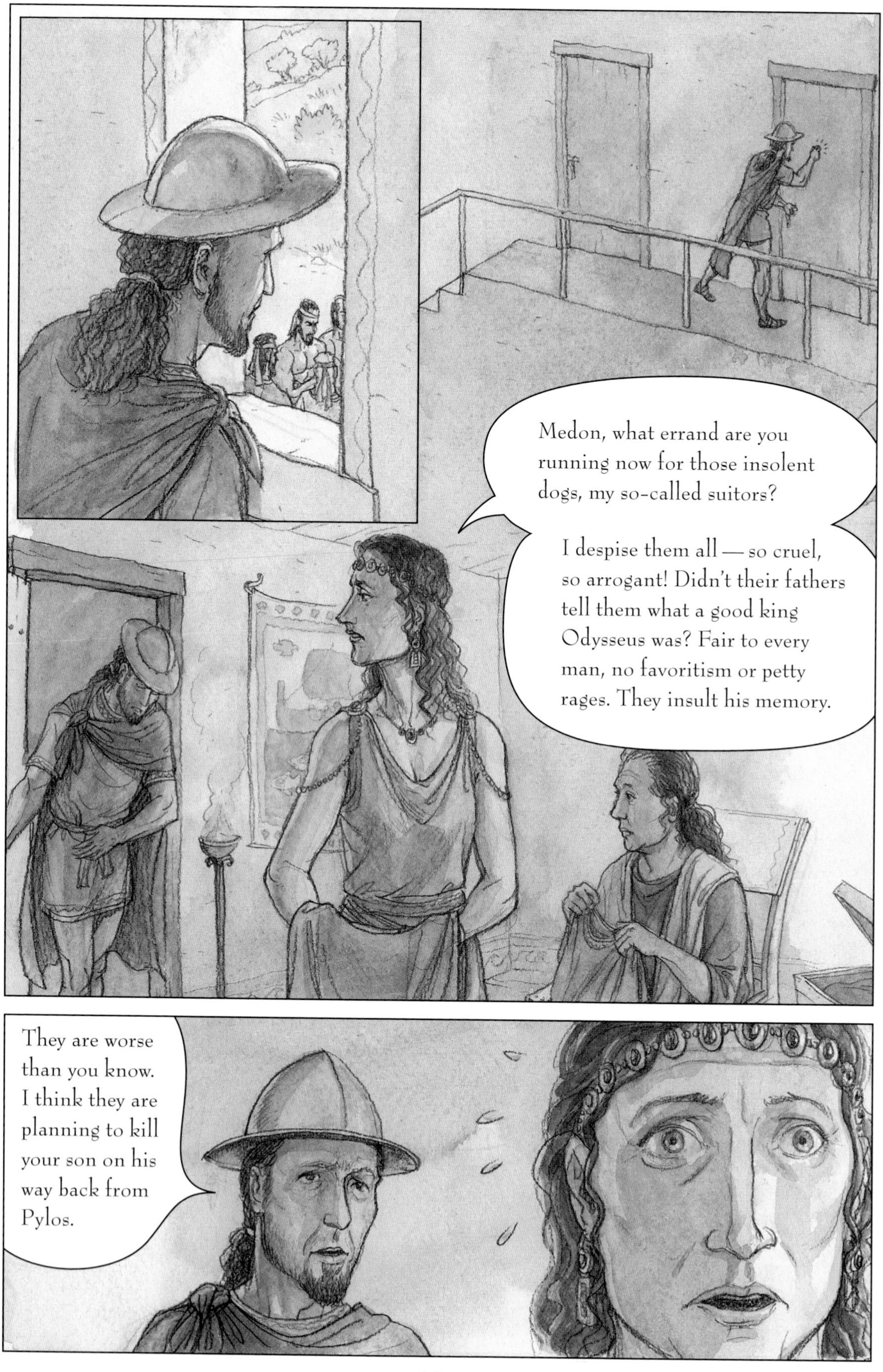
Medon, what errand are you running now for those insolent dogs, my so-called suitors?
I despise them all — so cruel, so arrogant! Didn't their fathers tell them what a good king Odysseus was? Fair to every man, no favoritism or petty rages. They insult his memory.
They are worse than you know. I think they are planning to kill your son on his way back from Pylos.

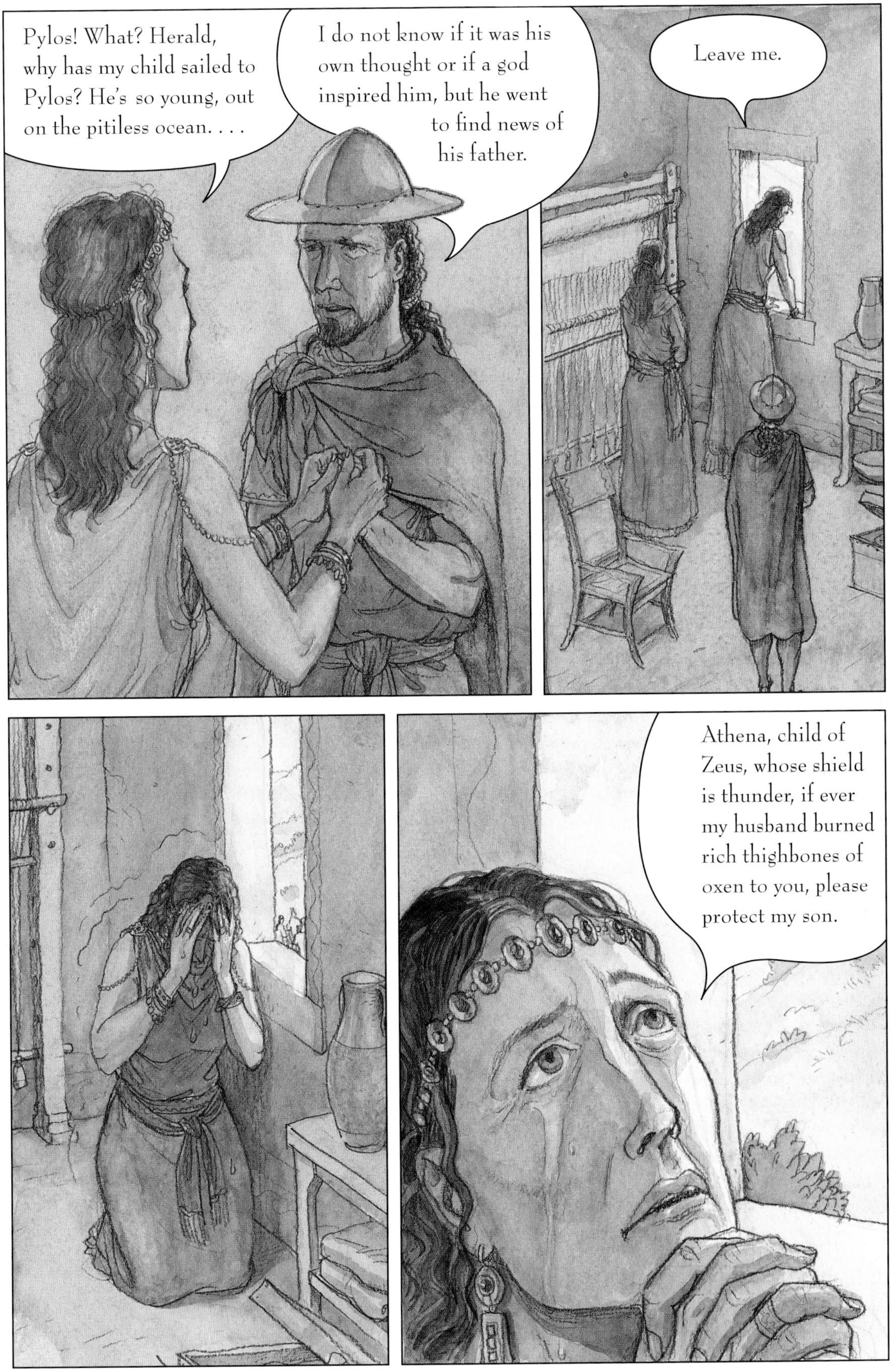
Pylos! What? Herald, why has my child sailed to Pylos? He's so young, out on the pitiless ocean. . . .
I do not know if it was his own thought or if a god inspired him, but he went to find news of his father.
Leave me.
Athena, child of Zeus, whose shield is thunder, if ever my husband burned rich thighbones of oxen to you, please protect my son.

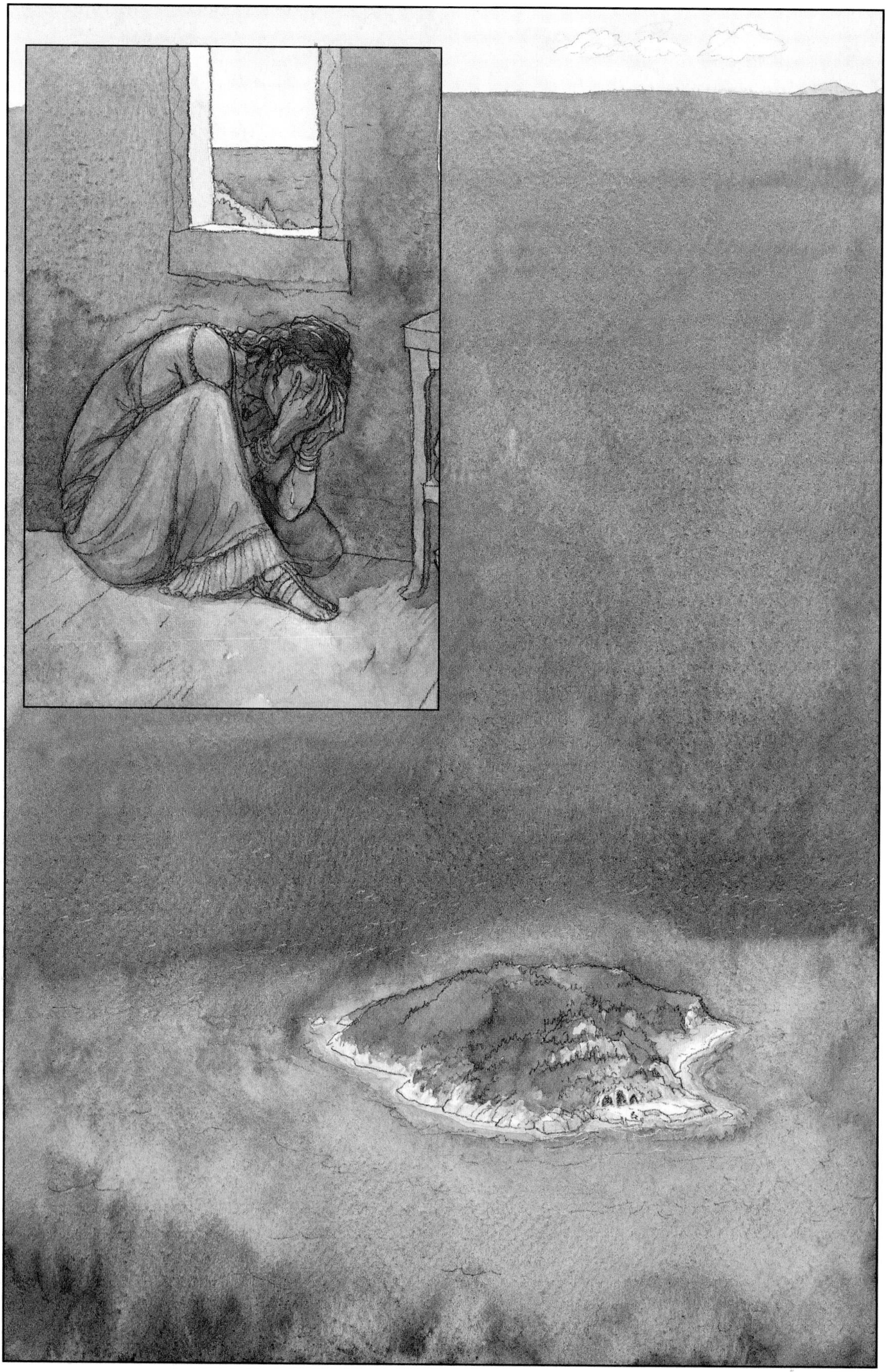

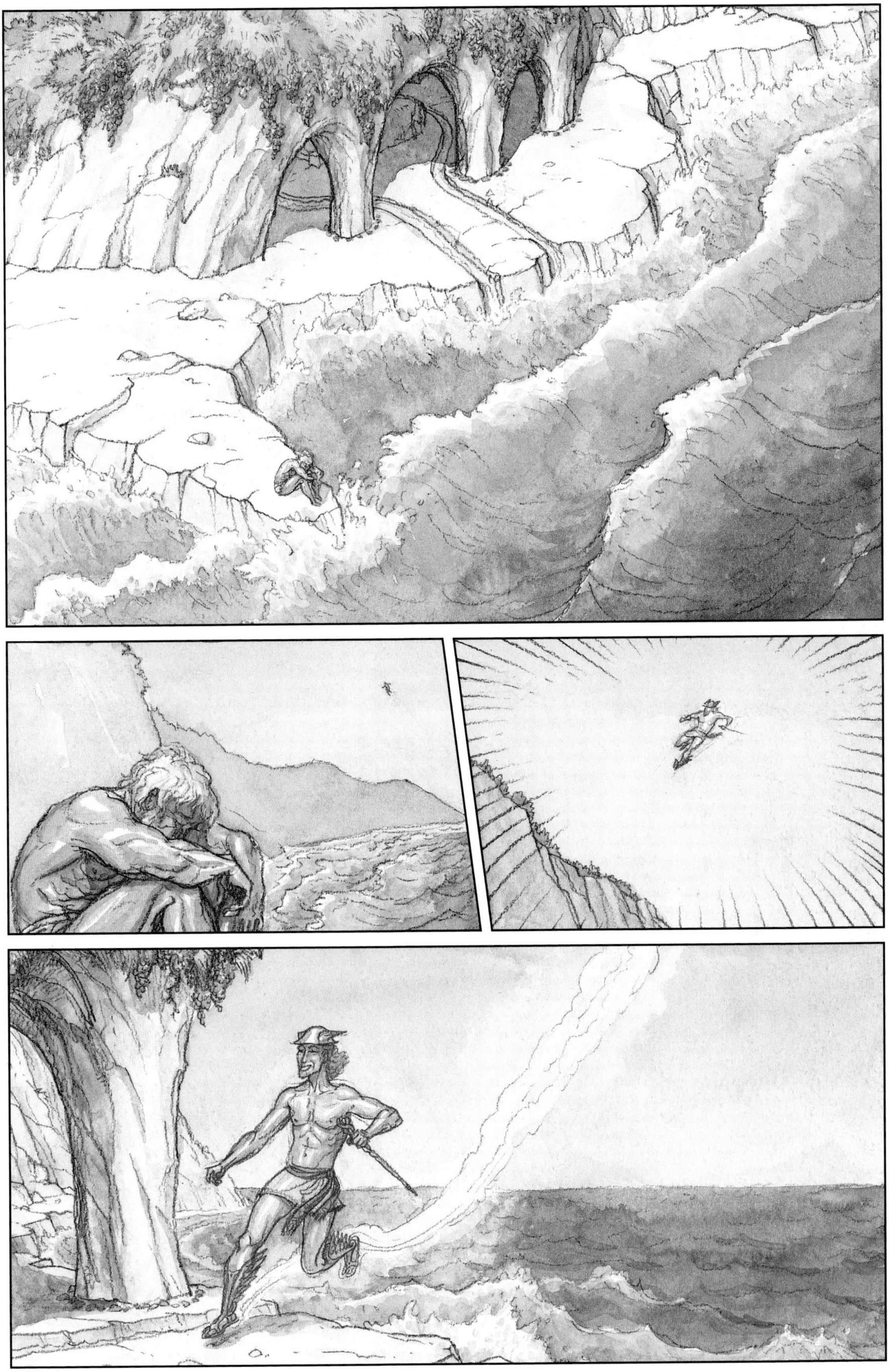

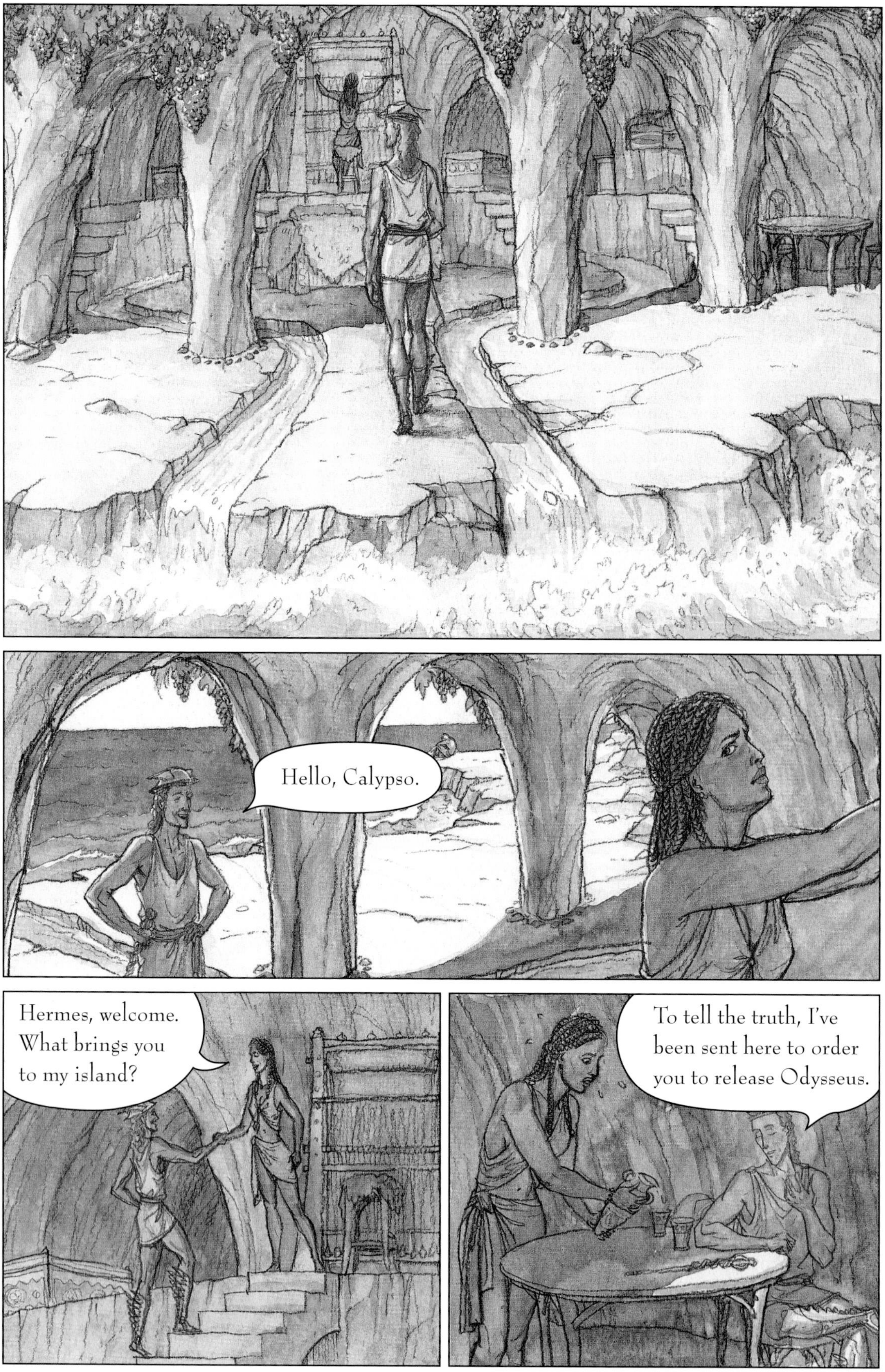
Hello, Calypso.
Hermes, welcome. What brings you to my island?
To tell the truth, I've been sent here to order you to release Odysseus.

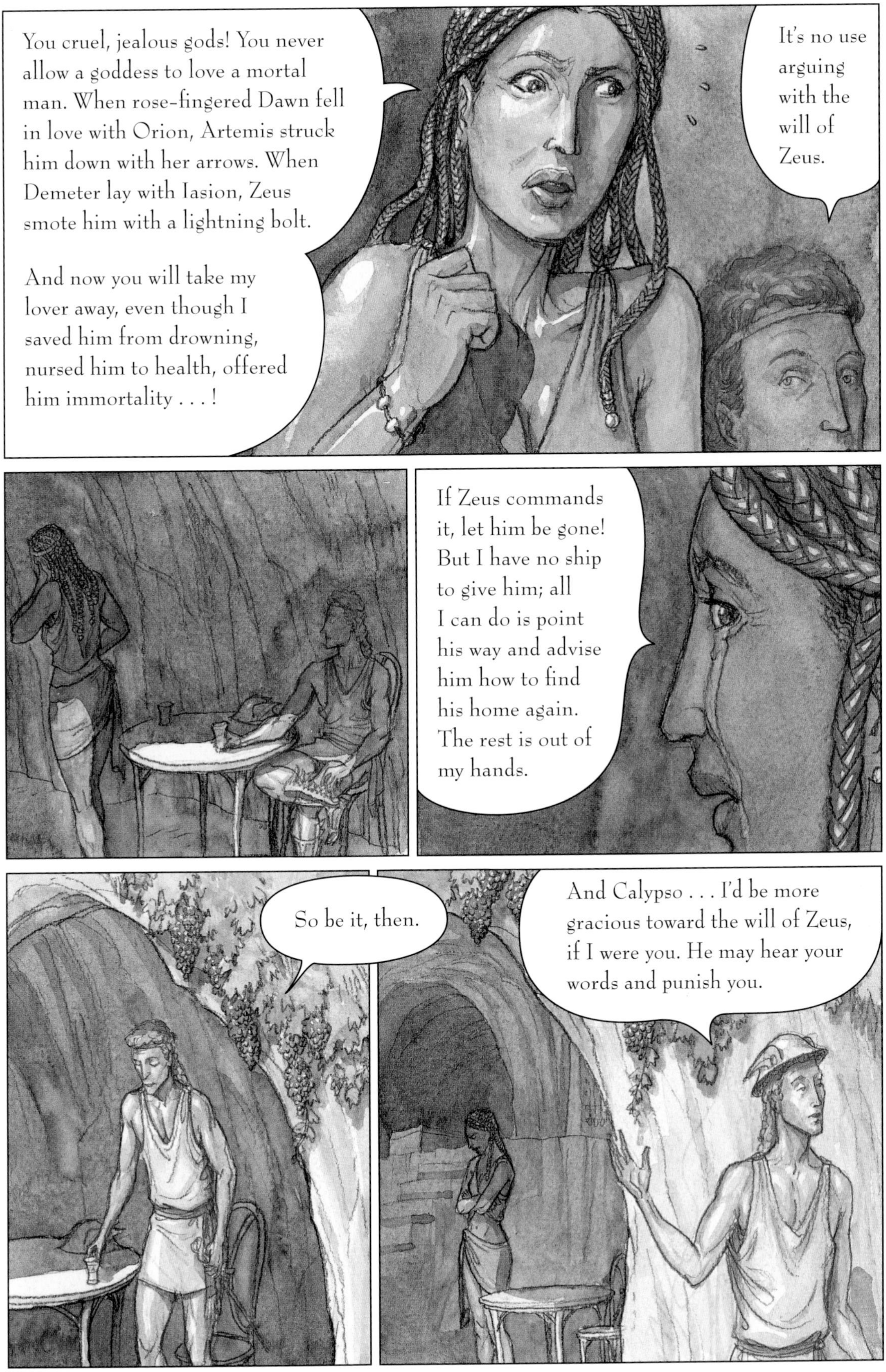
You cruel, jealous gods! You never allow a goddess to love a mortal man. When rose-fingered Dawn fell in love with Orion, Artemis struck him down with her arrows. When Demeter lay with Iasion, Zeus smote him with a lightning bolt.
And now you will take my lover away, even though I saved him from drowning, nursed him to health, offered him immortality . . . !
It's no use arguing with the will of Zeus.
If Zeus commands it, let him be gone! But I have no ship to give him; all I can do is point his way and advise him how to find his home again. The rest is out of my hands.
So be it, then.
And Calypso . . . I'd be more gracious toward the will of Zeus, if I were you. He may hear your words and punish you.

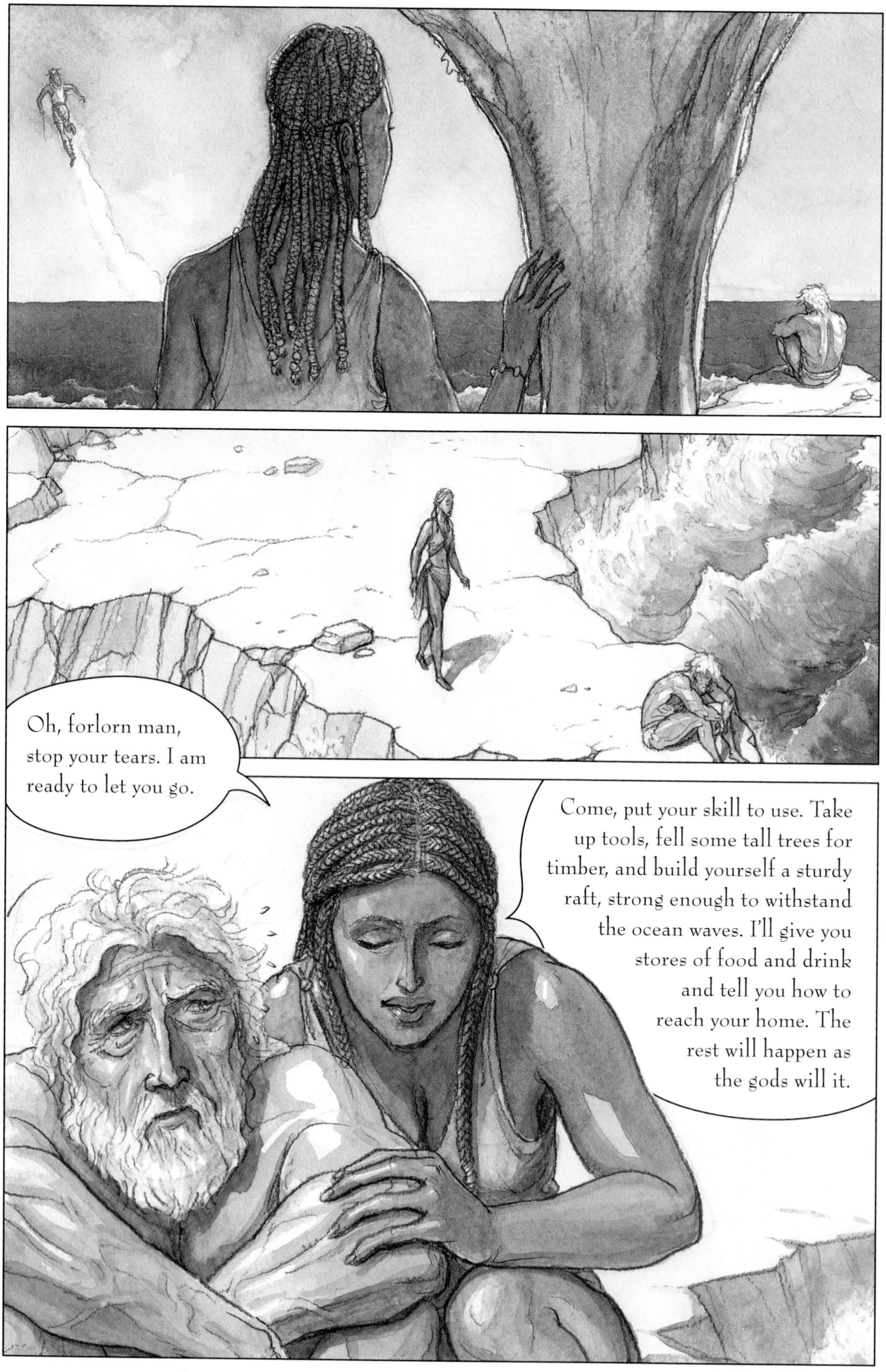
Oh, forlorn man, stop your tears. I am ready to let you go.
Come, put your skill to use. Take up tools, fell some tall trees for timber, and build yourself a sturdy raft, strong enough to withstand the ocean waves. I'll give you stores of food and drink and tell you how to reach your home. The rest will happen as the gods will it.

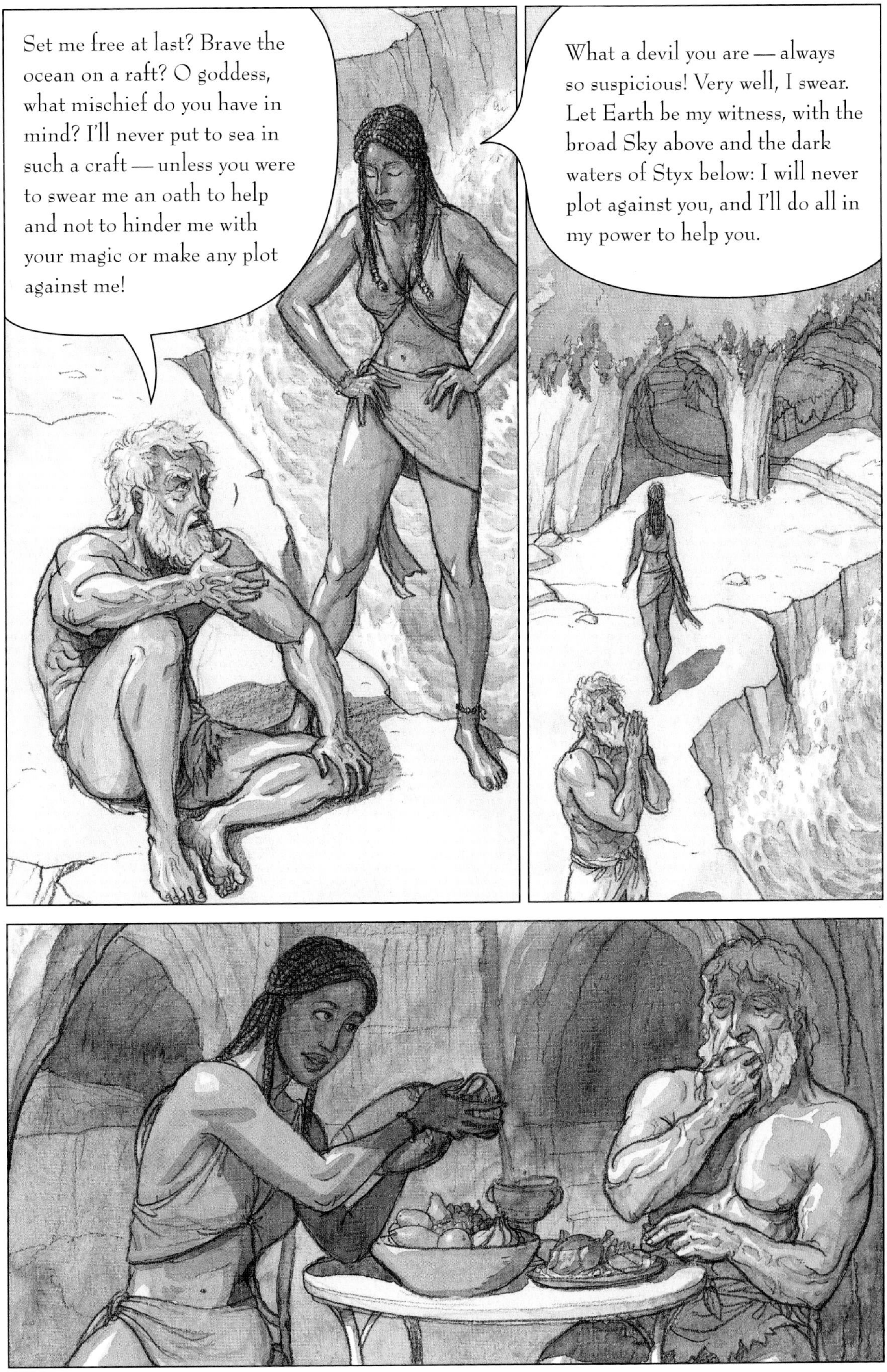
Set me free at last? Brave the ocean on a raft? O goddess, what mischief do you have in mind? I'll never put to sea in such a craft — unless you were to swear me an oath to help and not to hinder me with your magic or make any plot against me!
What a devil you are — always so suspicious! Very well, I swear. Let Earth be my witness, with the broad Sky above and the dark waters of Styx below: I will never plot against you, and I'll do all in my power to help you.

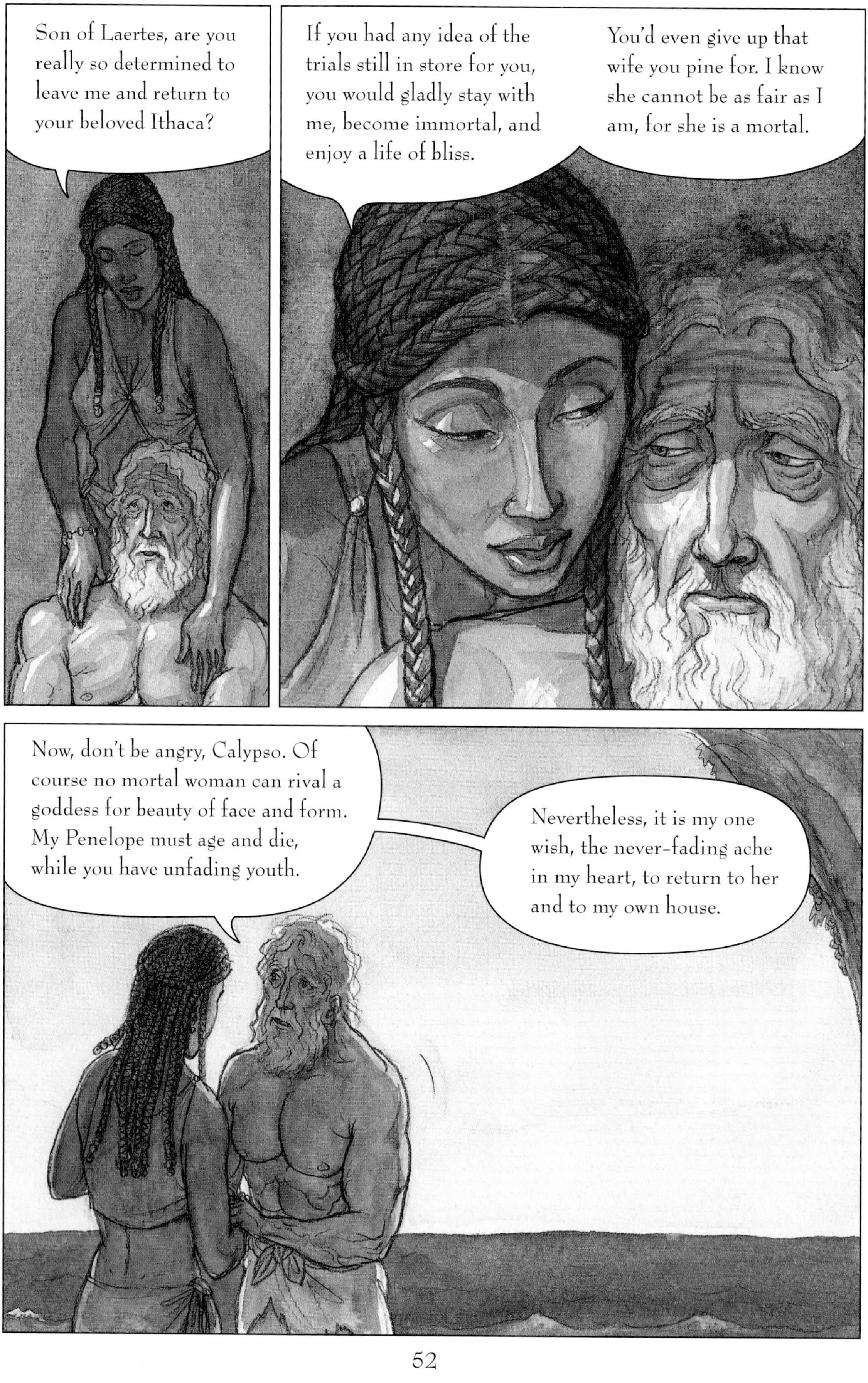
Son of Laertes, are you really so determined to leave me and return to your beloved Ithaca?
If you had any idea of the trials still in store for you, you would gladly stay with me, become immortal, and enjoy a life of bliss.
You'd even give up that wife you pine for. I know she cannot be as fair as I am, for she is a mortal.
Now, don't be angry, Calypso. Of course no mortal woman can rival a goddess for beauty of face and form. My Penelope must age and die, while you have unfading youth.
Nevertheless, it is my one wish, the never-fading ache in my heart, to return to her and to my own house.

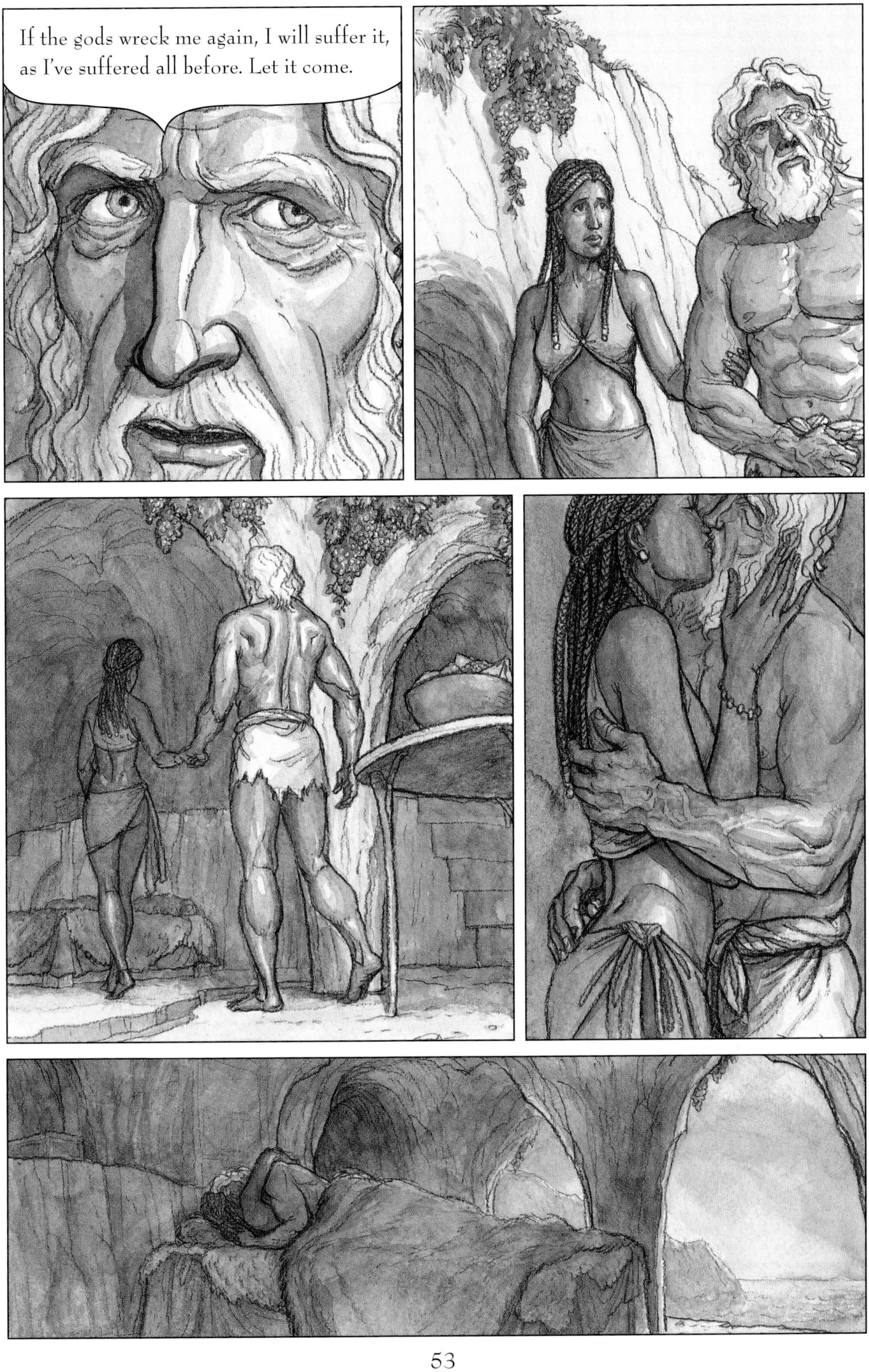
If the gods wreck me again, I will suffer it, as I've suffered all before. Let it come.

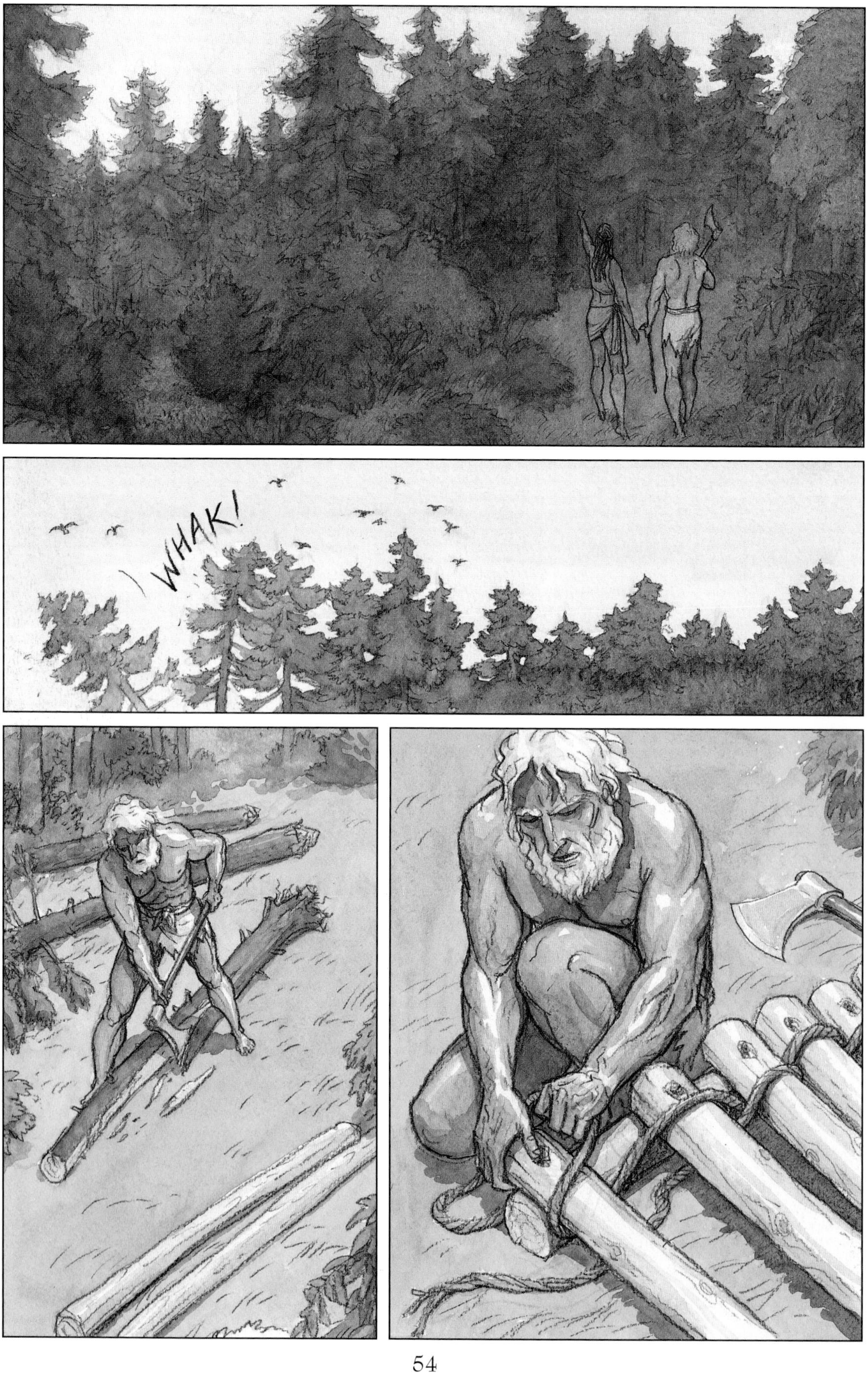
WHAK!

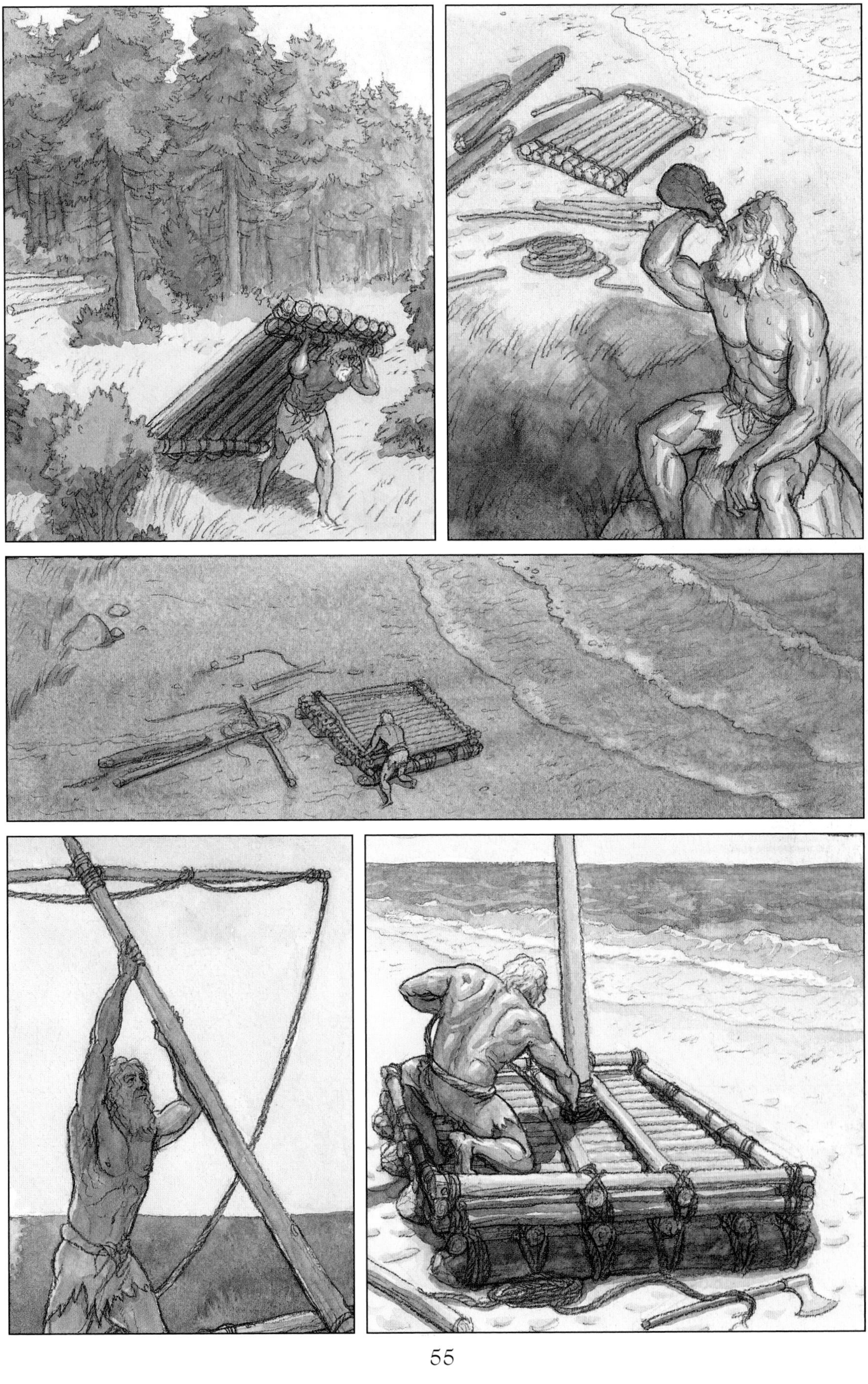

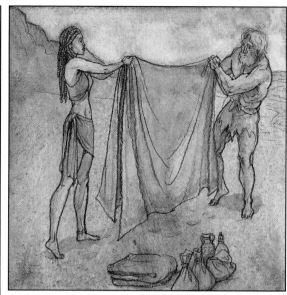

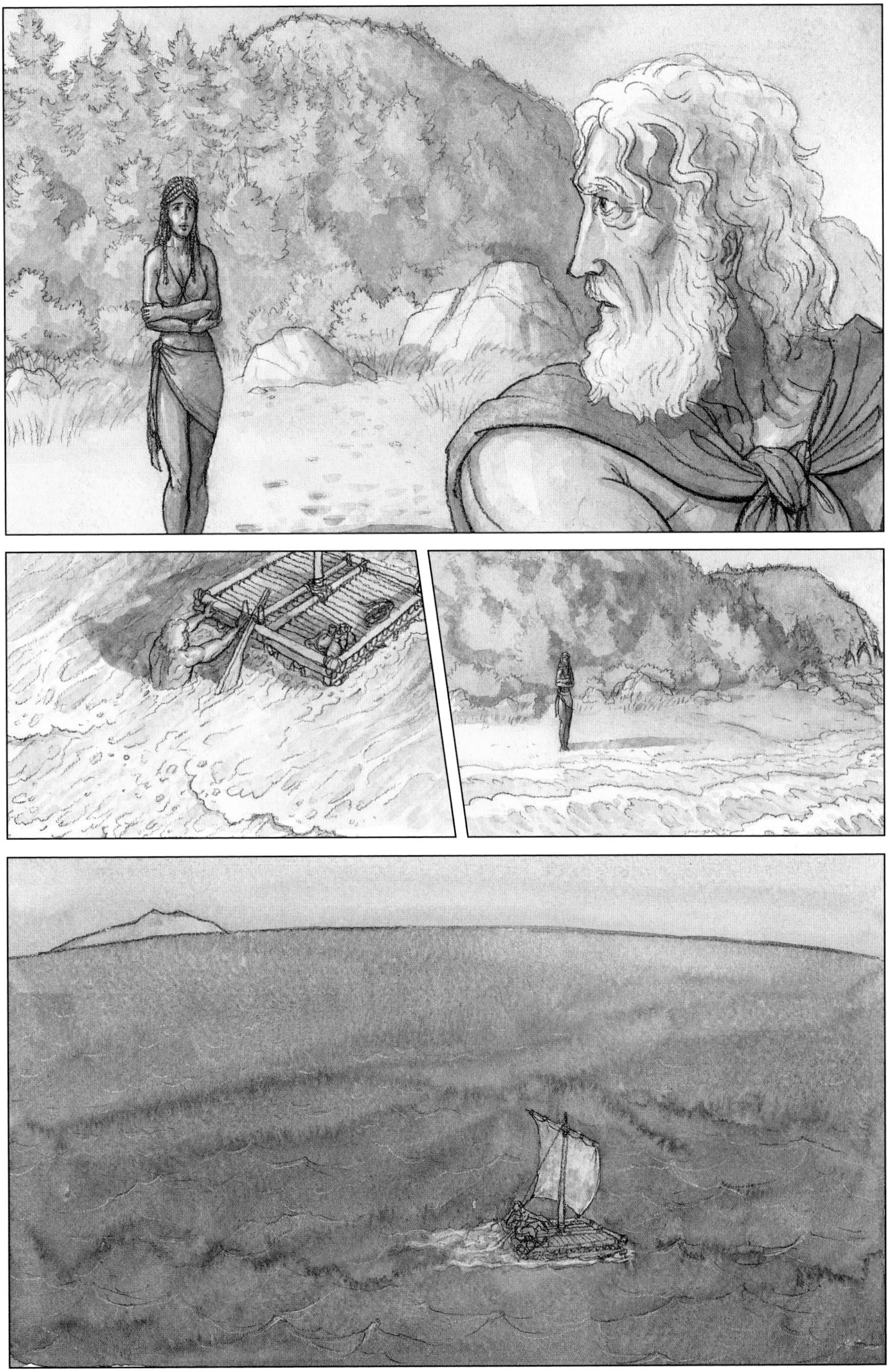

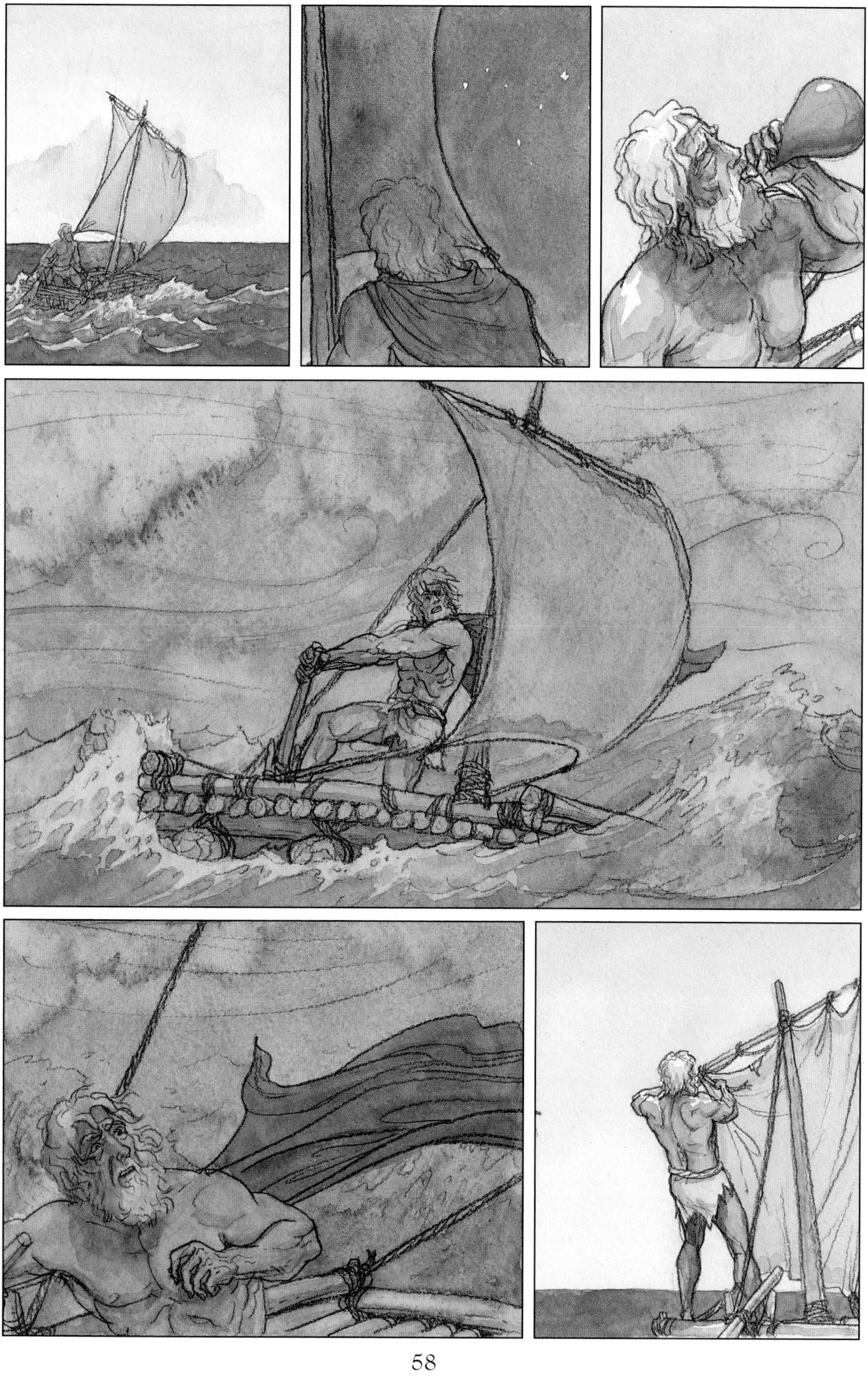

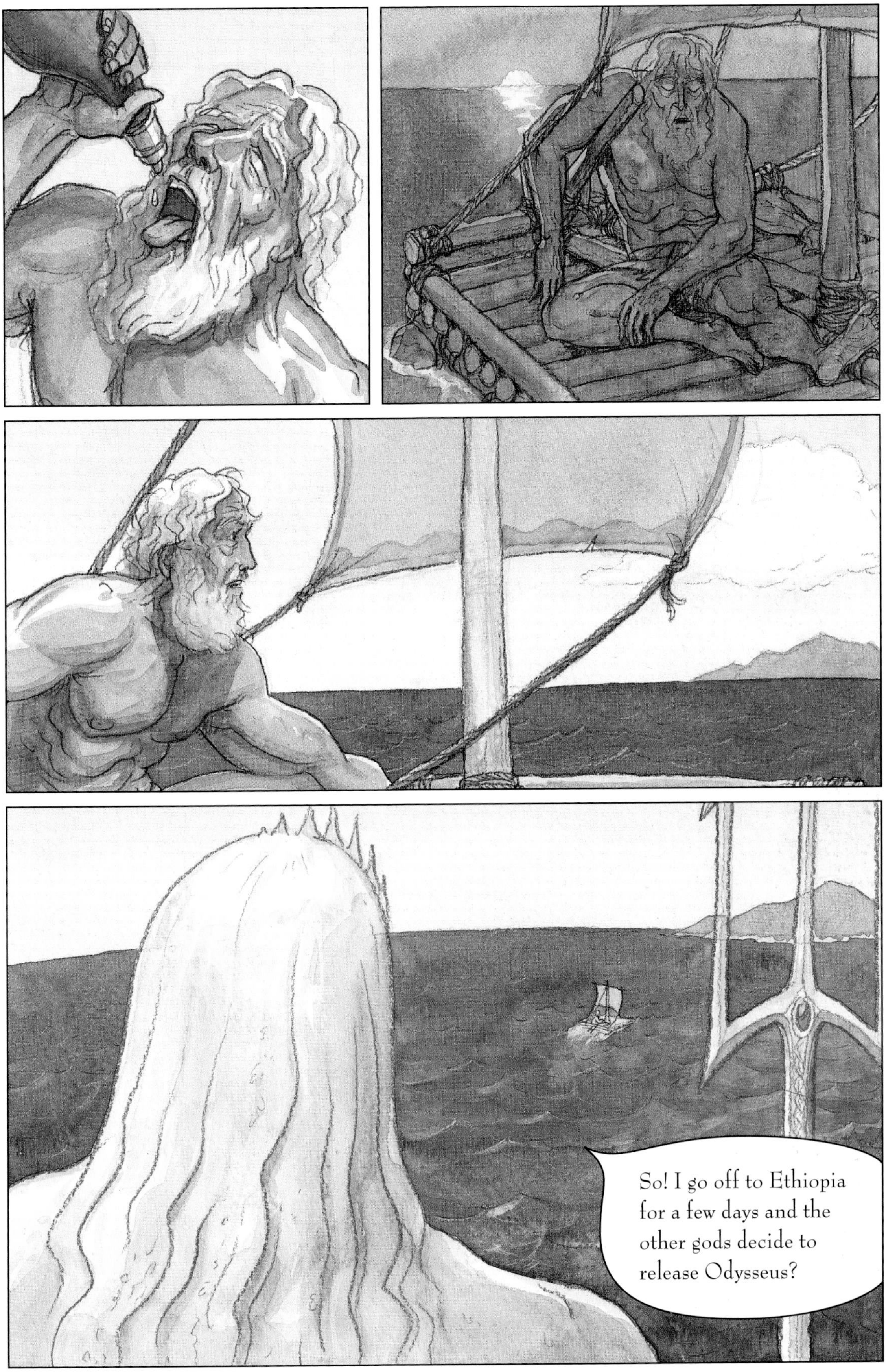
So! I go off to Ethiopia for a few days and the other gods decide to release Odysseus?

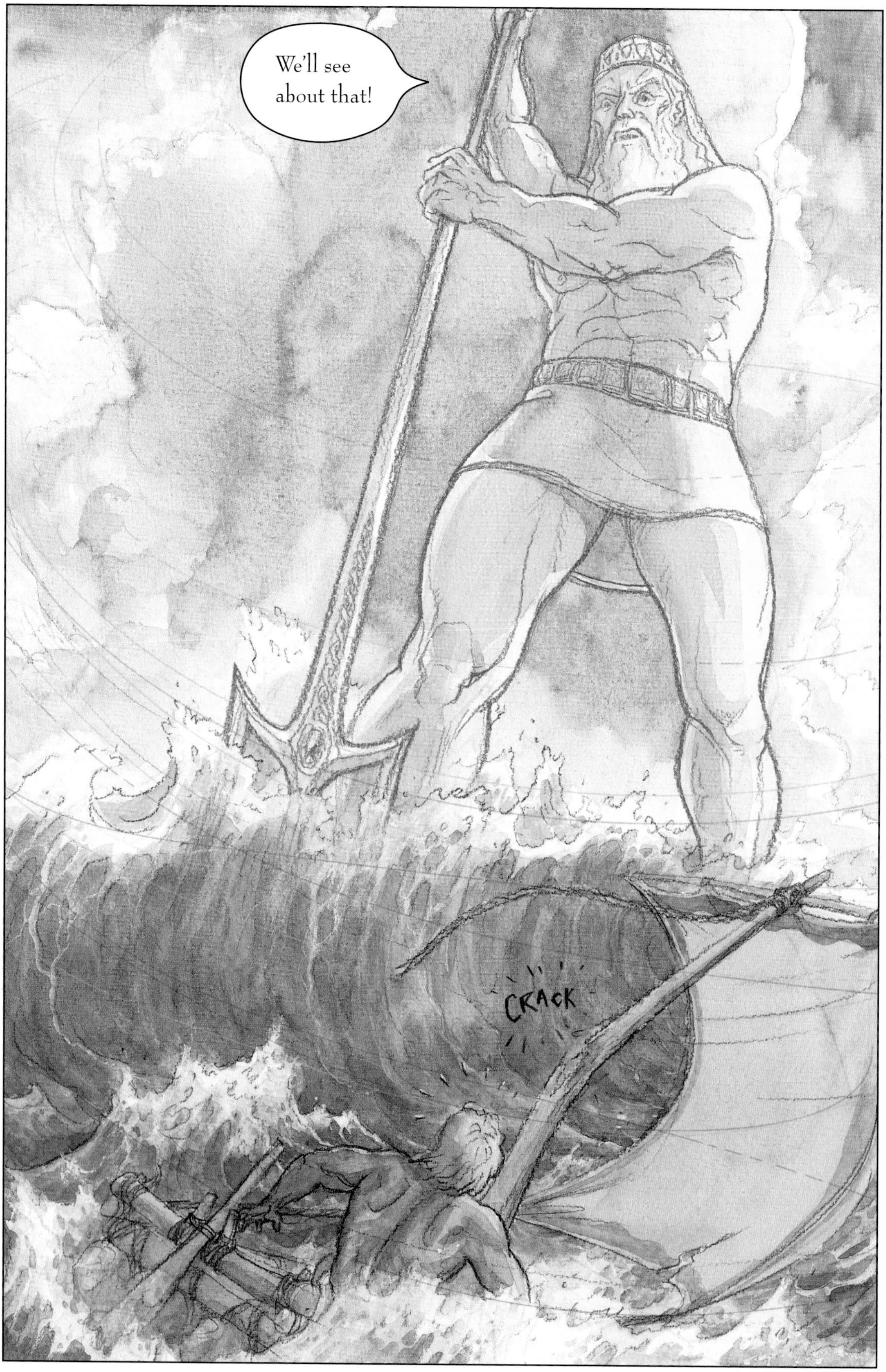
We'll see about that!
CRACK

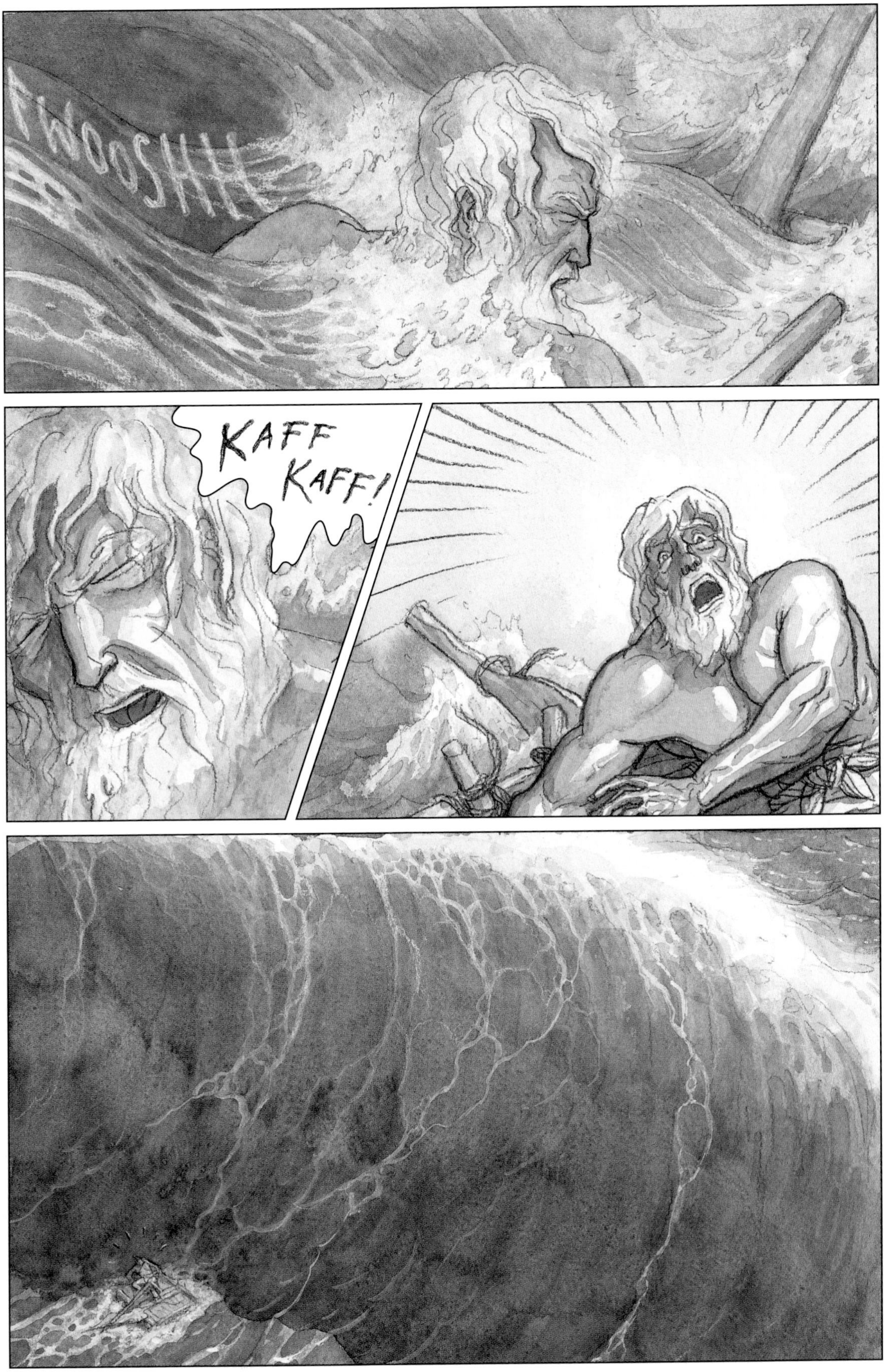
TWOOSHH
KAFF KAFF!

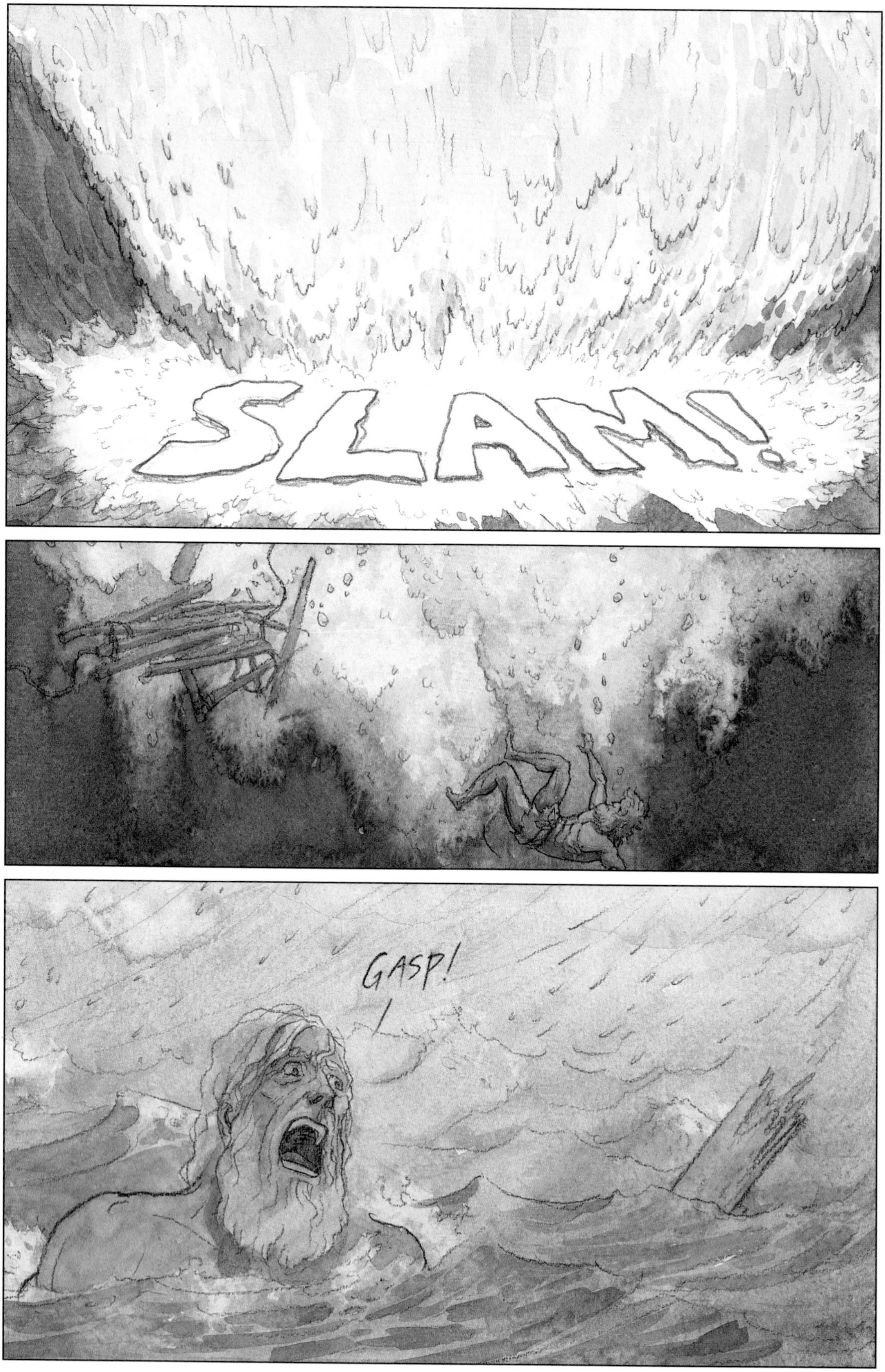
SLAM!
GASP!

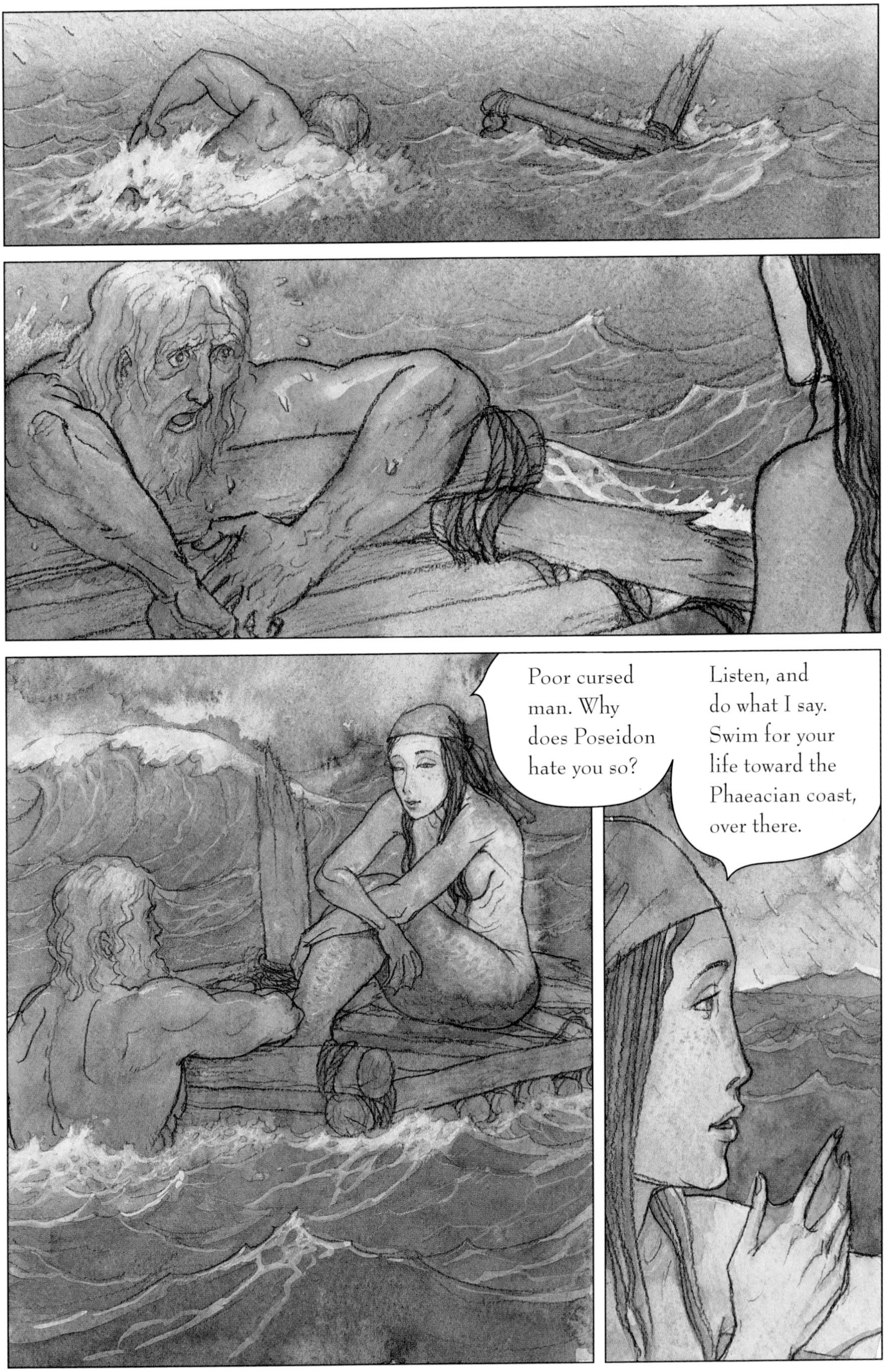
Poor cursed man. Why does Poseidon hate you so?
Listen, and do what I say. Swim for your life toward the Phaeacian coast, over there.

Here, take my veil and wind it around your waist. It will protect you. When you reach the shore, toss it back into the sea.

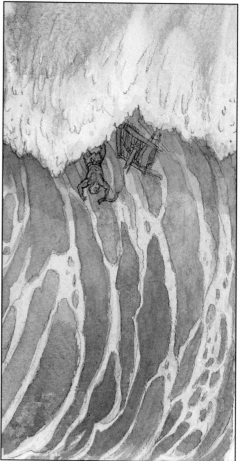

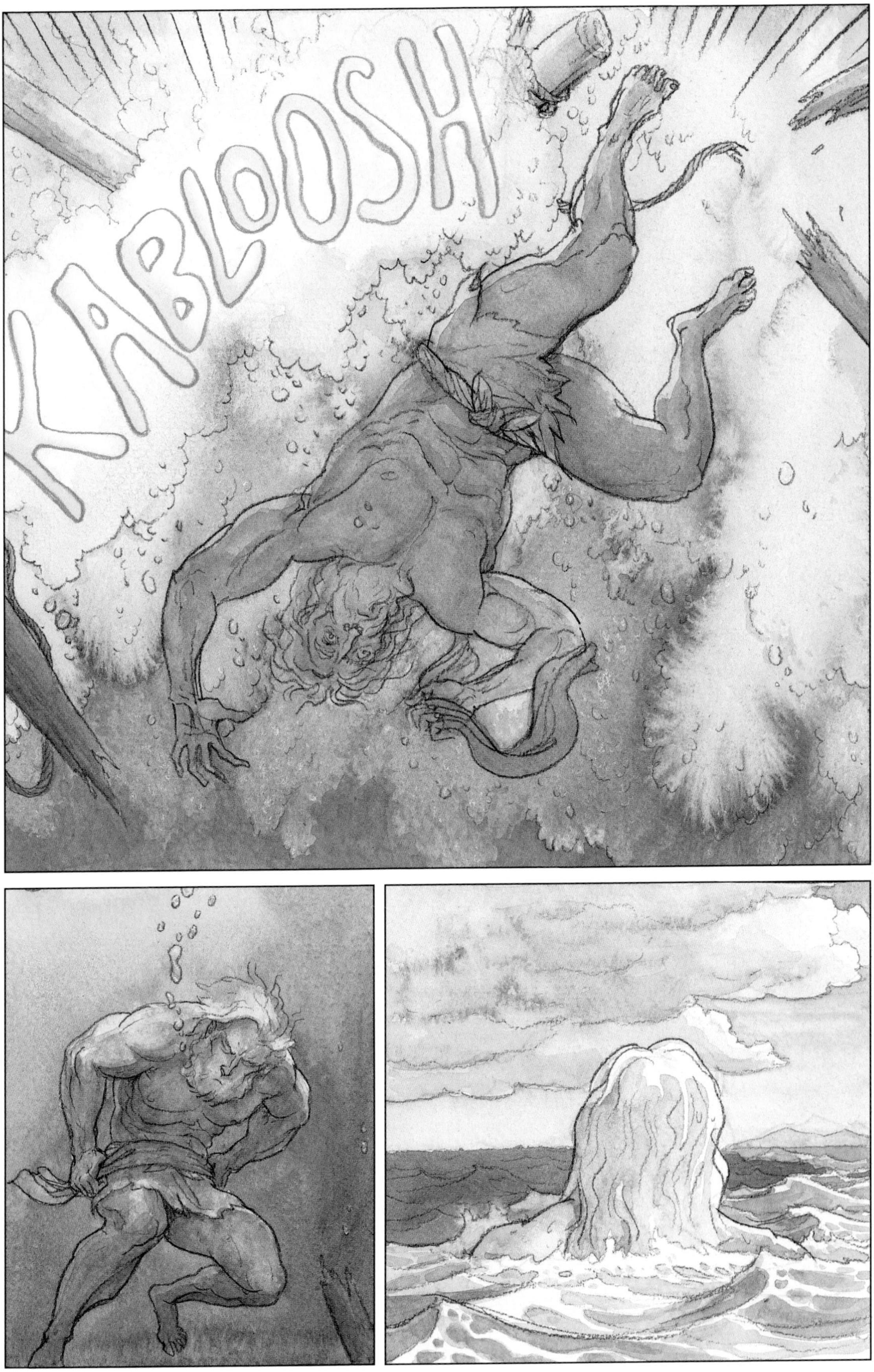
KABLOOSH

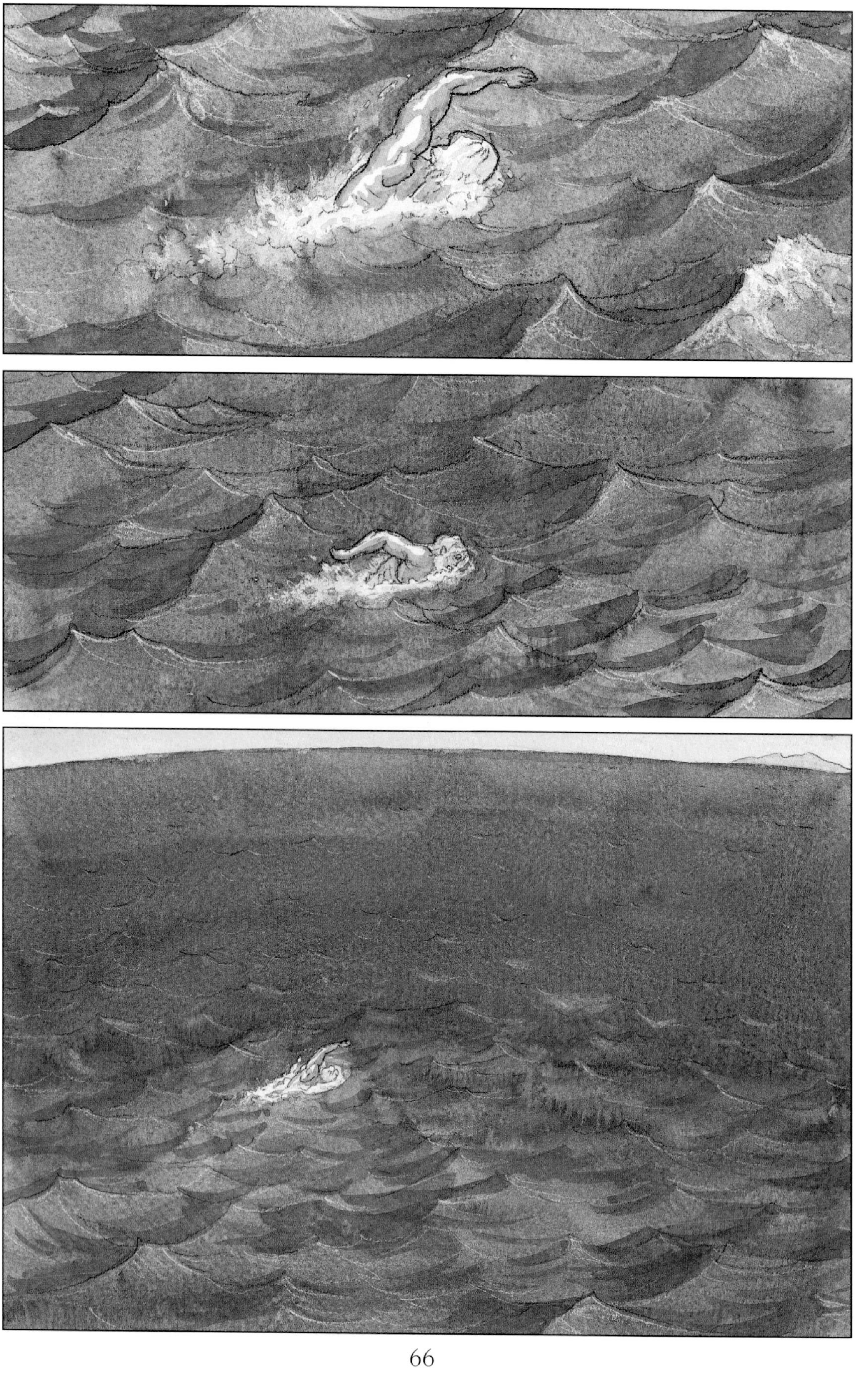

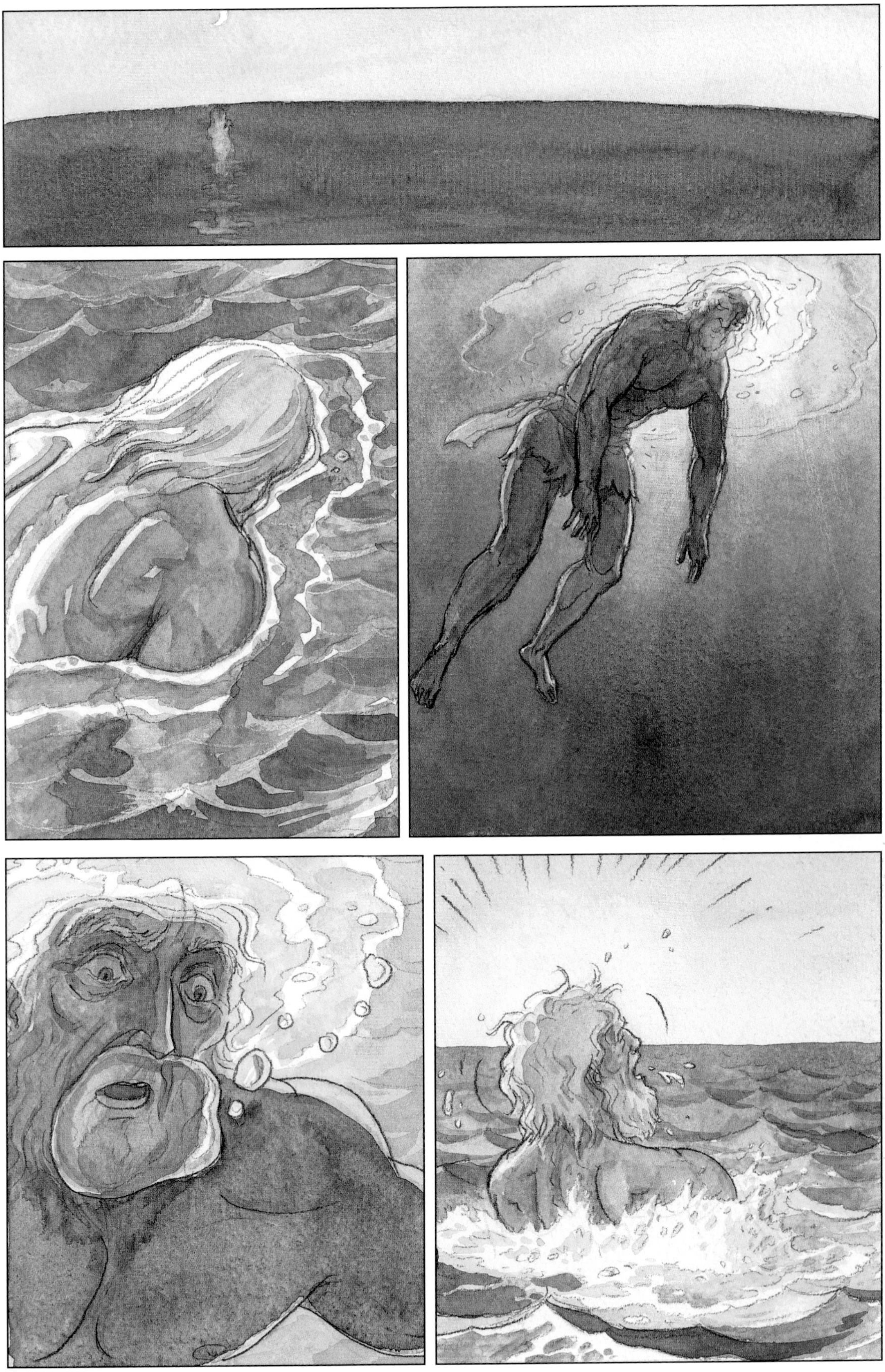

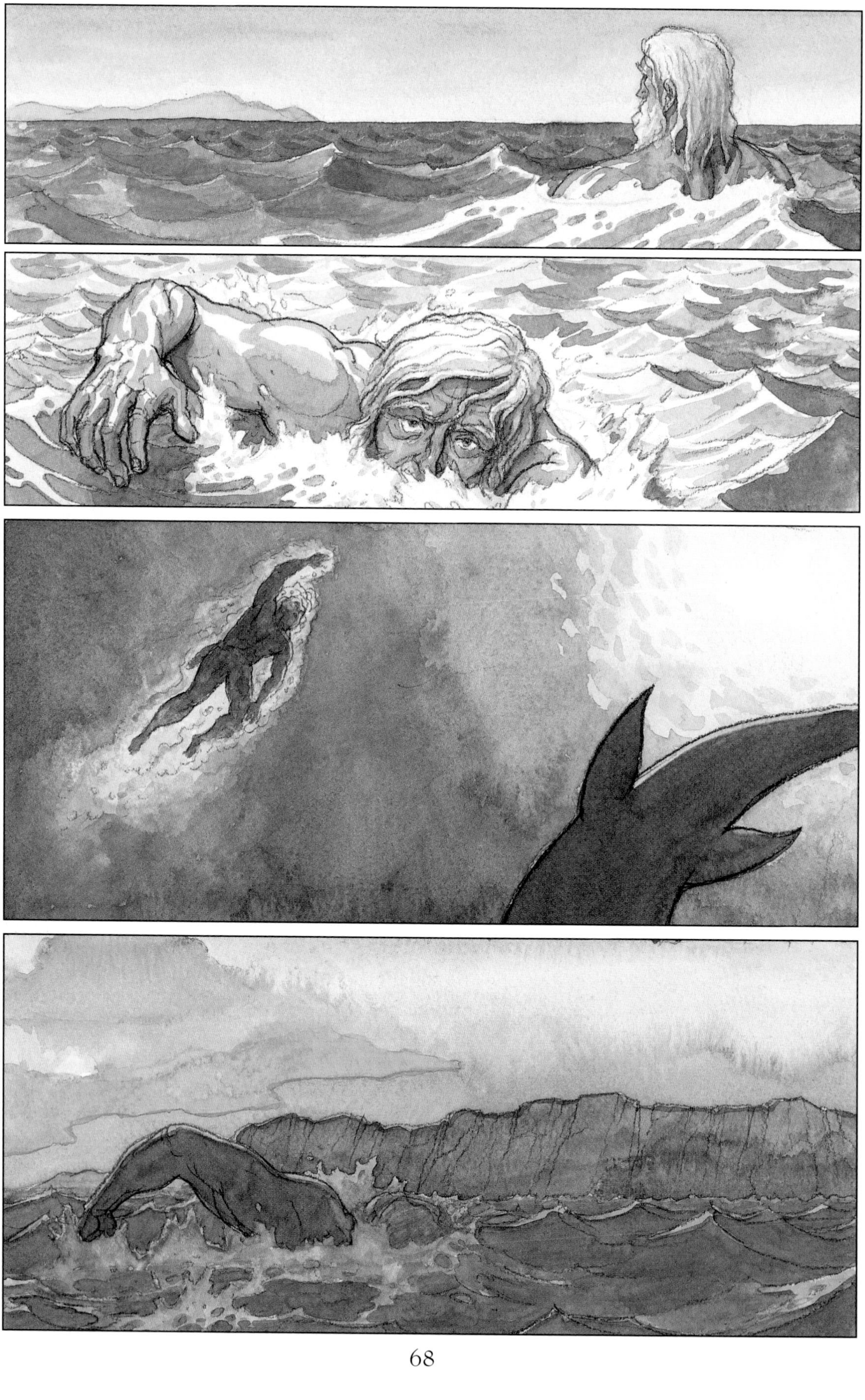

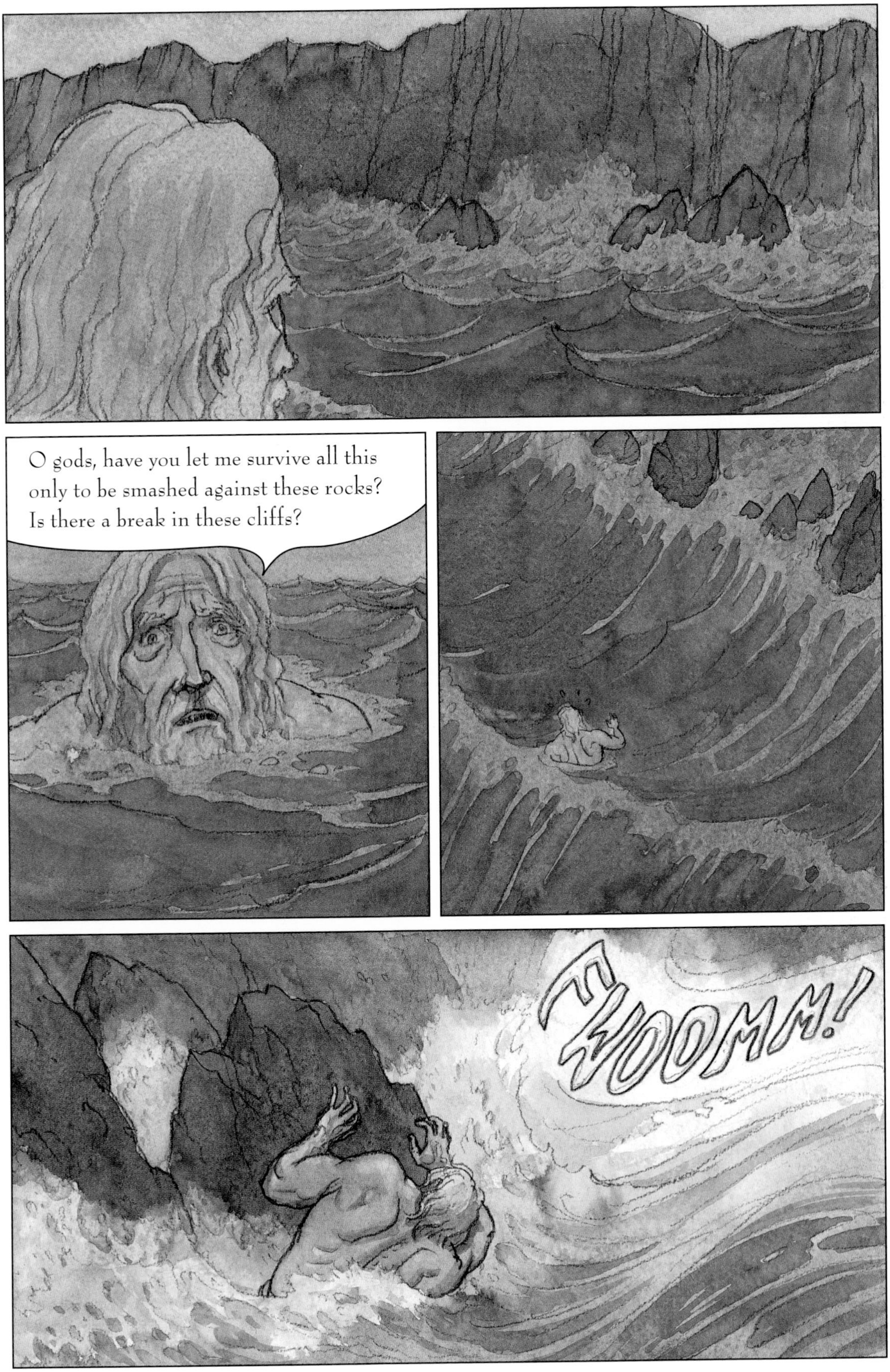
O gods, have you let me survive all this only to be smashed against these rocks? Is there a break in these cliffs?
FWOOMM!

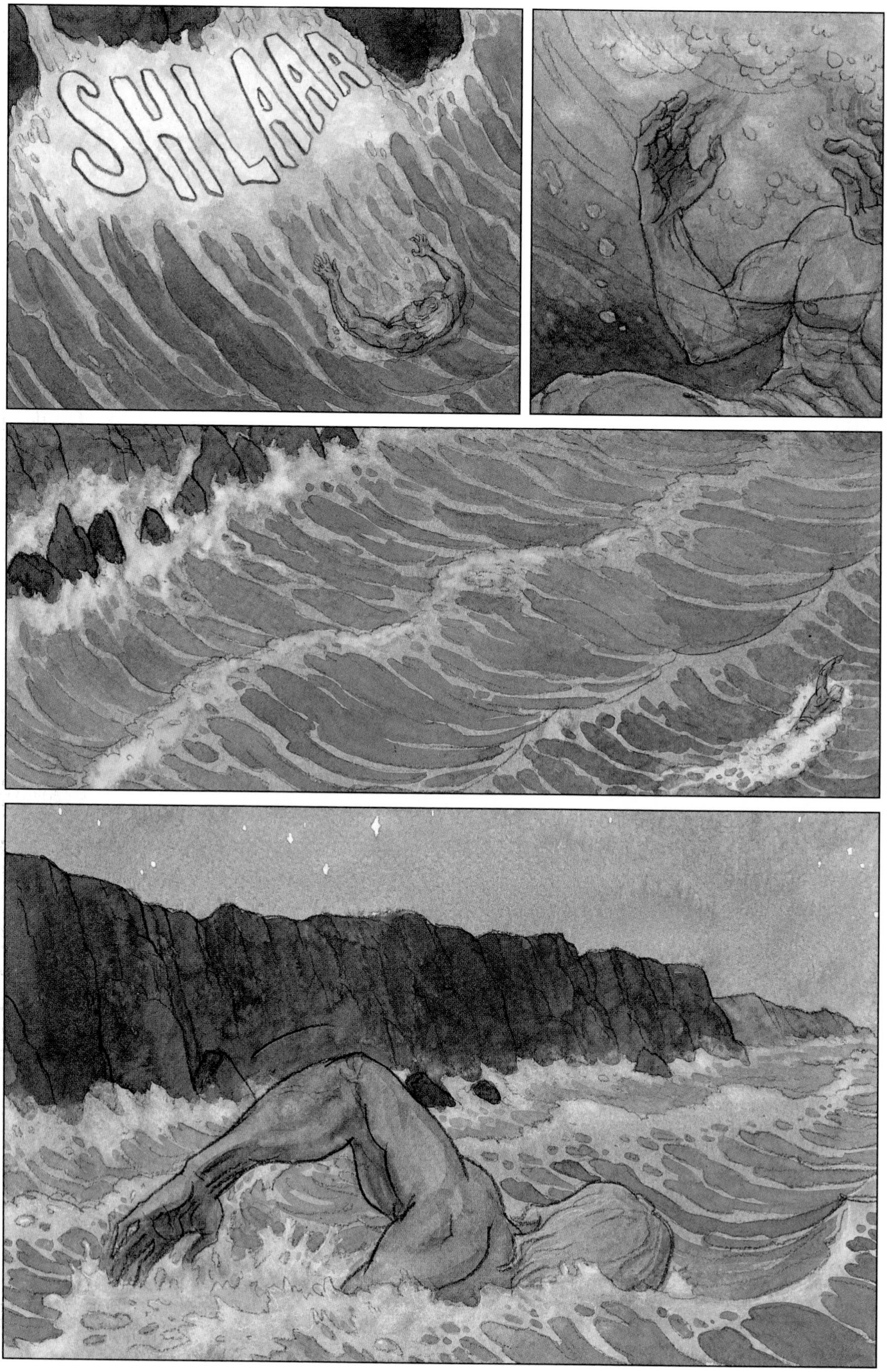
SHLAAA

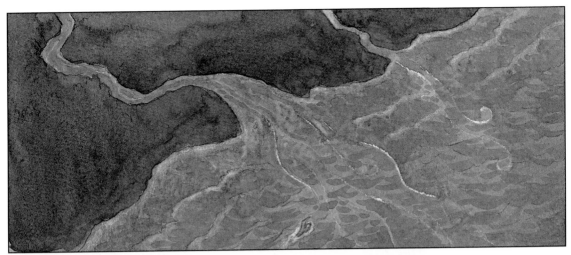

Hear me, lord of the river. I come to you in great need. Show mercy — calm your currents and let me swim to shore.

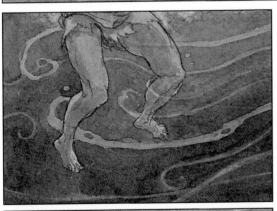

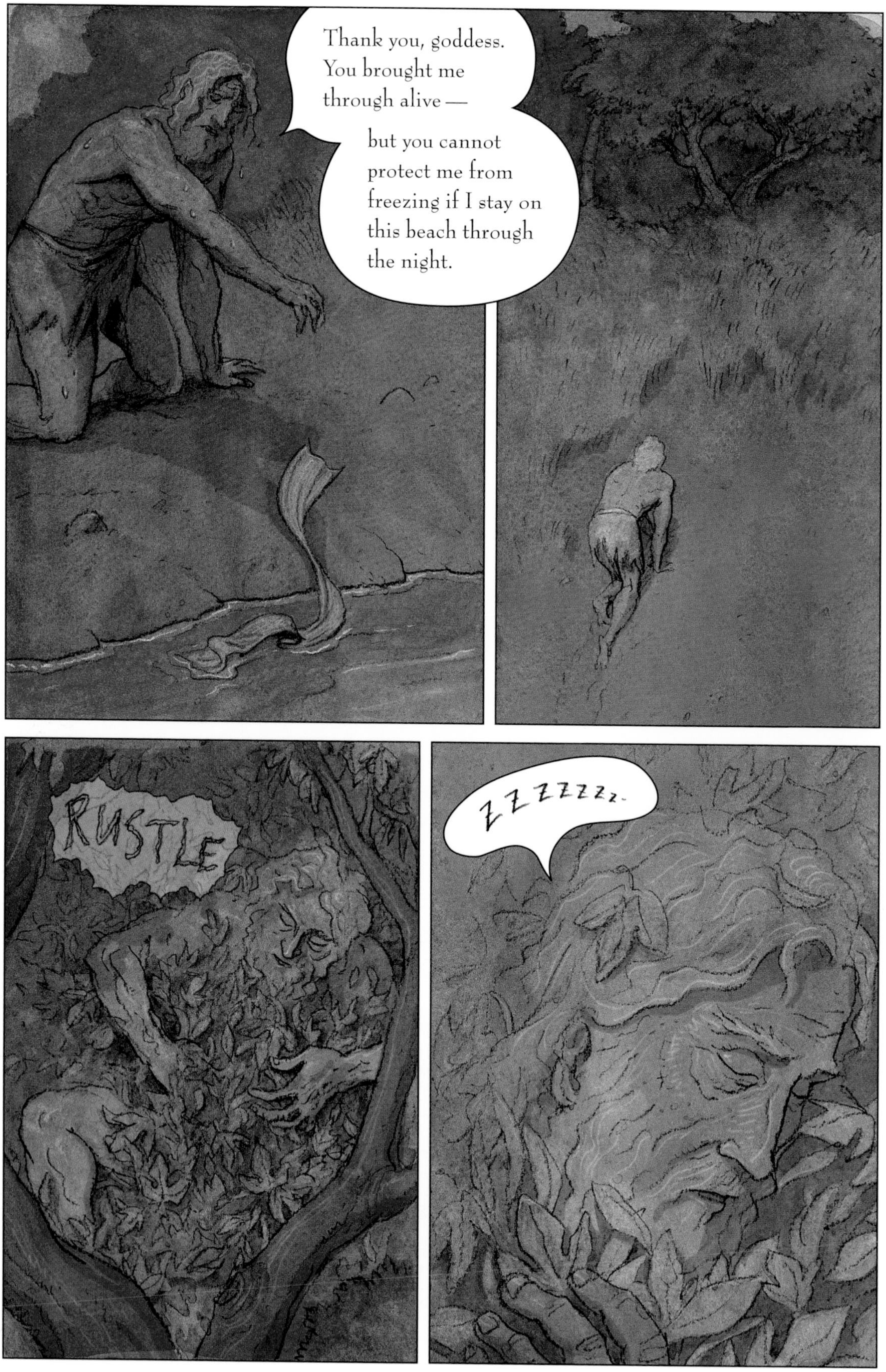

Thank you, goddess. You brought me through alive —
but you cannot protect me from freezing if I stay on this beach through the night.
RUSTLE
ZZZZZZz

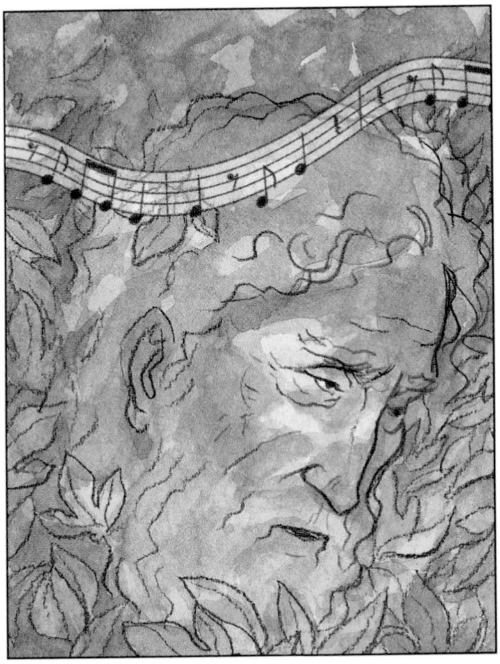

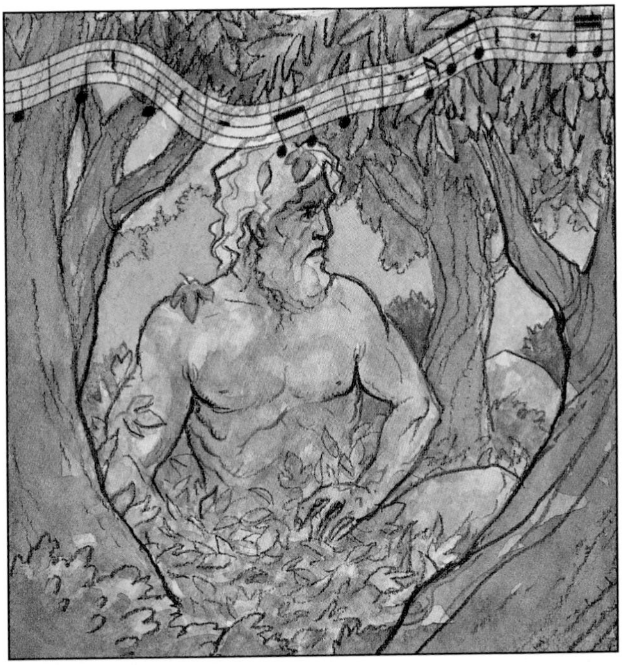

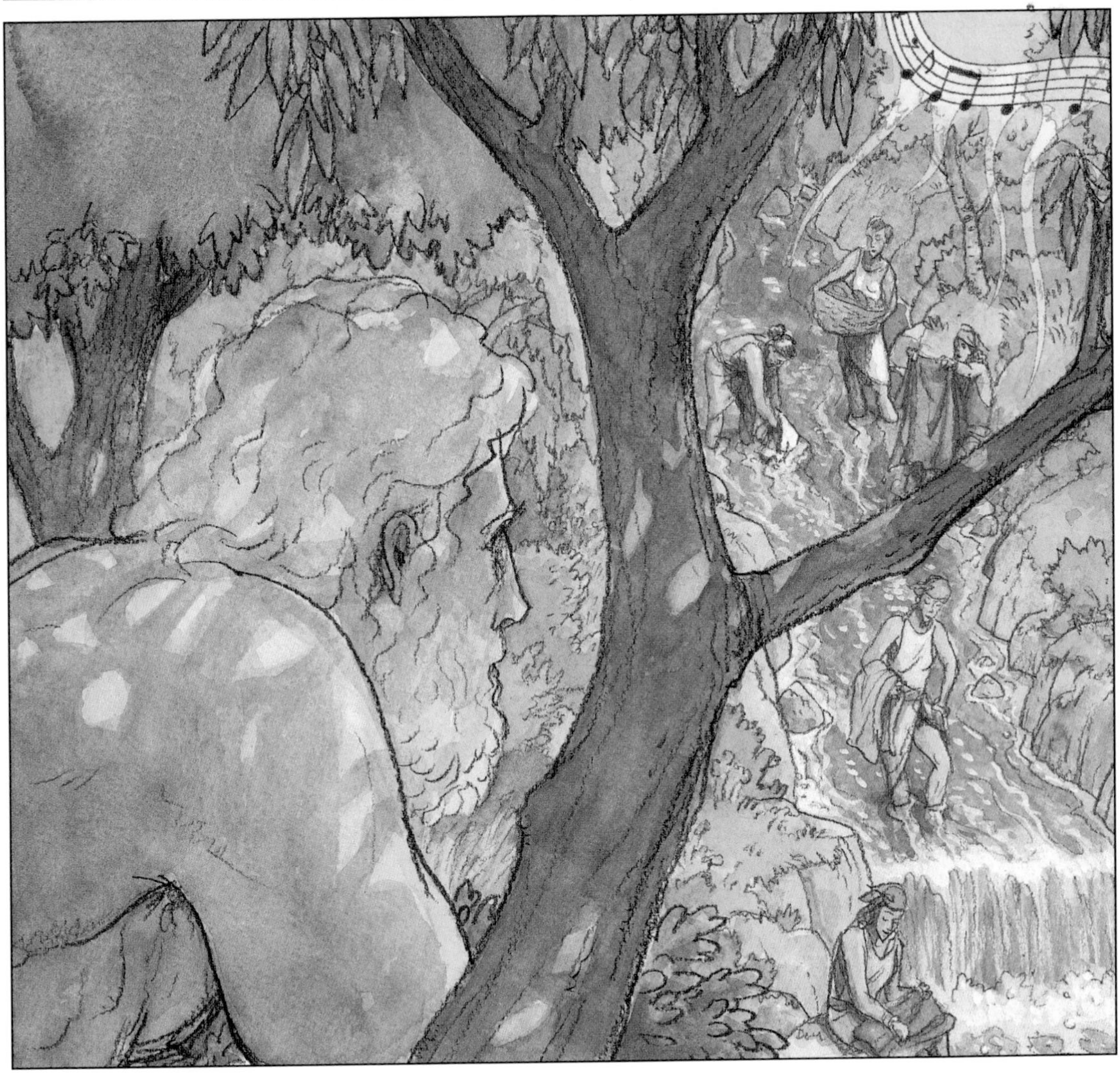

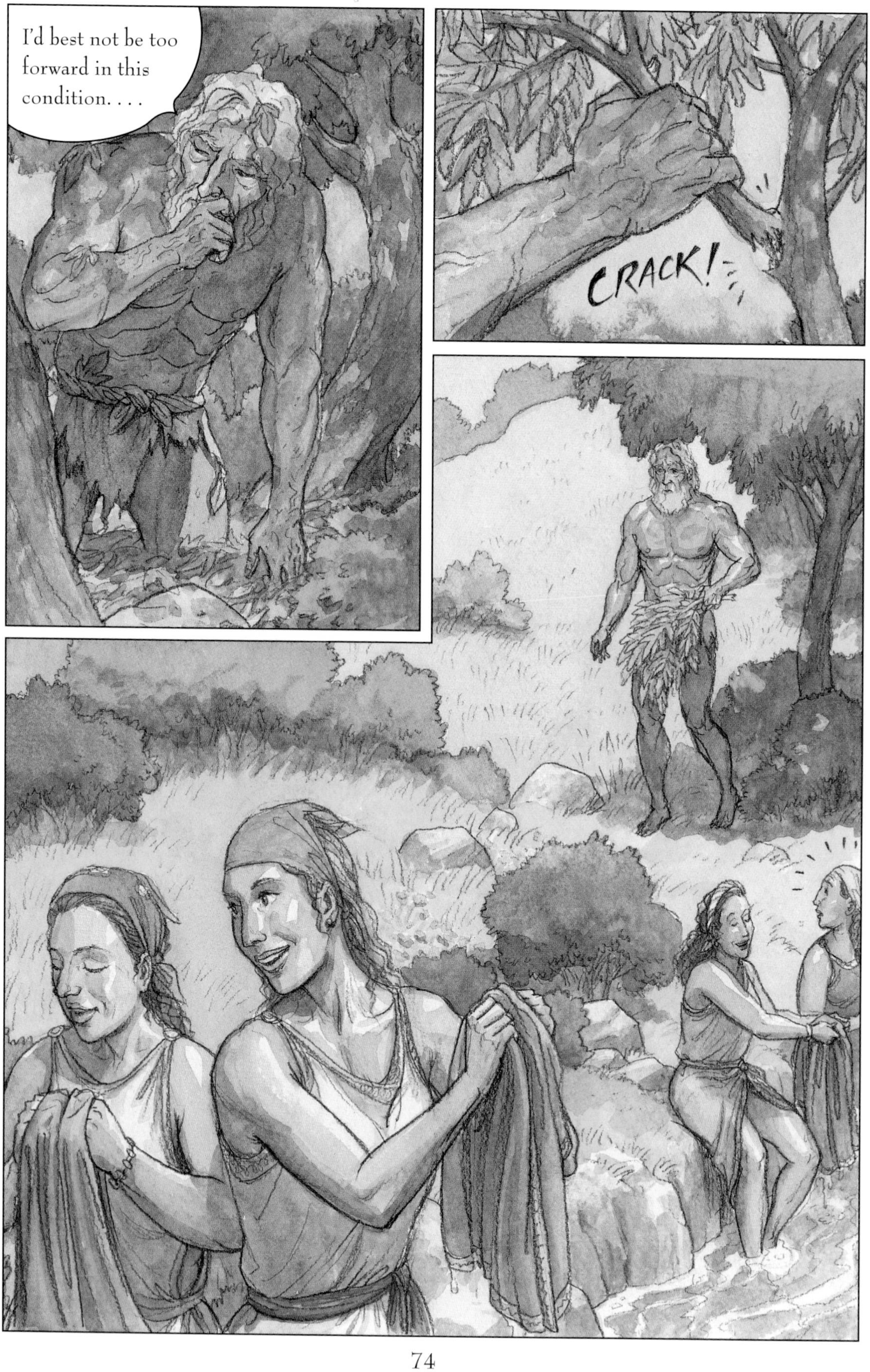
I'd best not be too forward in this condition. . . .
CRACK!

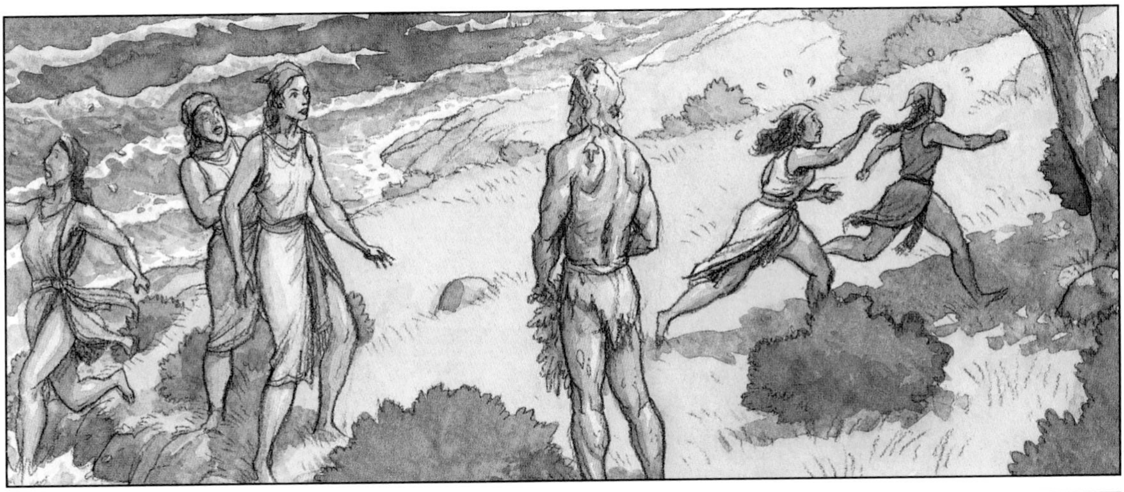

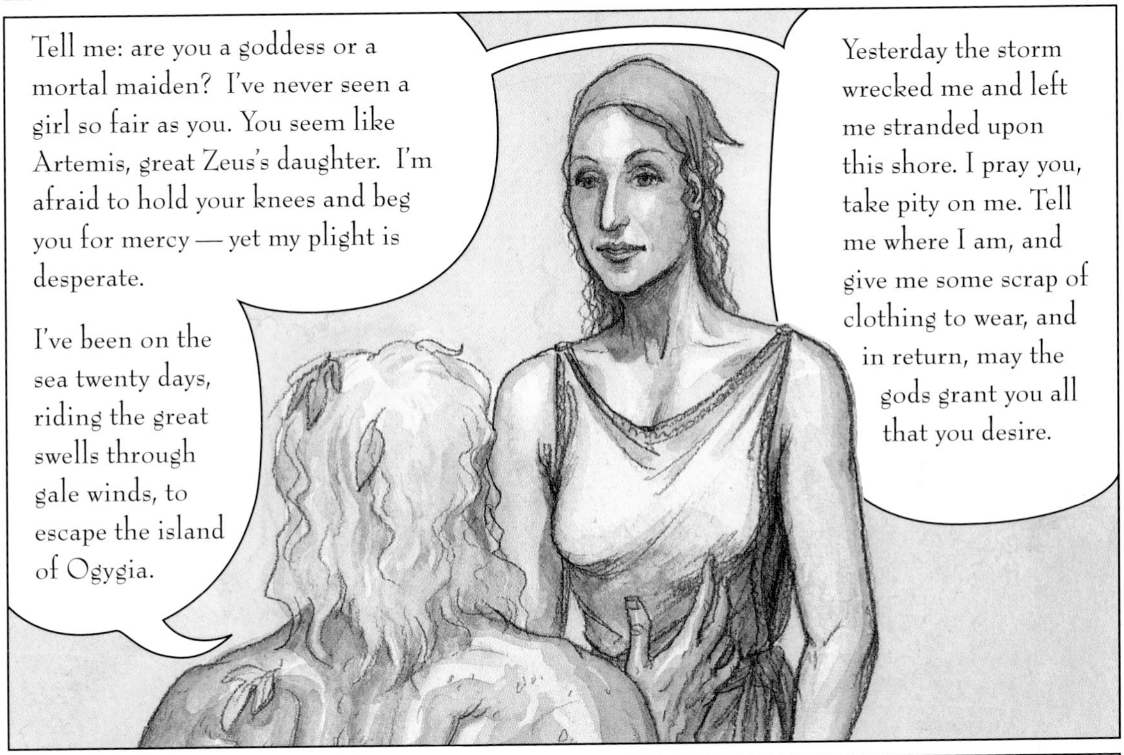
Tell me: are you a goddess or a mortal maiden? I've never seen a girl so fair as you. You seem like Artemis, great Zeus's daughter. I'm afraid to hold your knees and beg you for mercy — yet my plight is desperate.
I've been on the sea twenty days, riding the great swells through gale winds, to escape the island of Ogygia.
Yesterday the storm wrecked me and left me stranded upon this shore. I pray you, take pity on me. Tell me where I am, and give me some scrap of clothing to wear, and in return, may the gods grant you all that you desire.

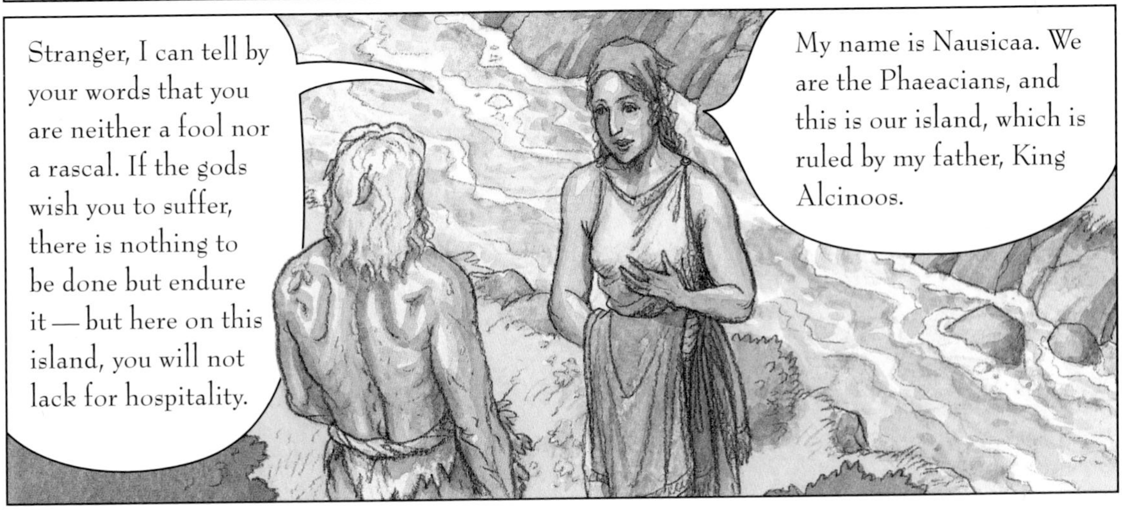
Stranger, I can tell by your words that you are neither a fool nor a rascal. If the gods wish you to suffer, there is nothing to be done but endure it — but here on this island, you will not lack for hospitality.
My name is Nausicaa. We are the Phaeacians, and this is our island, which is ruled by my father, King Alcinoos.

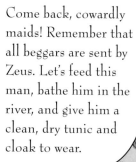

Come back, cowardly maids! Remember that all beggars are sent by Zeus. Let's feed this man, bathe him in the river, and give him a clean, dry tunic and cloak to wear.

Let me wash myself, princess. I'm embarrassed to let any high-born women touch my wrinkled skin and salt-caked hair.

Well, then, when you've bathed and eaten, we will show you the way to town.

I'll lead you partway, but when we approach the town, you must wait — if you followed me by the docks, the sailors would gossip.

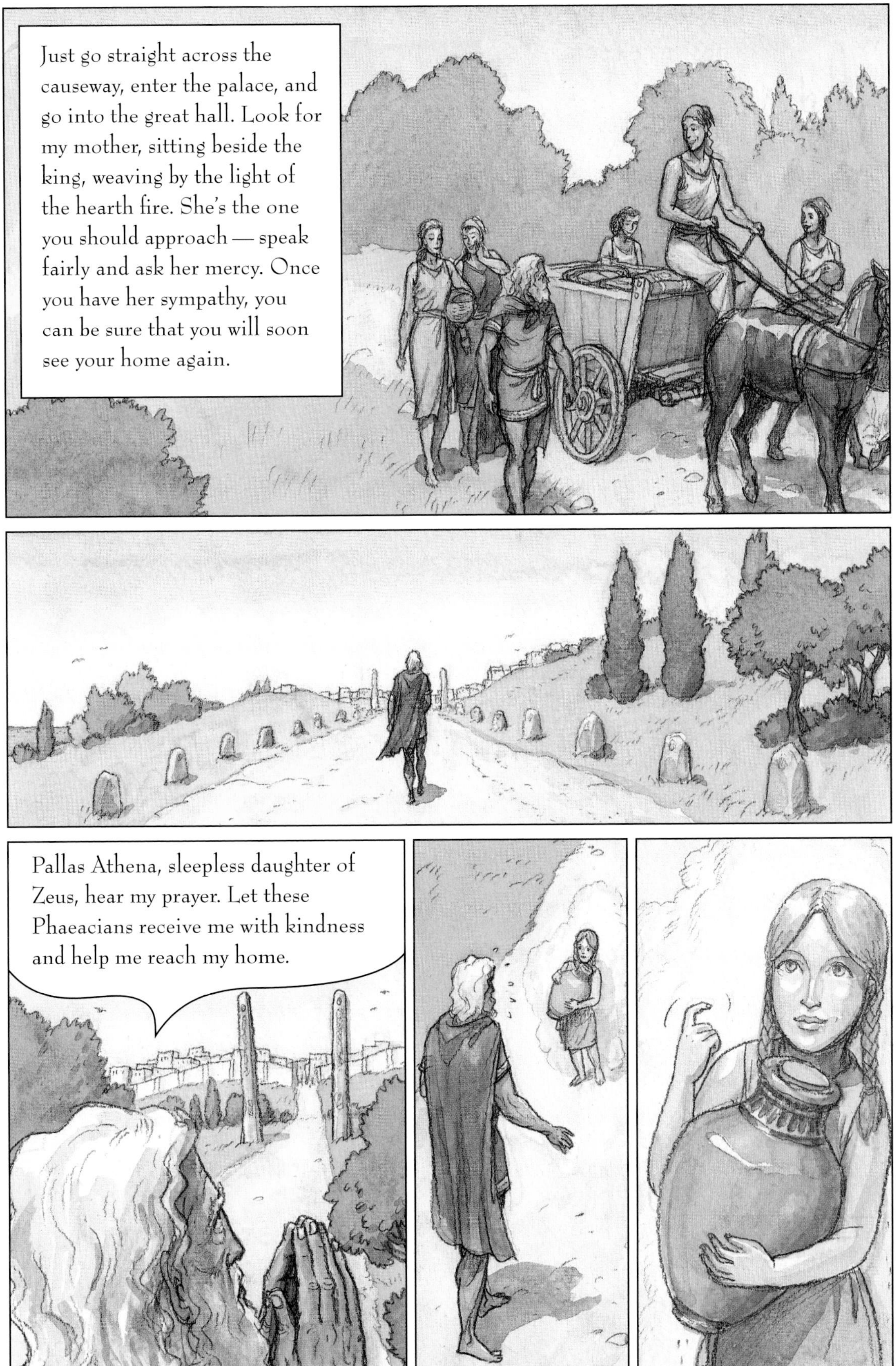
Just go straight across the causeway, enter the palace, and go into the great hall. Look for my mother, sitting beside the king, weaving by the light of the hearth fire. She's the one you should approach — speak fairly and ask her mercy. Once you have her sympathy, you can be sure that you will soon see your home again.
Pallas Athena, sleepless daughter of Zeus, hear my prayer. Let these Phaeacians receive me with kindness and help me reach my home.

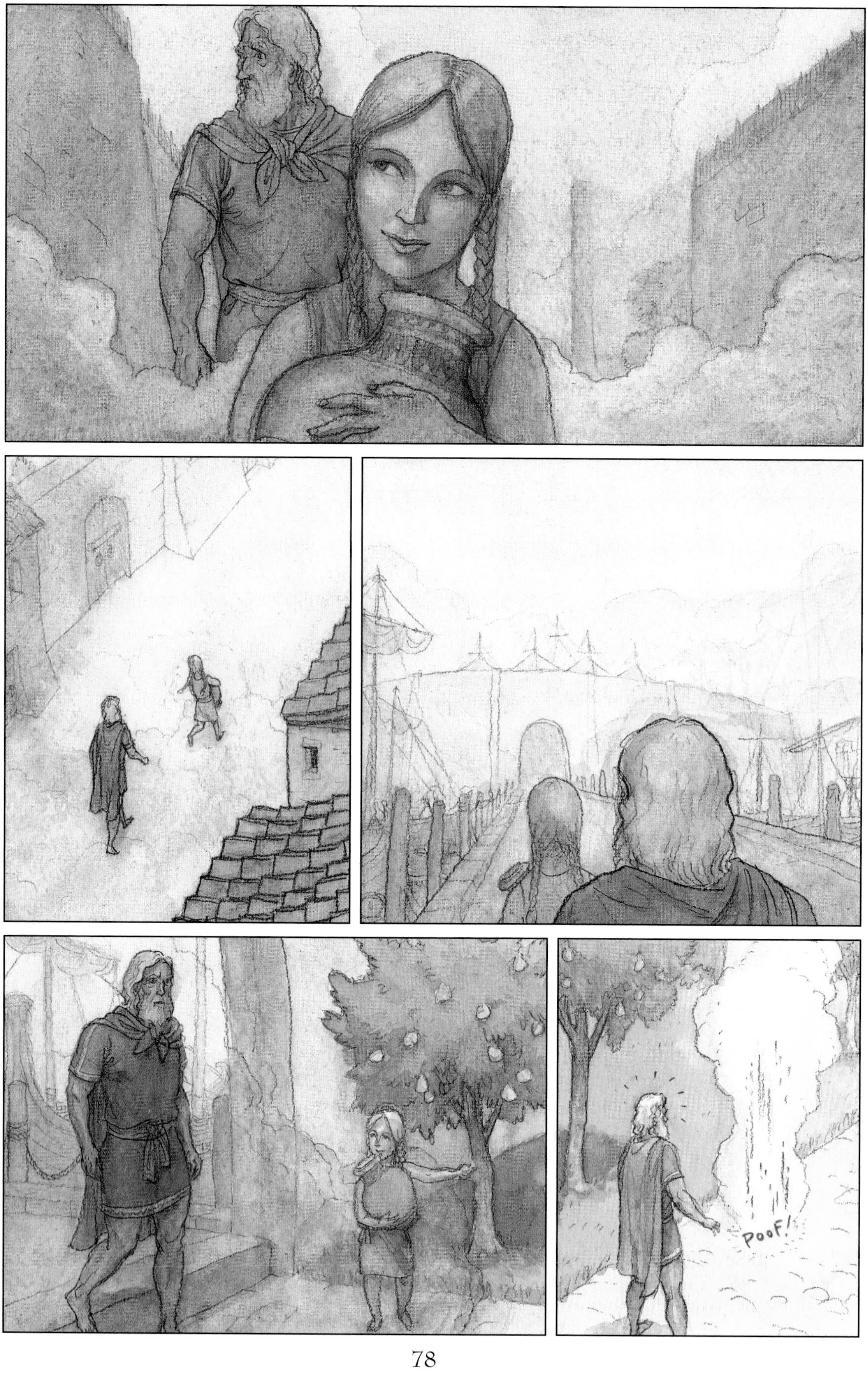
POOF!

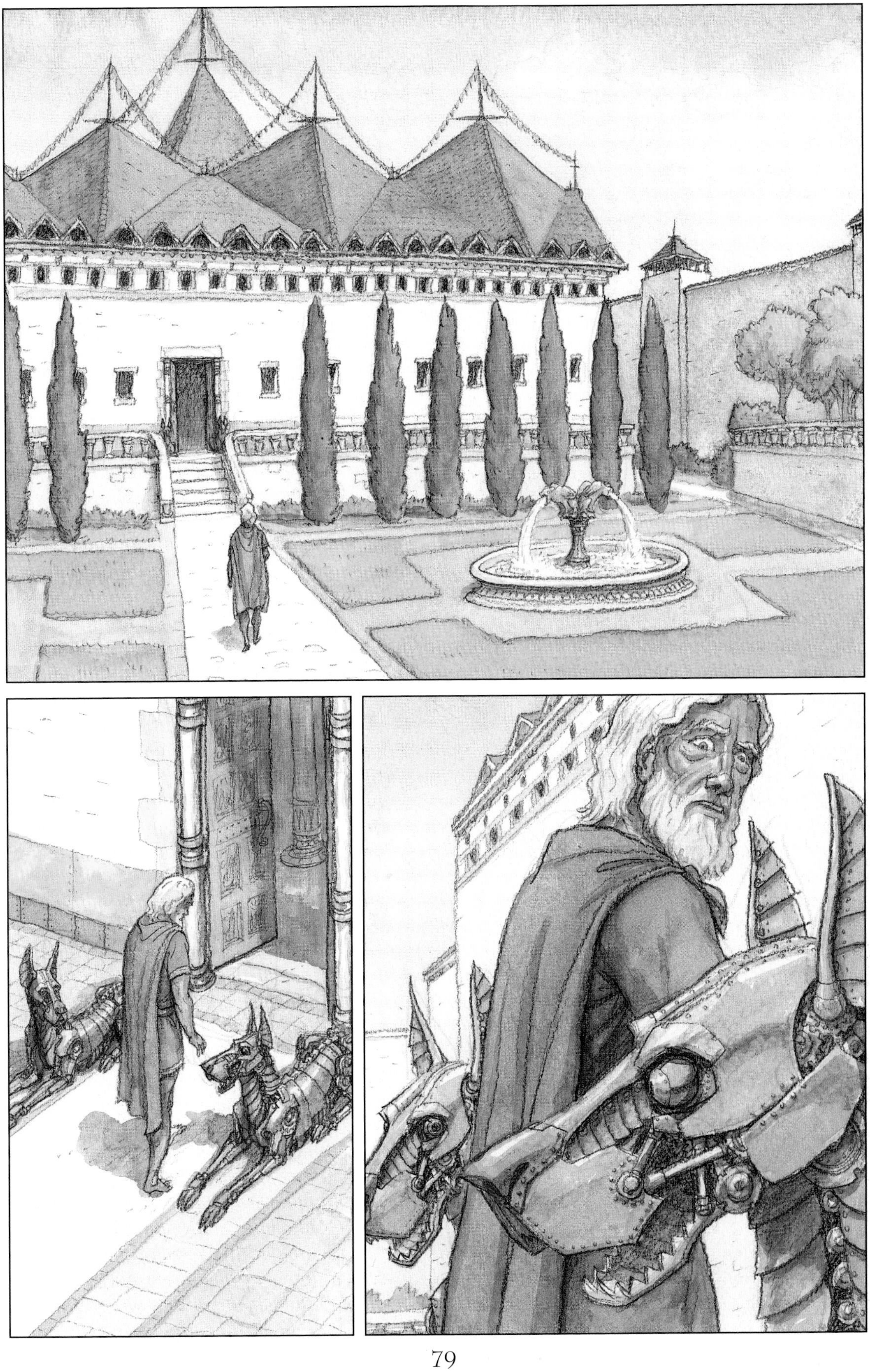

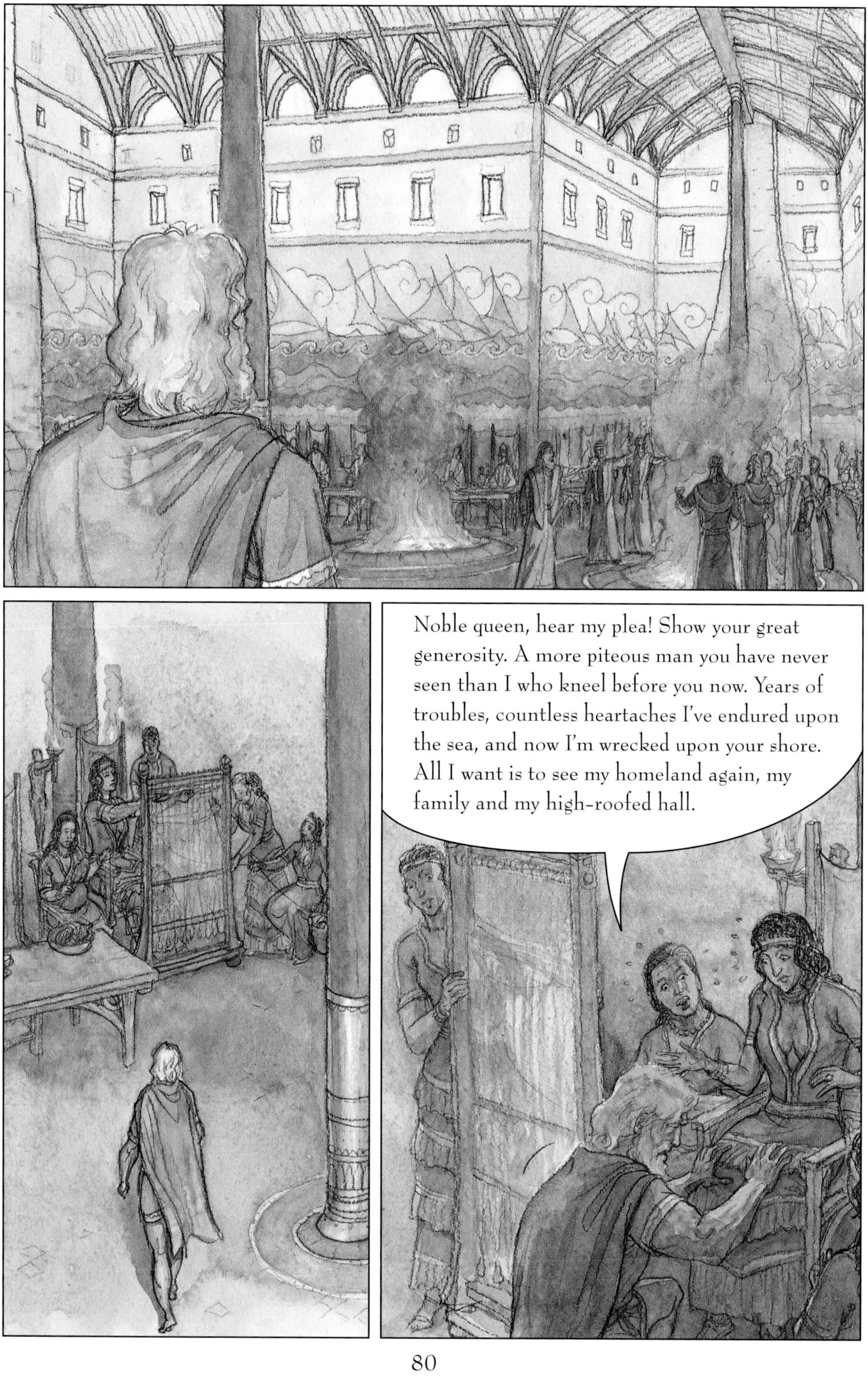
Noble queen, hear my plea! Show your great generosity. A more piteous man you have never seen than I who kneel before you now. Years of troubles, countless heartaches I've endured upon the sea, and now I'm wrecked upon your shore. All I want is to see my homeland again, my family and my high-roofed hall.

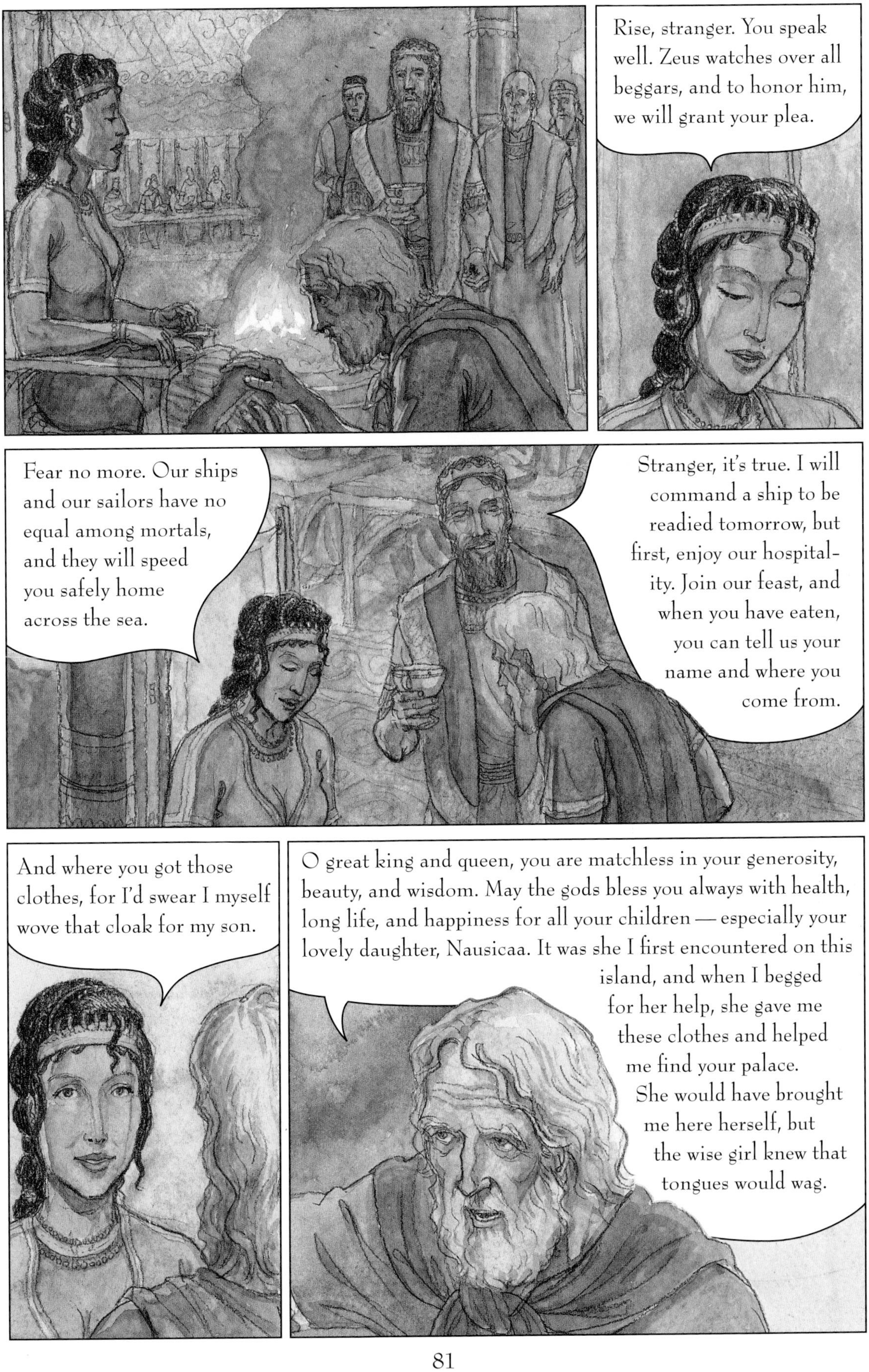
Rise, stranger. You speak well. Zeus watches over all beggars, and to honor him, we will grant your plea.
Fear no more. Our ships and our sailors have no equal among mortals, and they will speed you safely home across the sea.
Stranger, it's true. I will command a ship to be readied tomorrow, but first, enjoy our hospital-ity. Join our feast, and when you have eaten, you can tell us your name and where you come from.
And where you got those clothes, for I'd swear I myself wove that cloak for my son.
O great king and queen, you are matchless in your generosity, beauty, and wisdom. May the gods bless you always with health, long life, and happiness for all your children — especially your lovely daughter, Nausicaa. It was she I first encountered on this island, and when I begged for her help, she gave me these clothes and helped me find your palace. She would have brought me here herself, but the wise girl knew that tongues would wag.

As for the rest of my story, it is long and weary, painful for me even to think of.

Friends, our guest is tired. Let's go to bed. Tomorrow we will ready a ship, and hold a farewell feast for him with games, dancing, and gifts.

I will have my servants prepare a bed for you.

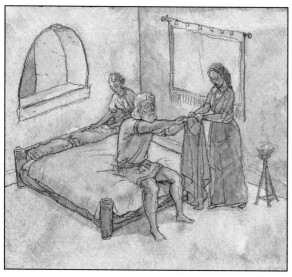

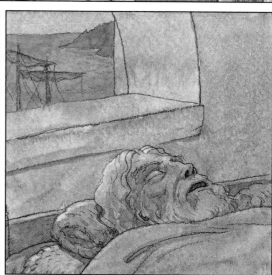

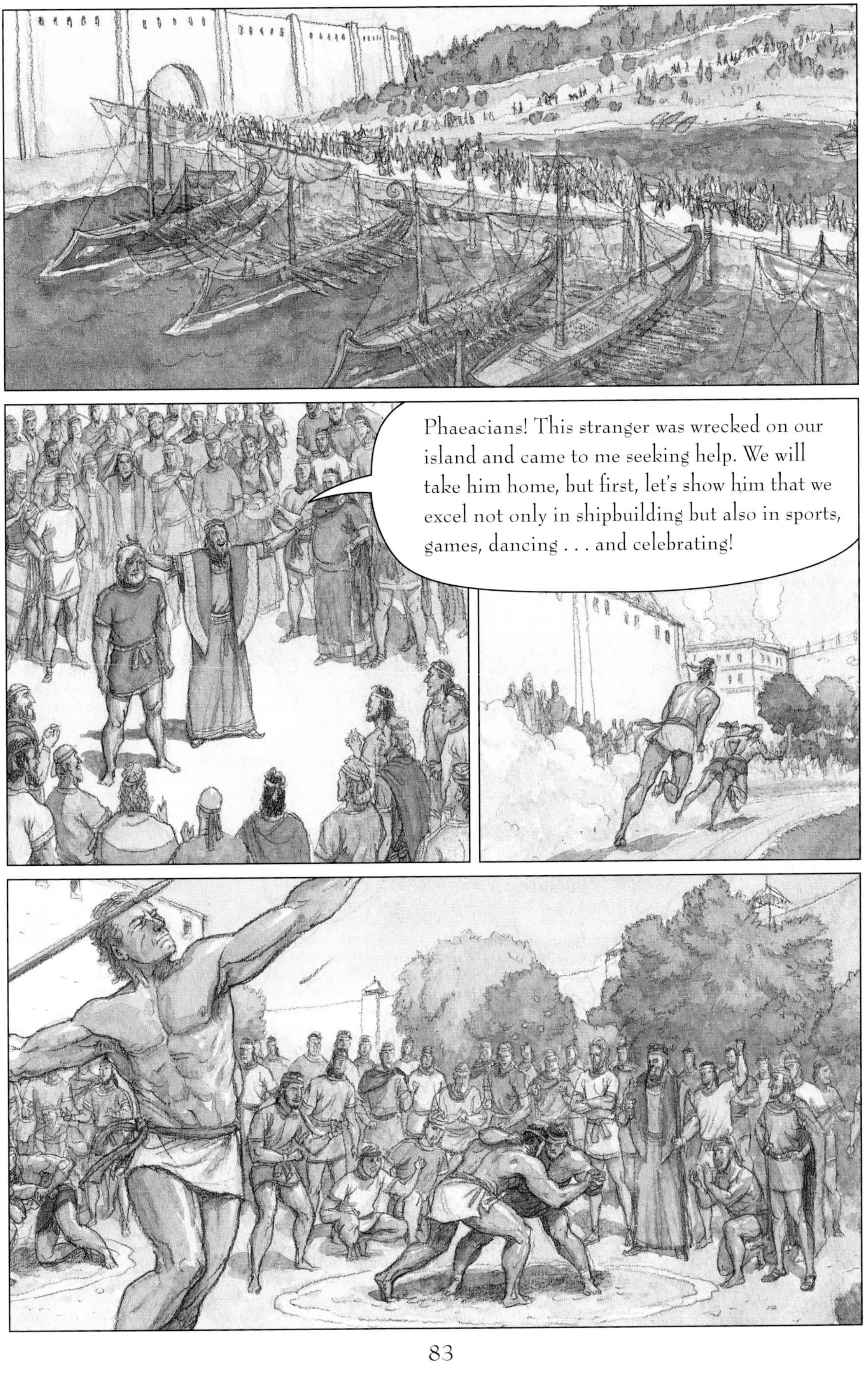
Phaeacians! This stranger was wrecked on our island and came to me seeking help. We will take him home, but first, let's show him that we excel not only in shipbuilding but also in sports, games, dancing . . . and celebrating!

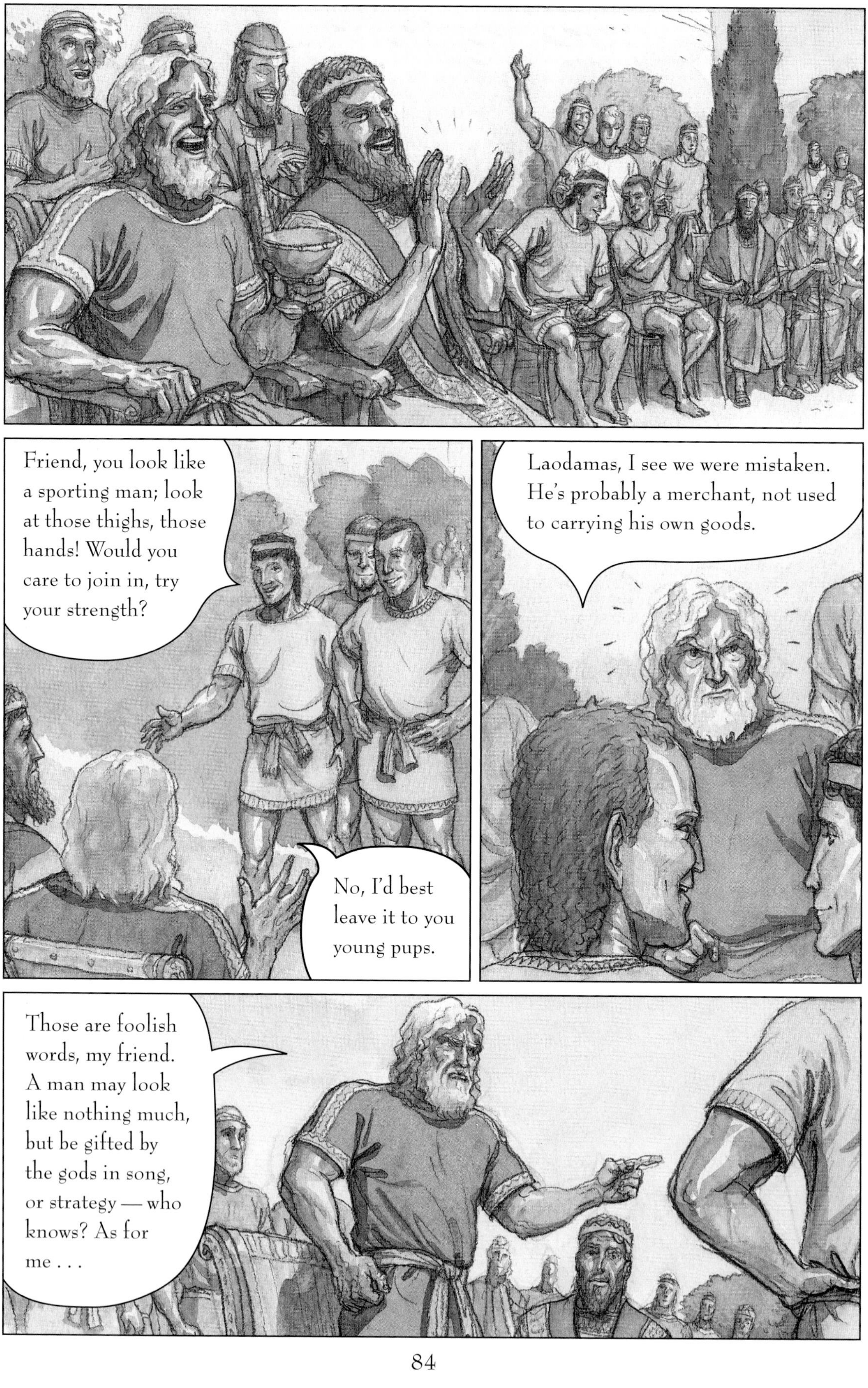
Friend, you look like a sporting man; look at those thighs, those hands! Would you care to join in, try your strength?
No, I'd best leave it to you young pups.
Laodamas, I see we were mistaken. He's probably a merchant, not used to carrying his own goods.
Those are foolish words, my friend. A man may look like nothing much, but be gifted by the gods in song, or strategy — who knows? As for me . . .

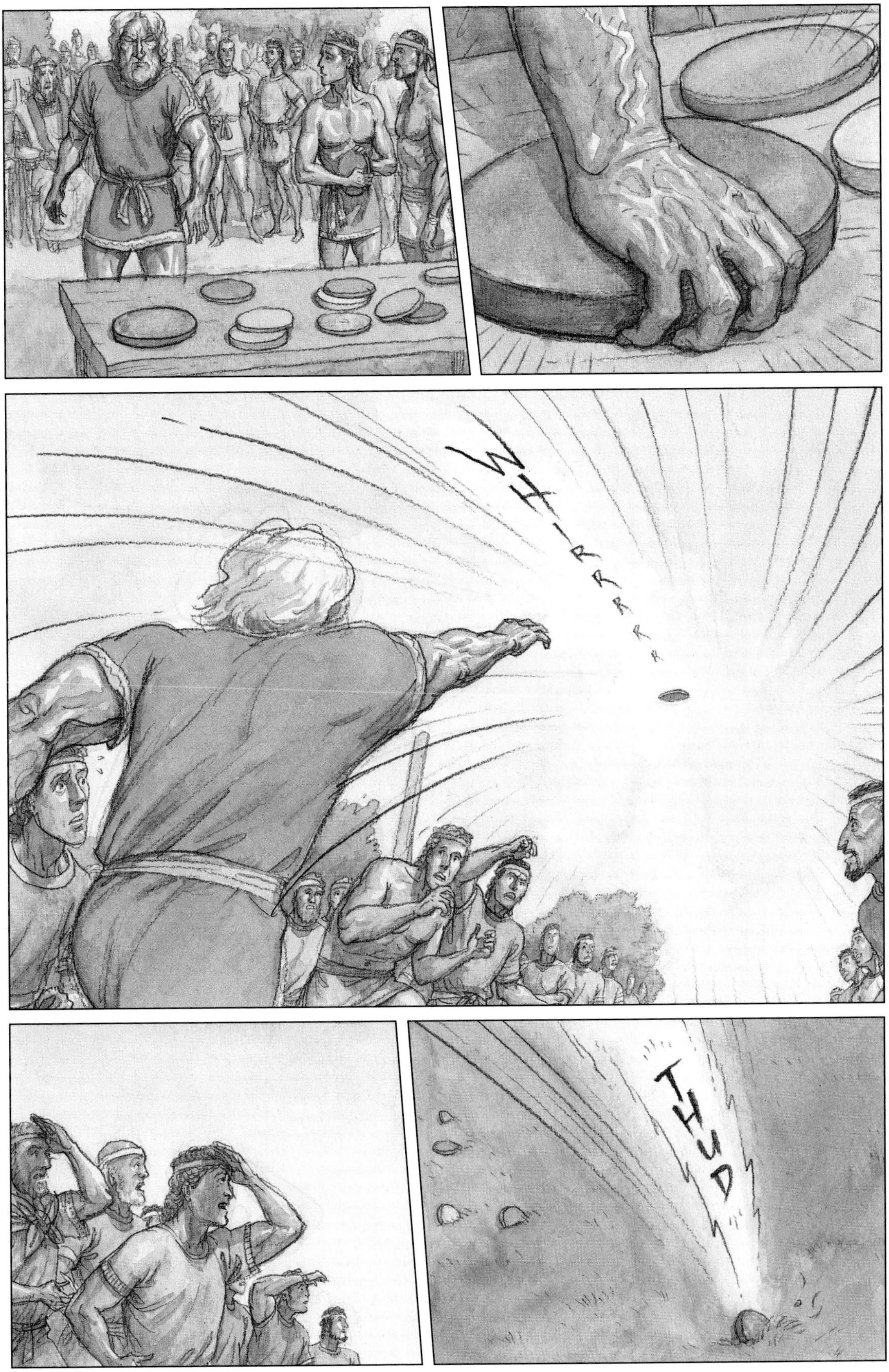
WHIRRRRRR
THUD

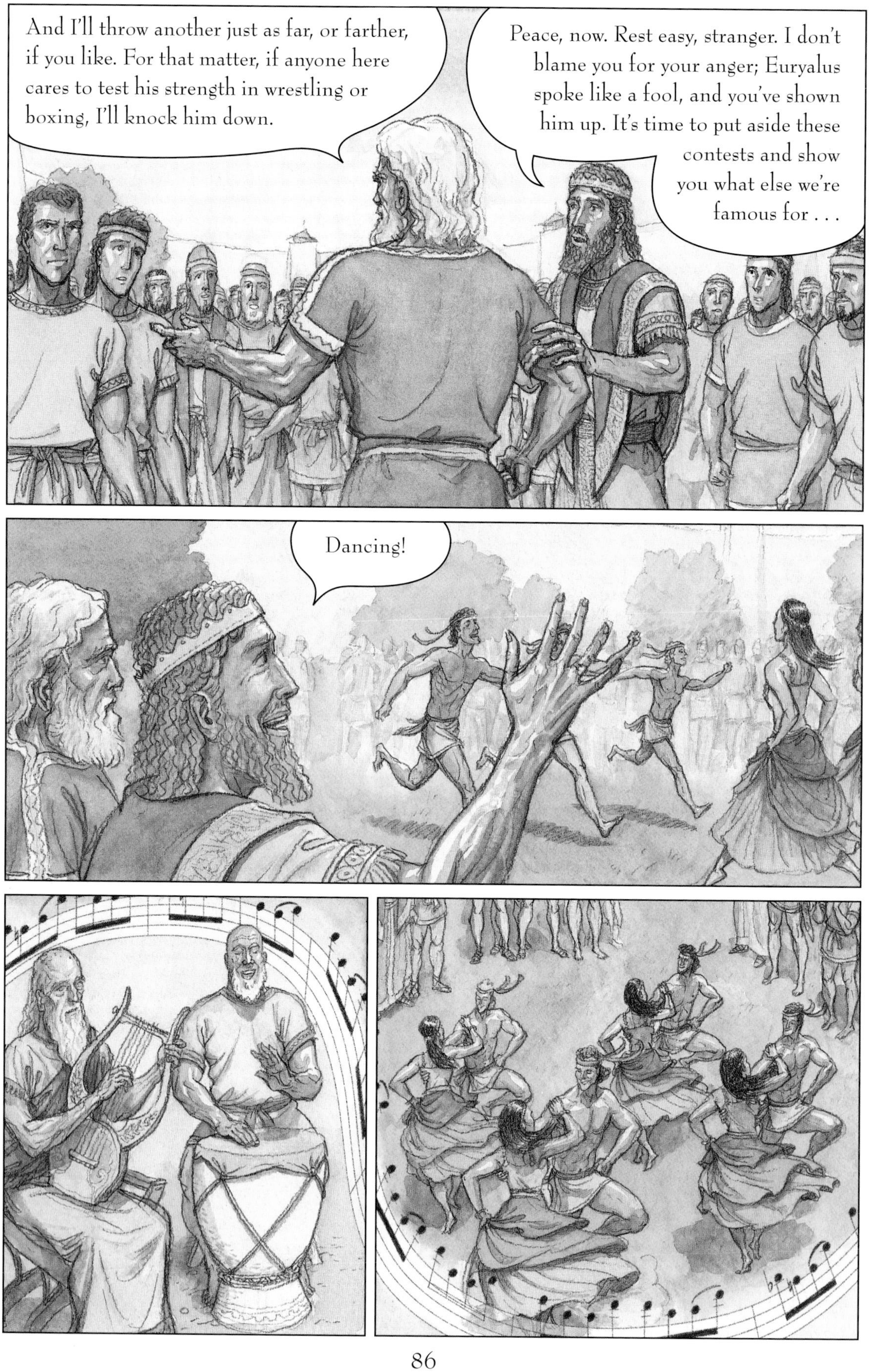
And I'll throw another just as far, or farther, if you like. For that matter, if anyone here cares to test his strength in wrestling or boxing, I'll knock him down.
Peace, now. Rest easy, stranger. I don't blame you for your anger; Euryalus spoke like a fool, and you've shown him up. It's time to put aside these contests and show you what else we're famous for . . .
Dancing!

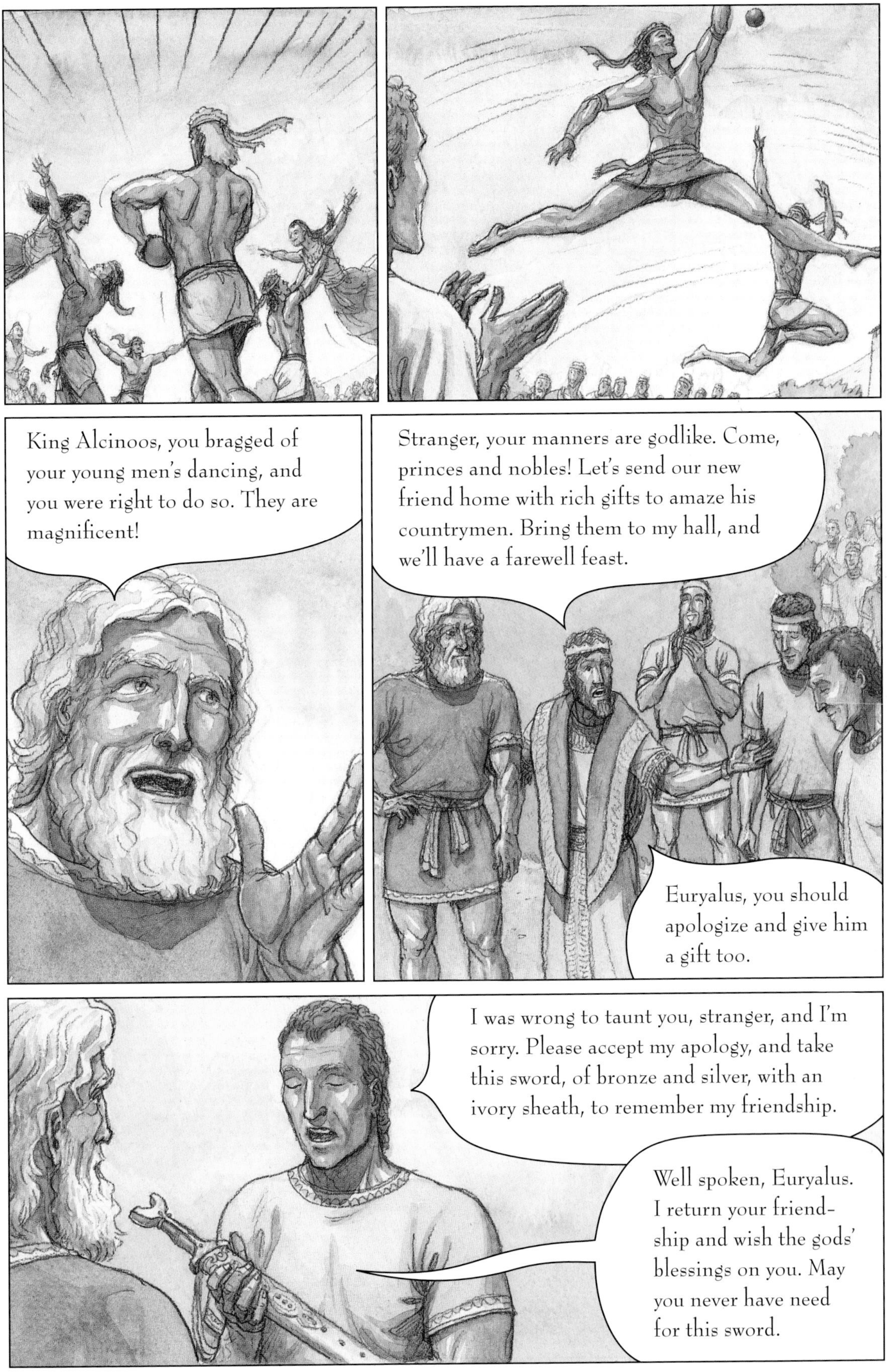
King Alcinoos, you bragged of your young men's dancing, and you were right to do so. They are magnificent!
Stranger, your manners are godlike. Come, princes and nobles! Let's send our new friend home with rich gifts to amaze his countrymen. Bring them to my hall, and we'll have a farewell feast.
Euryalus, you should apologize and give him a gift too.
I was wrong to taunt you, stranger, and I'm sorry. Please accept my apology, and take this sword, of bronze and silver, with an ivory sheath, to remember my friendship.
Well spoken, Euryalus. I return your friend-ship and wish the gods' blessings on you. May you never have need for this sword.

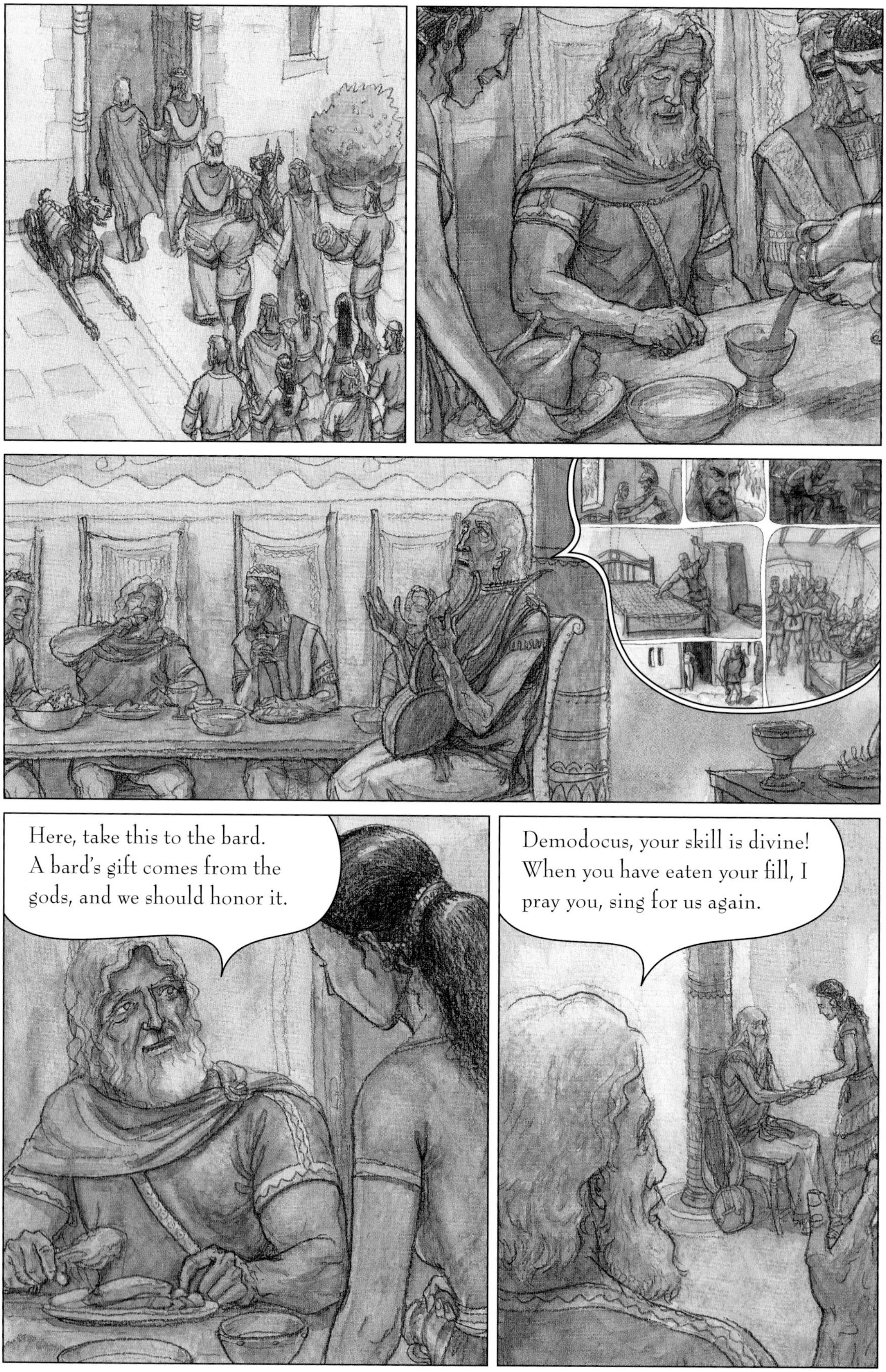
Here, take this to the bard.
A bard's gift comes from the gods, and we should honor it.
Demodocus, your skill is divine! When you have eaten your fill, I pray you, sing for us again.

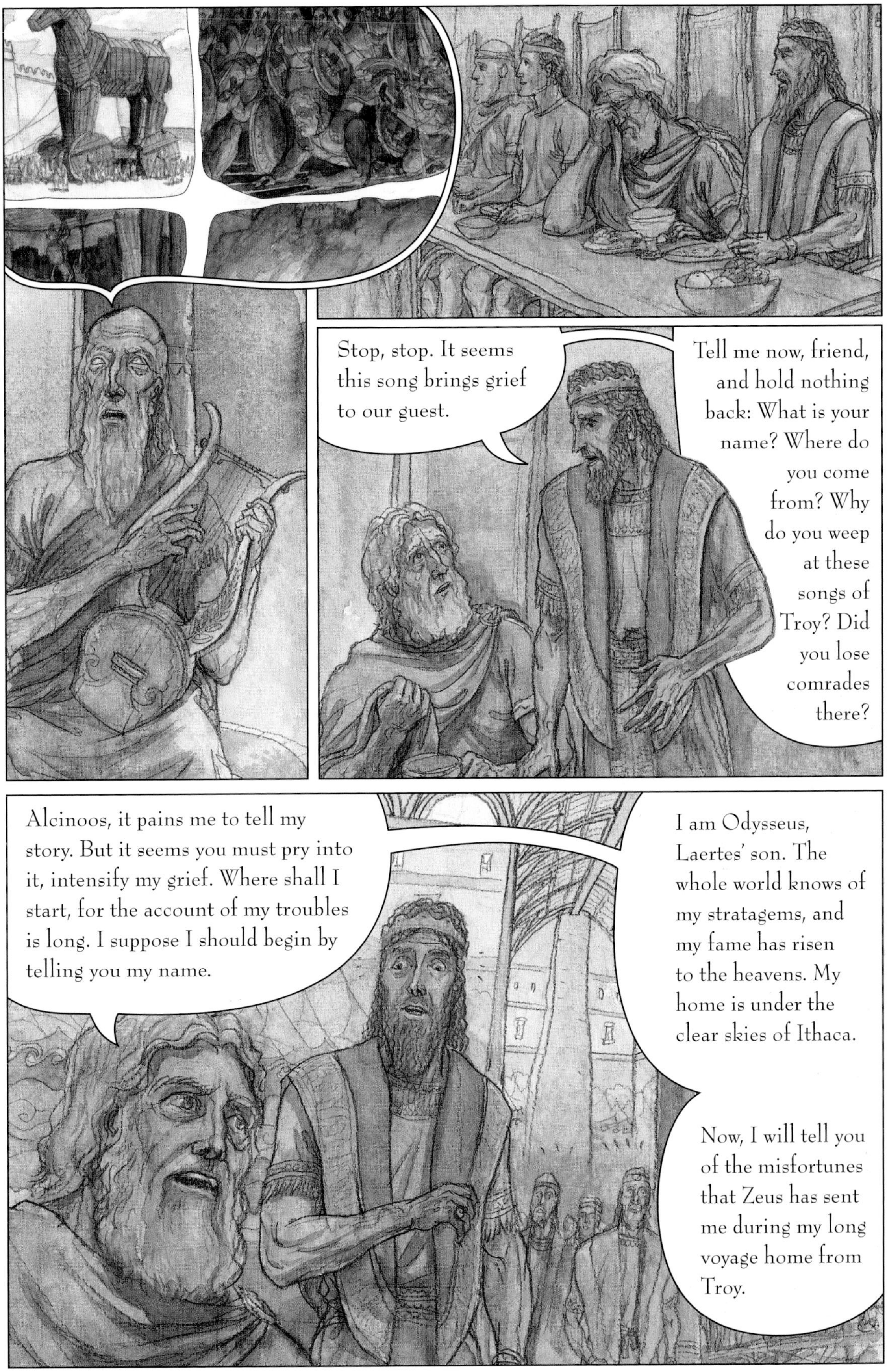
Stop, stop. It seems this song brings grief to our guest.
Tell me now, friend, and hold nothing back: What is your name? Where do you come from? Why do you weep at these songs of Troy? Did you lose comrades there?
Alcinoos, it pains me to tell my story. But it seems you must pry into it, intensify my grief. Where shall I start, for the account of my troubles is long. I suppose I should begin by telling you my name.
I am Odysseus, Laertes' son. The whole world knows of my stratagems, and my fame has risen to the heavens. My home is under the clear skies of Ithaca.
Now, I will tell you of the misfortunes that Zeus has sent me during my long voyage home from Troy.

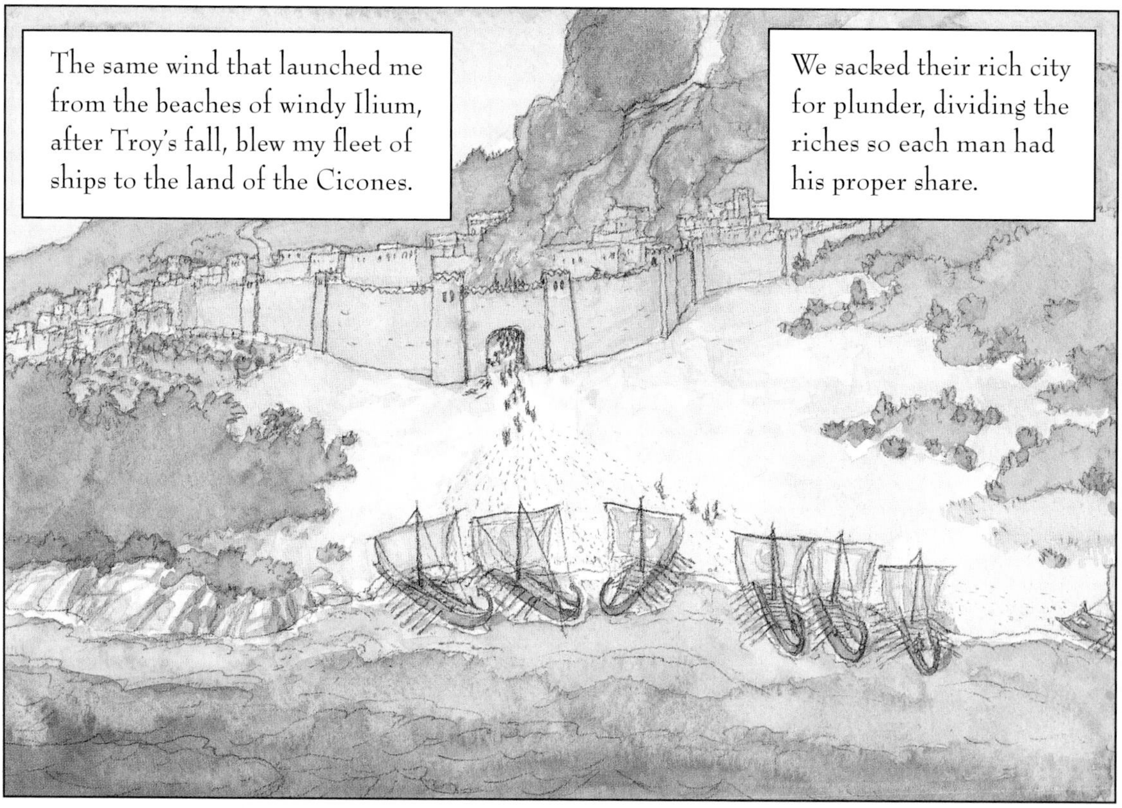
The same wind that launched me from the beaches of windy Ilium, after Troy's fall, blew my fleet of ships to the land of the Cicones.
We sacked their rich city for plunder, dividing the riches so each man had his proper share.

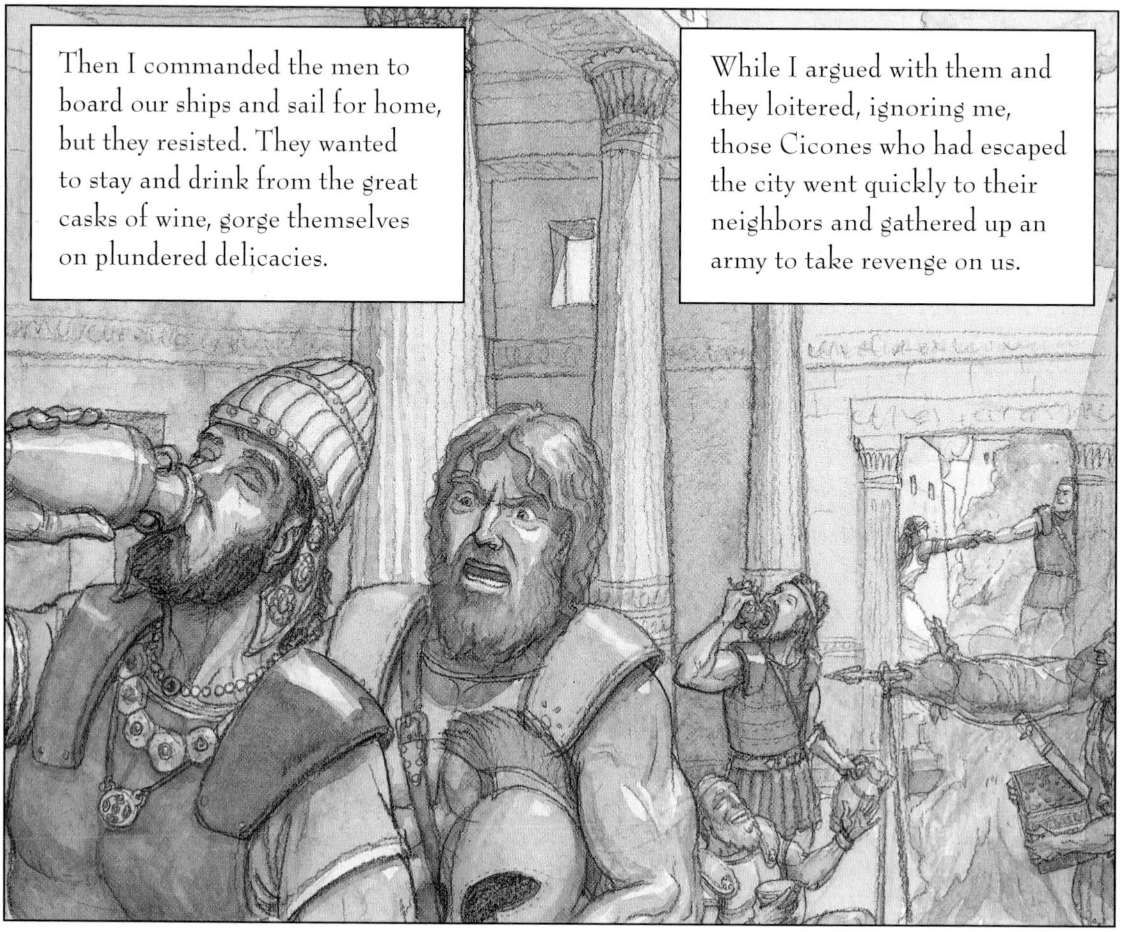
Then I commanded the men to board our ships and sail for home, but they resisted. They wanted to stay and drink from the great casks of wine, gorge themselves on plundered delicacies.
While I argued with them and they loitered, ignoring me, those Cicones who had escaped the city went quickly to their neighbors and gathered up an army to take revenge on us.

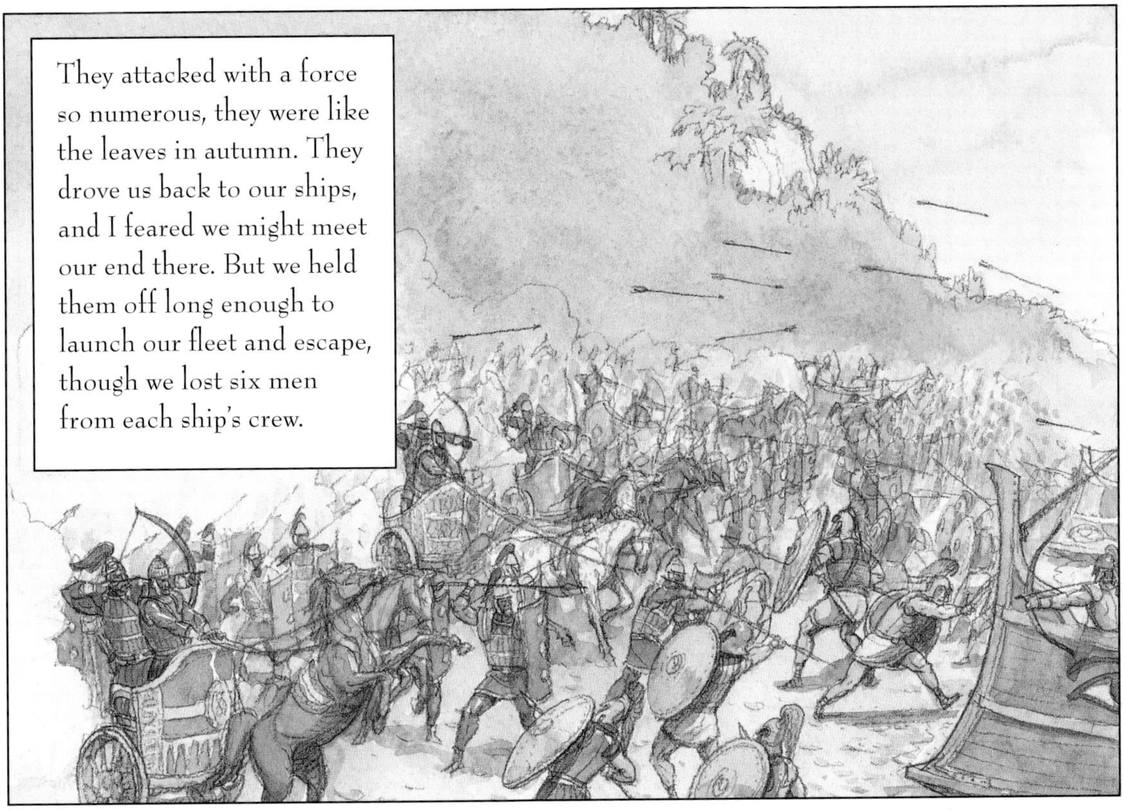
They attacked with a force so numerous, they were like the leaves in autumn. They drove us back to our ships, and I feared we might meet our end there. But we held them off long enough to launch our fleet and escape, though we lost six men from each ship's crew.

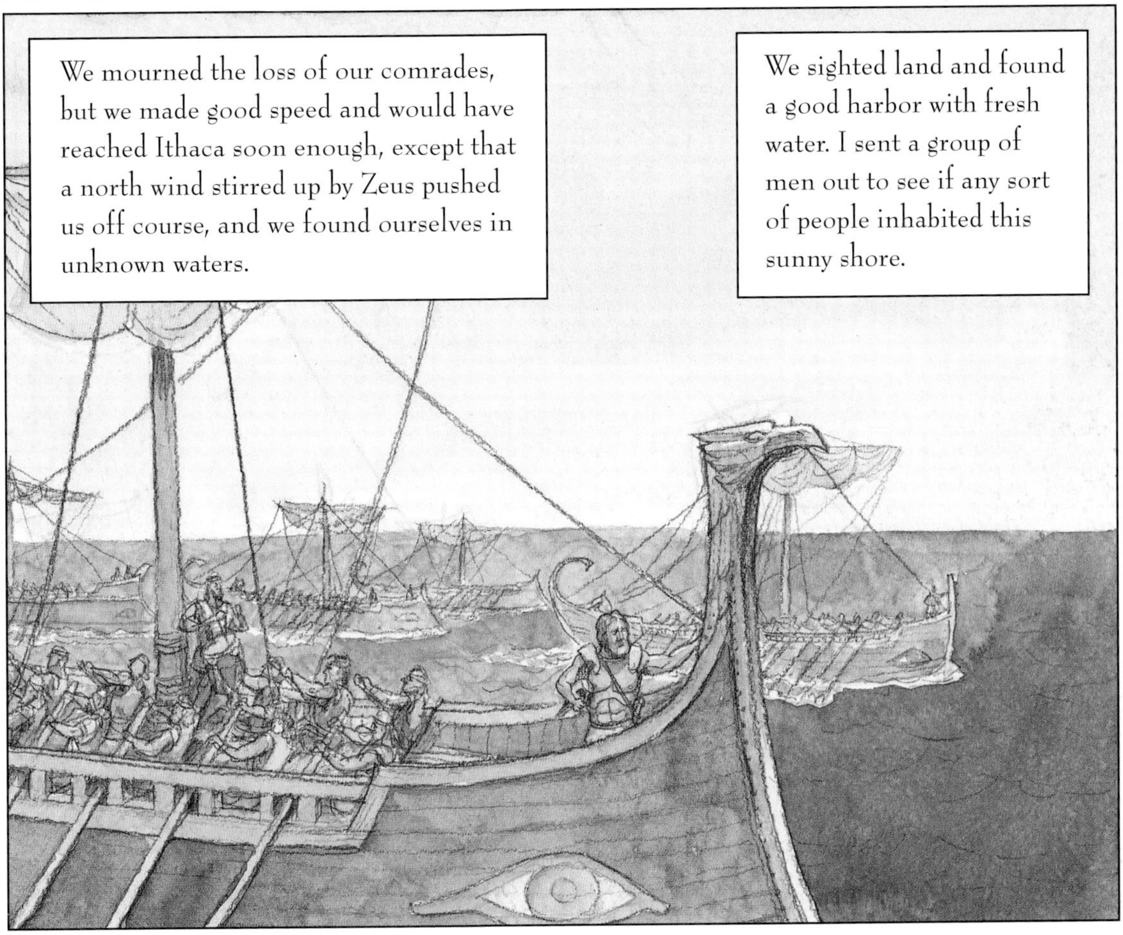
We mourned the loss of our comrades, but we made good speed and would have reached Ithaca soon enough, except that a north wind stirred up by Zeus pushed us off course, and we found ourselves in unknown waters.
We sighted land and found a good harbor with fresh water. I sent a group of men out to see if any sort of people inhabited this sunny shore.

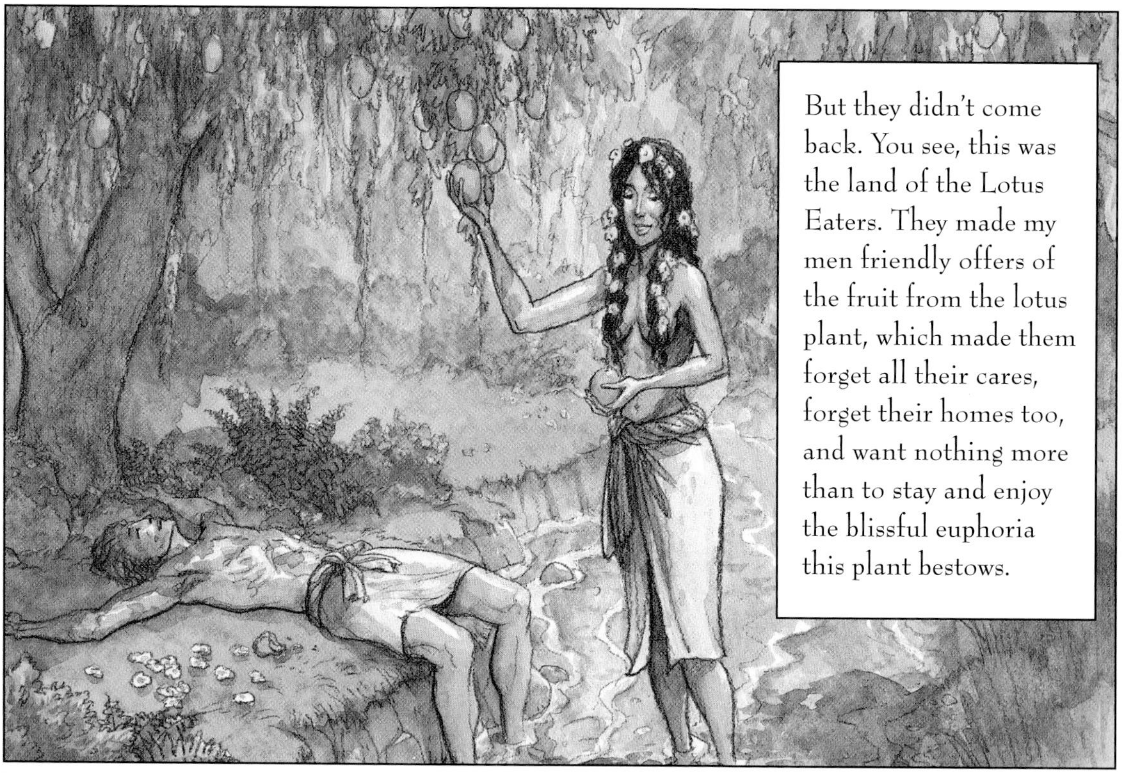
But they didn't come back. You see, this was the land of the Lotus Eaters. They made my men friendly offers of the fruit from the lotus plant, which made them forget all their cares, forget their homes too, and want nothing more than to stay and enjoy the blissful euphoria this plant bestows.

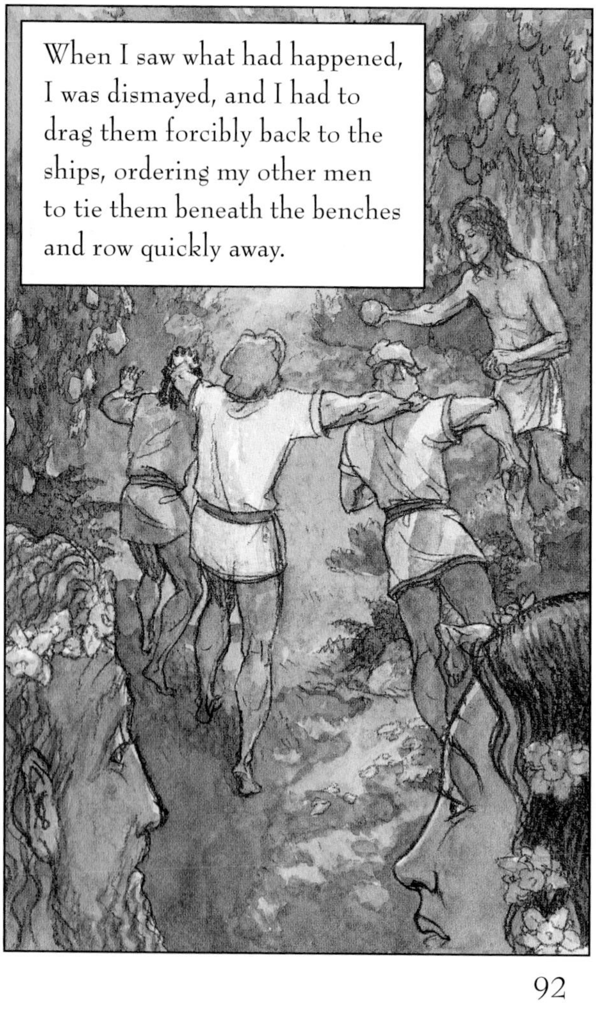
When I saw what had happened, I was dismayed, and I had to drag them forcibly back to the ships, ordering my other men to tie them beneath the benches and row quickly away.

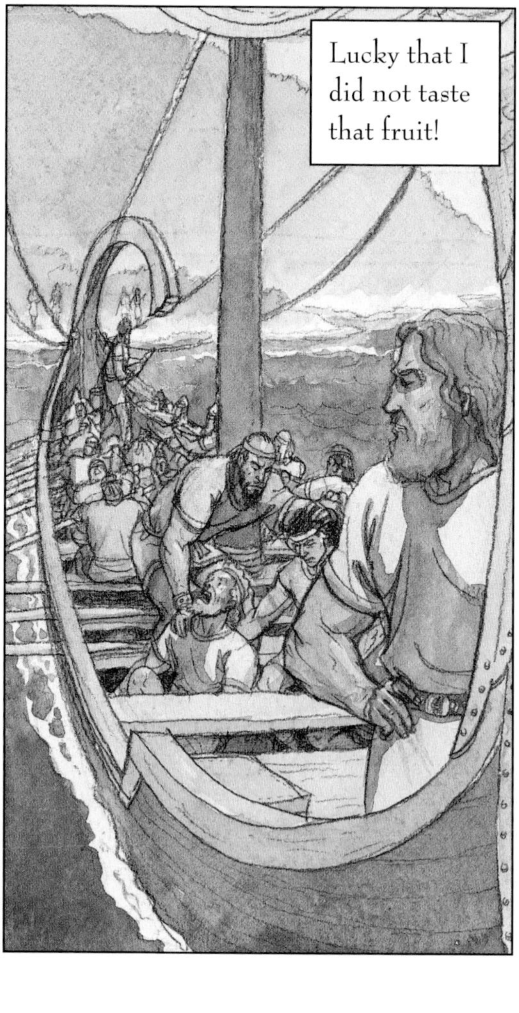
Lucky that I did not taste that fruit!

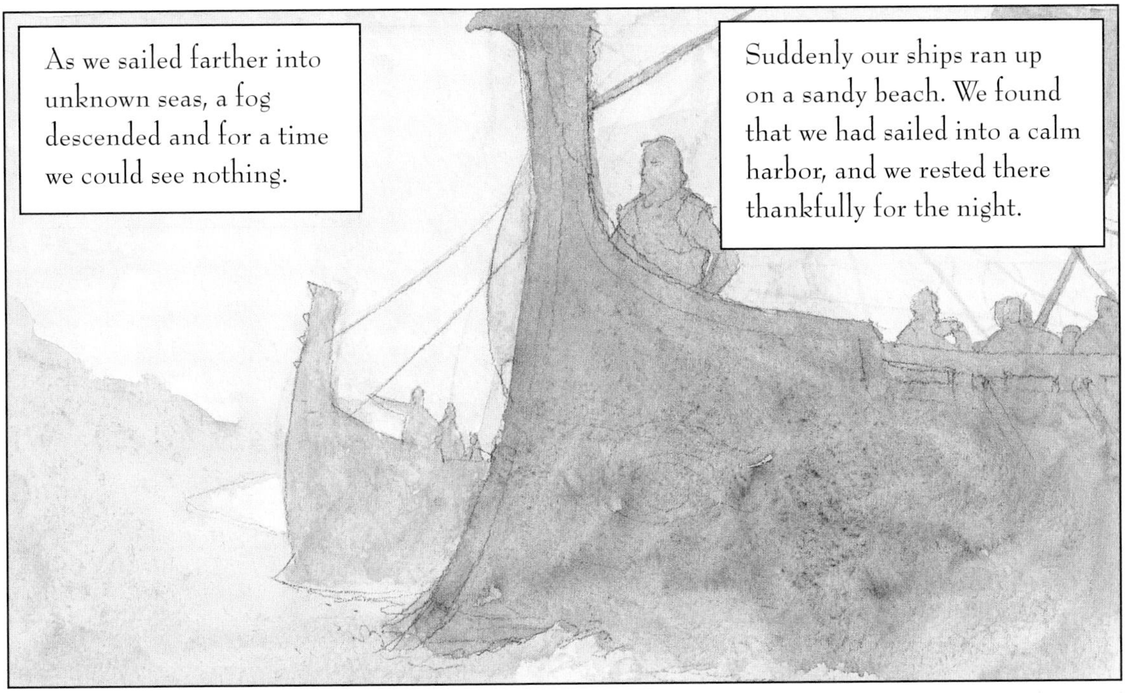
As we sailed farther into unknown seas, a fog descended and for a time we could see nothing.
Suddenly our ships ran up on a sandy beach. We found that we had sailed into a calm harbor, and we rested there thankfully for the night.

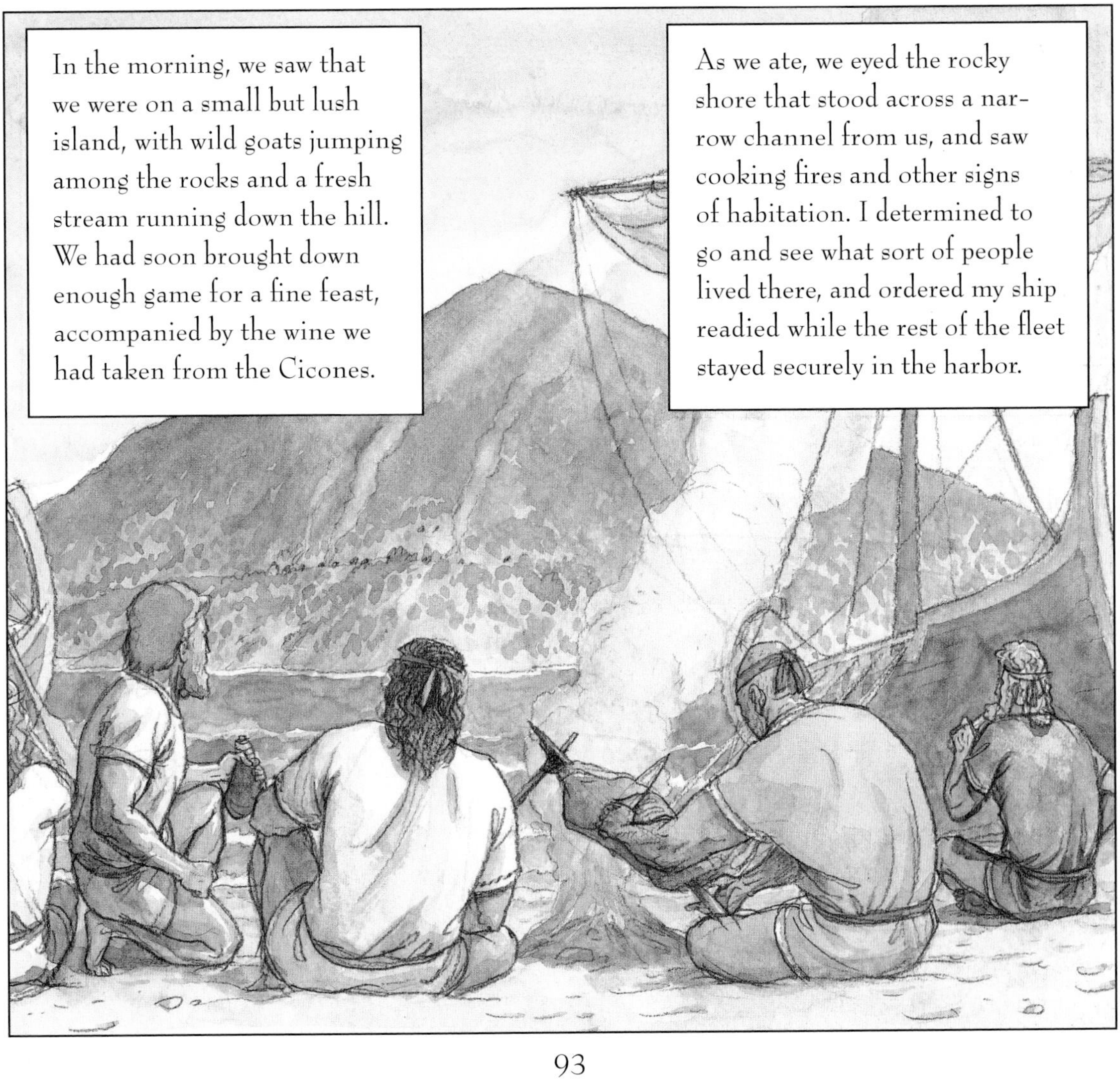
In the morning, we saw that we were on a small but lush island, with wild goats jumping among the rocks and a fresh stream running down the hill. We had soon brought down enough game for a fine feast, accompanied by the wine we had taken from the Cicones.
As we ate, we eyed the rocky shore that stood across a narrow channel from us, and saw cooking fires and other signs of habitation. I determined to go and see what sort of people lived there, and ordered my ship readied while the rest of the fleet stayed securely in the harbor.

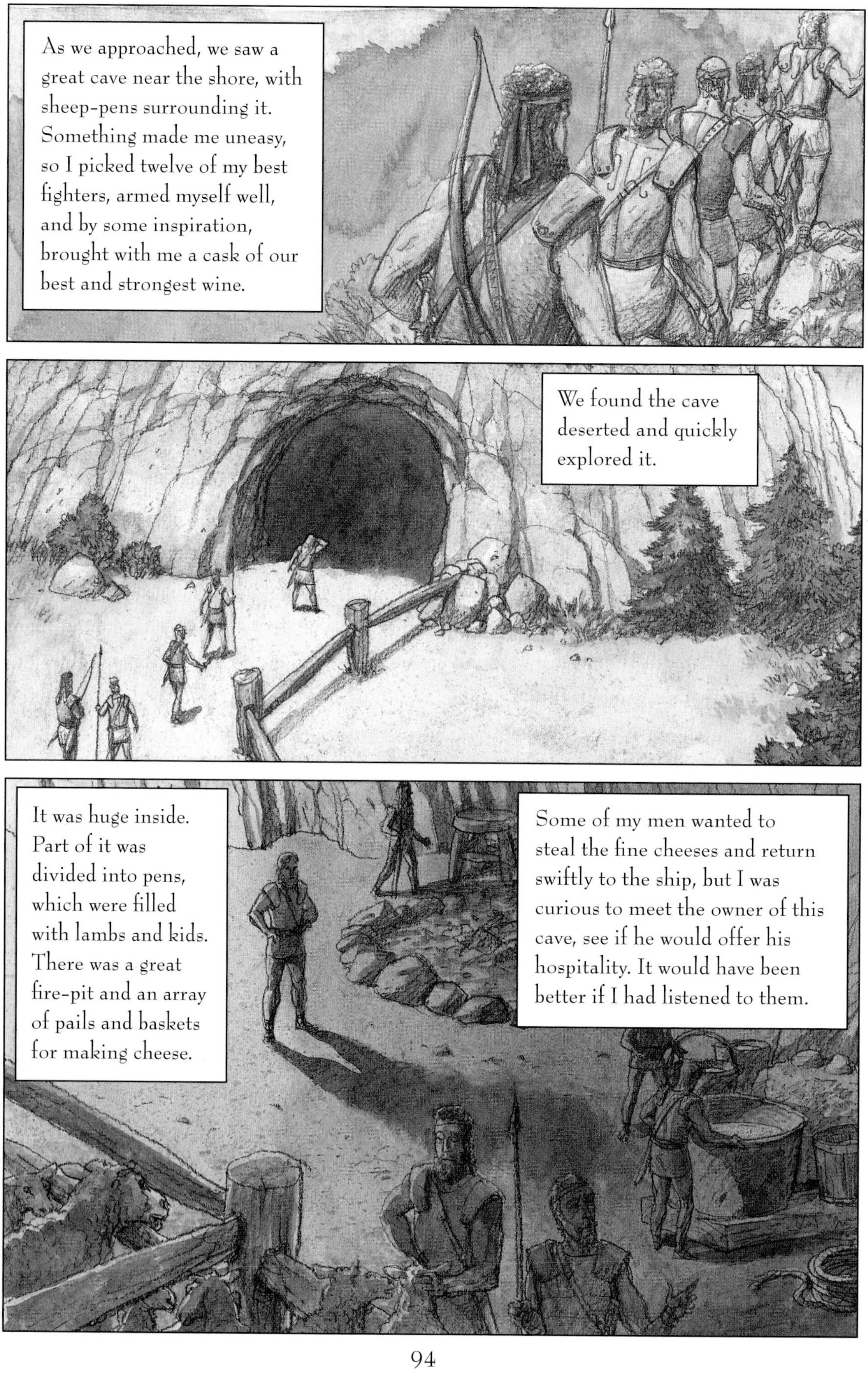
As we approached, we saw a great cave near the shore, with sheep-pens surrounding it. Something made me uneasy, so I picked twelve of my best fighters, armed myself well, and by some inspiration, brought with me a cask of our best and strongest wine.
We found the cave deserted and quickly explored it.
It was huge inside. Part of it was divided into pens, which were filled with lambs and kids. There was a great fire-pit and an array of pails and baskets for making cheese.
Some of my men wanted to steal the fine cheeses and return swiftly to the ship, but I was curious to meet the owner of this cave, see if he would offer his hospitality. It would have been better if I had listened to them.

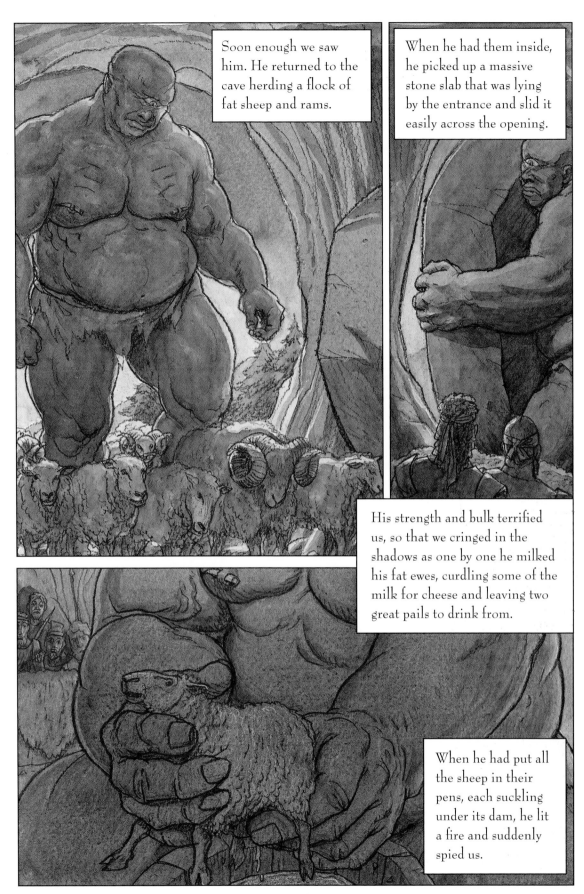

Soon enough we saw him. He returned to the cave herding a flock of fat sheep and rams.

When he had them inside, he picked up a massive stone slab that was lying by the entrance and slid it easily across the opening.

His strength and bulk terrified us, so that we cringed in the shadows as one by one he milked his fat ewes, curdling some of the milk for cheese and leaving two great pails to drink from.

When he had put all the sheep in their pens, each suckling under its dam, he lit a fire and suddenly spied us.

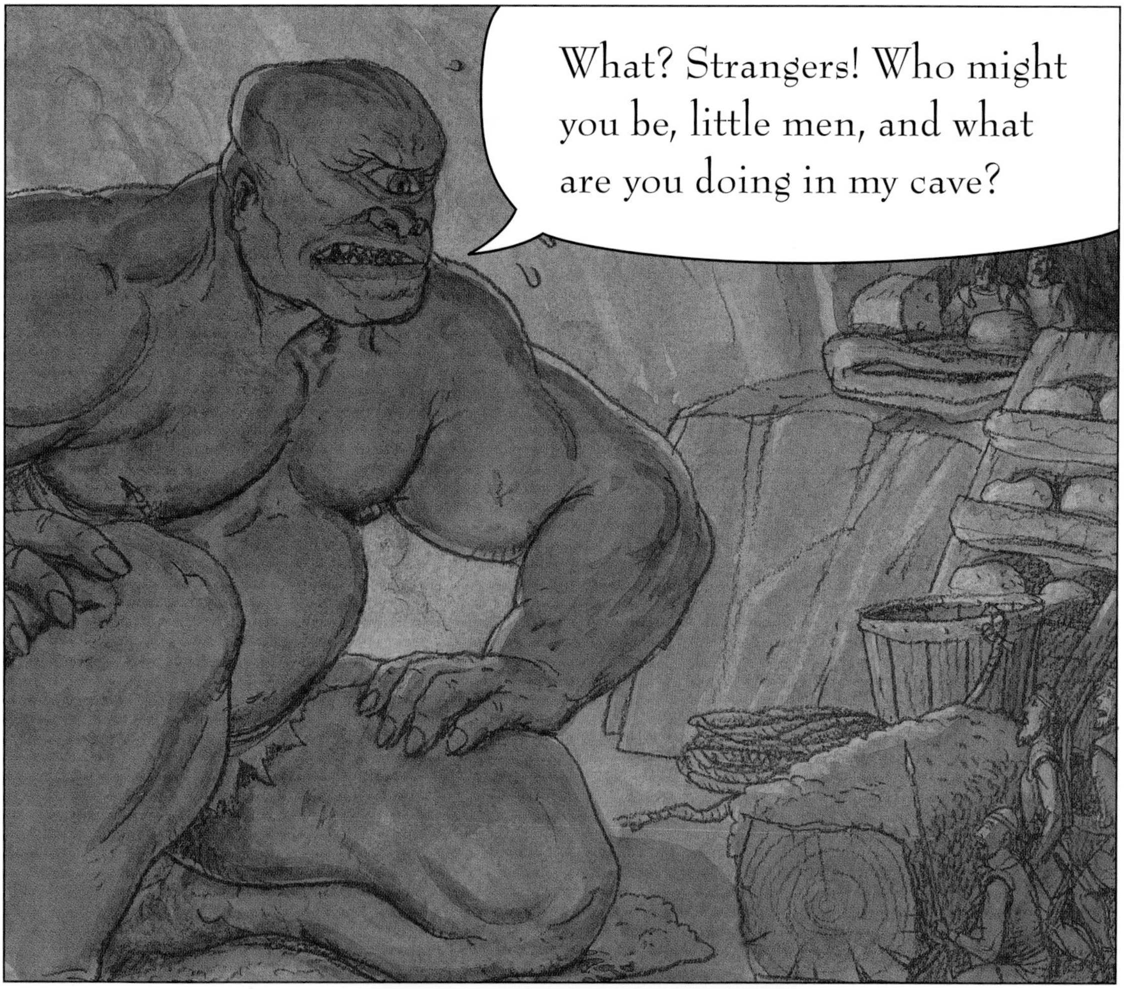
What? Strangers! Who might you be, little men, and what are you doing in my cave?

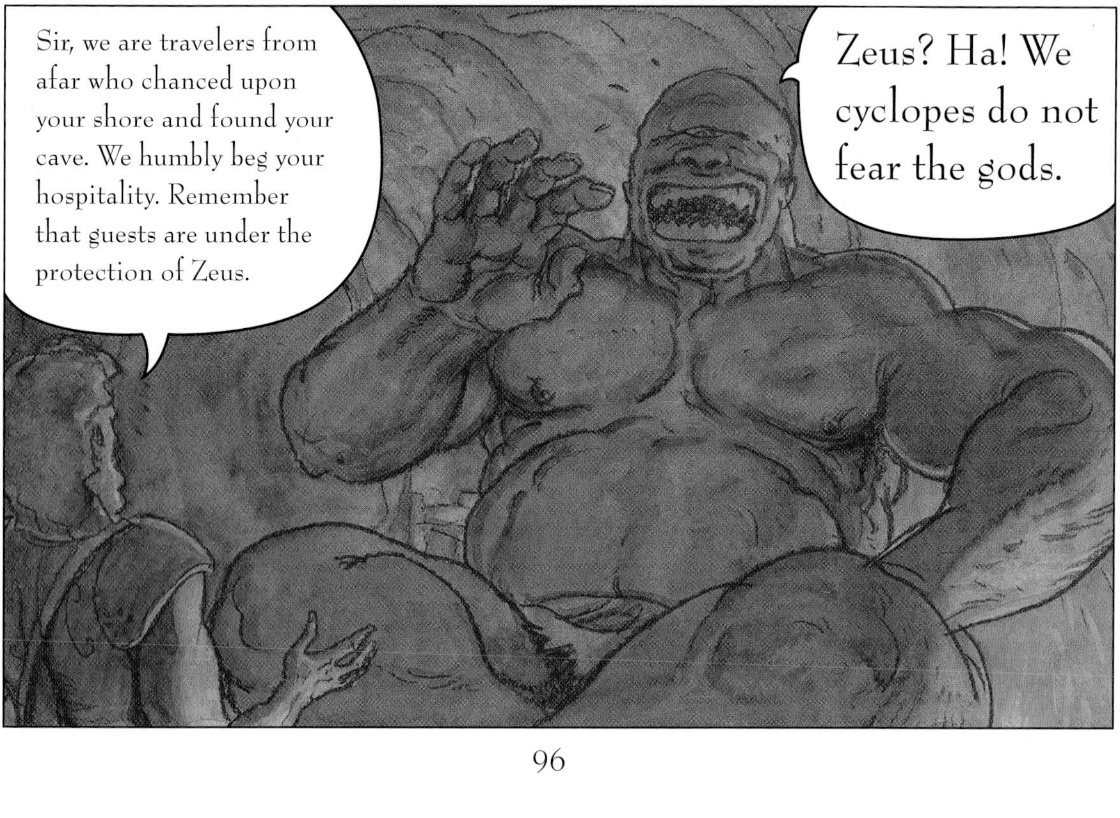
Sir, we are travelers from afar who chanced upon your shore and found your cave. We humbly beg your hospitality. Remember that guests are under the protection of Zeus.
Zeus? Ha! We cyclopes do not fear the gods.

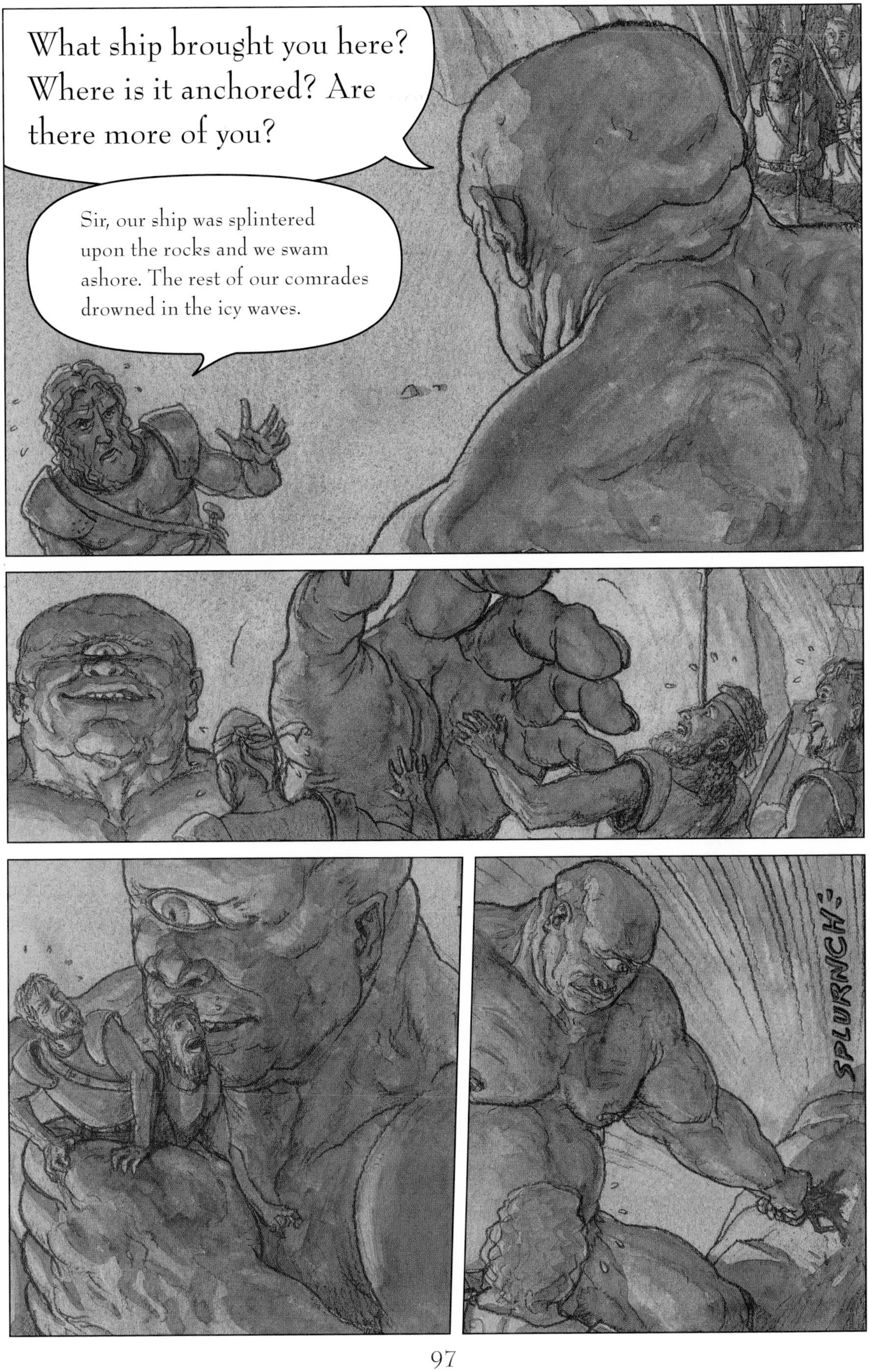
What ship brought you here? Where is it anchored? Are there more of you?
Sir, our ship was splintered upon the rocks and we swam ashore. The rest of our comrades drowned in the icy waves.
SPLURNCH!

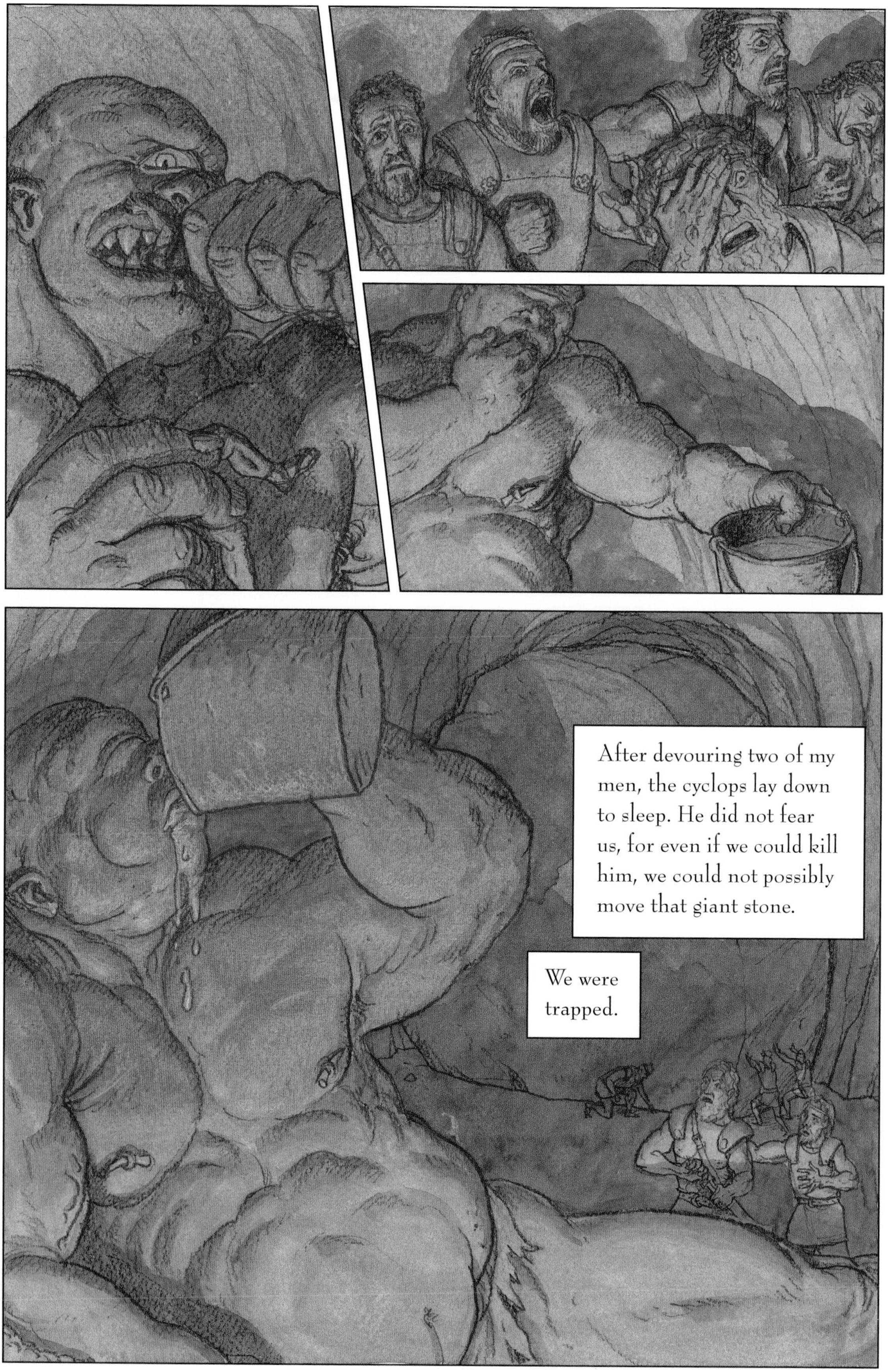
After devouring two of my men, the cyclops lay down to sleep. He did not fear us, for even if we could kill him, we could not possibly move that giant stone.
We were trapped.

In the morning, the cyclops killed two more men for his breakfast, then drove his sheep outside and replaced the stone across the entrance as easily as a man might cap a quiver of arrows.

I racked my brain for a plan that would let us escape alive from the clutches of that brute, and this was what seemed best to me:

There was a massive staff of green wood lying in the cave, and I whittled this down to a sharp point and hid it in the back of the cave. I picked four of my strongest men to help me wield it when the time came.

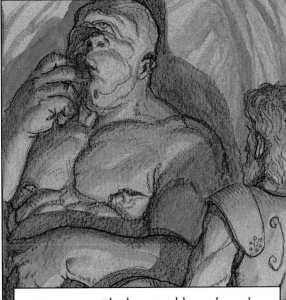

Once again I had to stand by and watch as he killed two more of my men to make his dinner. When he had devoured them, I approached him.

Here, have some wine, monster. I brought it as a gift, though that means nothing to you. I'll wager it's finer than anything you have here.
GULP!
Give me some more, stranger!
And tell me your name, for I will make you a gift in return for this magnificent wine.
Three times I filled the bowl, and he drained it empty. Then, when his wits were addled, I answered him.

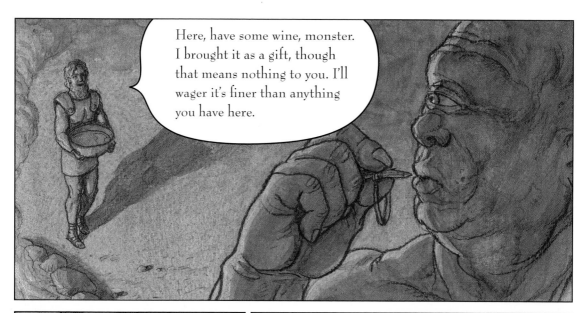

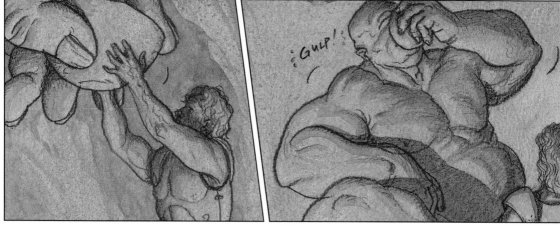

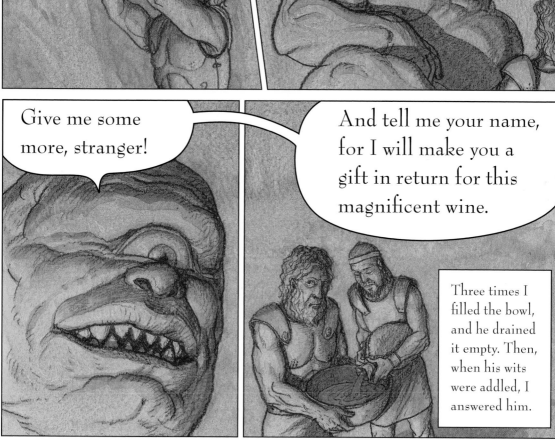

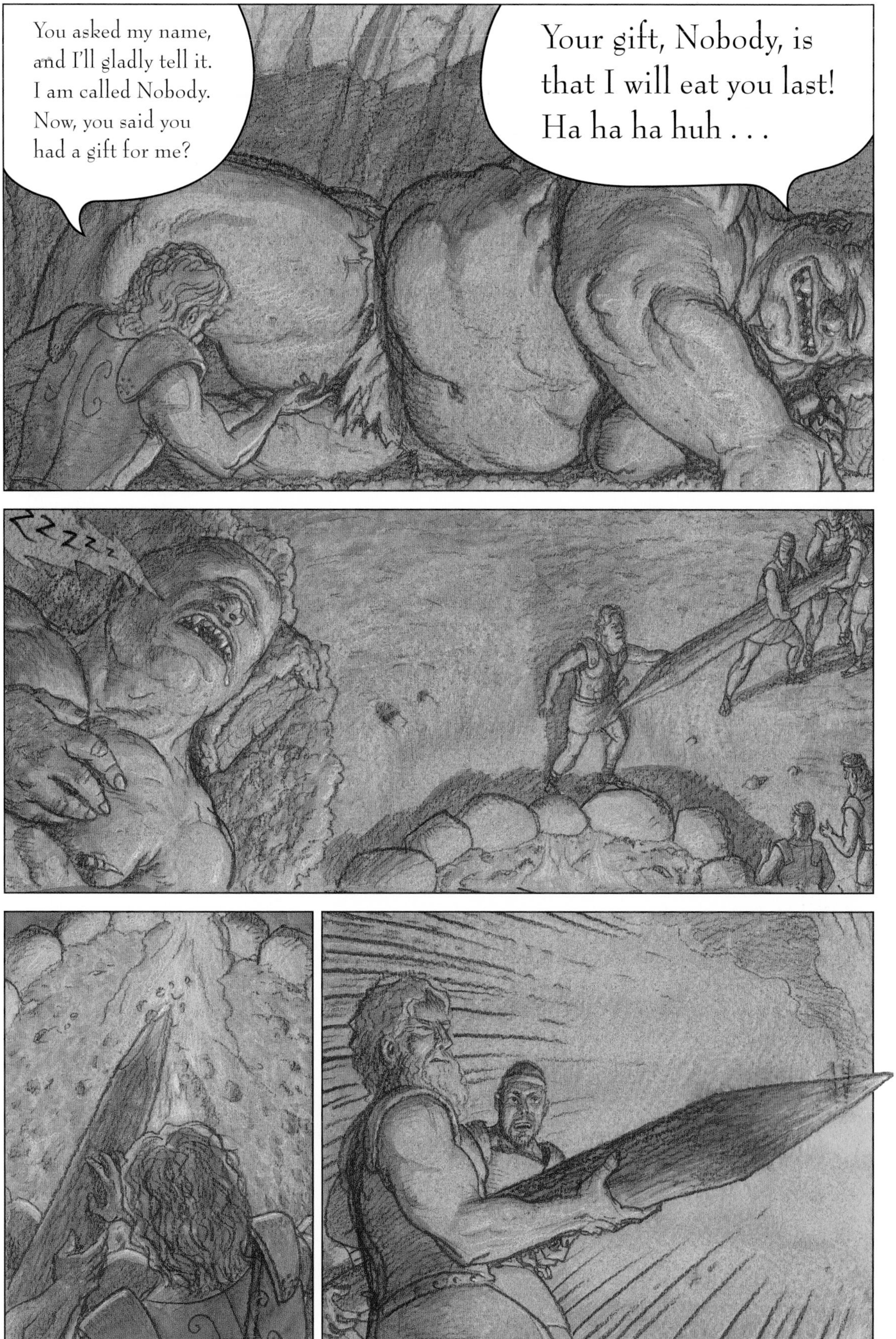
You asked my name, and I'll gladly tell it. I am called Nobody. Now, you said you had a gift for me?
Your gift, Nobody, is that I will eat you last! Ha ha ha huh . . .
ZZZZZ

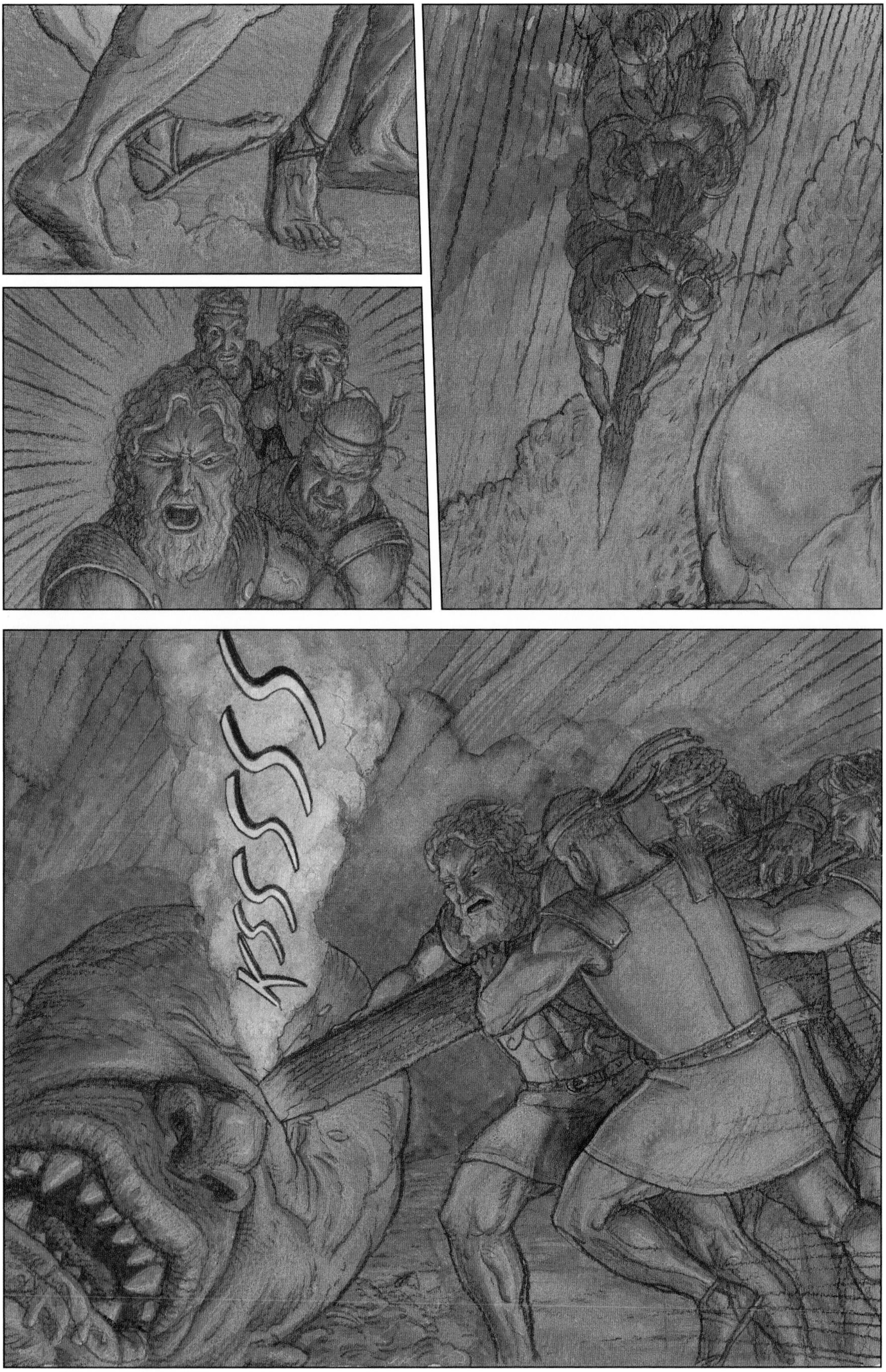
KSSSSS

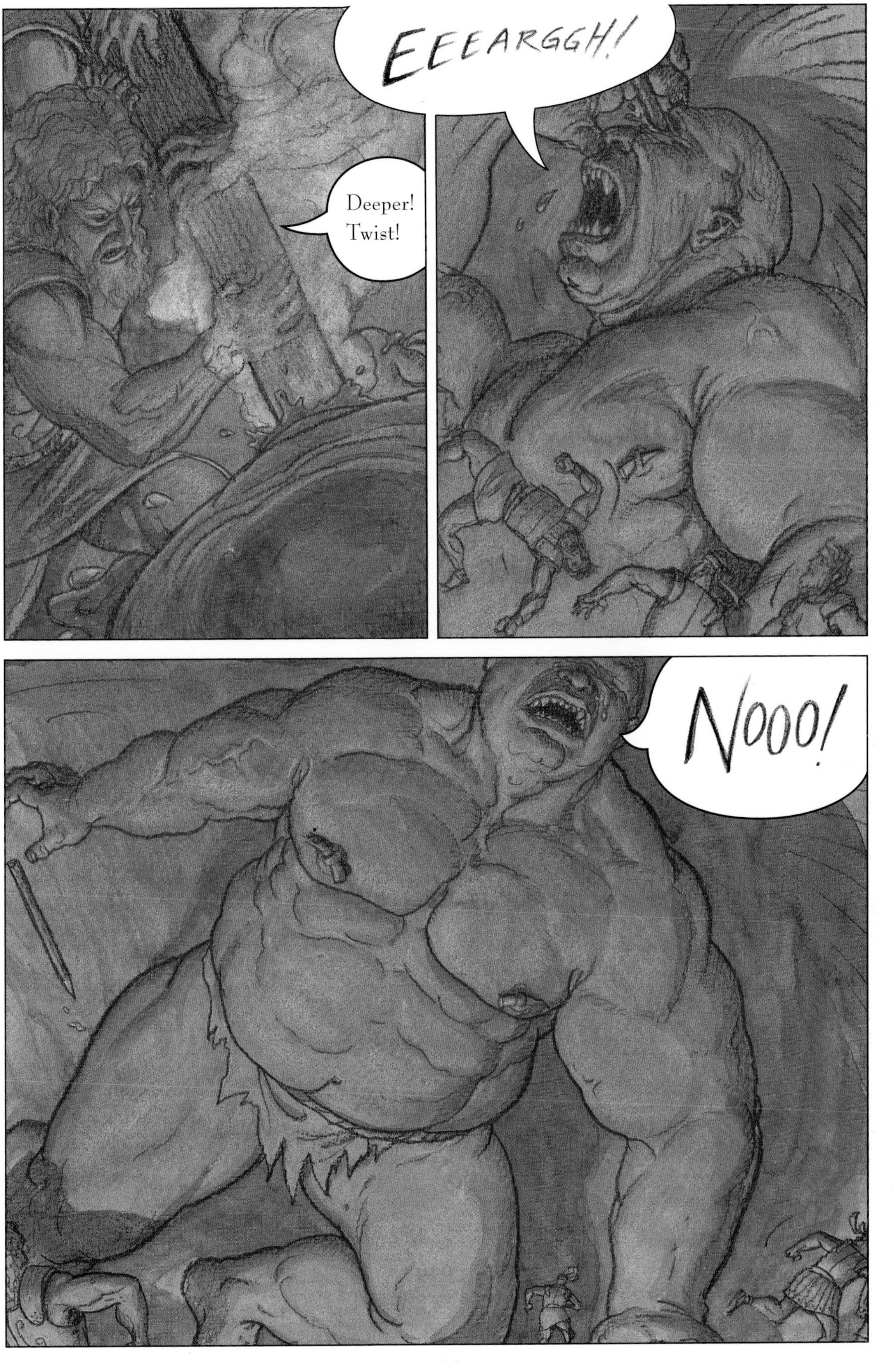
Deeper!
Twist!
EEEARGGH!
NOOO!

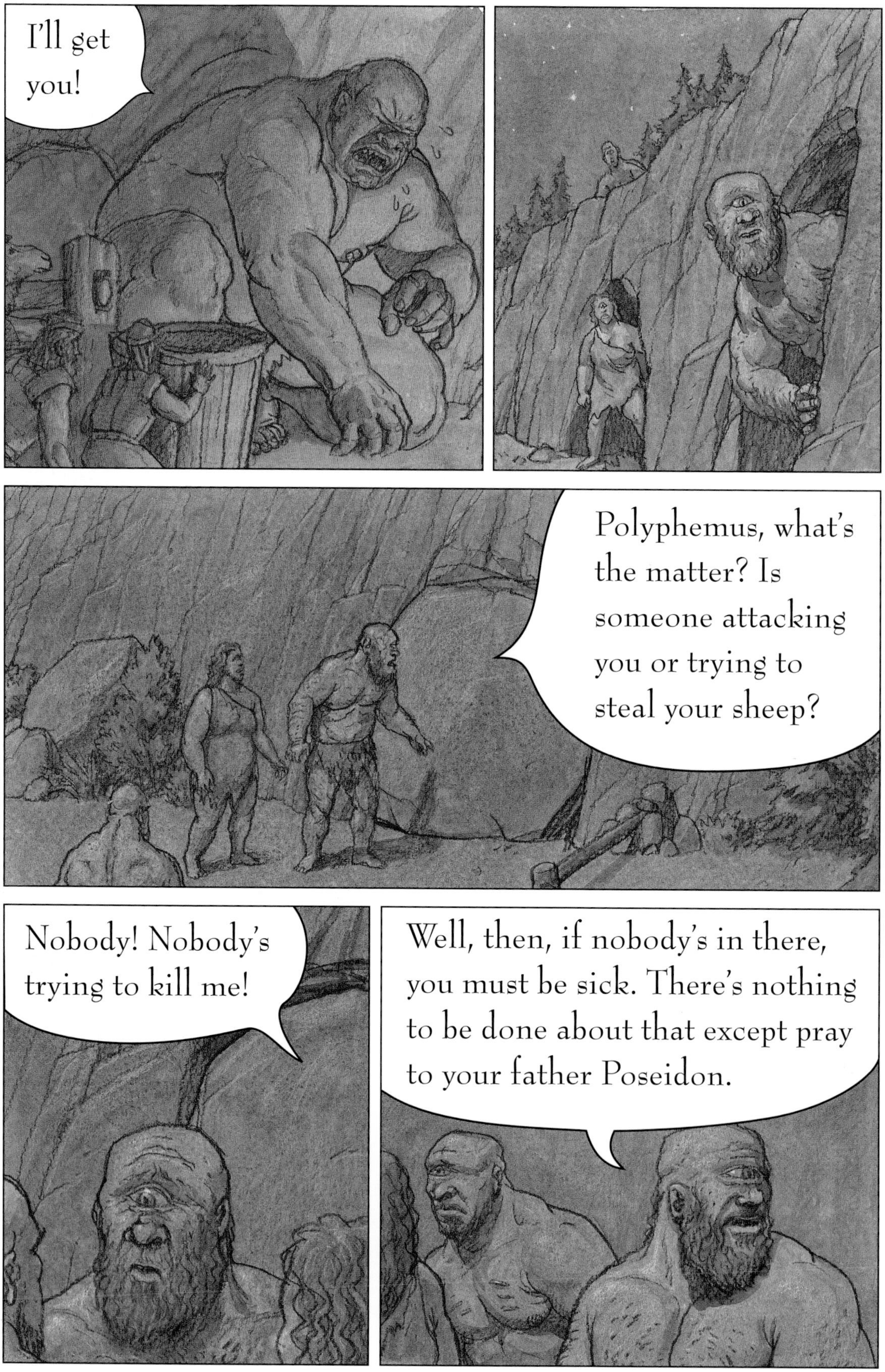
I'll get you!
Polyphemus, what's the matter? Is someone attacking you or trying to steal your sheep?
Nobody! Nobody's trying to kill me!
Well, then, if nobody's in there, you must be sick. There's nothing to be done about that except pray to your father Poseidon.

No! Idiots! Aaargh!
CRUNCH
Come on, now, Nobody, try to escape!

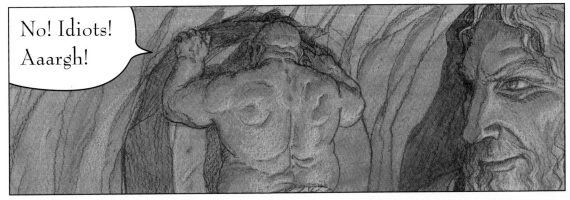

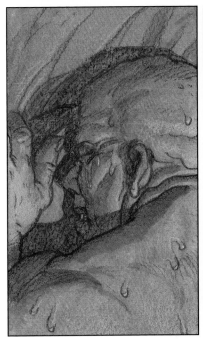

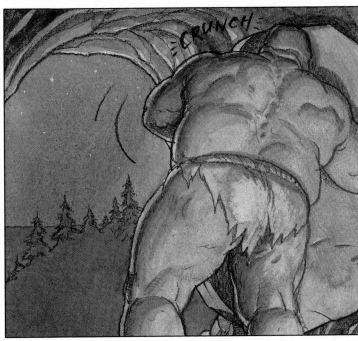

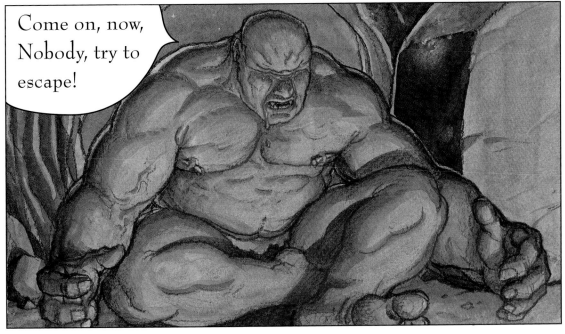

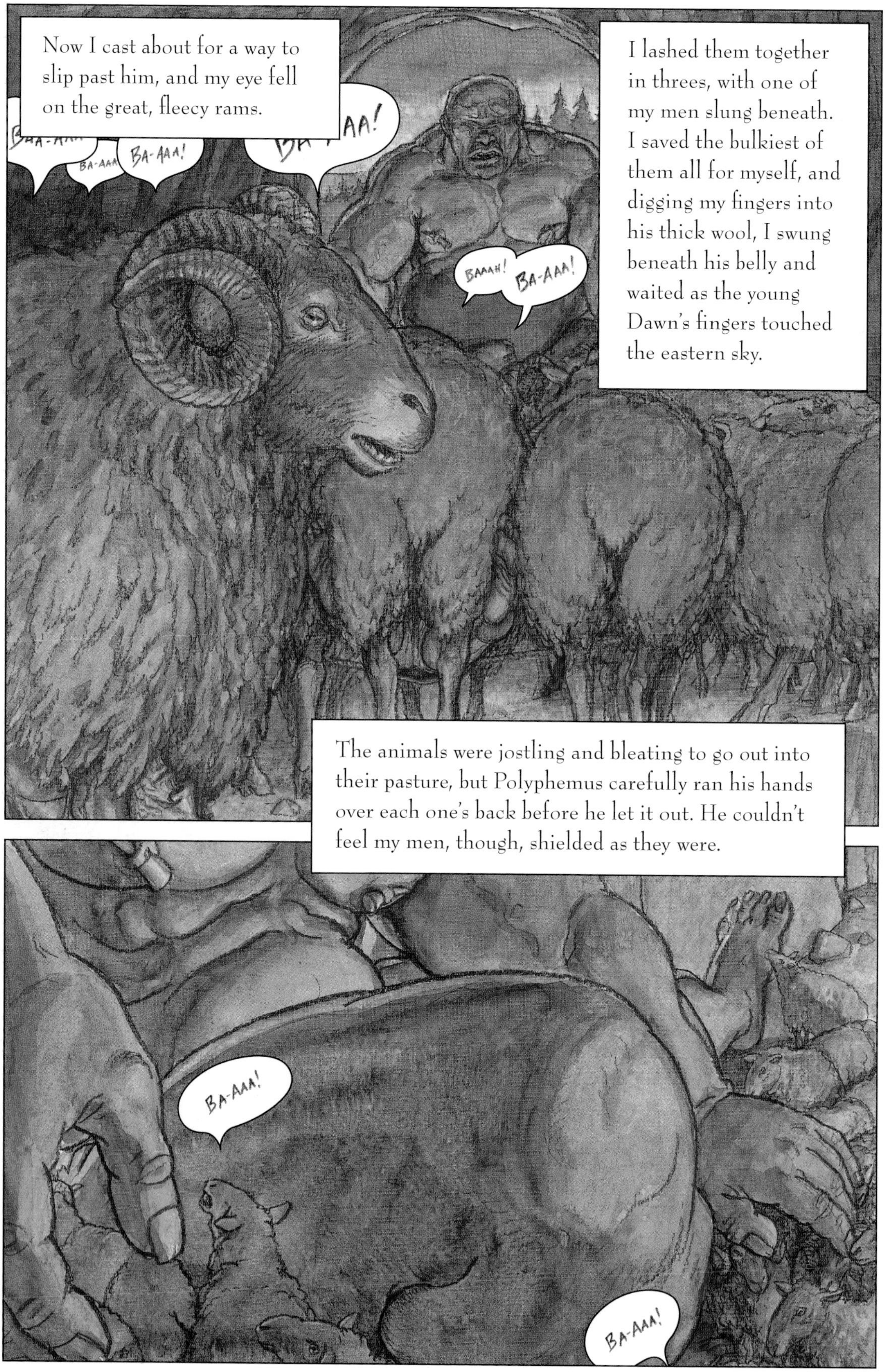
Now I cast about for a way to slip past him, and my eye fell on the great, fleecy rams.
BA-AAA
BA-AAA!
I lashed them together in threes, with one of my men slung beneath. I saved the bulkiest of them all for myself, and digging my fingers into his thick wool, I swung beneath his belly and waited as the young Dawn's fingers touched the eastern sky.
BAAAH!
BA-AAA!
The animals were jostling and bleating to go out into their pasture, but Polyphemus carefully ran his hands over each one's back before he let it out. He couldn't feel my men, though, shielded as they were.
BA-AAA!
BA-AAA!

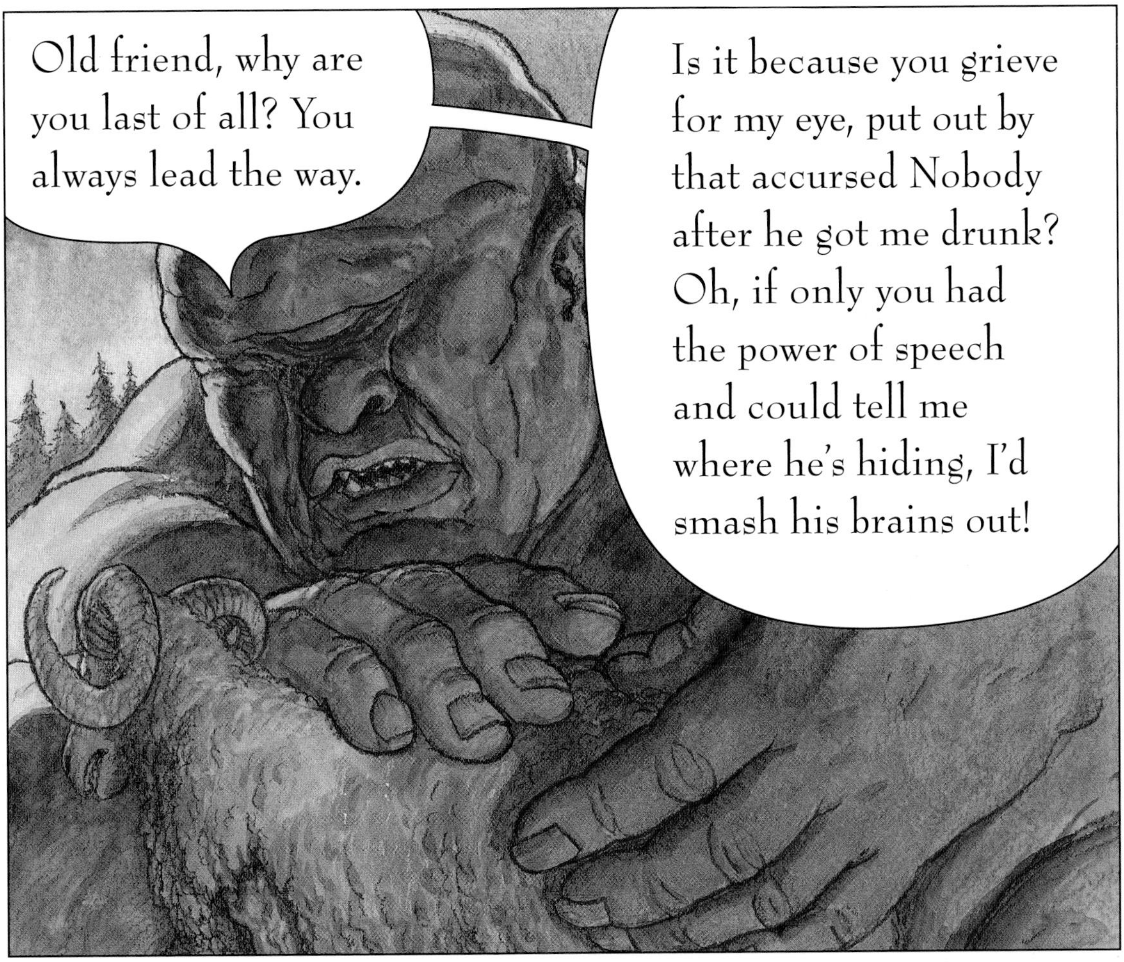
Old friend, why are you last of all? You always lead the way.
Is it because you grieve for my eye, put out by that accursed Nobody after he got me drunk? Oh, if only you had the power of speech and could tell me where he's hiding, I'd smash his brains out!

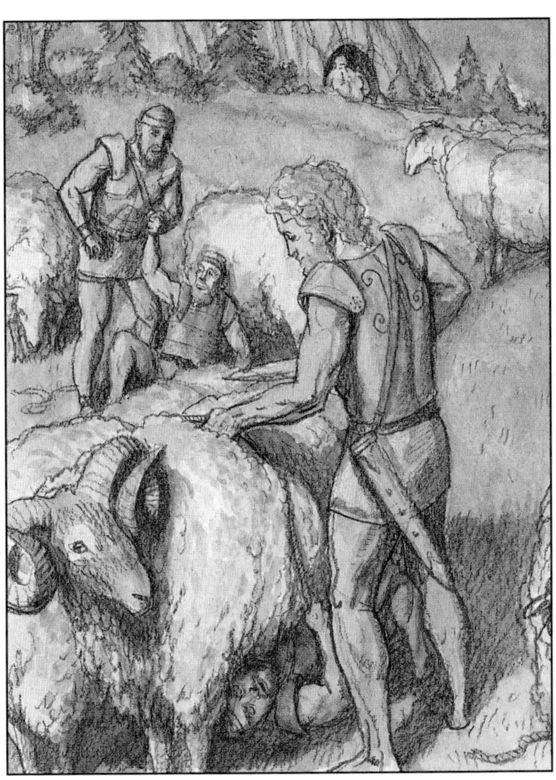

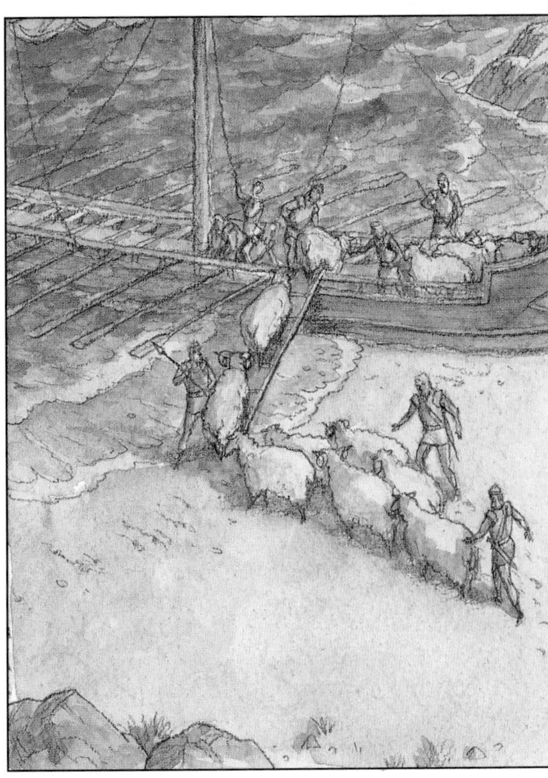

Cyclops! Your victims have escaped, and the gods have paid you back for your crimes!

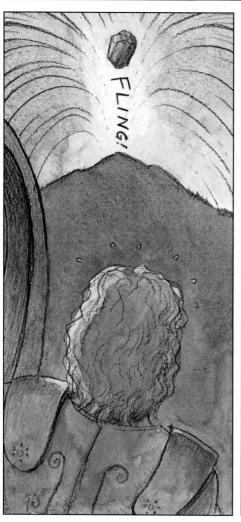

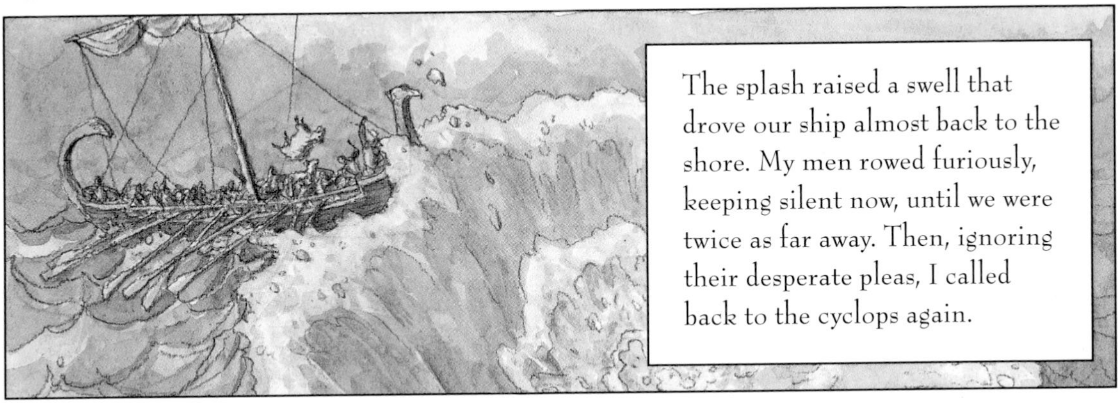
The splash raised a swell that drove our ship almost back to the shore. My men rowed furiously, keeping silent now, until we were twice as far away. Then, ignoring their desperate pleas, I called back to the cyclops again.

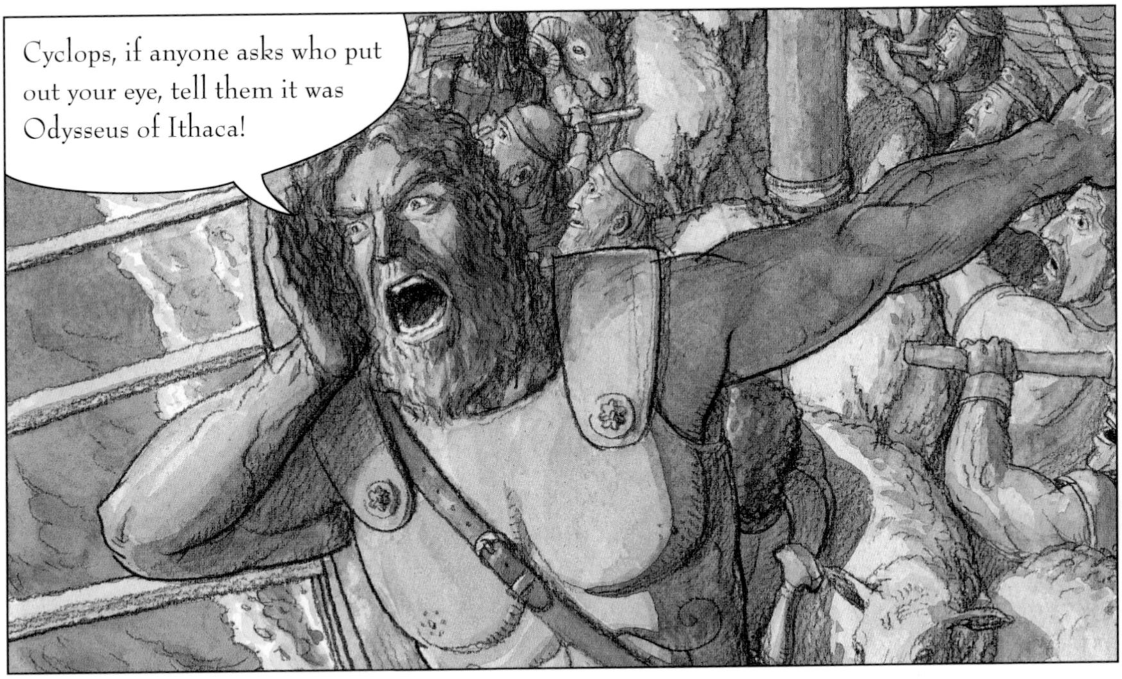
Cyclops, if anyone asks who put out your eye, tell them it was Odysseus of Ithaca!

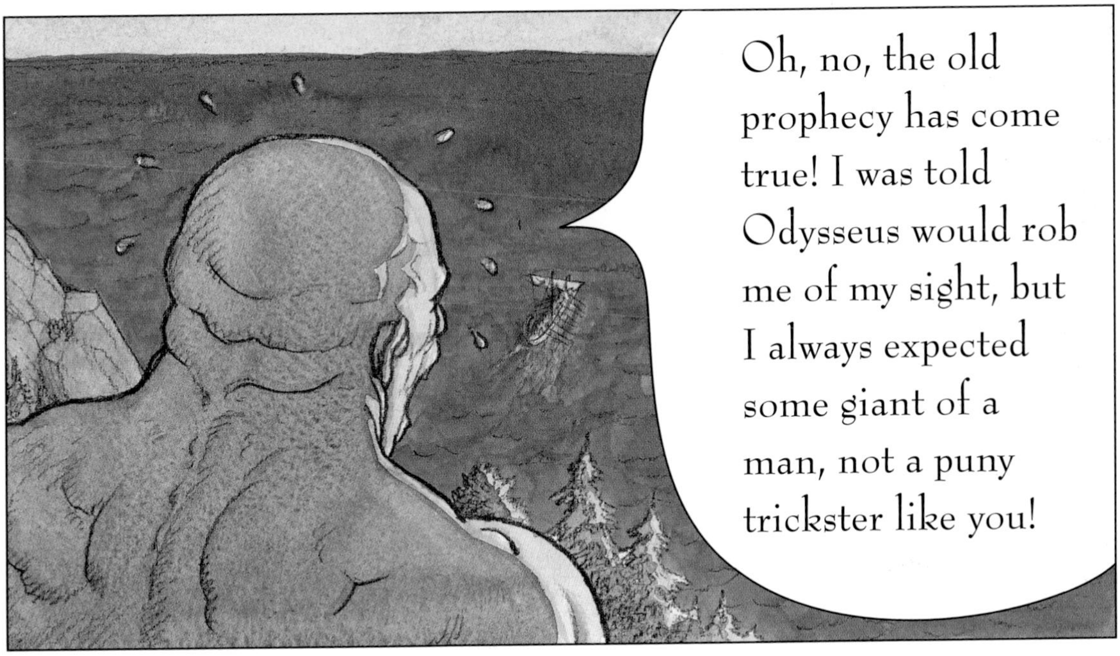
Oh, no, the old prophecy has come true! I was told Odysseus would rob me of my sight, but I always expected some giant of a man, not a puny trickster like you!

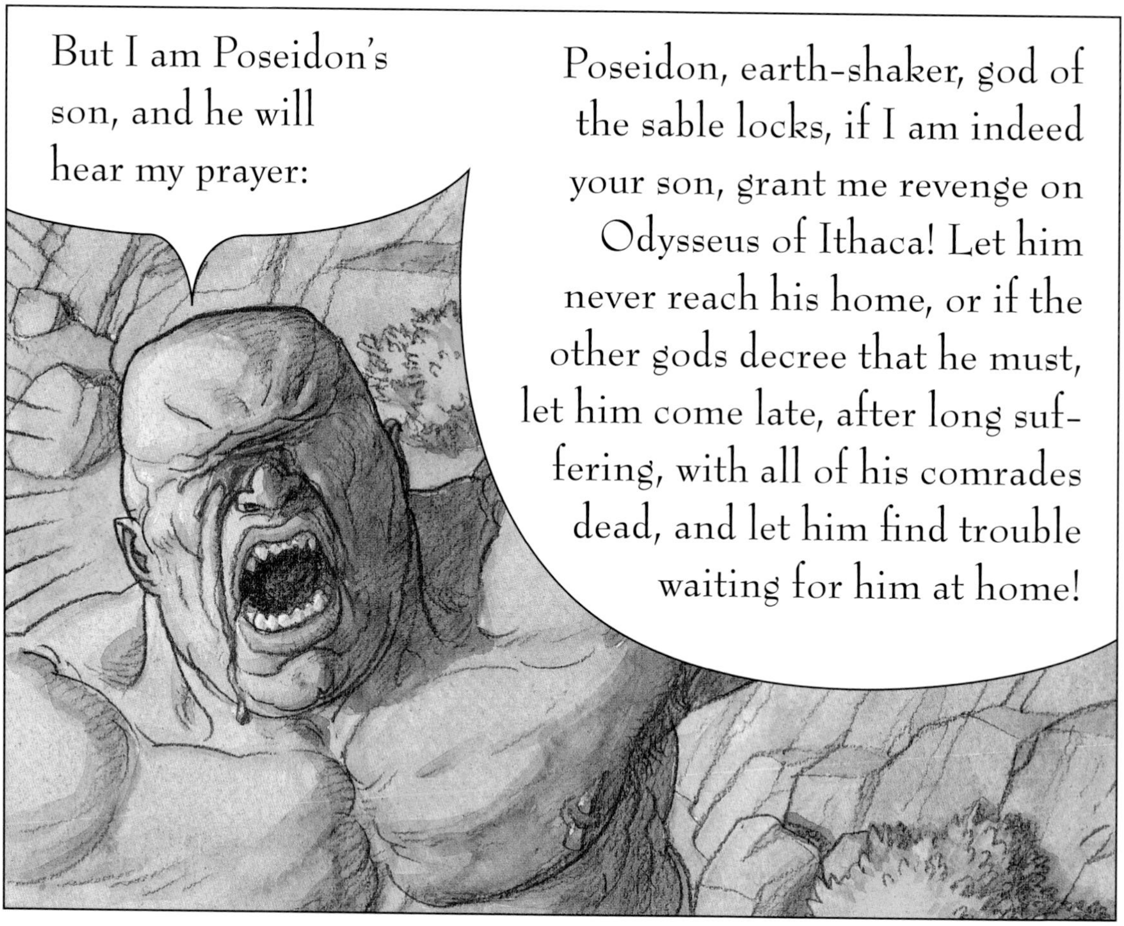
But I am Poseidon's son, and he will hear my prayer:
Poseidon, earth-shaker, god of the sable locks, if I am indeed your son, grant me revenge on Odysseus of Ithaca! Let him never reach his home, or if the other gods decree that he must, let him come late, after long suffering, with all of his comrades dead, and let him find trouble waiting for him at home!

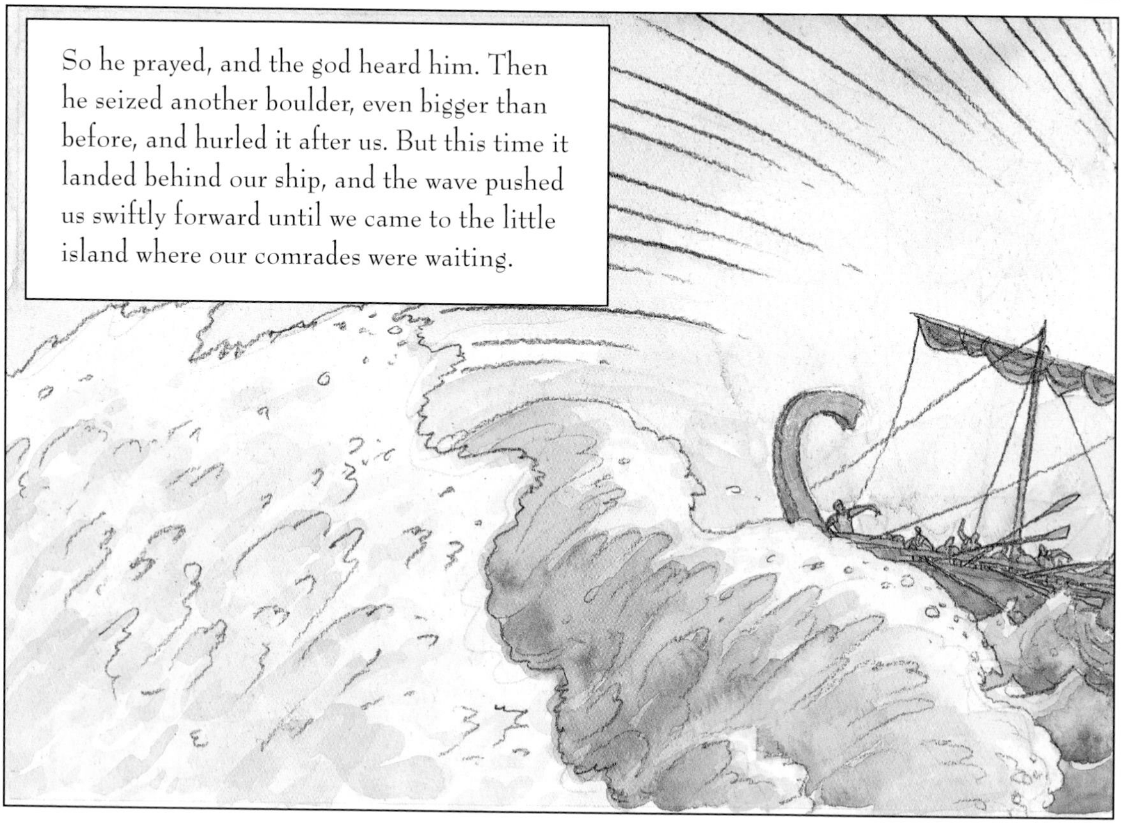
So he prayed, and the god heard him. Then he seized another boulder, even bigger than before, and hurled it after us. But this time it landed behind our ship, and the wave pushed us swiftly forward until we came to the little island where our comrades were waiting.

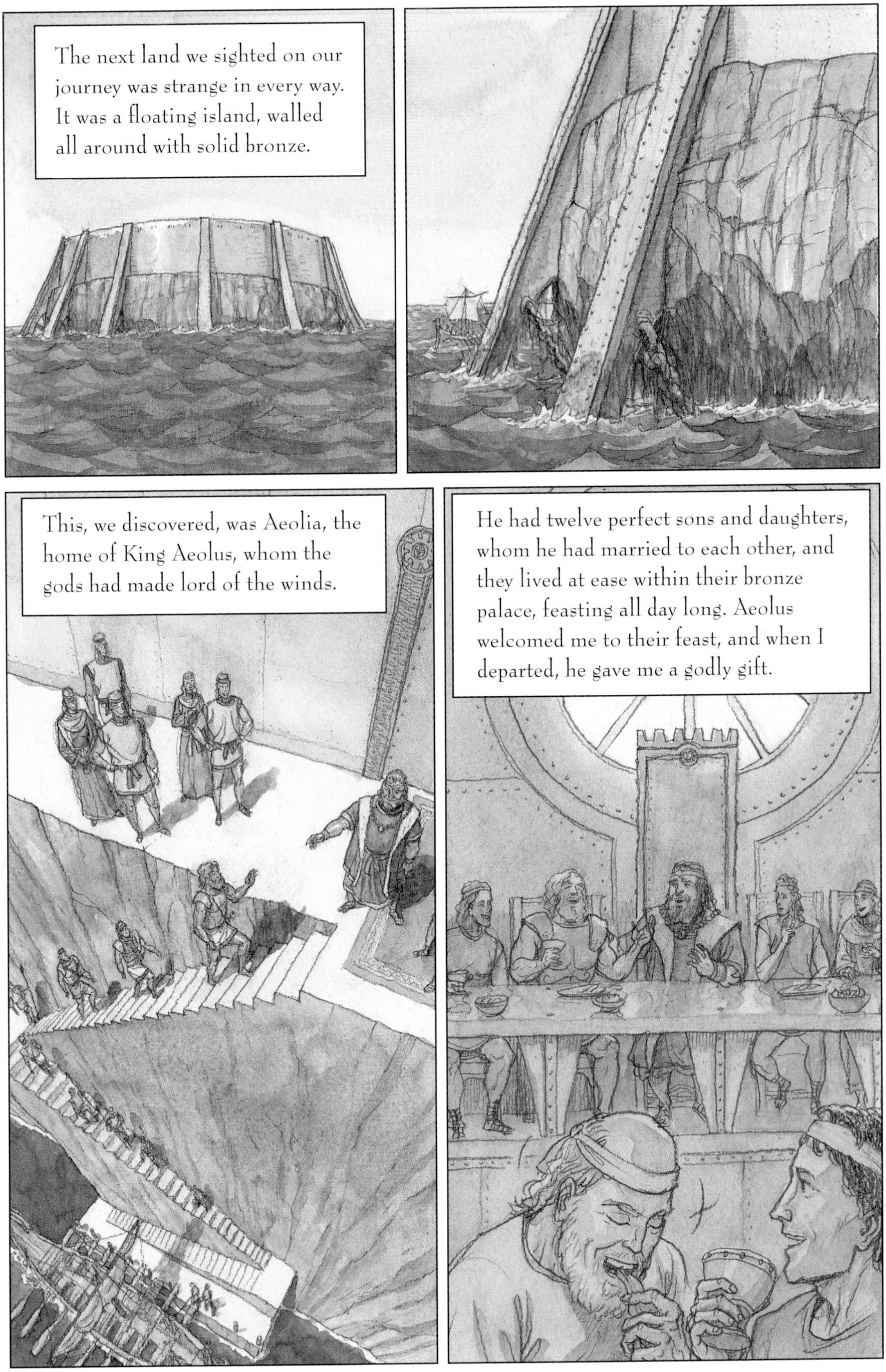
The next land we sighted on our journey was strange in every way. It was a floating island, walled all around with solid bronze.
This, we discovered, was Aeolia, the home of King Aeolus, whom the gods had made lord of the winds.
He had twelve perfect sons and daughters, whom he had married to each other, and they lived at ease within their bronze palace, feasting all day long. Aeolus welcomed me to their feast, and when I departed, he gave me a godly gift.

He captured the winds and bound them up in a great bag made from the hide of a full-grown ox, sealing the neck tight with wire so nothing could escape. But he left the west wind free to blow us straight on our course for home.

I stayed up for nine days without a rest, manning the helm myself, for I was determined that nothing would stop me reaching home now.

We sighted land — Ithaca! I thought my troubles were over, and I left the helm to sit and rest my legs. But sleep overcame me, and as soon as my eyes were closed, mischief erupted among my crew.

They took it into their heads that the bag Aeolus gave me must contain gold and riches, which I planned to keep all for myself. The fools! Mad with jealousy, they decided to open the bag and see.

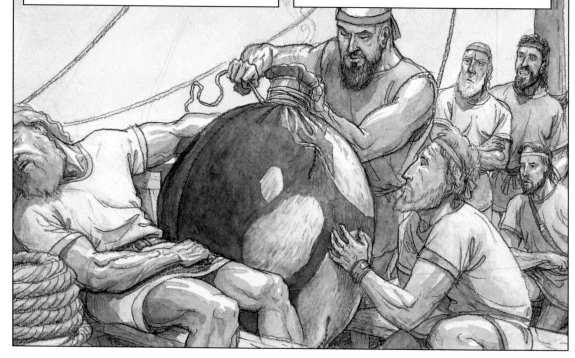

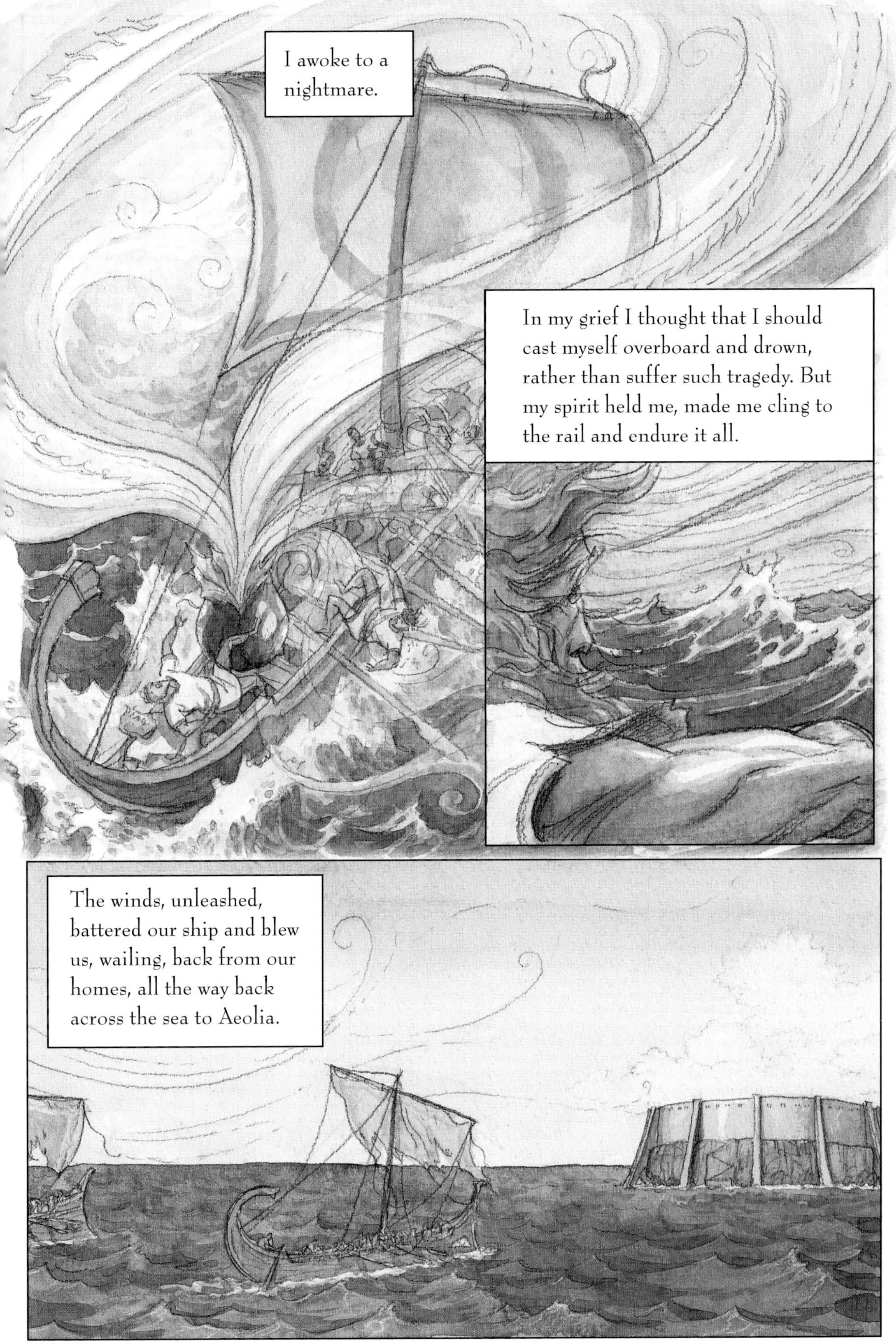
I awoke to a nightmare.
In my grief I thought that I should cast myself overboard and drown, rather than suffer such tragedy. But my spirit held me, made me cling to the rail and endure it all.
The winds, unleashed, battered our ship and blew us, wailing, back from our homes, all the way back across the sea to Aeolia.

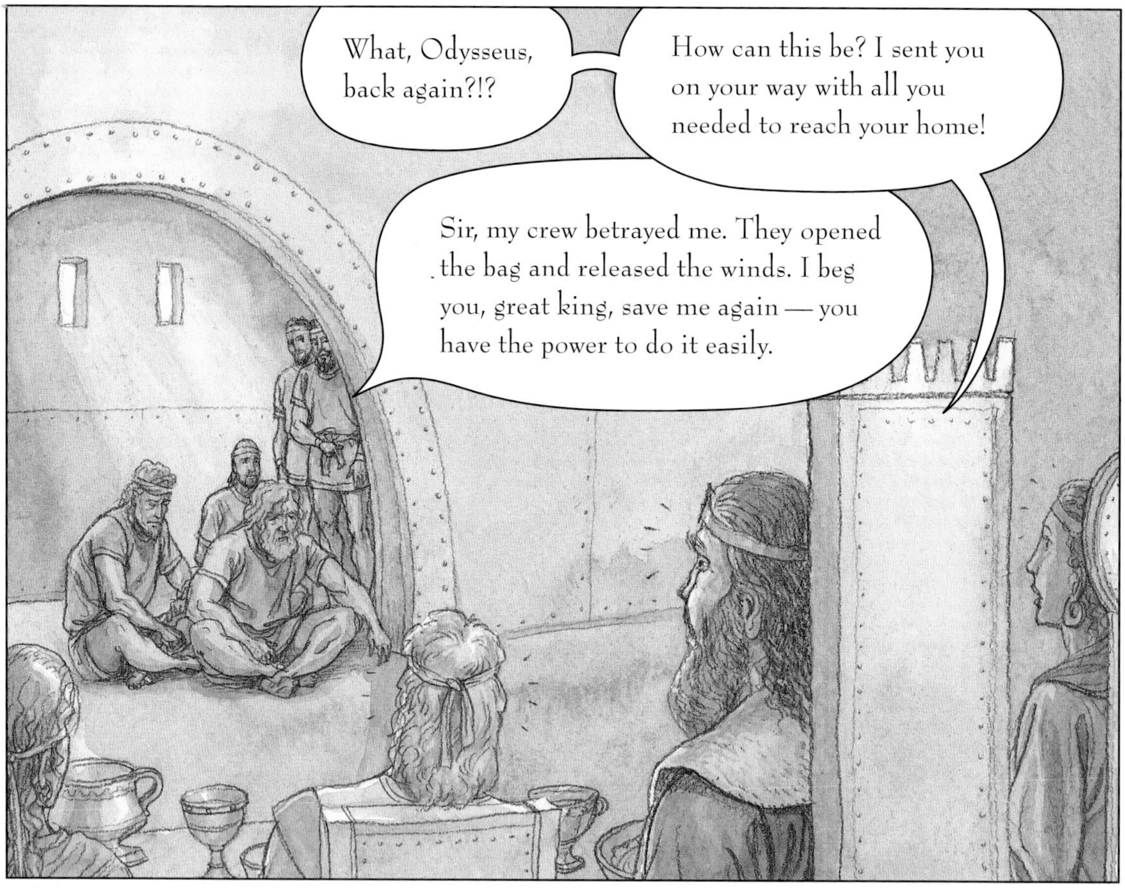
What, Odysseus, back again?!?
How can this be? I sent you on your way with all you needed to reach your home!
Sir, my crew betrayed me. They opened the bag and released the winds. I beg you, great king, save me again — you have the power to do it easily.

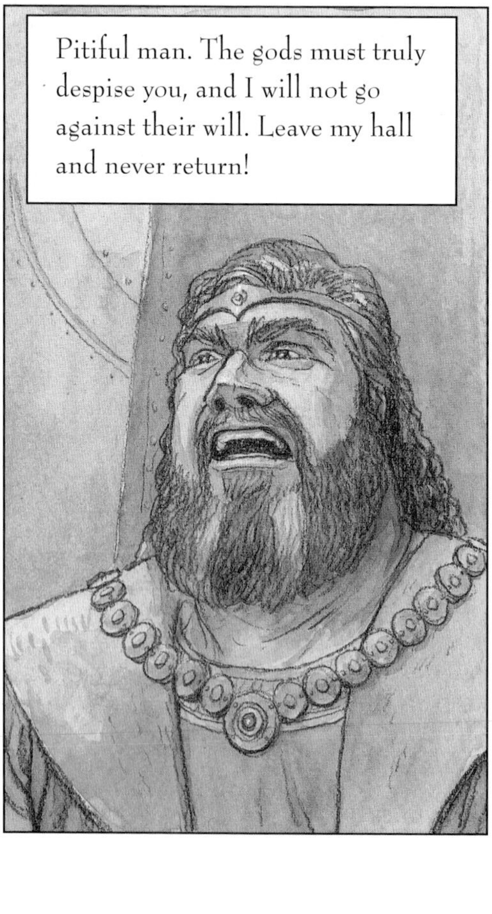
Pitiful man. The gods must truly despise you, and I will not go against their will. Leave my hall and never return!

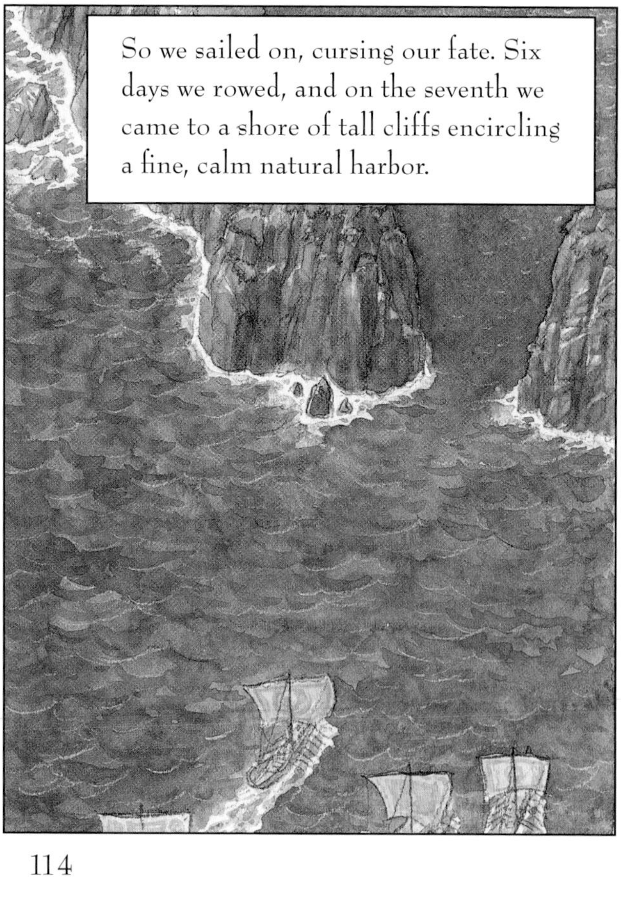
So we sailed on, cursing our fate. Six days we rowed, and on the seventh we came to a shore of tall cliffs encircling a fine, calm natural harbor.

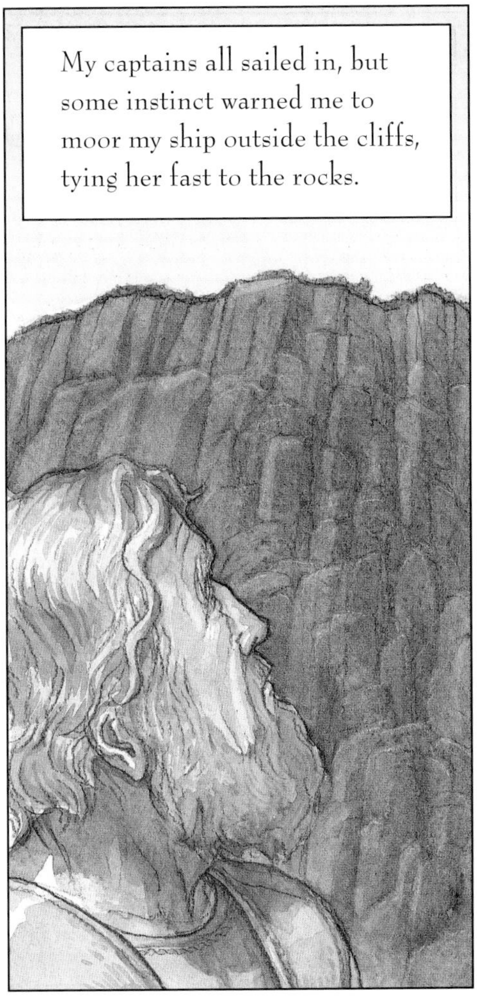
My captains all sailed in, but some instinct warned me to moor my ship outside the cliffs, tying her fast to the rocks.

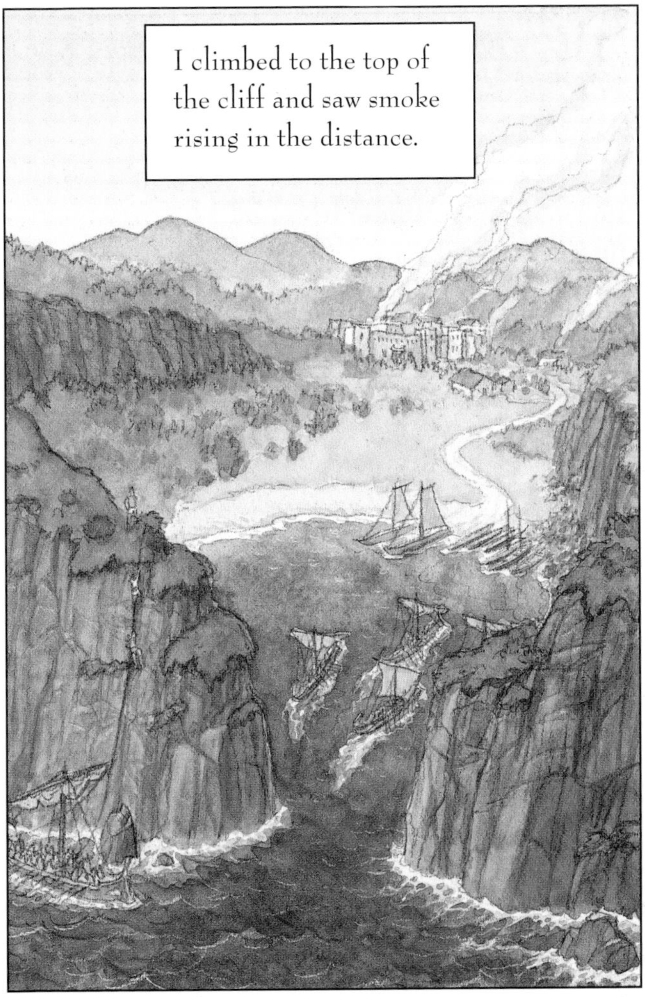
I climbed to the top of the cliff and saw smoke rising in the distance.

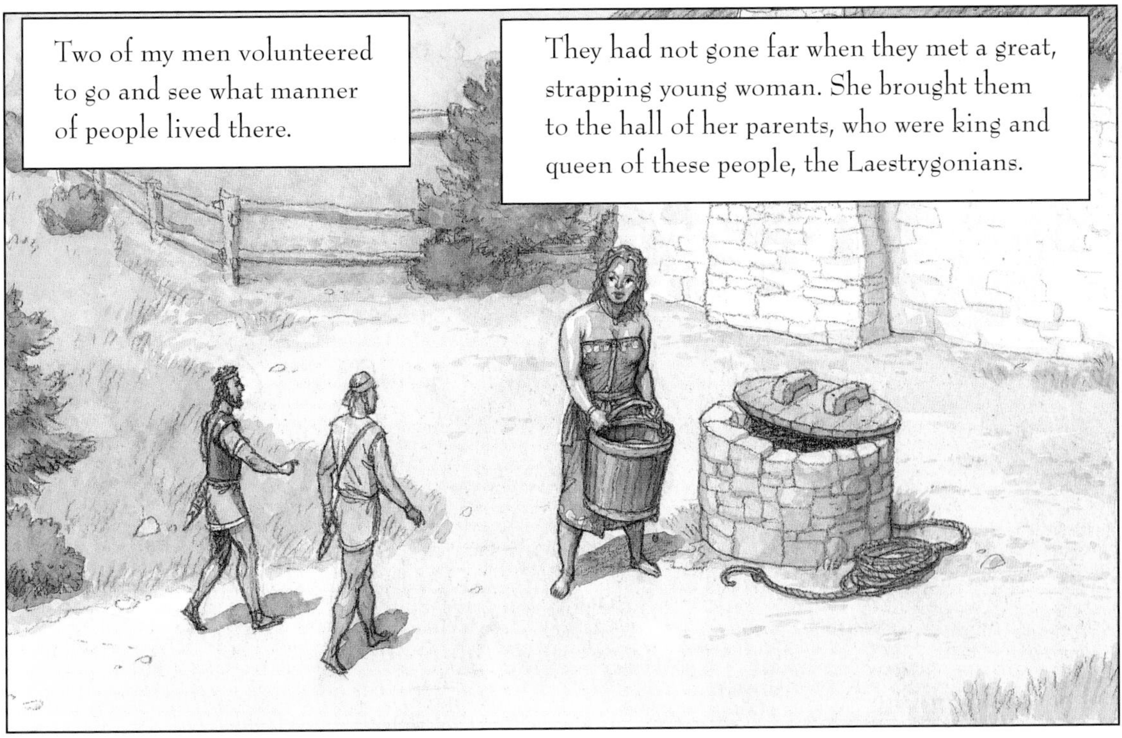
Two of my men volunteered to go and see what manner of people lived there.
They had not gone far when they met a great, strapping young woman. She brought them to the hall of her parents, who were king and queen of these people, the Laestrygonians.

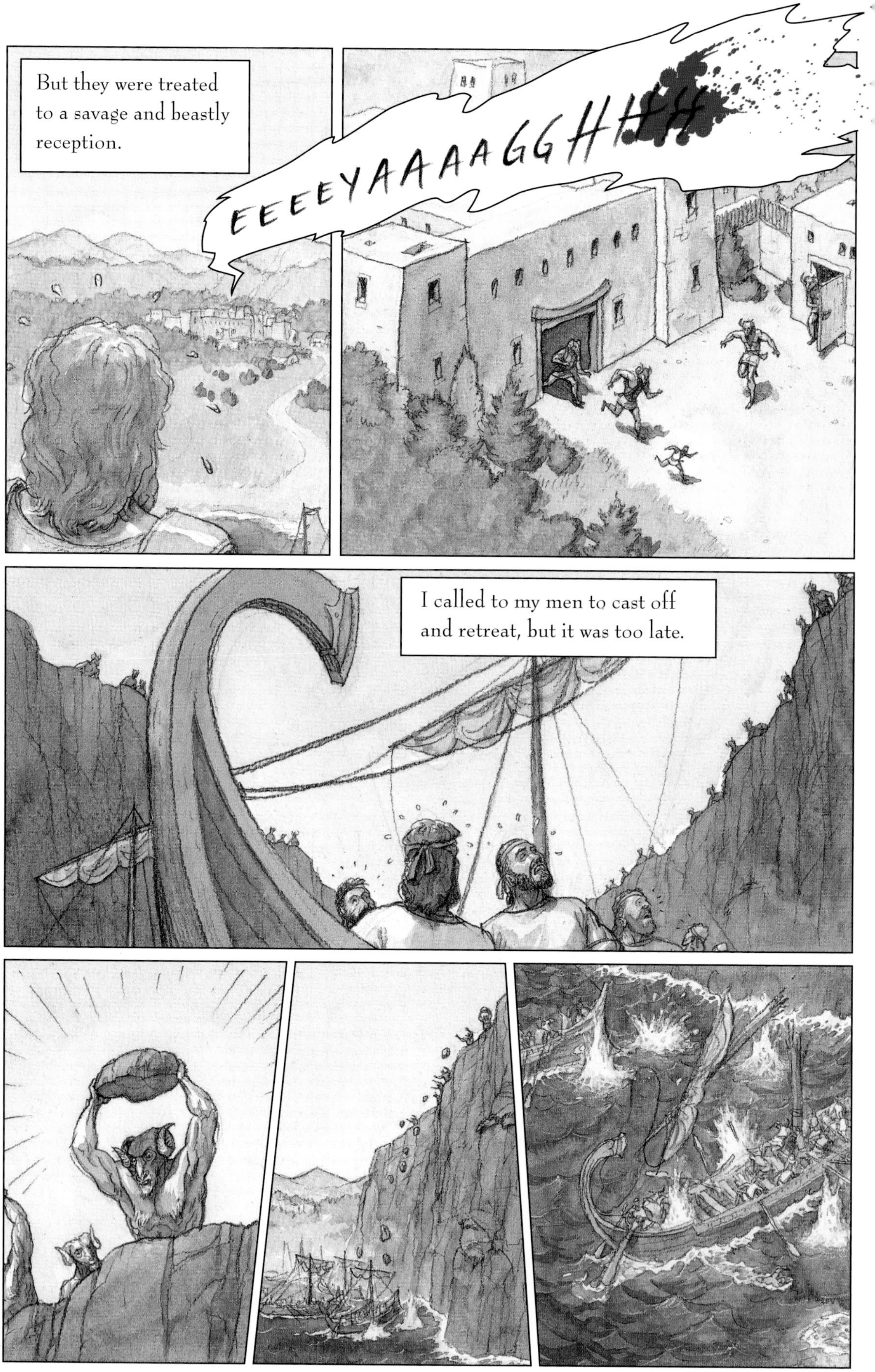
But they were treated to a savage and beastly reception.
EEEEYAAAAAGGHHH
I called to my men to cast off and retreat, but it was too late.

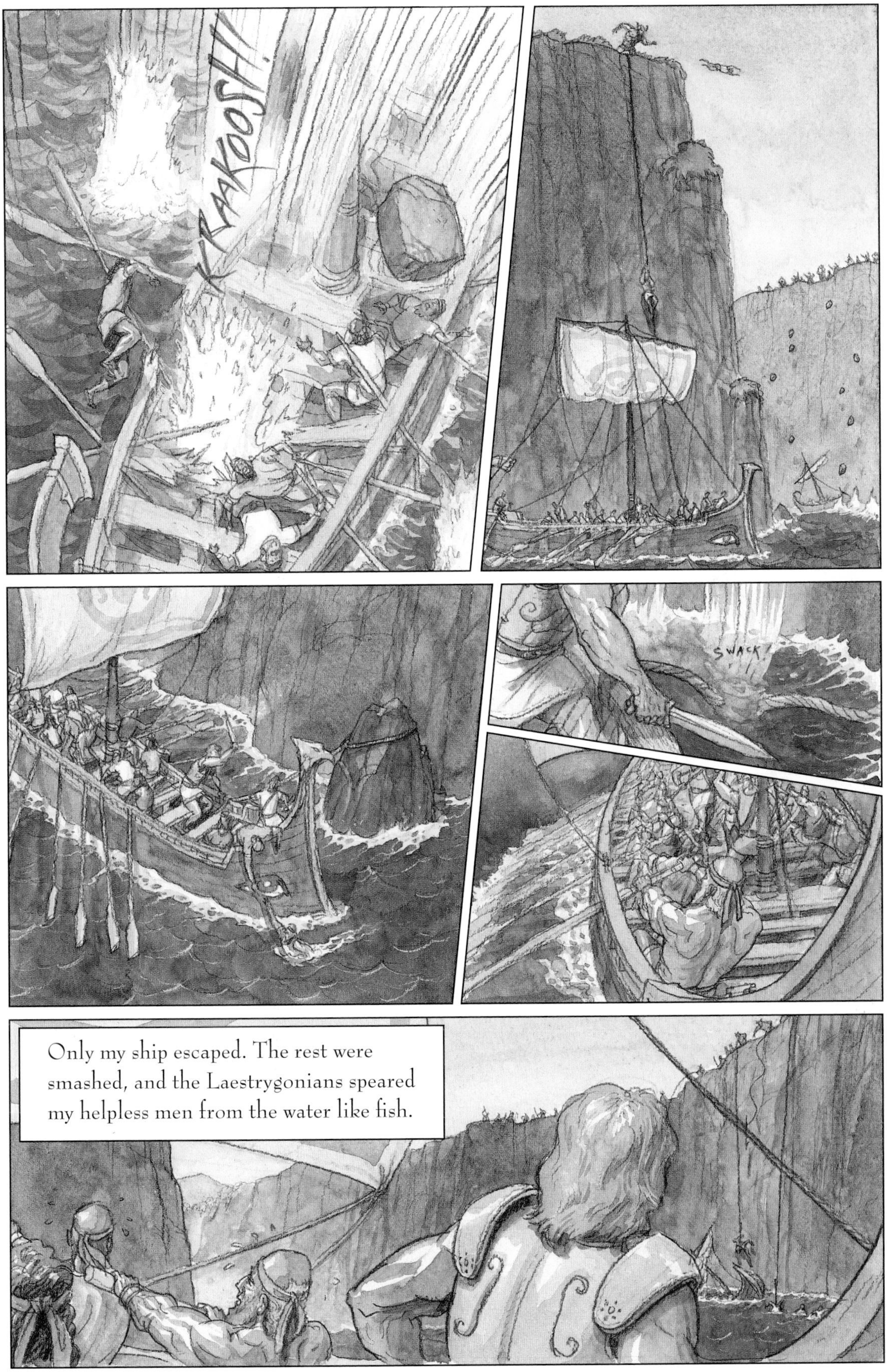
KRAAKOOSH!
SWACK!
Only my ship escaped. The rest were smashed, and the Laestrygonians speared my helpless men from the water like fish.

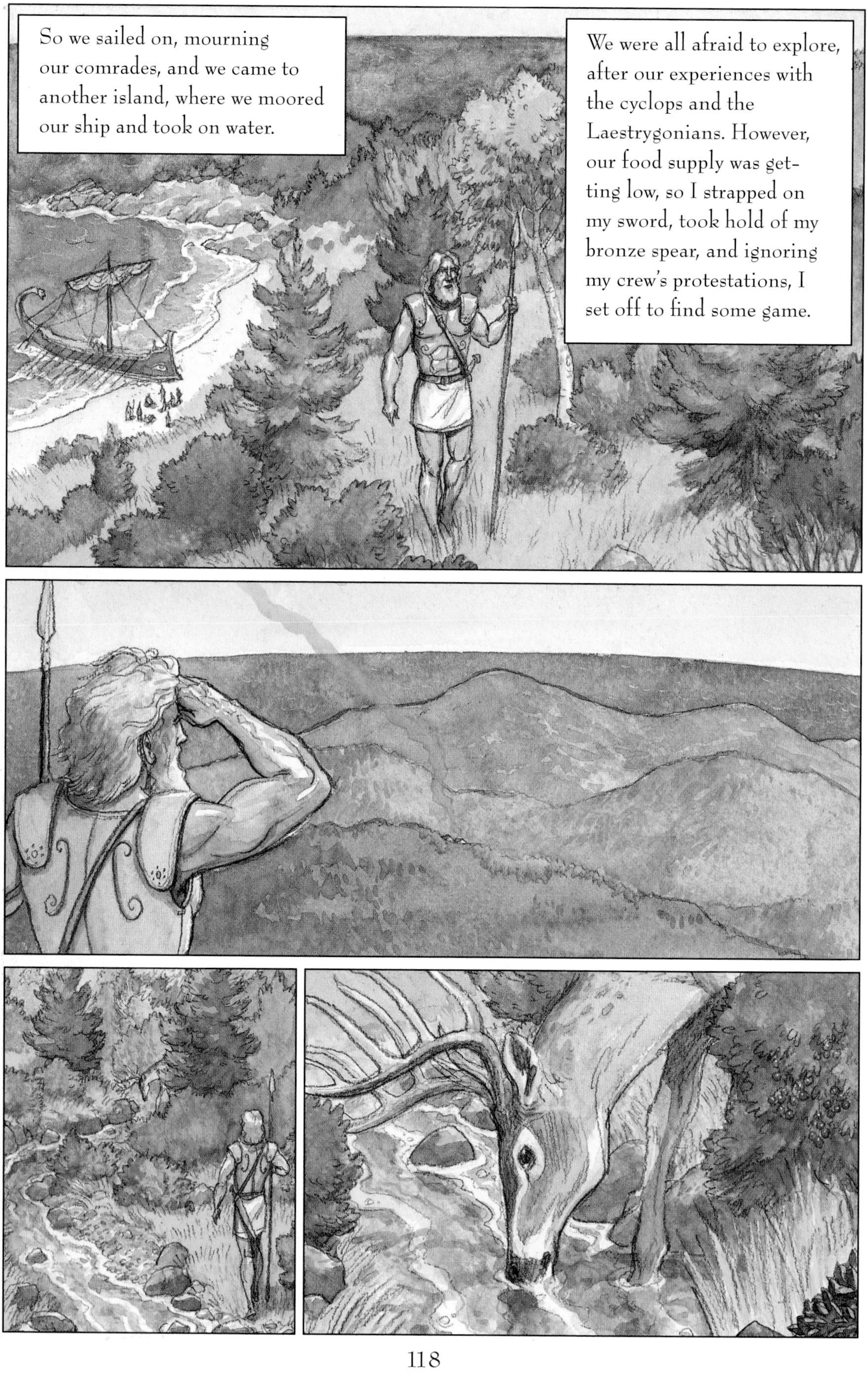
So we sailed on, mourning our comrades, and we came to another island, where we moored our ship and took on water.
We were all afraid to explore, after our experiences with the cyclops and the Laestrygonians. However, our food supply was getting low, so I strapped on my sword, took hold of my bronze spear, and ignoring my crew's protestations, I set off to find some game.

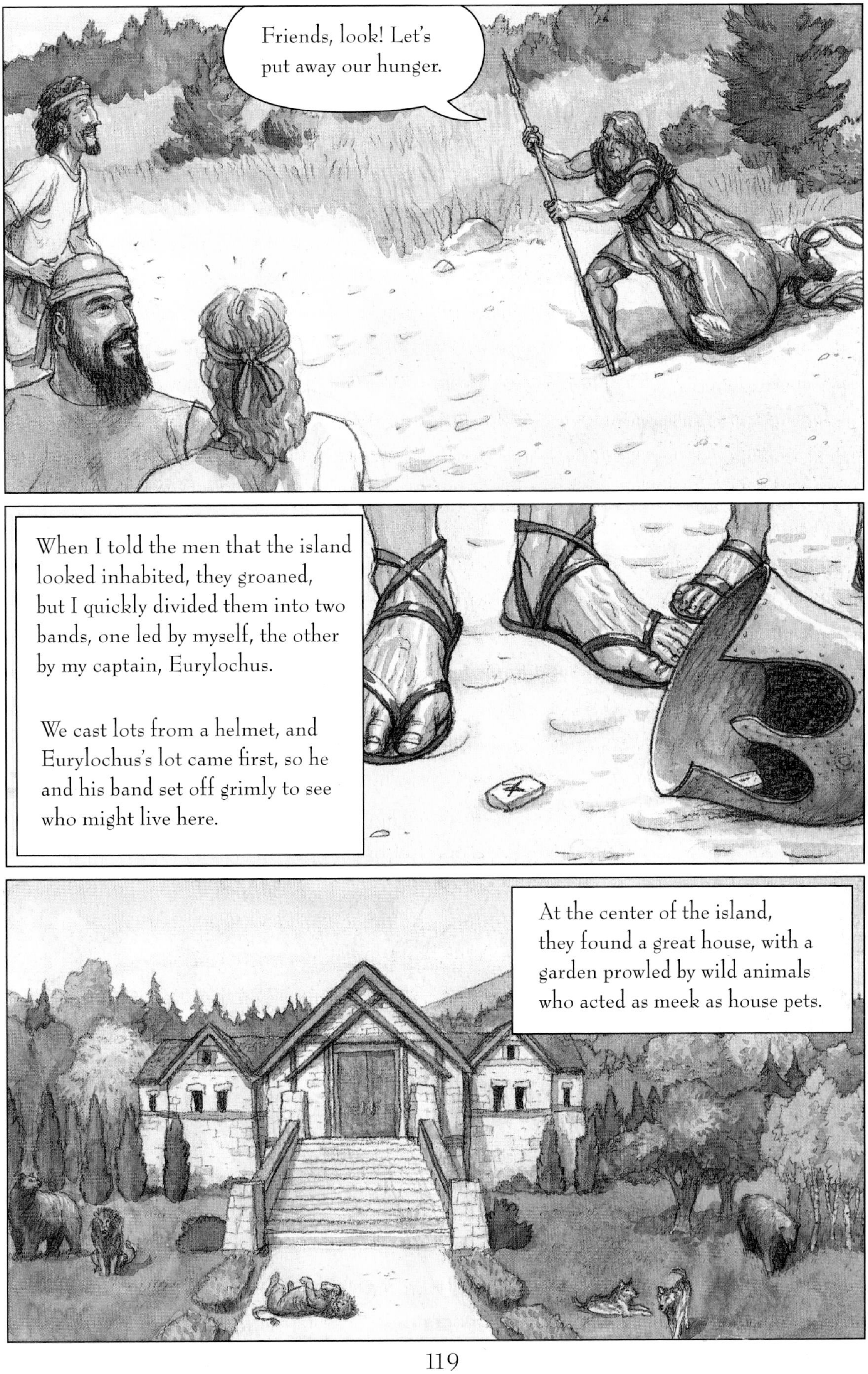
Friends, look! Let's put away our hunger.
When I told the men that the island looked inhabited, they groaned, but I quickly divided them into two bands, one led by myself, the other by my captain, Eurylochus.
We cast lots from a helmet, and Eurylochus's lot came first, so he and his band set off grimly to see who might live here.
At the center of the island, they found a great house, with a garden prowled by wild animals who acted as meek as house pets.

They heard a beautiful voice singing within. Drawn by her song, my men went to the door and hailed her, and she came out at once to greet them — the bewitching queen Circe.

Only Eurylochus held back, sensing a trap.

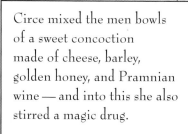

Circe mixed the men bowls of a sweet concoction made of cheese, barley, golden honey, and Pramnian wine — and into this she also stirred a magic drug.

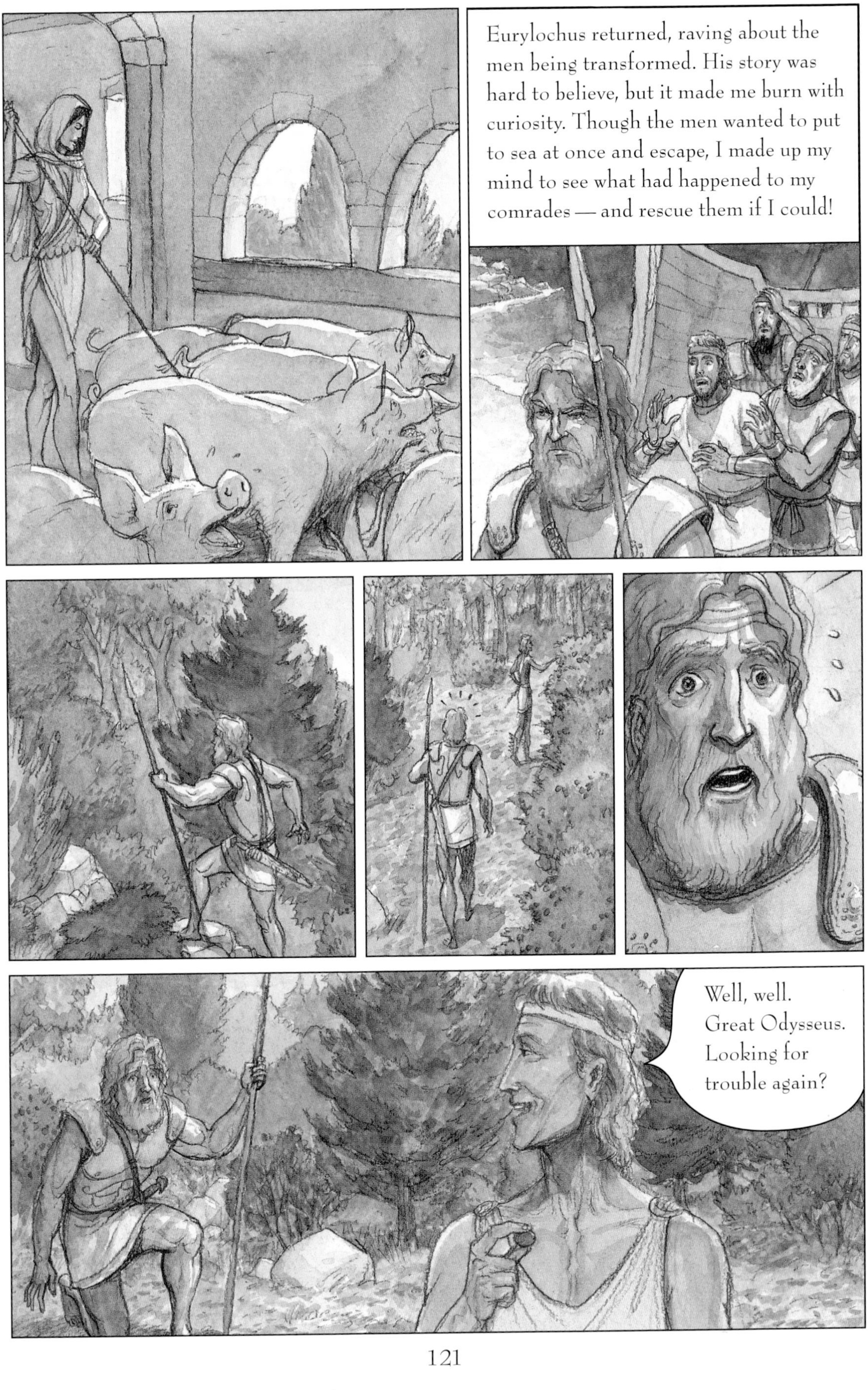
Eurylochus returned, raving about the men being transformed. His story was hard to believe, but it made me burn with curiosity. Though the men wanted to put to sea at once and escape, I made up my mind to see what had happened to my comrades — and rescue them if I could!
Well, well. Great Odysseus. Looking for trouble again?

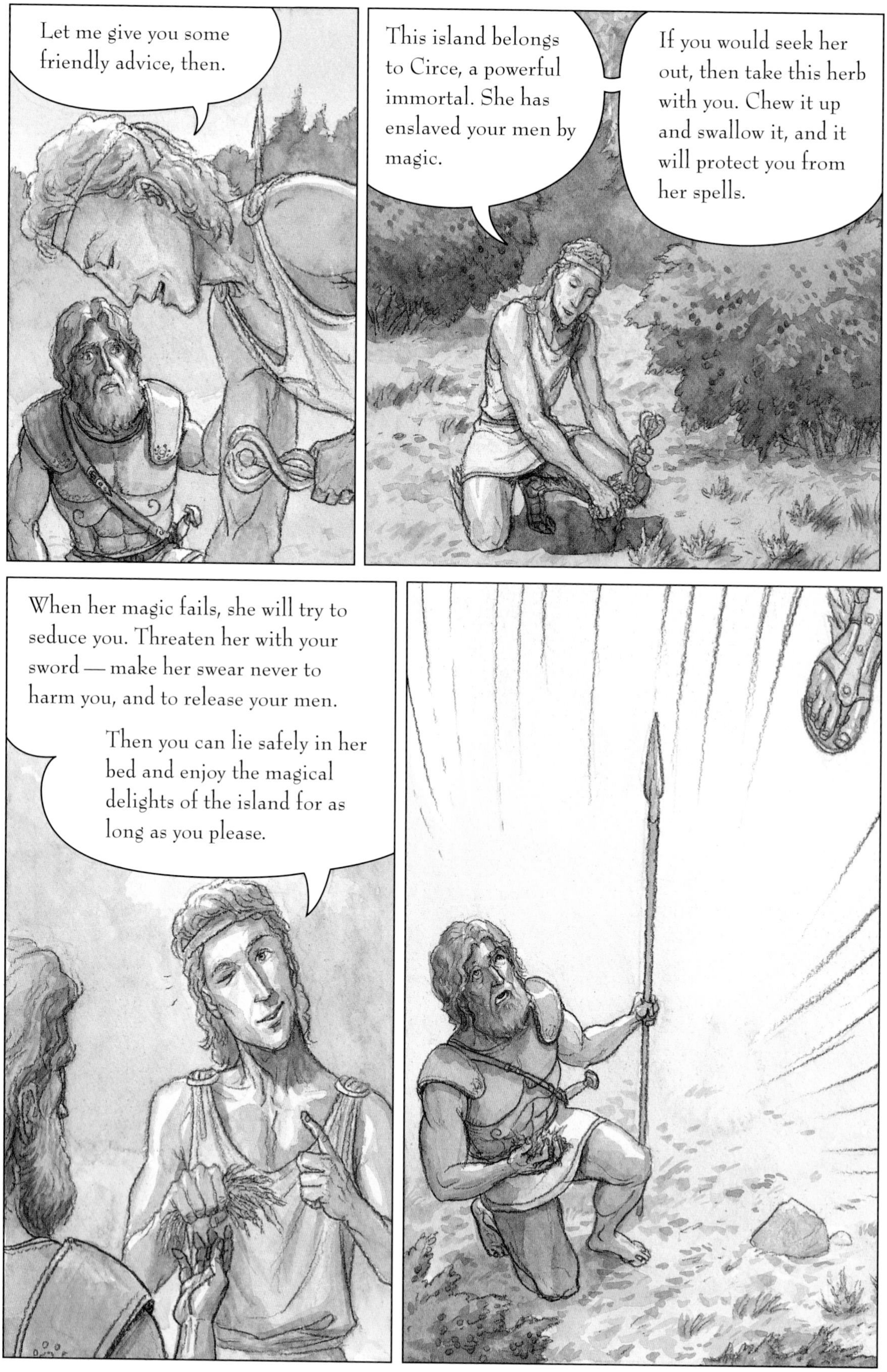
Let me give you some friendly advice, then.
This island belongs to Circe, a powerful immortal. She has enslaved your men by magic.
If you would seek her out, then take this herb with you. Chew it up and swallow it, and it will protect you from her spells.
When her magic fails, she will try to seduce you. Threaten her with your sword — make her swear never to harm you, and to release your men.
Then you can lie safely in her bed and enjoy the magical delights of the island for as long as you please.

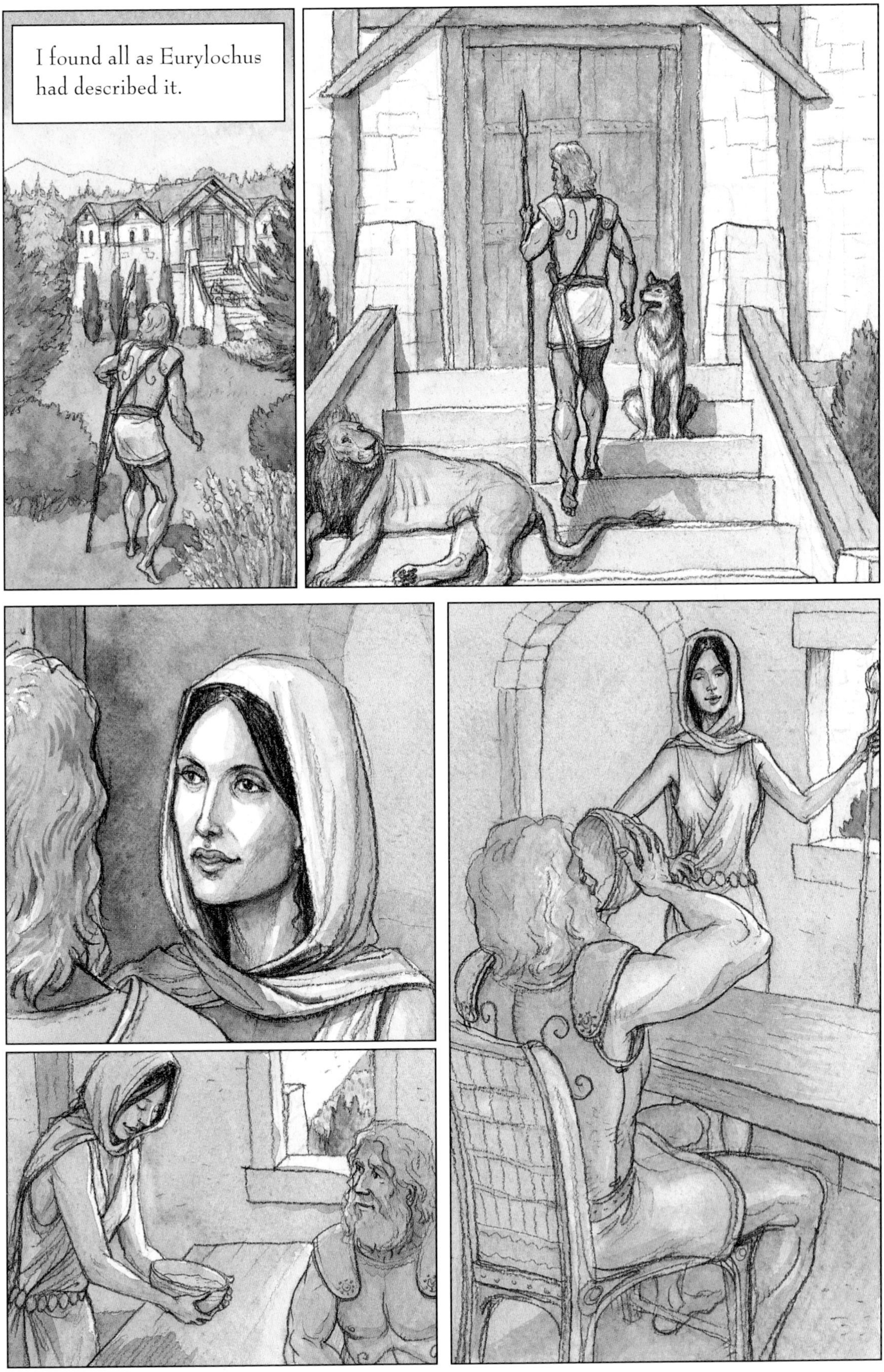
I found all as Eurylochus had described it.

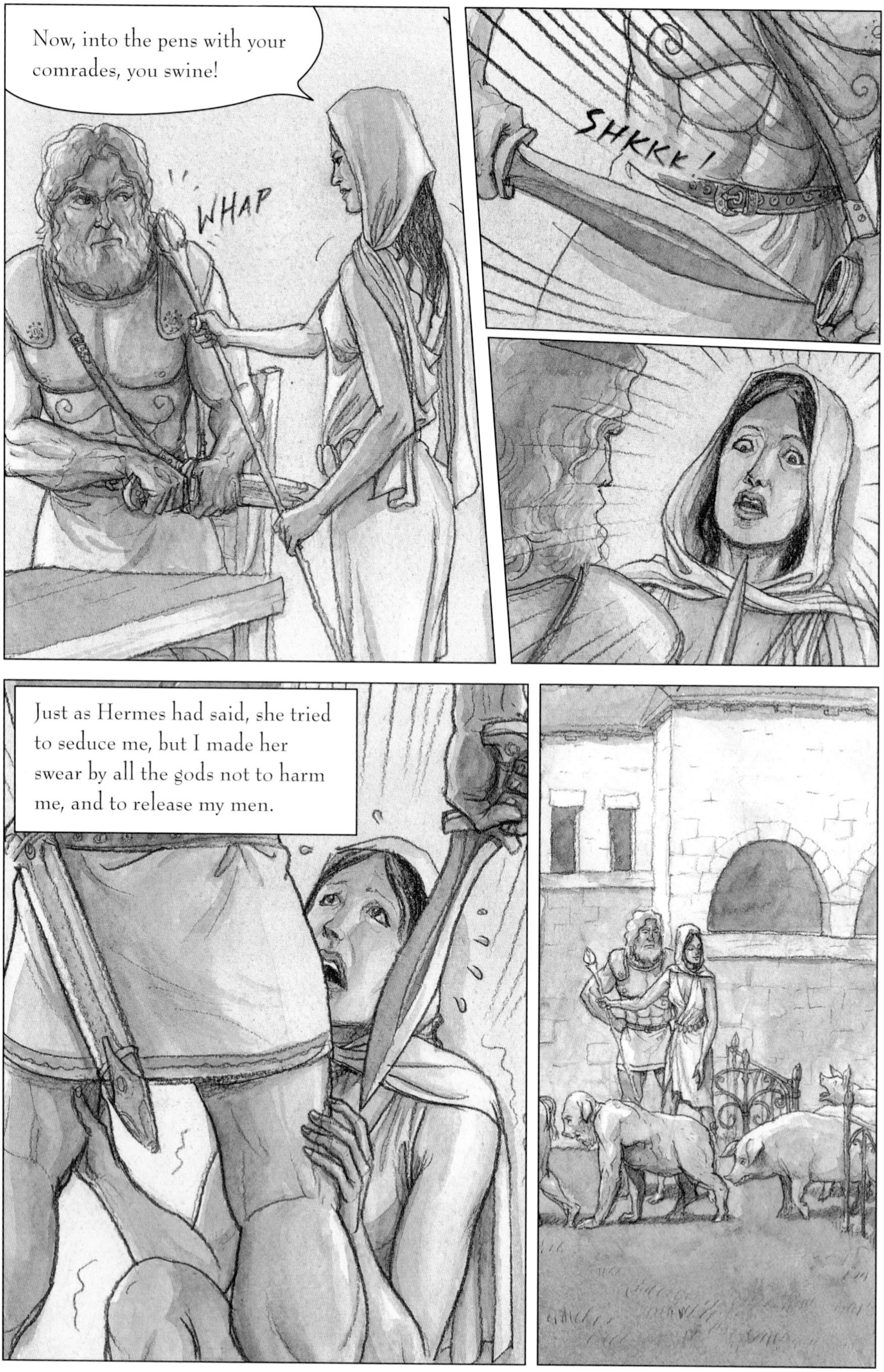
Now, into the pens with your comrades, you swine!
WHAP
SHKKK!
Just as Hermes had said, she tried to seduce me, but I made her swear by all the gods not to harm me, and to release my men.

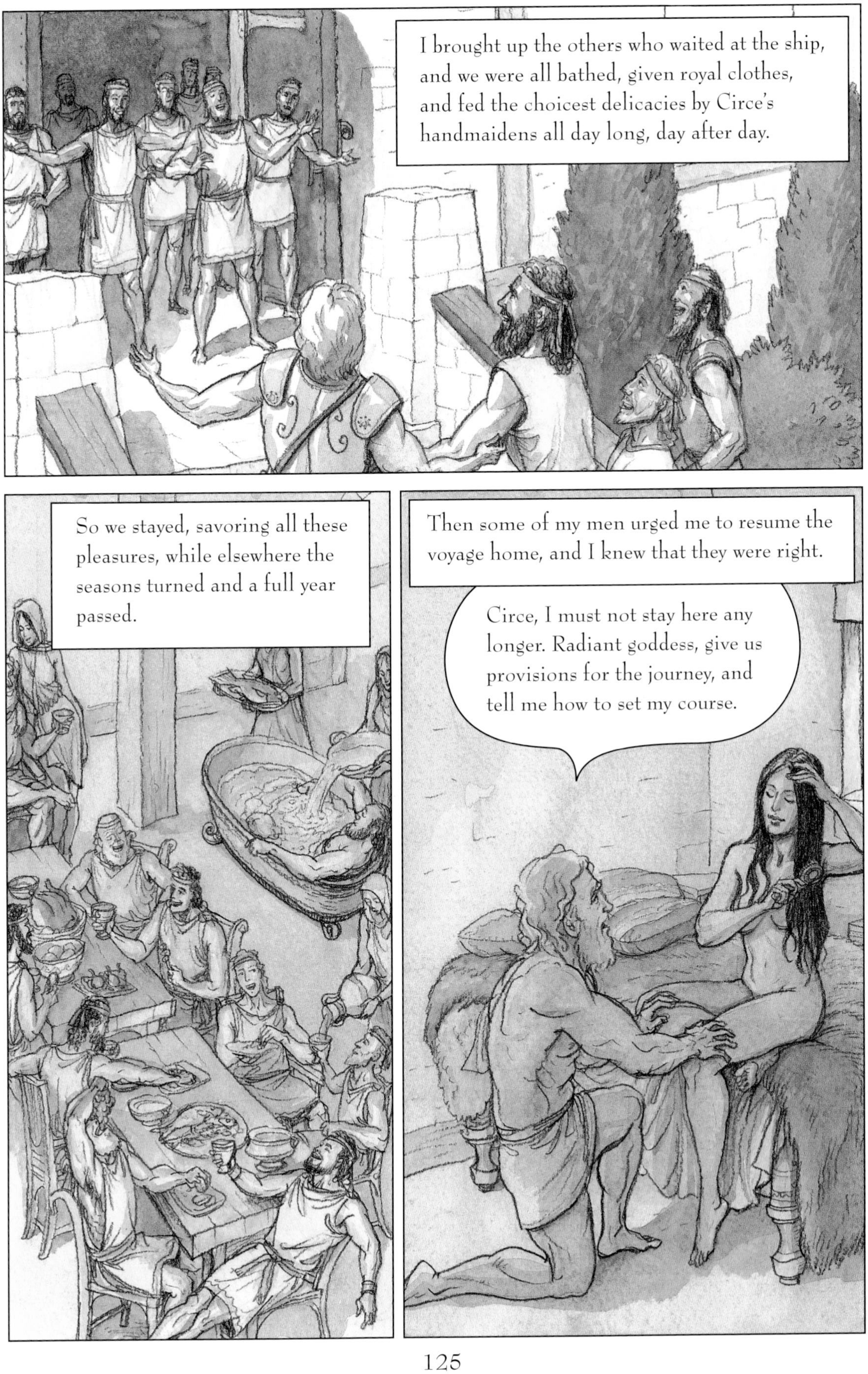
I brought up the others who waited at the ship, and we were all bathed, given royal clothes, and fed the choicest delicacies by Circe's handmaidens all day long, day after day.
So we stayed, savoring all these pleasures, while elsewhere the seasons turned and a full year passed.
Then some of my men urged me to resume the voyage home, and I knew that they were right.
Circe, I must not stay here any longer. Radiant goddess, give us provisions for the journey, and tell me how to set my course.

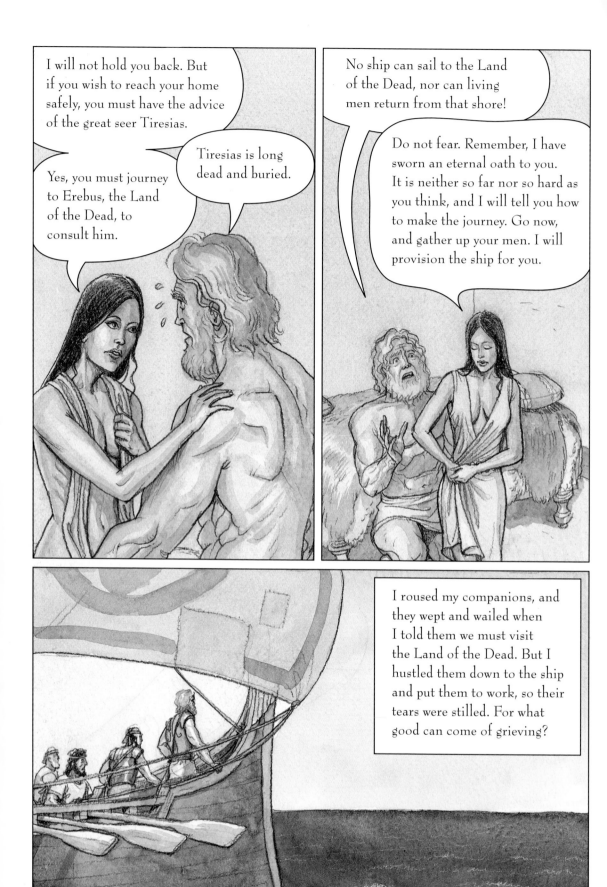

I will not hold you back. But if you wish to reach your home safely, you must have the advice of the great seer Tiresias.

Tiresias is long dead and buried.

Yes, you must journey to Erebus, the Land of the Dead, to consult him.

No ship can sail to the Land of the Dead, nor can living men return from that shore!

Do not fear. Remember, I have sworn an eternal oath to you. It is neither so far nor so hard as you think, and I will tell you how to make the journey. Go now, and gather up your men. I will provision the ship for you.

I roused my companions, and they wept and wailed when I told them we must visit the Land of the Dead. But I hustled them down to the ship and put them to work, so their tears were stilled. For what good can come of grieving?

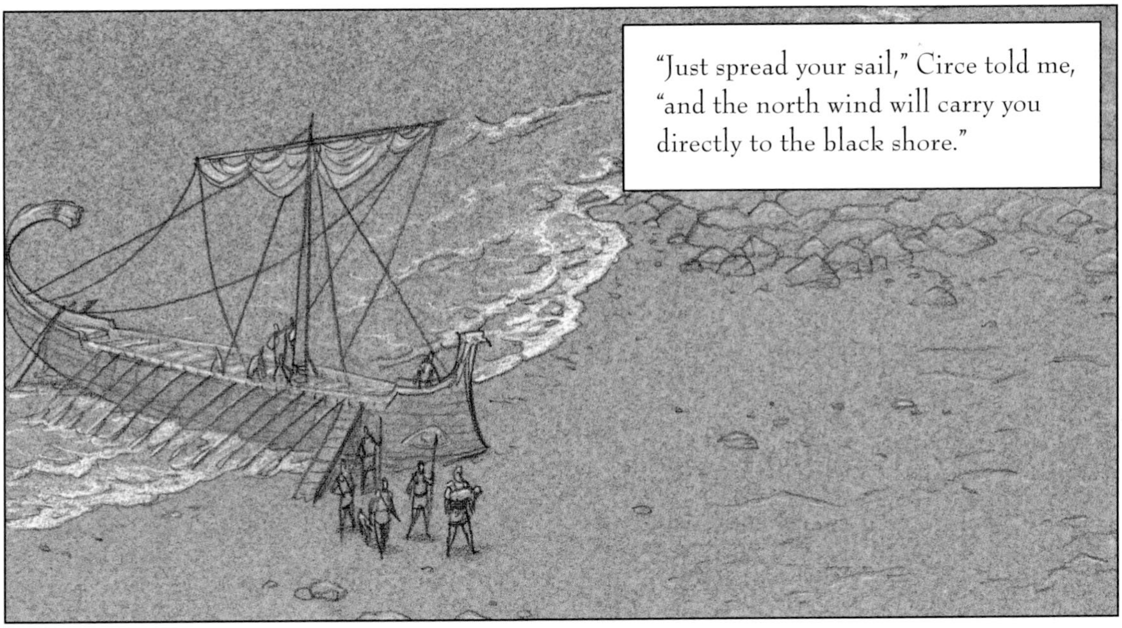
"Just spread your sail," Circe told me, "and the north wind will carry you directly to the black shore."

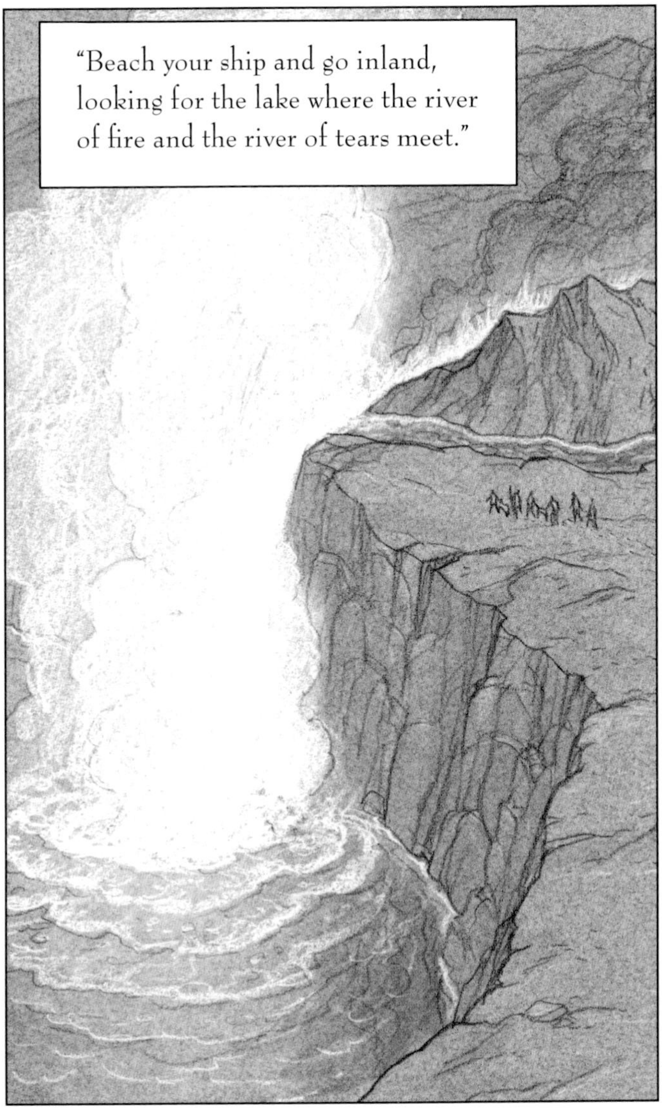
"Beach your ship and go inland, looking for the lake where the river of fire and the river of tears meet."

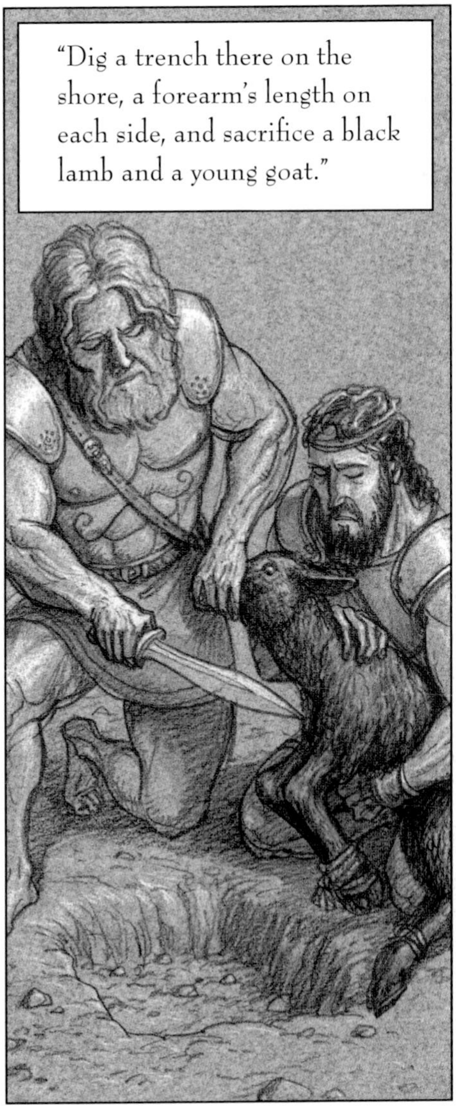
"Dig a trench there on the shore, a forearm's length on each side, and sacrifice a black lamb and a young goat."

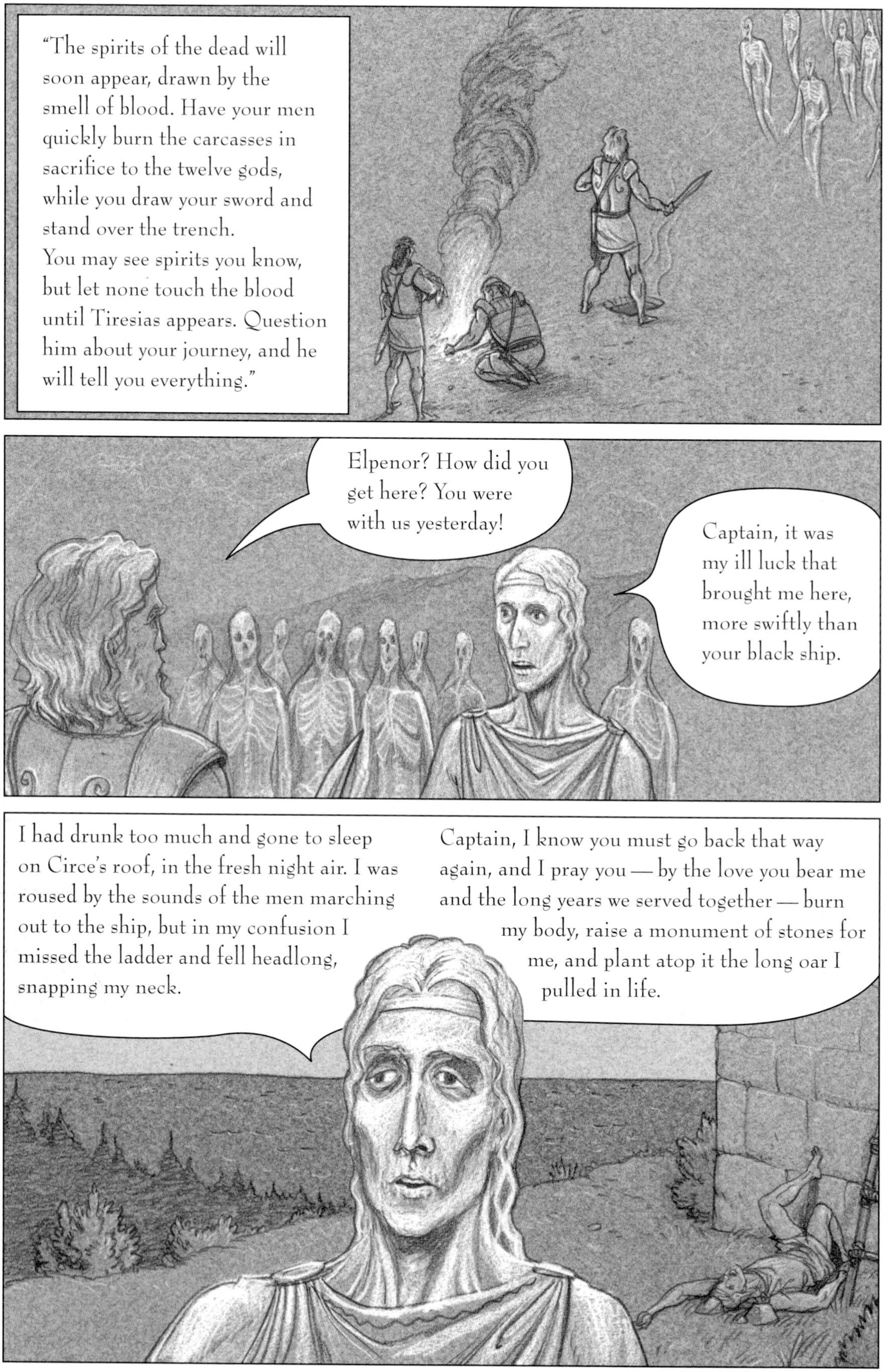
"The spirits of the dead will soon appear, drawn by the smell of blood. Have your men quickly burn the carcasses in sacrifice to the twelve gods, while you draw your sword and stand over the trench.
You may see spirits you know, but let none touch the blood until Tiresias appears. Question him about your journey, and he will tell you everything."
Elpenor? How did you get here? You were with us yesterday!
Captain, it was my ill luck that brought me here, more swiftly than your black ship.
I had drunk too much and gone to sleep on Circe's roof, in the fresh night air. I was roused by the sounds of the men marching out to the ship, but in my confusion I missed the ladder and fell headlong, snapping my neck.
Captain, I know you must go back that way again, and I pray you — by the love you bear me and the long years we served together — burn my body, raise a monument of stones for me, and plant atop it the long oar I pulled in life.

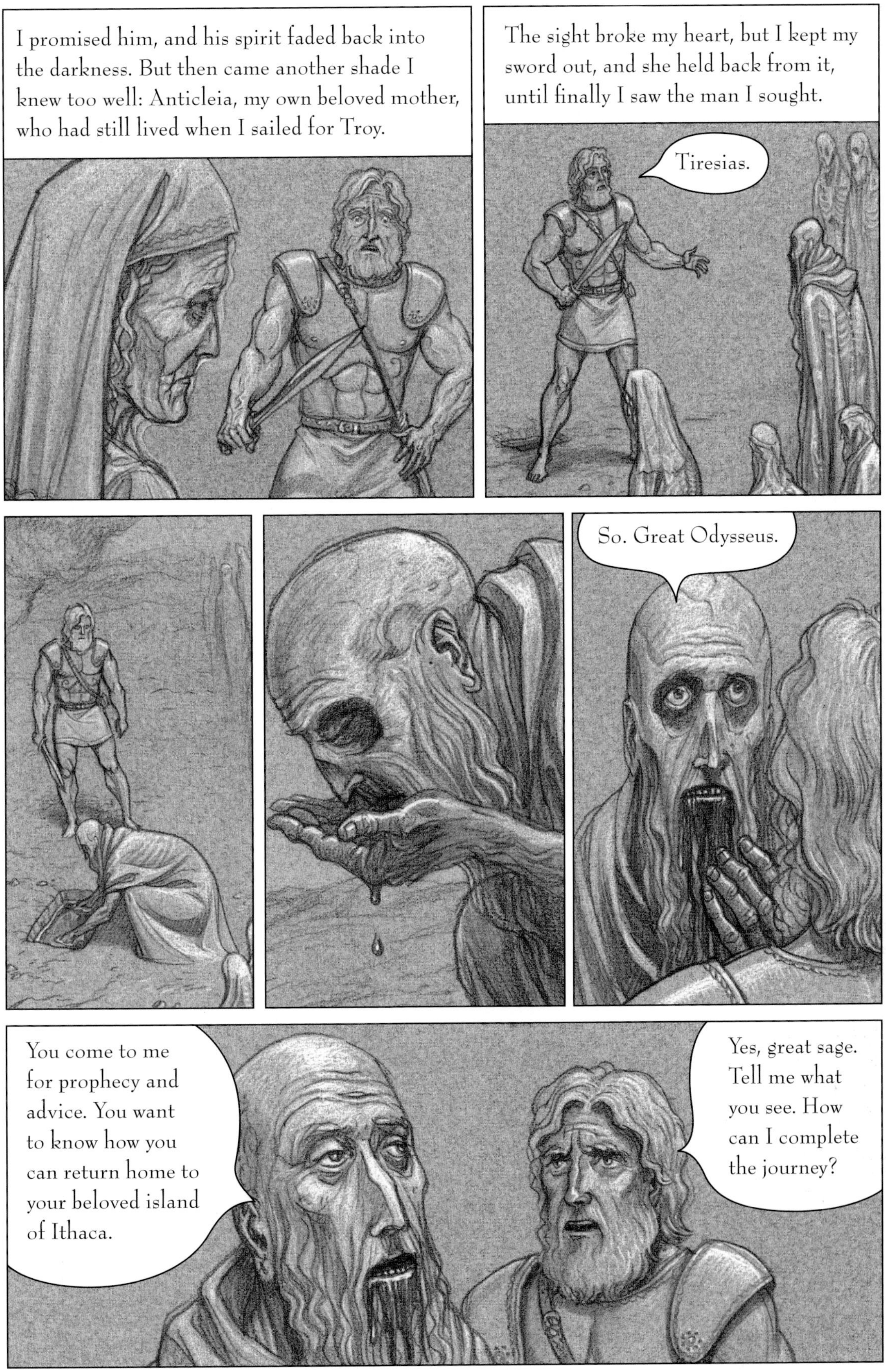
I promised him, and his spirit faded back into the darkness. But then came another shade I knew too well: Anticleia, my own beloved mother, who had still lived when I sailed for Troy.
The sight broke my heart, but I kept my sword out, and she held back from it, until finally I saw the man I sought.
Tiresias.
So. Great Odysseus.
You come to me for prophecy and advice. You want to know how you can return home to your beloved island of Ithaca.
Yes, great sage. Tell me what you see. How can I complete the journey?

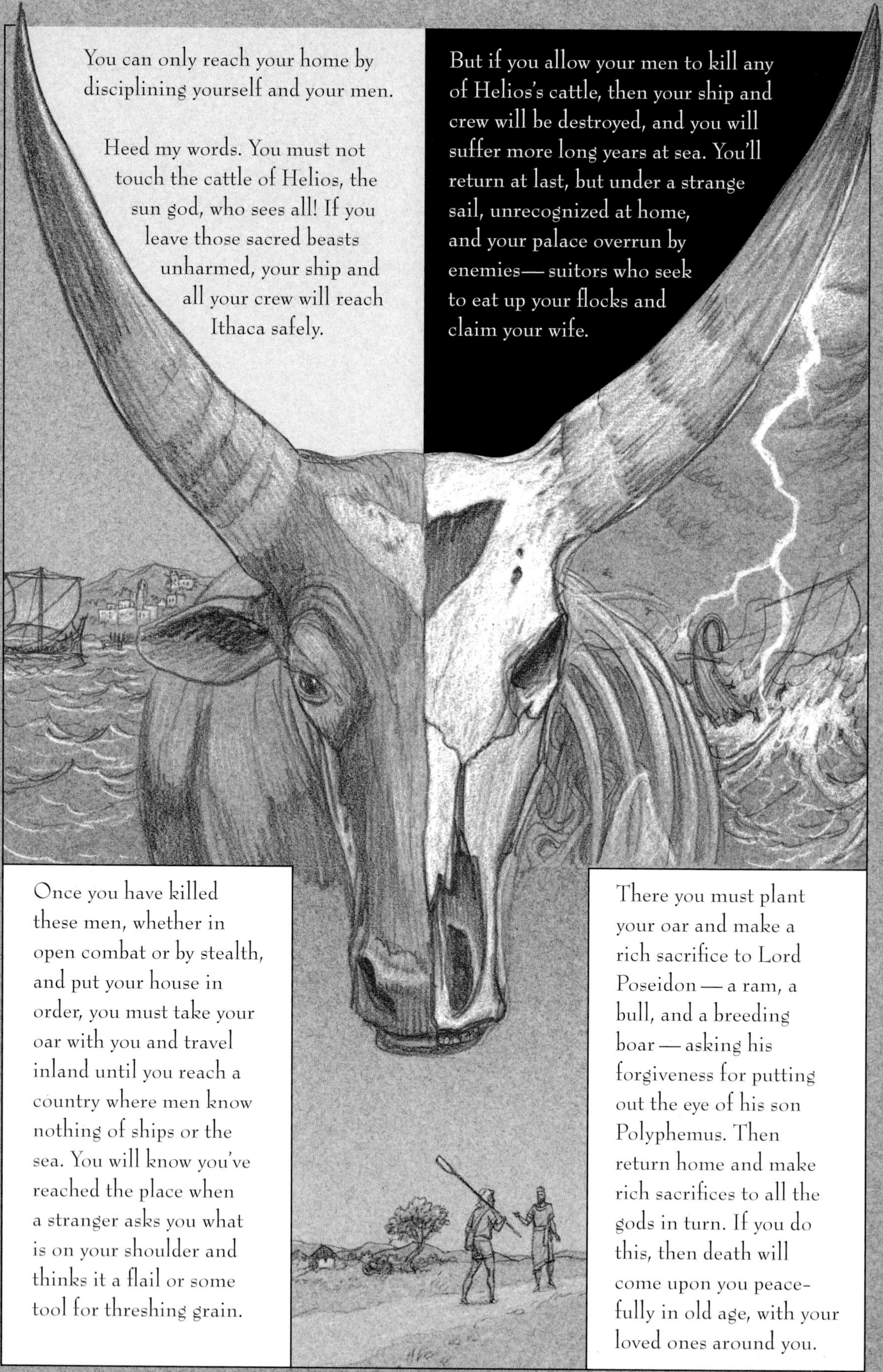
You can only reach your home by disciplining yourself and your men.
Heed my words. You must not touch the cattle of Helios, the sun god, who sees all! If you leave those sacred beasts unharmed, your ship and all your crew will reach Ithaca safely.
But if you allow your men to kill any of Helios's cattle, then your ship and crew will be destroyed, and you will suffer more long years at sea. You'll return at last, but under a strange sail, unrecognized at home, and your palace overrun by enemies— suitors who seek to eat up your flocks and claim your wife.
Once you have killed these men, whether in open combat or by stealth, and put your house in order, you must take your oar with you and travel inland until you reach a country where men know nothing of ships or the sea. You will know you've reached the place when a stranger asks you what is on your shoulder and thinks it a flail or some tool for threshing grain.
There you must plant your oar and make a rich sacrifice to Lord Poseidon — a ram, a bull, and a breeding boar — asking his forgiveness for putting out the eye of his son Polyphemus. Then return home and make rich sacrifices to all the gods in turn. If you do this, then death will come upon you peacefully in old age, with your loved ones around you.

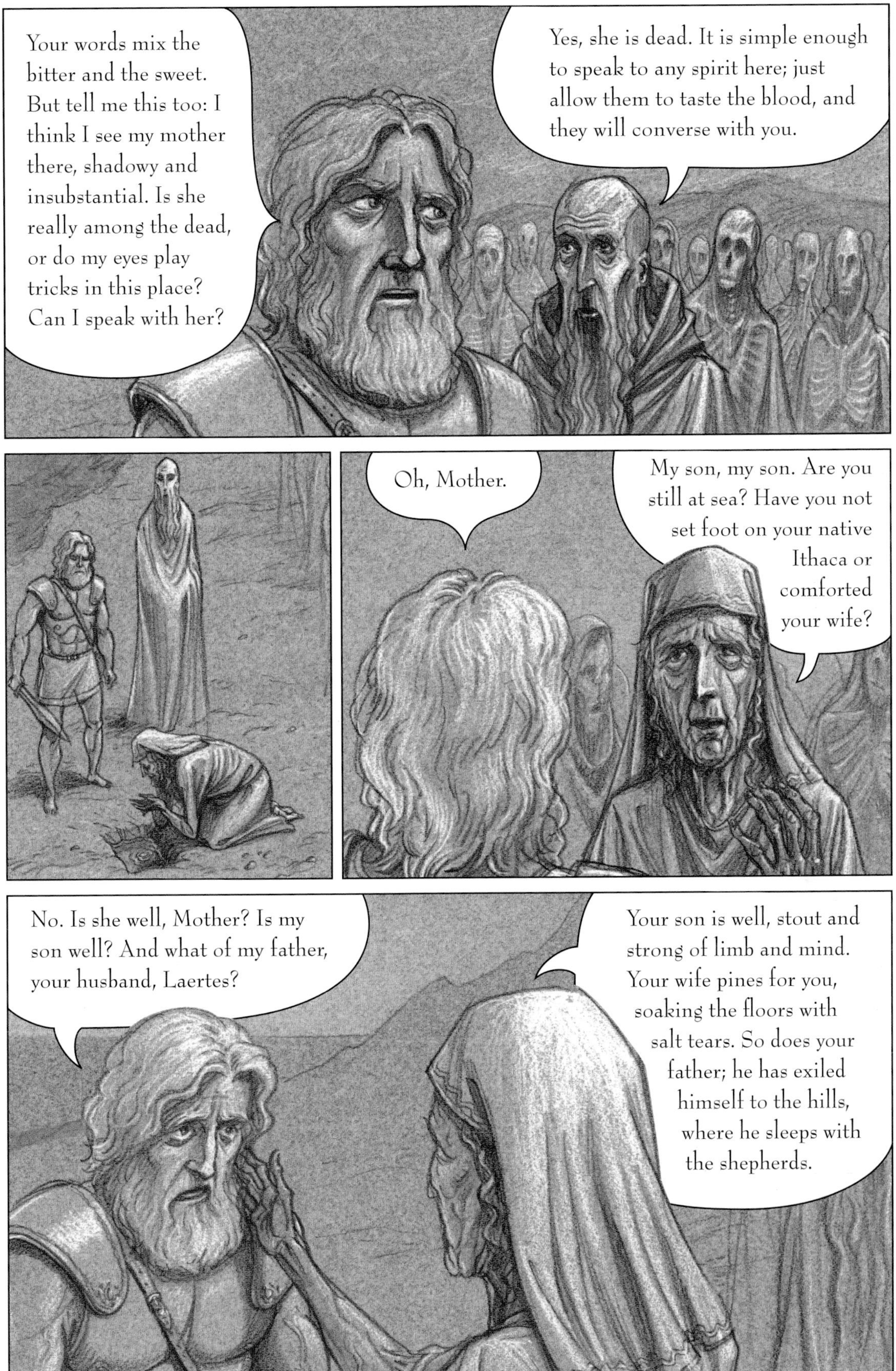
Your words mix the bitter and the sweet. But tell me this too: I think I see my mother there, shadowy and insubstantial. Is she really among the dead, or do my eyes play tricks in this place? Can I speak with her?
Yes, she is dead. It is simple enough to speak to any spirit here; just allow them to taste the blood, and they will converse with you.
Oh, Mother.
My son, my son. Are you still at sea? Have you not set foot on your native Ithaca or comforted your wife?
No. Is she well, Mother? Is my son well? And what of my father, your husband, Laertes?
Your son is well, stout and strong of limb and mind. Your wife pines for you, soaking the floors with salt tears. So does your father; he has exiled himself to the hills, where he sleeps with the shepherds.

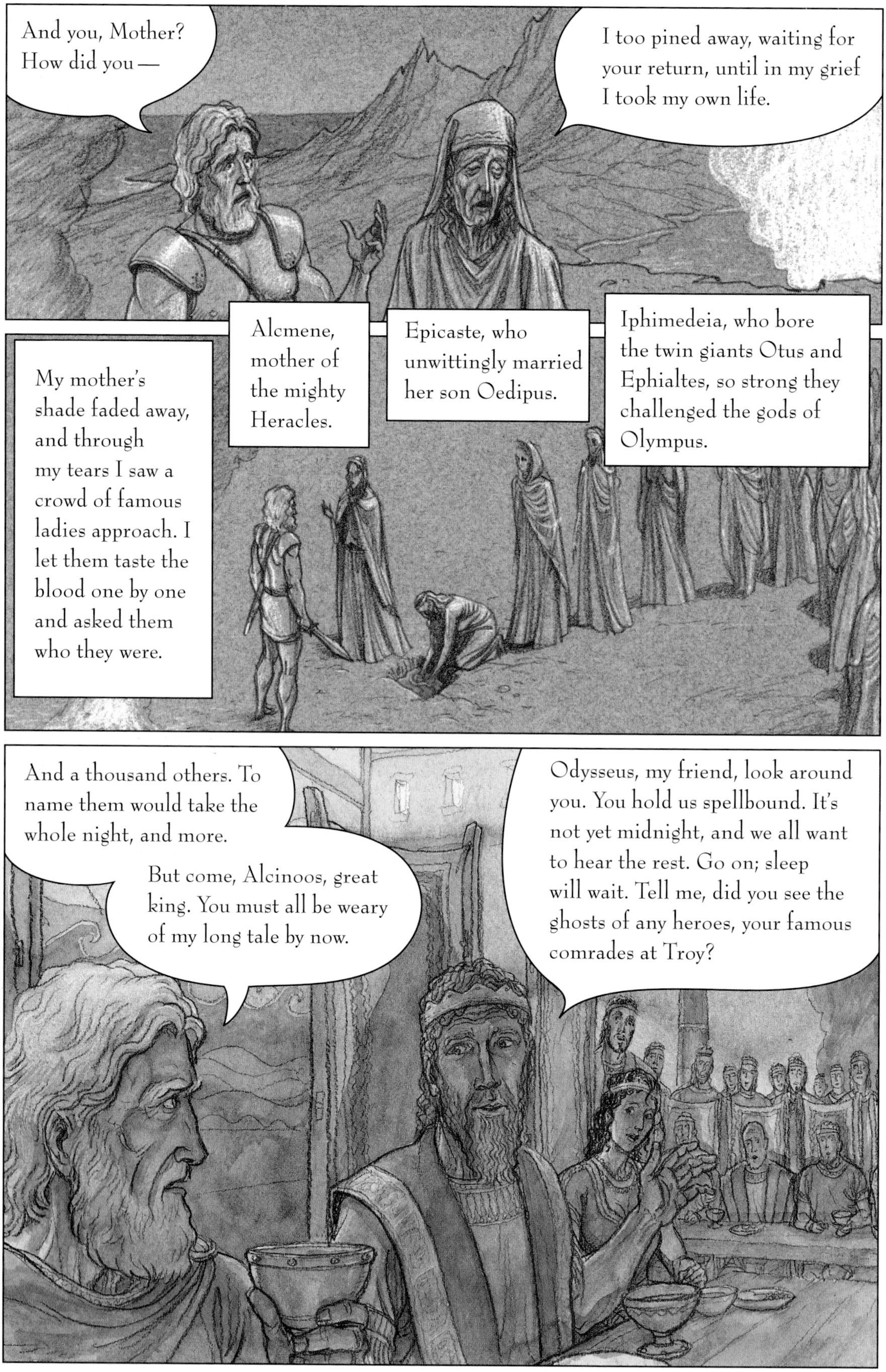
And you, Mother? How did you —
I too pined away, waiting for your return, until in my grief I took my own life.
My mother's shade faded away, and through my tears I saw a crowd of famous ladies approach. I let them taste the blood one by one and asked them who they were.
Alcmene, mother of the mighty Heracles.
Epicaste, who unwittingly married her son Oedipus.
Iphimedeia, who bore the twin giants Otus and Ephialtes, so strong they challenged the gods of Olympus.
And a thousand others. To name them would take the whole night, and more.
But come, Alcinoos, great king. You must all be weary of my long tale by now.
Odysseus, my friend, look around you. You hold us spellbound. It's not yet midnight, and we all want to hear the rest. Go on; sleep will wait. Tell me, did you see the ghosts of any heroes, your famous comrades at Troy?

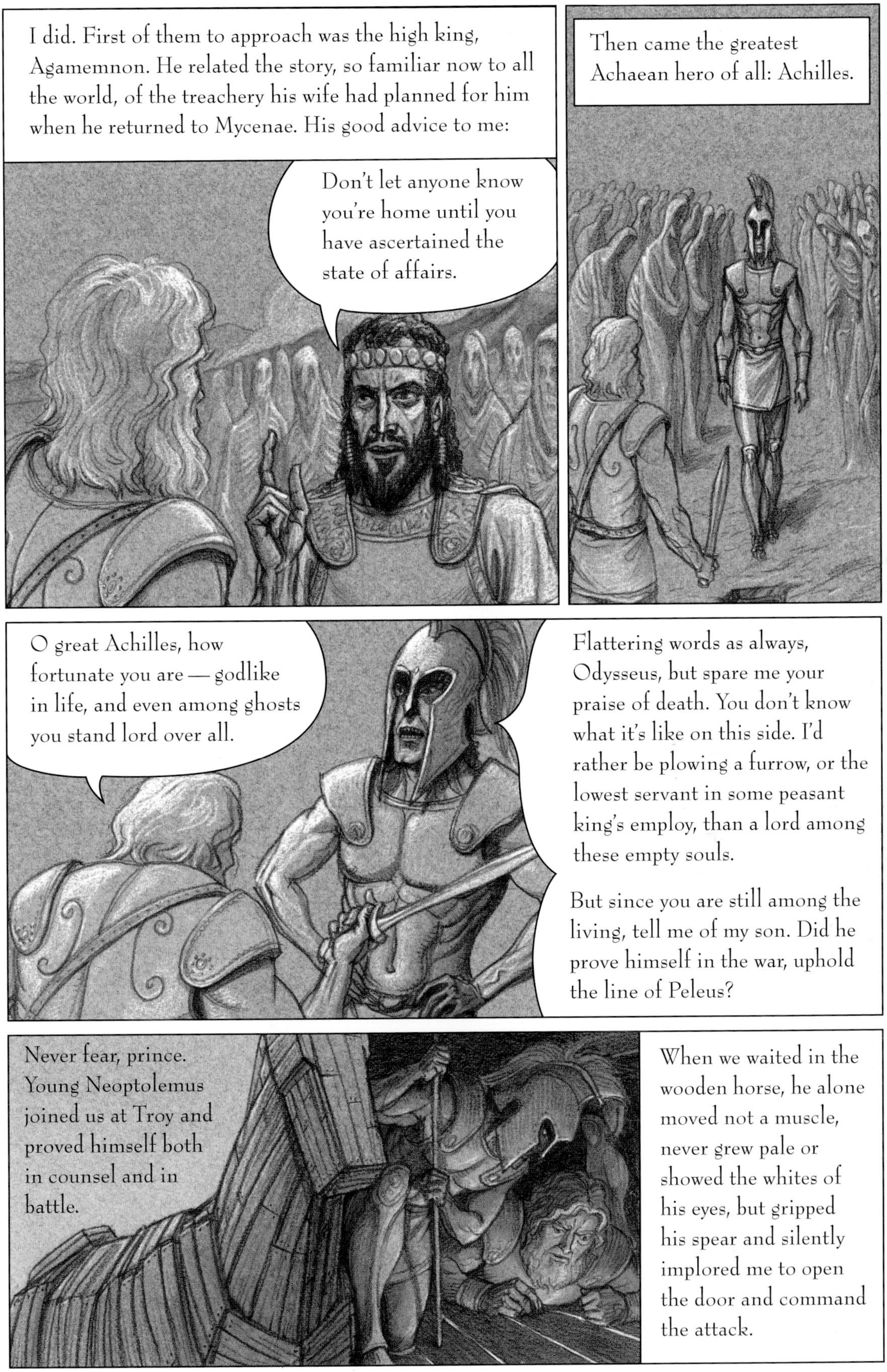
I did. First of them to approach was the high king, Agamemnon. He related the story, so familiar now to all the world, of the treachery his wife had planned for him when he returned to Mycenae. His good advice to me:
Don't let anyone know you're home until you have ascertained the state of affairs.
Then came the greatest Achaean hero of all: Achilles.
O great Achilles, how fortunate you are — godlike in life, and even among ghosts you stand lord over all.
Flattering words as always, Odysseus, but spare me your praise of death. You don't know what it's like on this side. I'd rather be plowing a furrow, or the lowest servant in some peasant king's employ, than a lord among these empty souls.
But since you are still among the living, tell me of my son. Did he prove himself in the war, uphold the line of Peleus?
Never fear, prince. Young Neoptolemus joined us at Troy and proved himself both in counsel and in battle.
When we waited in the wooden horse, he alone moved not a muscle, never grew pale or showed the whites of his eyes, but gripped his spear and silently implored me to open the door and command the attack.

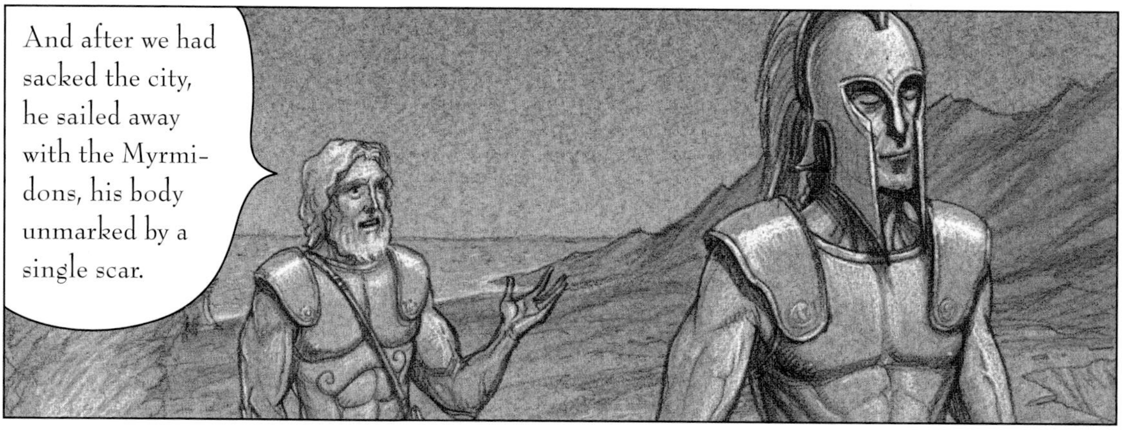
And after we had sacked the city, he sailed away with the Myrmidons, his body unmarked by a single scar.

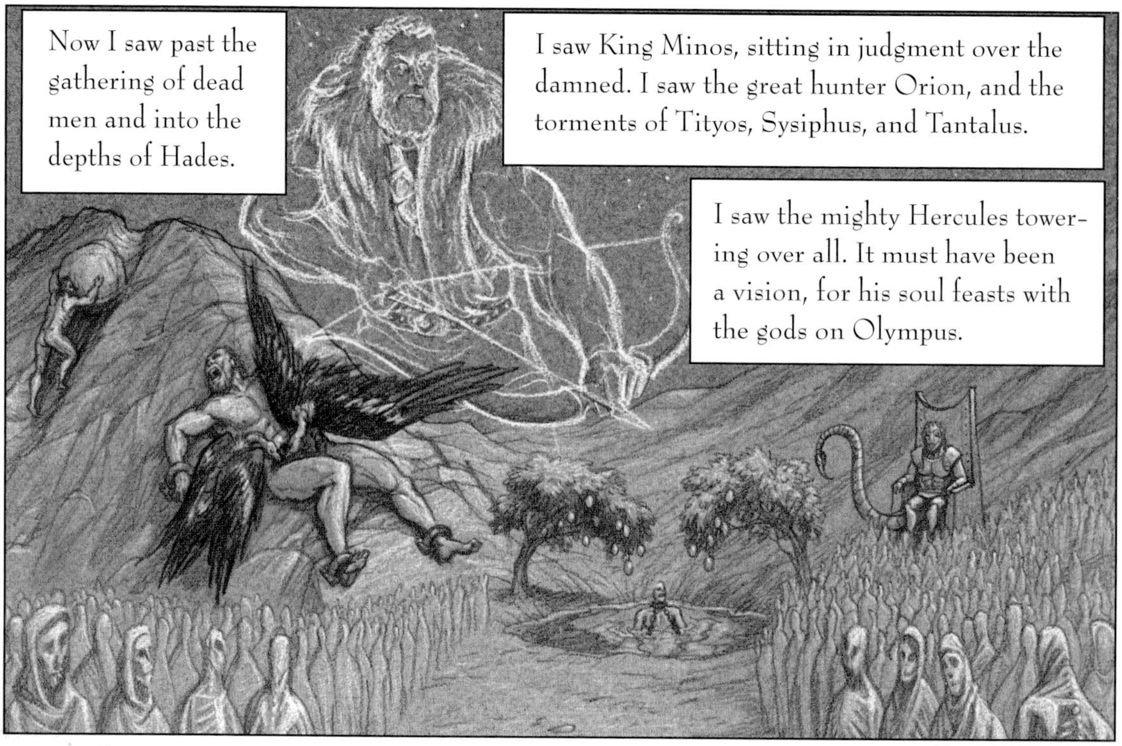
Now I saw past the gathering of dead men and into the depths of Hades.
I saw King Minos, sitting in judgment over the damned. I saw the great hunter Orion, and the torments of Tityos, Sysiphus, and Tantalus.
I saw the mighty Hercules towering over all. It must have been a vision, for his soul feasts with the gods on Olympus.

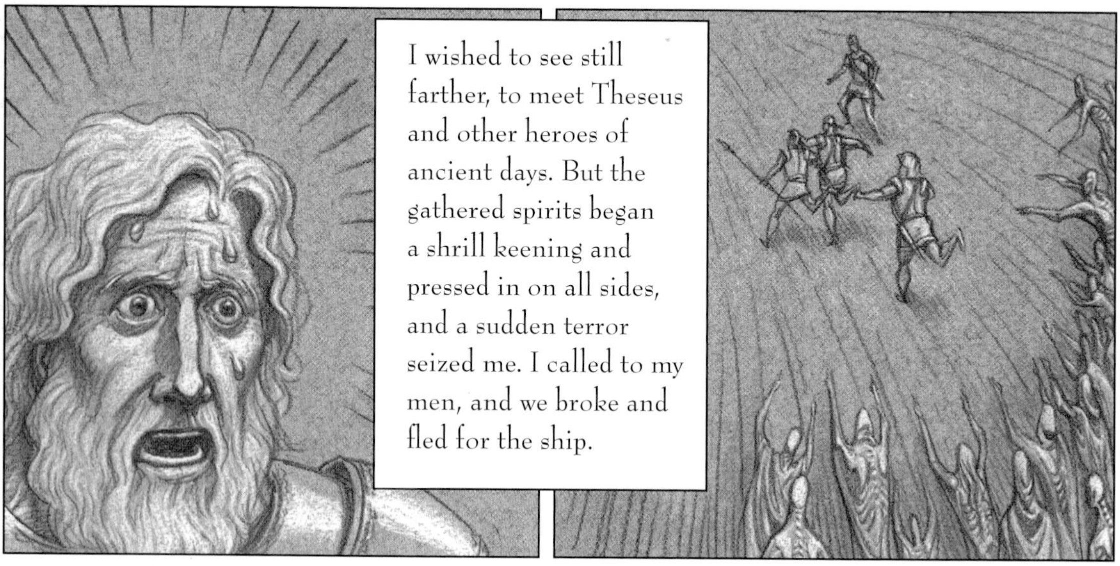
I wished to see still farther, to meet Theseus and other heroes of ancient days. But the gathered spirits began a shrill keening and pressed in on all sides, and a sudden terror seized me. I called to my men, and we broke and fled for the ship.

We returned to Aeaea and burned the body of Elpenor.

The next morning, Circe sent us on our way, with good provisions and a following breeze.

She also warned me about the dangers that lay on our route, and I informed the crew of all but one. . . .

"First," she told me, "you will come near the island of the sirens, whose sweet song lures sailors to certain doom."

"You must plug your crew's ears with beeswax and tell them to row on without stopping. But if you alone wish to hear their song, tell your men to tie you firmly to the mast. If you cry out for release, they must only bind you tighter."

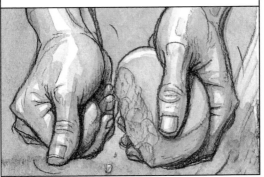

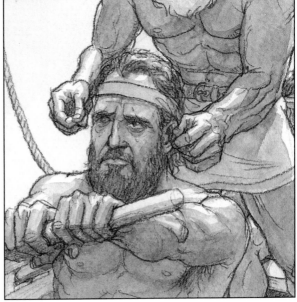

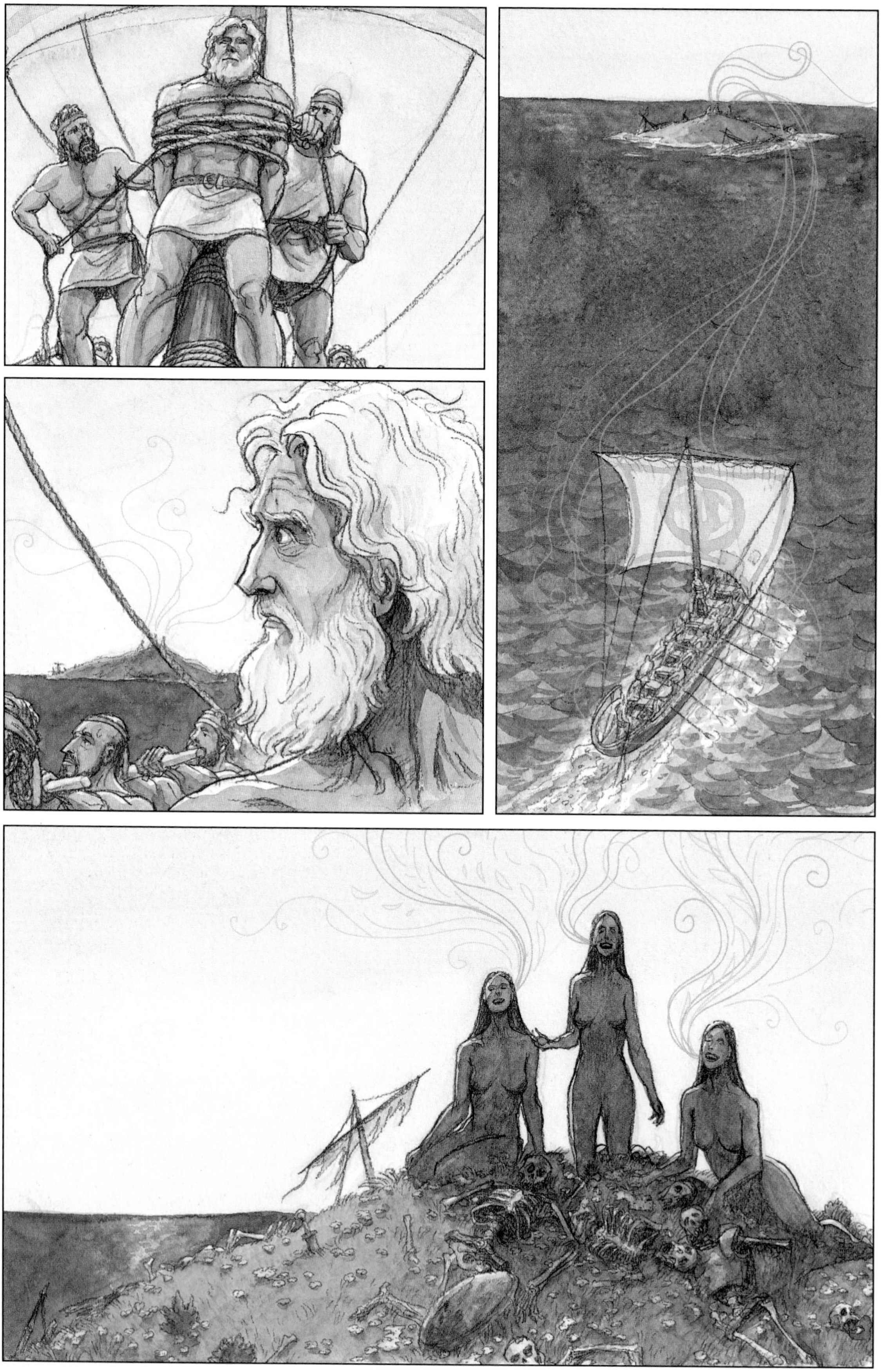

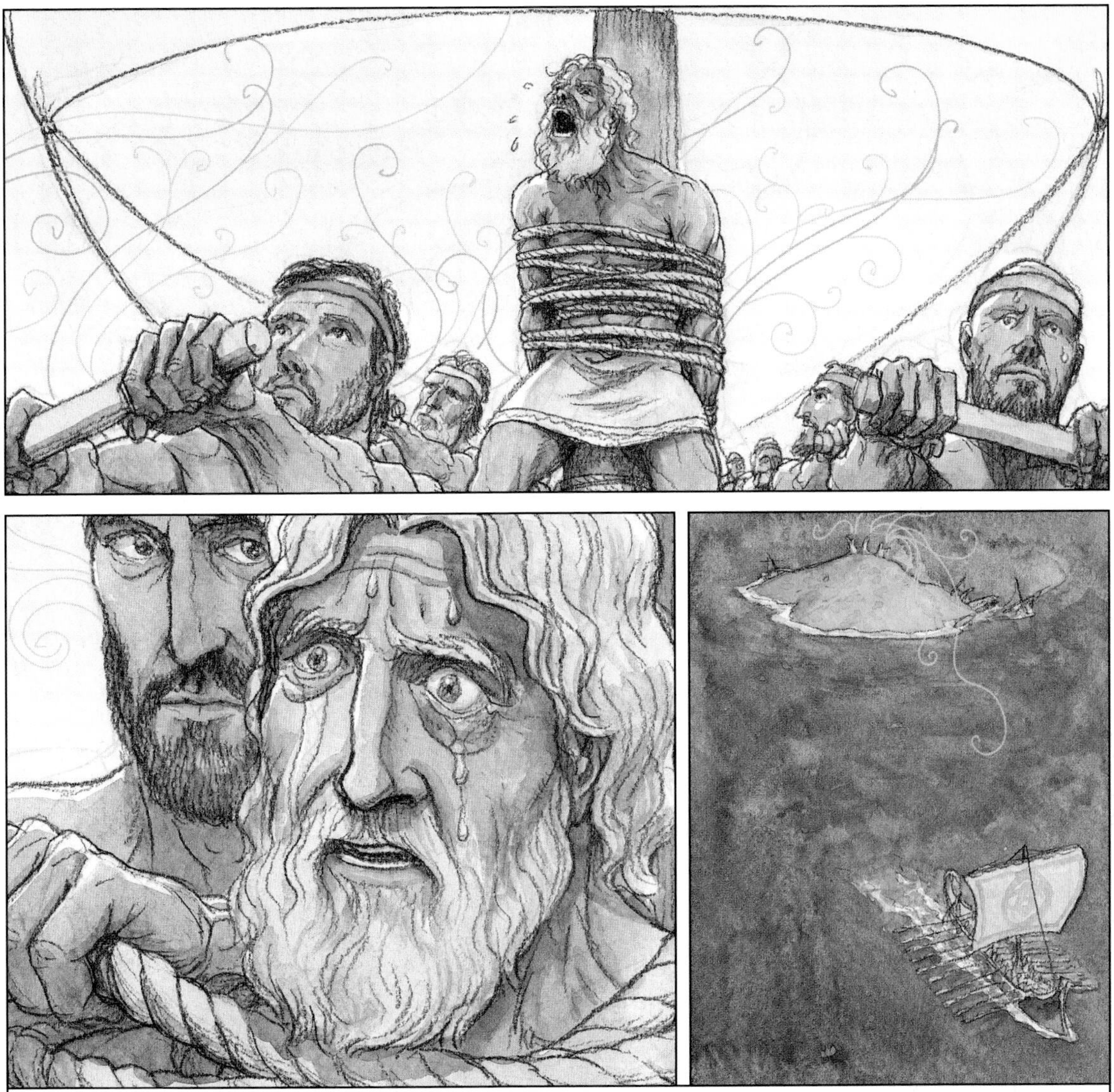

"After you pass the sirens, you will have to make a choice. You will come in sight of an unbroken line of jagged cliffs, where the sea rages and boils on sharp rocks. Steer well clear of this, for no ship that approaches can avoid being wrecked. Even birds who try to pass that way are caught in downdrafts and perish in the spray."

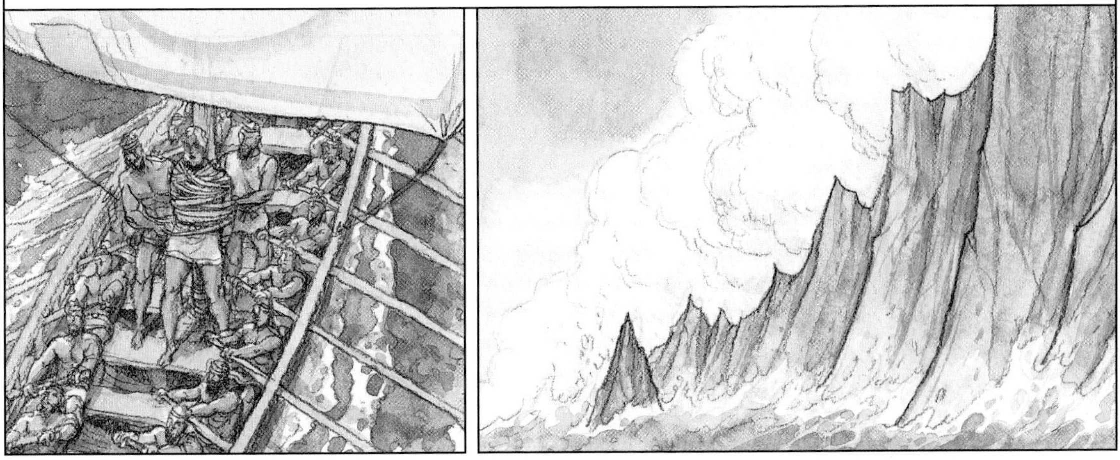

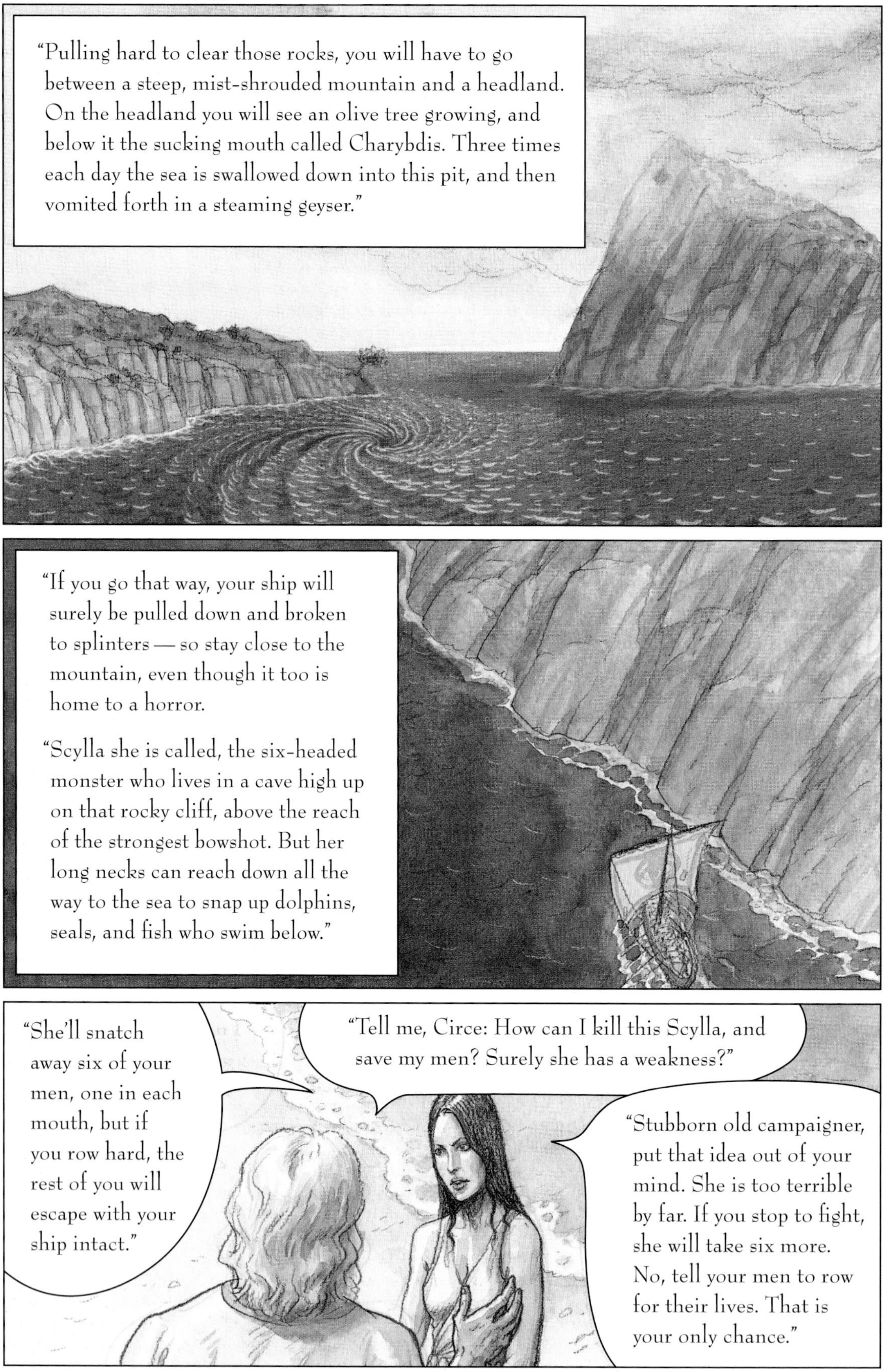
"Pulling hard to clear those rocks, you will have to go between a steep, mist-shrouded mountain and a headland. On the headland you will see an olive tree growing, and below it the sucking mouth called Charybdis. Three times each day the sea is swallowed down into this pit, and then vomited forth in a steaming geyser."
"If you go that way, your ship will surely be pulled down and broken to splinters — so stay close to the mountain, even though it too is home to a horror.
"Scylla she is called, the six-headed monster who lives in a cave high up on that rocky cliff, above the reach of the strongest bowshot. But her long necks can reach down all the way to the sea to snap up dolphins, seals, and fish who swim below."
"She'll snatch away six of your men, one in each mouth, but if you row hard, the rest of you will escape with your ship intact."
"Tell me, Circe: How can I kill this Scylla, and save my men? Surely she has a weakness?"
"Stubborn old campaigner, put that idea out of your mind. She is too terrible by far. If you stop to fight, she will take six more. No, tell your men to row for their lives. That is your only chance."

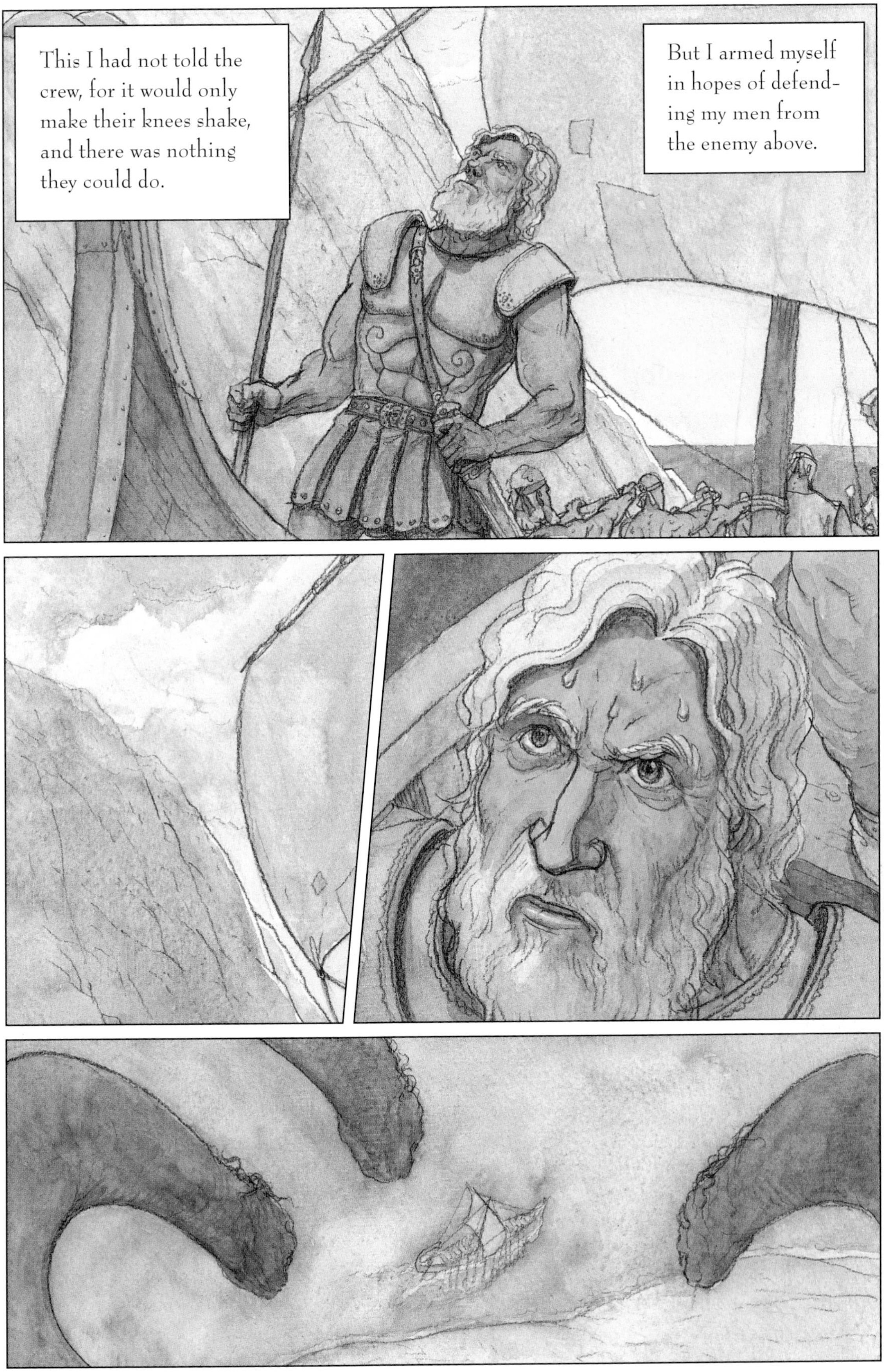
This I had not told the crew, for it would only make their knees shake, and there was nothing they could do.
But I armed myself in hopes of defending my men from the enemy above.

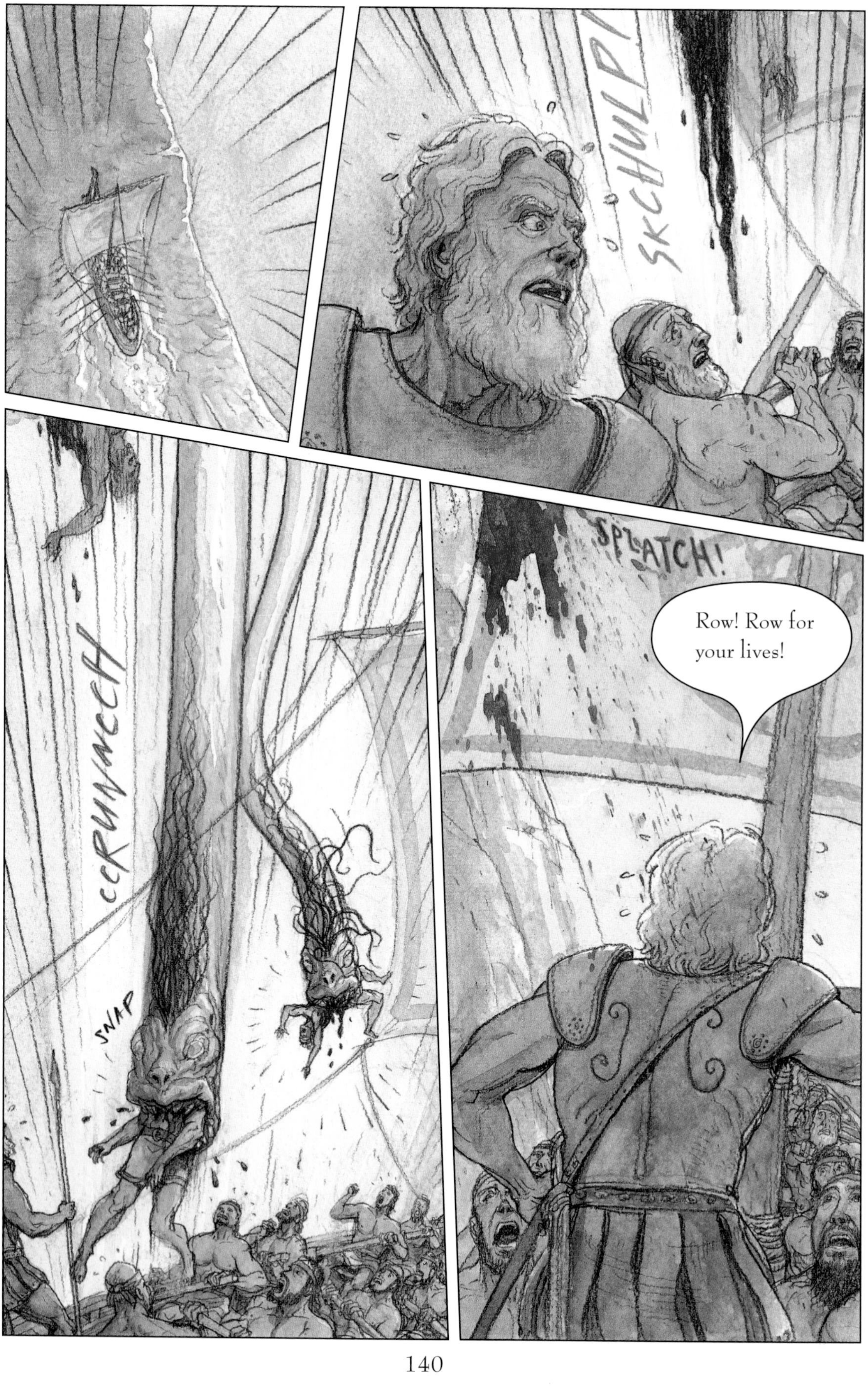
SKCHULP!
CCRUNNCCH
SNAP
SPLATCH!
Row! Row for your lives!

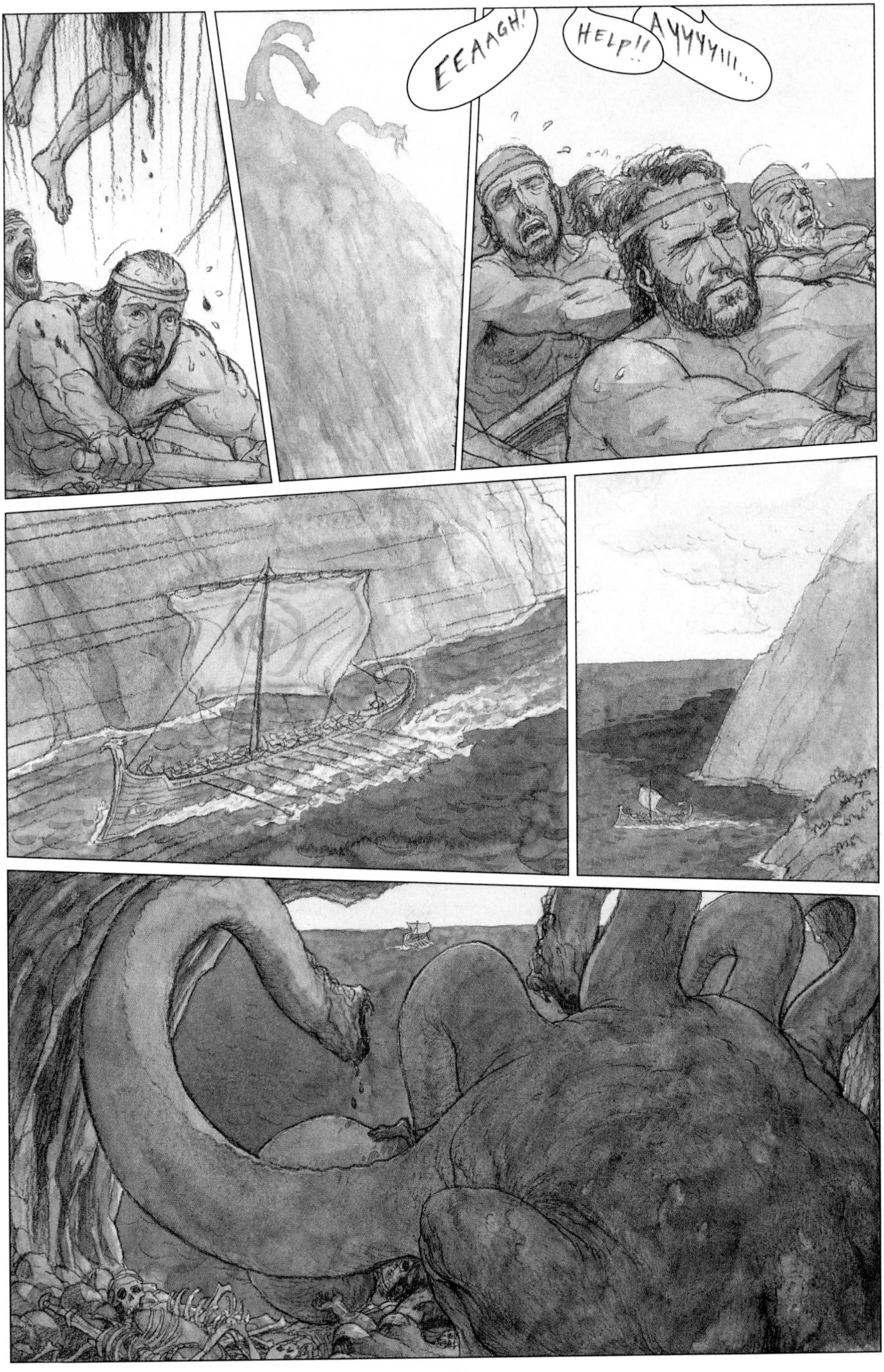
EEAAGH!
HELP!!
AYYYY!!!...

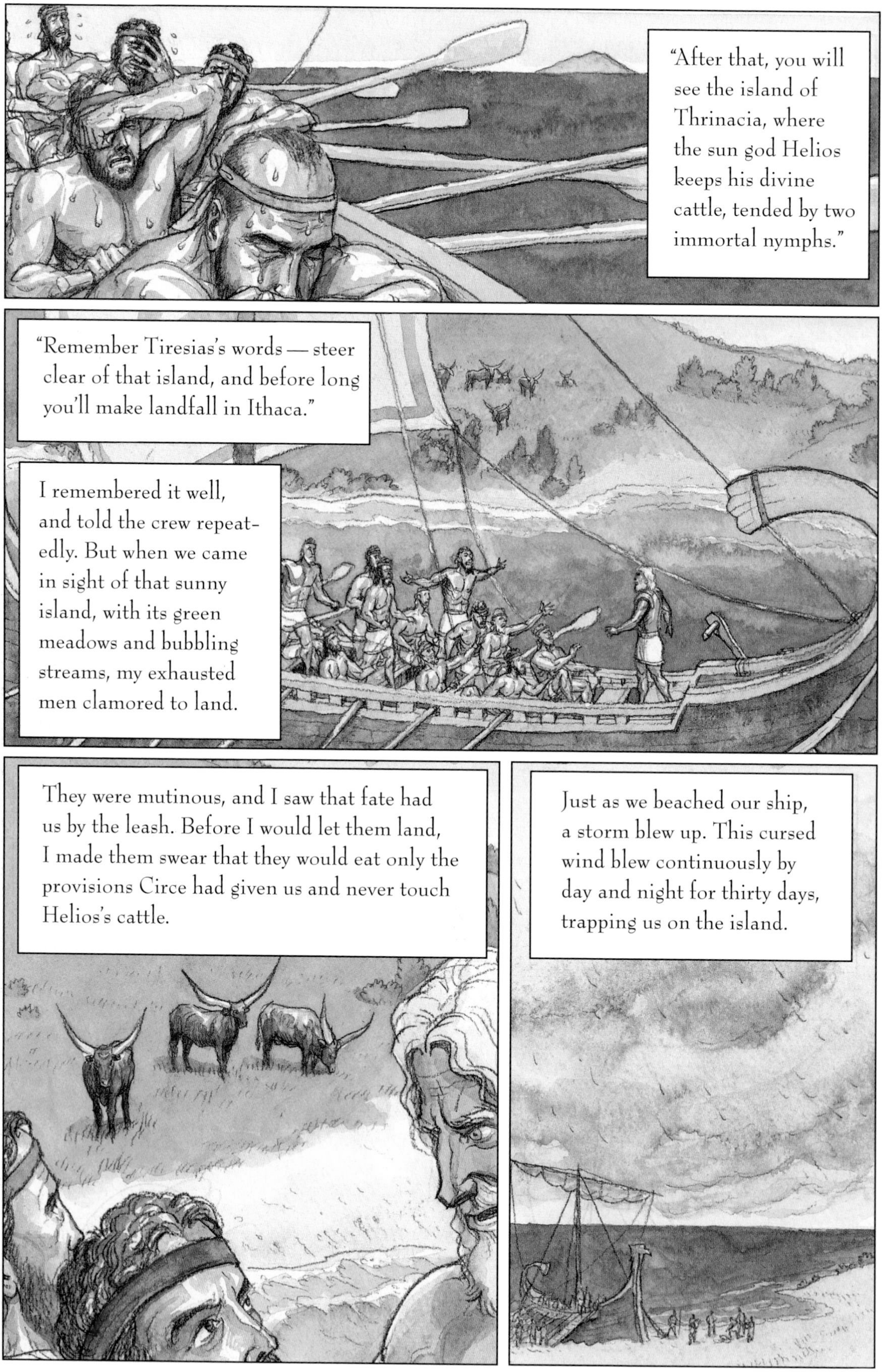
"After that, you will see the island of Thrinacia, where the sun god Helios keeps his divine cattle, tended by two immortal nymphs."
"Remember Tiresias's words — steer clear of that island, and before long you'll make landfall in Ithaca."
I remembered it well, and told the crew repeatedly. But when we came in sight of that sunny island, with its green meadows and bubbling streams, my exhausted men clamored to land.
They were mutinous, and I saw that fate had us by the leash. Before I would let them land, I made them swear that they would eat only the provisions Circe had given us and never touch Helios's cattle.
Just as we beached our ship, a storm blew up. This cursed wind blew continuously by day and night for thirty days, trapping us on the island.

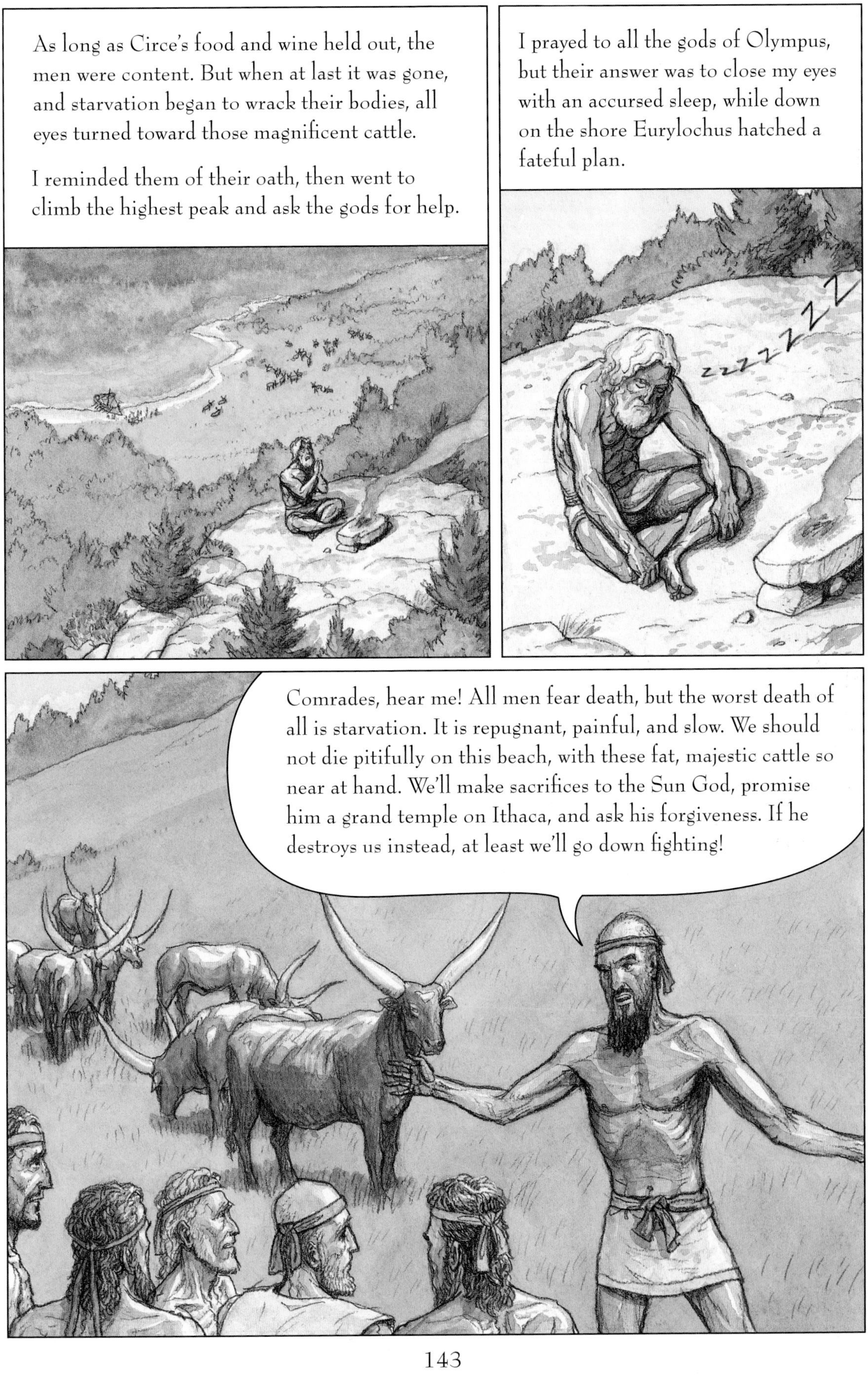
As long as Circe's food and wine held out, the men were content. But when at last it was gone, and starvation began to wrack their bodies, all eyes turned toward those magnificent cattle.
I reminded them of their oath, then went to climb the highest peak and ask the gods for help.
I prayed to all the gods of Olympus, but their answer was to close my eyes with an accursed sleep, while down on the shore Eurylochus hatched a fateful plan.
ZZZZZZZZ
Comrades, hear me! All men fear death, but the worst death of all is starvation. It is repugnant, painful, and slow. We should not die pitifully on this beach, with these fat, majestic cattle so near at hand. We'll make sacrifices to the Sun God, promise him a grand temple on Ithaca, and ask his forgiveness. If he destroys us instead, at least we'll go down fighting!

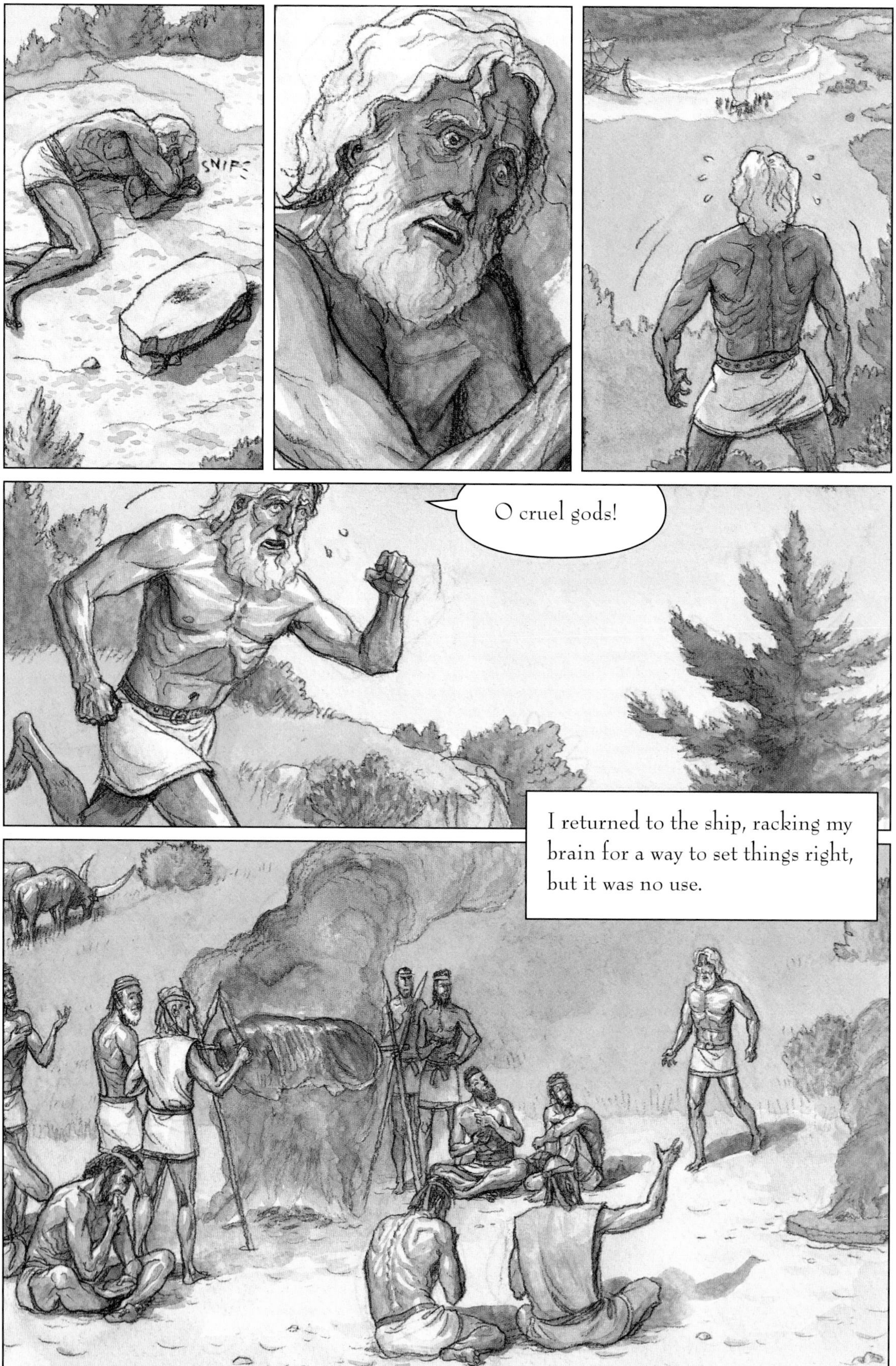
SNIFF
O cruel gods!
I returned to the ship, racking my brain for a way to set things right, but it was no use.

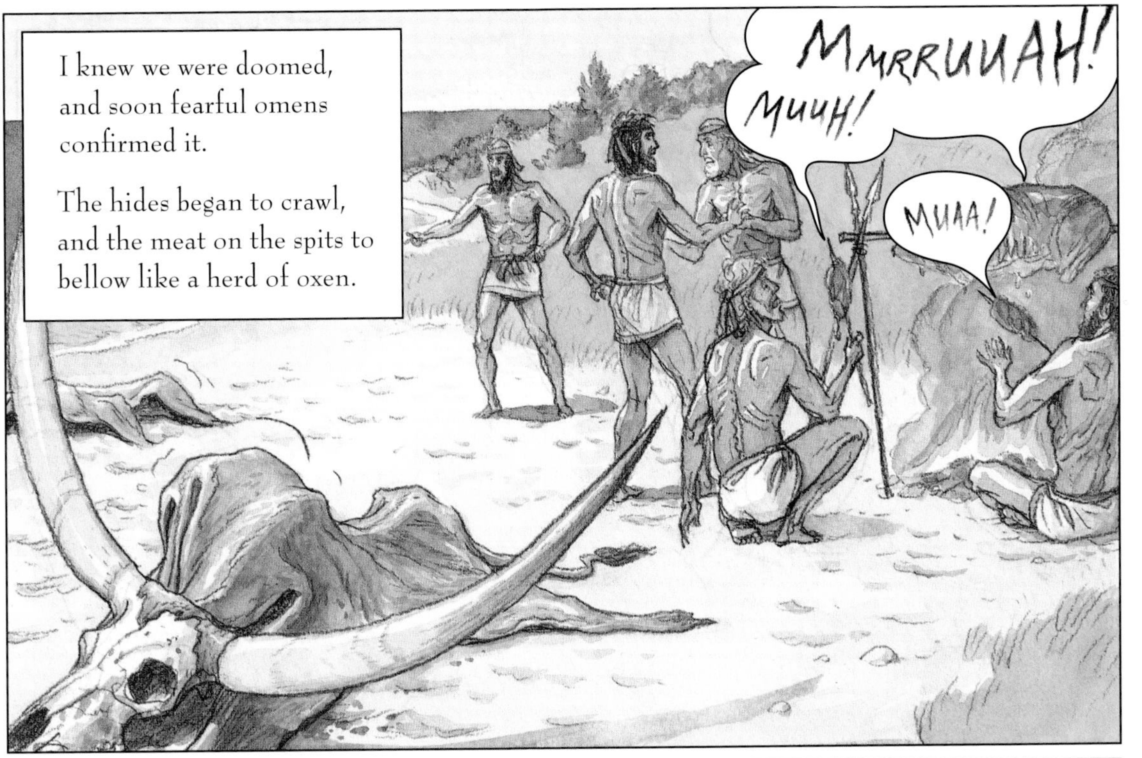
I knew we were doomed, and soon fearful omens confirmed it.
The hides began to crawl, and the meat on the spits to bellow like a herd of oxen.
MMRRUUAH!
MUUH!
MUAA!

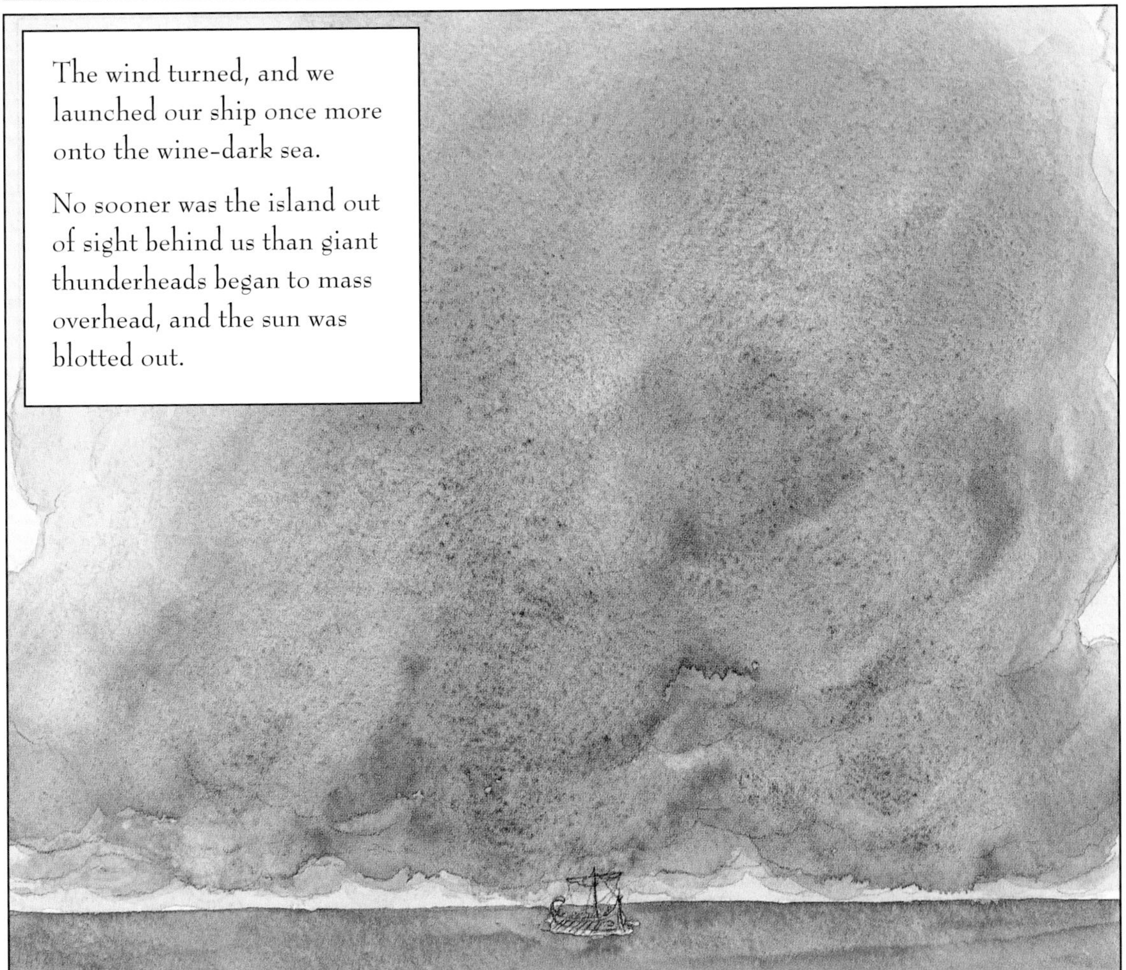
The wind turned, and we launched our ship once more onto the wine-dark sea.
No sooner was the island out of sight behind us than giant thunderheads began to mass overhead, and the sun was blotted out.

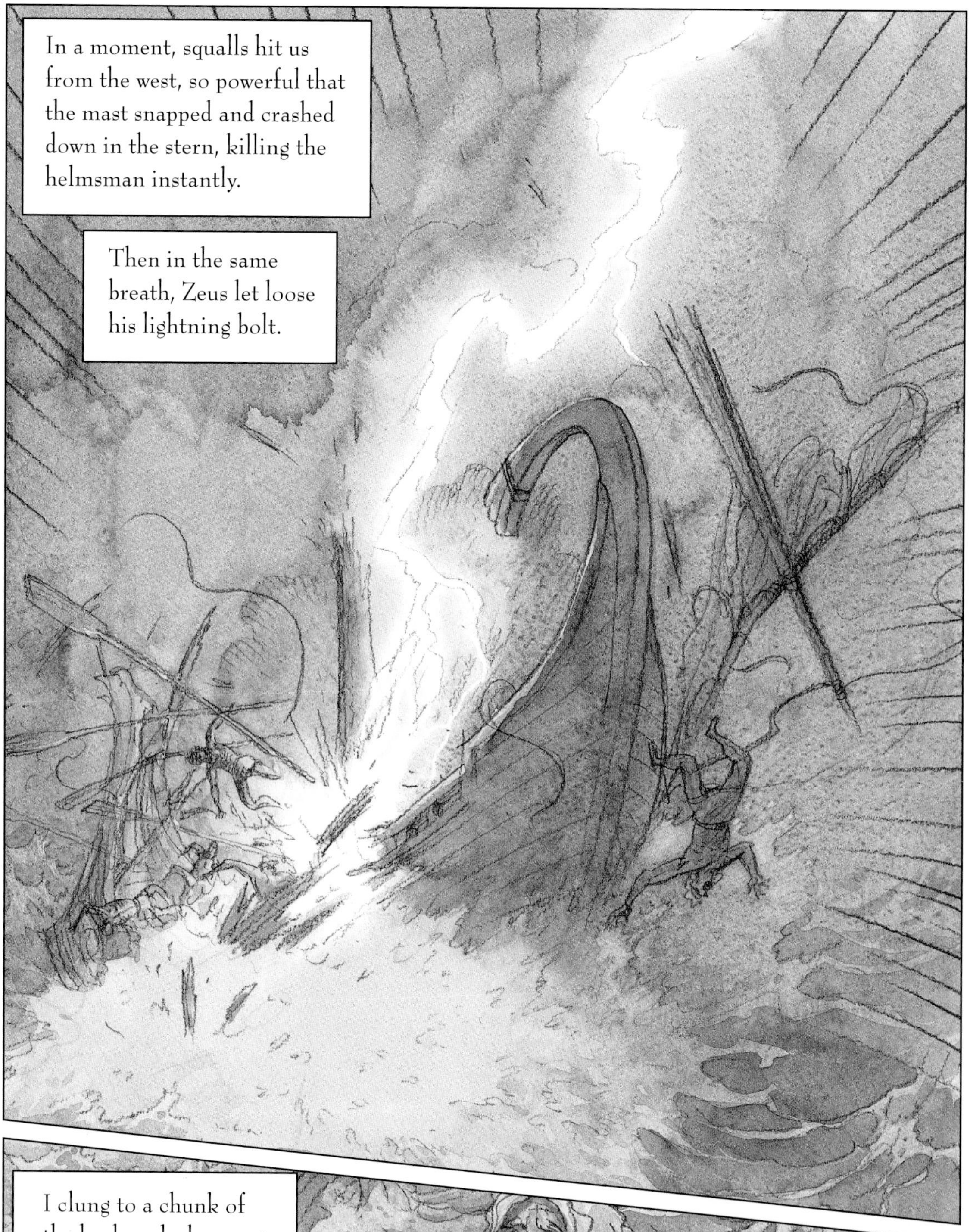
In a moment, squalls hit us from the west, so powerful that the mast snapped and crashed down in the stern, killing the helmsman instantly.
Then in the same breath, Zeus let loose his lightning bolt.

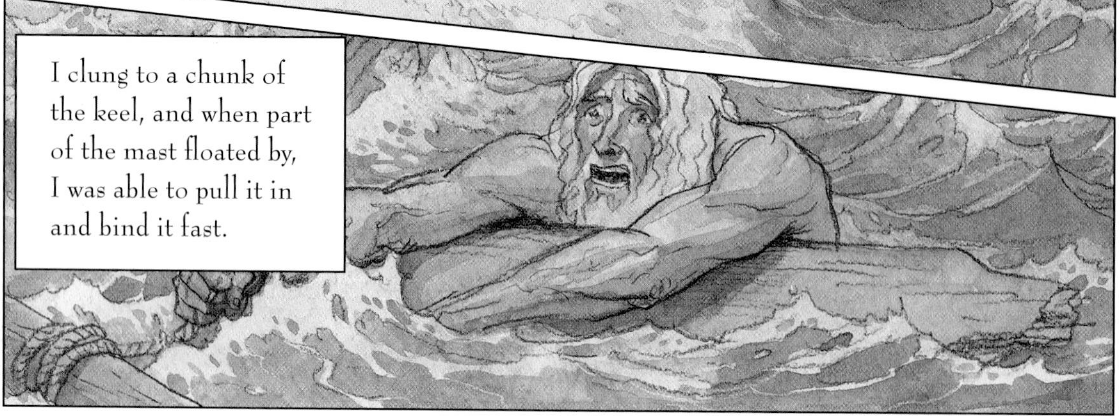
I clung to a chunk of the keel, and when part of the mast floated by, I was able to pull it in and bind it fast.

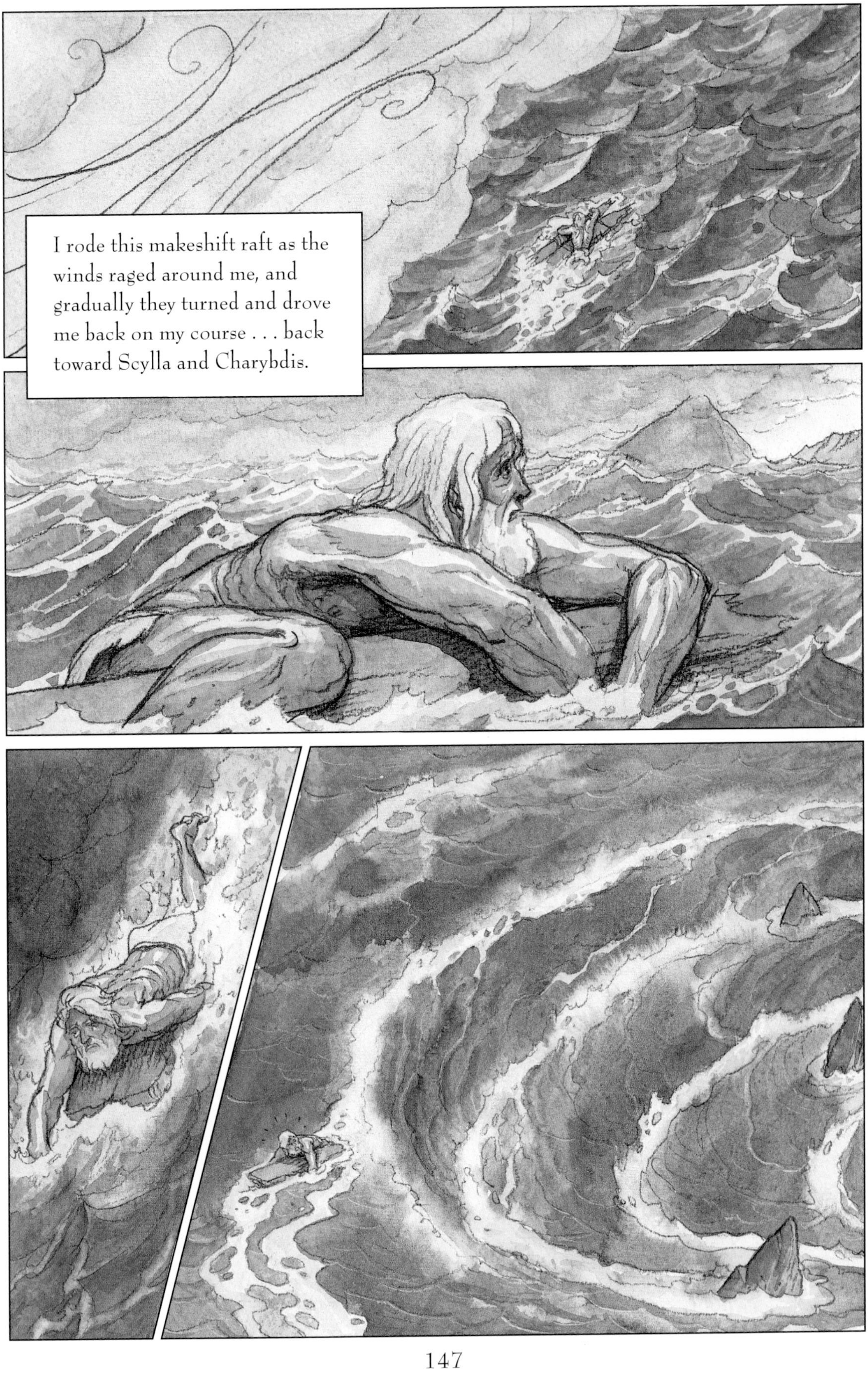
I rode this makeshift raft as the winds raged around me, and gradually they turned and drove me back on my course . . . back toward Scylla and Charybdis.

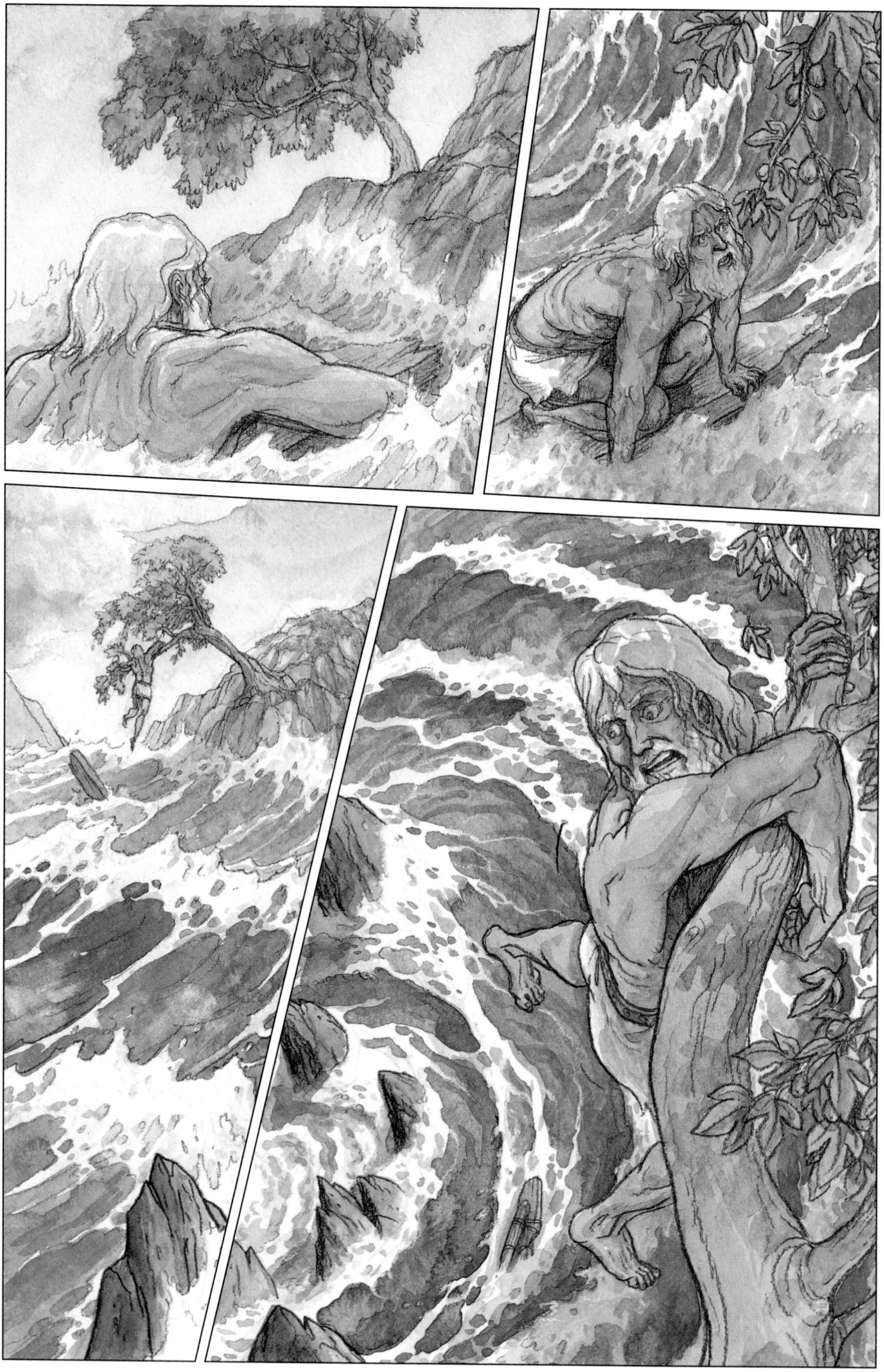

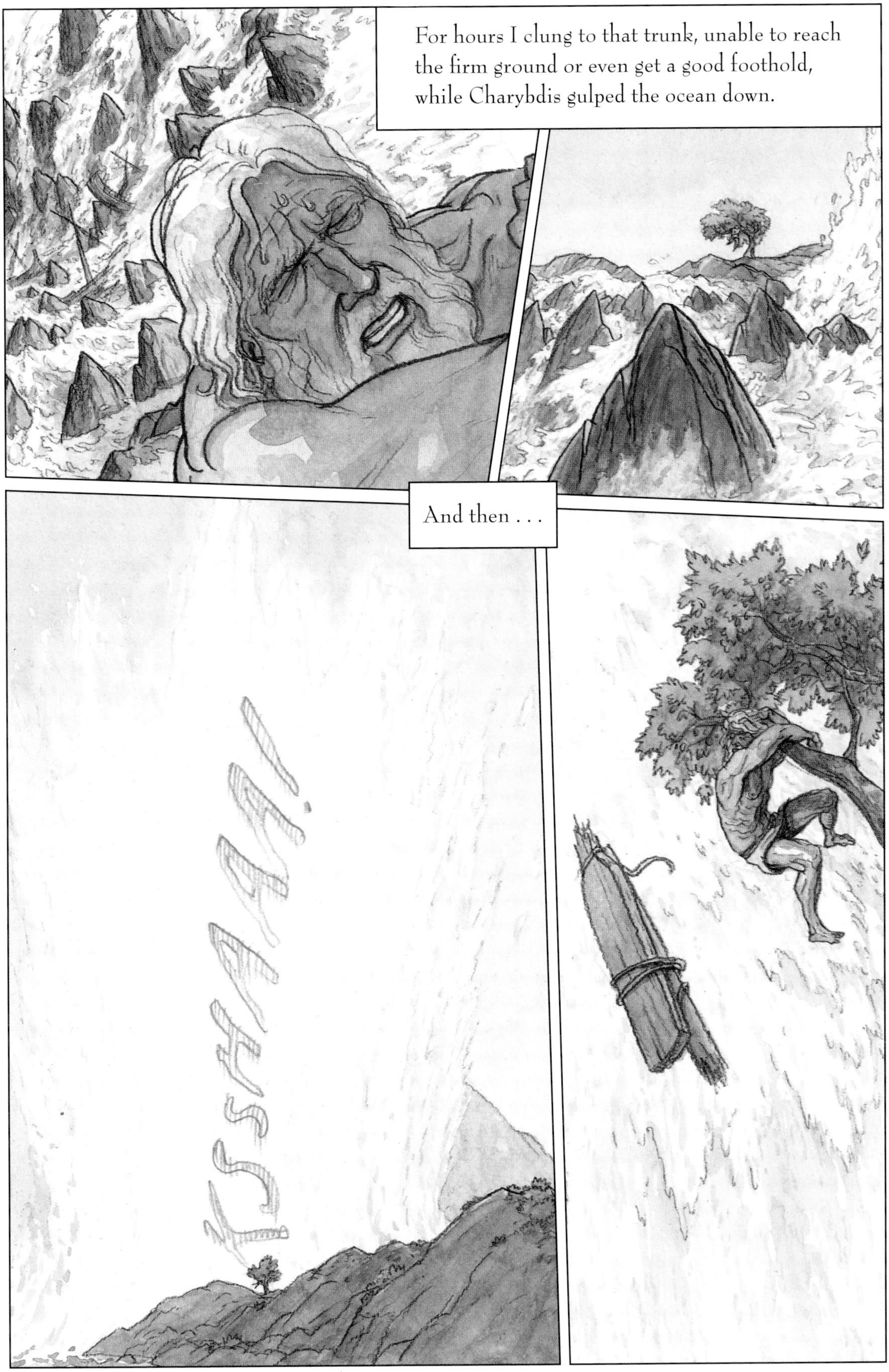
For hours I clung to that trunk, unable to reach the firm ground or even get a good foothold, while Charybdis gulped the ocean down.
And then . . .

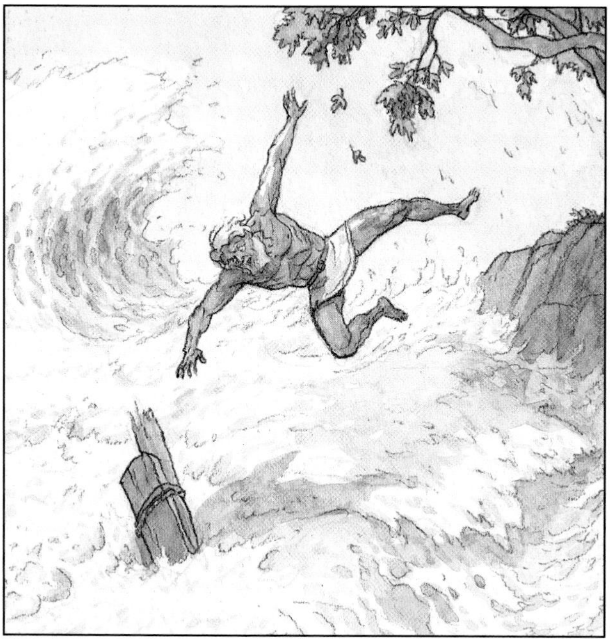

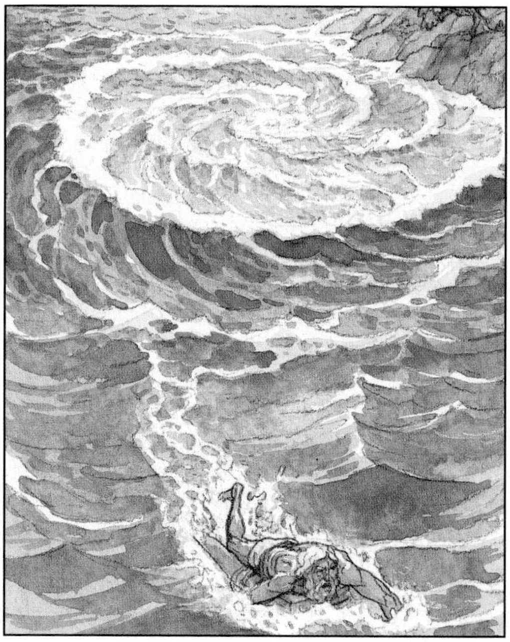

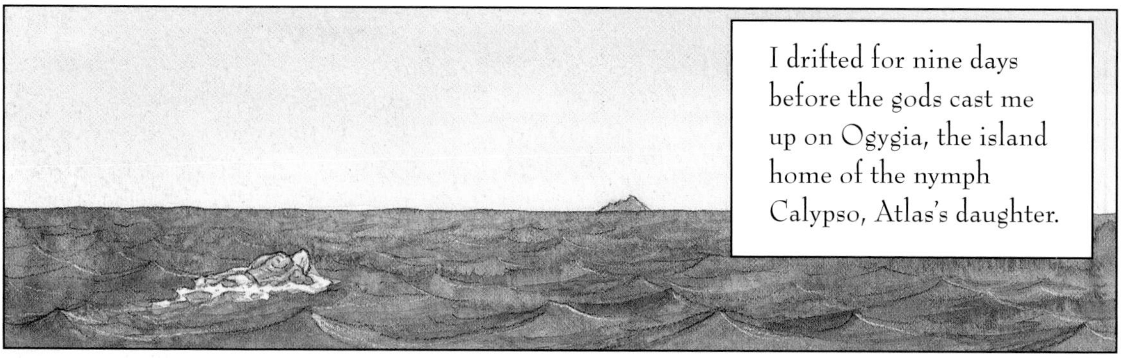
I drifted for nine days before the gods cast me up on Ogygia, the island home of the nymph Calypso, Atlas's daughter.

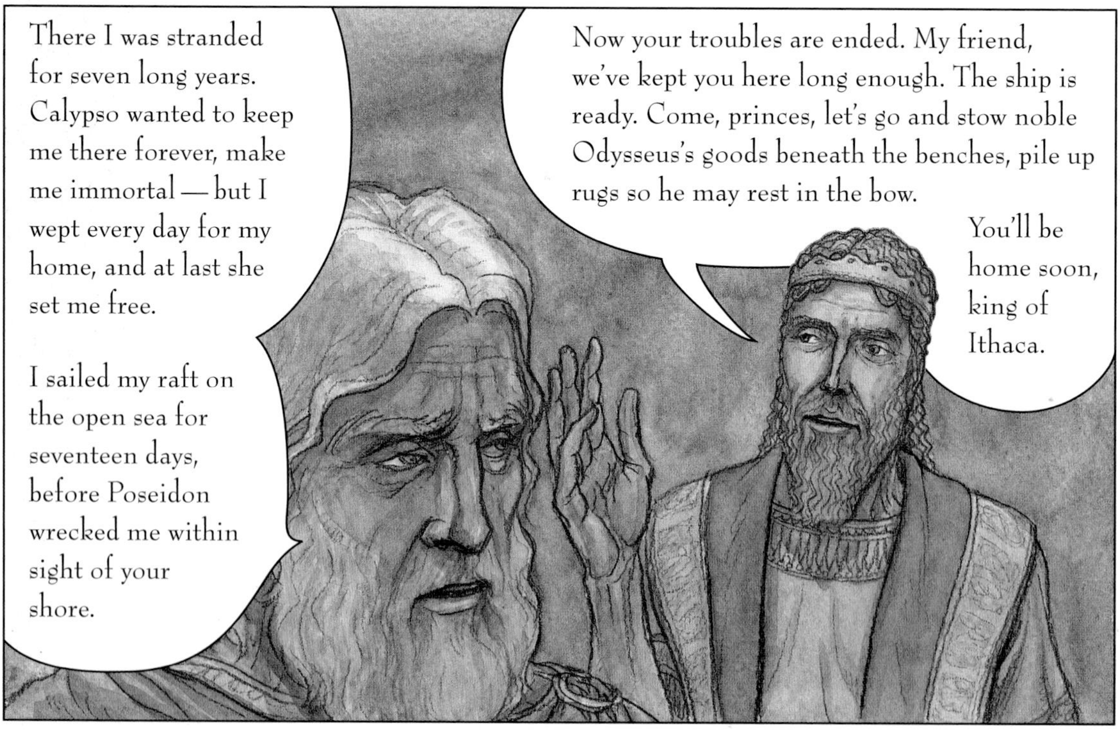
There I was stranded for seven long years. Calypso wanted to keep me there forever, make me immortal — but I wept every day for my home, and at last she set me free.
I sailed my raft on the open sea for seventeen days, before Poseidon wrecked me within sight of your shore.
Now your troubles are ended. My friend, we've kept you here long enough. The ship is ready. Come, princes, let's go and stow noble Odysseus's goods beneath the benches, pile up rugs so he may rest in the bow.
You'll be home soon, king of Ithaca.

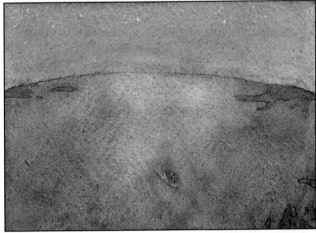

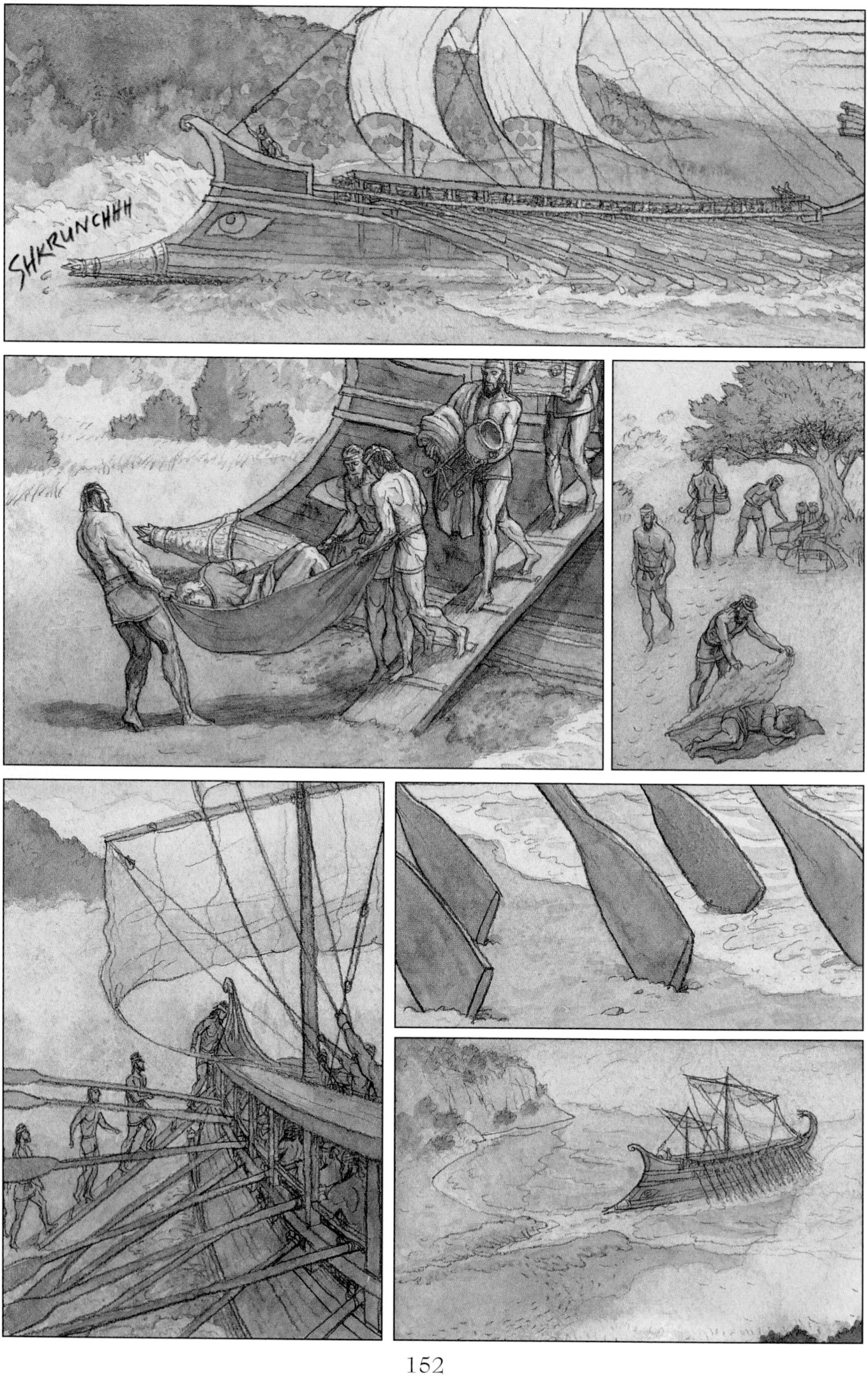
SHKRUNCHHH

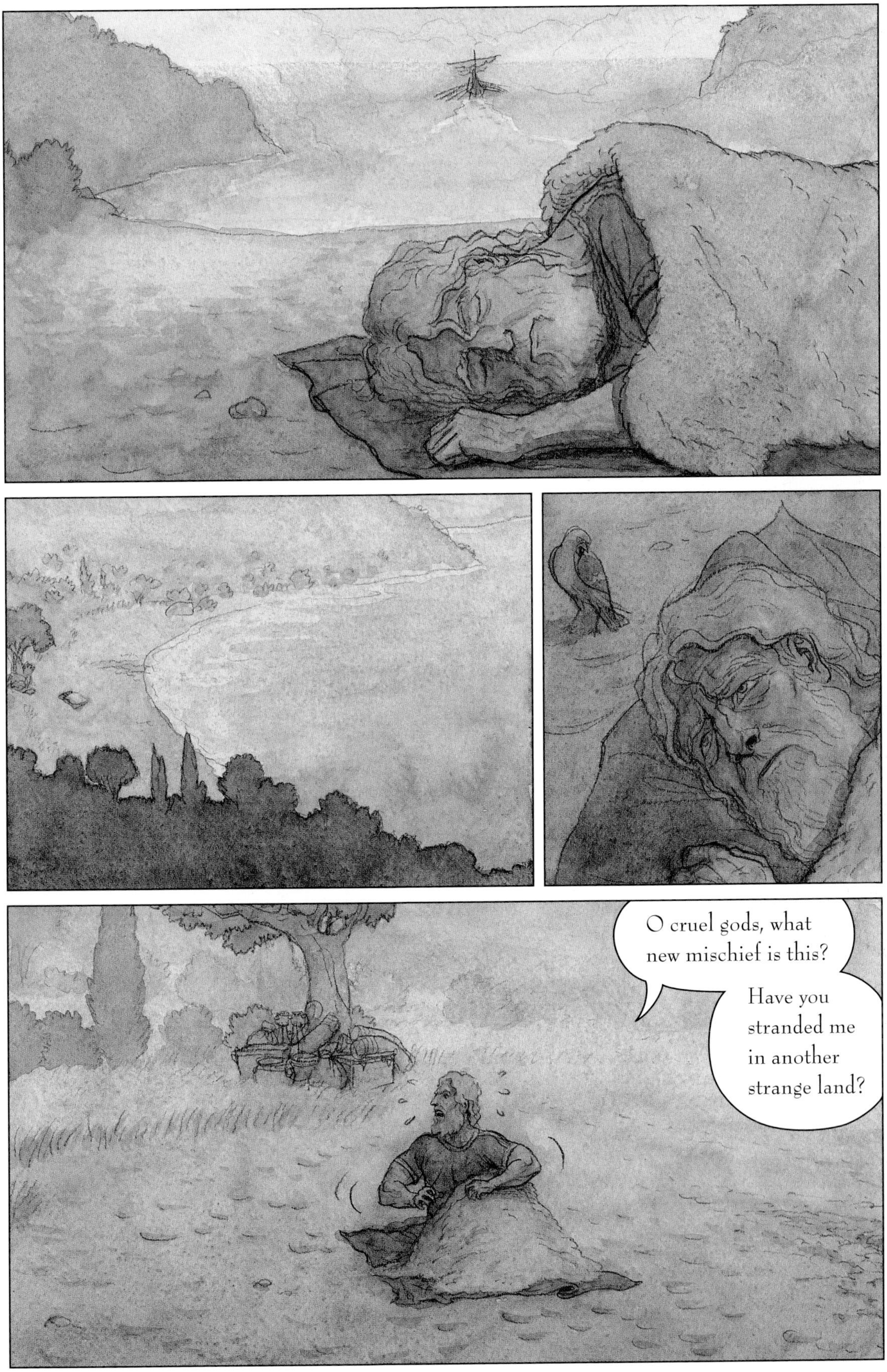
O cruel gods, what new mischief is this?
Have you stranded me in another strange land?

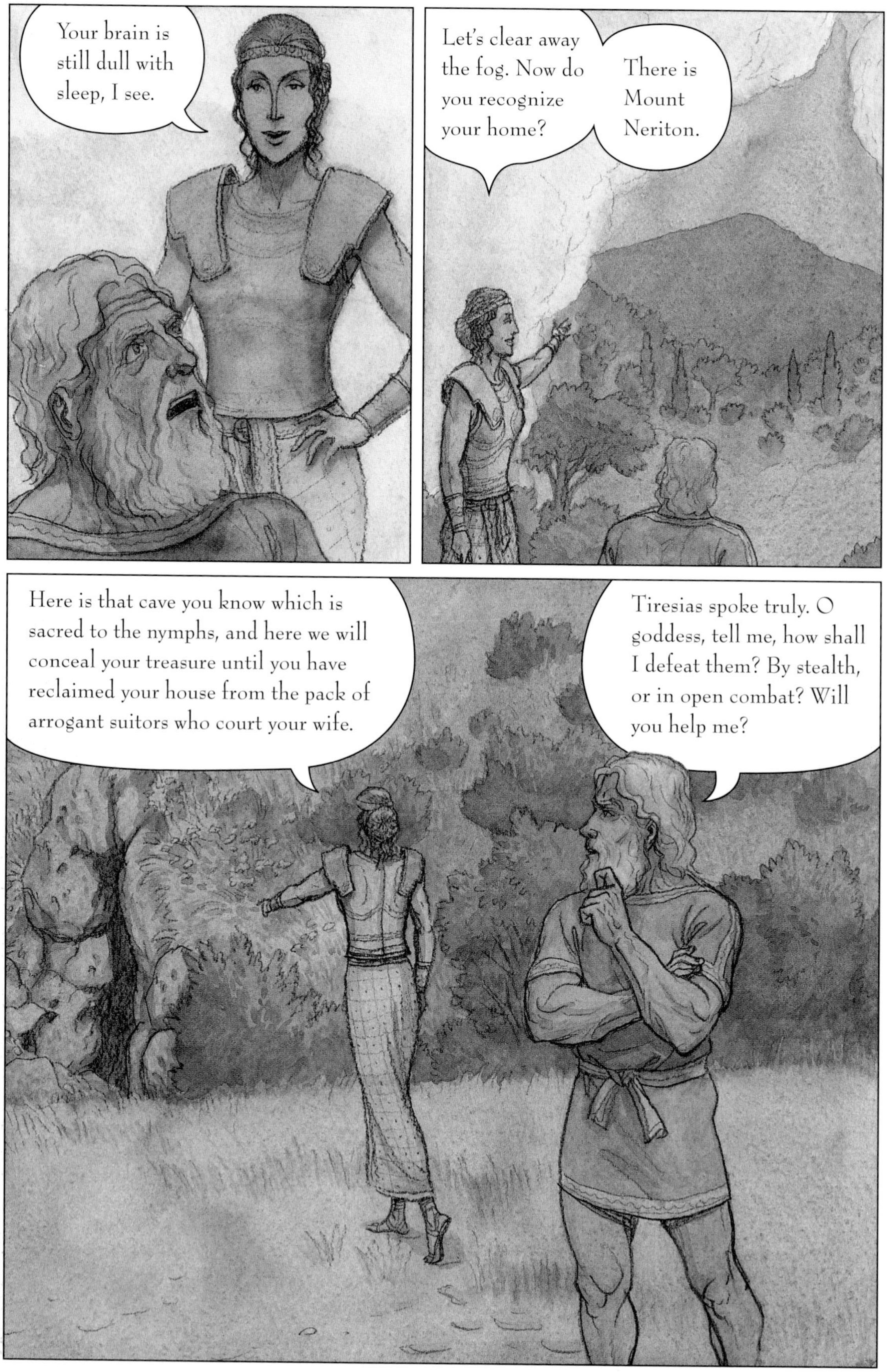
Your brain is still dull with sleep, I see.
Let's clear away the fog. Now do you recognize your home?
There is Mount Neriton.
Here is that cave you know which is sacred to the nymphs, and here we will conceal your treasure until you have reclaimed your house from the pack of arrogant suitors who court your wife.
Tiresias spoke truly. O goddess, tell me, how shall I defeat them? By stealth, or in open combat? Will you help me?

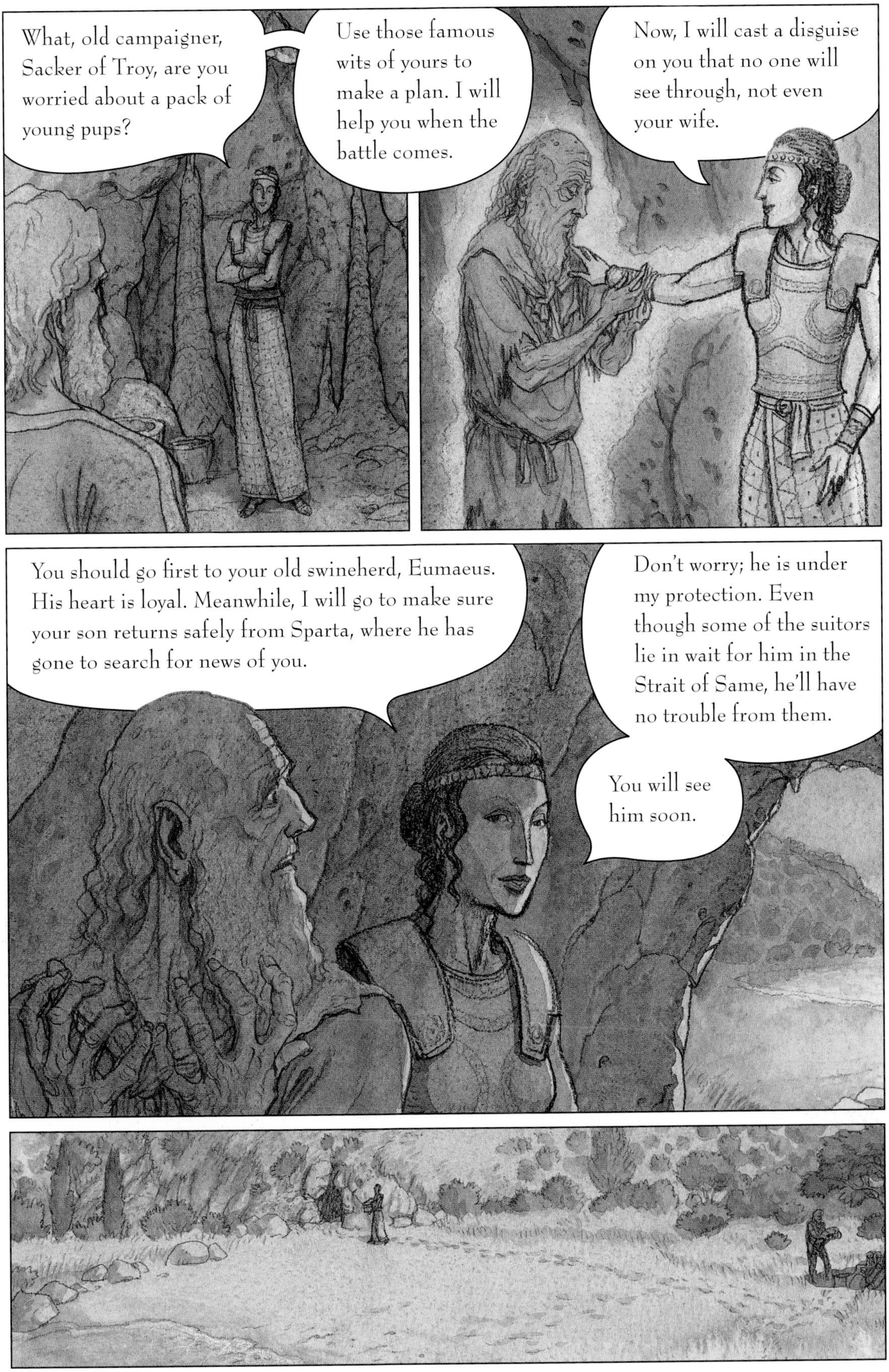
What, old campaigner, Sacker of Troy, are you worried about a pack of young pups?
Use those famous wits of yours to make a plan. I will help you when the battle comes.
Now, I will cast a disguise on you that no one will see through, not even your wife.
You should go first to your old swineherd, Eumaeus. His heart is loyal. Meanwhile, I will go to make sure your son returns safely from Sparta, where he has gone to search for news of you.
Don't worry; he is under my protection. Even though some of the suitors lie in wait for him in the Strait of Same, he'll have no trouble from them.
You will see him soon.

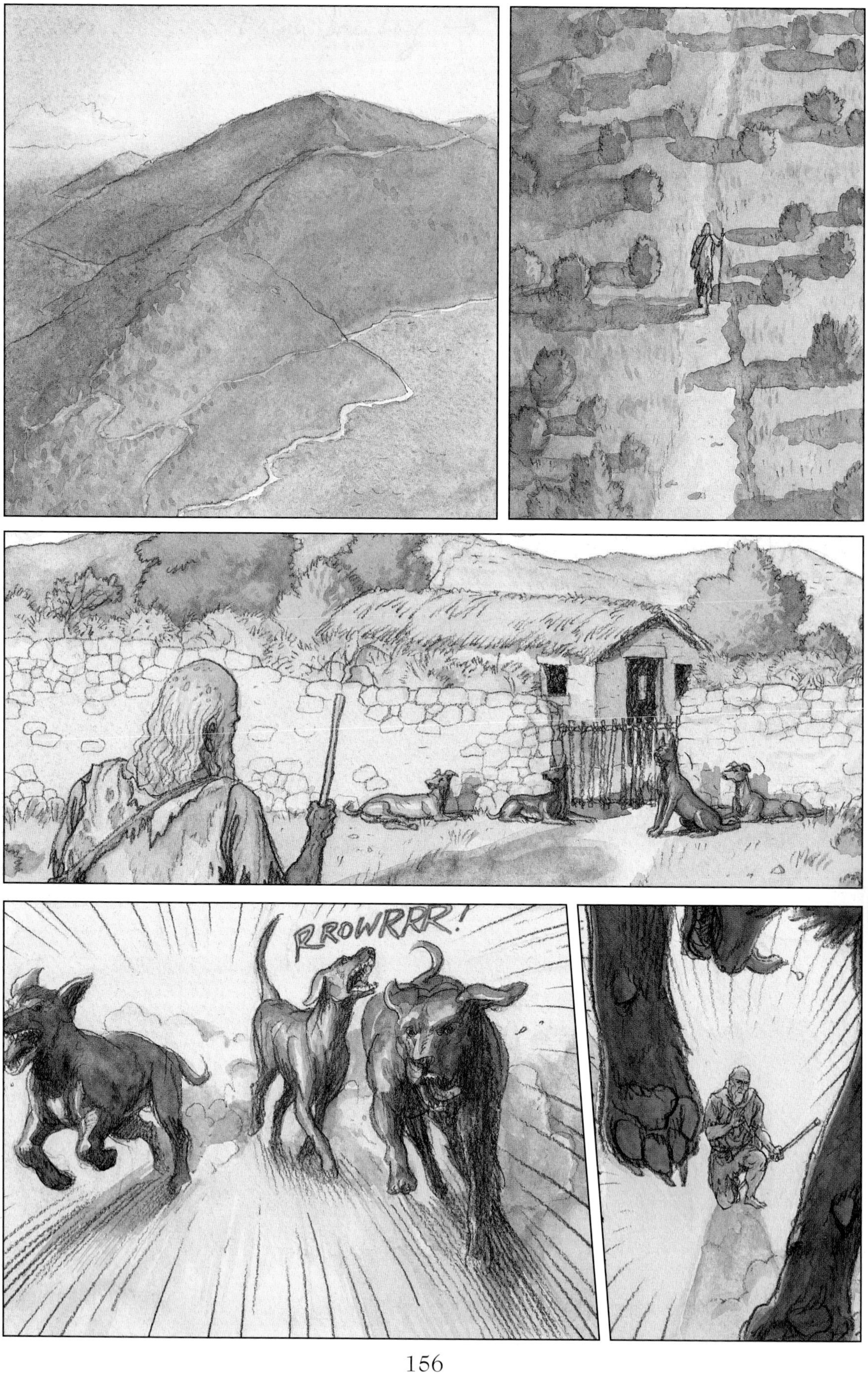
RROWRRR!

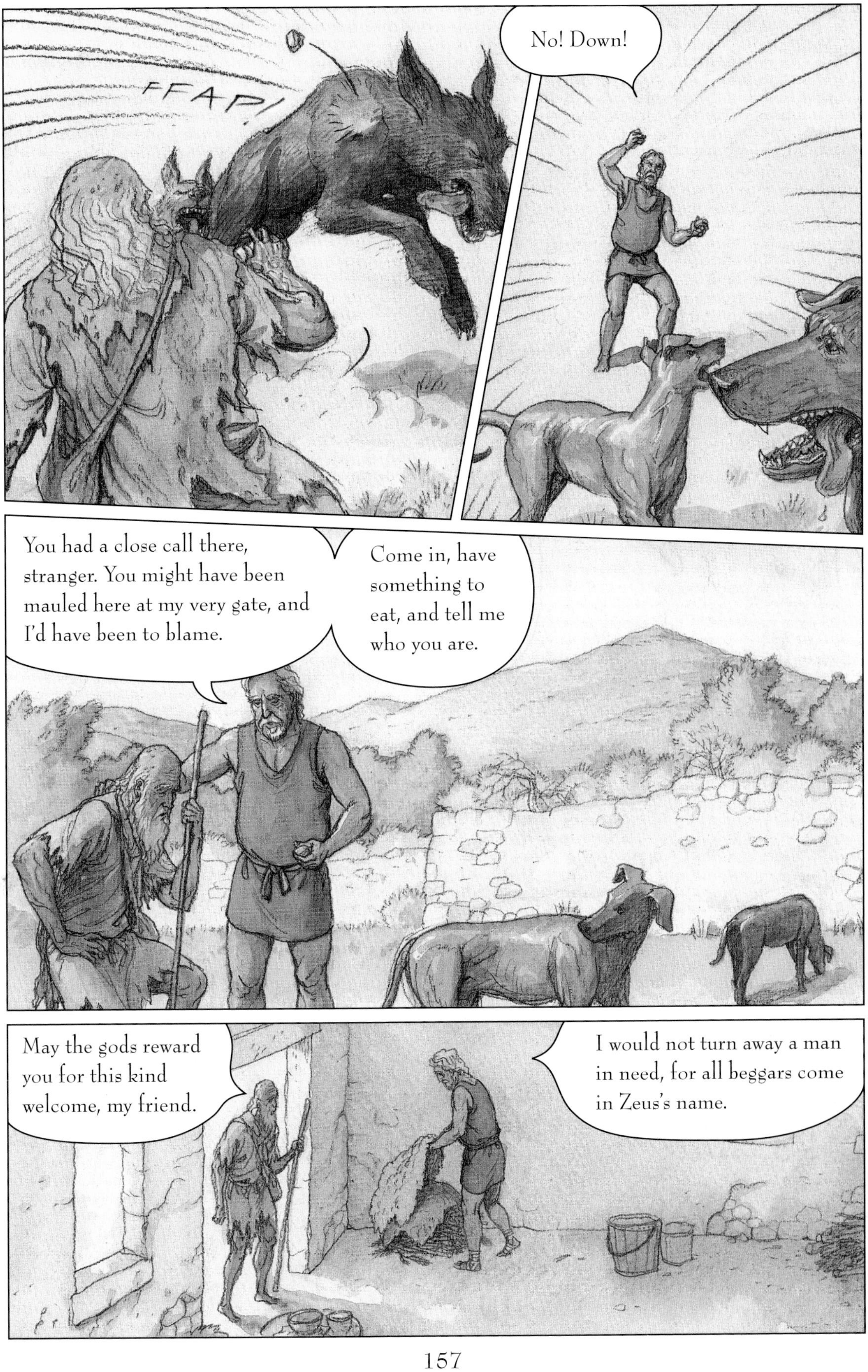
FFAP!
No! Down!
You had a close call there, stranger. You might have been mauled here at my very gate, and I'd have been to blame.
Come in, have something to eat, and tell me who you are.
May the gods reward you for this kind welcome, my friend.
I would not turn away a man in need, for all beggars come in Zeus's name.

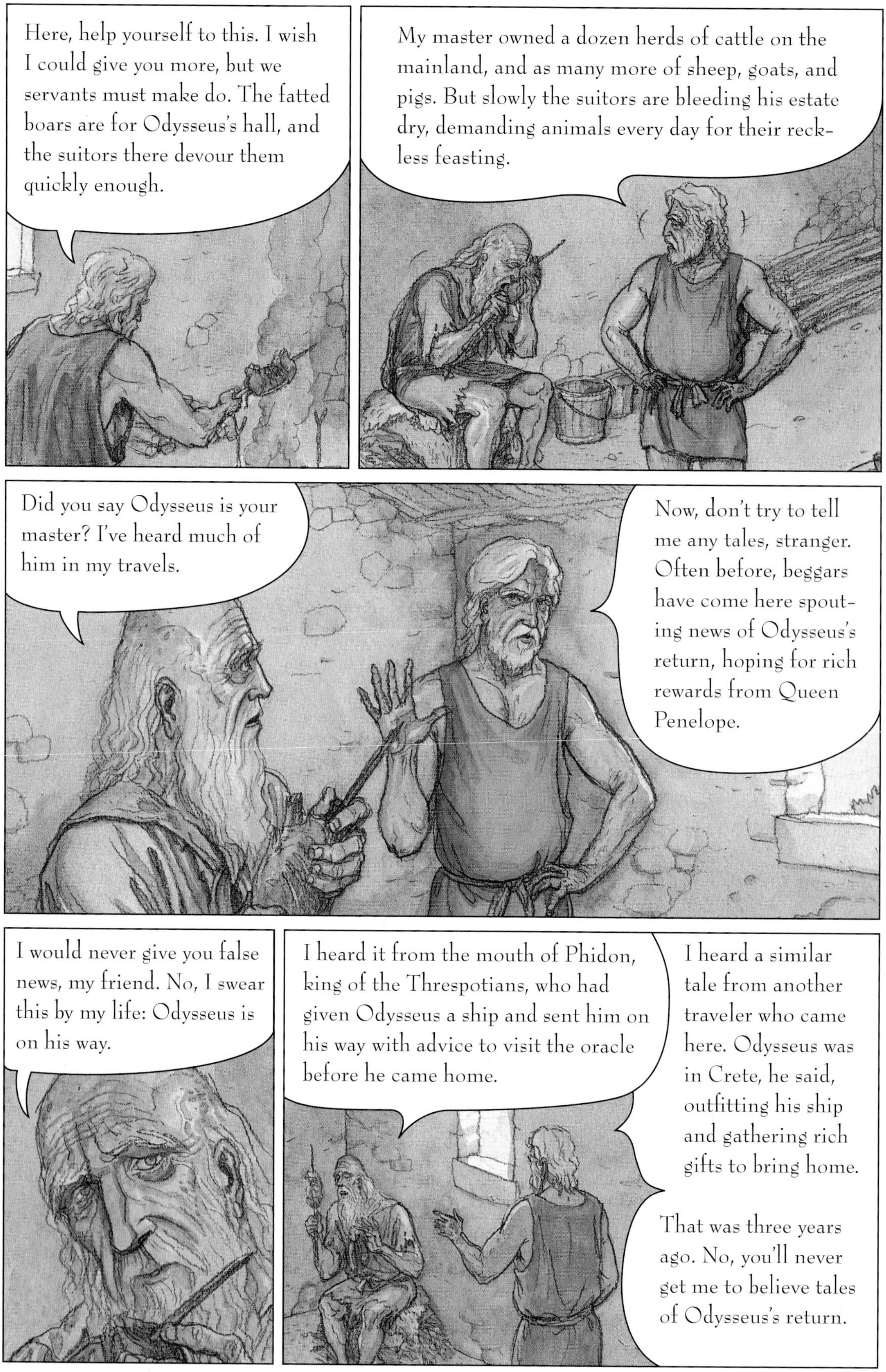
Here, help yourself to this. I wish I could give you more, but we servants must make do. The fatted boars are for Odysseus's hall, and the suitors there devour them quickly enough.
My master owned a dozen herds of cattle on the mainland, and as many more of sheep, goats, and pigs. But slowly the suitors are bleeding his estate dry, demanding animals every day for their reckless feasting.
Did you say Odysseus is your master? I've heard much of him in my travels.
Now, don't try to tell me any tales, stranger. Often before, beggars have come here spouting news of Odysseus's return, hoping for rich rewards from Queen Penelope.
I would never give you false news, my friend. No, I swear this by my life: Odysseus is on his way.
I heard it from the mouth of Phidon, king of the Threspotians, who had given Odysseus a ship and sent him on his way with advice to visit the oracle before he came home.
I heard a similar tale from another traveler who came here. Odysseus was in Crete, he said, outfitting his ship and gathering rich gifts to bring home.
That was three years ago. No, you'll never get me to believe tales of Odysseus's return.

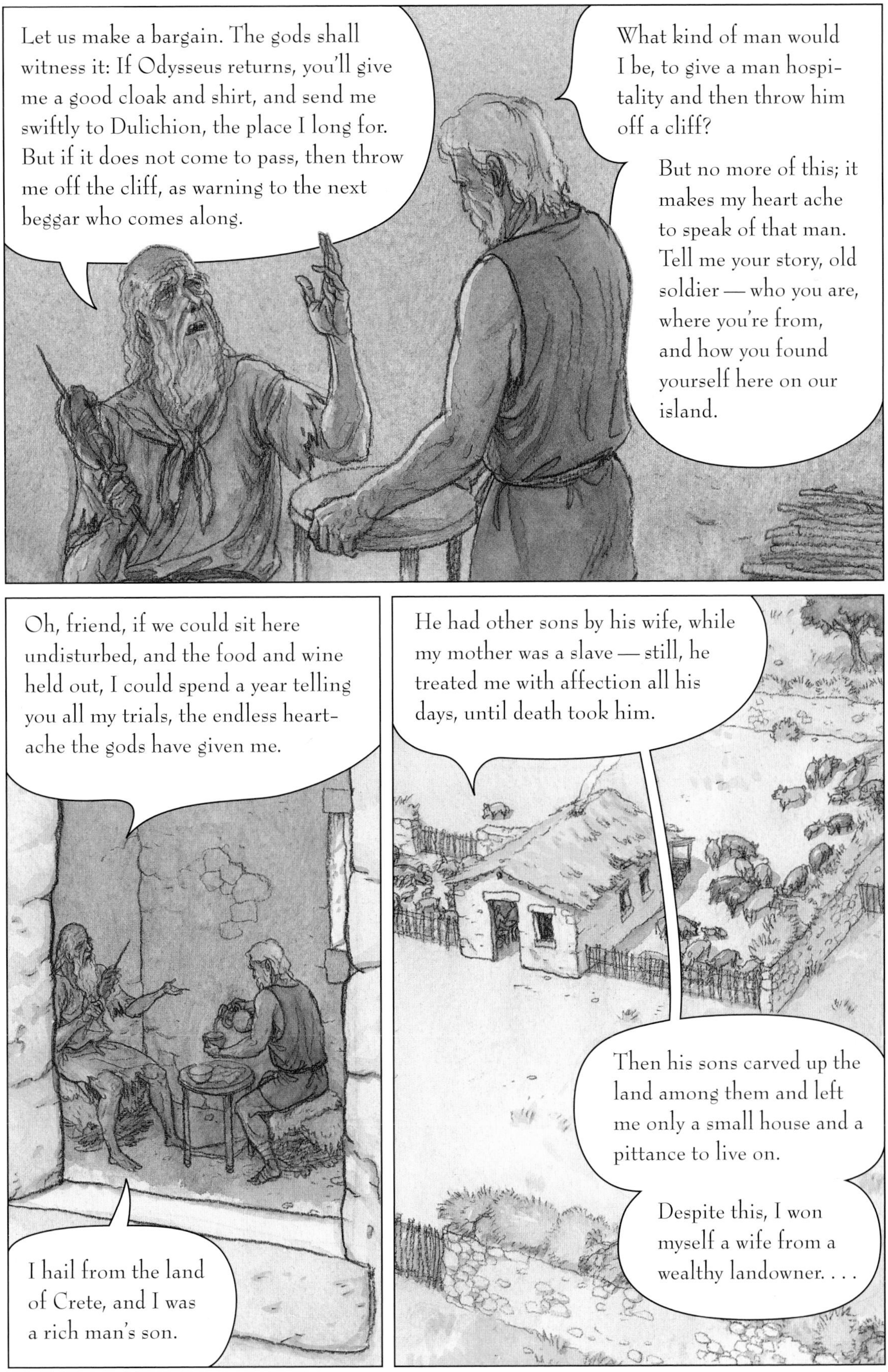
Let us make a bargain. The gods shall witness it: If Odysseus returns, you'll give me a good cloak and shirt, and send me swiftly to Dulichion, the place I long for. But if it does not come to pass, then throw me off the cliff, as warning to the next beggar who comes along.
What kind of man would I be, to give a man hospitality and then throw him off a cliff?
But no more of this; it makes my heart ache to speak of that man. Tell me your story, old soldier — who you are, where you're from, and how you found yourself here on our island.
Oh, friend, if we could sit here undisturbed, and the food and wine held out, I could spend a year telling you all my trials, the endless heartache the gods have given me.
I hail from the land of Crete, and I was a rich man's son.
He had other sons by his wife, while my mother was a slave — still, he treated me with affection all his days, until death took him.
Then his sons carved up the land among them and left me only a small house and a pittance to live on.
Despite this, I won myself a wife from a wealthy landowner. . . .

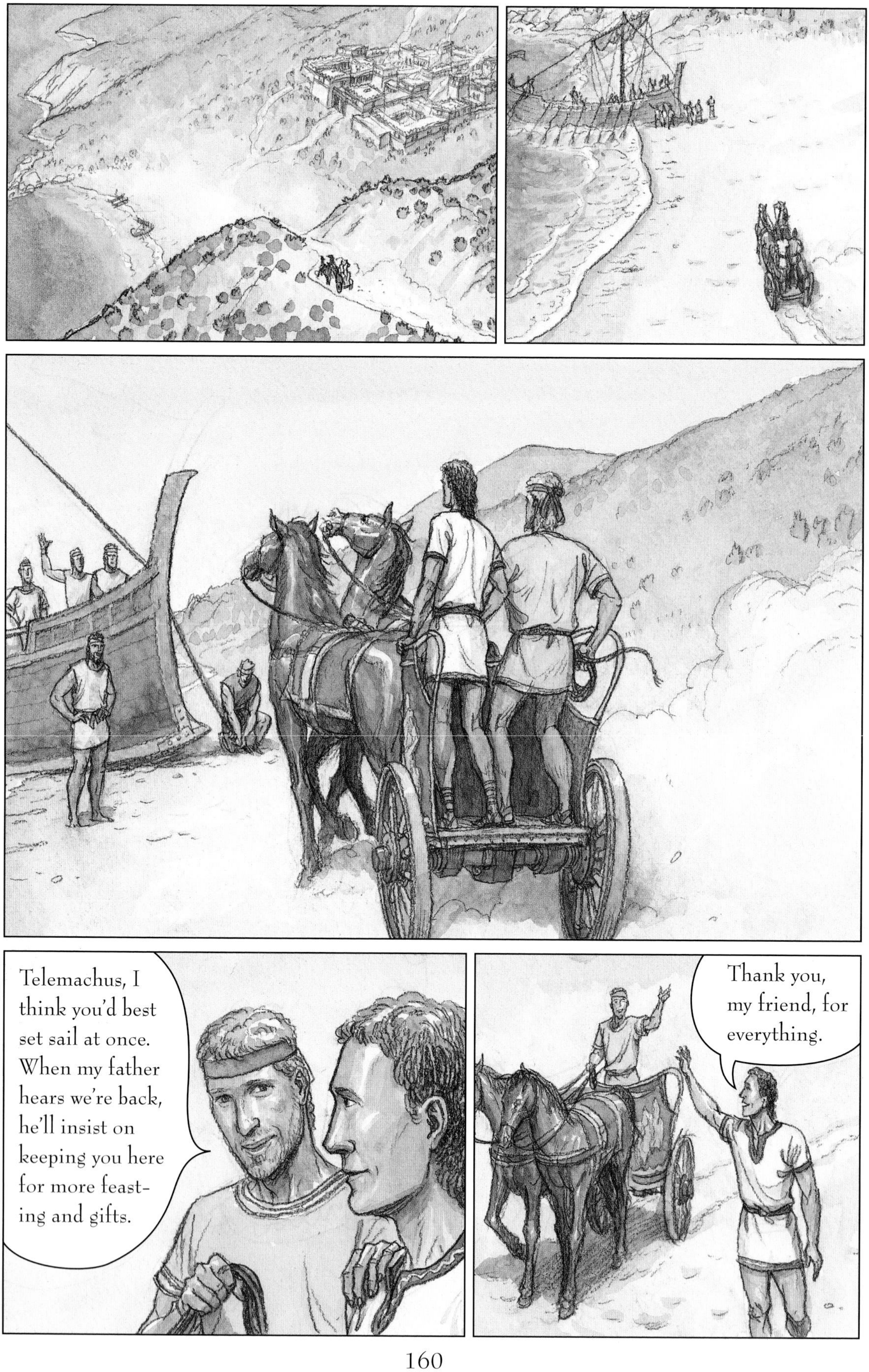
Telemachus, I think you'd best set sail at once. When my father hears we're back, he'll insist on keeping you here for more feasting and gifts.
Thank you, my friend, for everything.

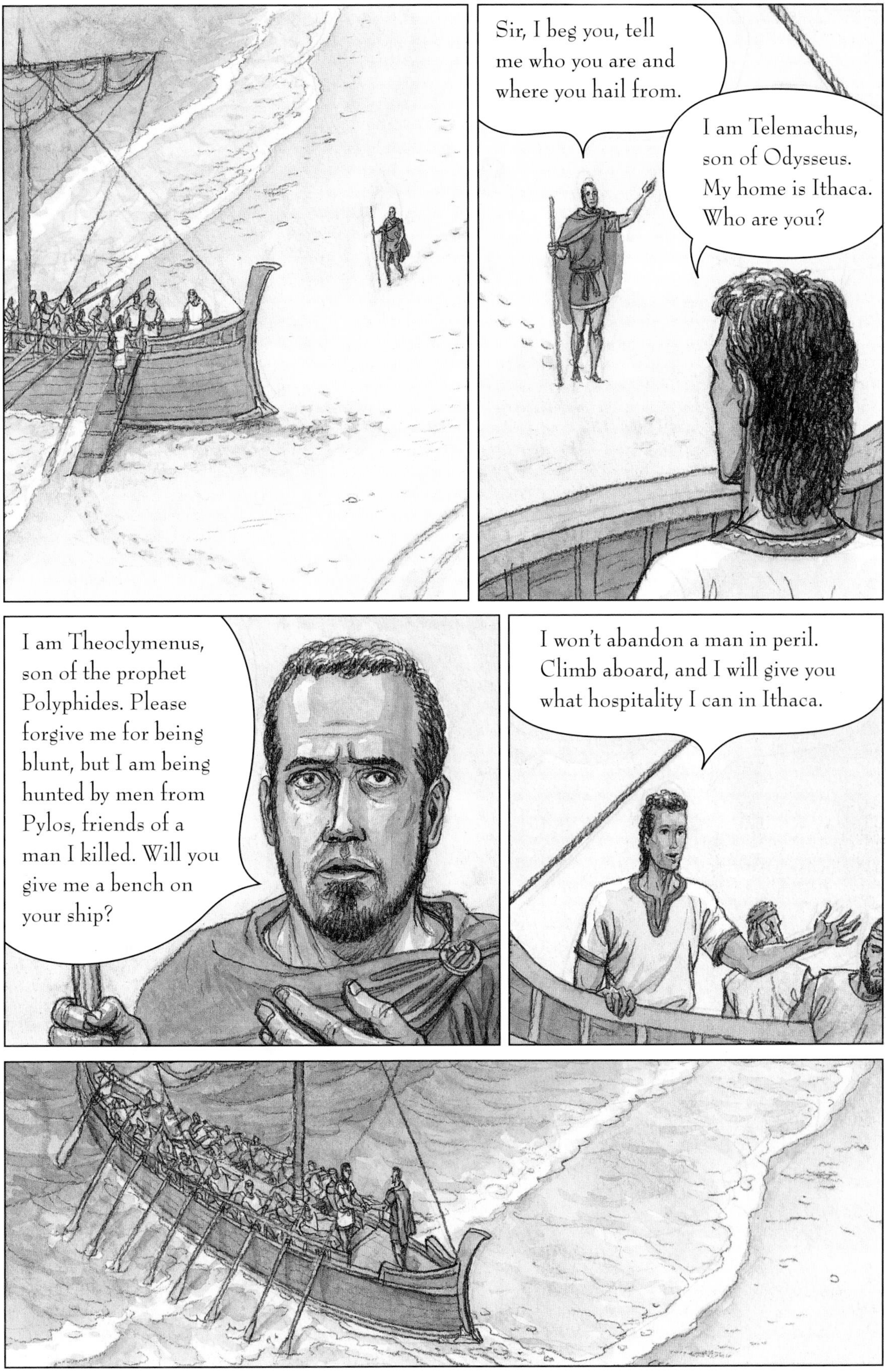
Sir, I beg you, tell me who you are and where you hail from.
I am Telemachus, son of Odysseus. My home is Ithaca. Who are you?
I am Theoclymenus, son of the prophet Polyphides. Please forgive me for being blunt, but I am being hunted by men from Pylos, friends of a man I killed. Will you give me a bench on your ship?
I won't abandon a man in peril. Climb aboard, and I will give you what hospitality I can in Ithaca.

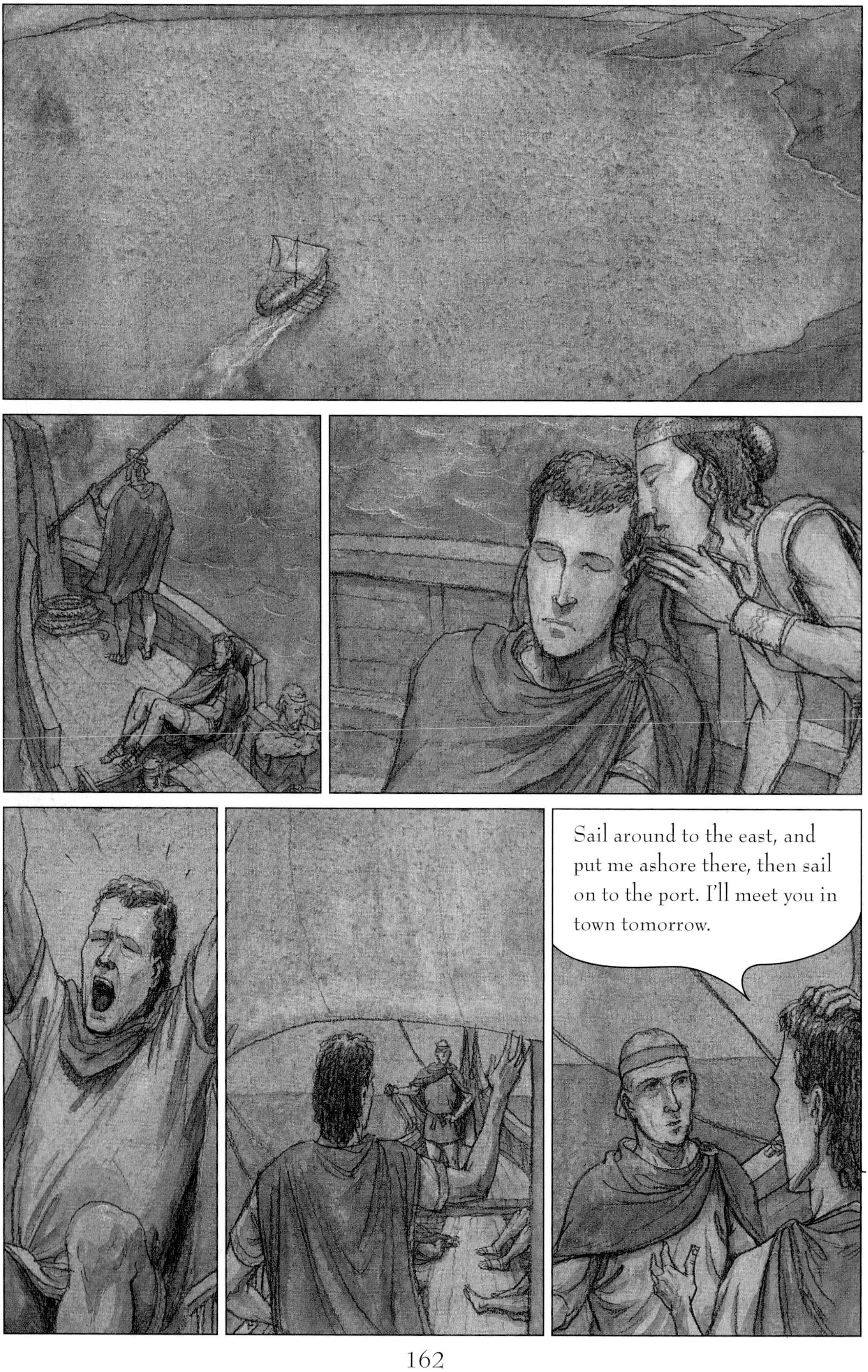
Sail around to the east, and put me ashore there, then sail on to the port. I'll meet you in town tomorrow.

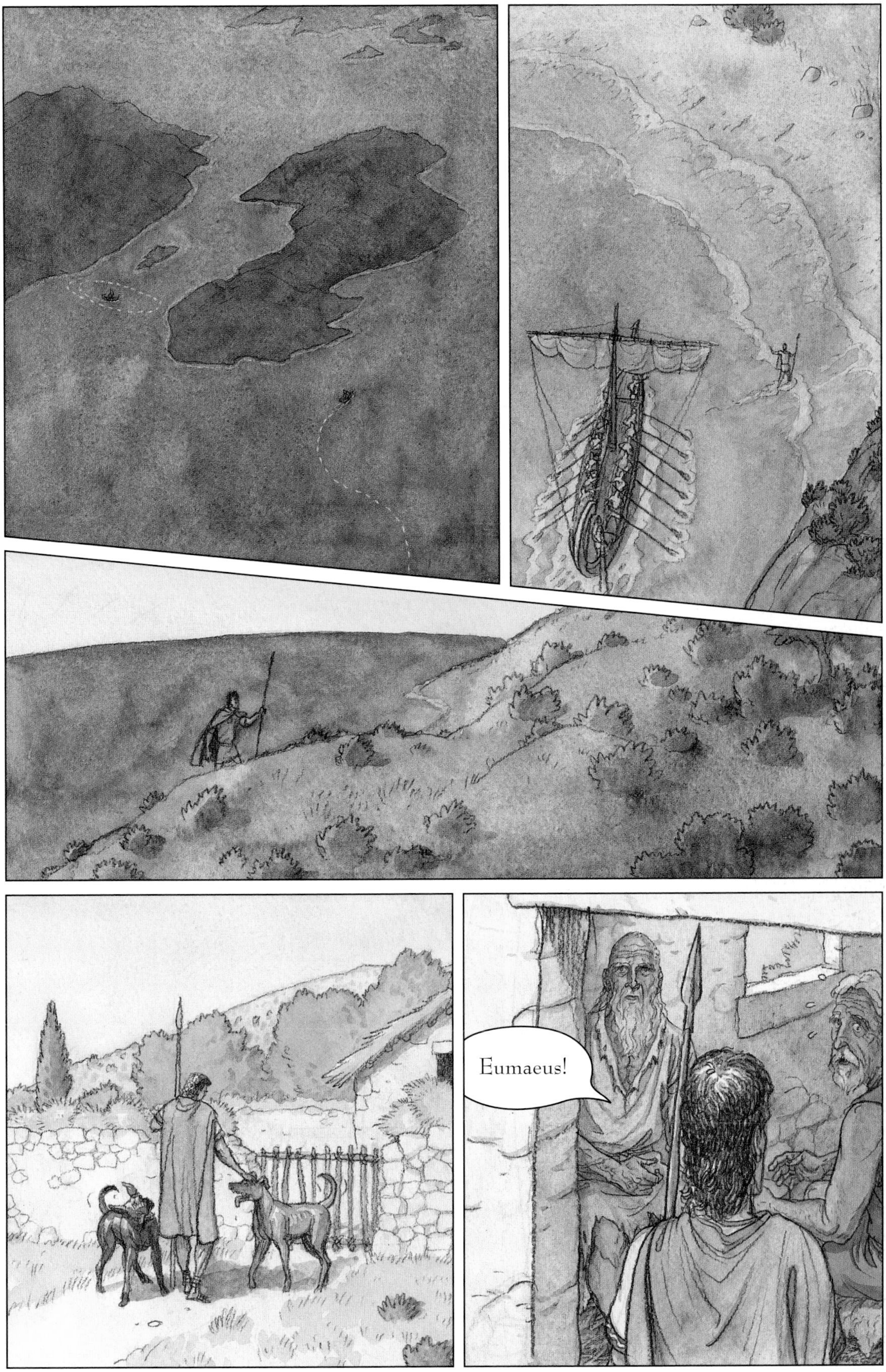
Eumaeus!

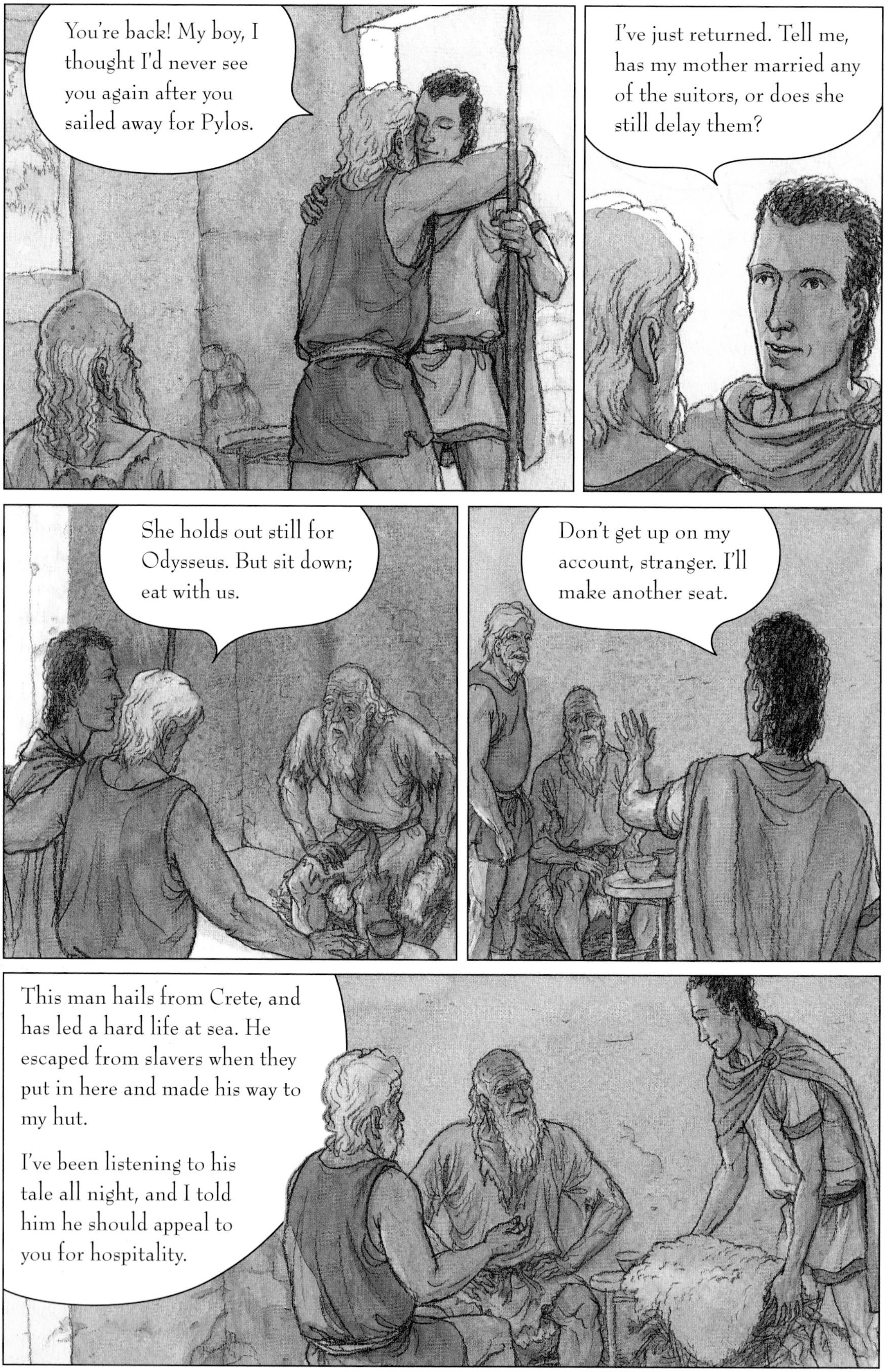
You're back! My boy, I thought I'd never see you again after you sailed away for Pylos.
I've just returned. Tell me, has my mother married any of the suitors, or does she still delay them?
She holds out still for Odysseus. But sit down; eat with us.
Don't get up on my account, stranger. I'll make another seat.
This man hails from Crete, and has led a hard life at sea. He escaped from slavers when they put in here and made his way to my hut.
I've been listening to his tale all night, and I told him he should appeal to you for hospitality.

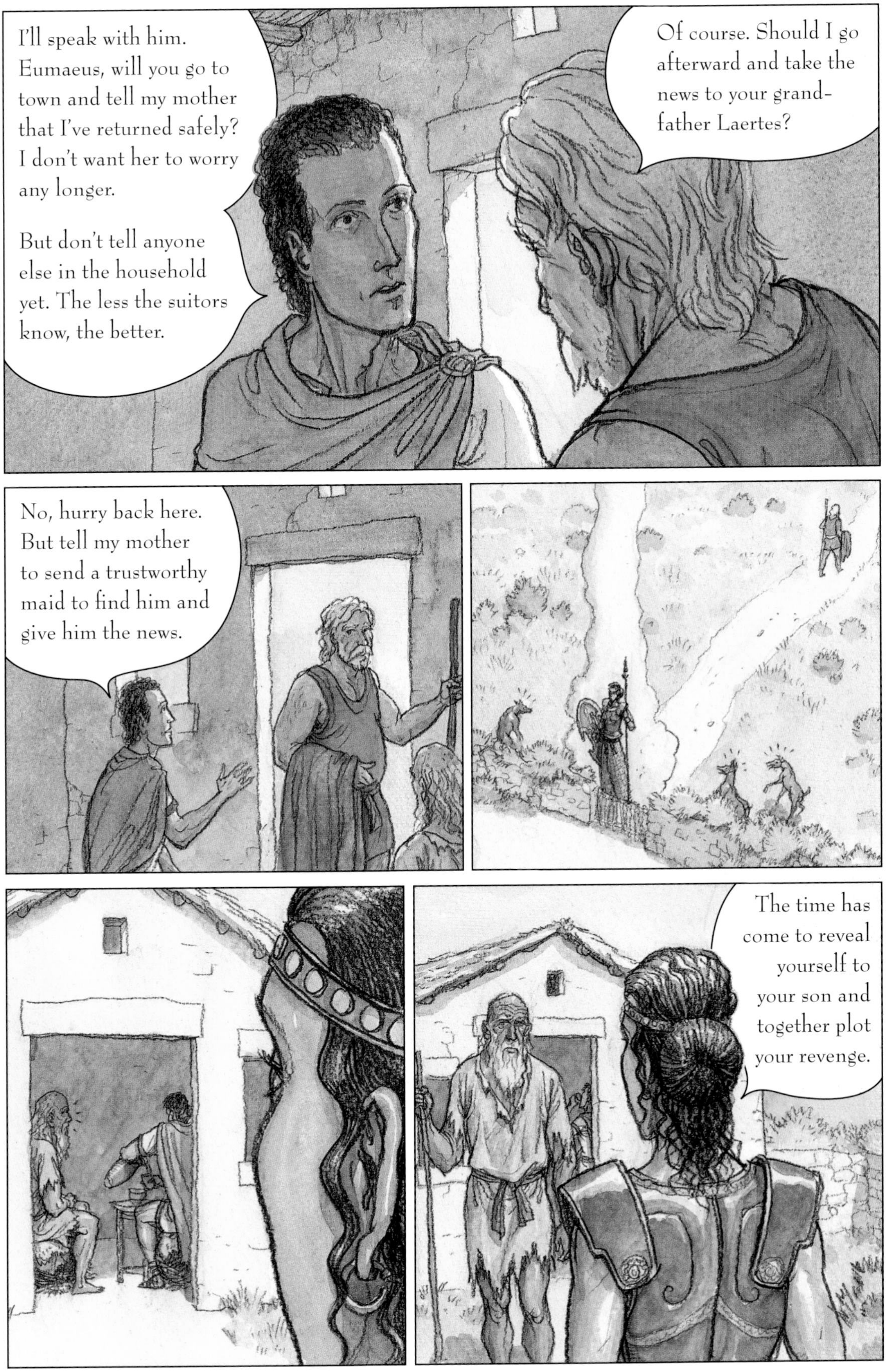
I'll speak with him. Eumaeus, will you go to town and tell my mother that I've returned safely? I don't want her to worry any longer.
But don't tell anyone else in the household yet. The less the suitors know, the better.
Of course. Should I go afterward and take the news to your grand-father Laertes?
No, hurry back here. But tell my mother to send a trustworthy maid to find him and give him the news.
The time has come to reveal yourself to your son and together plot your revenge.

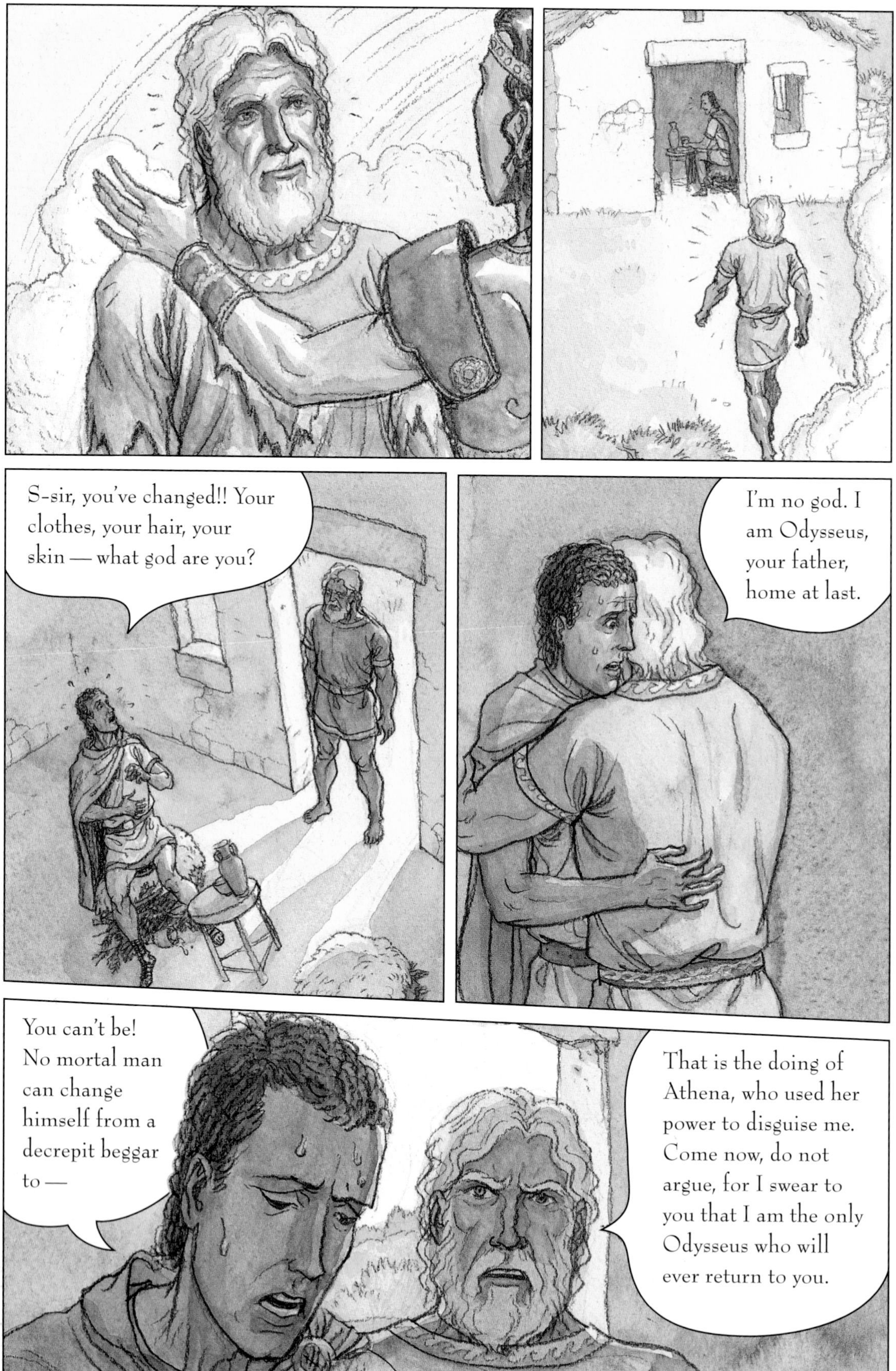
S-sir, you've changed!! Your clothes, your hair, your skin — what god are you?
I'm no god. I am Odysseus, your father, home at last.
You can't be! No mortal man can change himself from a decrepit beggar to —
That is the doing of Athena, who used her power to disguise me. Come now, do not argue, for I swear to you that I am the only Odysseus who will ever return to you.

. . . . .

Father?!

My son . . . my son.

Father, how—

No questions yet. I must make a plan to slay the vermin who infest my palace. Tell me, how many are there?

Too many, Father. Oh, I have wished this for so long, but it is madness to talk of killing them all—just the two of us against over a hundred!

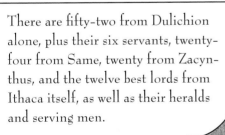

There are fifty-two from Dulichion alone, plus their six servants, twenty-four from Same, twenty from Zacynthus, and the twelve best lords from Ithaca itself, as well as their heralds and serving men.

If we pit ourselves against all these, I fear our revenge will come back on our own heads. We need allies, men-at-arms to help us.

Tell me, then: will Athena and Zeus do, to stand beside us?

! — but will they help us?

Yes. Trust me.

But now you should return to the palace and mingle with the suitors. The swineherd will bring me down presently to beg.

If the suitors abuse me, you must steel yourself and endure it. Try to win them over with friendly words, but don't raise a hand to defend me.

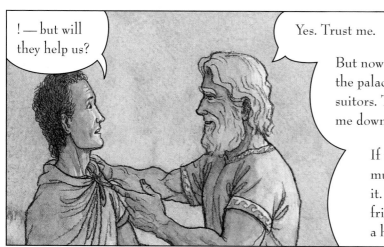

One more thing: When it is time, I will give you a nod. At that signal, gather up all the weapons from the hall and lock them in the storeroom. If anyone asks you why you took them away, say they were getting dark with soot from the fire.

Just stow two sets of gear close at hand for the two of us — swords, spears, and oxhide shields.

Let no one know I'm home, not even your mother. We must find out which of the servants and field hands are loyal and which side with the suitors.

I'm ready, Father. Let's not waste time now with the field hands — not until we have reclaimed your hall!

168

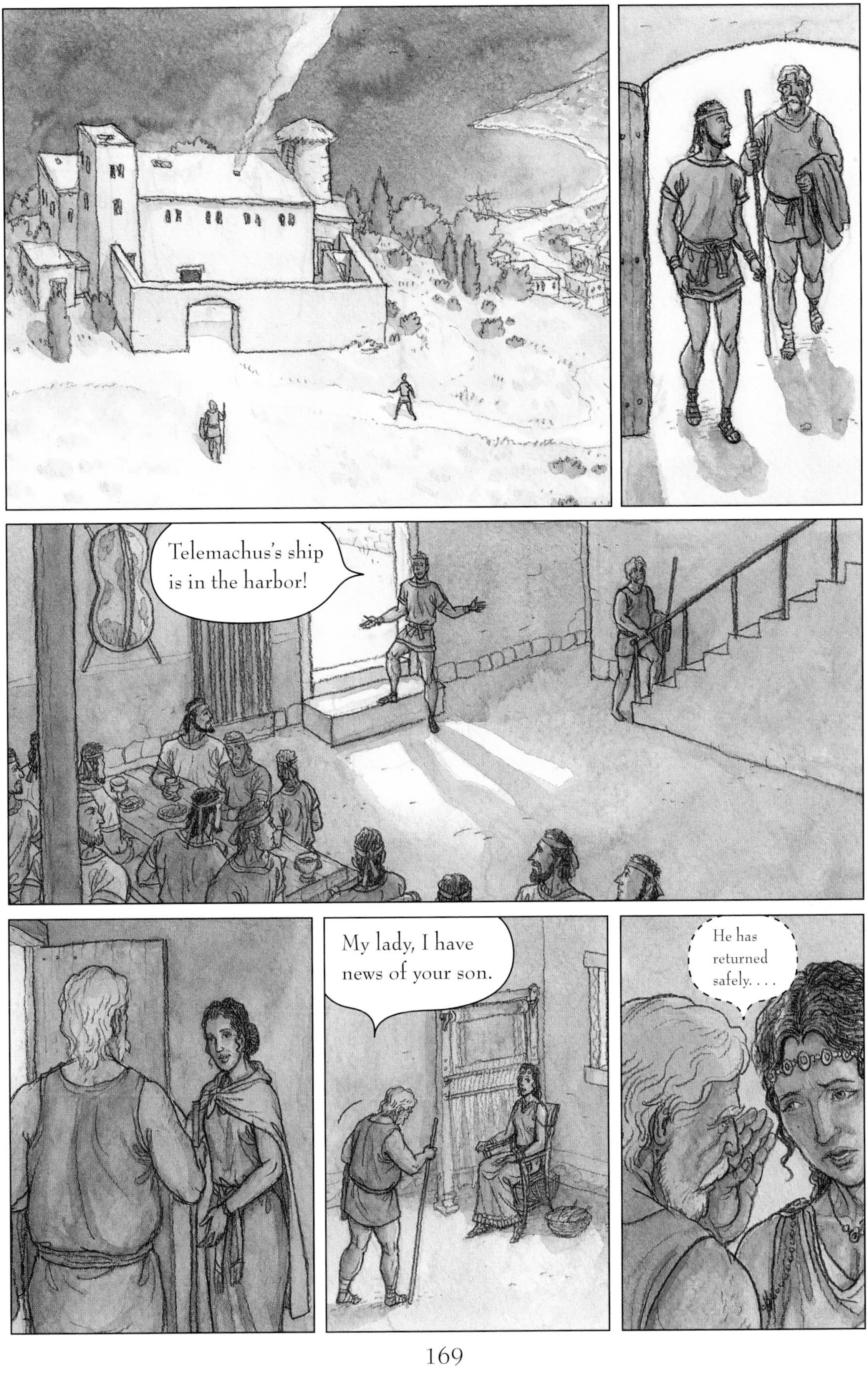
Telemachus's ship is in the harbor!
My lady, I have news of your son.
He has returned safely. . . .

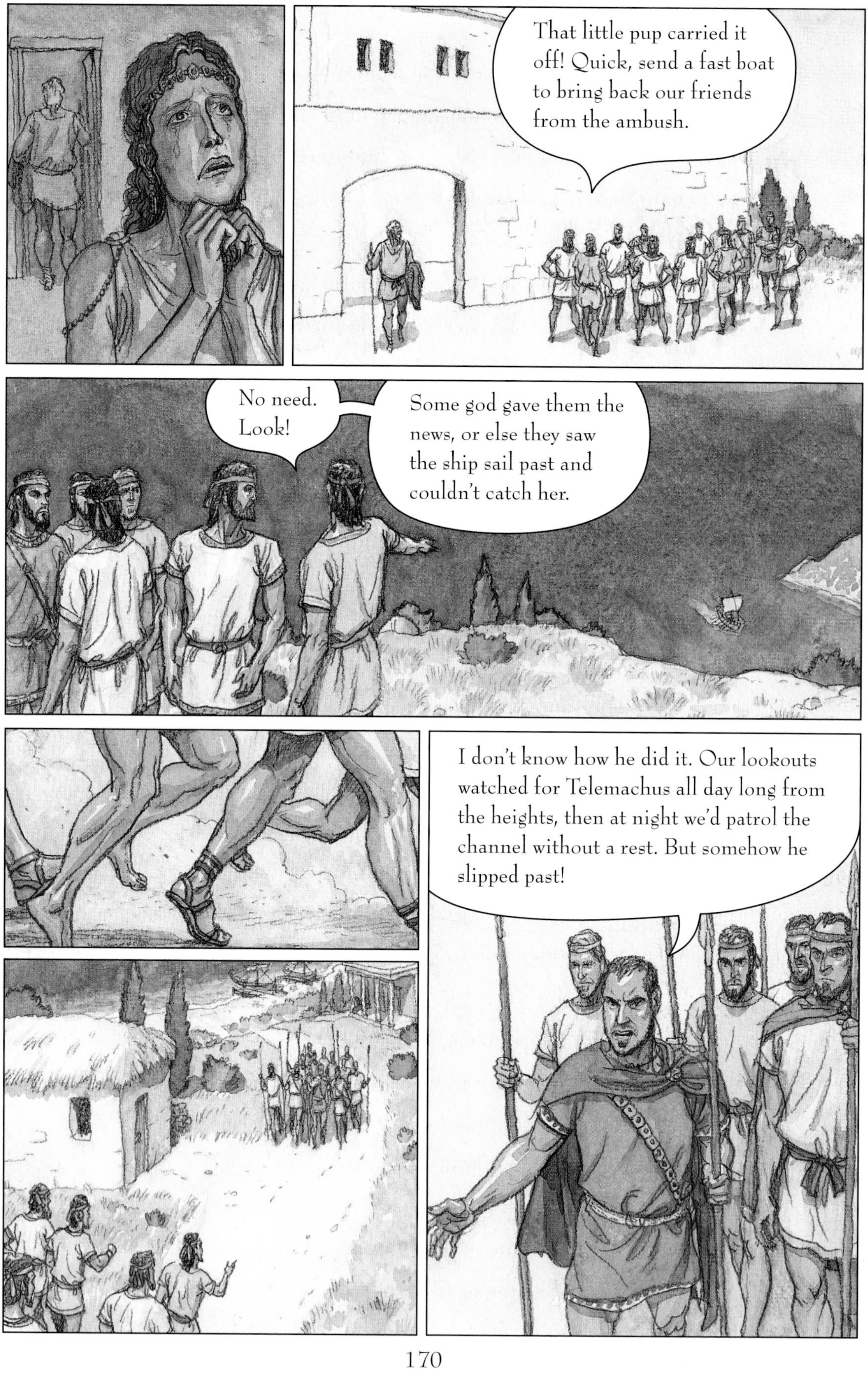
That little pup carried it off! Quick, send a fast boat to bring back our friends from the ambush.
No need. Look!
Some god gave them the news, or else they saw the ship sail past and couldn't catch her.
I don't know how he did it. Our lookouts watched for Telemachus all day long from the heights, then at night we'd patrol the channel without a rest. But somehow he slipped past!

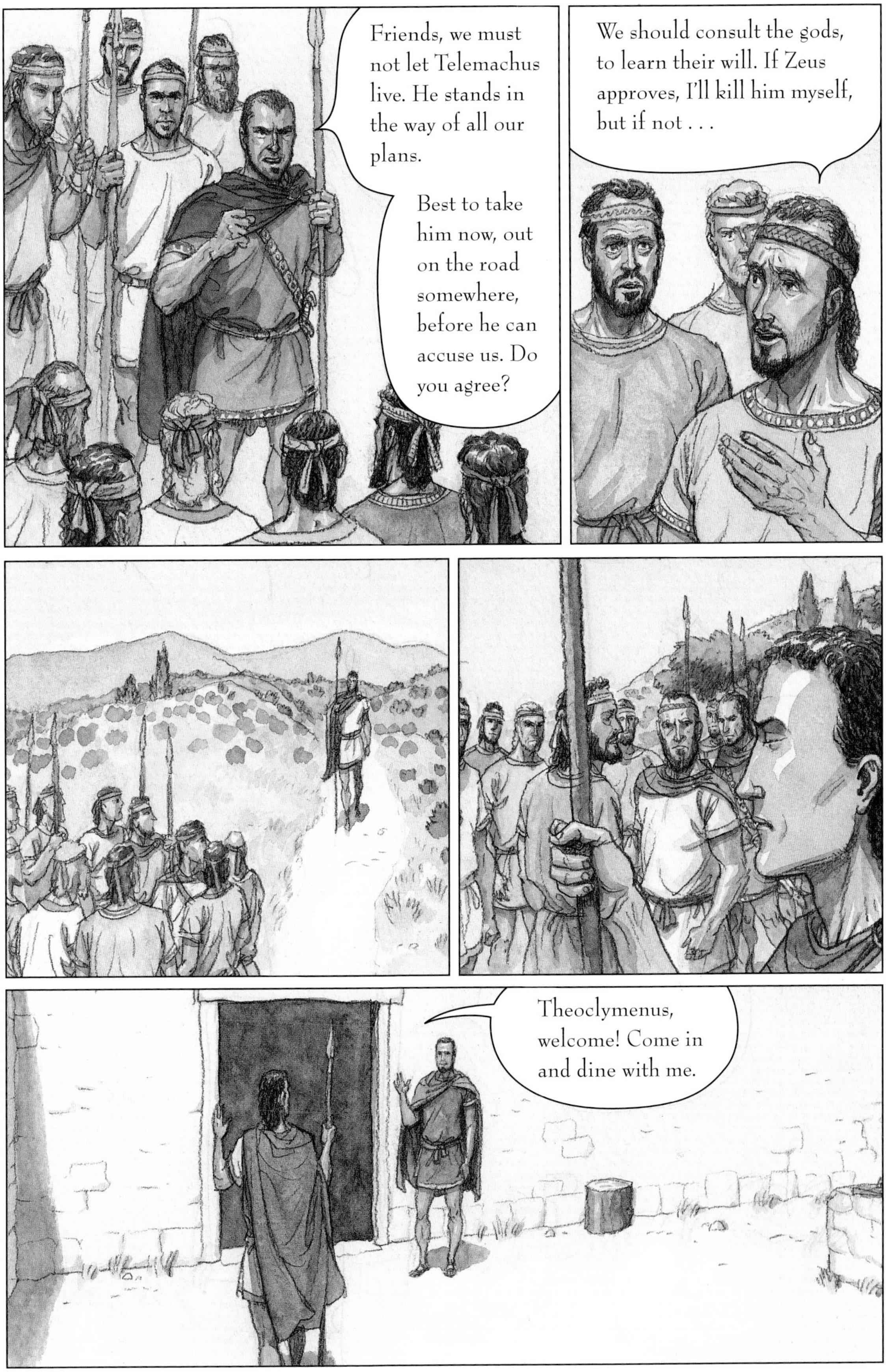
Friends, we must not let Telemachus live. He stands in the way of all our plans.
Best to take him now, out on the road somewhere, before he can accuse us. Do you agree?
We should consult the gods, to learn their will. If Zeus approves, I'll kill him myself, but if not . . .
Theoclymenus, welcome! Come in and dine with me.

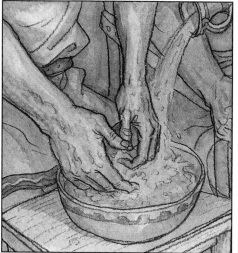

So, Telemachus. Were you going to tell me what you learned on your journey? Or would you rather leave me wondering?

Mother, I'll tell you everything about my travels soon — but as to my father, King Menelaus told me he heard from the Old Man of the Sea that Odysseus is stranded on an island, with no ship to bring him home.

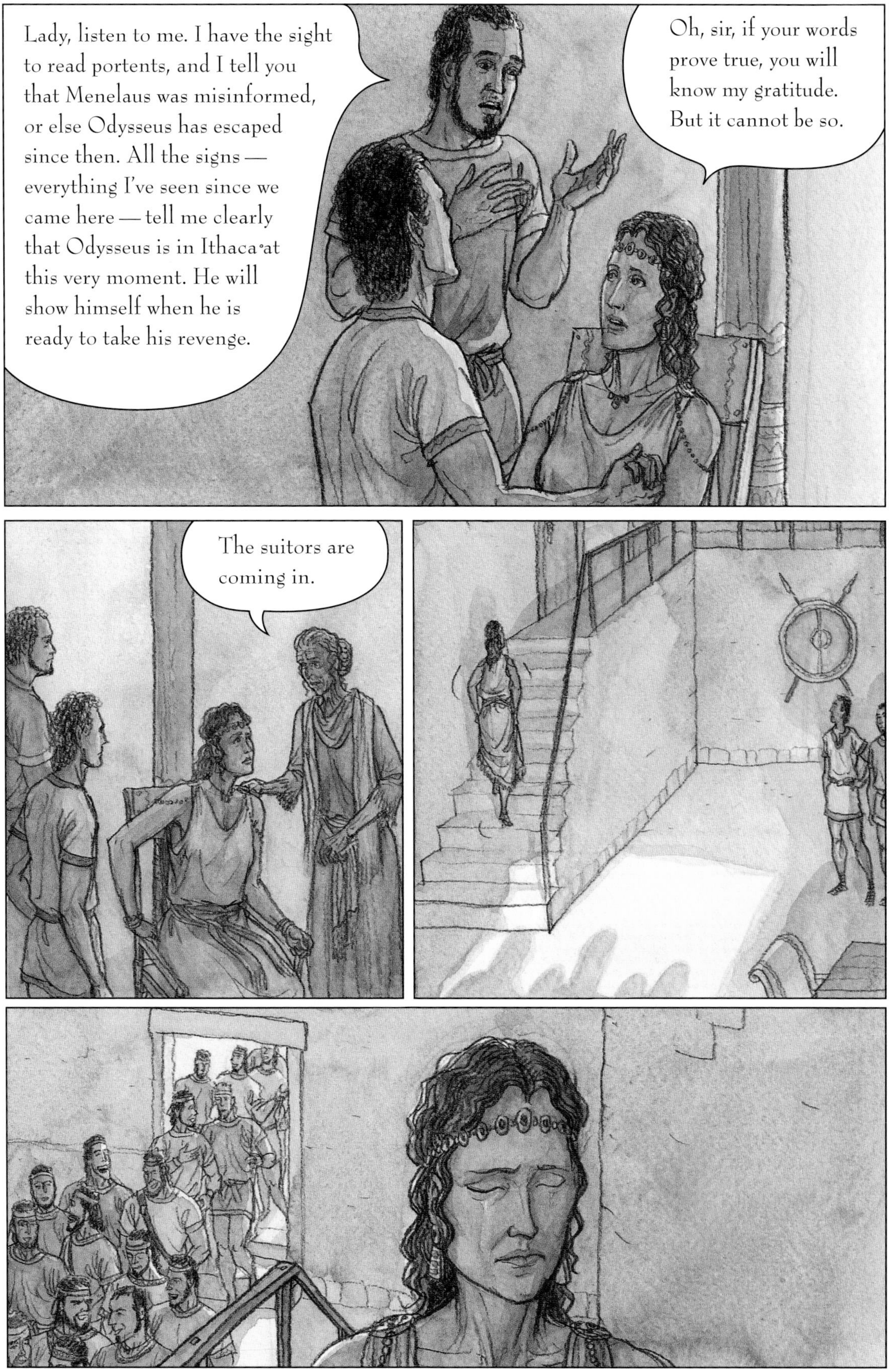
Lady, listen to me. I have the sight to read portents, and I tell you that Menelaus was misinformed, or else Odysseus has escaped since then. All the signs — everything I've seen since we came here — tell me clearly that Odysseus is in Ithaca at this very moment. He will show himself when he is ready to take his revenge.
Oh, sir, if your words prove true, you will know my gratitude. But it cannot be so.
The suitors are coming in.

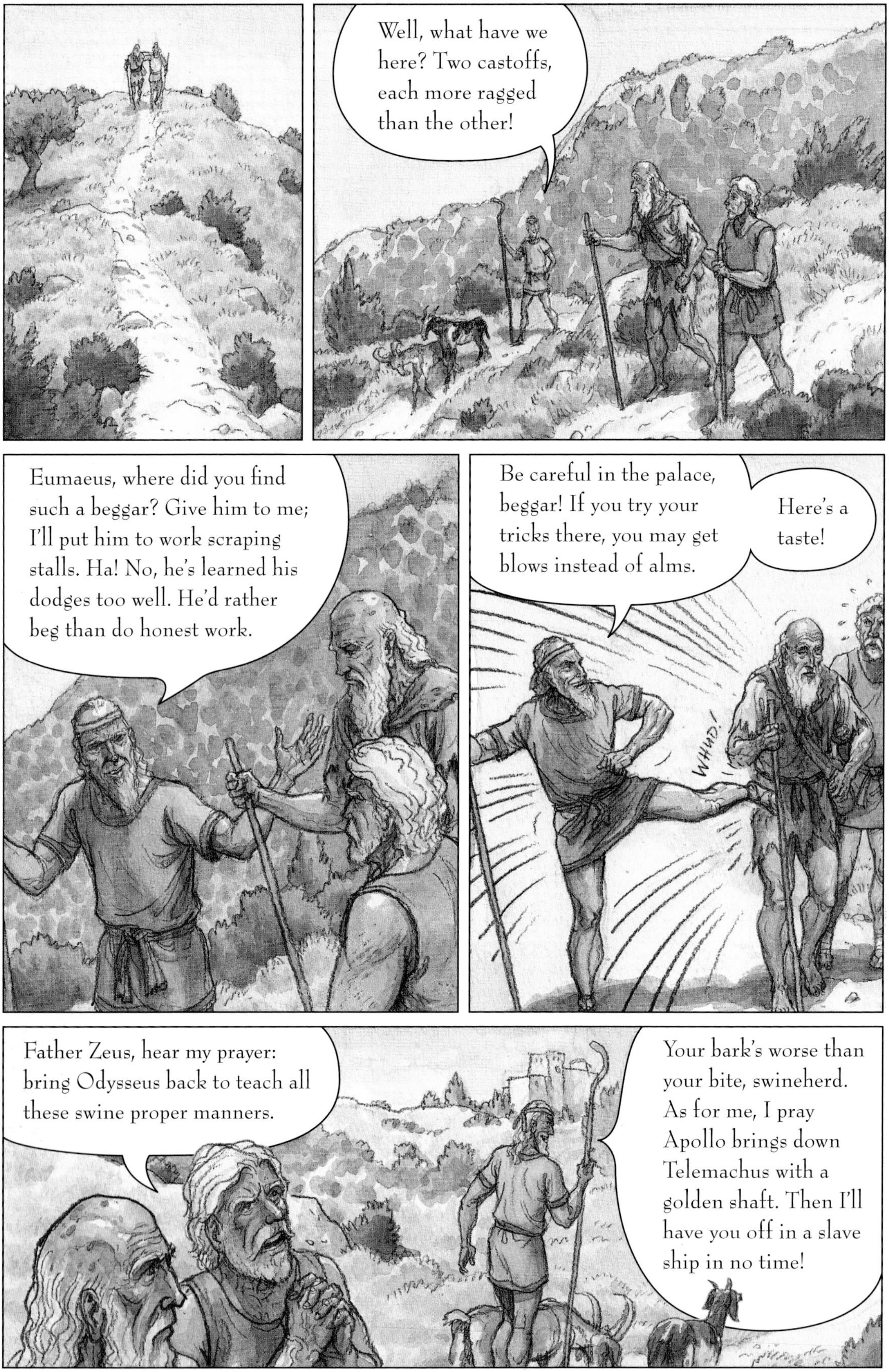
Well, what have we here? Two castoffs, each more ragged than the other!
Eumaeus, where did you find such a beggar? Give him to me; I'll put him to work scraping stalls. Ha! No, he's learned his dodges too well. He'd rather beg than do honest work.
Be careful in the palace, beggar! If you try your tricks there, you may get blows instead of alms.
Here's a taste!
WHUD!
Father Zeus, hear my prayer: bring Odysseus back to teach all these swine proper manners.
Your bark's worse than your bite, swineherd. As for me, I pray Apollo brings down Telemachus with a golden shaft. Then I'll have you off in a slave ship in no time!

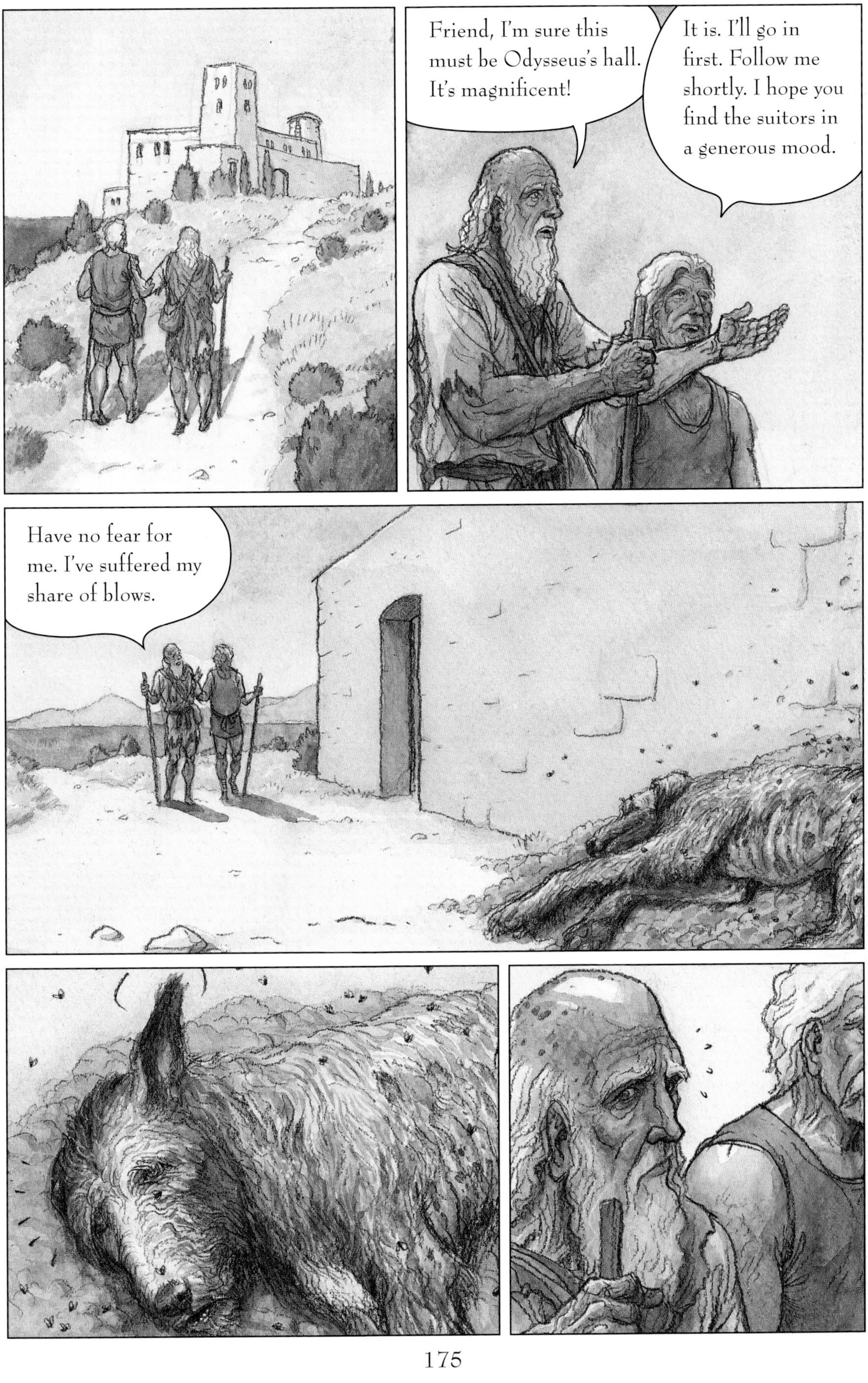
Friend, I'm sure this must be Odysseus's hall. It's magnificent!
It is. I'll go in first. Follow me shortly. I hope you find the suitors in a generous mood.
Have no fear for me. I've suffered my share of blows.

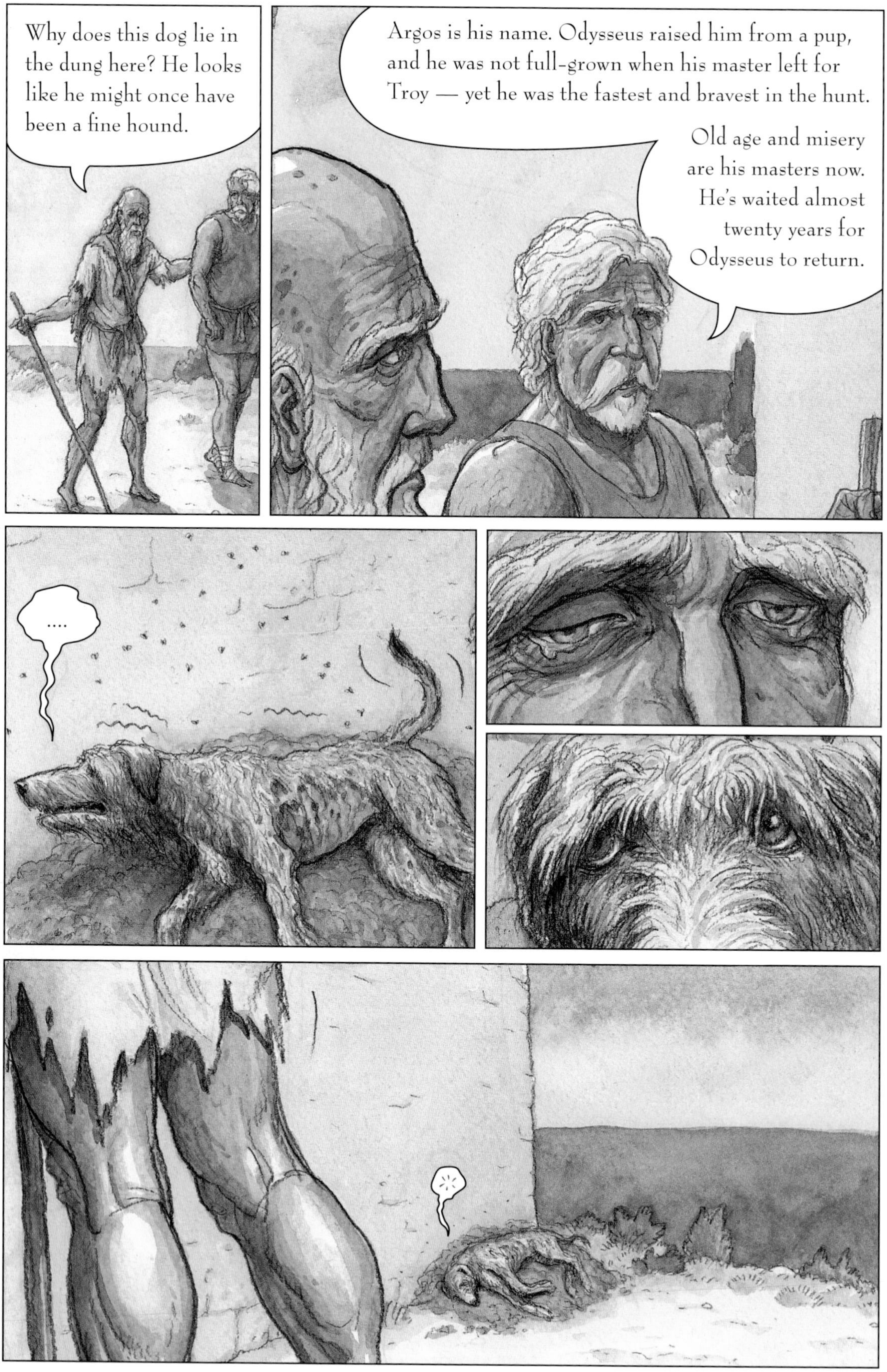
Why does this dog lie in the dung here? He looks like he might once have been a fine hound.
Argos is his name. Odysseus raised him from a pup, and he was not full-grown when his master left for Troy — yet he was the fastest and bravest in the hunt.
Old age and misery are his masters now. He's waited almost twenty years for Odysseus to return.
....

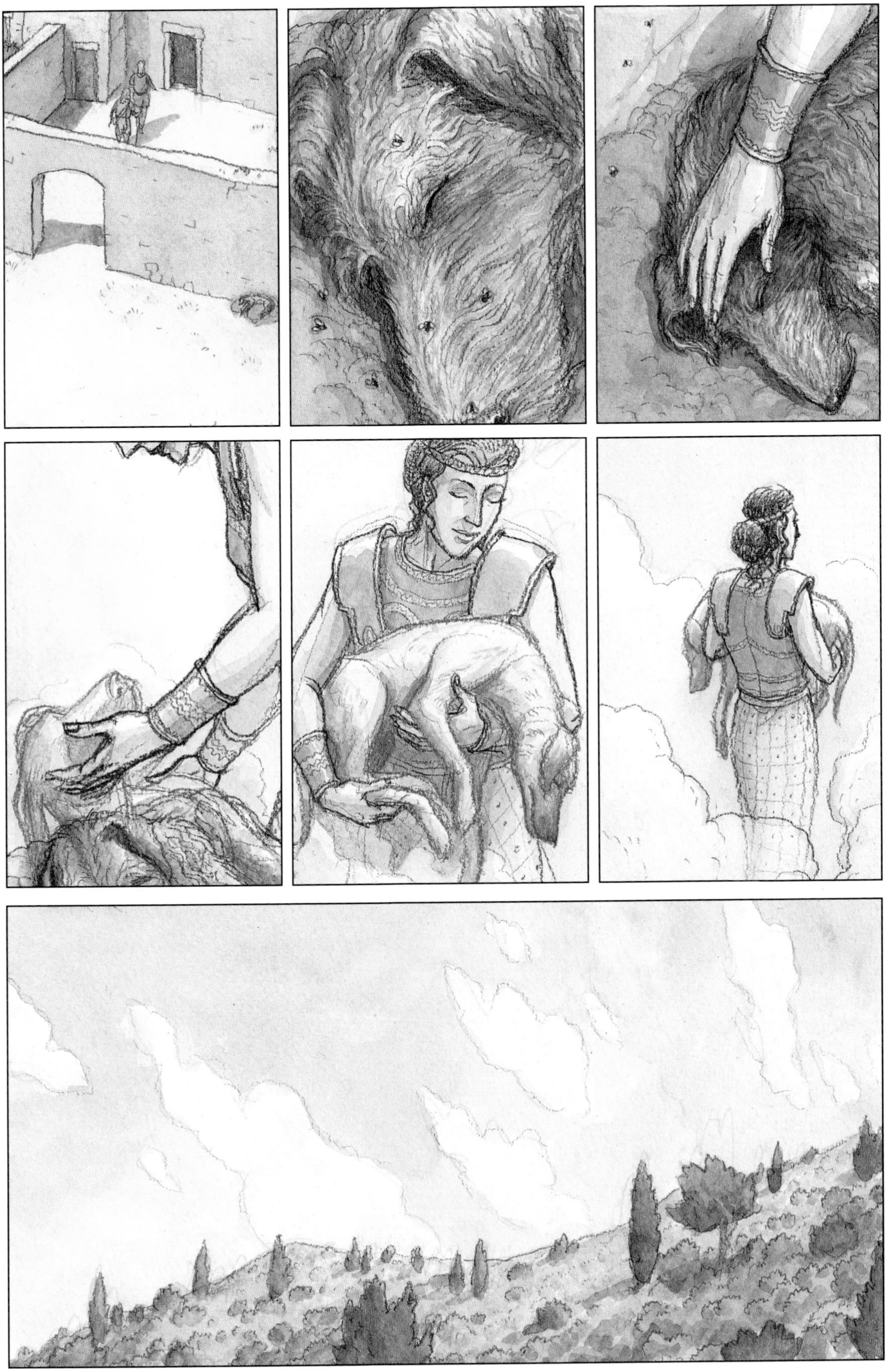

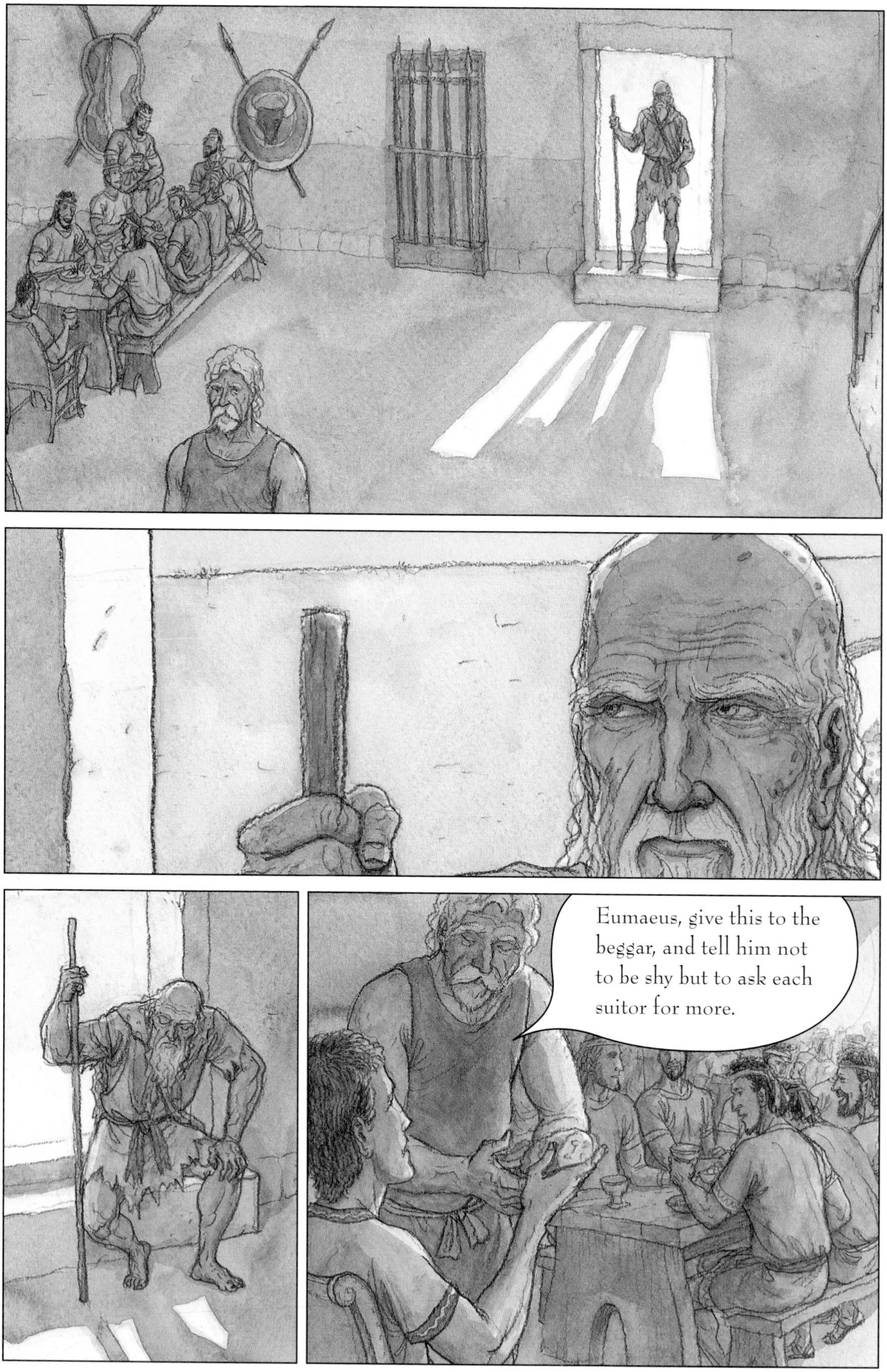
Eumaeus, give this to the beggar, and tell him not to be shy but to ask each suitor for more.

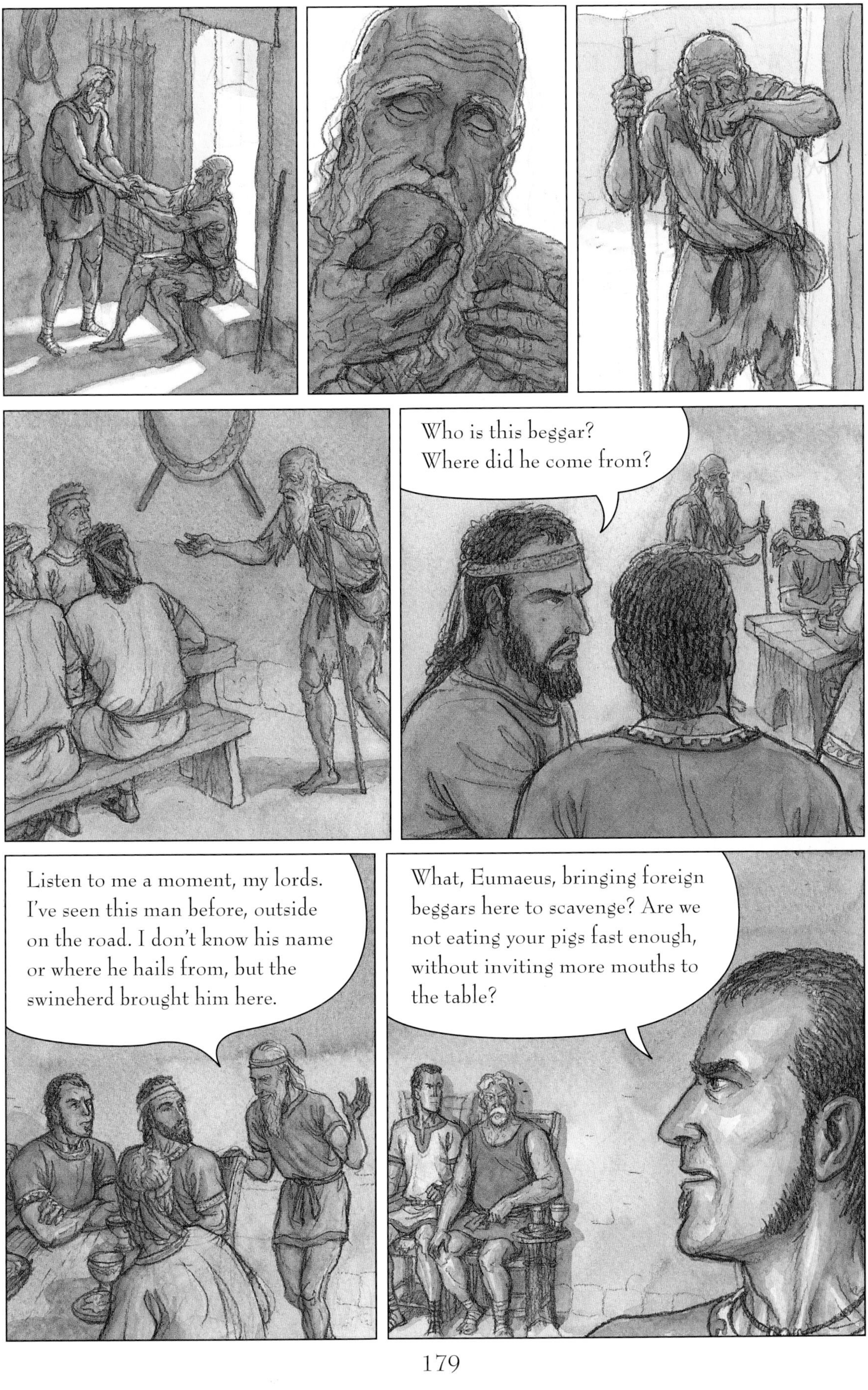
Who is this beggar? Where did he come from?
Listen to me a moment, my lords. I've seen this man before, outside on the road. I don't know his name or where he hails from, but the swineherd brought him here.
What, Eumaeus, bringing foreign beggars here to scavenge? Are we not eating your pigs fast enough, without inviting more mouths to the table?

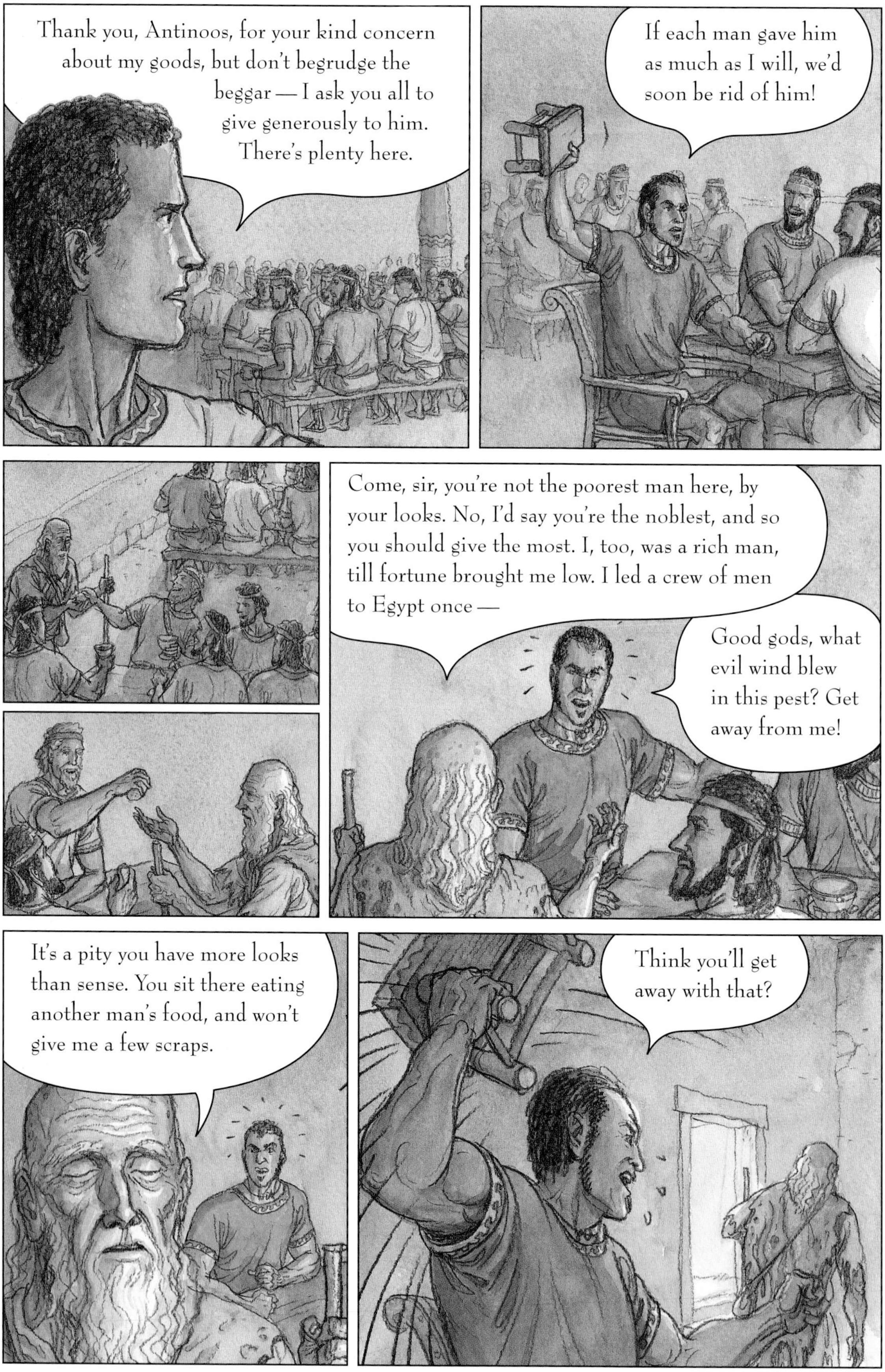
Thank you, Antinoos, for your kind concern about my goods, but don't begrudge the beggar — I ask you all to give generously to him. There's plenty here.
If each man gave him as much as I will, we'd soon be rid of him!
Come, sir, you're not the poorest man here, by your looks. No, I'd say you're the noblest, and so you should give the most. I, too, was a rich man, till fortune brought me low. I led a crew of men to Egypt once —
Good gods, what evil wind blew in this pest? Get away from me!
It's a pity you have more looks than sense. You sit there eating another man's food, and won't give me a few scraps.
Think you'll get away with that?

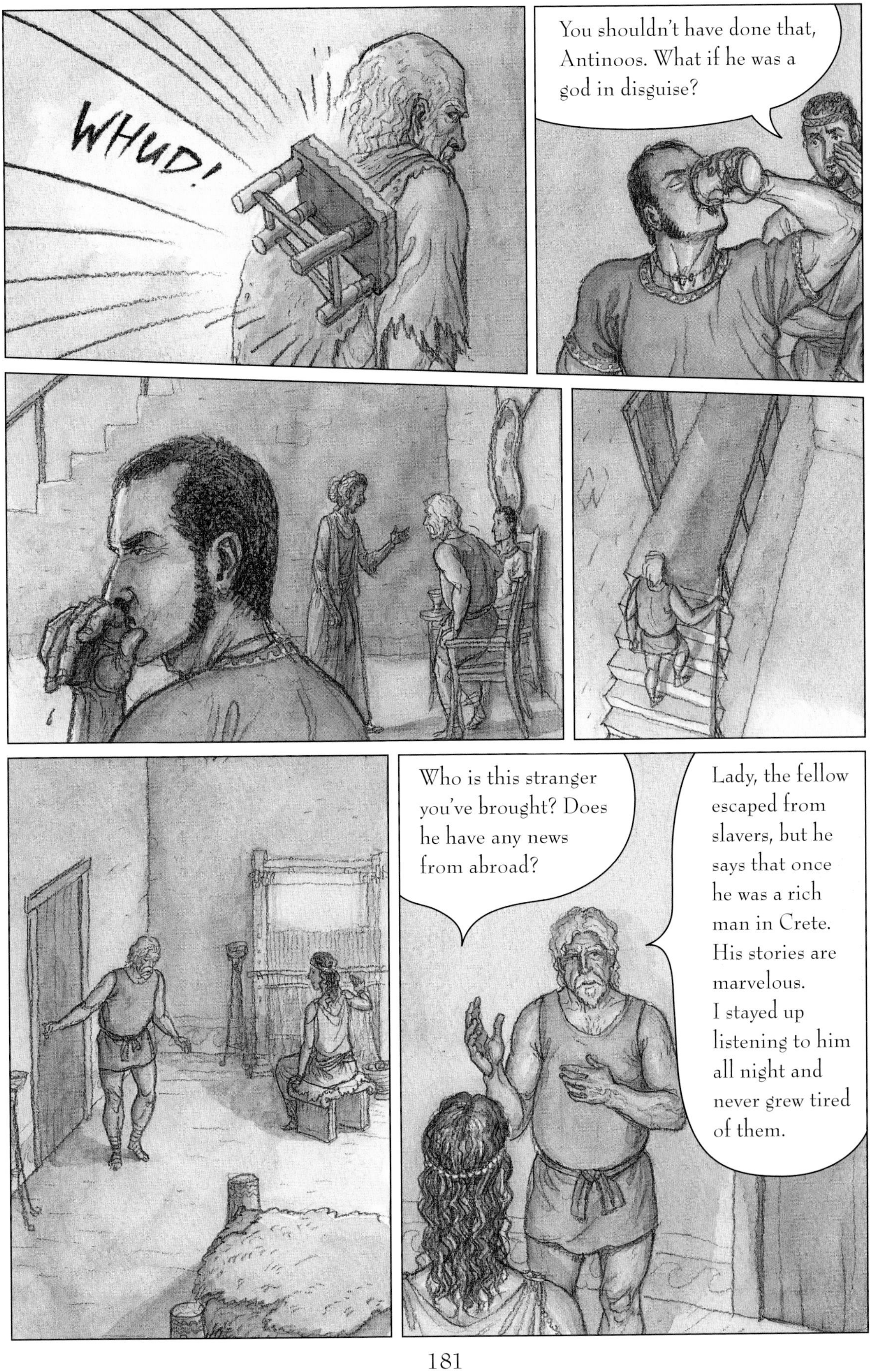
WHUD!
You shouldn't have done that, Antinoos. What if he was a god in disguise?
Who is this stranger you've brought? Does he have any news from abroad?
Lady, the fellow escaped from slavers, but he says that once he was a rich man in Crete. His stories are marvelous. I stayed up listening to him all night and never grew tired of them.

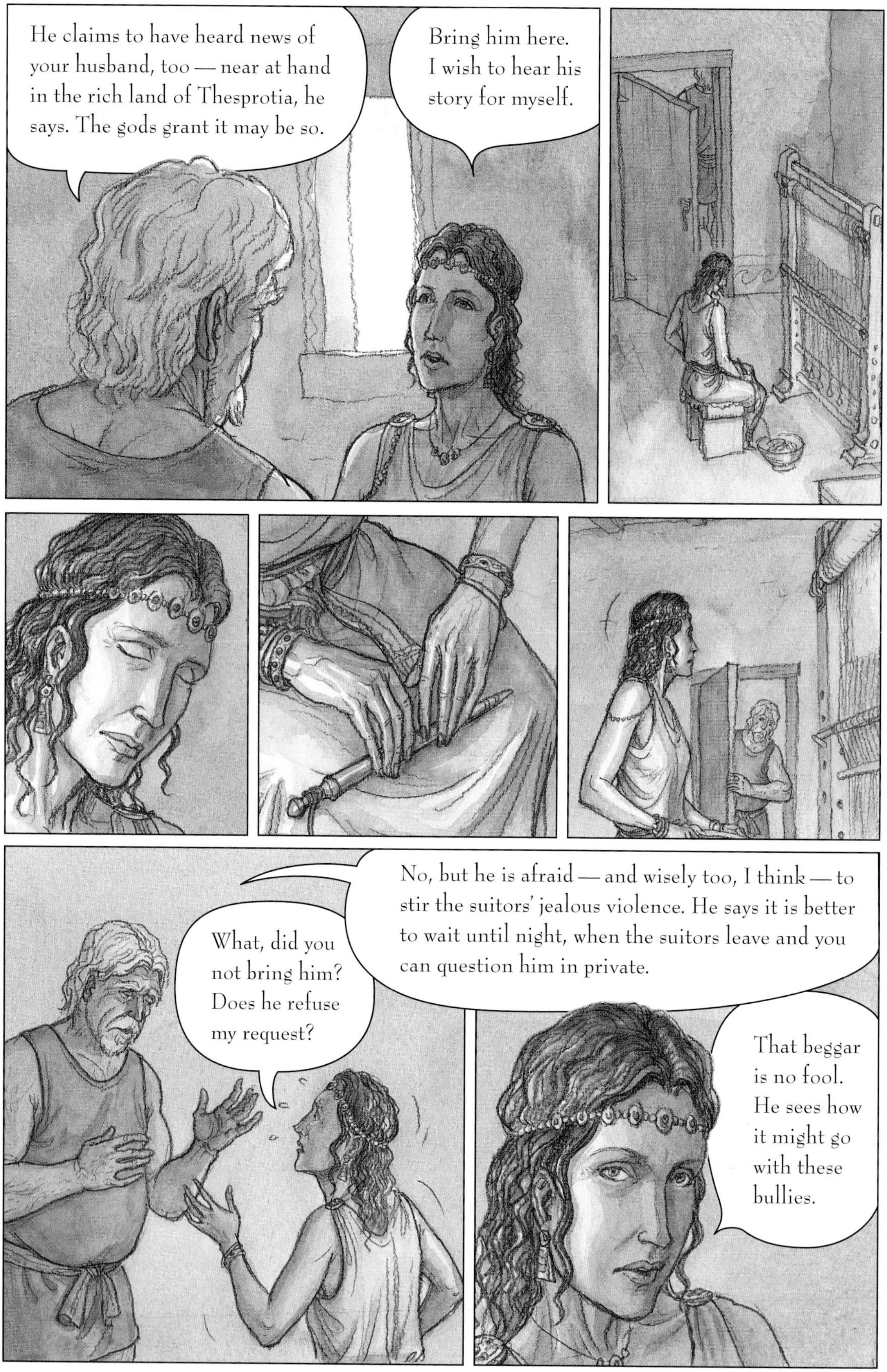
He claims to have heard news of your husband, too — near at hand in the rich land of Thesprotia, he says. The gods grant it may be so.
Bring him here. I wish to hear his story for myself.
What, did you not bring him? Does he refuse my request?
No, but he is afraid — and wisely too, I think — to stir the suitors' jealous violence. He says it is better to wait until night, when the suitors leave and you can question him in private.
That beggar is no fool. He sees how it might go with these bullies.

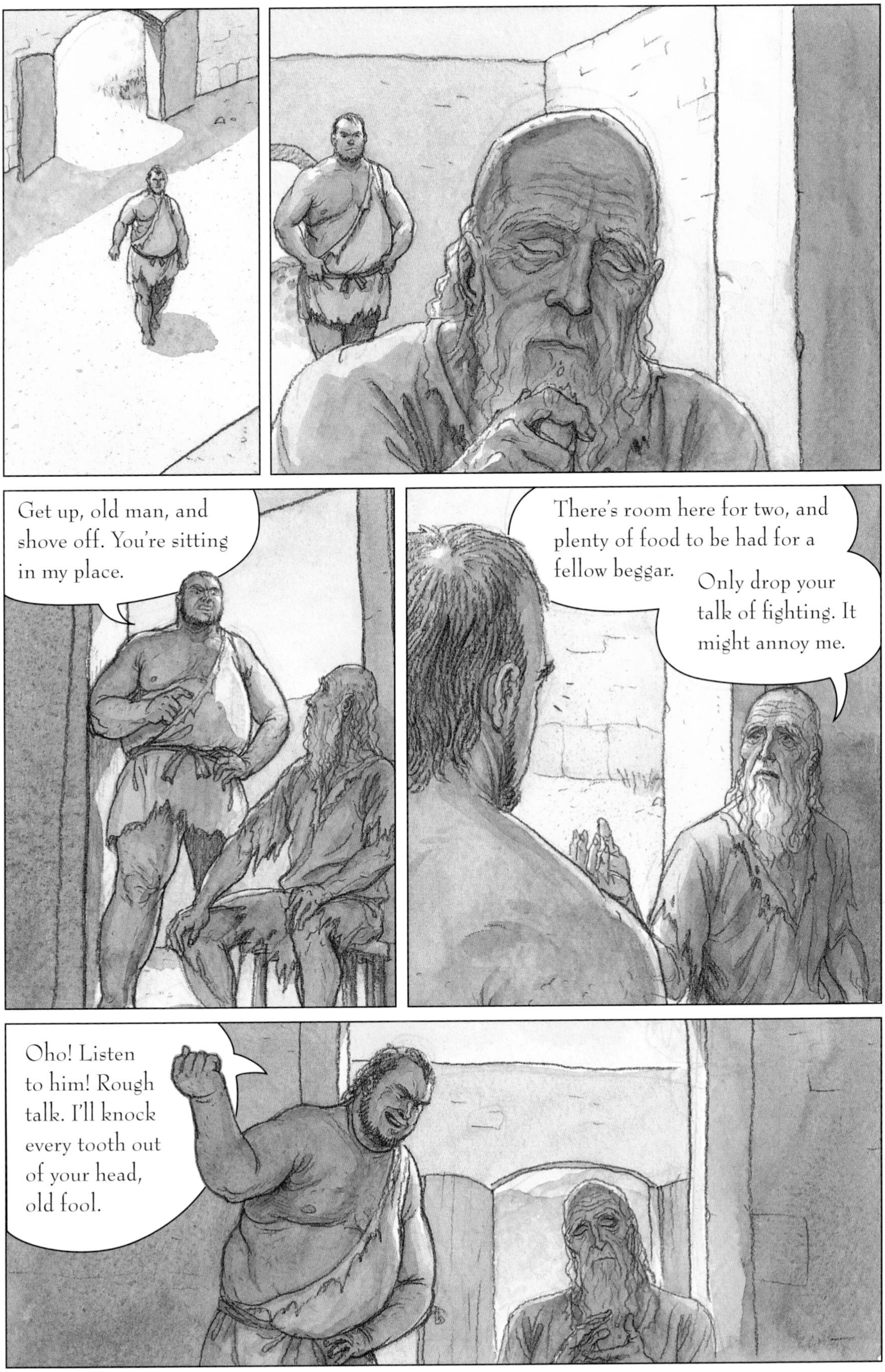
Get up, old man, and shove off. You're sitting in my place.
There's room here for two, and plenty of food to be had for a fellow beggar.
Only drop your talk of fighting. It might annoy me.
Oho! Listen to him! Rough talk. I'll knock every tooth out of your head, old fool.

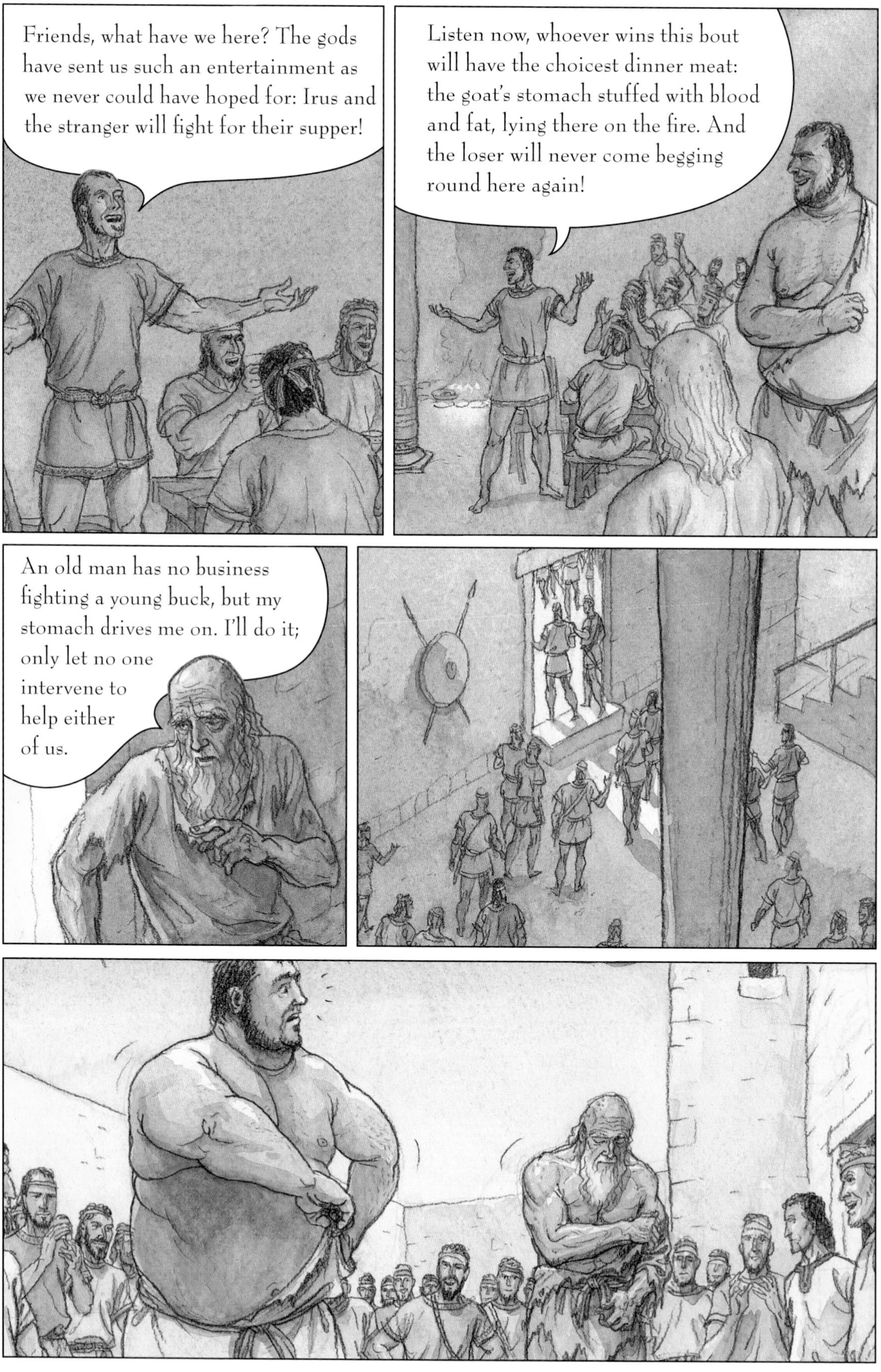
Friends, what have we here? The gods have sent us such an entertainment as we never could have hoped for: Irus and the stranger will fight for their supper!
Listen now, whoever wins this bout will have the choicest dinner meat: the goat's stomach stuffed with blood and fat, lying there on the fire. And the loser will never come begging round here again!
An old man has no business fighting a young buck, but my stomach drives me on. I'll do it; only let no one intervene to help either of us.

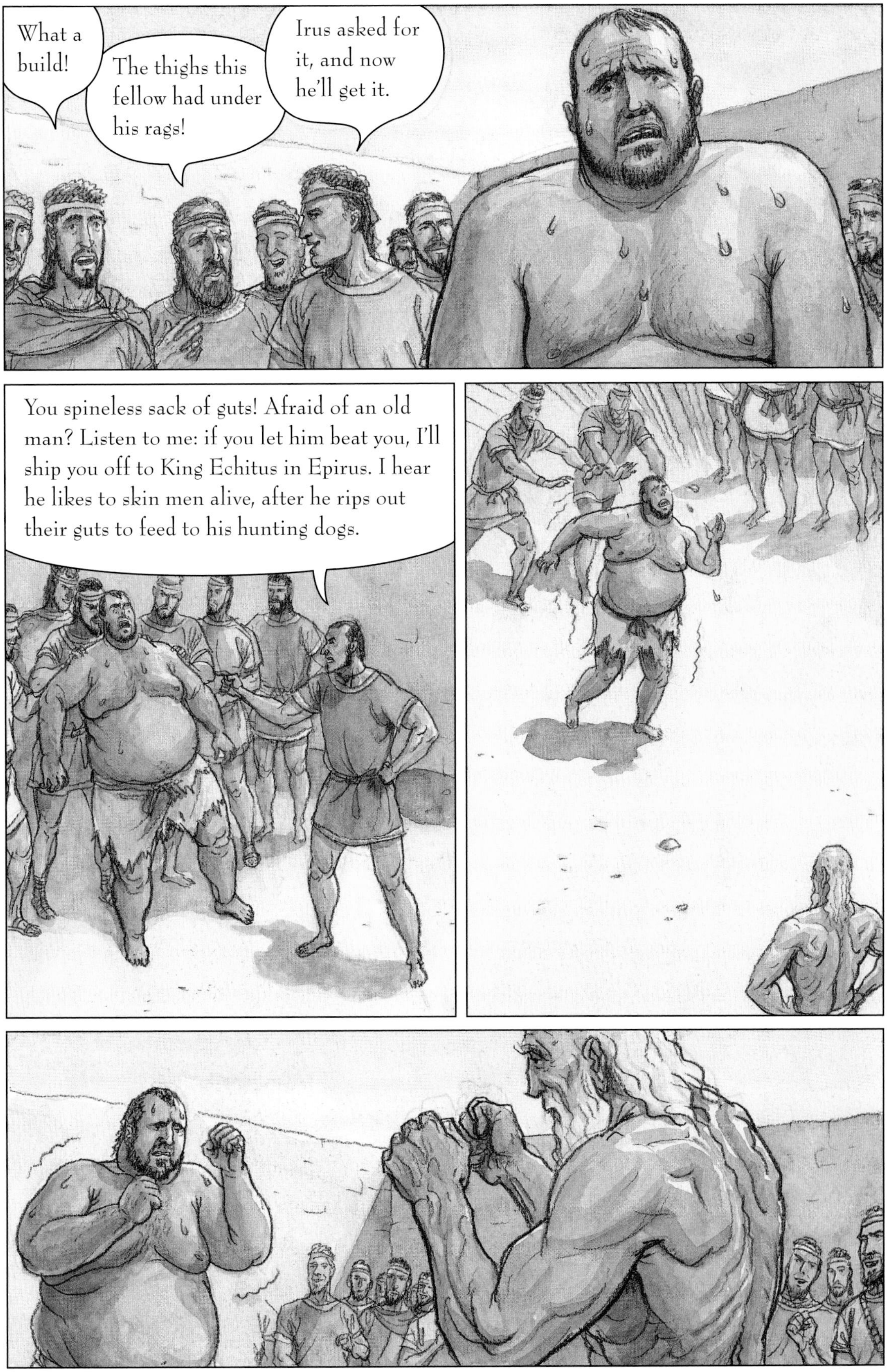
What a build!
The thighs this fellow had under his rags!
Irus asked for it, and now he'll get it.
You spineless sack of guts! Afraid of an old man? Listen to me: if you let him beat you, I'll ship you off to King Echitus in Epirus. I hear he likes to skin men alive, after he rips out their guts to feed to his hunting dogs.

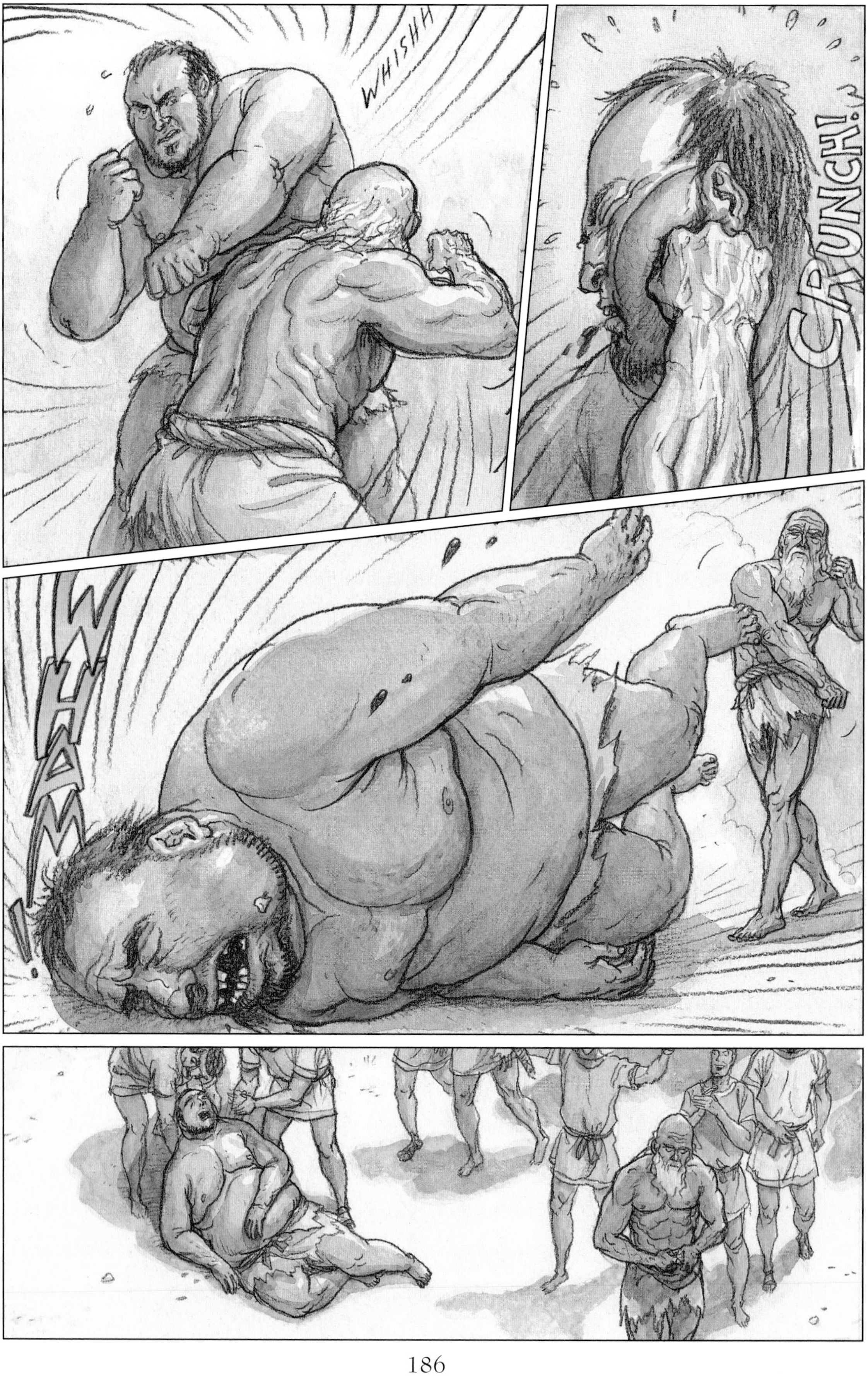
WHISHH
CRUNCH!
WHAM!

Well done, old man!

You put that parasite out of business.

May Zeus fill your pouch and grant your desires.

Here you go, old-timer. Good fortune to you.

You are Amphinomus, son of Nisus of Dulichion, are you not?

You seem like a sensible lad. Why not quit the company of these vultures? Mark my words: if you keep on like this, some catastrophe will befall you all.

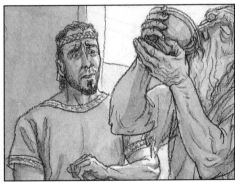

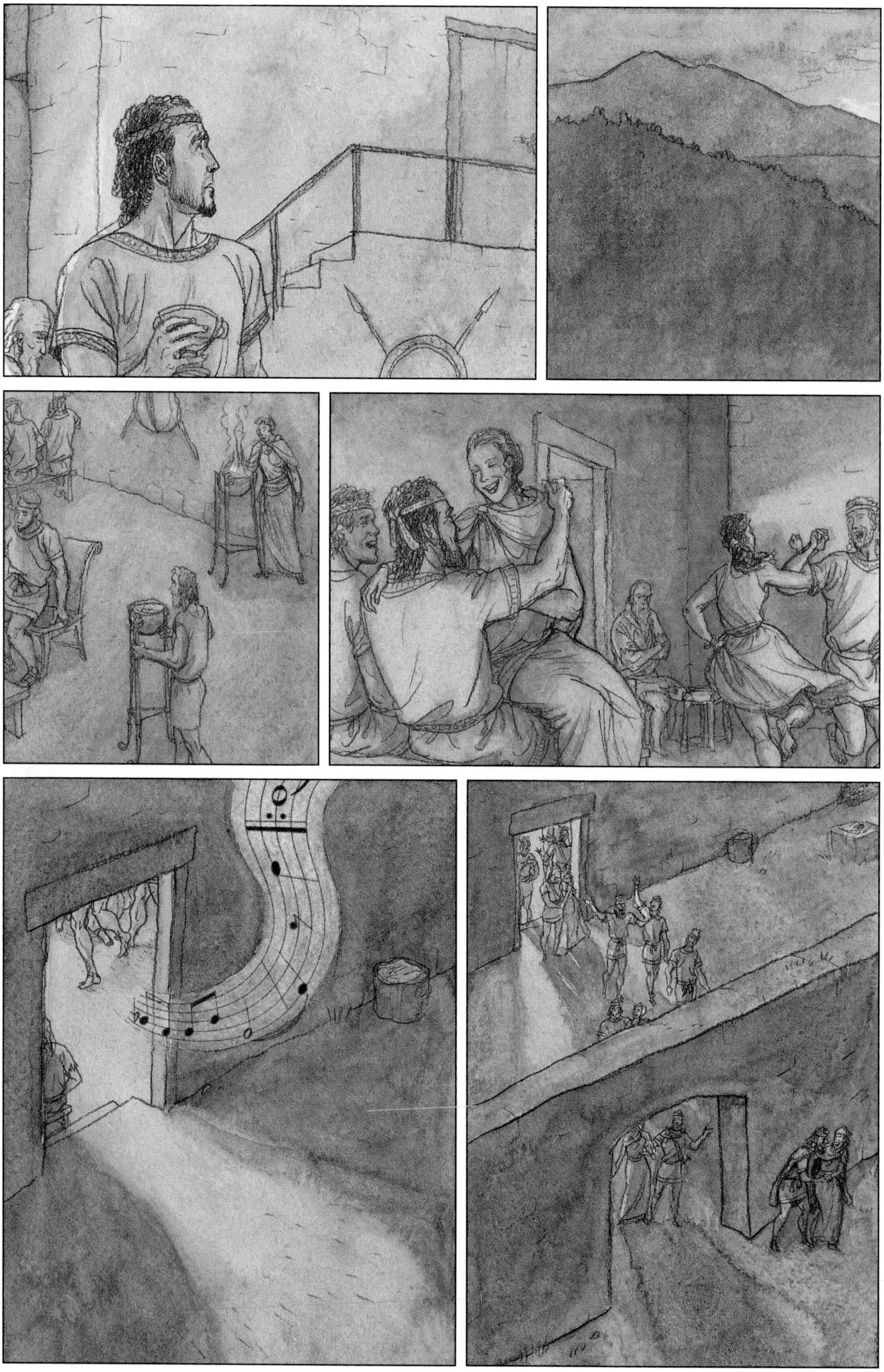

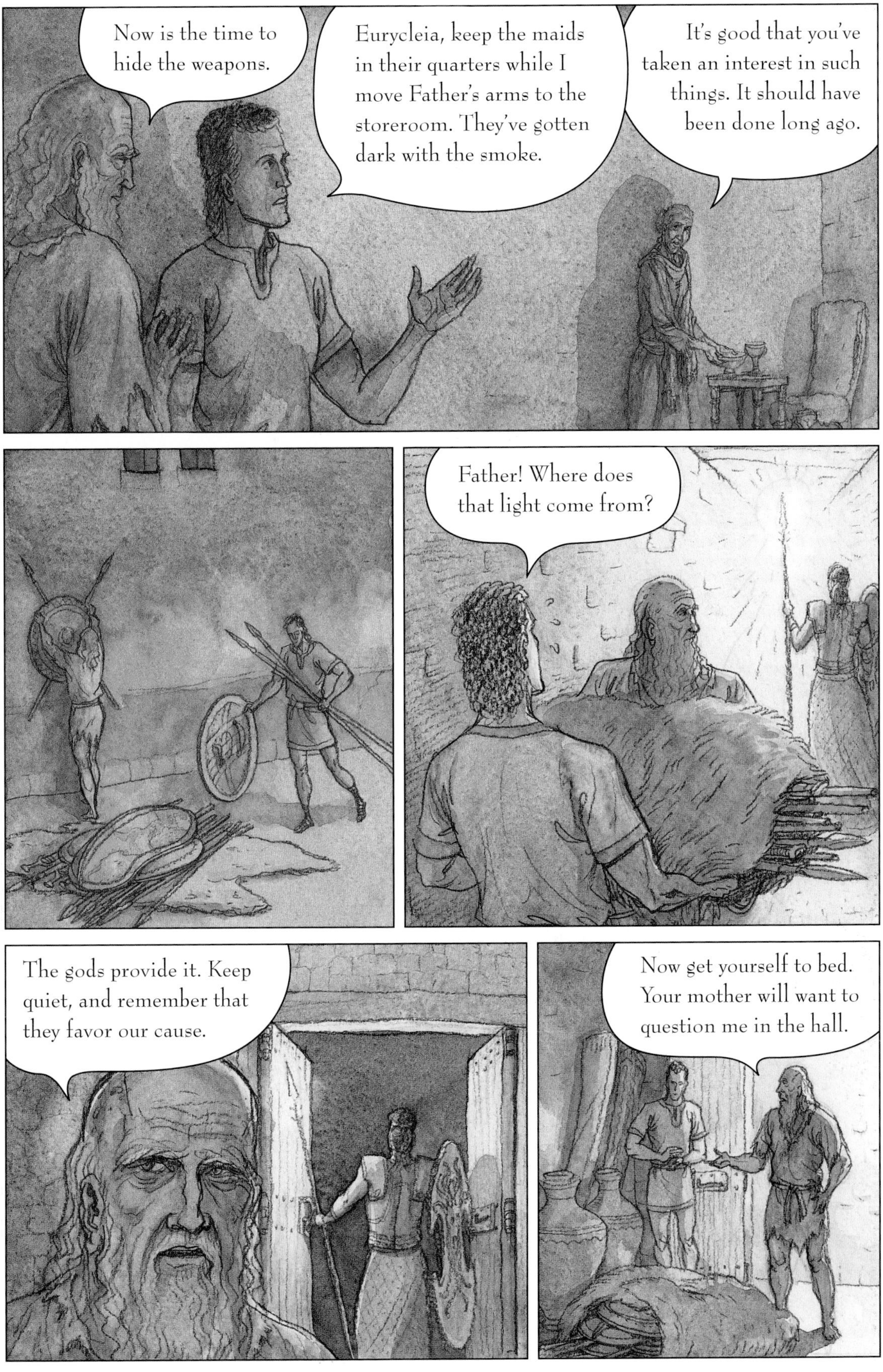
Now is the time to hide the weapons.
Eurycleia, keep the maids in their quarters while I move Father's arms to the storeroom. They've gotten dark with the smoke.
It's good that you've taken an interest in such things. It should have been done long ago.
Father! Where does that light come from?
The gods provide it. Keep quiet, and remember that they favor our cause.
Now get yourself to bed. Your mother will want to question me in the hall.

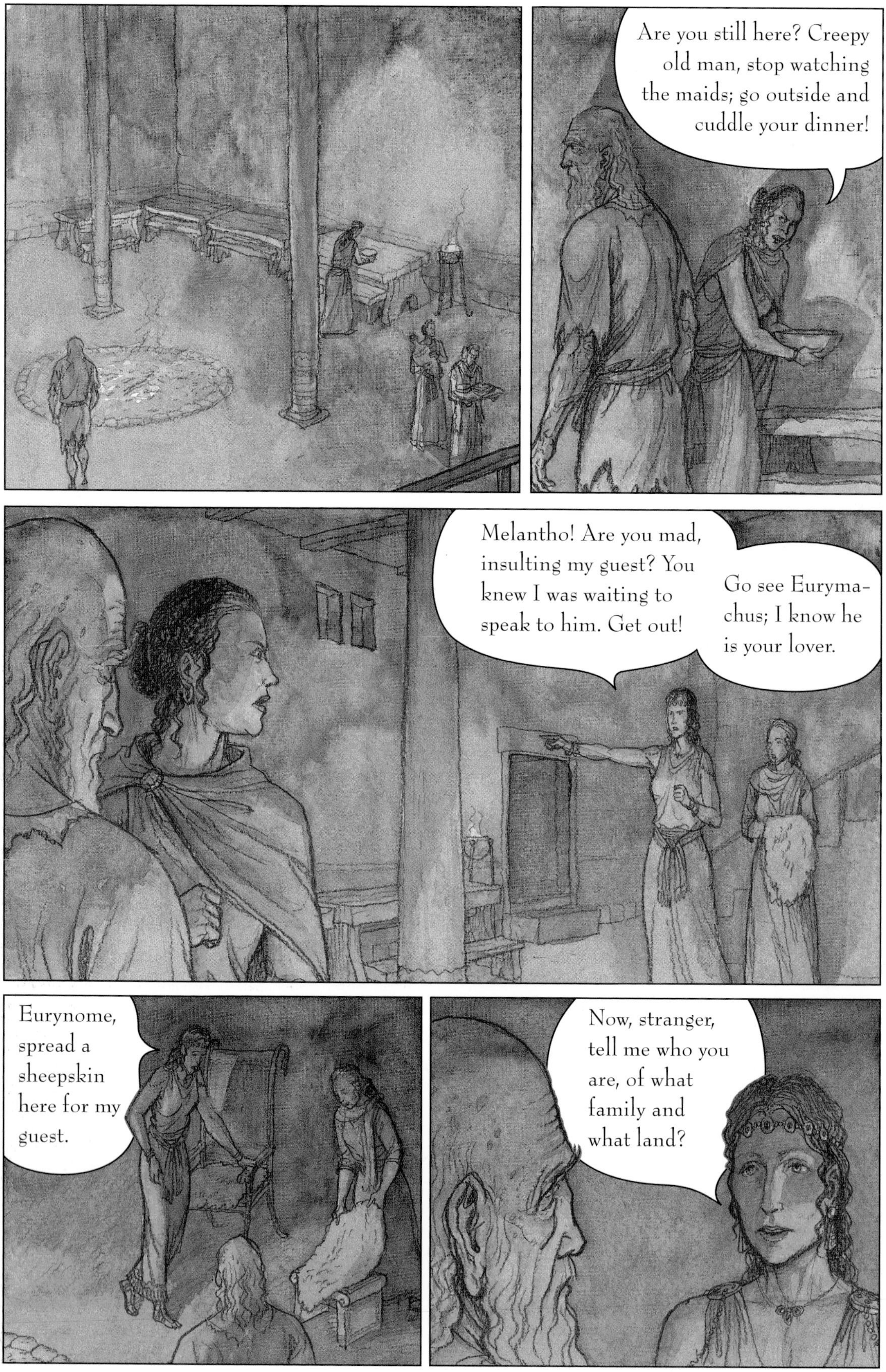
Are you still here? Creepy old man, stop watching the maids; go outside and cuddle your dinner!
Melantho! Are you mad, insulting my guest? You knew I was waiting to speak to him. Get out!
Go see Eurymachus; I know he is your lover.
Eurynome, spread a sheepskin here for my guest.
Now, stranger, tell me who you are, of what family and what land?

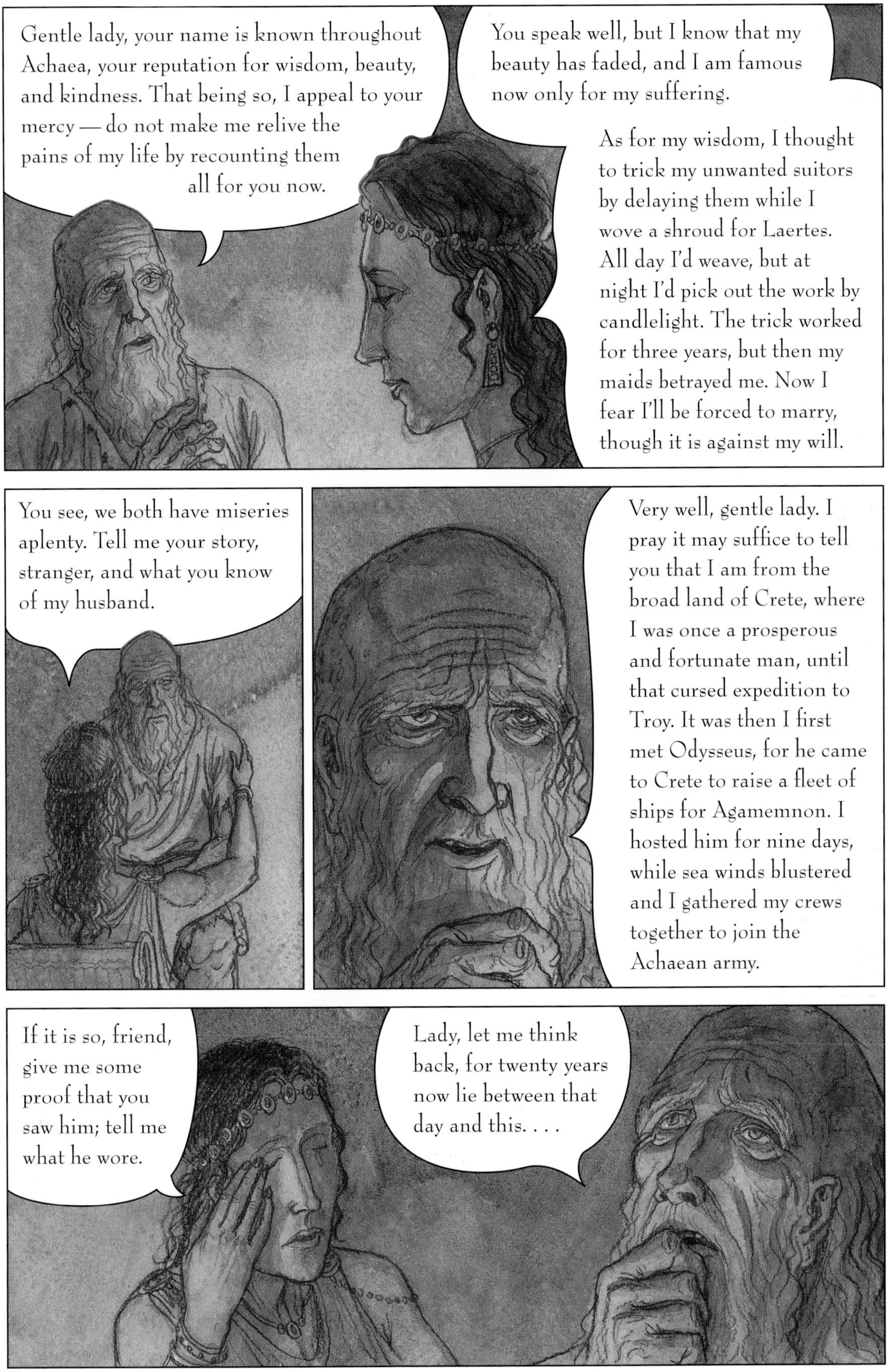
Gentle lady, your name is known throughout Achaea, your reputation for wisdom, beauty, and kindness. That being so, I appeal to your mercy — do not make me relive the pains of my life by recounting them all for you now.
You speak well, but I know that my beauty has faded, and I am famous now only for my suffering.
As for my wisdom, I thought to trick my unwanted suitors by delaying them while I wove a shroud for Laertes. All day I'd weave, but at night I'd pick out the work by candlelight. The trick worked for three years, but then my maids betrayed me. Now I fear I'll be forced to marry, though it is against my will.
You see, we both have miseries aplenty. Tell me your story, stranger, and what you know of my husband.
Very well, gentle lady. I pray it may suffice to tell you that I am from the broad land of Crete, where I was once a prosperous and fortunate man, until that cursed expedition to Troy. It was then I first met Odysseus, for he came to Crete to raise a fleet of ships for Agamemnon. I hosted him for nine days, while sea winds blustered and I gathered my crews together to join the Achaean army.
If it is so, friend, give me some proof that you saw him; tell me what he wore.
Lady, let me think back, for twenty years now lie between that day and this. . . .

He had a purple cloak, lined with fleece, double thick. There was a brooch upon it, wondrous workmanship — a hound pinning a fawn, all in gold. And a fine, close-fitting tunic, marvelously soft.

But then, I don't know if he brought these things from Ithaca or if some lord gave them to him as a guest gift.

Now you have won my thanks. I put that tunic and cloak on his shoulders myself and fastened it with that pin.

But lady, you do not need to stain your cheeks any longer with tears. I have something else to tell you.

Your husband is on his way, near at hand.

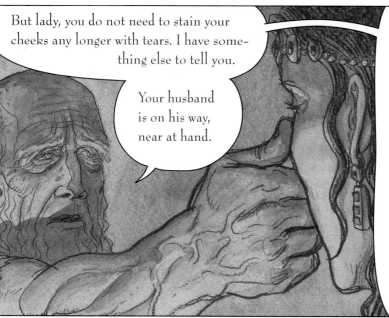

I heard this from the king of the Thesprotians, who had sent him on his way in a good ship. The man had been lost at sea for years, because his crew devoured the cattle of Helios, and so Zeus destroyed his ship and stranded him. But he escaped and made his way back here, gathering treasure as he came. I got here first only because Odysseus had gone to consult the oracle.

If only what you say could prove true, you would know my gratitude and any man would count you blessed. But it will never be. We have no master here to furnish a ship and send you on your way with rich gifts, no man like Odysseus.

Or did I dream him?

192

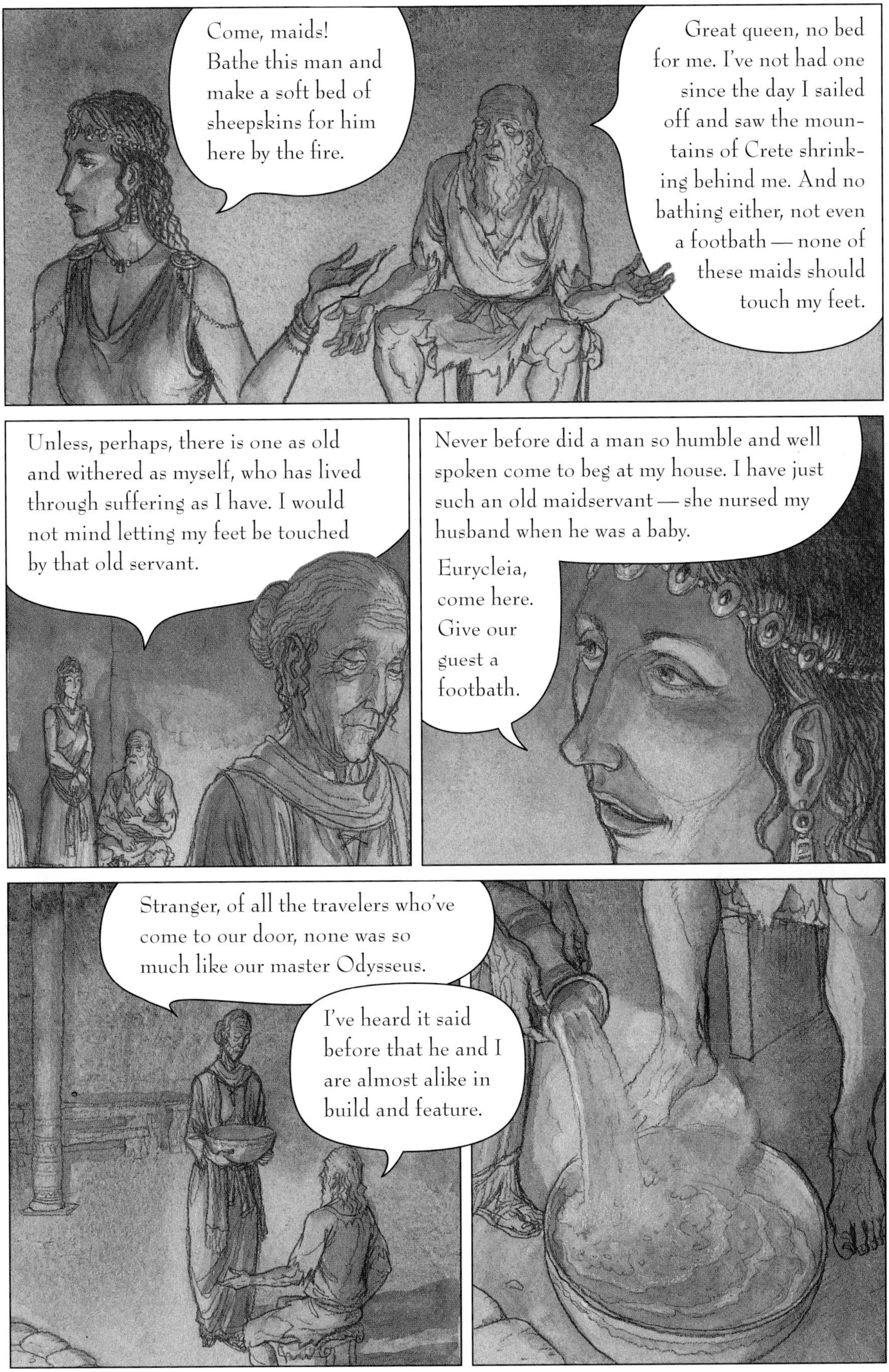
Come, maids! Bathe this man and make a soft bed of sheepskins for him here by the fire.
Great queen, no bed for me. I've not had one since the day I sailed off and saw the mountains of Crete shrinking behind me. And no bathing either, not even a footbath — none of these maids should touch my feet.
Unless, perhaps, there is one as old and withered as myself, who has lived through suffering as I have. I would not mind letting my feet be touched by that old servant.
Never before did a man so humble and well spoken come to beg at my house. I have just such an old maidservant — she nursed my husband when he was a baby.
Eurycleia, come here. Give our guest a footbath.
Stranger, of all the travelers who've come to our door, none was so much like our master Odysseus.
I've heard it said before that he and I are almost alike in build and feature.

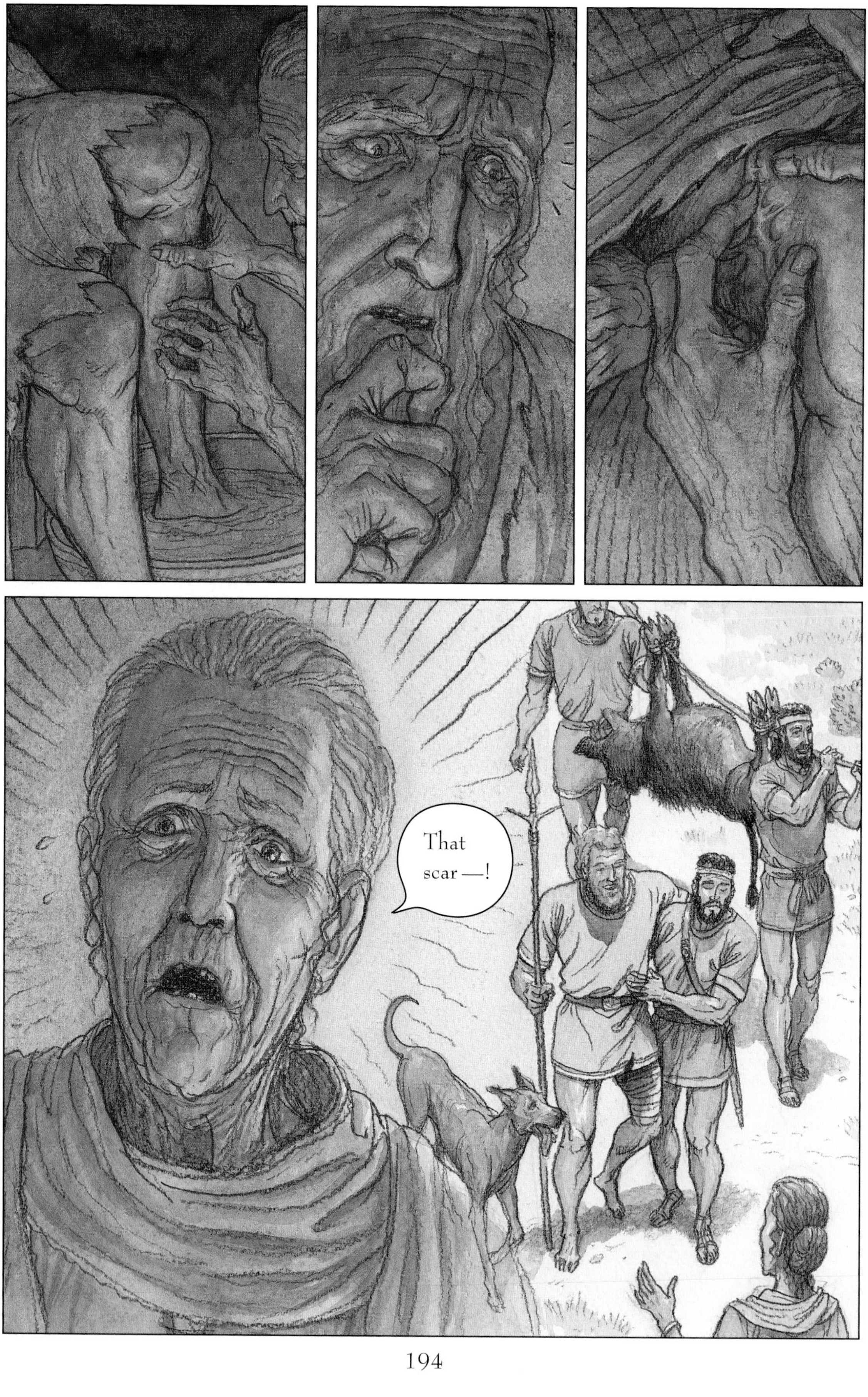
That scar —!

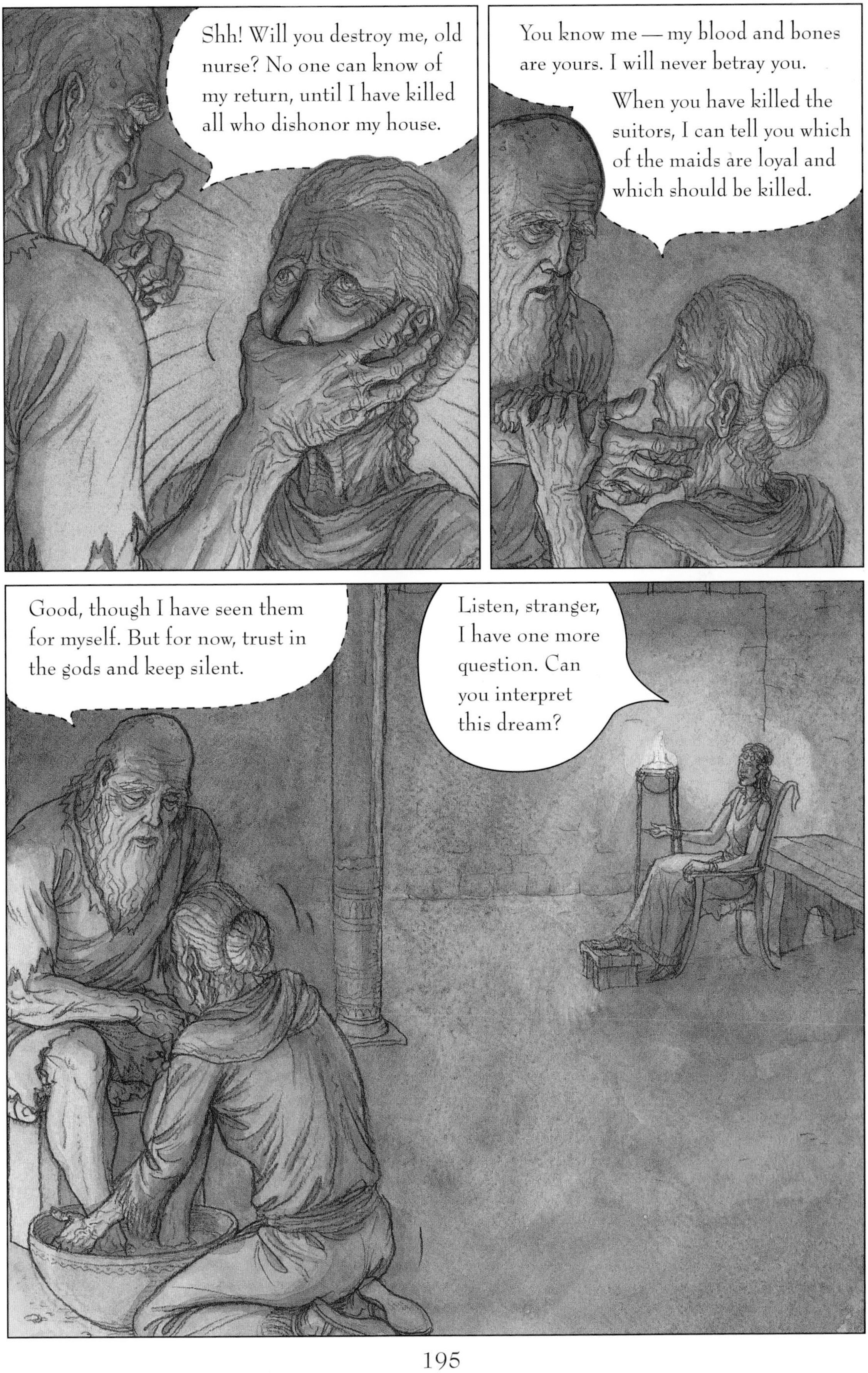
Shh! Will you destroy me, old nurse? No one can know of my return, until I have killed all who dishonor my house.
You know me — my blood and bones are yours. I will never betray you.
When you have killed the suitors, I can tell you which of the maids are loyal and which should be killed.
Good, though I have seen them for myself. But for now, trust in the gods and keep silent.
Listen, stranger, I have one more question. Can you interpret this dream?

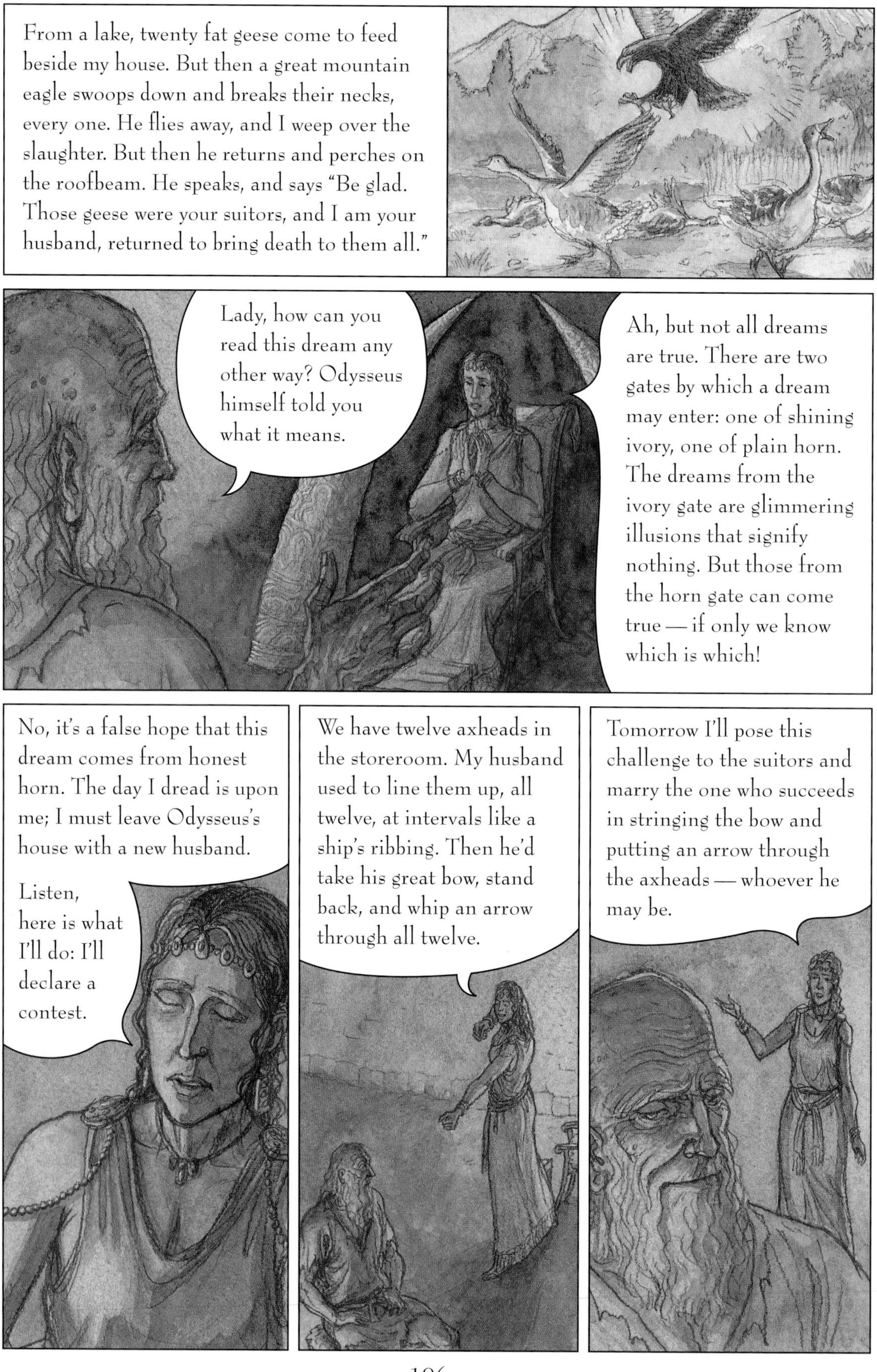
From a lake, twenty fat geese come to feed beside my house. But then a great mountain eagle swoops down and breaks their necks, every one. He flies away, and I weep over the slaughter. But then he returns and perches on the roofbeam. He speaks, and says "Be glad. Those geese were your suitors, and I am your husband, returned to bring death to them all."
Lady, how can you read this dream any other way? Odysseus himself told you what it means.
Ah, but not all dreams are true. There are two gates by which a dream may enter: one of shining ivory, one of plain horn. The dreams from the ivory gate are glimmering illusions that signify nothing. But those from the horn gate can come true — if only we know which is which!
No, it's a false hope that this dream comes from honest horn. The day I dread is upon me; I must leave Odysseus's house with a new husband.
Listen, here is what I'll do: I'll declare a contest.
We have twelve axheads in the storeroom. My husband used to line them up, all twelve, at intervals like a ship's ribbing. Then he'd take his great bow, stand back, and whip an arrow through all twelve.
Tomorrow I'll pose this challenge to the suitors and marry the one who succeeds in stringing the bow and putting an arrow through the axheads — whoever he may be.

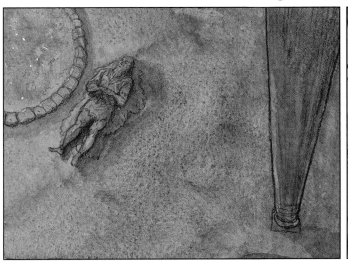

Still awake? What troubles you?

The odds are strong against us. But more than that — after the suitors are killed, what then? Their kin will come for revenge too.

Another man would put his trust in some mortal, but not you; no, even with a god as your guardian, still you mistrust everything.

Let me make it plain, then: even if fifty such bands of men crowded around you, screaming for your blood, you would emerge victorious.

Now, rest.

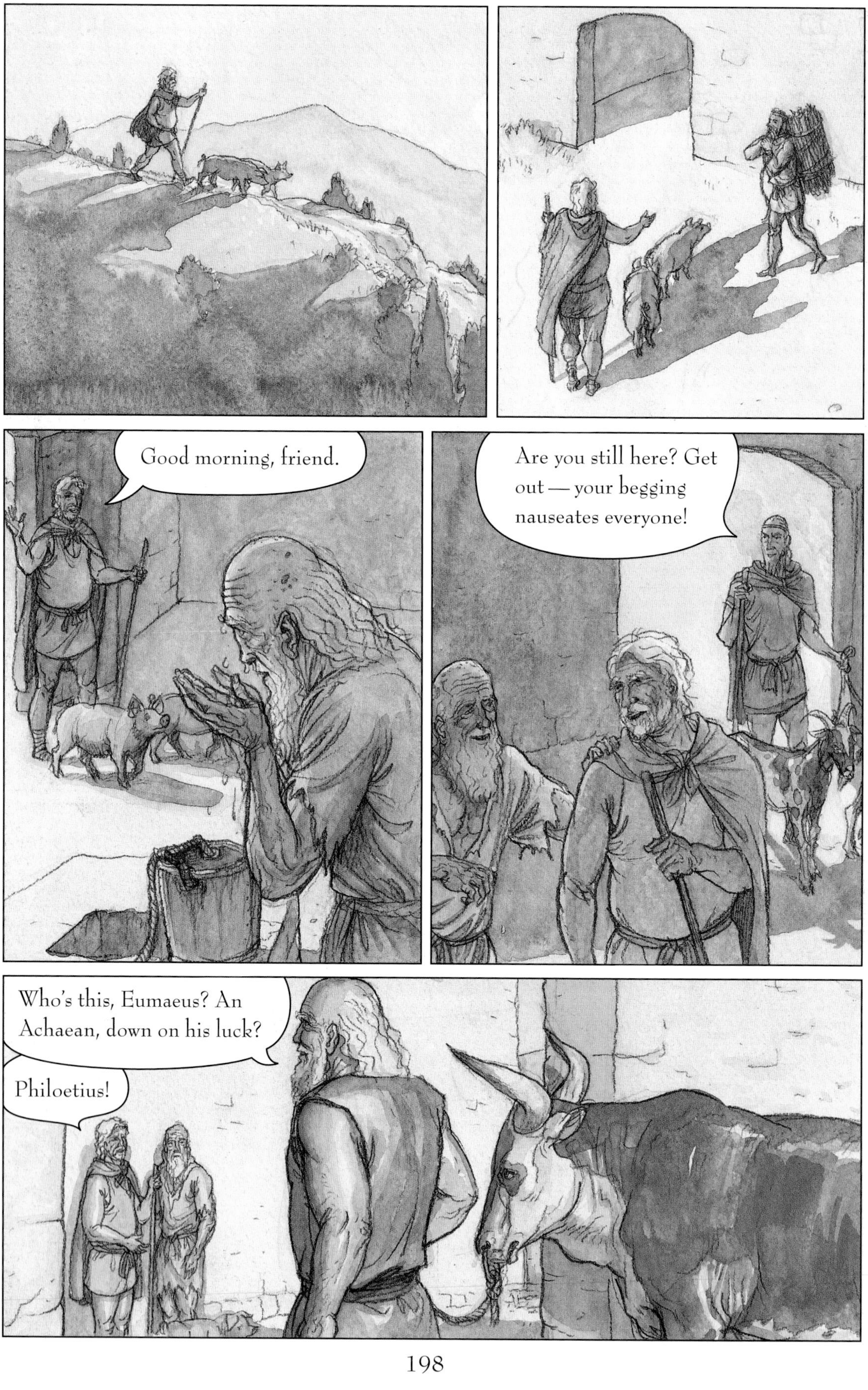
Good morning, friend.
Are you still here? Get out — your begging nauseates everyone!
Who's this, Eumaeus? An Achaean, down on his luck?
Philoetius!

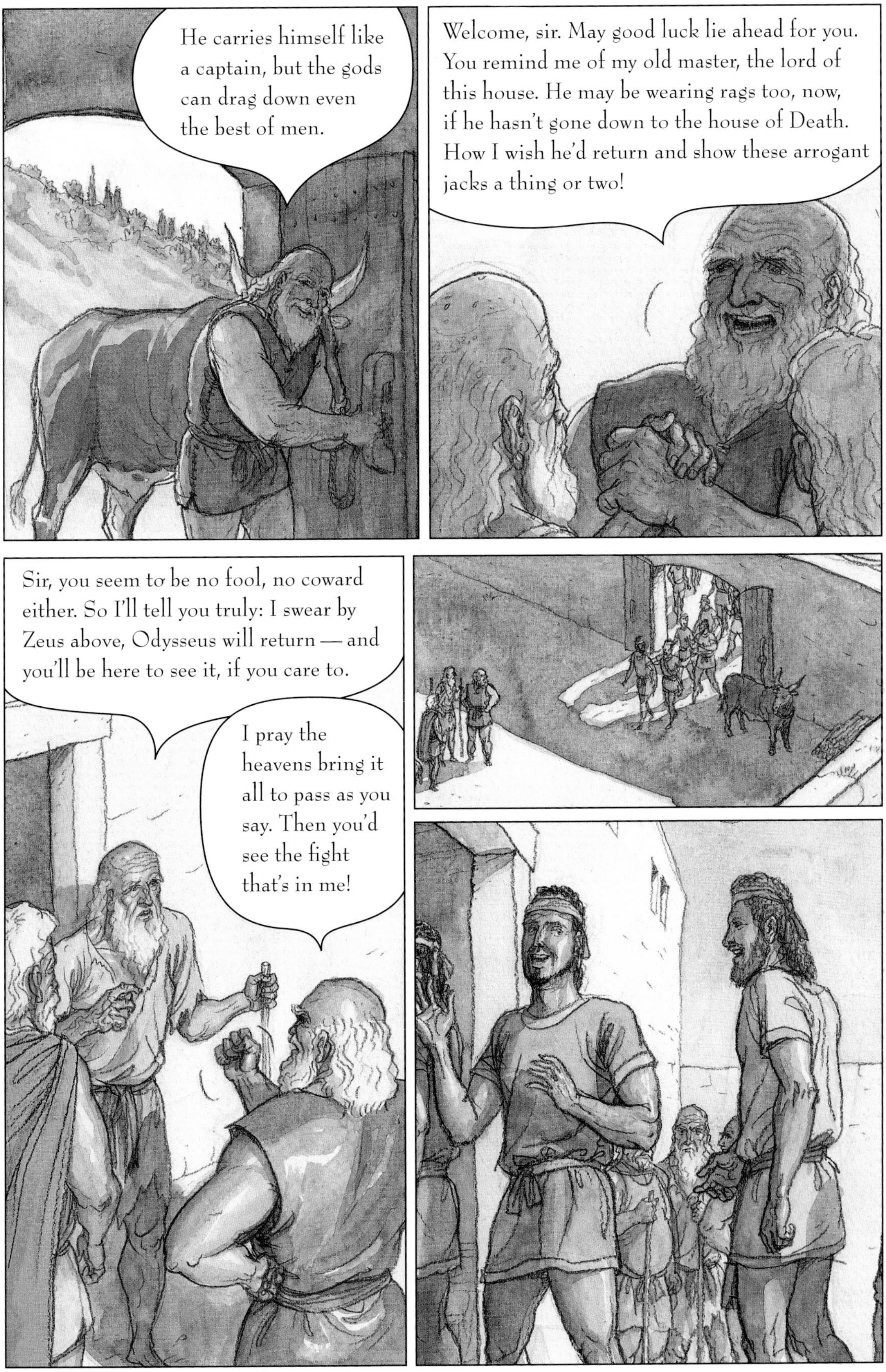
He carries himself like a captain, but the gods can drag down even the best of men.
Welcome, sir. May good luck lie ahead for you. You remind me of my old master, the lord of this house. He may be wearing rags too, now, if he hasn't gone down to the house of Death. How I wish he'd return and show these arrogant jacks a thing or two!
Sir, you seem to be no fool, no coward either. So I'll tell you truly: I swear by Zeus above, Odysseus will return — and you'll be here to see it, if you care to.
I pray the heavens bring it all to pass as you say. Then you'd see the fight that's in me!

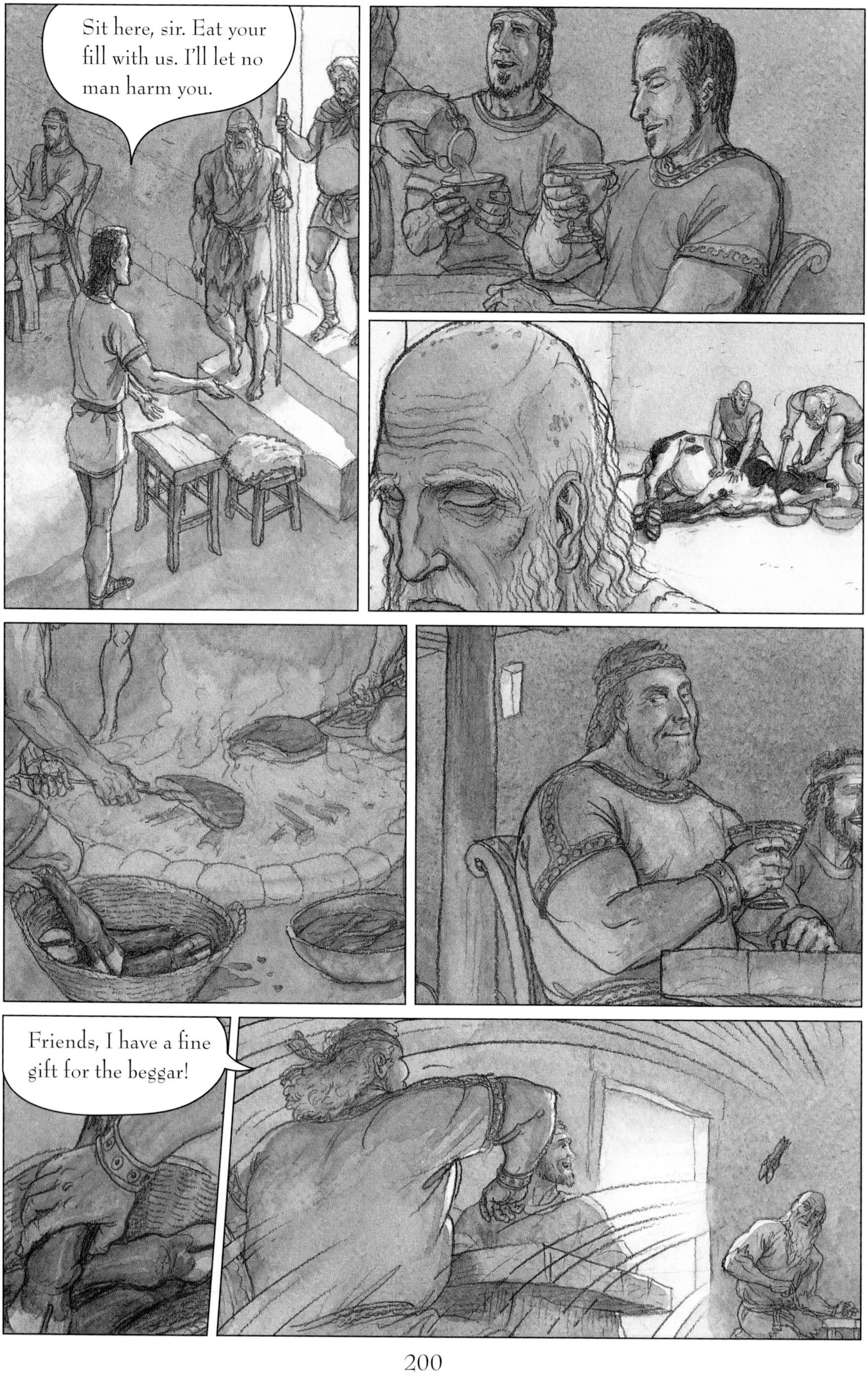
Sit here, sir. Eat your fill with us. I'll let no man harm you.
Friends, I have a fine gift for the beggar!

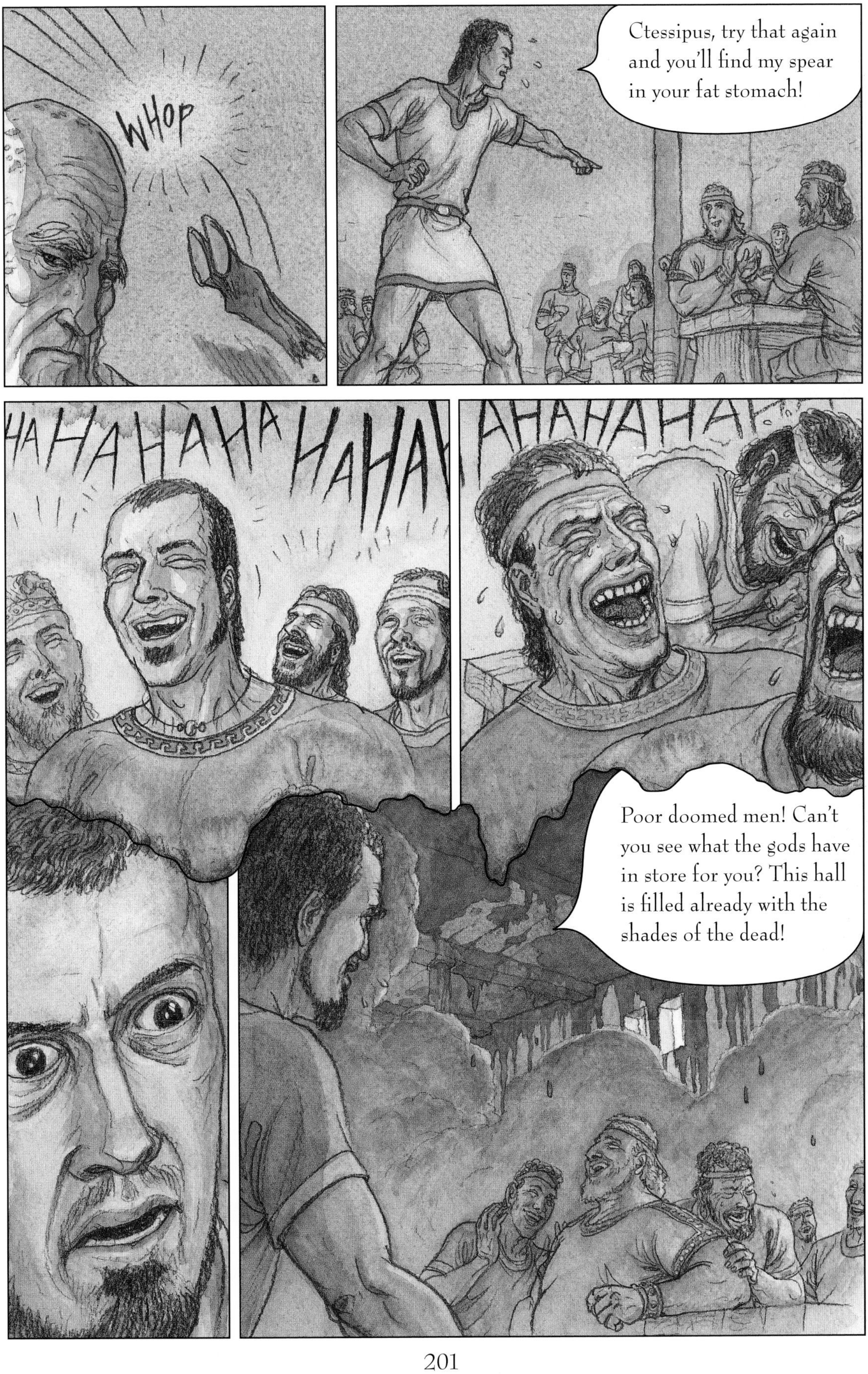
WHOP
Ctessipus, try that again and you'll find my spear in your fat stomach!
HAHAHAHAHAHAHA
AHAHAHAHA
Poor doomed men! Can't you see what the gods have in store for you? This hall is filled already with the shades of the dead!

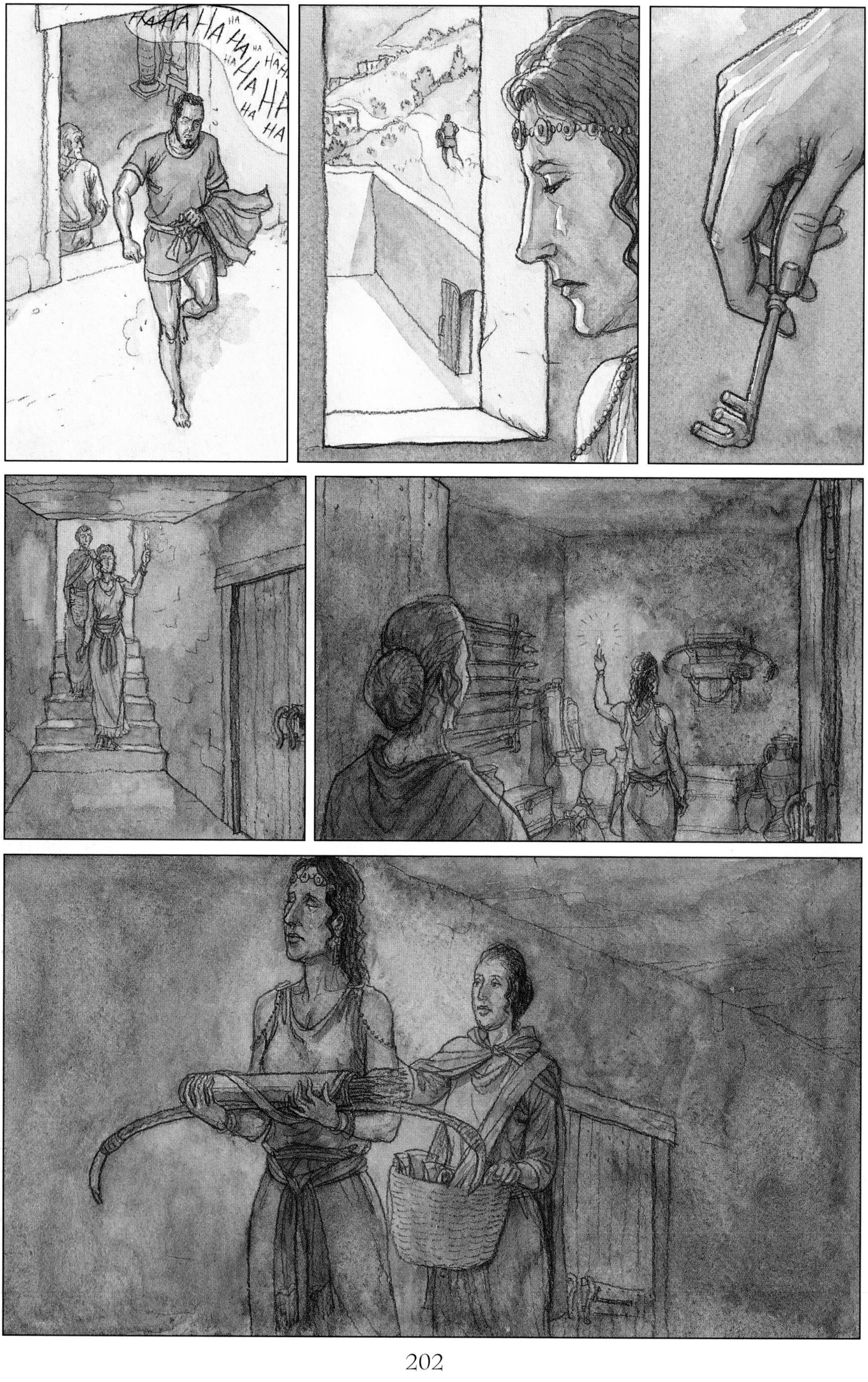
HA HA HA HA HA HA HA HA HA HA HA HA

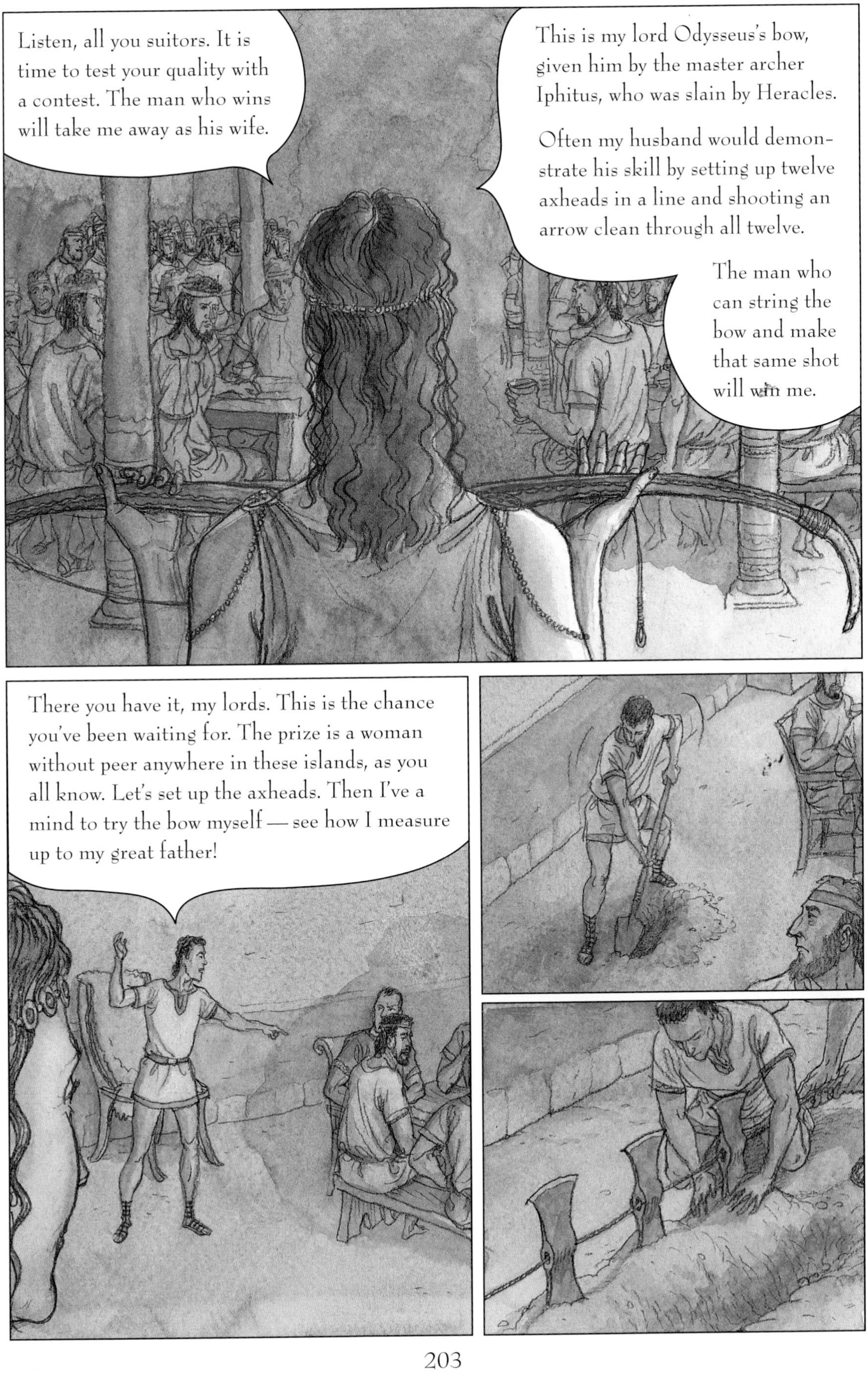
Listen, all you suitors. It is time to test your quality with a contest. The man who wins will take me away as his wife.
This is my lord Odysseus's bow, given him by the master archer Iphitus, who was slain by Heracles.
Often my husband would demonstrate his skill by setting up twelve axheads in a line and shooting an arrow clean through all twelve.
The man who can string the bow and make that same shot will win me.
There you have it, my lords. This is the chance you've been waiting for. The prize is a woman without peer anywhere in these islands, as you all know. Let's set up the axheads. Then I've a mind to try the bow myself — see how I measure up to my great father!

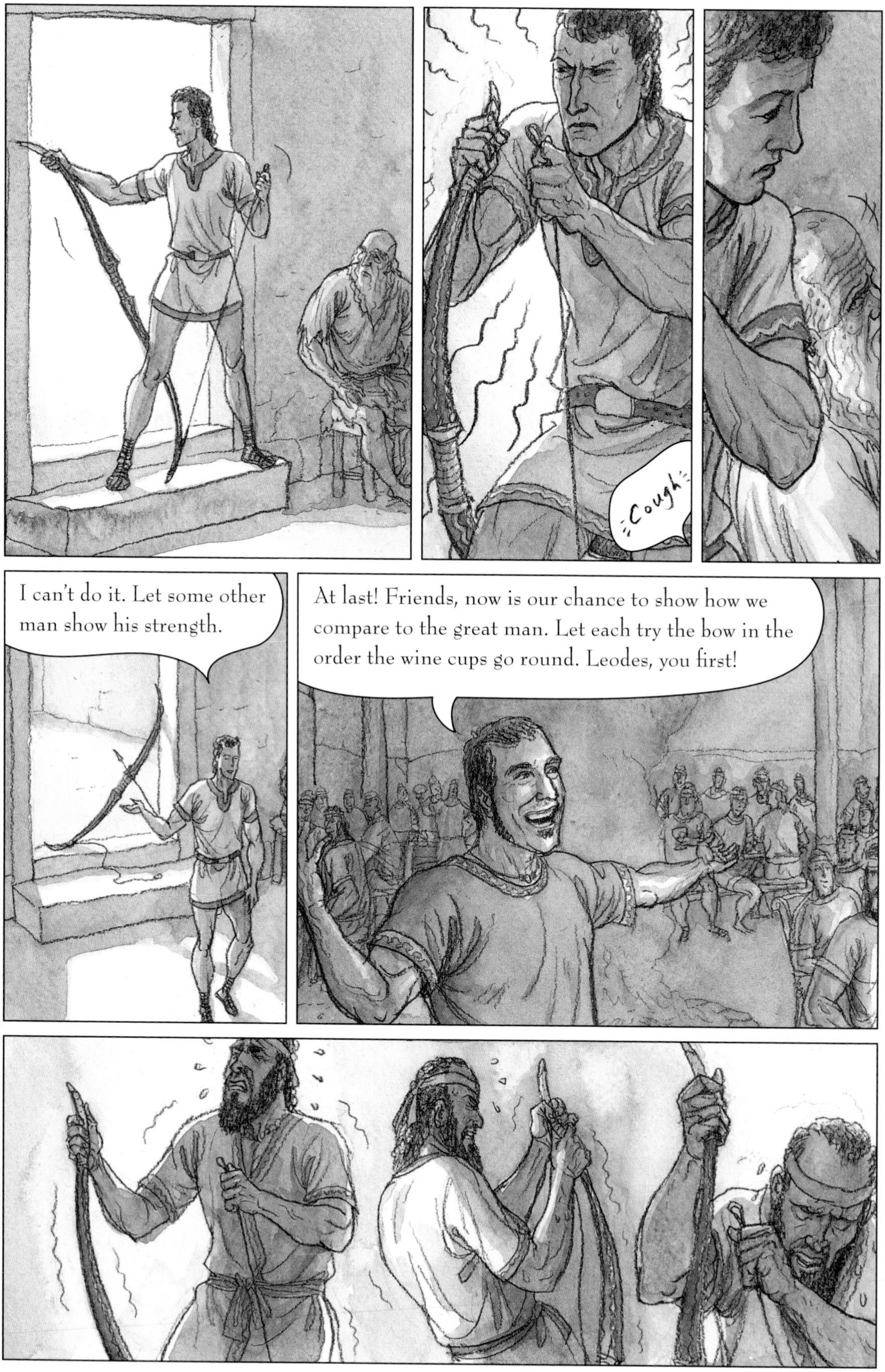
Cough
I can't do it. Let some other man show his strength.
At last! Friends, now is our chance to show how we compare to the great man. Let each try the bow in the order the wine cups go round. Leodes, you first!

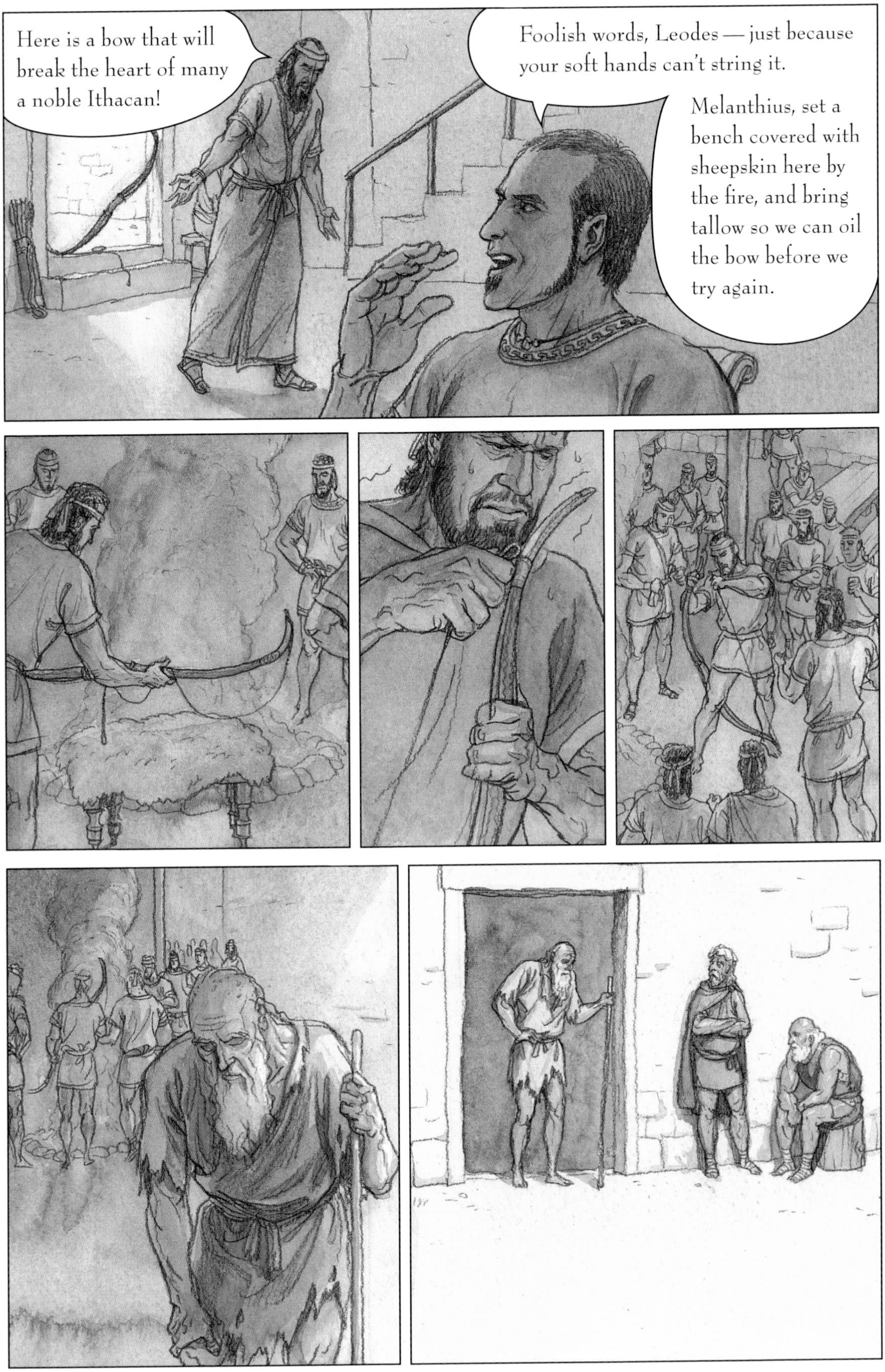
Here is a bow that will break the heart of many a noble Ithacan!
Foolish words, Leodes — just because your soft hands can't string it.
Melanthius, set a bench covered with sheepskin here by the fire, and bring tallow so we can oil the bow before we try again.

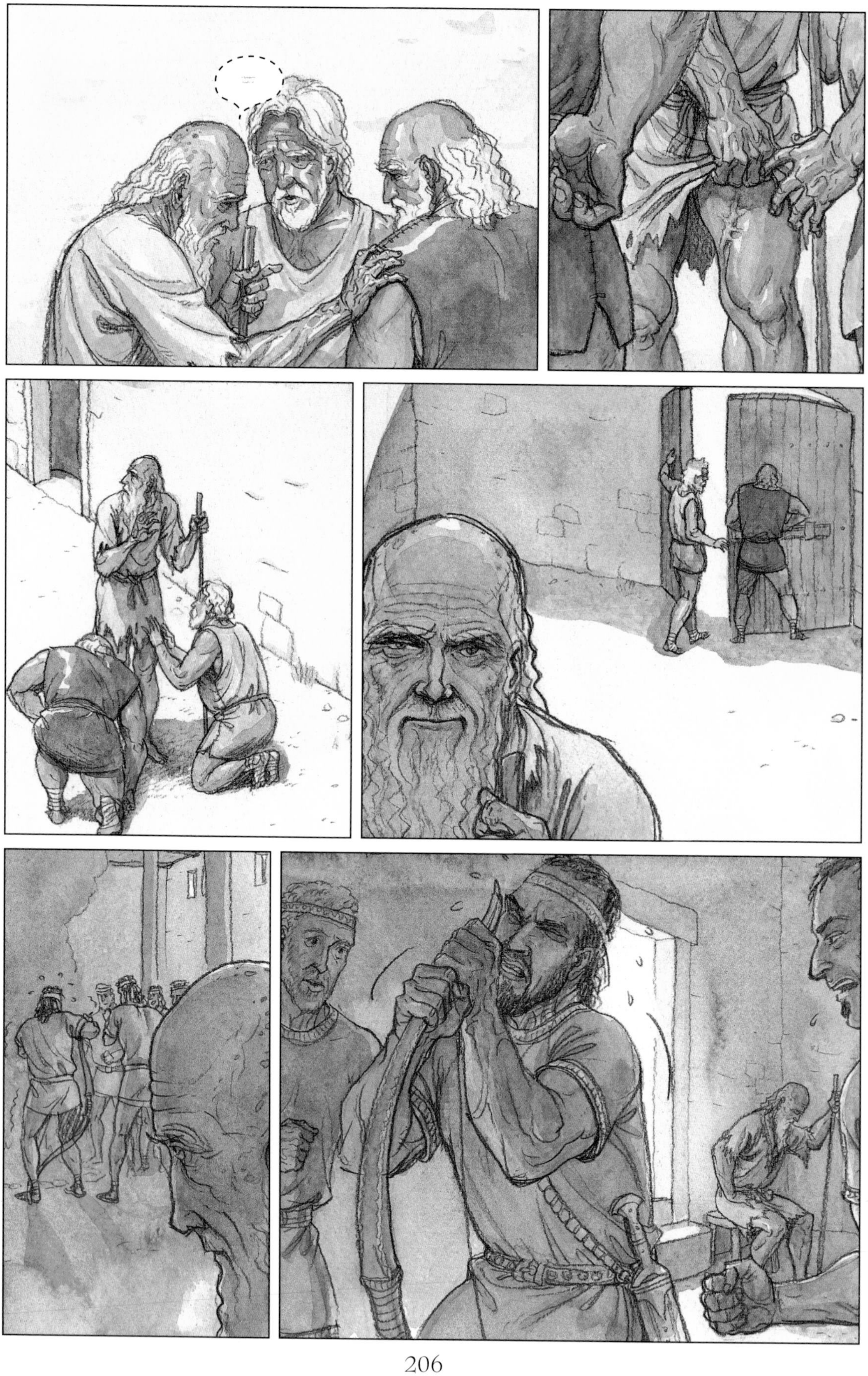

This is a cursed day for the island nobles. Odysseus's bow has made us all look like weaklings.

Never fear, Eurymachus and all you noble gentlemen. Today is Apollo's sacred holiday — no bow should be drawn today. Let's wait until morning, then offer up sacrifices to the archer god. Then we'll see who he favors to string the bow and make the shot.

Good princes, I must beg your leave to ask a favor.

Seeing all this has given me a keen desire to test my strength against the great bow of Odysseus, to see if I still have any muscle left in these old arms.

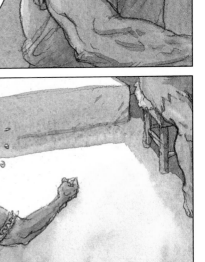

What gall! Quiet, beggar, or we'll drag you out of here.

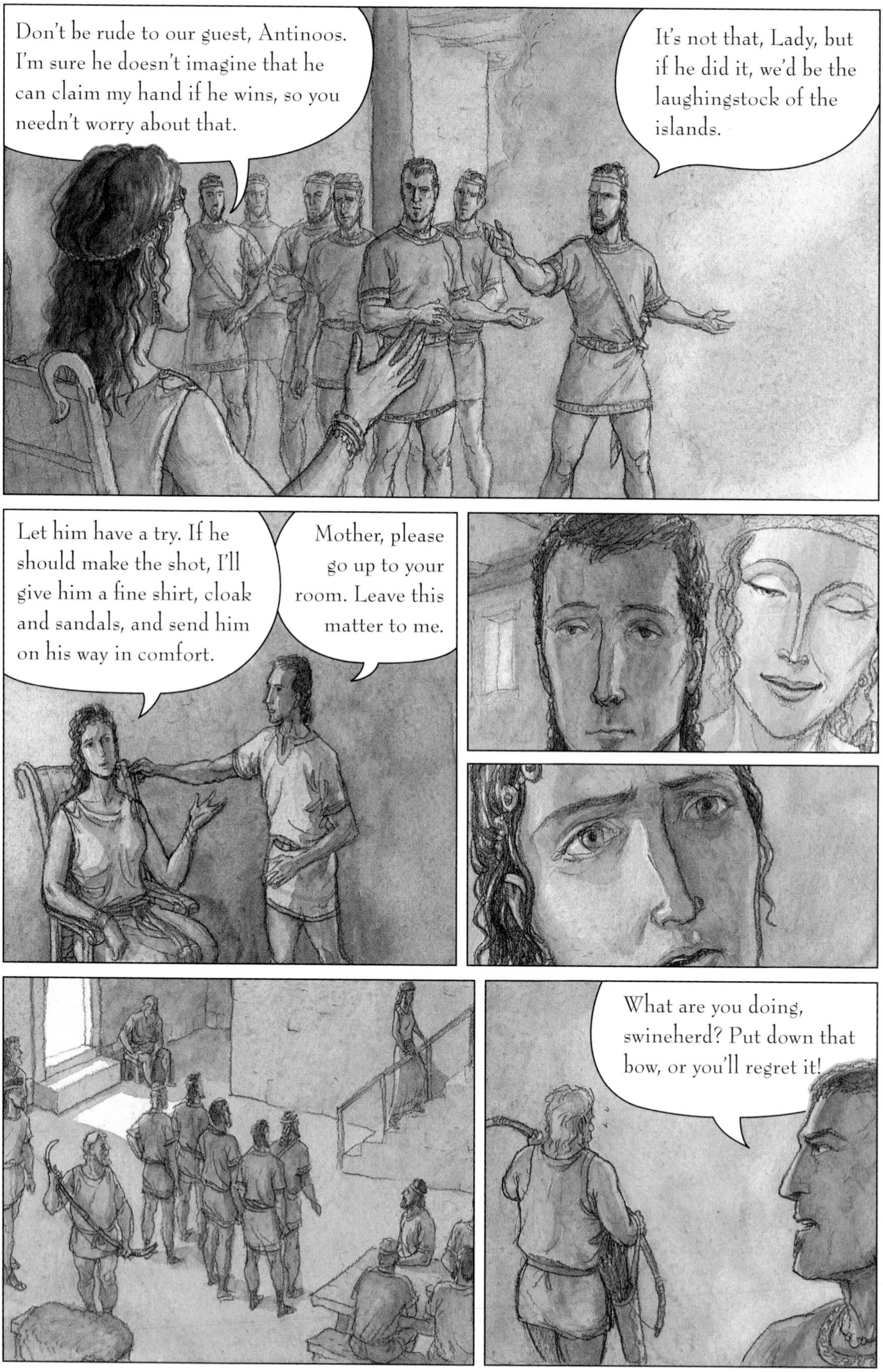
Don't be rude to our guest, Antinoos. I'm sure he doesn't imagine that he can claim my hand if he wins, so you needn't worry about that.
It's not that, Lady, but if he did it, we'd be the laughingstock of the islands.
Let him have a try. If he should make the shot, I'll give him a fine shirt, cloak and sandals, and send him on his way in comfort.
Mother, please go up to your room. Leave this matter to me.
What are you doing, swineherd? Put down that bow, or you'll regret it!

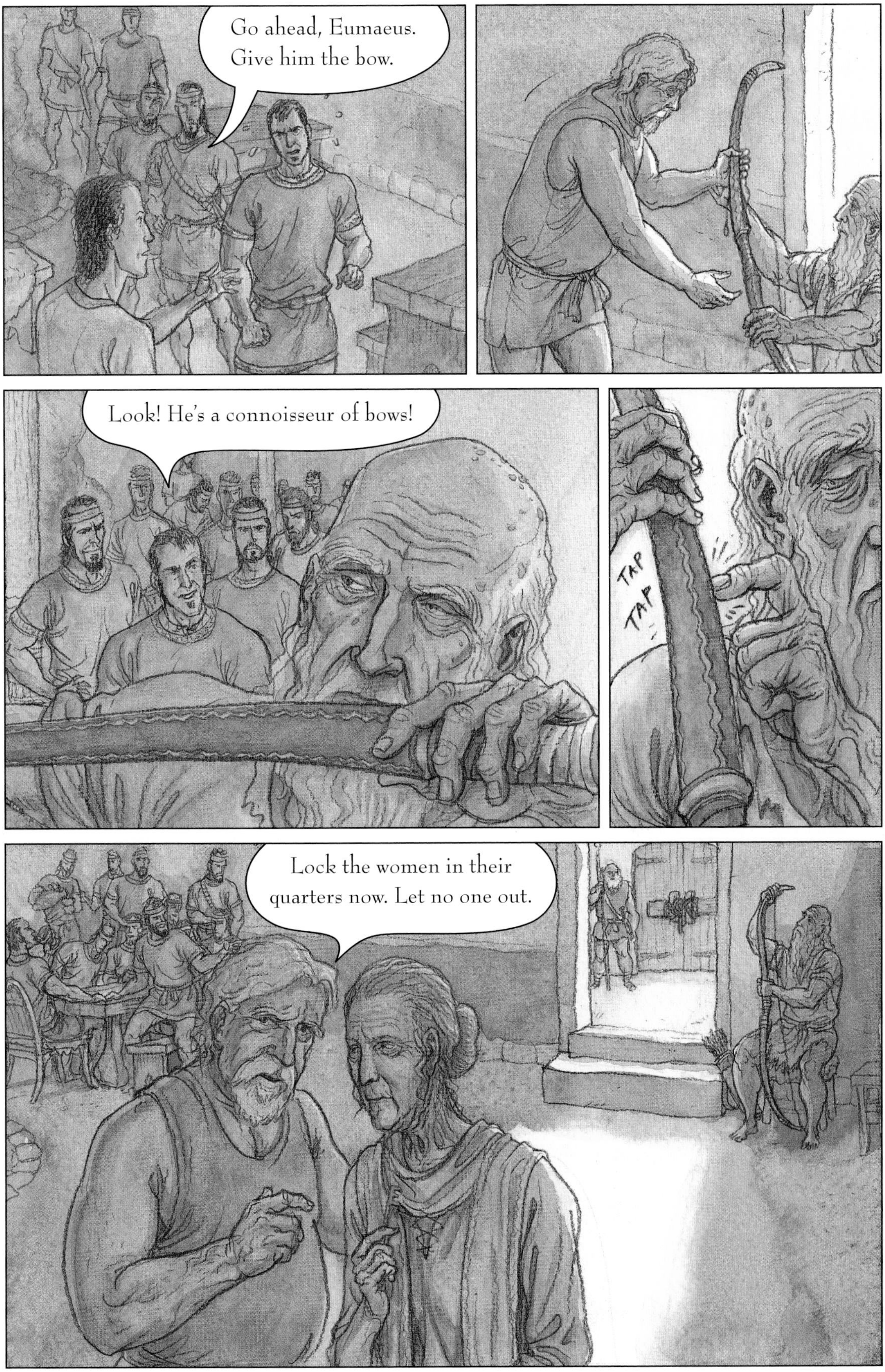
Go ahead, Eumaeus.
Give him the bow.
Look! He's a connoisseur of bows!
TAP
TAP
Lock the women in their
quarters now. Let no one out.

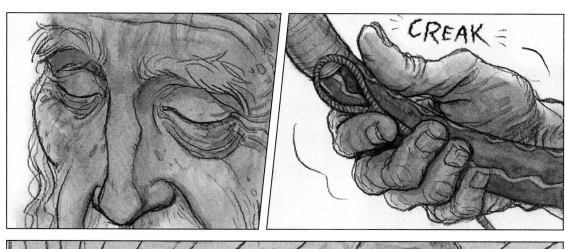

CREAK

SHICK

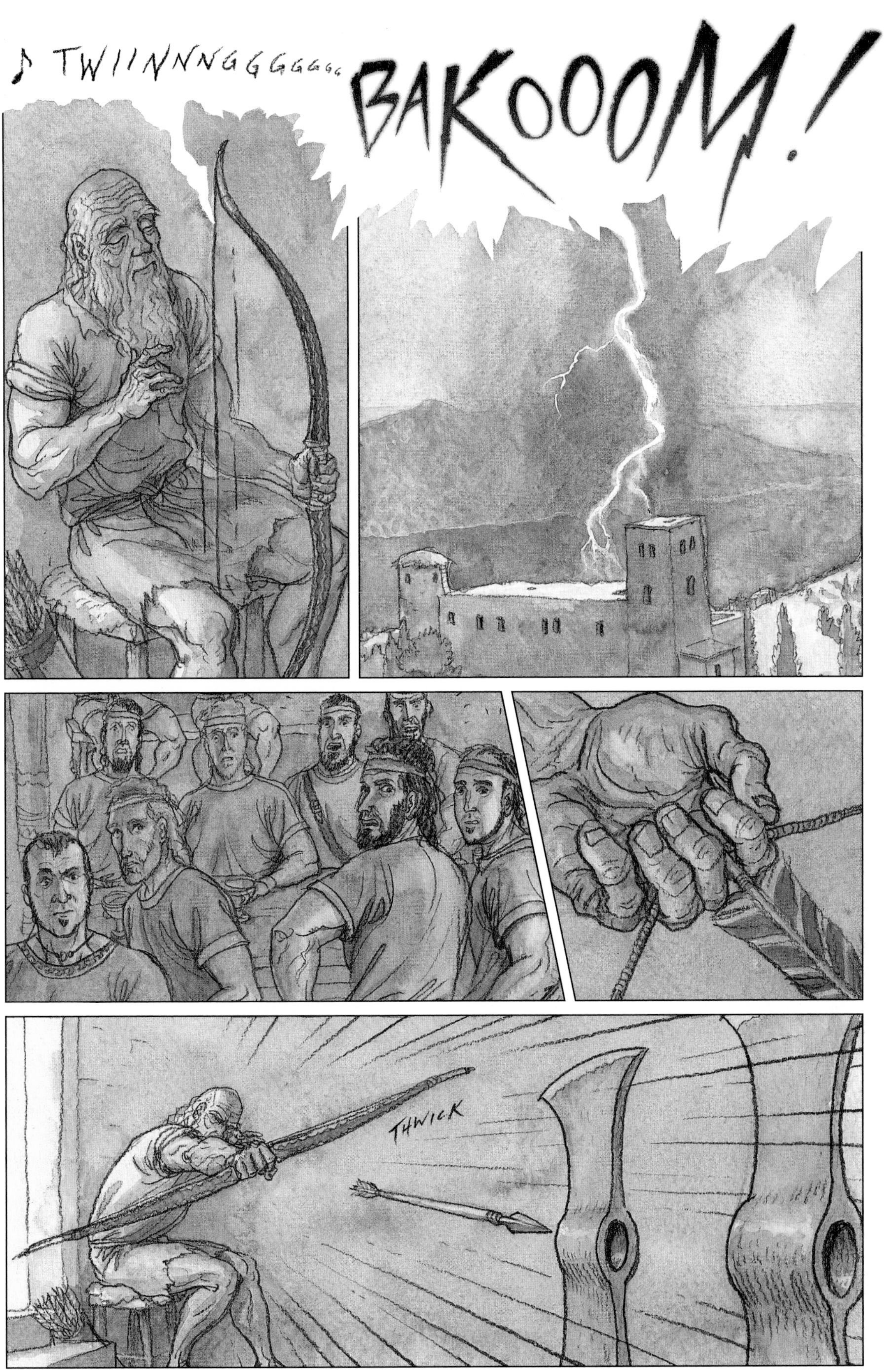
♪ TWIINNNGGGGGG...
BAKOOOM!
THWICK

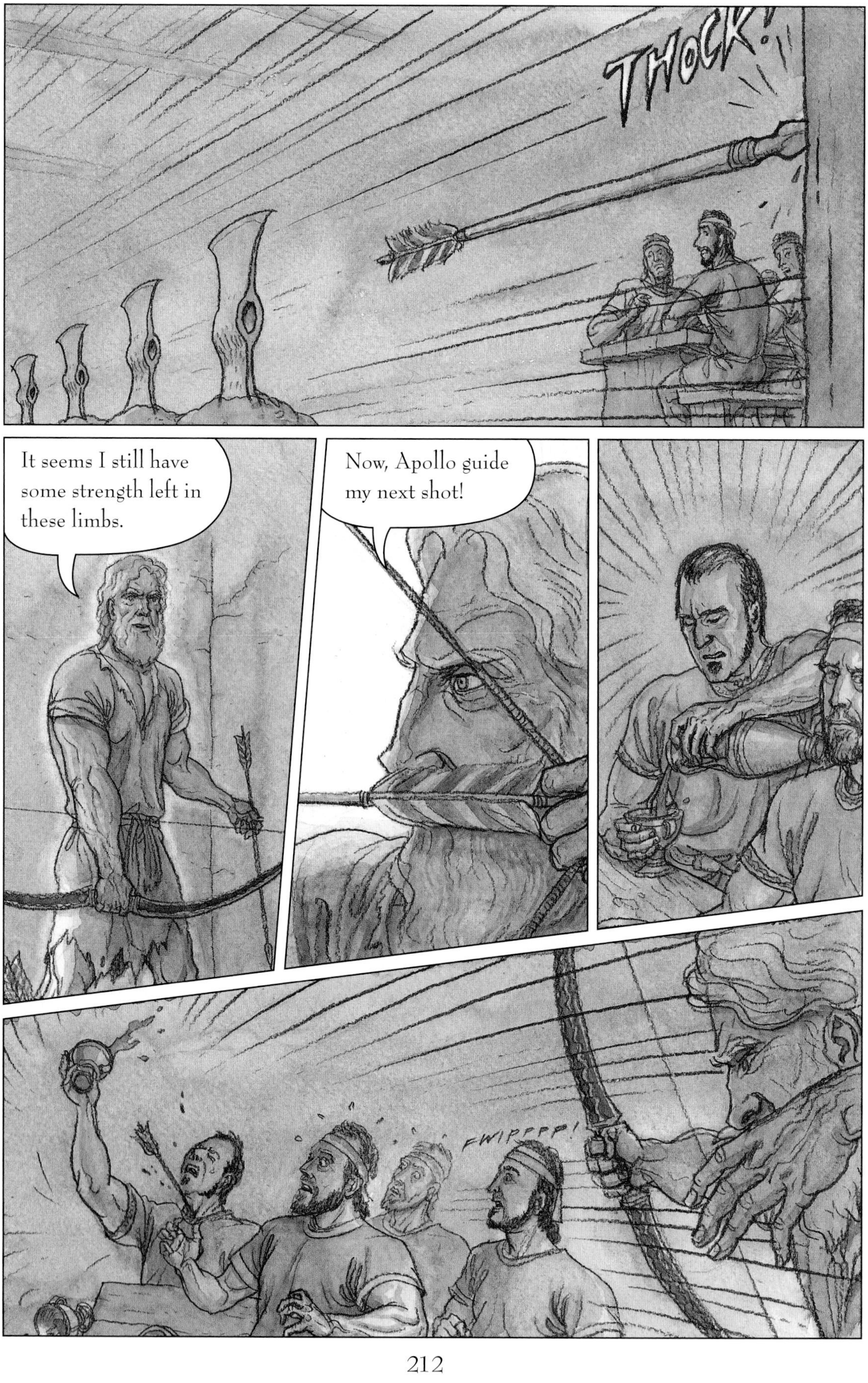
THOCK!
It seems I still have some strength left in these limbs.
Now, Apollo guide my next shot!
FWIPPPP!

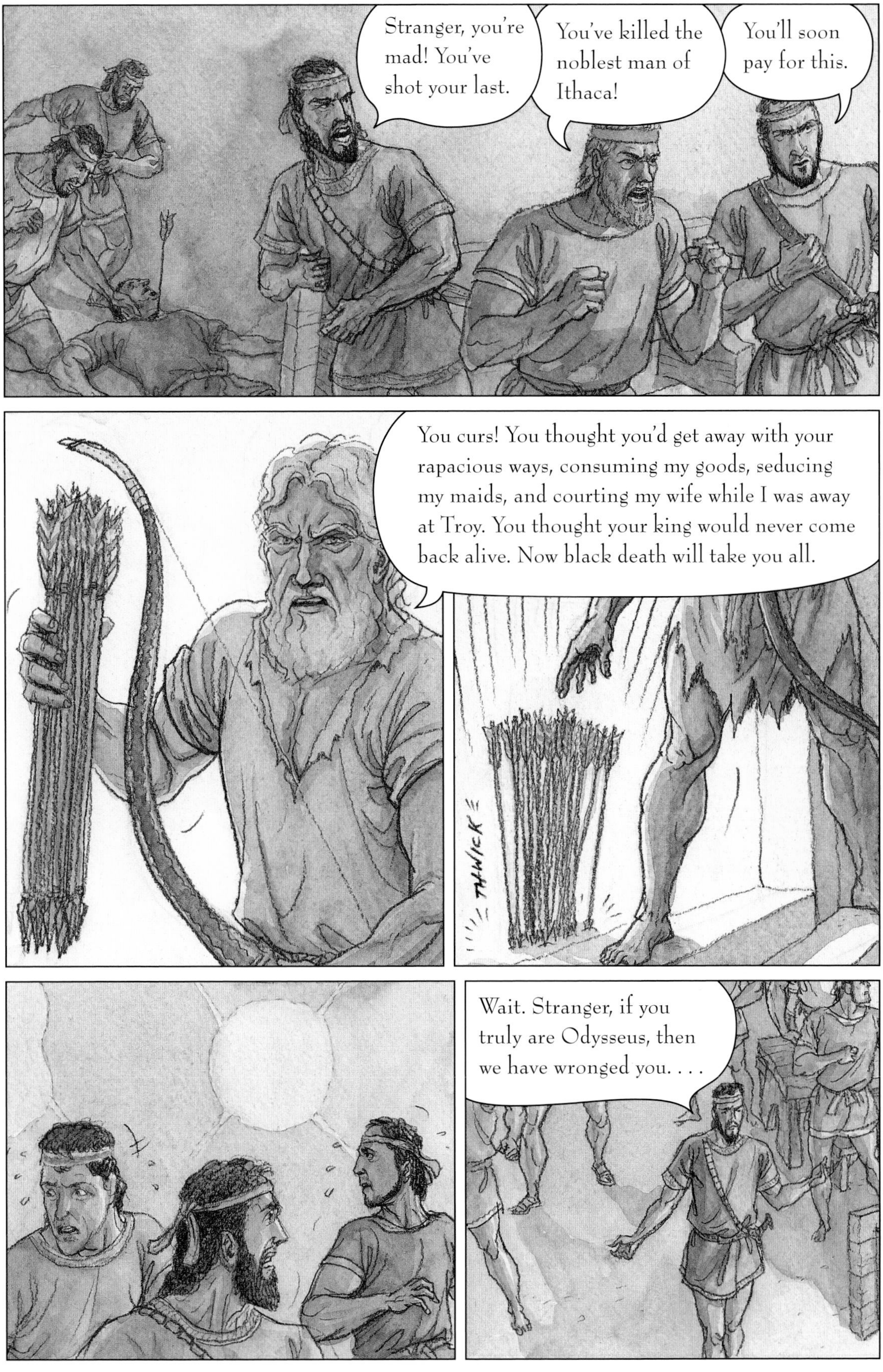
Stranger, you're mad! You've shot your last.
You've killed the noblest man of Ithaca!
You'll soon pay for this.
You curs! You thought you'd get away with your rapacious ways, consuming my goods, seducing my maids, and courting my wife while I was away at Troy. You thought your king would never come back alive. Now black death will take you all.
THWICK
Wait. Stranger, if you truly are Odysseus, then we have wronged you. . . .

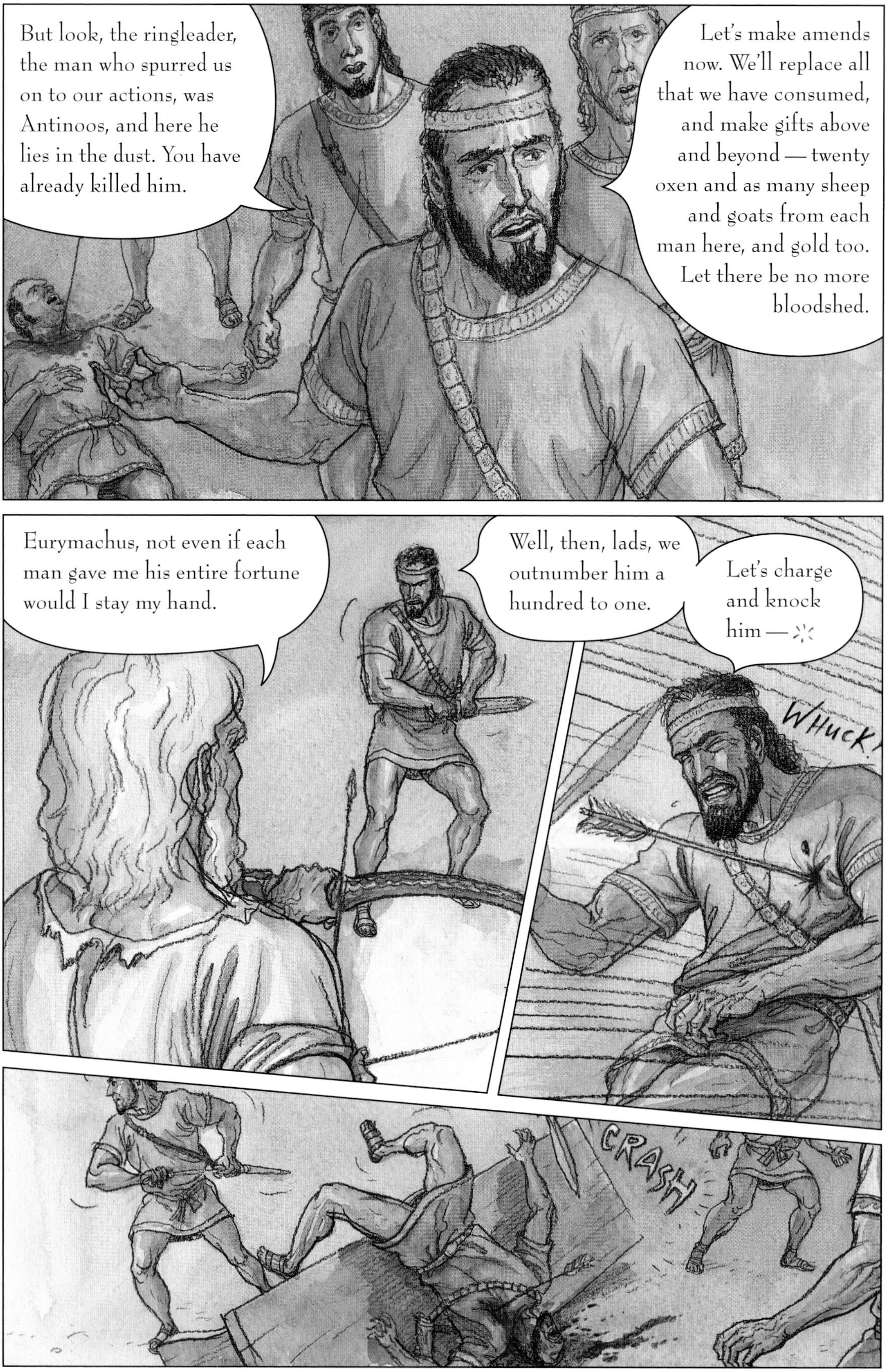
But look, the ringleader, the man who spurred us on to our actions, was Antinoos, and here he lies in the dust. You have already killed him.
Let's make amends now. We'll replace all that we have consumed, and make gifts above and beyond — twenty oxen and as many sheep and goats from each man here, and gold too. Let there be no more bloodshed.
Eurymachus, not even if each man gave me his entire fortune would I stay my hand.
Well, then, lads, we outnumber him a hundred to one.
Let's charge and knock him —
WHUCK!
CRASH

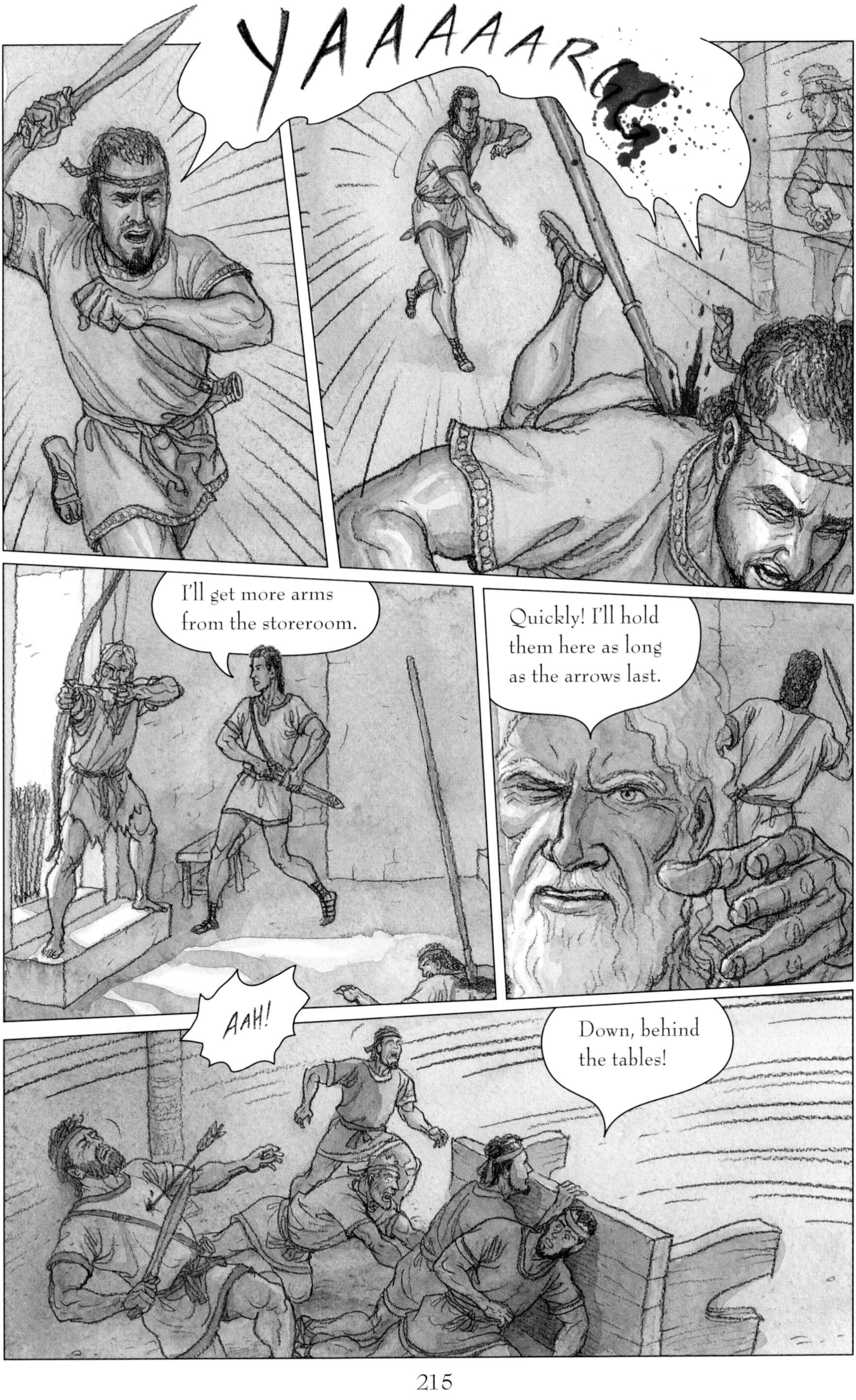
YAAAARG
I'll get more arms from the storeroom.
Quickly! I'll hold them here as long as the arrows last.
AAH!
Down, behind the tables!

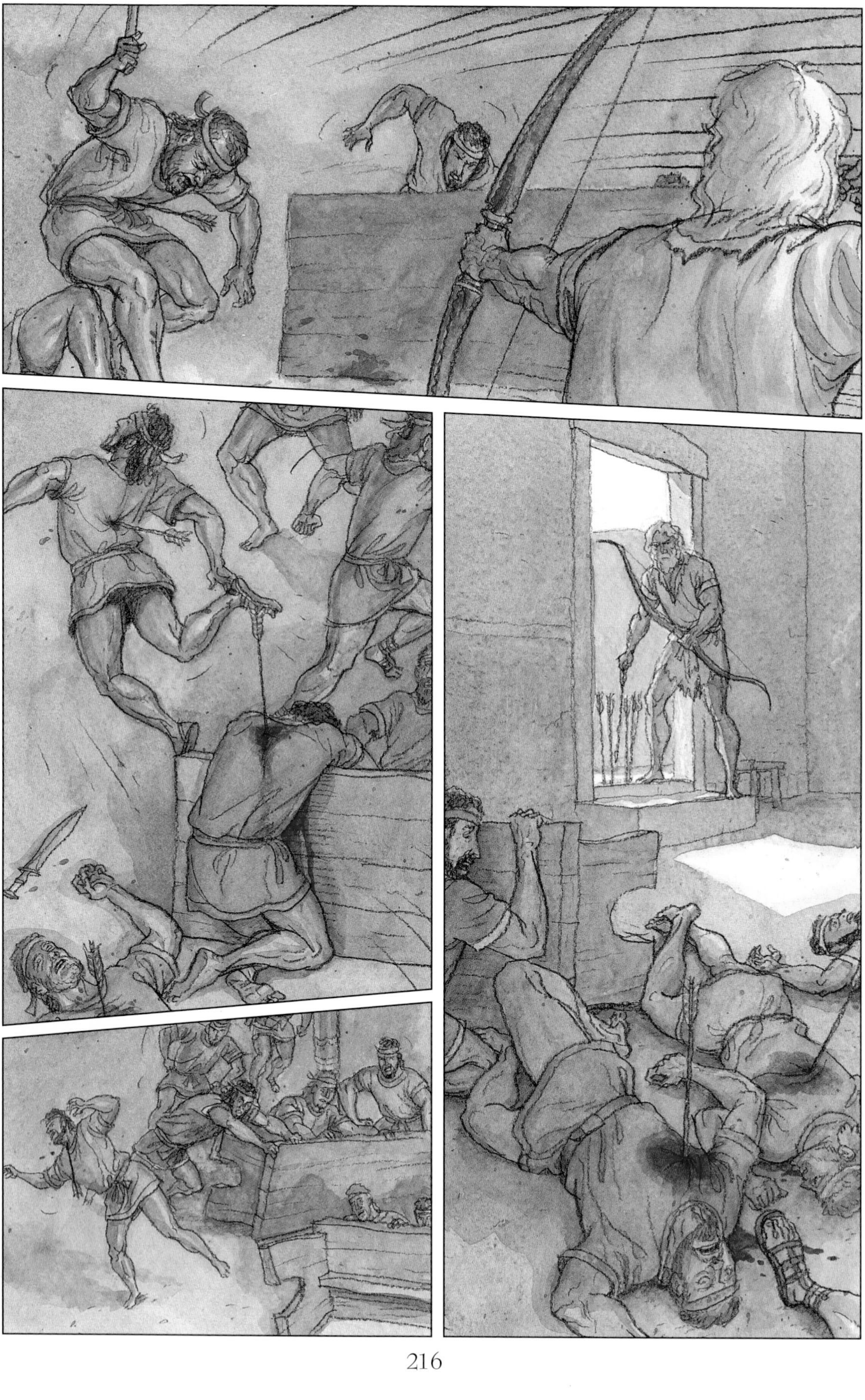

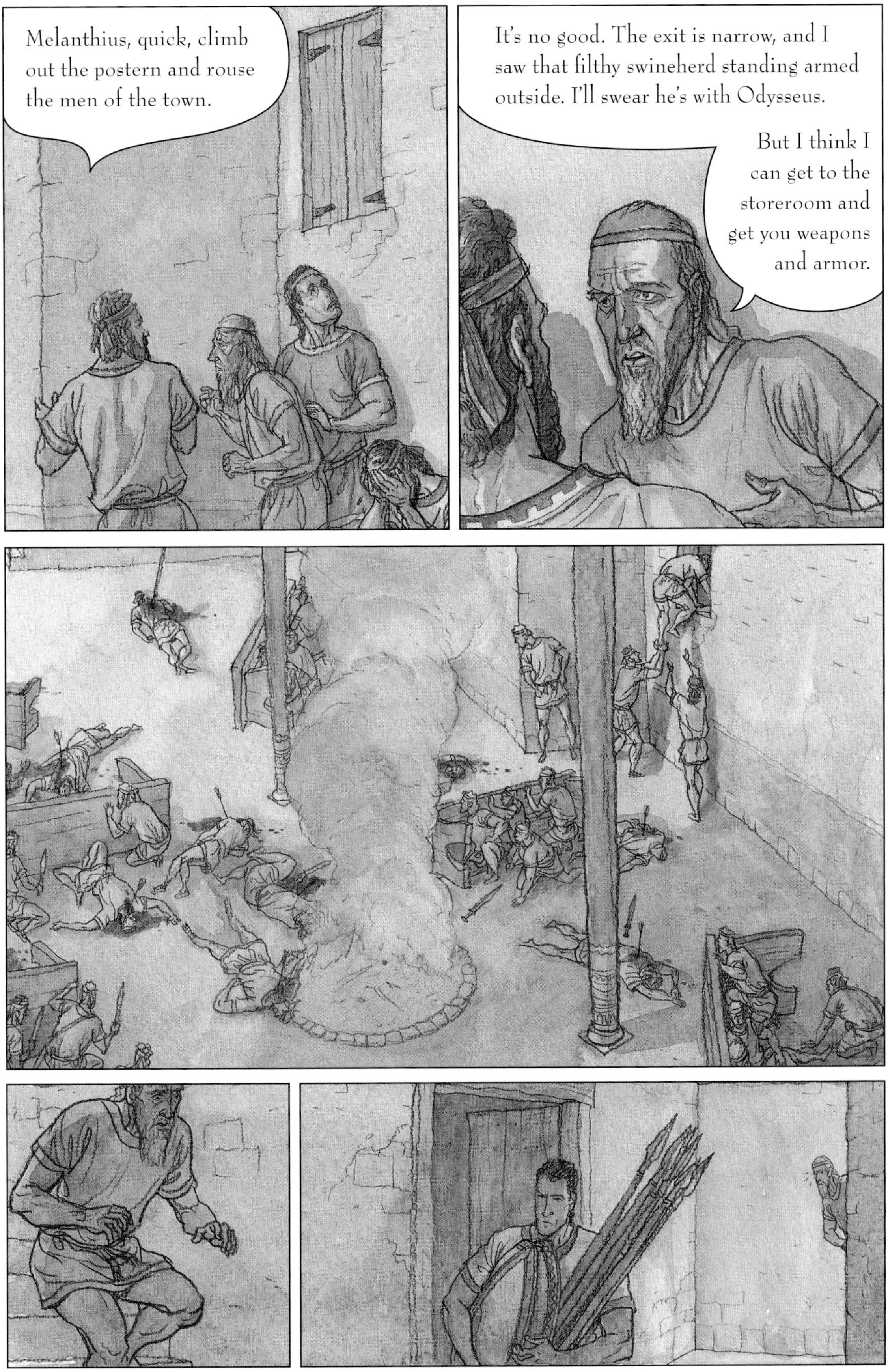
Melanthius, quick, climb out the postern and rouse the men of the town.
It's no good. The exit is narrow, and I saw that filthy swineherd standing armed outside. I'll swear he's with Odysseus.
But I think I can get to the storeroom and get you weapons and armor.

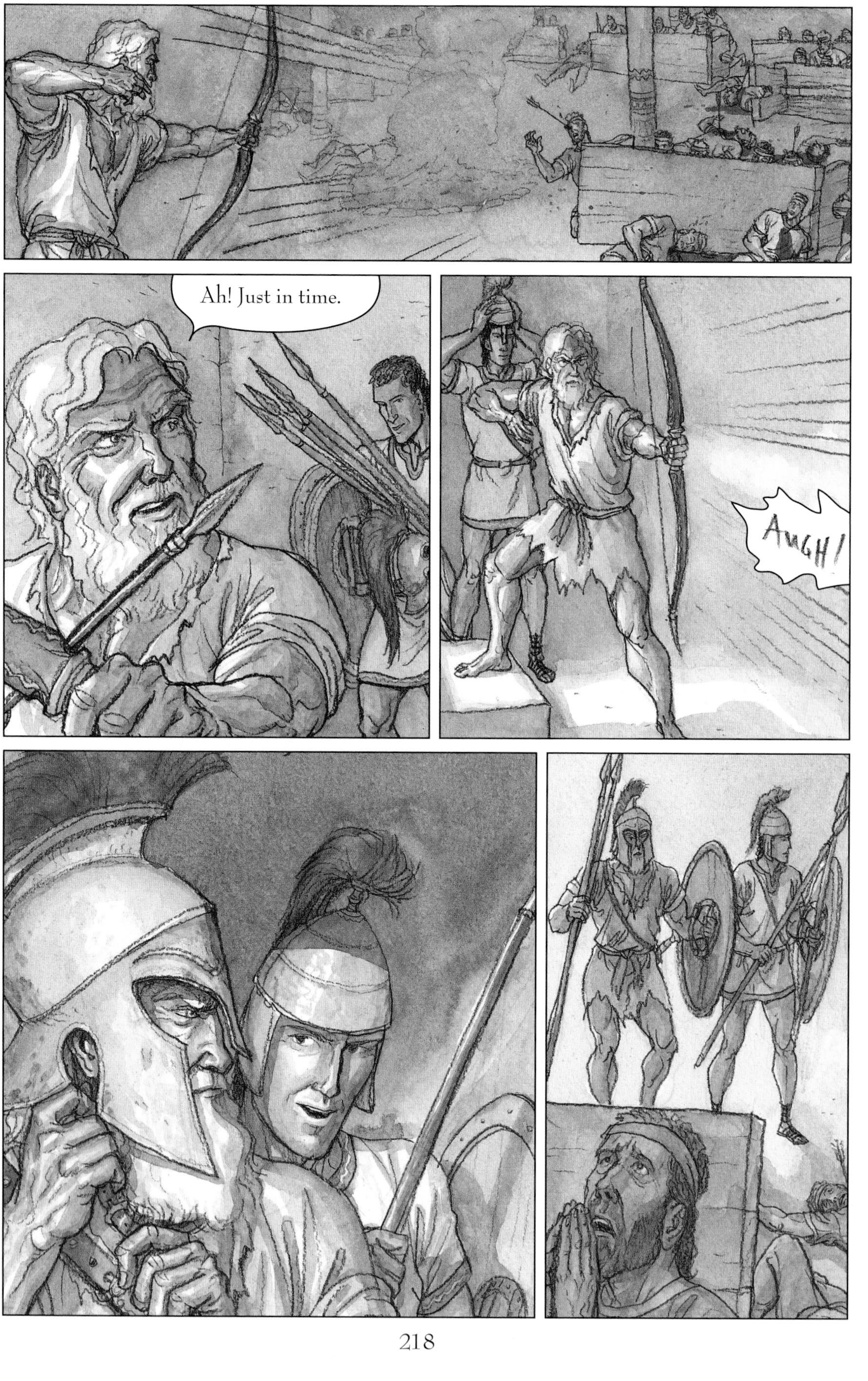
Ah! Just in time.
AUGH!

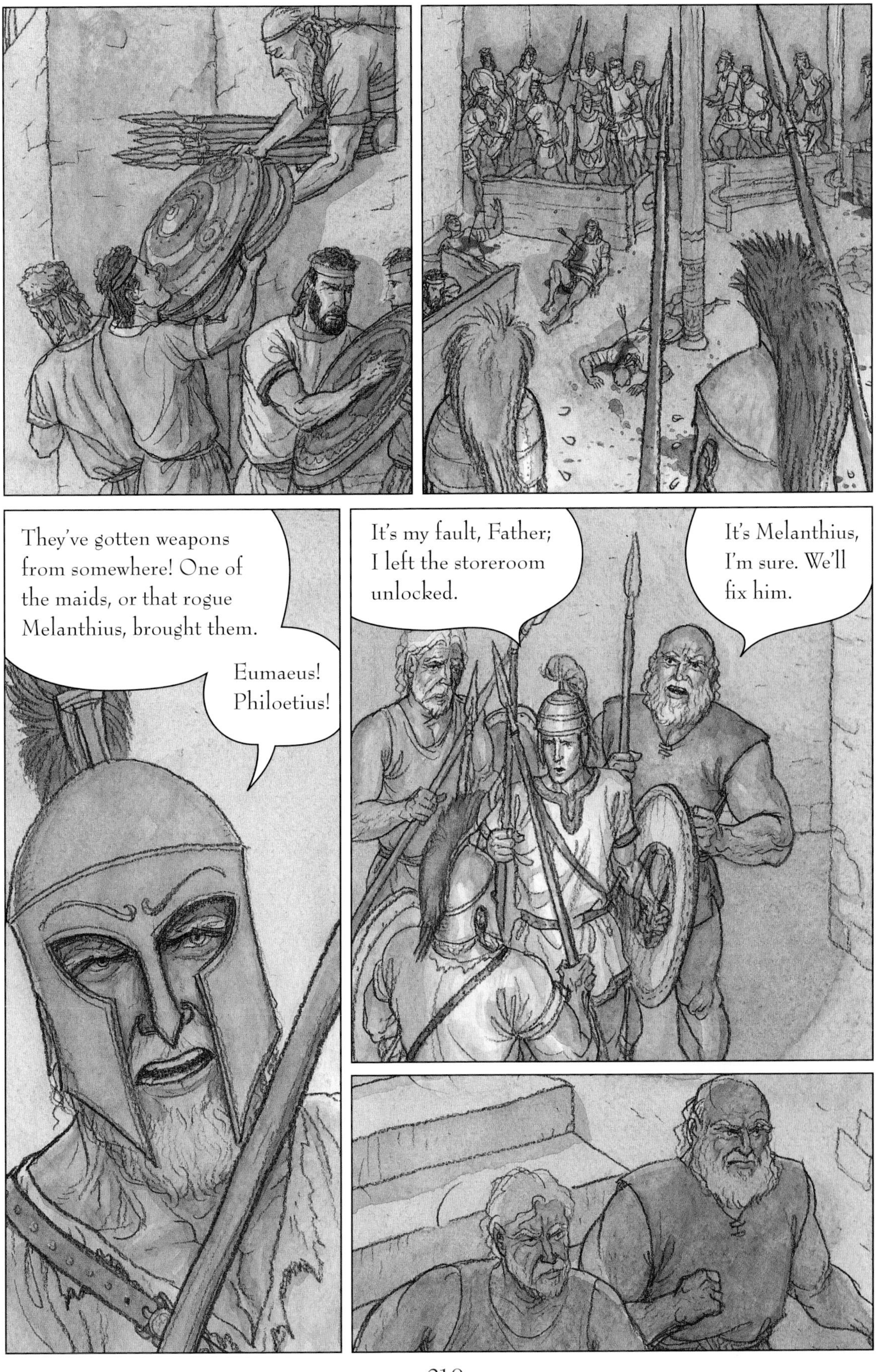
They've gotten weapons from somewhere! One of the maids, or that rogue Melanthius, brought them.
Eumaeus! Philoetius!
It's my fault, Father; I left the storeroom unlocked.
It's Melanthius, I'm sure. We'll fix him.

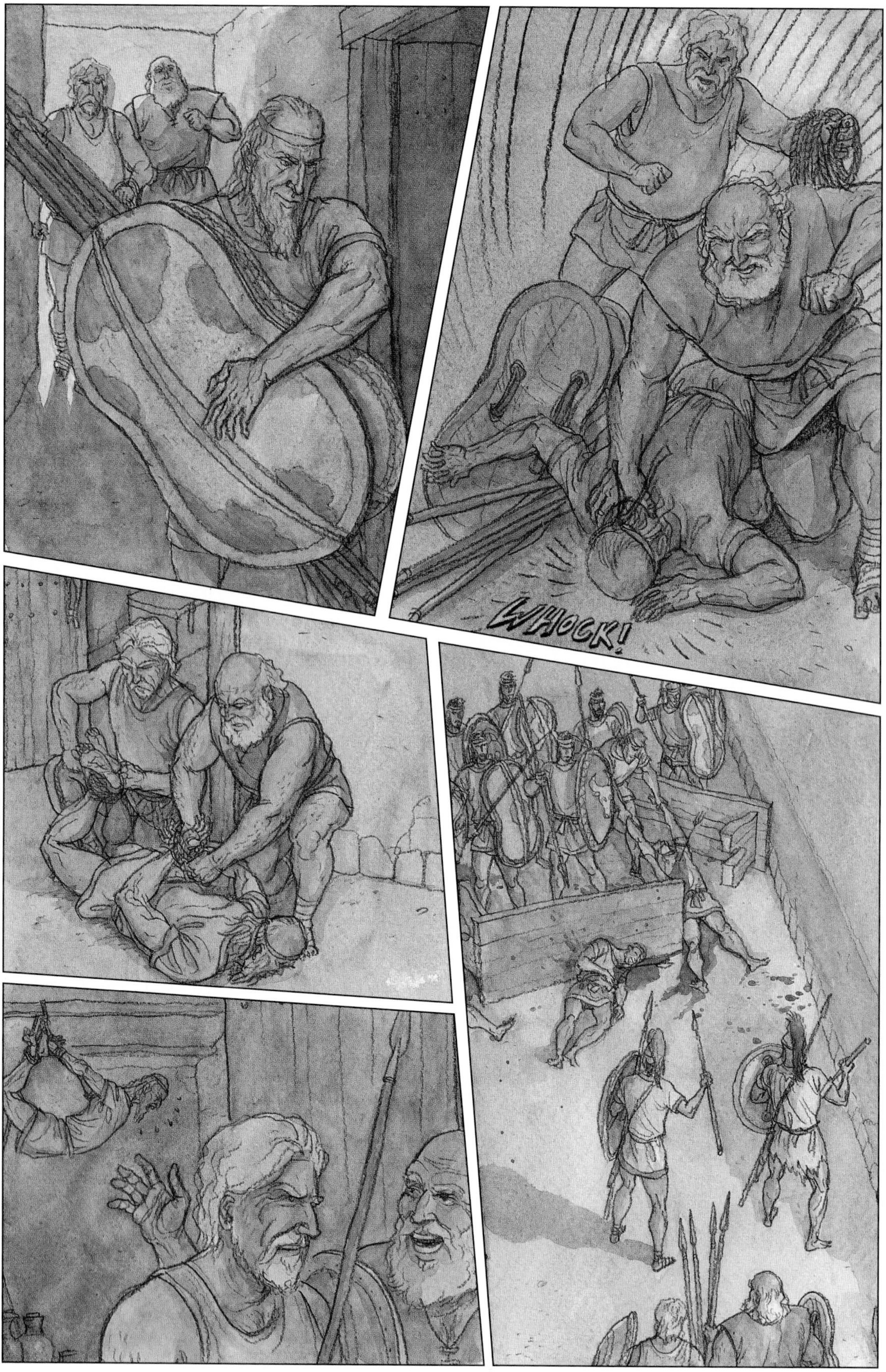
WHOCK!

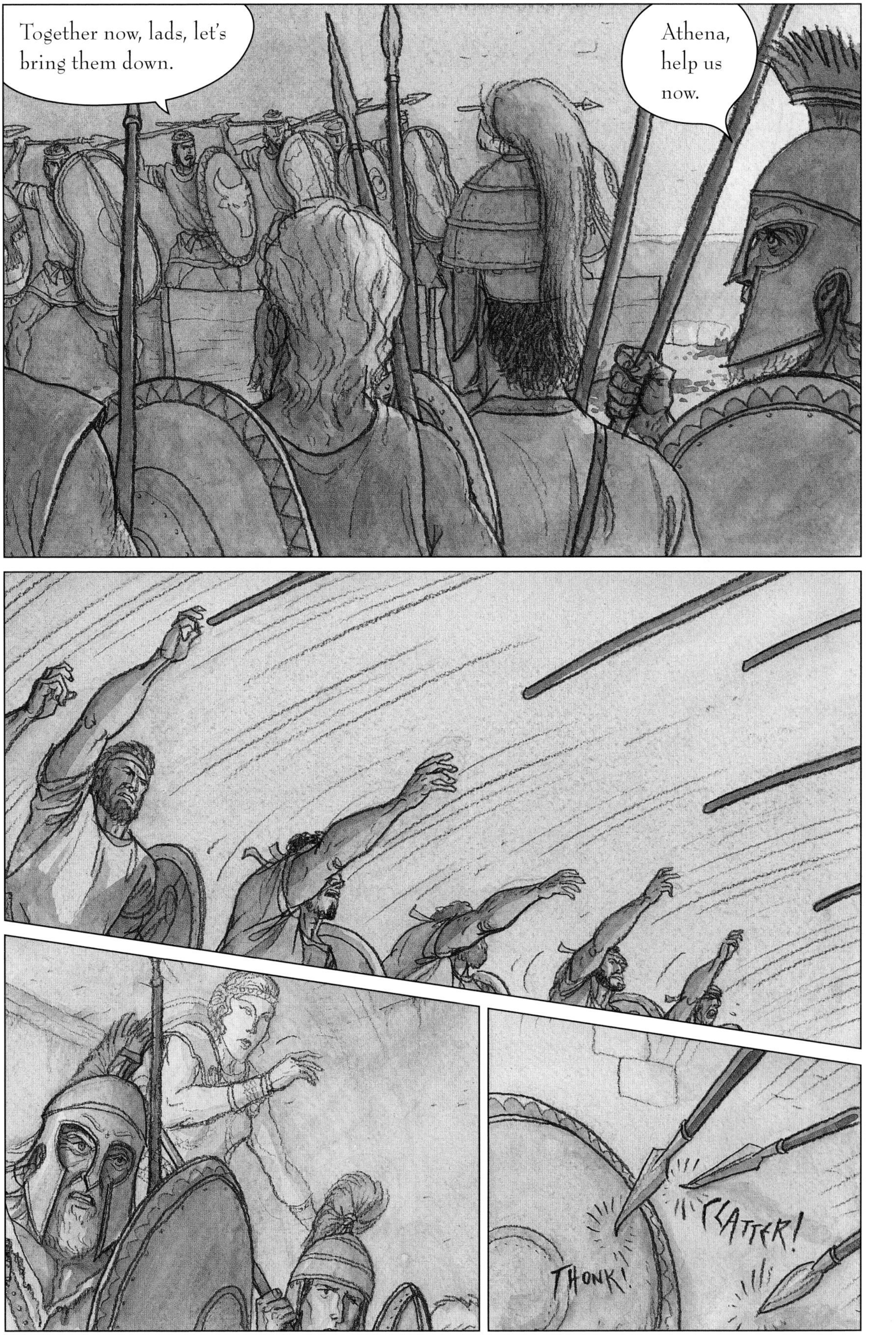
Together now, lads, let's bring them down.
Athena, help us now.
CLATTER!
THONK!

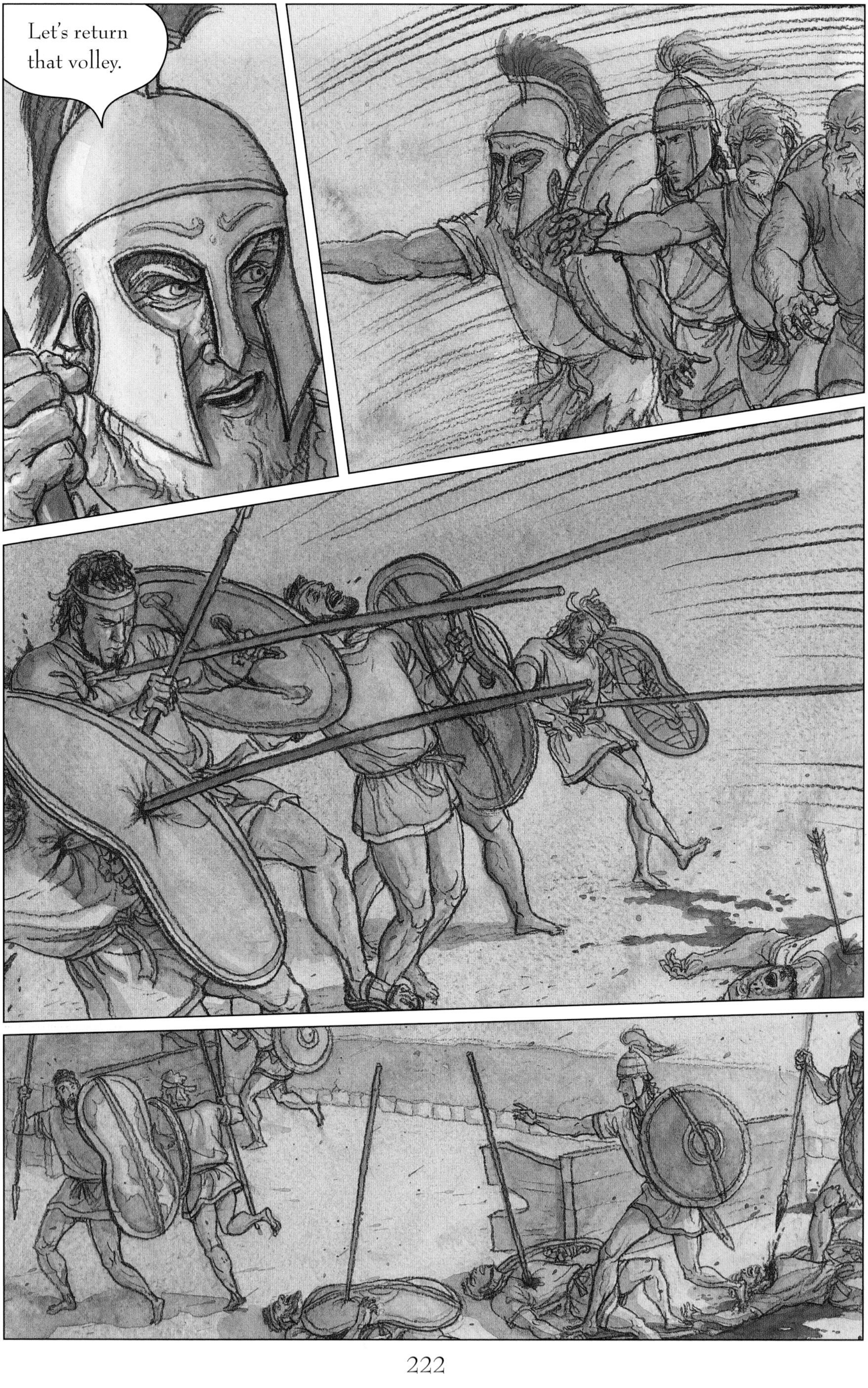
Let's return that volley.

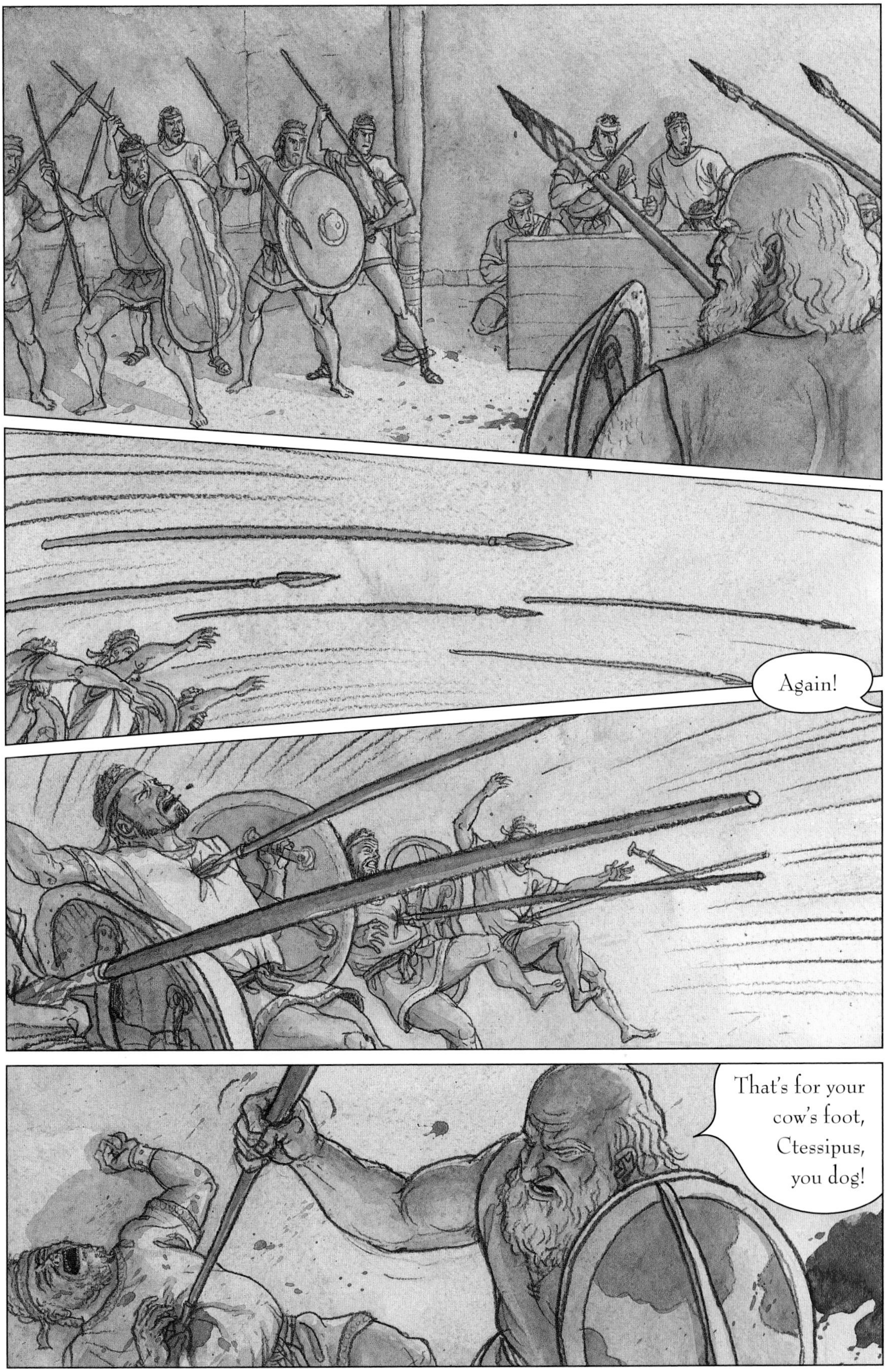
Again!
That's for your cow's foot, Ctessipus, you dog!

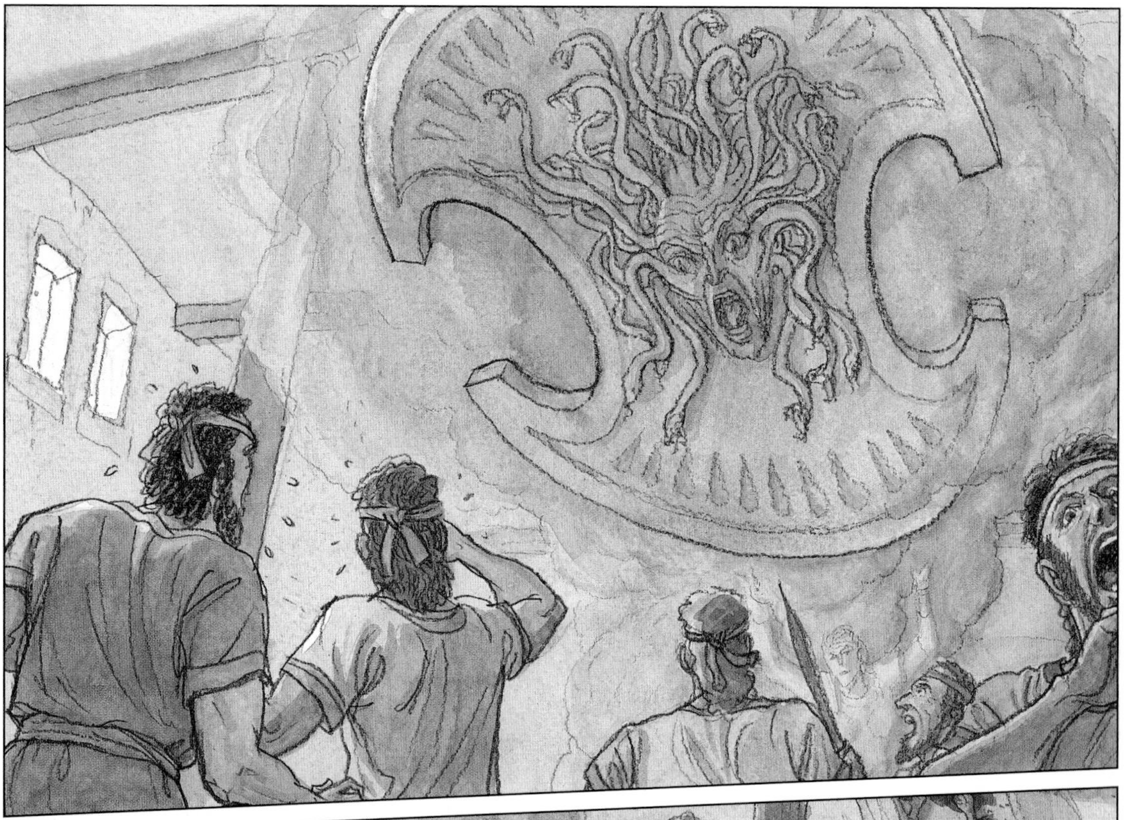

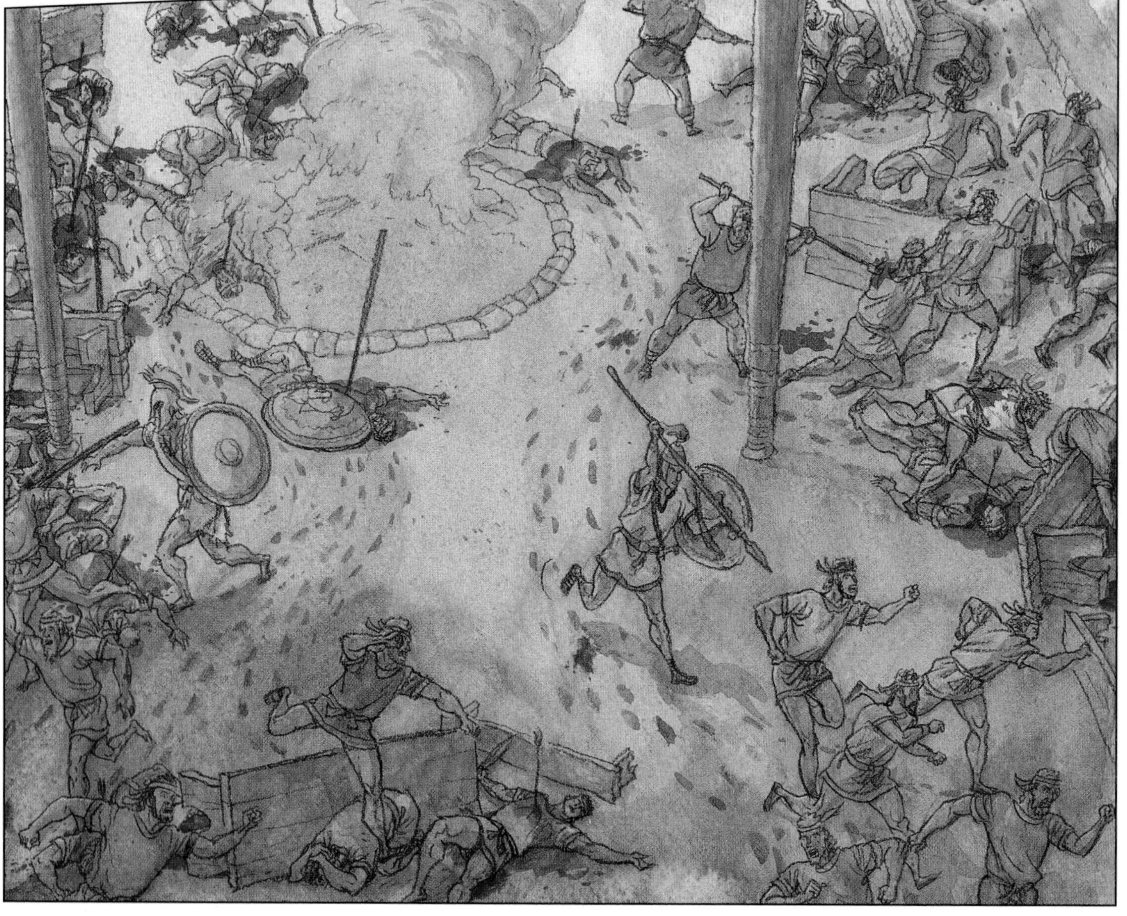

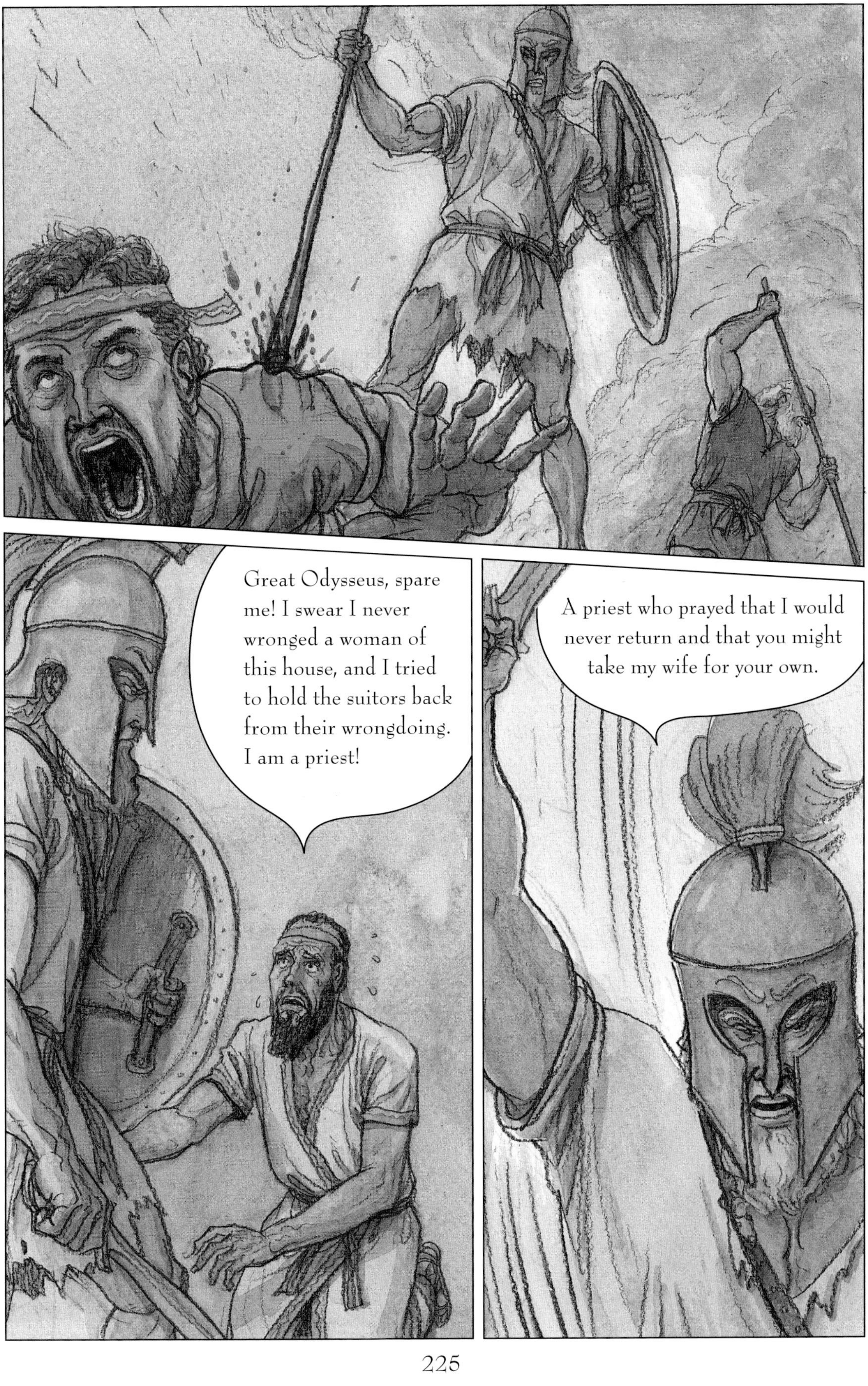
Great Odysseus, spare me! I swear I never wronged a woman of this house, and I tried to hold the suitors back from their wrongdoing. I am a priest!
A priest who prayed that I would never return and that you might take my wife for your own.

SWOCK!

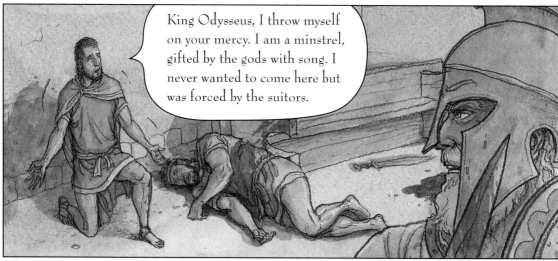

King Odysseus, I throw myself on your mercy. I am a minstrel, gifted by the gods with song. I never wanted to come here but was forced by the suitors.

Don't kill him! He speaks truly.

And there's another we should spare, if he's still alive — Medon, the herald. He's loyal to us.

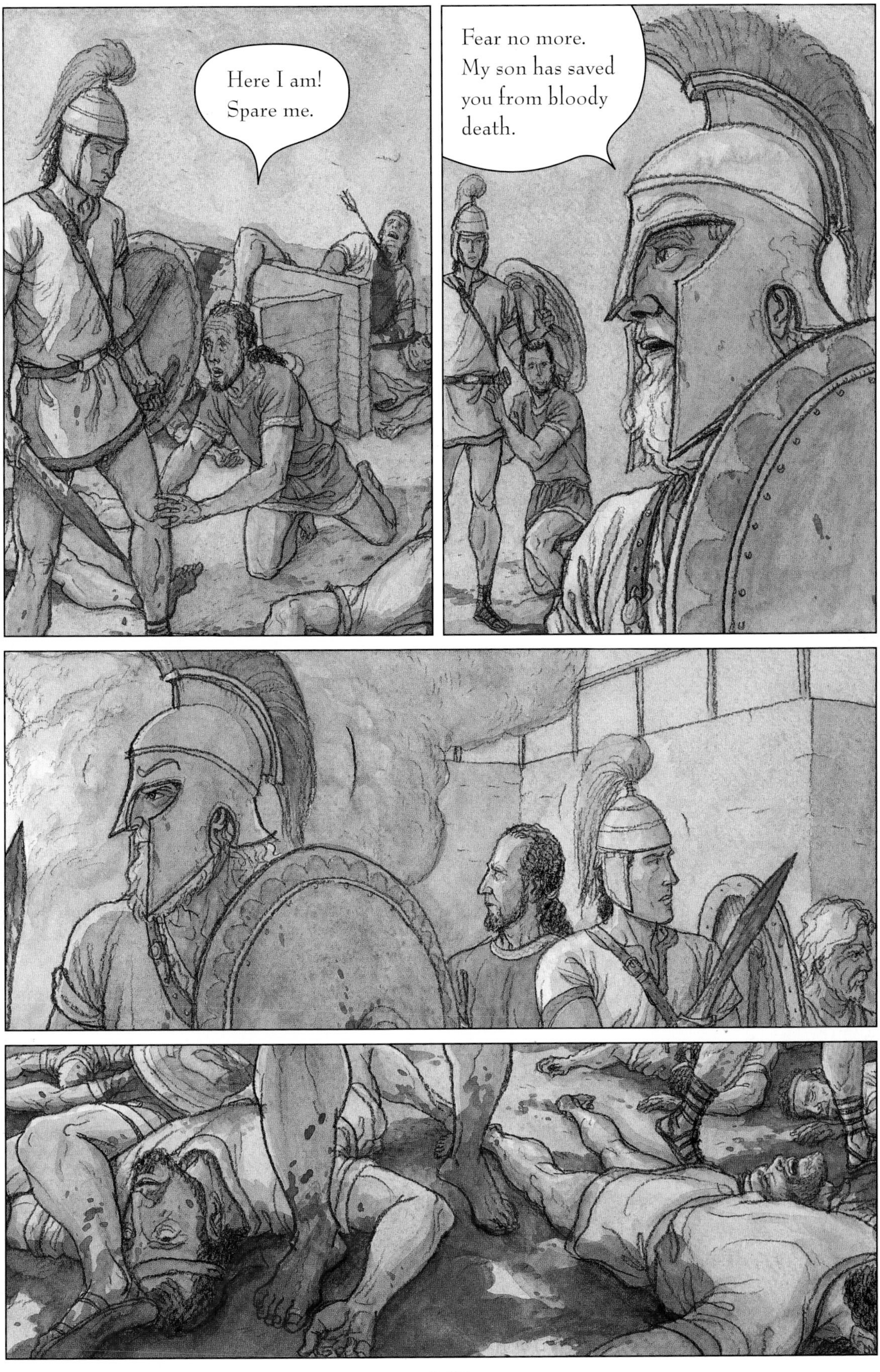
Here I am!
Spare me.
Fear no more.
My son has saved
you from bloody
death.

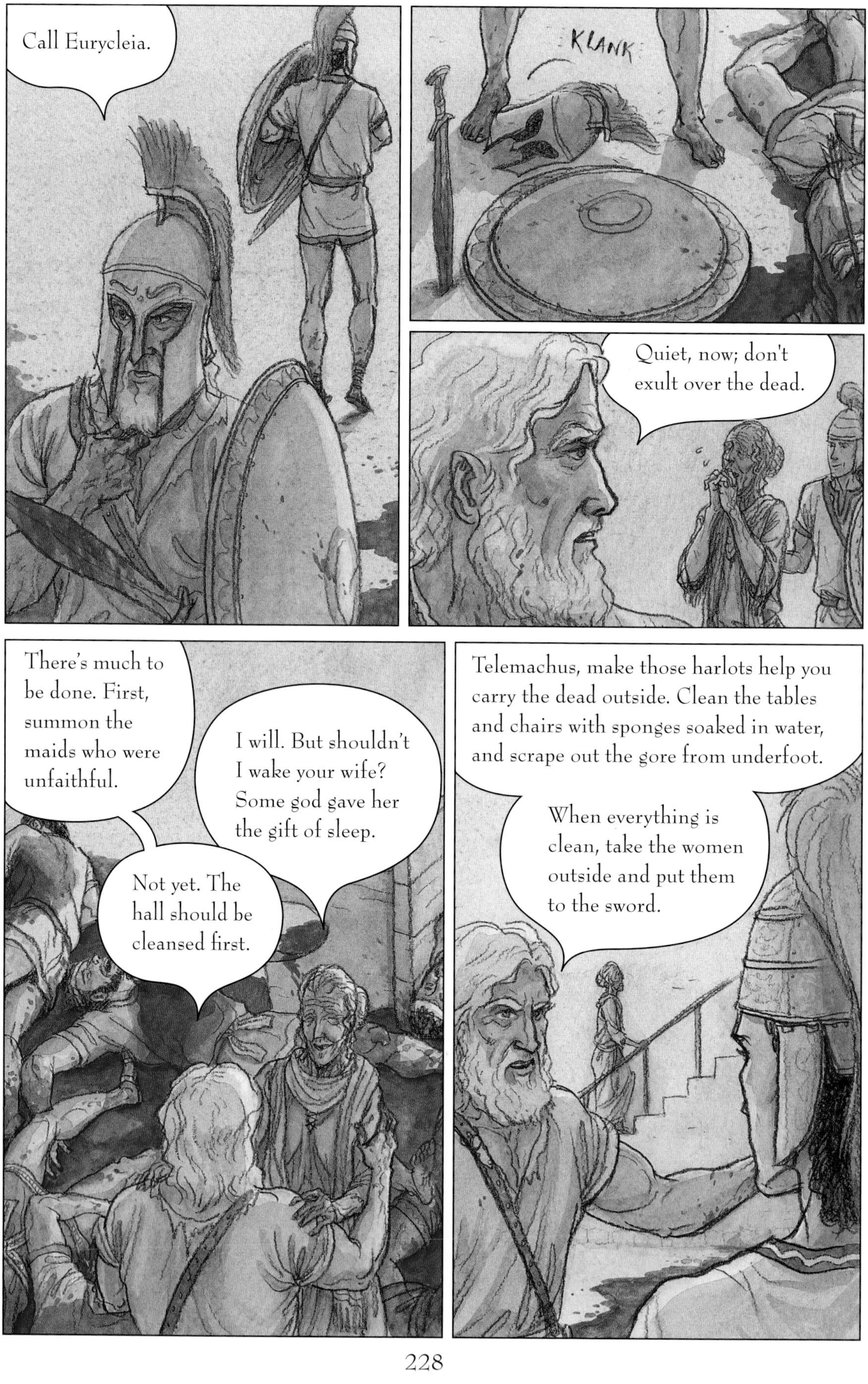

Call Eurycleia.
KLANK
Quiet, now; don't exult over the dead.
There's much to be done. First, summon the maids who were unfaithful.
I will. But shouldn't I wake your wife? Some god gave her the gift of sleep.
Not yet. The hall should be cleansed first.
Telemachus, make those harlots help you carry the dead outside. Clean the tables and chairs with sponges soaked in water, and scrape out the gore from underfoot.
When everything is clean, take the women outside and put them to the sword.

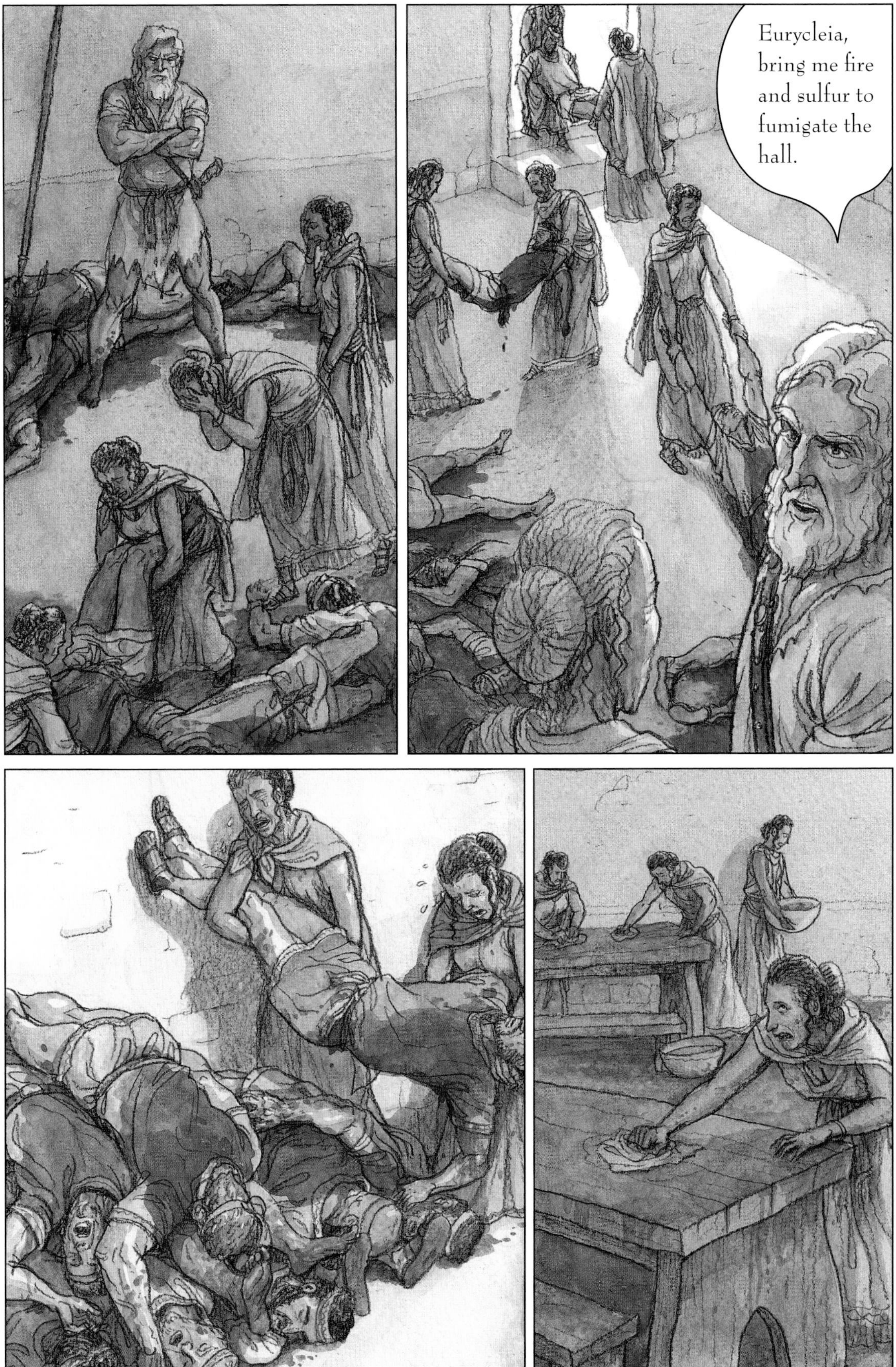
Eurycleia, bring me fire and sulfur to fumigate the hall.

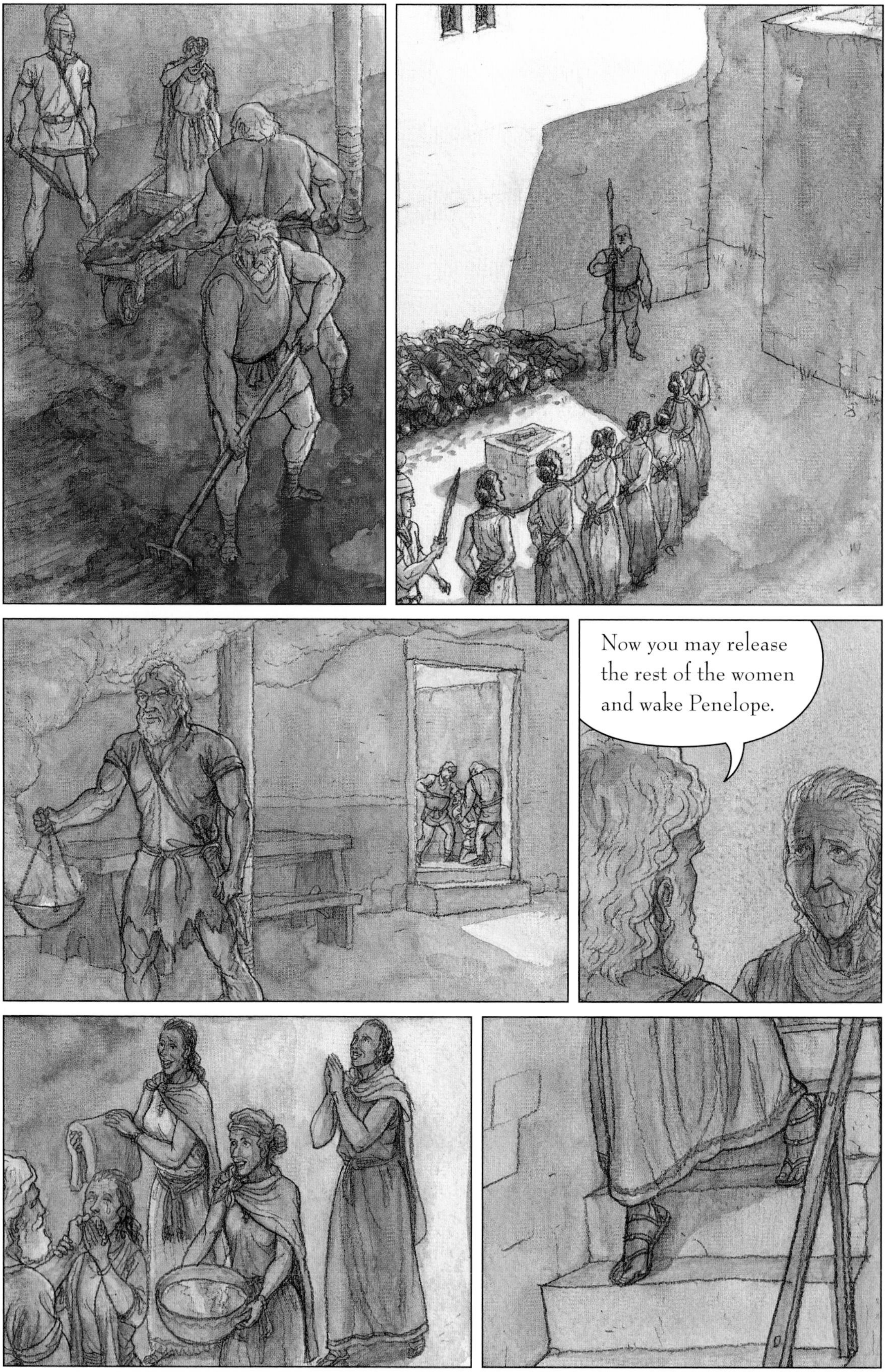
Now you may release
the rest of the women
and wake Penelope.

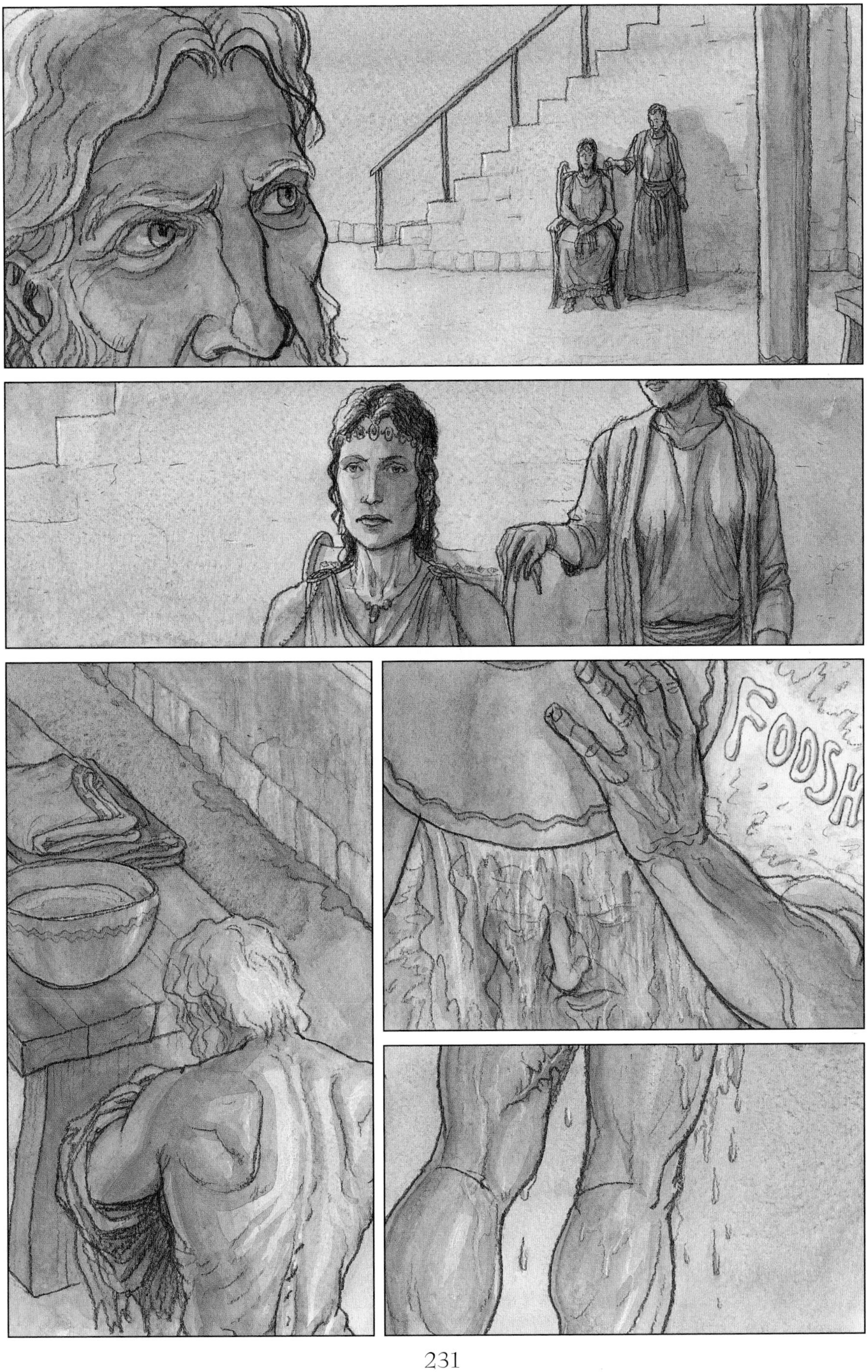
FOOSH

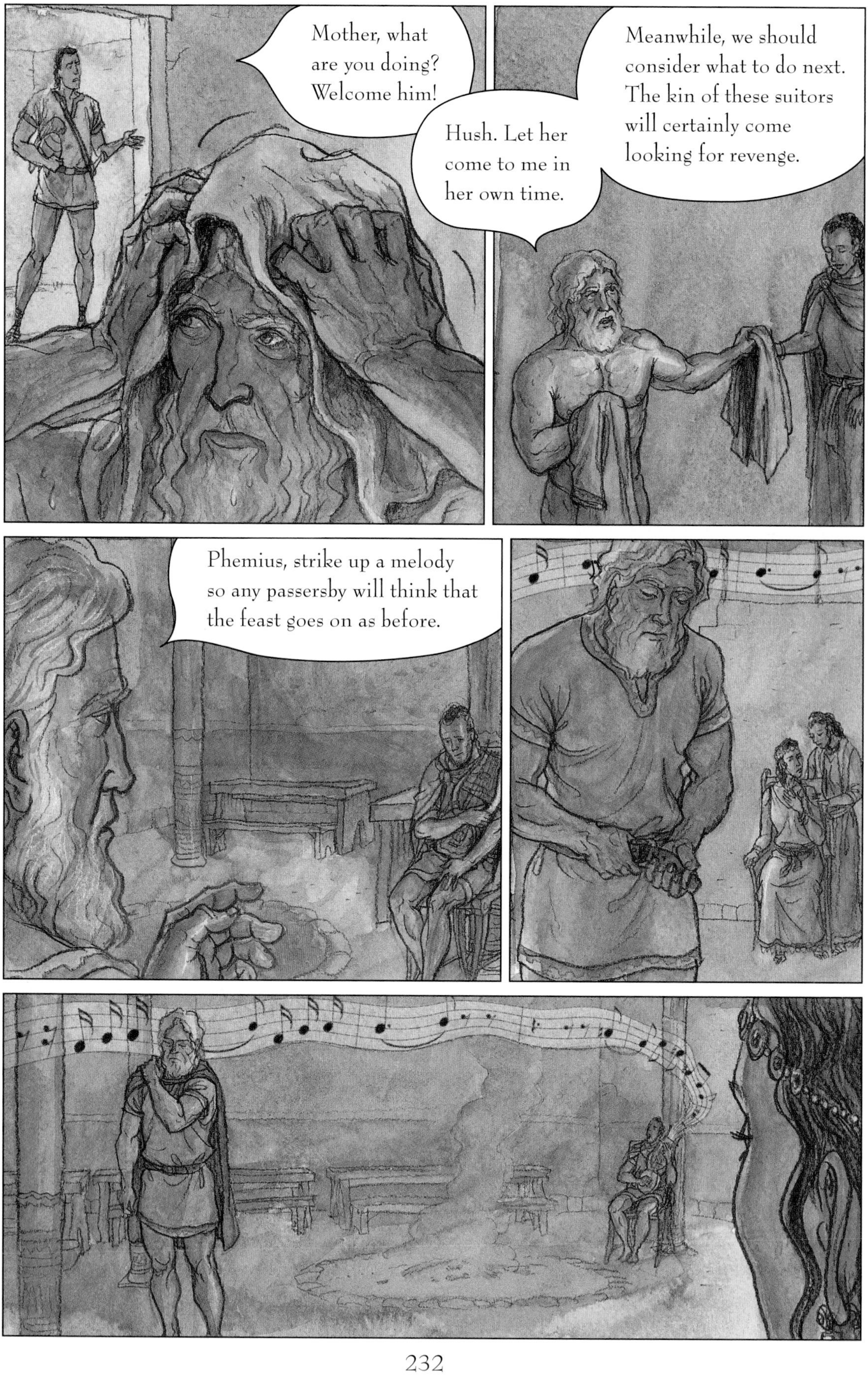
Mother, what are you doing? Welcome him!
Hush. Let her come to me in her own time.
Meanwhile, we should consider what to do next. The kin of these suitors will certainly come looking for revenge.
Phemius, strike up a melody so any passersby will think that the feast goes on as before.

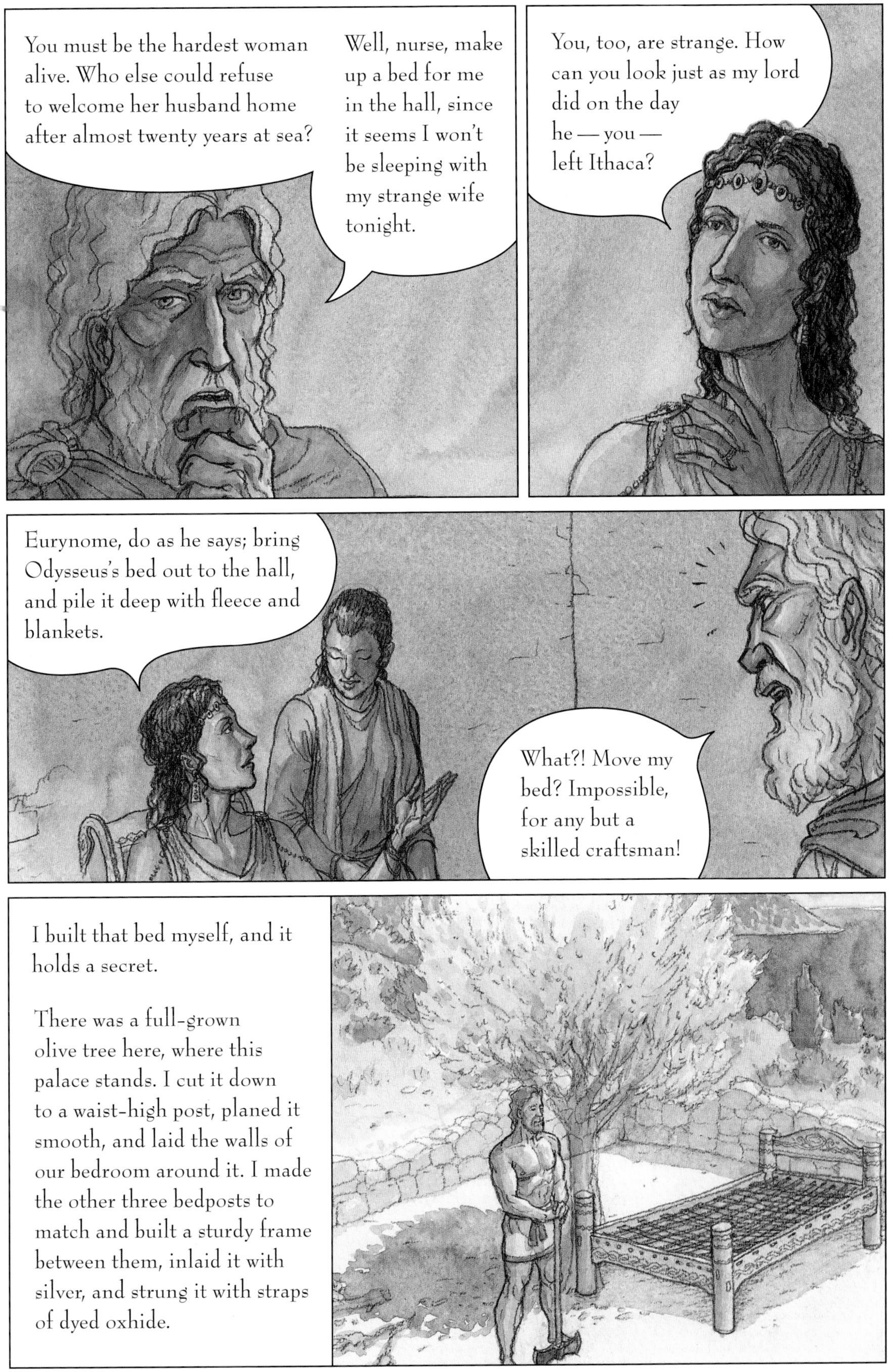
You must be the hardest woman alive. Who else could refuse to welcome her husband home after almost twenty years at sea?
Well, nurse, make up a bed for me in the hall, since it seems I won't be sleeping with my strange wife tonight.
You, too, are strange. How can you look just as my lord did on the day he — you — left Ithaca?
Eurynome, do as he says; bring Odysseus's bed out to the hall, and pile it deep with fleece and blankets.
What?! Move my bed? Impossible, for any but a skilled craftsman!
I built that bed myself, and it holds a secret.
There was a full-grown olive tree here, where this palace stands. I cut it down to a waist-high post, planed it smooth, and laid the walls of our bedroom around it. I made the other three bedposts to match and built a sturdy frame between them, inlaid it with silver, and strung it with straps of dyed oxhide.

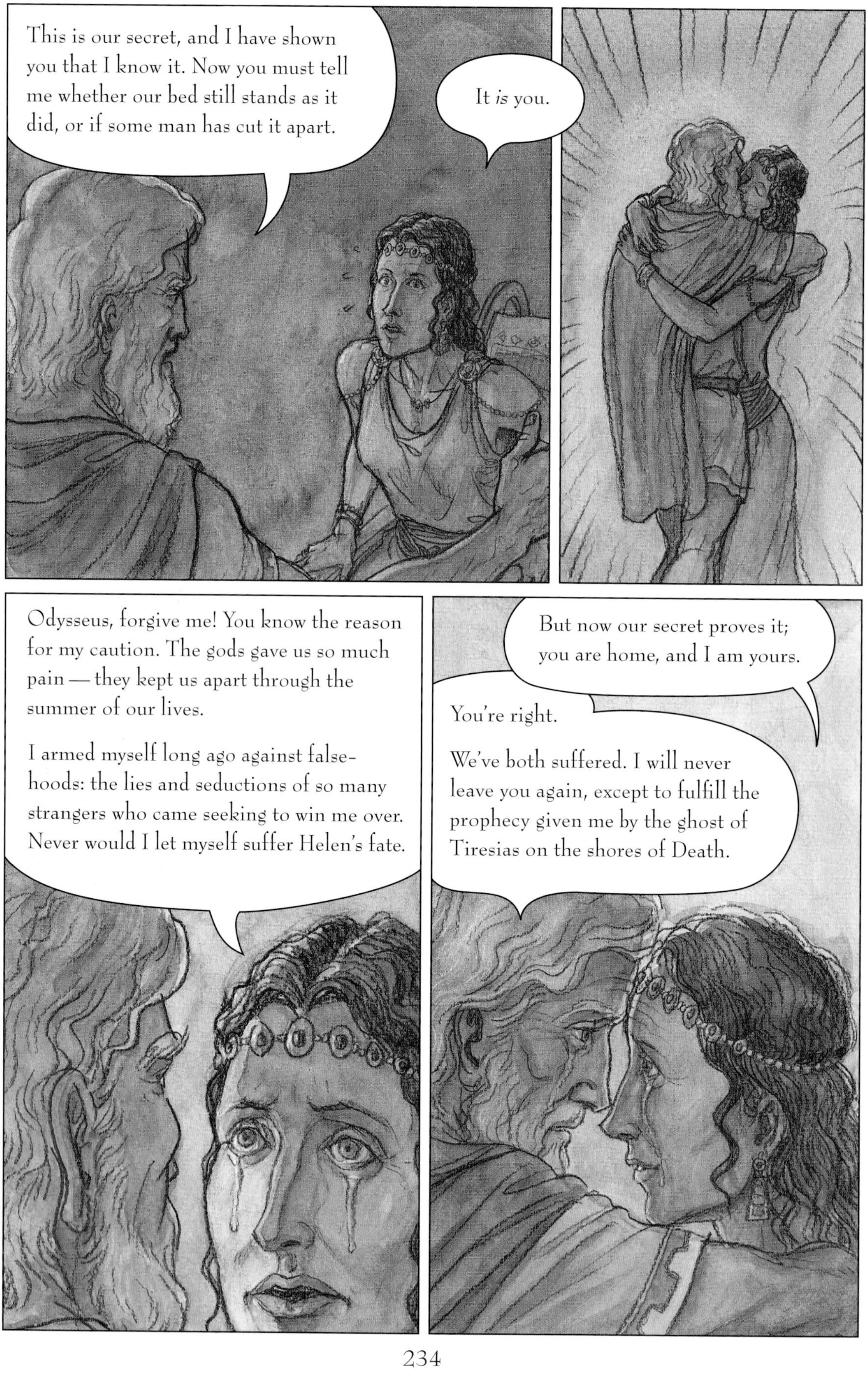
This is our secret, and I have shown you that I know it. Now you must tell me whether our bed still stands as it did, or if some man has cut it apart.
It *is* you.
Odysseus, forgive me! You know the reason for my caution. The gods gave us so much pain — they kept us apart through the summer of our lives.
I armed myself long ago against falsehoods: the lies and seductions of so many strangers who came seeking to win me over. Never would I let myself suffer Helen's fate.
But now our secret proves it; you are home, and I am yours.
You're right.
We've both suffered. I will never leave you again, except to fulfill the prophecy given me by the ghost of Tiresias on the shores of Death.

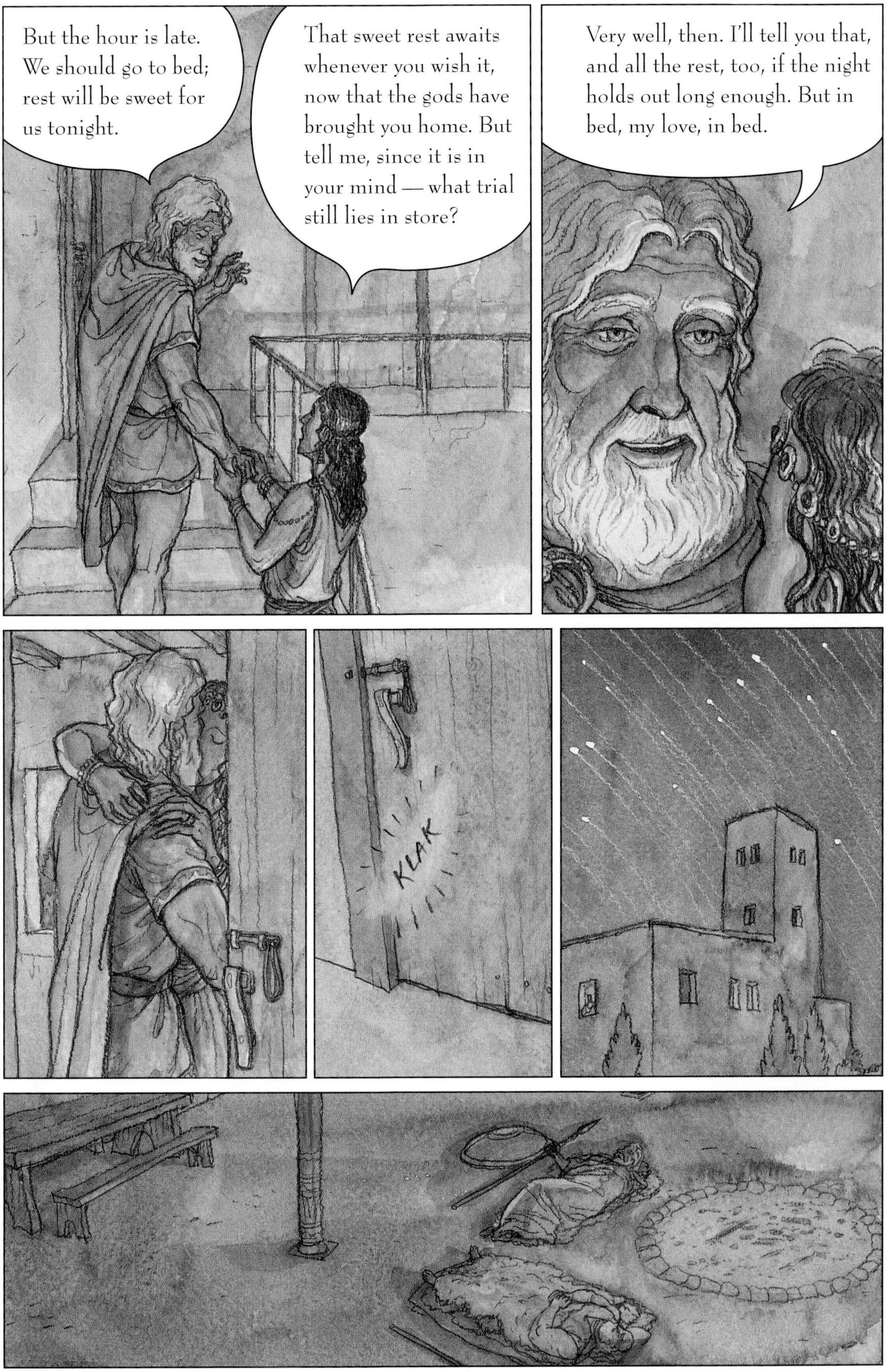
But the hour is late. We should go to bed; rest will be sweet for us tonight.
That sweet rest awaits whenever you wish it, now that the gods have brought you home. But tell me, since it is in your mind — what trial still lies in store?
Very well, then. I'll tell you that, and all the rest, too, if the night holds out long enough. But in bed, my love, in bed.
KLAK

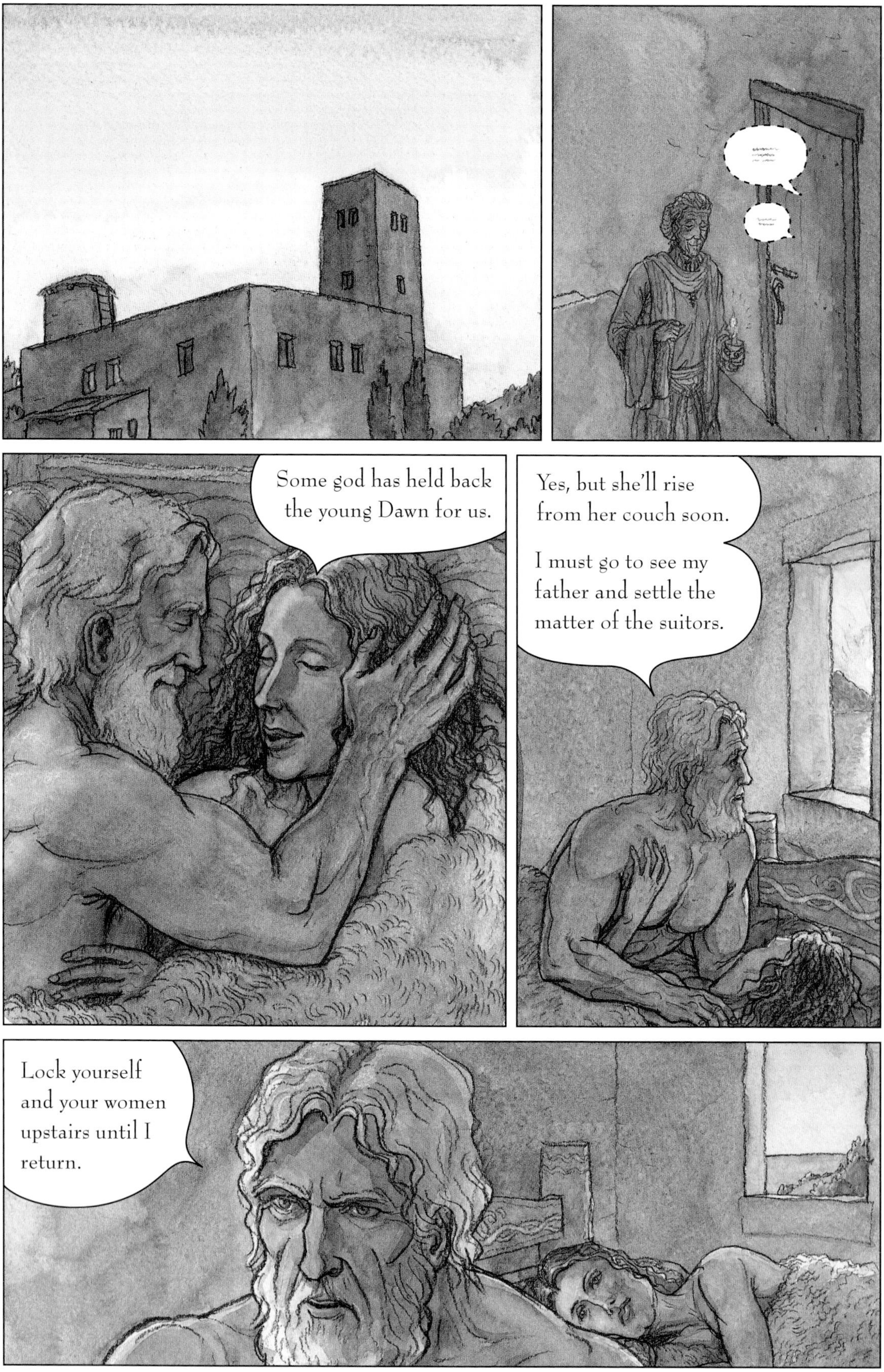
Some god has held back the young Dawn for us.
Yes, but she'll rise from her couch soon.
I must go to see my father and settle the matter of the suitors.
Lock yourself and your women upstairs until I return.

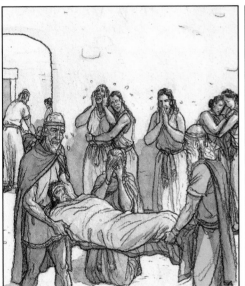

Friends, what kind of king takes all the best young men of his country away to perish on foreign shores, then comes back and slaughters the next generation? He's nothing but a murderer, and we must catch him before he flees to some ally on the mainland!

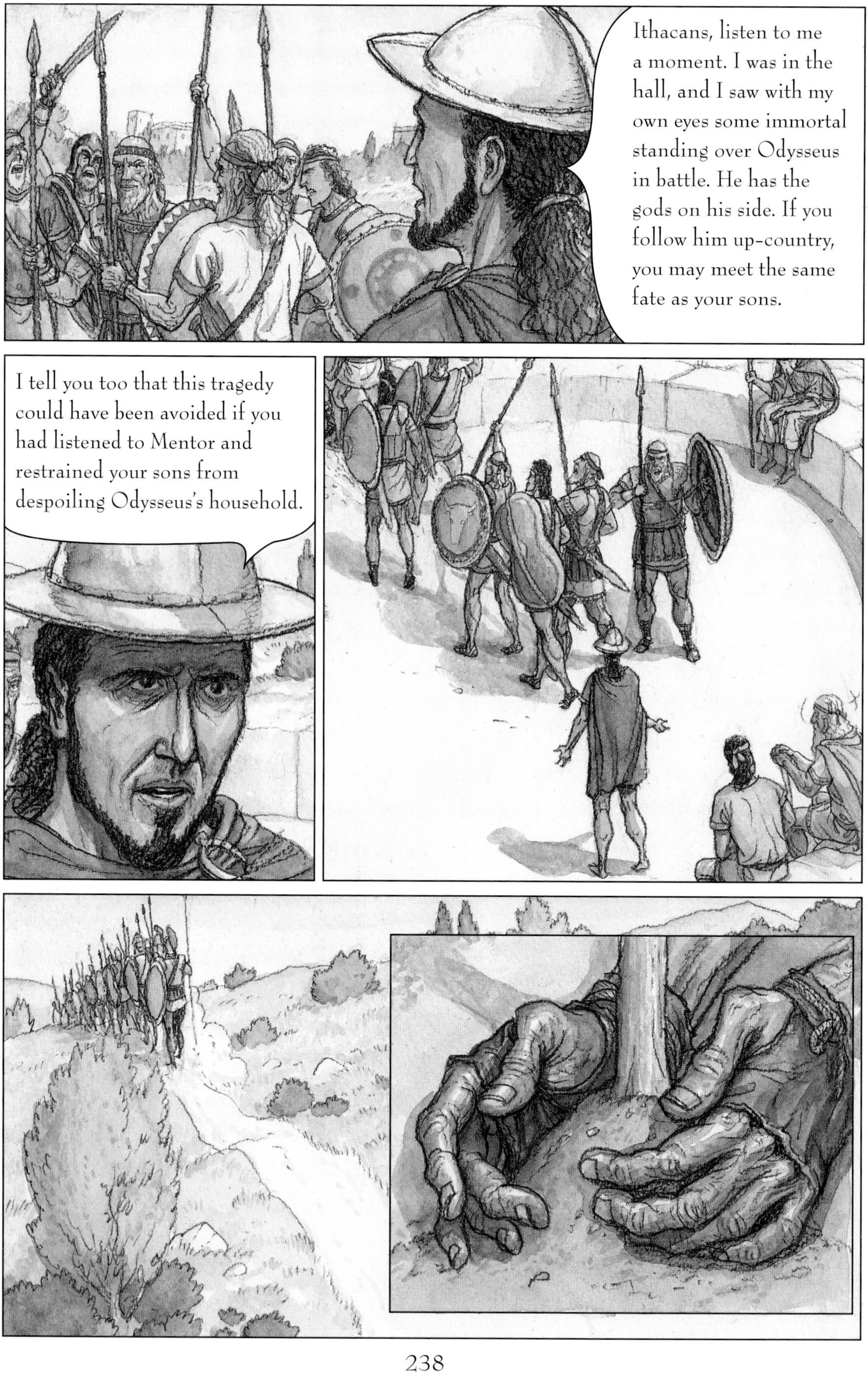
Ithacans, listen to me a moment. I was in the hall, and I saw with my own eyes some immortal standing over Odysseus in battle. He has the gods on his side. If you follow him up-country, you may meet the same fate as your sons.
I tell you too that this tragedy could have been avoided if you had listened to Mentor and restrained your sons from despoiling Odysseus's household.

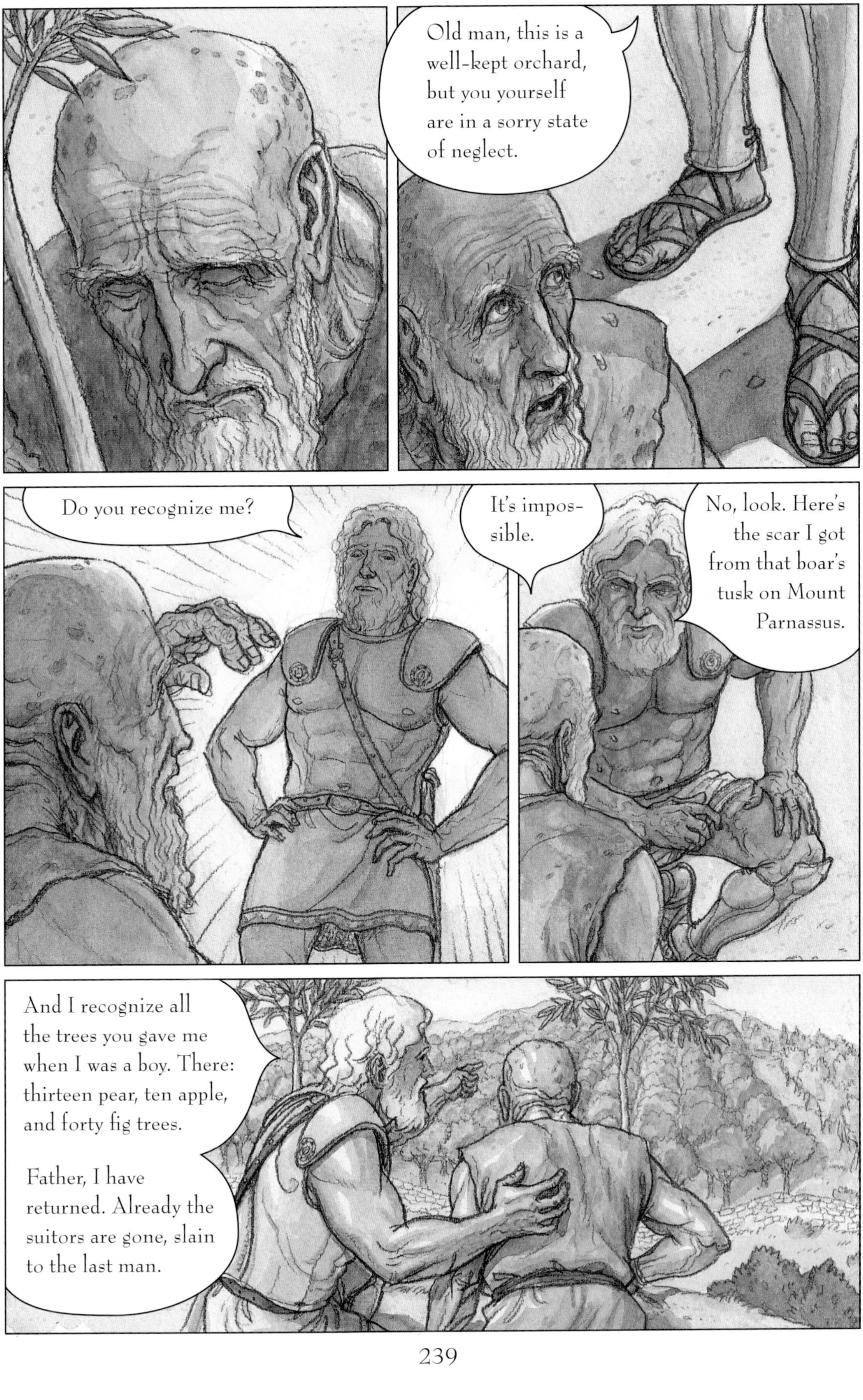
Old man, this is a well-kept orchard, but you yourself are in a sorry state of neglect.
Do you recognize me?
It's impossible.
No, look. Here's the scar I got from that boar's tusk on Mount Parnassus.
And I recognize all the trees you gave me when I was a boy. There: thirteen pear, ten apple, and forty fig trees.
Father, I have returned. Already the suitors are gone, slain to the last man.

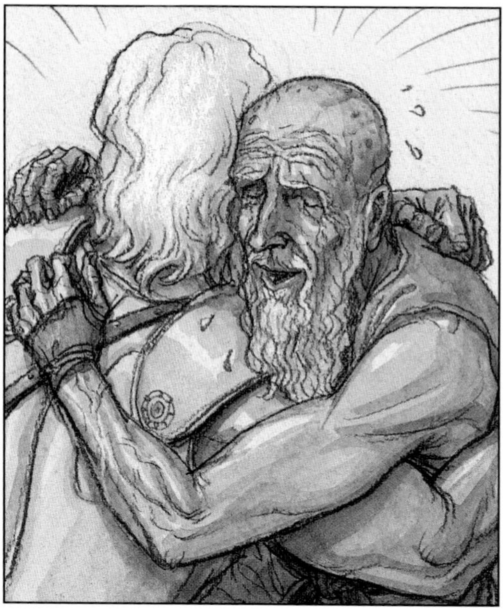

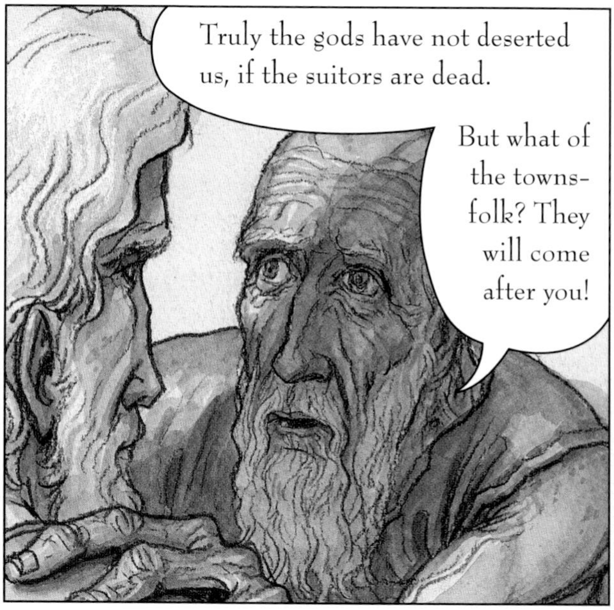
Truly the gods have not deserted us, if the suitors are dead.
But what of the towns-folk? They will come after you!

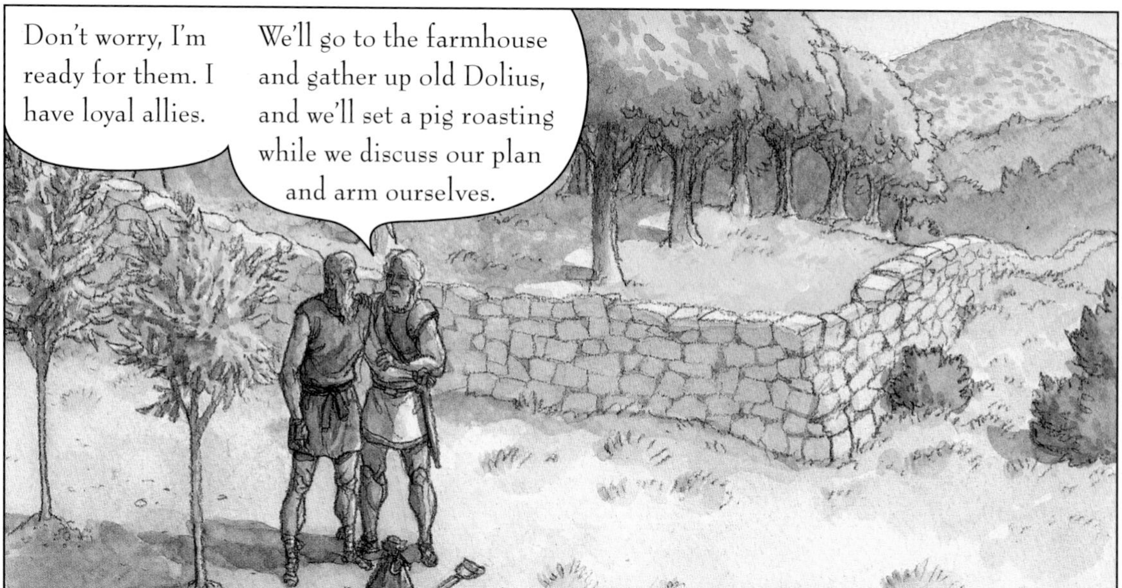
Don't worry, I'm ready for them. I have loyal allies.
We'll go to the farmhouse and gather up old Dolius, and we'll set a pig roasting while we discuss our plan and arm ourselves.

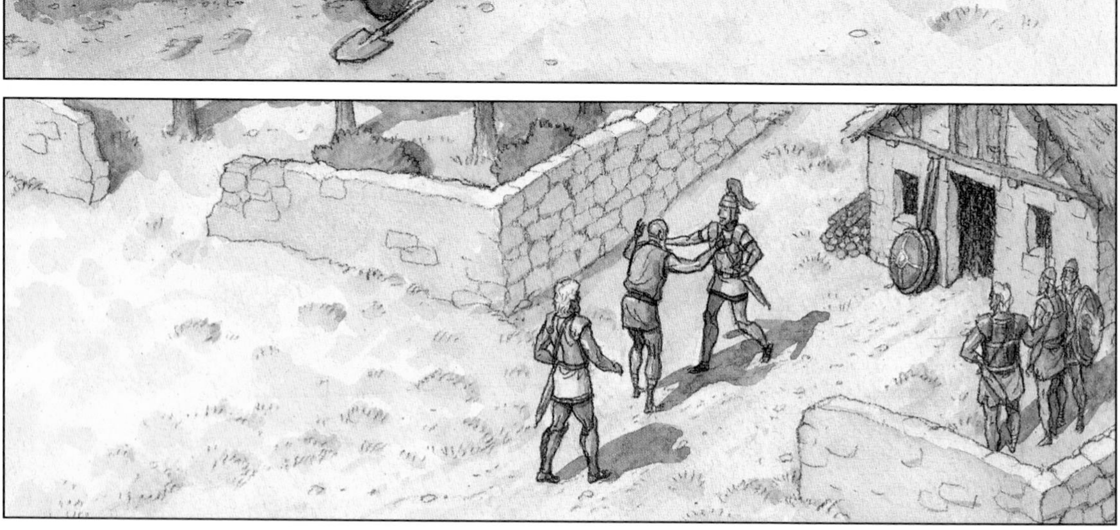

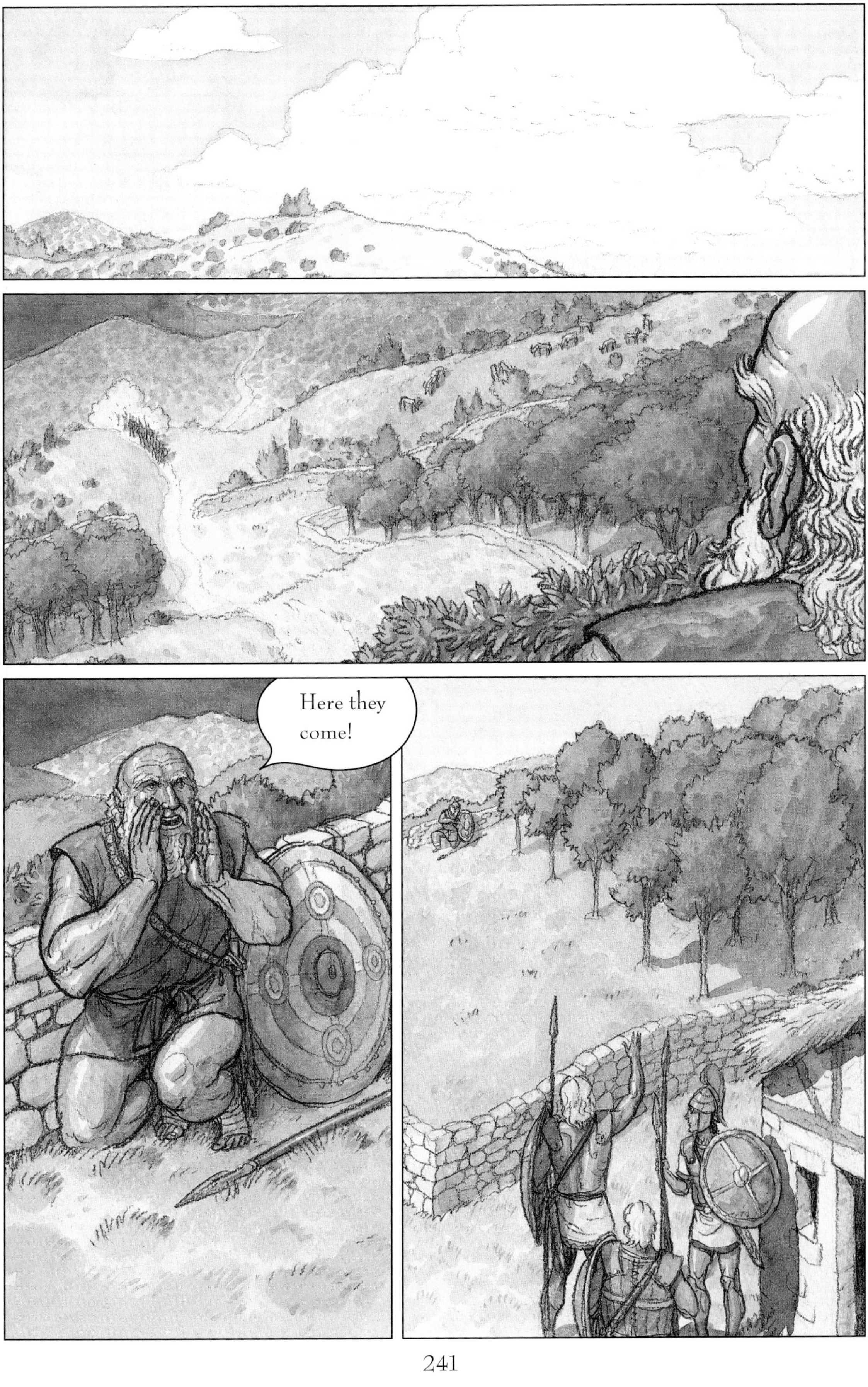
Here they come!

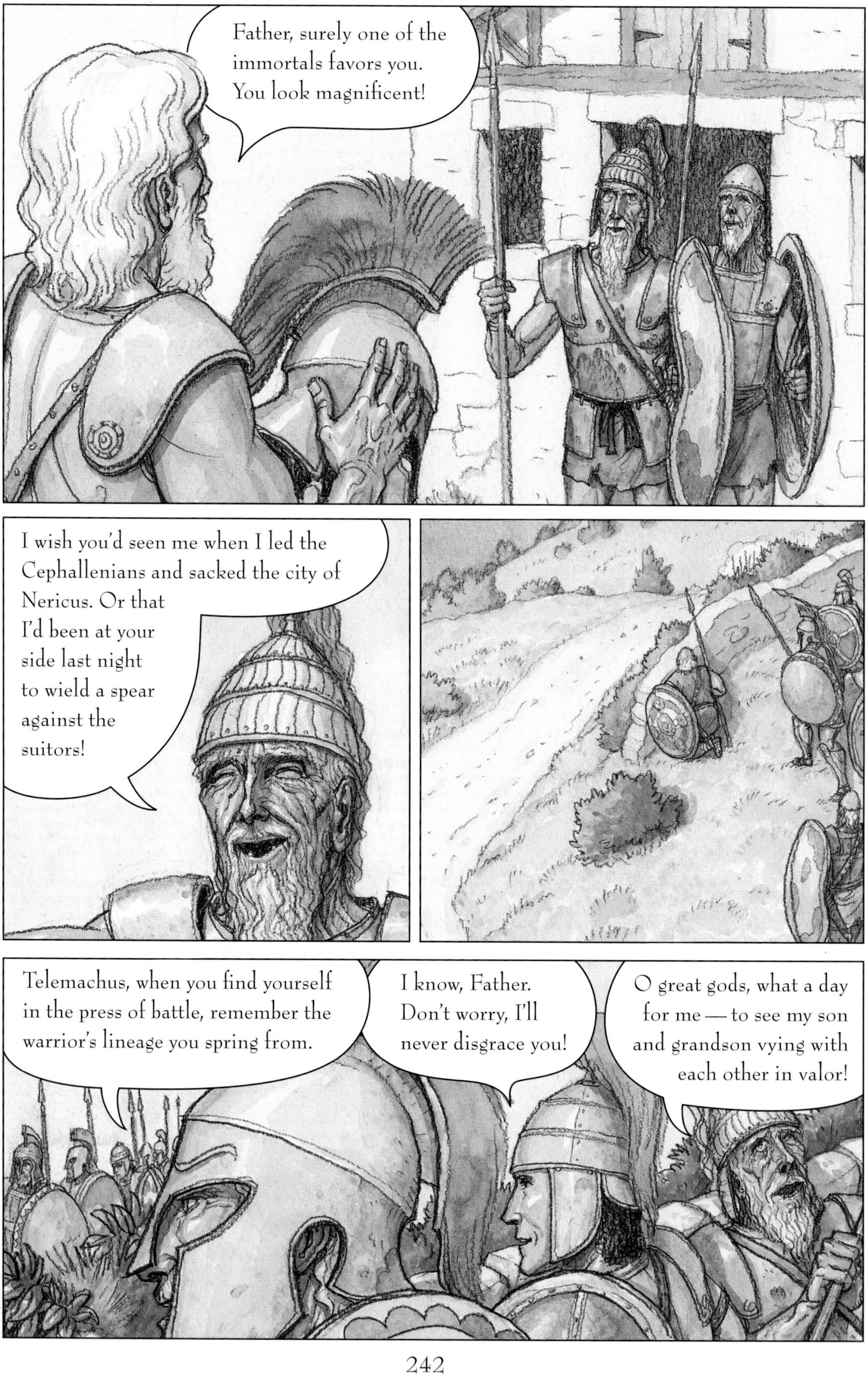
Father, surely one of the immortals favors you. You look magnificent!
I wish you'd seen me when I led the Cephallenians and sacked the city of Nericus. Or that I'd been at your side last night to wield a spear against the suitors!
Telemachus, when you find yourself in the press of battle, remember the warrior's lineage you spring from.
I know, Father. Don't worry, I'll never disgrace you!
O great gods, what a day for me — to see my son and grandson vying with each other in valor!

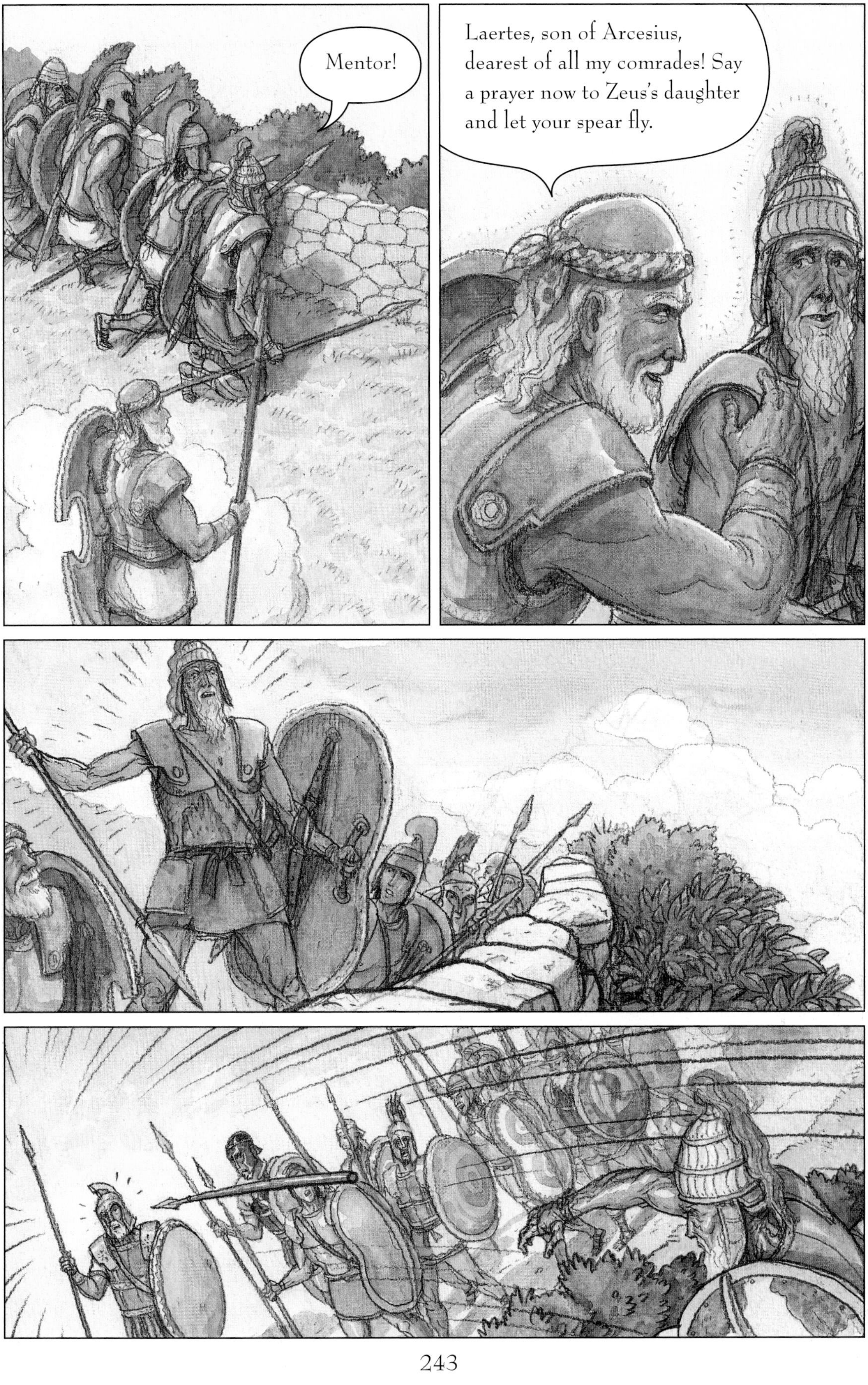
Mentor!
Laertes, son of Arcesius, dearest of all my comrades! Say a prayer now to Zeus's daughter and let your spear fly.

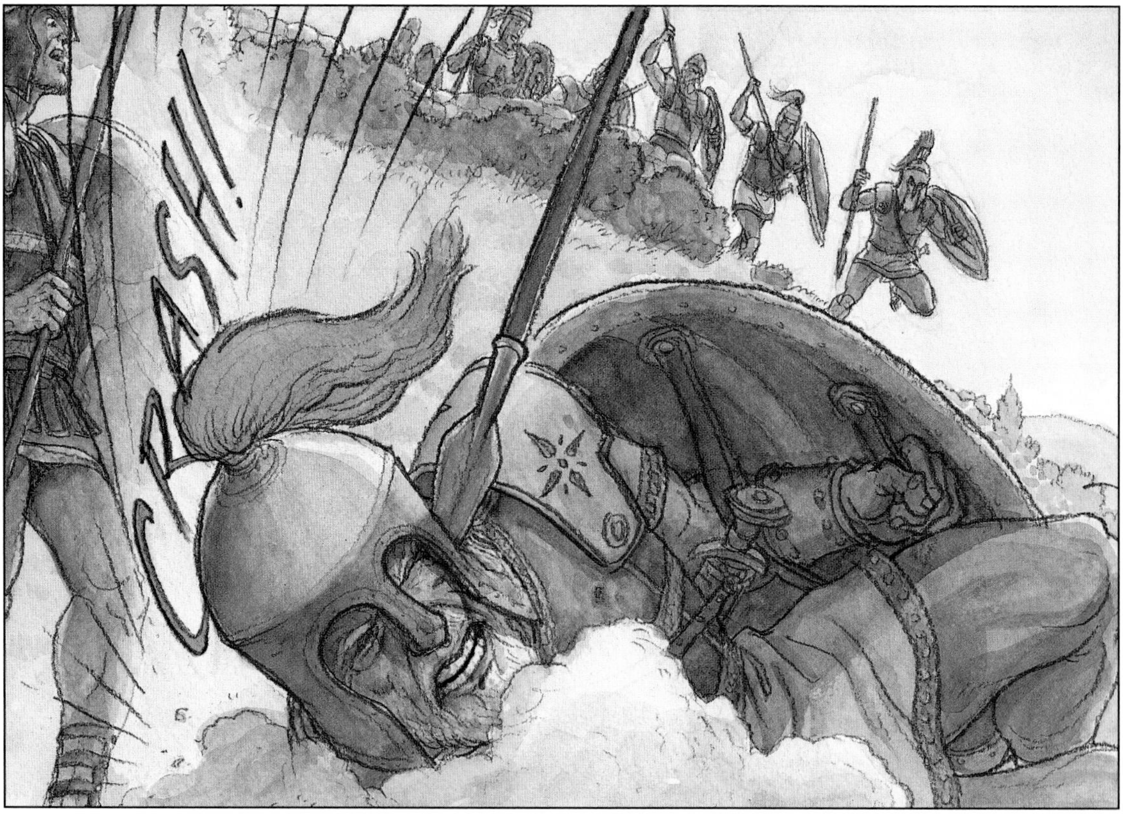
CRASH!

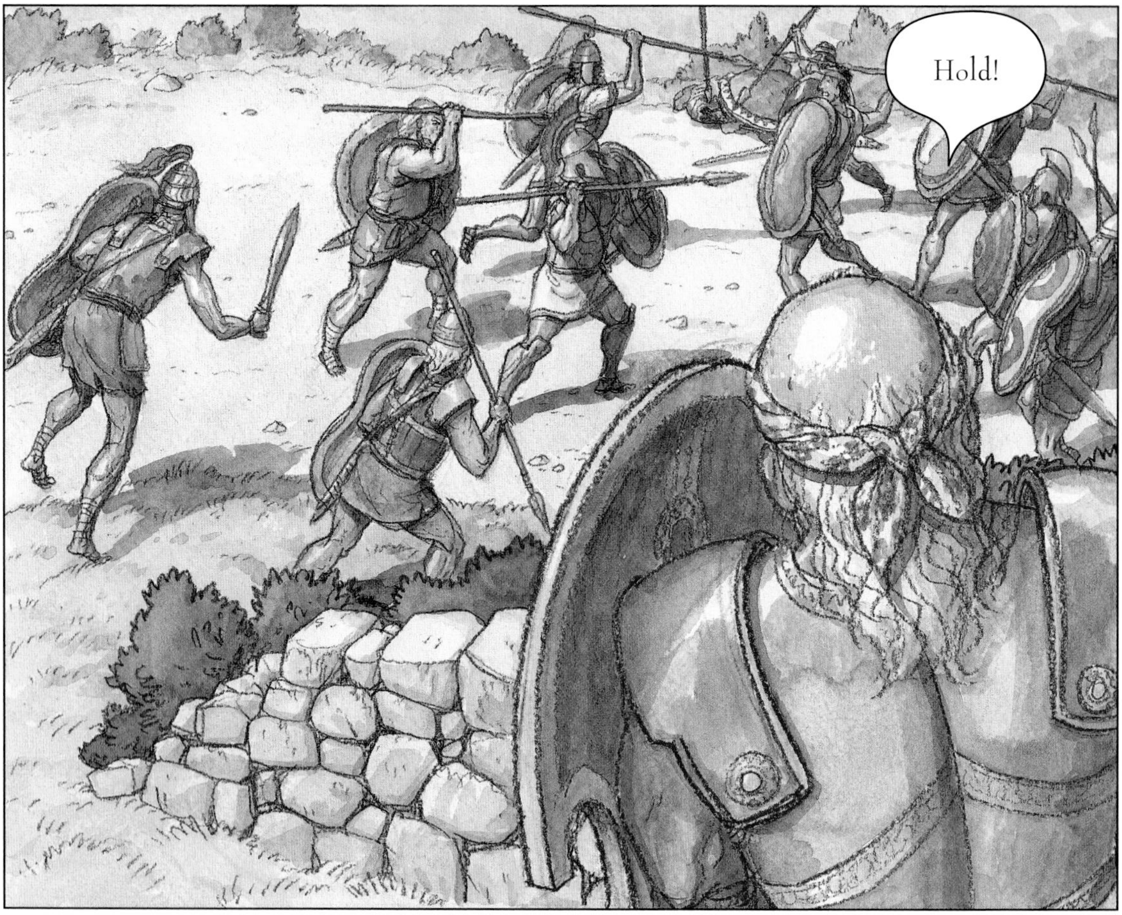
Hold!

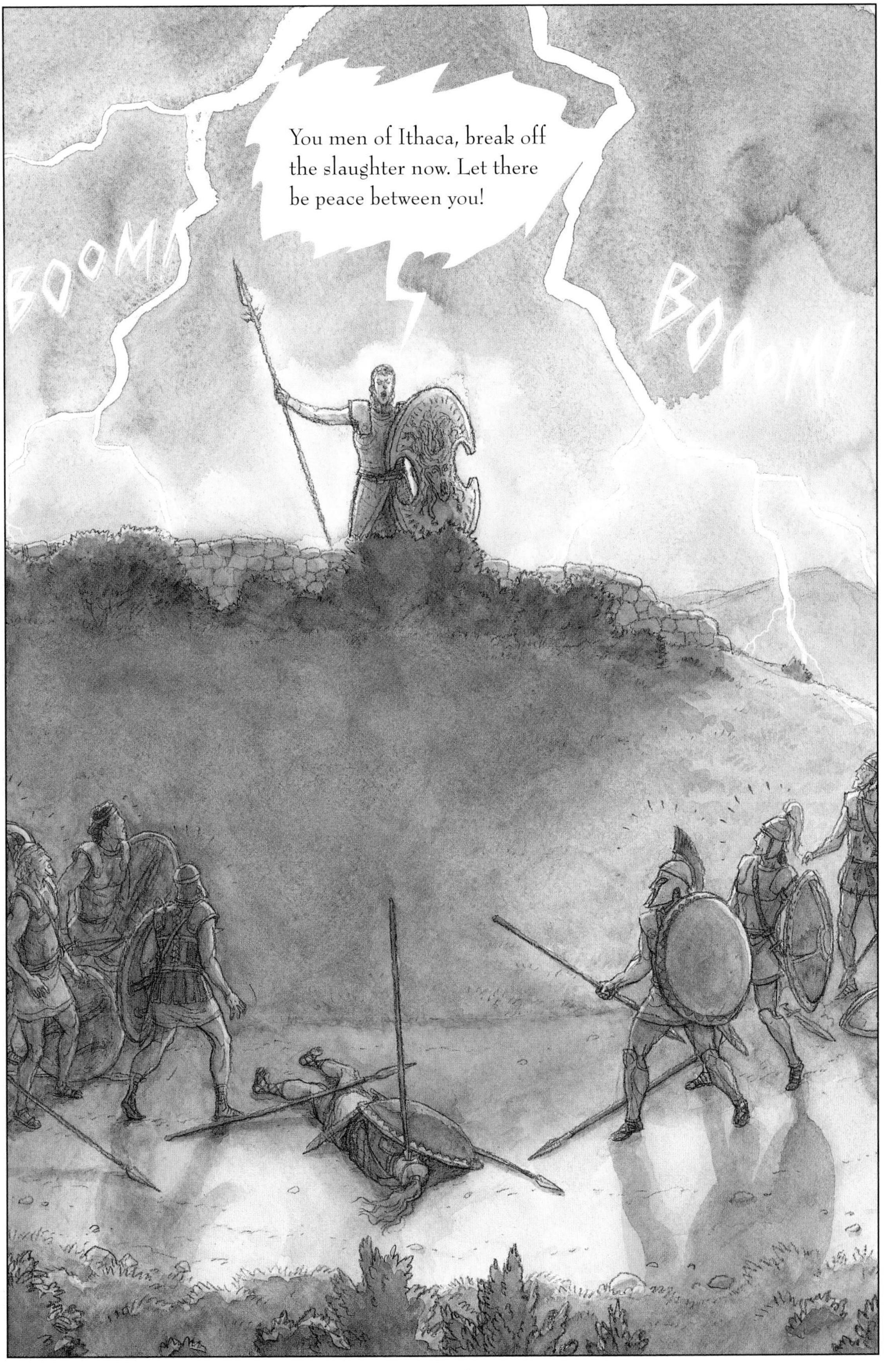

You men of Ithaca, break off the slaughter now. Let there be peace between you!
BOOM!
BOOOM!

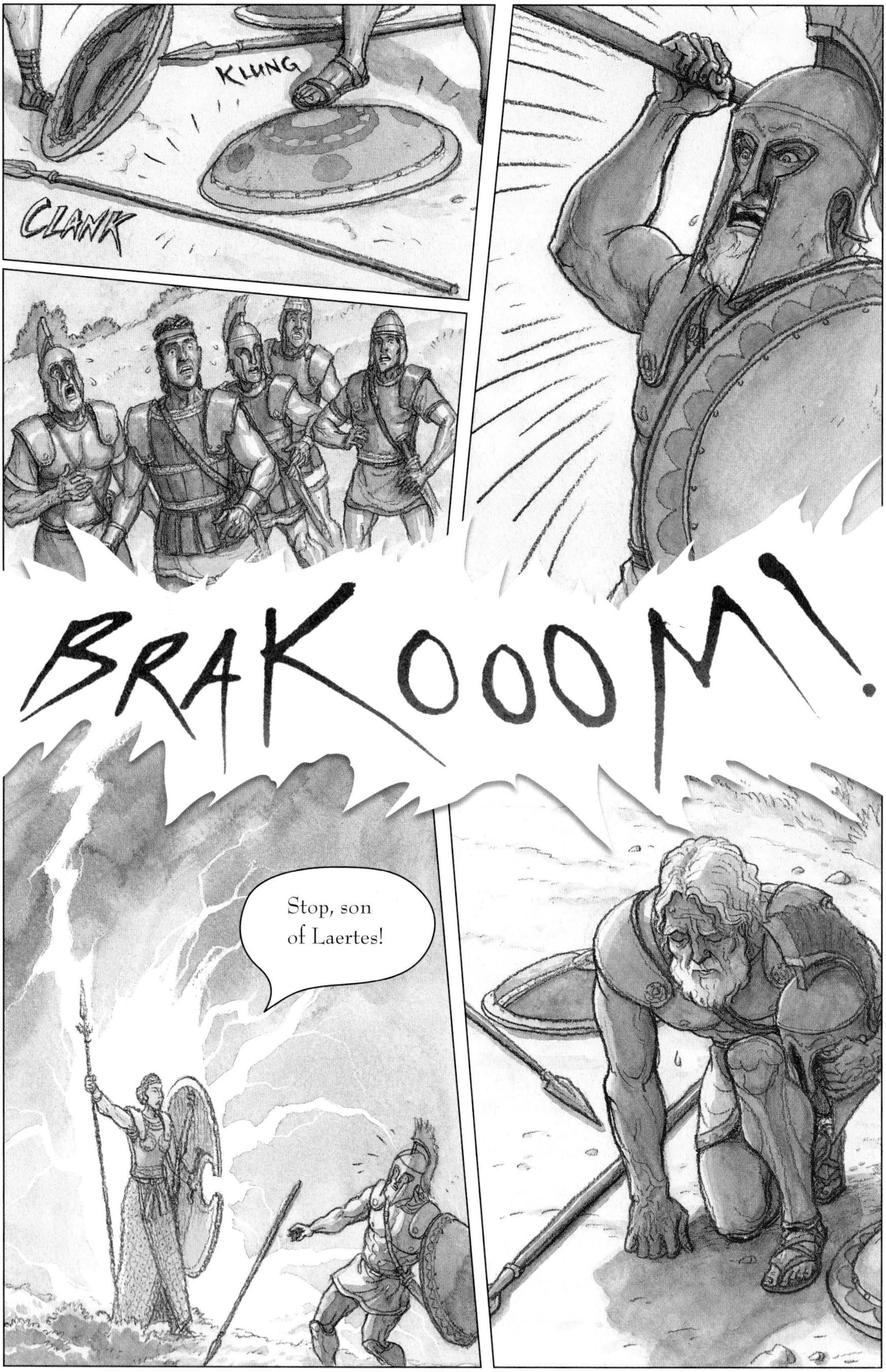
KLUNG
CLANK
BRAKOOOM!
Stop, son of Laertes!

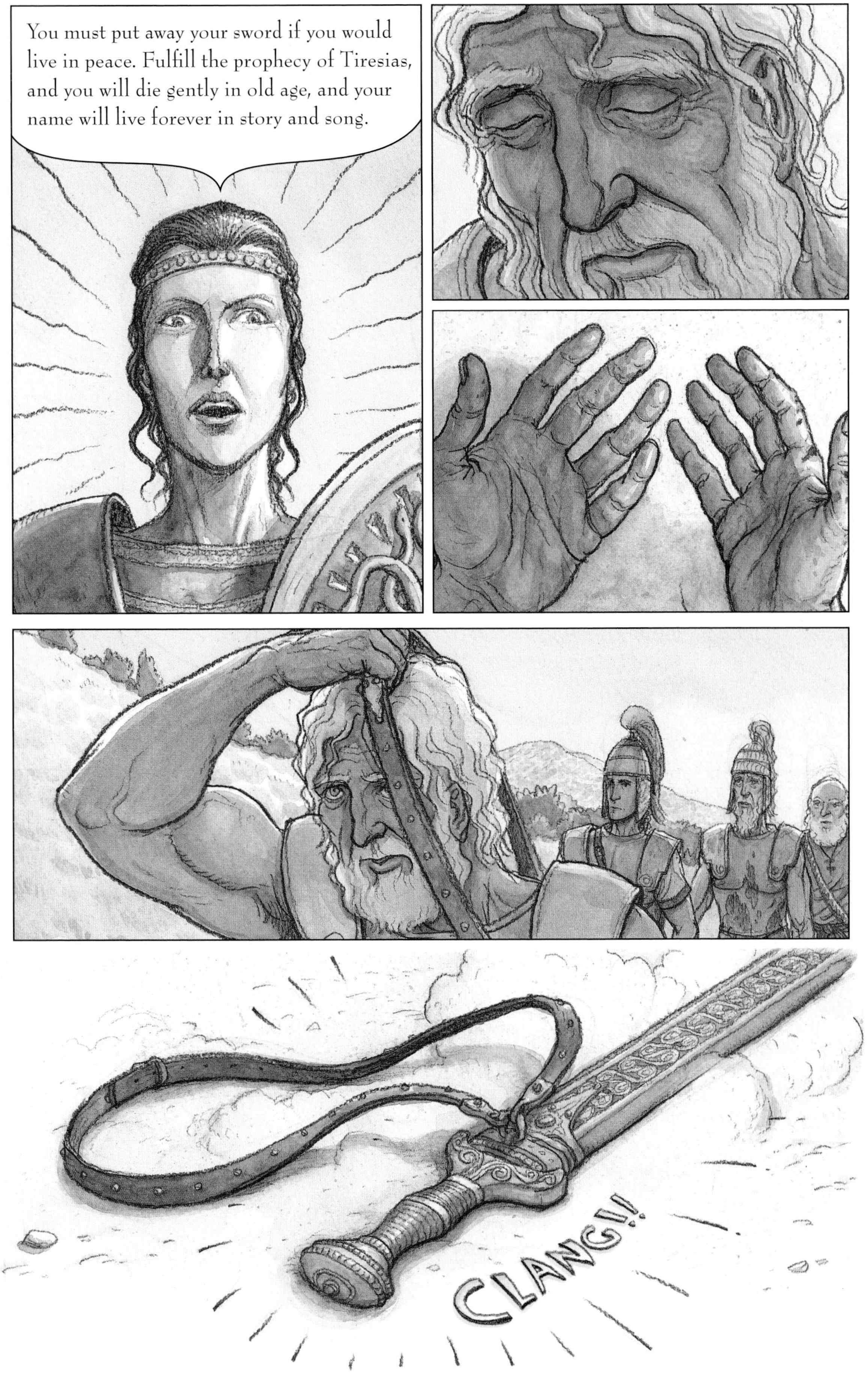
You must put away your sword if you would live in peace. Fulfill the prophecy of Tiresias, and you will die gently in old age, and your name will live forever in story and song.
CLANG!!

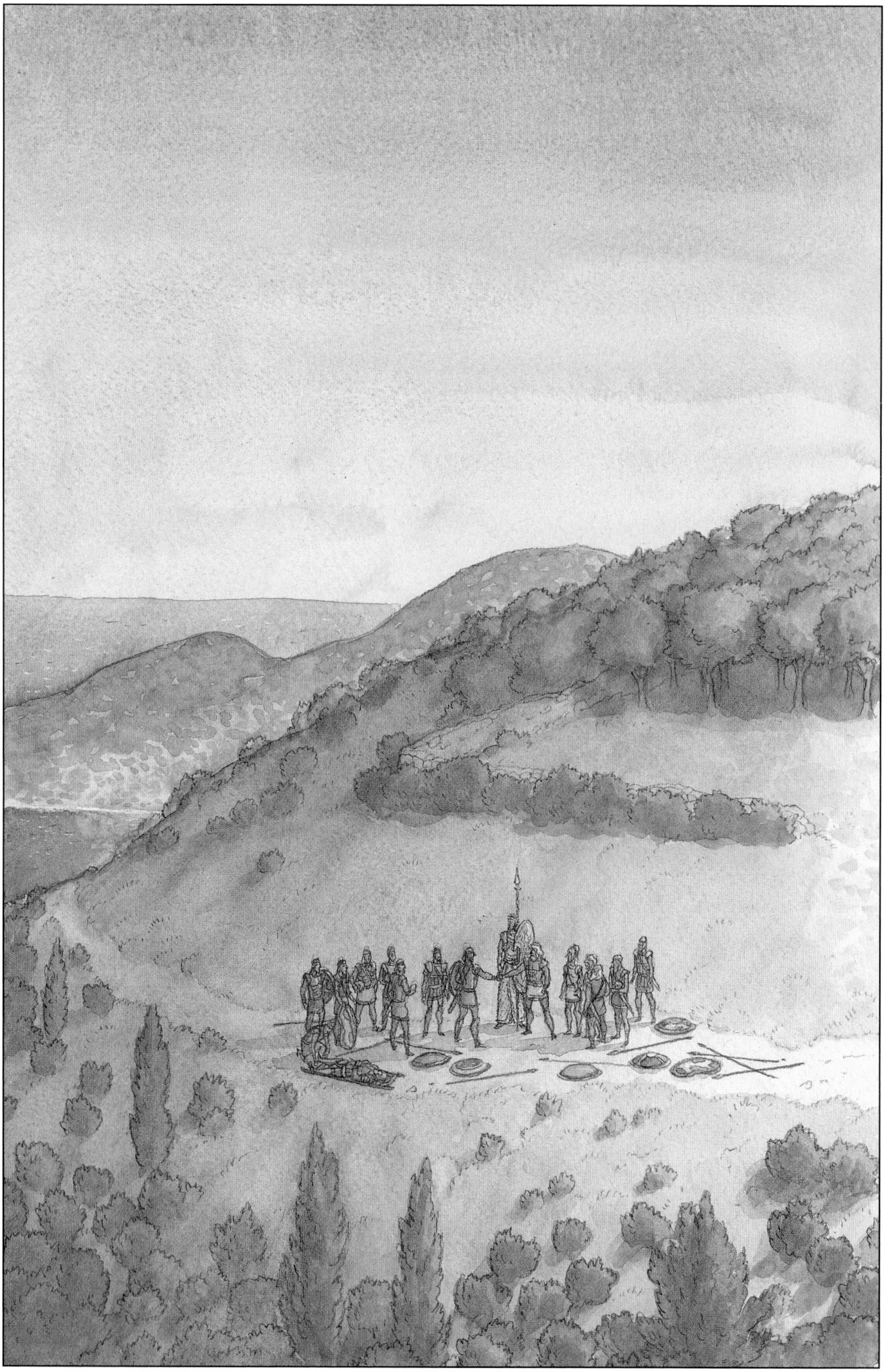

Here ends the story of Odysseus, as it has been passed down since the age of gods and monsters.

NOTES

Very little is known about Homer, the composition of his epic poems, or even the Bronze Age itself. In my research I encountered open questions and scholarly disagreement at every turn. Luckily *The Odyssey* is a rather fantastic story, so I didn't feel I needed to be one-hundred-percent historically accurate. In fact, after researching the history pretty thoroughly, I opted to break from realism in most of my designs, while preserving just enough historical touches to give Odysseus's world a ring of authenticity.

My favorite translation of *The Odyssey* is that of Robert Fitzgerald, closely followed by Robert Fagles. I like the balance of poetry and readability that these two translations offer. However, in adapting and abridging Homer to the graphic-novel format, I had to rewrite most of the material for brevity, and for this purpose it was more useful to work from the plainer prose of Samuel Butler's and E. V. Rieu's translations — with frequent reference to Fagles and Fitzgerald, and to a lesser extent Lattimore, Lawrence, Cowper, and Chapman. I also admire Rodney Merrill's metrically correct verse translation, which I discovered partway through this project (thanks, Laura).

I have used near-direct quotes in a few cases where I really admired the translator's art, and those passages appear in this book as follows — Fagles: page 170. Fitzgerald: pages 12, 16, 18, 180, 187, 192, 193, 196 and 199. Rieu: pages 89, 90, and 91.

I don't think you need a full glossary to understand *The Odyssey*, but there are a few words that might trip you up if you haven't been reading your Greek classics. *Achaeans* and *Argives* both refer to the inhabitants of ancient Greece. A *hecatomb* is a religious sacrifice of one hundred cattle (as shown in chapter 3). The *Myrmidons* are Achilles' followers.

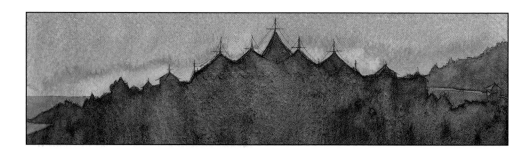

THANKS

I'd particularly like to thank my wonderful editor, Deb Wayshak, and all the other excellent folks at Candlewick who have been a delight to work with.

I'd also like to thank: Eric Shanower (author of *Age of Bronze,* an excellent, meticulously researched graphic retelling of the Trojan War) for sharing his expertise on Mycenaean archaeology, James Sturm (author of one of my favorite graphic novels, *Satchel Paige: Striking Out Jim Crow*) for excellent advice, Heather Glista for costuming, Mark Tsai for computer help, and Bob Ebener for modeling.

Many of my friends and colleagues took me up on the offer to use their likenesses, in whole or in part, for some of the hundreds of supporting characters in the story. Thanks to Dennis Bachman, Bill Ballard, Rafael Baptista, Toby Bazarnick, John Beauchemin, Kurt Bickenbach, Chris Bruser, Wes Carroll, Diane Cowan, Juan Diaz, Matt Edwards, Bill Farquhar, Mike Lamenzo, Mat MacKenzie, Andy Meuse, Pat McElhatton, Eric Orr, Margaret Ryding, Jim Vincent, Chris Yona, and Chris Zirpoli. I hope you all recognize yourselves, though I didn't always capture the likeness.

Special thanks to Joyce DeForge, who first introduced me to *The Odyssey.*

And of course, I give extra-special thanks to my #1 supporter and constant companion, the lovely and talented Alison Morris.

For my parents, Steven and Judith,
who set me on my creative odyssey

☙

First edition 2010

Library of Congress Cataloging-in-Publication Data

Hinds, Gareth, date.
The odyssey / Gareth Hinds. — 1st ed.
p.   cm.
Summary: Retells, in graphic novel format, Homer's epic tale of Odysseus, the ancient Greek hero who
encounters witches and other obstacles on his journey home after fighting in the Trojan War.

1. Graphic novels. 2. Odysseus (Greek mythology) — Juvenile fiction. [1. Graphic novels. 2. Odysseus
(Greek mythology) — Fiction. 3. Mythology, Greek — Fiction. 4. Adventure and adventurers — Fiction.
5. Heroes — Fiction.]
I. Homer. Odyssey. II. Title.
PZ7.7.H56Ody 2010
741.5'973 — dc22   2010007512

ISBN 978-0-7636-4266-2 (hardcover)
ISBN 978-0-7636-4268-6 (paperback)

16 17 18 19 20 CCP 10 9 8 7 6

Printed in Shenzhen, Guangdong, China

This book was typeset in Bernhard Modern.
The illustrations were done in pencil and watercolor.

Candlewick Press
99 Dover Street
Somerville, Massachusetts 02144

visit us at www.candlewick.com

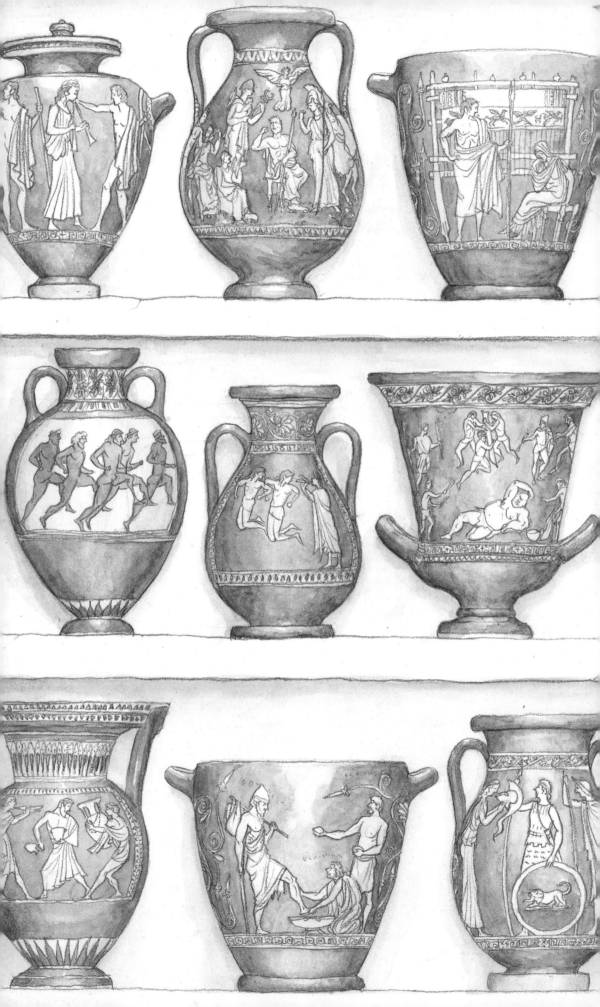